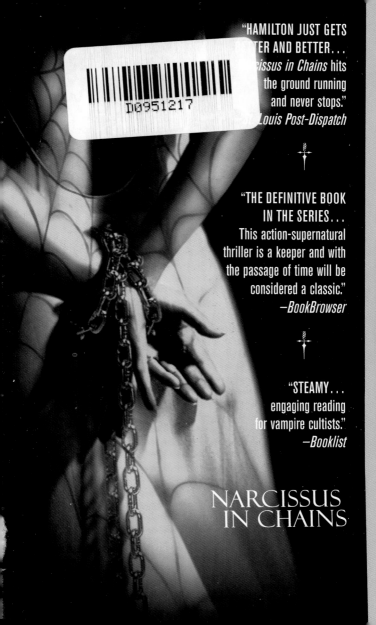

"HAMILTON JUST GETS
BETTER AND BETTER...
Narcissus in Chains hits
the ground running
and never stops."
—*St. Louis Post-Dispatch*

"THE DEFINITIVE BOOK
IN THE SERIES...
This action-supernatural
thriller is a keeper and with
the passage of time will be
considered a classic."
—*BookBrowser*

"STEAMY...
engaging reading
for vampire cultists."
—*Booklist*

NARCISSUS
IN CHAINS

D0951217

Men are men. Jean-Claude and Richard are each something else entirely. Anita Blake, Vampire Hunter, torn between them, has been avoiding both vampire and werewolf for months. But when a kidnapper targets innocents she has sworn to protect, Anita turns to them for help, which will require harnessing both their powers—and their hungers . . .

"The last thing on God's green earth that I needed was another man in my life . . .

"I didn't have a clue what to do with the two I had already. The fact that they were, respectively, a Master Vampire and an Ulfric, werewolf king, was only part of the problem . . . They both had my libido, but I was trying to decide who had my heart . . ."

Includes an excerpt from the Anita Blake novel, *Cerulean Sins*

Praise for the novels of

LAURELL K. HAMILTON

featuring Anita Blake, Vampire Hunter

Narcissus in Chains

"Laurell K. Hamilton's sexiest book, and that's saying something . . . The relationships between the characters take center stage." —*St. Louis Post-Dispatch*

"The definitive book in the series . . . Laurell K. Hamilton has written the best book of her career because she gives the audience the answers they have been waiting for. This action-supernatural thriller is a keeper and with the passage of time will be considered a classic." —*BookBrowser*

"In [this novel] tough, sarcastic Anita Blake . . . torn between her inner vamp and wolf makes a final mating choice that no fan will expect . . . Better pounce!"
—*Kirkus Reviews*

"Interesting . . . compelling." —*Locus*

"Amorous." —*Publishers Weekly*

Obsidian Butterfly

"An erotic, demonic thrill ride. Her sexy, edgy, wickedly ironic style sweeps the reader into her unique world and delivers red-hot entertainment. Hamilton's marvelous storytelling can be summed up in three words: Over the top. She blends the genres of romance, horror, and adventure with stunning panache. Great fun!" —Jayne Ann Krentz

"Just when I think that Laurell K. Hamilton can't possibly get any further out on the edge, along she comes with yet another eye-popping blend of hilarious sex, violence, and stuff that makes your hair stand on end. I've never read a writer with a more fertile imagination—and fewer inhibitions about using it!" —Diana Gabaldon

"A monstrously entertaining read." —*Publishers Weekly*

"Hamilton sets a good pace and weaves a nifty tapestry of glowy-eyed monsters against a background of blood."
—*Kirkus Reviews*

"A fast-paced, high-fire-power mix, a nice grisly vacation from Anita's usual relationship problems." —*Locus*

"An abundance of thrills, chills, violence, and sexual innuendo. Recommended." —*Library Journal*

"An R-rated *Buffy the Vampire Slayer* . . . the action never stops . . . the climax is an edge-of-your-seat cliffhanger . . . dessert for the mind, with sprinkles!"
—*The New York Review of Science Fiction*

"*Obsidian*'s greater attention to continuity and detail sharpens Hamilton's trademark intensity and nonstop action." —*Crescent Blues Book Views*

continued . . .

The Killing Dance

"As usual, the plot is full of red herrings . . . also as usual it's a lot of fun, with some significant new developments in Anita's personal life fans of the series won't want to miss."
—*Locus*

Burnt Offerings

"Filled with nonstop action, witty dialog, and steamy sex, this title will appeal to fans of Anne Rice and Tanya Huff."

—*Library Journal*

Blue Moon

"[This] series has to rank as one of the most addictive substances on earth . . . *Blue Moon* is the best book Laurell Hamilton has produced recently."   —*SF Site*

AND DON'T MISS LAURELL K. HAMILTON'S
DEBUT NOVEL

Nightseer

"Sorcerous intrigues, revenge, spellcraft . . . and rapid-fire action. Clever . . . refreshing . . . lively."   —*Dragon*

NARCISSUS IN CHAINS

LAURELL K. HAMILTON

JOVE BOOKS, NEW YORK

THE BERKLEY PUBLISHING GROUP
Published by the Penguin Group
Penguin Group (USA) Inc.
375 Hudson Street, New York, New York 10014, USA
Penguin Group (Canada), 90 Eglinton Avenue East, Suite 700, Toronto, Ontario M4P 2Y3, Canada
(a division of Pearson Penguin Canada Inc.)
Penguin Books Ltd., 80 Strand, London WC2R 0RL, England
Penguin Group Ireland, 25 St. Stephen's Green, Dublin 2, Ireland (a division of Penguin Books Ltd.)
Penguin Group (Australia), 250 Camberwell Road, Camberwell, Victoria 3124, Australia
(a division of Pearson Australia Group Pty. Ltd.)
Penguin Books India Pvt. Ltd., 11 Community Centre, Panchsheel Park, New Delhi—110 017, India
Penguin Group (NZ), Cnr. Airborne and Rosedale Roads, Albany, Auckland 1310, New Zealand
(a division of Pearson New Zealand Ltd.)
Penguin Books (South Africa) (Pty.) Ltd., 24 Sturdee Avenue, Rosebank, Johannesburg 2196,
South Africa

Penguin Books Ltd., Registered Offices: 80 Strand, London WC2R 0RL, England

NARCISSUS IN CHAINS

A Jove Book / published by arrangement with the author

PRINTING HISTORY
Berkley hardcover edition / October 2001
Jove mass-market edition / October 2002

Copyright © 2001 by Laurell K. Hamilton.
Excerpt from *Cerulean Sins* copyright © 2003 by Laurell K. Hamilton.
Cover art by Craig White.
Cover design by Judy Murello.

ISBN: 0-515-13387-6

JOVE®
Jove Books are published by The Berkley Publishing Group,
a division of Penguin Group (USA) Inc.,
375 Hudson Street, New York, New York 10014.
JOVE and the "J" design are trademarks belonging to Penguin Group (USA) Inc.

PRINTED IN THE UNITED STATES OF AMERICA

16 15 14 13 12 11 10 9 8

This one's for J., who renewed my faith in men, love, and happiness. Thank you.

Acknowledgments

To my writing group, who didn't get to see this one before it went to New York. Tom Drennan, Rett Mac-Pherson, Deborah Millitello, Marella Sands, Sharon Shinn, and Mark Sumner. May this be the last book that doesn't get to go through the group due to time constraints, or any other reason. Thanks to Joan-Marie Knappenberger for letting Trinity come over to play with Melissa while I did last-minute things. Thanks to Darla Cook, who helps keep me sane, and Robin Bell, for almost the same reason. Thanks to all the fans for their enthusiasm. Anita and I, both, appreciate it.

1

JUNE HAD COME in like its usual hot, sweaty self, but a freak cold front had moved in during the night and the car radio had been full of the record low temperatures. It was only in the low sixties, not that cold, but after weeks of eighty- and ninety-plus, it felt downright frigid. My best friend, Ronnie Sims, and I were sitting in my Jeep with the windows down, letting the unseasonably cool air drift in on us. Ronnie had turned thirty tonight. We were talking about how she felt about the big 3-0 and other girl talk. Considering that she's a private detective and I raise the dead for a living it was pretty ordinary talk. Sex, guys, turning thirty, vampires, werewolves. You know, the usual.

We could have gone inside the house, but there is something about the intimacy of a car after dark that makes you want to linger. Or maybe it was the sweet smell of springlike air coming through the windows like the caress of some half-remembered lover.

"Okay, so he's a werewolf. No one's perfect," Ronnie said. "Date him, sleep with him, marry him. My vote's for Richard."

"I know you don't like Jean-Claude."

"Don't like him!" Her hands gripped the passenger-side door handle, squeezing it until I could see the tension in her shoulders. I think she was counting to ten.

"If I killed as easily as you do, I'd have killed that son of a bitch two years ago and your life would be a lot less complicated now."

That last was an understatement. But . . . "I don't want him dead, Ronnie."

"He's a vampire, Anita. He *is* dead." She turned and looked at me in the dark. Her soft gray eyes and yellow hair had turned to silver and near white in the cold light of the stars. The shadows and bright reflected light left her face in bold relief, like some modern painting. But the look on her face was almost frightening. There was a fearful determination there.

If it had been me with that look on my face, I'd have warned me not to do anything stupid, like kill Jean-Claude. But Ronnie wasn't a shooter. She'd killed twice, both times to save my life. I owed her. But she wasn't a person who could hunt someone down in cold blood and kill him. Not even a vampire. I knew this about her, so I didn't have to caution her. "I used to think I knew what dead was or wasn't, Ronnie." I shook my head. "The line isn't so clear-cut."

"He seduced you," she said.

I looked away from her angry face and stared at the foil-wrapped swan in my lap. Deirdorfs and Hart, where we'd had dinner, got creative with their doggy bags: foil-wrapped animals. I couldn't argue with Ronnie, and I was getting tired of trying.

Finally, I said, "Every lover seduces you, Ronnie, that's the way it works."

She slammed her hands so hard onto the dashboard it startled me and must have hurt her. "Damn it, Anita, it's not the same."

I was starting to get angry, and I didn't want to be angry, not with Ronnie. I had taken her out to dinner to make her feel better, not to fight. Louis Fane, her steady boyfriend, was out of town at a conference, and she was bummed about that, and about turning thirty. So I'd tried to make her feel better, and she seemed determined to make me feel worse.

"Look, I haven't seen either Jean-Claude or Richard for six months. I'm not dating either of them, so we can skip the lecture on vampire ethics."

"Now that's an oxymoron," she said.

"What is?" I asked.

"Vampire ethics," she said.

I frowned at her. "That's not fair, Ronnie."

"You are a vampire executioner, Anita. You are the one

who taught me that they aren't just people with fangs. They are monsters."

I'd had enough. I opened the car door and slid to the edge of the seat. Ronnie grabbed my shoulder. "Anita, I'm sorry. I'm sorry. Please don't be mad."

I didn't turn around. I sat there with my feet hanging out the door, the cool air creeping into the closer warmth of the car.

"Then drop it, Ronnie. I mean drop it."

She leaned over and gave me a quick hug from behind. "I'm sorry. It's none of my business who you sleep with."

I leaned into the hug for a moment. "That's right, it's not." Then I pulled away and got out of the car. My high heels crunched on the gravel of my driveway. Ronnie had wanted us to dress up, so we had. It was her birthday. It wasn't until after dinner that I'd realized her diabolical scheme. She'd had me wear heels and a nice little black skirt outfit. The top was actually, gasp, a well-fitted halter top. Or would that be backless evening wear? However pricey it was, it was still a very short skirt and a halter top. Ronnie had helped me pick the outfit out about a week ago. I should have known her innocent "oh, let's just both dress up" was a ruse. There had been other dresses that covered more skin and had longer hemlines, but none that camouflaged the belly-band holster that cut across my lower waist. I'd actually taken the holster along with us on the shopping trip, just to be sure. Ronnie thought I was being paranoid, but I don't go anywhere after dark unarmed. Period.

The skirt was just roomy enough and black enough to hide the fact that I wore the belly band and a Firestar 9 mm. The top was heavy enough material, what there was of it, that you really couldn't see the handle of the gun under the cloth. All I had to do was lift the bottom of the top and the gun was right there, ready to be drawn. It was the most user-friendly dressy outfit I'd ever owned. Made me wish they made it in a different color so I could have two of them.

Ronnie's plan had been to go to a club on her birthday. A dance club. Eek. I never went to clubs. I did not dance. But I went in with her. Yes, she got me out on the floor, mainly because her dancing alone was attracting too much unwanted male attention. At least with both of us dancing together the would-be Casanovas stayed at a distance. Though saying I danced was inaccurate. I stood there and sort of swayed. Ronnie danced. She danced like it was her last night on Earth and she had to put every muscle to good use. It was spectacular, and a little frightening. There was something almost desperate to it, as if Ronnie felt the cold hand of time creeping up faster and faster. Or maybe that was just me projecting my own insecurities. I'd turned twenty-six early in the year, and, frankly, at the rate I was going, I probably wouldn't have to worry about hitting thirty. Death cures all ills. Well, most of them.

There had been one man who had attached himself to me instead of Ronnie. I didn't understand why. She was a tall leggy blond, dancing like she was having sex with the music. But he offered me drinks. I don't drink. He tried to slow dance. I refused. I finally had to be rude. Ronnie told me to dance with him, at least he was human. I told her that birthday guilt only went so far, and she'd used hers up.

The last thing on God's green earth that I needed was another man in my life. I didn't have a clue what to do with the two I had already. The fact that they were, respectively, a Master Vampire and an Ulfric, werewolf king, was only part of the problem. That fact alone should let you know just how deep a hole I was digging. Or would that be, already have dug? Yeah, already dug. I was about halfway to China and still throwing dirt up in the air.

I'd been celibate for six months. So, as far as I knew, had they. Everyone was waiting for me to make up my mind. Waiting for me to choose, or decide, something, anything.

I'd been a rock for half a year, because I'd stayed away from them. I hadn't seen them, in the flesh anyway. I had returned no phone calls. I had run for the hills at the first hint of cologne. Why such drastic measures? Frankly, because almost every time I saw them, I fell off the chastity wagon. They both had my libido, but I was trying to decide who had my heart. I still didn't know. The only thing I had decided was that it was time to stop hiding. I had to see them and figure out what we were all going to do. I'd decided two weeks ago that I needed to see them. It was the day that I refilled my birth-control pill prescription, and started taking it again. The very last thing I needed was a surprise pregnancy. That the first thing I thought of when I thought of Richard and Jean-Claude was to go back on birth control tells you something about the effect they had on me.

You needed to be on the pill for at least a month to be safe, or as safe as you ever got. Four more weeks, five to be sure, then I'd call. Maybe.

I heard Ronnie's heels running on the gravel. "Anita, Anita, wait, don't be angry."

The thing was, I wasn't angry with her. I was angry with me. Angry that after all these months I still couldn't decide between the two men. I stopped walking and waited for her, huddled in my little black skirt outfit, the little foil swan in my hands. The night had turned cool enough to make me wish I'd worn a jacket. When Ronnie caught up with me I started walking again.

"I'm not mad, Ronnie, just tired. Tired of you, my family, Dolph, Zerbrowski, everyone being so damned judgmental." My heels hit the sidewalk with sharp *clacks*. Jean-Claude had once said he could tell if I was angry just by the sound of my heels on the floor. "Watch your step. You're wearing higher heels than I am." Ronnie was five feet eight, which meant with heels she was nearly six feet.

I was wearing two-inch heels, which put me at five five. I get a much better workout when Ronnie and I jog together than she does.

The phone was ringing as I juggled the key and the foil-wrapped leftovers. Ronnie took the leftovers, and I shoved the door open with my shoulder. I was running across the floor in my high heels before I remembered that I was on vacation. Which meant whatever emergency was calling at 2:05 in the morning was not my problem, not for another two weeks at least. But old habits die hard, and I was at the phone before I remembered. I actually let the machine pick up while I stood there, heart pounding. I was planning on ignoring it, but . . . but I still stood ready to grab the receiver just in case.

Loud, booming music, and a man's voice. I didn't recognize the music, but I recognized the voice. "Anita, it's Gregory. Nathaniel's in trouble."

Gregory was one of the wereleopards I'd inherited when I killed their alpha, their leader. As a human, I wasn't really up to the job, but until I found a replacement, even I was better than nothing. Wereanimals without a dominant to protect them were anyone's meat, and if someone moved in and slaughtered them, it would sort of be my fault. So I acted as their protector, but the job was more complicated than I'd ever dreamed. Nathaniel was the problem. All the others were rebuilding their lives since their old leader had been killed, but not Nathaniel. He'd had a hard life: abused, raped, pimped out, and topped. Topped meant he'd been someone's slave—as in sex and pain. He was one of the few true submissives I'd ever met, though, admittedly, my pool of acquaintance was limited.

I cursed softly and picked up the phone. "I'm here, Gregory, what's happened now?" Even to me, my voice sounded tired and half-angry.

"If I had anyone else to call, Anita, I'd call them, but you're it." He sounded tired and angry, too. Great.

"Where's Elizabeth? She was supposed to be riding herd on Nathaniel tonight." I'd finally agreed that Nathaniel could start going out to the dominance and submission clubs if he was accompanied by Elizabeth and at least one other wereleopard. Tonight it had been Gregory riding shotgun, but without Elizabeth, Gregory wasn't dominant enough to keep Nathaniel safe. A normal submissive would have been safe in one of the clubs with someone there to simply say, "no thanks, we'll pass." But Nathaniel was one of those rare subs who are almost incapable of saying no, and there had been hints made that his idea of pain and sex could be very extreme. Which meant that he might say yes to things that were very, very bad for him. Wereanimals can take a lot of injury and not be permanently damaged, but there is a limit. A healthy bottom will say *stop* when he's had too much or he feels something bad happening, but Nathaniel wasn't that healthy. So he had keepers with him to make sure no one really bad got ahold of him. But it was more than that. A good dominant trusts his sub to say *when* before the damage is too great. The dom trusts the sub to know his own body and have enough self-preservation to call out before he is in past what his body can take. Nathaniel did not come with that safety feature, which meant a dominant with the best of intentions could end up hurting him badly before realizing Nathaniel wouldn't help himself.

I actually had accompanied Nathaniel a few times. As his Nimir-ra it was sort of my job to interview prospective . . . keepers. I'd gone prepared for the clubs to be one of the lower circles of hell and had been pleasantly shocked. I'd had more trouble with sexual propositions in a normal bar on a Saturday night. In the clubs everyone was very careful not to impose on you or to be seen as pushy. It was a small community, and if you got a reputation for being obnoxious, you could find yourself blacklisted, with no one to play with. I'd found the people in the scene were polite, and once you made it clear you were not there to play, no one bothered you, except tourists. Tourists were posers, people not really into the scene, who liked to dress up and frequent the clubs. They didn't know the rules, and hadn't bothered to ask. They probably thought a woman who would come to a place like this would do anything. I'd persuaded them differently. But I'd had to stop going with Nathaniel. The other wereleopards said I gave off so much dominant vibe that no dominant would ever approach Nathaniel while I was with him. Though we'd had offers for ménage à trois of every description. I felt like I needed a button that said, "No, I don't want to have a bondage three-way with you, thanks for asking, though."

Elizabeth had supposedly been dominant, but not too much to take Nathaniel out and try to pick him up a . . . date.

"Elizabeth left," Gregory said.

"Without Nathaniel?" I made it a question.

"Yes."

"Well, that just fries my bacon," I said.

"What?" he asked.

"I'm angry with Elizabeth."

"It gets better," he said.

"How much better can it be, Gregory? You all assured me that these clubs were safe. A little bondage, a little light slap and tickle. You all convinced me that I couldn't keep Nathaniel away from it indefinitely. You said that they had ways to monitor the area so no one could possibly get hurt. That's what you and Zane and Cherry told me. Hell, I've seen it myself. There are safety monitors everywhere, it's safer than some dates I've had, so what could have possibly gone wrong?"

"We couldn't have anticipated this," he said.

"Just get to the end of the story, Gregory, the foreplay is getting tedious."

There was silence for longer than there should have been, just the overly loud music. "Gregory, are you still there?"

"Gregory is indisposed," a man's voice said.

"Who is this?"

"I am Marco, if that helps you, though I doubt that it does." His voice was cultured—American, but upper crusty.

"New in town are you?" I asked.

"Something like that," he said.

"Welcome to town. Make sure you go up in the Arch while you're here, it's a nice view. But what has your recent arrival in St. Louis got to do with me and mine?"

"We didn't realize it was your pet we had at first. He wasn't the one we were hunting for, but now that we have him, we're keeping him."

"You can't 'keep' him," I said.

"Come down and take him away from us, if you can." That strangely smooth voice made the threat all the more effective. There was no anger, nothing personal. It sounded like business, and I had no clue what it was about.

"Put Gregory back on," I said.

"I don't think so. He's enjoying some personal time with my friends right now."

"How do I know he's still alive?" My voice was as unemotional as his. I wasn't feeling anything yet; it was too sudden, too unexpected, like coming in on the middle of a movie.

"No one's dead, yet," the man said.

"How do I know that?"

He was quiet for a second, then, "What sort of people are you used to dealing with, that you would ask if we've killed him first thing?"

"It's been a rough year. Now put Gregory on the phone, because until I know he's alive, and he tells me the others are, this negotiation is stalled."

"How do you know we are negotiating?" Marco asked.

"Call it a hunch."

"My, you are direct."

"You have no idea how direct I can be, Marco. Put Gregory on the phone."

There was the music-filled silence, and more music, but no voices. "Gregory, Gregory, are you there? Is anyone there?" Shit, I thought.

"I'm afraid that your kitty-cat won't squawl for us. A point of pride, I think."

"Put the reciever to his ear and let me talk to him."

"As you wish."

More of the loud music. I spoke as if I was sure that Gregory was listening. "Gregory, I need to know you're alive. I need to know that Nathaniel and everyone else is alive. Talk to me, Gregory."

His voice came squeezed tight, as if he were gritting his teeth. "Yesss."

"Yes, what, they're all alive?"

"Yess."

"What are they doing to you?"

He screamed into the phone, and the sound raised the hairs on my neck and danced down my arms in goosebumps. The sound stopped abruptly. "Gregory, Gregory!" I was yelling against the techno-beat of the music, but no one was answering.

Marco came back on the line. "They are all alive, if not quite well. The one they call Nathaniel is a lovely young man, all that long auburn hair and the most extraordinary violet eyes. So pretty, it would be a shame to spoil all that beauty. Of course, this one is lovely too, blond, blue-eyed. Someone told me that they both work as strippers? Is that true?"

I wasn't numb anymore, I was scared, and angry, and I still had not a clue to why this was happening. My voice came out almost even, almost calm. "Yeah, it's true. You're new in town, Marco, so you don't know me. But trust me, you don't want to do this."

"Perhaps not, but my alpha does."

Ah, shapeshifter politics. I hated shapeshifter politics. "Why? The wereleopards are no threat to anyone."

"Ours is not to reason why, ours is but to do and die."

A literate kidnapper, refreshing. "What do you want, Marco?"

"My alpha wants you to come down and rescue your cats, if you can."

"What club are you at?"

"Narcissus in Chains." And he hung up.

2

"DAMN IT!"

"What's happened?" Ronnie asked. I'd almost forgotten her. She didn't belong in this part of my life, but there she was, leaning against the kitchen cabinets, searching my face, looking worried.

"I'll take care of it."

She gripped my arm. "You gave me this speech about wanting your friends back, about not wanting to push us all away. Did you mean it, or was it just talk?"

I took a deep breath and let it out. I told her what the other side of the conversation had been.

"And you don't have any clue what this is about?" she asked.

"No, I don't."

"That's odd. Usually stuff like this builds up, it doesn't just drop out of the blue."

I nodded. "I know."

"Star 69 will ring back whatever number just called you."

"What good will that do?"

"It will let you know if they're really at this club, or whether it's just a trap for you."

"Not just another pretty face, are you?" I said.

She smiled. "I'm a trained detective. We know about these things." The humor didn't quite reach her eyes, but she was trying.

I dialed, and the phone rang for what seemed forever, then another male voice answered, "Yeah."

"Is this Narcissus in Chains?"

"Yeah, who's this?"

"I need to speak with Gregory?"

"Don't know any Gregory," he said.

"Who is this?" I asked.

"This is a freaking pay phone, lady. I just picked up." Then he hung up, too. It seemed to be my night for it.

"They called from a pay phone at the club," I said.

"Well, at least you know where they are," Ronnie said.

"Do you know where the club is?" I asked.

Ronnie shook her head. "Not my kind of scene."

"Mine either." In fact the only card-carrying dominance and submission players that I knew personally were all at the club waiting to be saved.

Who did I know that might know where the club was, and something about its reputation? I couldn't trust what the wereleopards had told me about it being a safe place. Obviously, they'd been wrong.

One name sprang to mind. The only one I knew to call that might know where Narcissus in Chains was, and what kind of trouble I'd be in if I went inside. Jean-Claude. Since I was dealing with shapeshifter politics it might have made sense to call Richard, with him being a werewolf and all. But the shapeshifters were a very clannish lot. One type of animal rarely crossed boundaries to help another. Frustrating, but true. The exception was the treaty between the werewolves and the wererats, but everyone else was left to fend, and squabble, and bleed, among themselves. Oh, if some small group got out of hand and attracted too much unwanted police attention, the wolves and rats would discipline them, but short of that, no one seemed to want to interfere with each other. That was one of the reasons I was still stuck baby-sitting the wereleopards.

Also, Richard didn't know any more about the D and S subculture than I did, maybe less. If you're wanting to ask questions about the sexual fringe, Jean-Claude is definitely your guy. He may not participate, but he seems to know who's doing what, and to whom, and where. Or I hoped he did. If it had just been my life at stake, I probably wouldn't have called either of the boys, but if I got killed doing this, that left no one to rescue Nathaniel and the rest. Unacceptable.

Ronnie had kicked off her high heels. "I didn't bring my gun, but I'm sure you have a spare."

I shook my head. "You're not going."

Anger makes her gray eyes the color of storm clouds. "The hell I'm not."

"Ronnie, these are shapeshifters, and you're human."

"So are you," she said.

"Because of Jean-Claude's vampire marks, I'm a little more than that. I can take damage that would kill you."

"You can't go in there alone," she said. Her arms were crossed under her breasts, her face set in angry, stubborn lines.

"I don't plan on going in alone."

"It's because I'm not a shooter, isn't it?"

"You don't kill easily, Ronnie, no shame in that, but I can't take you into a gang of shapeshifters unless I know that you'll shoot to kill if you have to." I gripped her upper arms. She stayed stiff and angry under my touch. "It would kill a piece of me to lose you, Ronnie. It would kill a bigger piece to know that you died because of some shit of mine. You can't hesitate with these people. You can't treat them like they're human. If you do, you die."

She was shaking her head. "Call the police."

I stepped away from her. "No."

"Damn it, Anita, damn it!"

"Ronnie, there are rules, and one of those rules is you don't take pack or pard business to the police." The main reason for that rule was that the police tended to frown on fights for dominance that ended with dead bodies on the ground, but no need to tell Ronnie that.

"It's a stupid rule," she said.

"Maybe, but it's still the way business is done with the shifters, no matter what flavor they are."

She sat down at the small two-seater breakfast table, on its little raised platform. "Who's going to be your backup then? Richard doesn't kill any easier than I do."

That was half true, but I let it slide. "No, I want someone at my back tonight who will do what needs doing, no flinching."

Her eyes were dark, dark with anger. "Jean-Claude." She made his name a curse.

I nodded.

"Are you sure he didn't plan this to get you back into his life, excuse me, death?"

"He knows me too well to screw with my people. He knows what I'd do if he hurt them."

Puzzlement flowed through the anger, softening her eyes, her face. "I hate him, but I know you love him. Could you really kill him? Could you really stare down the barrel of a gun and pull the trigger on him?"

I just looked at her, and I knew without a mirror that my eyes had grown distant, cold. It's hard for brown eyes to be cold, but I'd been managing it lately.

Something very like fear slid behind her eyes. I don't know if she was afraid for me, or of me. I preferred the first to the last. "You could do it. Jesus, Anita. You've known Jean-Claude longer than I've known Louie. I could never hurt Louie, no matter what he did."

I shrugged. "It would destroy me to do it, I think. It's not like I'd live happily ever after, if I survived at all. There's a very real chance that the vampire marks would drag me down to the grave with him."

"Another good reason not to kill him," she said.

"If he's behind the scream that Gregory gave over the phone, then he'll need better reasons to keep breathing than love, or lust, or my possible death."

"I don't understand that, Anita. I don't understand that at all."

"I know," I said. And I thought to myself it was one of the reasons Ronnie and I hadn't been seeing as much of each other as we once had. I got tired of explaining myself to her. No, of justifying myself to her.

You're my friend, my best friend, I thought. But I don't understand you anymore.

"Ronnie, I can't arm wrestle shapeshifters and vampires. I will lose a fair fight. The only way I survive, the only way my leopards survive, is because the other shifters fear me. They fear my threat. I'm only as good as my threat, Ronnie."

"So you'll go down there and kill them."

"I didn't say that."

"But you will."

"I'll try to avoid it," I said.

She tucked her knees up, wrapping her arms around those long legs. She'd managed to get a tiny prick in one of the hose; the hole was shiny with clear nail polish. She'd carried the polish in her purse for just such emergencies. I'd carried a gun and hadn't even taken a purse.

"If you get arrested, call, and I'll bail you out."

I shook my head. "If I get caught wasting three or more people in a public area, there won't be any bail tonight. The police probably won't even finish questioning me until long past dawn."

"How can you be so calm about this?" she asked.

I was beginning to remember why Ronnie and I had started drifting apart. I'd had almost the exact conversation with Richard once when an assassin had come to town to kill me. I gave the same answer. "Having hysterics won't help anything, Ronnie."

"But you're not angry about it."

"Oh, I am angry," I said.

She shook her head. "No, I mean you're not outraged that this is happening. You don't seem surprised, not like . . ." She shrugged. "Not like you should be."

"You mean not like you would be." I held up a hand before she could answer. "I don't have time to debate moral philosophy, Ronnie." I picked up the phone. "I'm going to call Jean-Claude."

"I keep urging you to dump the vampire and marry Richard, but maybe there's more than one reason why you can't let him go."

I dialed the number for Circus of the Damned from memory, and Ronnie just kept talking to my back. "Maybe you're not willing to give up a lover who's colder than you are."

The phone was ringing. "There are clean sheets on the guest bed, Ronnie. Sorry I won't be able to share girl talk tonight." I kept my back to her.

I heard her stand in a crinkle of skirts and knew when she walked out. I kept my back facing the room until I knew she was gone. It wouldn't do either of us any good to let her see me cry.

3

JEAN-CLAUDE WASN'T AT the Circus of the Damned. The voice on the other end of the phone at the Circus didn't recognize me and wouldn't believe I was Anita Blake, Jean-Claude's sometimes sweetie. So I'd been reduced to calling his other businesses. I'd tried Guilty Pleasures, his strip club, but he wasn't there. I tried Danse Macabre, his newest enterprise, but I was beginning to wonder if Jean-Claude had simply told everyone that he wasn't in if I called.

The thought bothered me a lot. I'd worried that after so long Richard might finally tell me to go to hell, that he'd had enough of my indecision. It had never occurred to me that Jean-Claude might not wait. If I was so unsure how I felt about him, why was my stomach squeezed tight with a growing sense of loss? The feeling had nothing to do with the wereleopards and their problems. It had everything to do with me and the fact that I suddenly felt lost. But it turned out he was at Danse Macabre, and he took my call. I had a moment for my stomach to unclench and my breath to ease out, then he was on the phone, and I was struggling to keep my metaphysical shields in place.

I hated metaphysics. Preternatural biology is still biology, metaphysics is magic, and I'm still not comfortable with it. For six months when I wasn't working, I was meditating, studying with a very wise psychic named Marianne, learning ritual magic, so I could control my God-given abilities. And so I could block the marks that bound me to Richard and Jean-Claude. An aura is like your personal protection, your personal energy. When it's healthy it keeps you safe like skin, but you get a hole in it, and infection can get inside. My aura had two holes in it, one for each of the men. I suspected that their auras had holes in them, too. Which put us all at risk. I'd blocked up my holes. Then only a few weeks ago, I'd come up against a nasty creature, a would-be god, a new category, even for me. It had been powerful enough to strip all my careful work away, leaving me raw and open again. Only the intervention of a local witch had saved me from being eaten from the aura down. I didn't have six more months of celibacy, meditation, and patience in me. The holes were there, and the only way to fill them was with Jean-Claude and Richard. That's what Marianne said, and I trusted her in a way that I trusted few others.

Jean-Claude's voice hit me over the phone like a velvet slap. My breath caught in my throat, and I could do nothing but feel the flow of his voice, the presence of him, like something alive, flowing over my skin. His voice has always been one of Jean-Claude's best things, but this was ridiculous. This was over the phone. How could I possibly see him in person and maintain my shields, let alone my composure?

"I know you are there, *ma petite*. Did you call merely to hear the sound of my voice?"

That was closer to the truth than was comfortable. "No, no." I still couldn't gather my thoughts. I was like an athlete who had let her training go. I just couldn't lift the same amount of weight, and there was weight to wading through Jean-Claude's power.

When I still didn't say anything, he spoke again. "*Ma petite,* to what do I owe this honor? Why have you deigned to call me?" His voice was bland, but there was a hint of something in it. Reproach perhaps.

I guess I had it coming. I rallied the troops and tried to sound like an intelligent human being, not always one of my best things. "It's been six months . . ."

"I am aware of that, *ma petite*."

He was being condescending. I hated that. It made me a little angry. The anger helped clear my head a little. "If you'll stop interrupting, I'll tell you why I called."

"My heart is all aflutter with anticipation."

I wanted to hang up. He was being an asshole, and part of me thought I might deserve the treatment, which made me even angrier. I'm always angriest when I think I'm in the wrong. I'd been a coward for months, and I was still a coward. I was afraid to be close to him, afraid of what I'd do. Damn it, Anita, get ahold of yourself. "Sarcasm is my department," I said.

"And what is my department?"

"I'm about to ask you for a favor," I said.

"Really?" He said it as if he might not grant it.

"Please, Jean-Claude, I'm asking for help. I don't do that often."

"That is certainly true. What would you have of me, *ma petite*? You know that you have but to ask, and it will be yours. No matter how angry I may be with you."

I let that comment go, because I didn't know what to do about it. "Do you know a club called Narcissus in Chains?"

He was quiet for a second or two. *"Oui."*

"Can you give me directions and meet me there?"

"Do you know what sort of a club this place is?"

"Yeah."

"Are you sure?"

"It's a bondage club, I know."

"Unless the last six months has changed you greatly, *ma petite,* that is not one of your preferences."

"Not mine, no."

"Your wereleopards are misbehaving again?"

"Something like that." I told him what had happened.

"I do not know this Marco."

"I didn't figure you did."

"But you did think that I knew where the club was?"

"I was hoping."

"I will meet you there with some of my people. Or will you allow only me to ride to your rescue?" He sounded amused now, which was better than angry, I guess.

"Bring who you need."

"You trust my judgment?"

"In this, yeah."

"But not in all things," he said softly.

"I don't trust anyone in all things, Jean-Claude."

He sighed. "So young to be so . . . jaded."

"I'm cynical, not jaded."

"And the difference is what, *ma petite*?"

"You're jaded."

He laughed then, the sound caressing me like the brush of a hand. It made things low in my body clench. "Ah," he said, "that explains all the differences."

"Just give me directions, please." I added the "please" to speed things along.

"They will not harm your wereleopards too greatly, I think. The club is run by shapeshifters, and they will smell too much blood and take matters into their own hands. It is one of the reasons Narcissus in Chains is no-man's-land, a neutral place for the fringe of our groups. Your leopards were right, it is usually a very safe place."

"Well, Gregory wasn't screaming because he felt safe."

"Perhaps not, but I know the owner. Narcissus would be very angry if someone became overzealous in his club."

"Narcissus, I don't know the name. Well, I know the Greek mythology stuff, but I don't recognize it as local."

"I would not expect you to. He does not often leave his club. But I will call him, and he will patrol your cats for you. He will not rescue them, but he will make sure no further damage is done."

"You trust Narcissus to do this?"

"Oui."

Jean-Claude had his faults, but if he trusted someone, he was usually right. "Okay. And thank you."

"You are most welcome." He drew a breath, then said quietly, "Would you have called if you had not needed my help? Would you ever have called?"

I'd been dreading this question from either Jean-Claude or Richard. But I finally had an answer. "I'll answer your question as best I can, but call it a hunch, it may be a long conversation. I need to know my people are safe before we start dissecting our relationship."

"Relationship? Is that what we have?" His voice was very dry.

"Jean-Claude."

"No, no, *ma petite,* I will call Narcissus now and save

your cats but only if you promise that when I call back we will finish this conversation."

"Promise."

"Your word," he said.

"Yes."

"Very well, *ma petite,* until we speak again." He hung up.

I hung up the phone and stood there. Was it cowardly to want to call someone else, anyone else, so the phone would be busy and we wouldn't have to have our little talk? Yeah, it was cowardly, but tempting. I hated talking about my personal life, especially to the people most intimately involved in it. I had just about enough time to change out of the skirt outfit when the phone rang. I jumped and answered it with my pulse in my throat. I was really dreading this conversation.

"Hello," I said.

"Narcissus will see to your cats' safety. Now, where were we?" He was silent for a heartbeat. "Oh, yes, would you ever have called if you had not needed my help?"

"The woman I'm studying with . . ."

"Marianne," he said.

"Yes, Marianne. Anyway, she says that I can't keep blocking the holes in my aura. That the only way to be safe from preternatural creepy-crawlies is to fill the holes with what they were meant to hold."

Silence on the other end of the phone. Silence for so long that I said, "Jean-Claude, you still there?"

"I am here."

"You don't sound happy about this."

"Do you know what you are saying, Anita?" It was always a bad sign when he used my real name.

"I think so."

"I want this very clear between us, *ma petite.* I do not want you coming back to me later, crying that you did not understand how tightly this would bind us. If you allow Richard and me to truly fill the marks upon your . . . body, we will share our auras. Our energy. Our magic."

"We're already doing that, Jean-Claude."

"In part, *ma petite,* but those are side effects of the marks. This will be a willing, knowledgeable joining. Once done, I do not think it can be undone without great damage to all of us."

It was my turn to sigh. "How many vampire challenges to your authority have there been while I've been off meditating?"

"A few," he said, voice cautious.

"More than a few I'd bet, because they sensed that your defenses are not complete. You had trouble backing them down without killing them, didn't you?"

"Let us say that I am glad that there were no serious challengers over the last year."

"You'd have lost without Richard and me to back you up, and you couldn't shield yourself without us there to touch. That worked when I was in town with you. Touching, being with each other helped us plug in to each other's power. It offset the problem."

"Oui," he said, softly.

"I didn't know, Jean-Claude. I'm not sure it would have made a difference, but I didn't know. God, Richard must be desperate—he doesn't kill like we do. His bluff is all that keeps the werewolves from tearing each other apart, and with two gaping holes in his most intimate defenses . . ." I let my voice trail off, but I still remembered the cold horror I'd felt when I realized how much I'd endangered all of us.

"Richard has had difficulties, *ma petite.* But we each have only one chink in our armor, the one that only you can heal. He was driven to merge his energies with mine. As you say, his bluff is very important to him."

"I didn't know, and I'm sorry for that. All I've been thinking about was how scared I was of being overwhelmed by the two of you. Marianne told me the truth when she thought I was ready to hear it."

"And are you done being frightened of us, *ma petite*?" His voice was careful when he asked, as if he were carrying a very full cup of very hot liquid up a long and narrow staircase.

I shook my head, realized he couldn't see it, and said,

"I'm not brave. I'm pretty much terrified. Terrified that if I do this, there is no going back, that maybe I'm fooling myself about a choice. Maybe there is no choice and hasn't been for a long time. But however we end up arranging the bedrooms, I can't let us all go around with gaping metaphysical wounds. Too many things will sense the weakness and exploit it."

"Like the creature you met in New Mexico," he said, voice still as cautious as I'd ever heard it.

"Yeah," I said.

"Are you saying that tonight you will agree to letting us merge the marks, that we will at last close these, as you so colorfully put it, wounds?"

"If it doesn't endanger my leopards, yeah. We need to do it as soon as possible. I'd hate to make the big decision and then have one of us get killed before we could batten down the hatches."

I heard him sigh, as if some great tension had left him. "You do not know how long I have waited for you to understand all this."

"You could have told me."

"You would not have believed me. You would have thought it was another trick to bind you closer to me."

"You're right, I wouldn't have believed you."

"Will Richard be meeting us at the club, as well?"

I was quiet for a heartbeat. "No, I'm not going to call him."

"Why ever not? It is a shapeshifter difficulty more than a vampire one."

"You know why not."

"You fear he will be too squeamish to allow you to do what needs doing to save your leopards."

"Yeah."

"Perhaps," Jean-Claude said.

"You aren't going to tell me to call him?"

"Why would I ask you to invite my chief rival for your affections to this little tête-à-tête? That would be foolish. I am many things, but foolish is not one of them."

That was certainly true. "Okay, give me directions, and I'll meet you and your people at the club."

"First, *ma petite,* what are you wearing?"

"Excuse me?"

"Clothes, *ma petite,* what clothes are you wearing?"

"Is this a joke? Because I don't have time . . ."

"It is not an idle question, *ma petite.* The sooner you answer, the sooner we can all leave."

I wanted to argue, but if Jean-Claude said he had a point he probably did. I told him what I was wearing.

"You surprise me, *ma petite.* With a little effort it should do nicely."

"What effort?"

"I suggest you add boots to your ensemble. The ones I purchased for you would do very well."

"I am not wearing five-inch spikes anywhere, Jean-Claude. I'd break an ankle."

"I planned on you wearing those boots just for me, *ma petite.* I was thinking of the other boots with the milder heels that I bought when you were so very angry about the others."

Oh. "Why do I have to change shoes?"

"Because, delicate flower that you are, you have the eyes of a policeman, and so it would be better if you wore leather boots instead of high heels. It would be better if you remember that you are trying to move through the club as quickly and smoothly as possible. No one will help you find your leopards if they think you are an outsider, especially a policeman."

"Nobody ever mistakes me for a cop."

"No, but they begin to mistake you for something that smells of guns and death. Look harmless tonight, *ma petite,* until it is time to be dangerous."

"I thought this friend of yours, this Narcissus, would just escort us in."

"He is not my friend, and I told you the club is neutral ground. Narcissus will see that no great harm comes to your cats, but that is all. He will not let you come barging in to his world like the proverbial bull in the china shop. That, he will not allow, nor will he allow us to bring in a small army of our own. He is the leader of the werehyenas, and they are the only army allowed inside the club. There is no Ulfric, or

Master of the City, within its walls. You have only the dominance you bring with you and your body to see you through."

"I'll have a gun," I said.

"But a gun will not get you into the upper rooms."

"What will?"

"Trust me, I will find a way."

I didn't like the sound of that at all. "Why is it that most of the time whenever I ask you for help, it's never a case where we can just run in and start shooting?"

"And why is it, *ma petite,* that when you do not invite me that it is almost always a case where you run in and shoot everything that moves?"

"Point taken," I said.

"What are your priorities for the night?" he asked.

I knew what he meant. "I want the wereleopards safe."

"And if they have been harmed?"

"I want vengeance."

"More than their safety?"

"No, safety first, vengeance is a luxury."

"Good. And if one, or more, is dead?"

"I don't want any of us going to jail, but eventually if not tonight, another night, they die." I listened to myself say it, and knew that I meant it.

"There is no mercy in you, *ma petite.*"

"You say that like it's a bad thing."

"No, it is merely an observation."

I stood there, holding the phone, waiting to be shocked at what I was proposing. But I wasn't. I said, "I don't want to kill anyone if I don't have to."

"That is not true, *ma petite.*"

"Fine, if they've killed my people, I want them dead. But I decided in New Mexico that I didn't want to be a sociopath, so I'm trying to act as if I'm not. So let's try to keep the body count low tonight, okay?"

"As you wish," he said. Then he added, "Do you really think that you can change the nature of what you are merely by wishing it?"

"Are you asking if I can stop being a sociopath, since I already am one?"

A moment of silence, then, "I think that is what I'm asking."

"I don't know, but if I don't pull myself back from the brink soon, Jean-Claude, there won't be any going back."

"I hear fear in your voice, *ma petite*."

"Yeah, you do."

"What do you fear?"

"I fear that by giving in to you and Richard that I'll lose myself. I fear that by not giving in to you and Richard I'll lose one of you. I fear that I'll get us killed because I'm thinking too much. I fear that I'm already a sociopath and there *is* no going back. Ronnie said that one of the reasons that I can't give you up and just settle down with Richard is that I can't give up a boyfriend who's colder than I am."

"I am sorry, *ma petite*." I wasn't sure exactly what he was apologizing for, but I accepted it anyway.

"Me, too. Give me directions to the club, I'll meet you there."

He gave me directions, and I read them back to him. We hung up. Neither of us said good-bye. Once upon a time we'd have ended the conversation with *je t'aime,* I love you. Once upon a time.

4

THE CLUB WAS over the river on the Illinois side, along with most of the other questionable clubs. Vampire-run businesses got a grandfather clause to operate in St. Louis proper, but the rest of the human-run clubs—and lycanthropes still counted legally as human—had to go into Illinois to avoid pesky zoning problems. Some of the zoning problems weren't even on the books, weren't even laws at all. But it was strange how many problems the bureaucrats could find when they didn't want a club in their fair city. If the vampires weren't such a big draw for tourists, the bureaucrats'd have probably found a way to get rid of them, too.

I finally found parking about two blocks from the club. It meant a walk to the club in an area of town that most women wouldn't want to be alone in after dark. Of course, most women wouldn't be armed. A gun doesn't cure all ills, but it's a start. I also had a knife sheath around each calf, very high up, so that the hilts came up on the side of my knees. I wasn't really comfortable that way, but I couldn't think of any other place to put knives so I could get to them easily. There was a very good chance I'd have bruises on my knees after tonight. Oh, well. I also had a black belt in Judo, and was making progress in Kenpo, a type of karate, one with fewer power moves and more moves using balance. I was as prepared as I could get for the wilds of the big city.

Of course, I usually don't walk around looking like bait. My skirt was so short that even with boots that came up to mid-thigh there was a good inch between the hem and the top of the boots. I'd put a jacket on for the drive, but had left it in the car because I didn't want to be carrying it around all night. I'd been in just enough clubs, whatever flavor they were, to know that inside it would be hot. So the goosebumps that traveled over my bare back and arms weren't from fear, but from the damp, chill air. I forced myself not to rub my arms as I walked and to at least look like I wasn't cold or uncomfortable. Actually the boots only had two-inch heels, and they were comfortable to walk in. Not as comfortable as my Nikes, but then, what is? But for dress shoes, the boots weren't bad. If I could have left the knives home, they'd have been peachy.

There was one other bit of protection that I'd added. Metaphysical shields come in different varieties. You can shield yourself with almost anything: metal, rock, plants, fire, water, wind, earth, etc. . . . Everyone has different shields because it's a very individual choice. It has to work for your own personal mind-set. You can have two psychics both using stone, but the shields won't be the same. Some people simply visualize rock, the thought of it, its essence, and that's sufficient. If something tries to attack them, they are safe behind the thought of rock. Another psychic might see a stone wall, like a garden wall around an old house, and that would do the same thing. For me, the shield had to be a tower. All shields are like bubbles that surround you completely, just like circles of power. I'd always understood this when I raised the dead, but for shielding I needed to see it in my head. So I imagined a stone tower, completely enclosed, no windows, no chinks, smooth and dark inside with only what I allowed in or out. Talking about shielding always made me feel like I was having a psychotic break and sharing my delusions. But it worked, and when I didn't shield, things tried to hurt me. It had only been in the last two weeks that Marianne had discovered that I hadn't really understood shielding at all. I'd thought it was just a matter of how powerful your aura was and how you could reinforce it. She said the only reason I'd been able to get by with that for as long as I had was that I was simply that powerful. But the shielding goes *outside* the aura like a wall around a castle, an extra defense. The innermost defense is a healthy aura. Hopefully by the end of the night I'd have one of those.

I turned the corner and found a line of people that stretched down the block. Great, just what I needed. I didn't stop at the end of the line, I kept walking towards the door, hoping I'd think of something to tell the doorperson when I got there. I didn't have time to wait through all this. I was about halfway up the line when a figure pushed out of the crowd and called my name.

It took me a second to recognize Jason. First, he'd cut his baby-fine blond hair short, businessman short. Second, he was wearing a sheer silver mesh shirt and a pair of pants that seemed mostly made of the same stuff. Only a thin line of solid silver ran over his groin. The outfit was so eye-catching that it took me a moment to realize just how sheer the cloth was. What I was really seeing wasn't the silver, but Jason's skin through a veil of glitter. The outfit, which left precious little to the imagination, ended in calf-high gray boots.

I had to make myself look at his face, because I was still shaking my head over the outfit. The outfit didn't look comfortable, but of course, Jason rarely complained about his clothes. He was like Jean-Claude's little dress-up werewolf, as well as morning snack. Sometimes bodyguard and sometimes a fetch-and-carry boy. Who else could Jean-Claude get to stand out in the cold, nearly naked?

Jason's eyes looked bigger, bluer somehow, without all the hair to distract your eye. His face looked older with the shorter hair, the bone structure cleaner, and I realized that Jason was perilously close to that line between cute and handsome. He'd been nineteen when we met. Twenty-two looked better on him. But the outfit—there was nothing to do but grin at the outfit.

He was grinning at me, too. I think we were both happy to see each other. In leaving Richard and Jean-Claude I'd left their people behind, too. Jason was Richard's pack member, and Jean-Claude's lap wolf.

"You look like a pornographic space man. If you were wearing street clothes, you might have gotten a hug," I said.

His smile flashed even wider. "I guess I'm dressed for punishment. Jean-Claude told me to wait for you and take you in. My hand's already got a stamp on it so we can just go straight inside."

"A little cold for the clothes, isn't it?"

"Why do you think I was standing deep in the crowd?" He offered me his arm. "May I escort you inside, my lady?"

I took his arm with my left hand. Jason put his free hand on top of mine, doing a double hold. If that was the worst teasing he did tonight, then he'd grown up some. The silver cloth was rougher than it looked, scratchy where it rubbed against my arm.

As Jason led me up the steps, I had to look behind him. The cloth that covered his groin was only a thin thong at the back, leaving nothing but a fine glitter over his butt. The shirt was not attached to the pants, so as he moved I got glimpses of his stomach. In fact the shirt was loose enough through the shoulders that when he took my arm the shirt pulled to one side, revealing his smooth, pale shoulder.

The music hit me at the door like a giant's slap. It was almost a wall we had to move through. I hadn't expected Narcissus in Chains to be a dance club. But except for the patrons' clothing being more exotic and running high to leather, it looked like a lot of other clubs. The place was large, dimly lit, dark in the corners, with too many people pushed into too small a space, moving their bodies frantically to music that was way too loud.

My hand tightened just a touch on Jason's arm, because truthfully I always feel a little overwhelmed by places like this. At least for the first few minutes. It's like I need a depth chamber between the outside world and the inside world, a moment to breath deep and adjust. But these clubs are not designed to give you time. They just bombard you with sensory overload and figure you'll survive.

Speaking of sensory overload, Jean-Claude was standing near the wall just to one side of the dance floor. His long black hair fell in soft curls around his shoulders, nearly to his waist. I didn't remember his hair being that long. He had his head turned away from me, watching the dancers, so I couldn't really see his face, but it gave me time to look at the rest of him. He was dressed in a black vinyl shirt that looked poured on. It left his arms bare, and I realized I'd never seen him in anything that bared his arms before. His skin looked unbelievably white against the shiny black vinyl, almost as if it glowed with some inner light. I knew it didn't, though it could. Jean-Claude would never be so déclassé as to show such power in a public place. His pants were made of the same shiny vinyl, making the long lines of his body look like they had been dipped into liquid patent leather. Vinyl boots came up just over his knees, gleaming as if they'd been spit polished. Everything about him gleamed, the dark glow of his clothes, the shining whiteness of his skin. Then abruptly he turned as if he felt me gazing at him.

Staring full into his face, even from across a room, made me catch my breath. He was beautiful. That heartrending beauty that was masculine but treaded the line between what was male and what was female. Not exactly androgynous, but close to it.

But as he moved towards me, the movement was utterly male, graceful as if he heard music in his head that he quietly danced to. But the walk, the movement of his shoulders—women did not move like that.

Jason patted my hand.

I jumped, staring at him.

He put his mouth close enough to my ear to whisper-shout above the music, "Breathe, Anita, remember to breathe."

I blushed, because that was how Jean-Claude affected me—like I was fourteen and was having the crush of my life. Jason tightened his grip on me, as if he thought I might make a run for it. Not a bad idea. I looked back, and saw that Jean-Claude was very near. The first time I saw the blue-green roil of the Caribbean, I cried, because it was so beautiful. Jean-Claude made me feel like that, like I should weep at his beauty. It was like being offered an original da Vinci, not just to hang on your wall and admire, but to roll around on top of. It seemed wrong. Yet I stood there, clutching Jason's arm, my heart hammering so hard I almost couldn't hear the music. I was scared, but it wasn't knife-in-the-dark scared, it was rabbit-in-the-headlights scared. I was caught, as I usually was with Jean-Claude, between two disparate instincts. Part of me wanted to run to him, to close the distance and climb his body and pull it around me. The other part wanted to run screaming into the night and pray he didn't follow.

He stood in front of me, but made no move to touch me, to close that last small space. He seemed as unwilling to touch me as I was to touch him. Was he afraid of me? Or did he sense my own fear and fear he might scare me off? We stood there simply staring at each other. His eyes were still the same dark, dark blue, with a wealth of black lashes lacing them.

Jason kissed my cheek, lightly, like you'd kiss your sister. It still made me jump. "I'm feeling like a third wheel. You two play nice." And he pulled away from me, leaving Jean-Claude and me staring at each other.

I don't know what we would have said, because three men joined us before we could decide. The shortest of the three was only about five feet seven, and he was wearing more makeup on his pale triangular face than I was. The makeup was well done, but he wasn't trying to look like a woman. His black hair was cut very short, though you could tell that it would be curly if it was long. He was wearing a black lace dress, long-sleeved, fitted at the waist, showing a slender but muscular chest. The skirt spilled out around him, almost June Cleaverish, and his stockings were black, with a very delicate spiderweb pattern. He wore open-toed sandals with spike heels, and both his toenails and his fingernails were painted black. He looked . . . lovely. But what made the outfit was the sense of power in him. It hung around him like an expensive perfume, and I knew he was an alpha something.

Jean-Claude spoke first. "This is Narcissus, owner of this establishment."

Narcissus held out his hand. I was momentarily confused about whether I was supposed to shake the hand or kiss it. If he'd been trying to pass for a woman, I'd have known the kiss would have been appropriate, but he wasn't. He wasn't so much cross-dressing as just dressing the way he wanted. I shook his hand. The grip was strong, but not too strong. He didn't try and test my strength, which some lycanthropes will do. He was secure, was Narcissus.

The two men behind him loomed over all of us, each well over six feet. One had a wide, muscular chest that was left mostly bare through a complicated crisscross of black leather straps. He had blond hair, cut very short on the sides and gelled into short spikes on top. His eyes were pale, and the look in them was not friendly. The second man was slimmer, built more like a professional basketball player than a weight-lifter. But the arms that showed from the leather vest were corded with muscle all the same. His skin was almost as dark as the leather he was wearing. All these two needed were a couple of tattoos apiece, and they would have screamed bad-ass.

Narcissus said, "This is Ulysses and Ajax." Ajax was the blond, and Ulysses was the oh-so brunette.

"Greek myths, nice naming convention," I said.

Narcissus blinked large dark eyes at me. Either he didn't think I was funny, or he simply didn't care. The music stopped abruptly. We were suddenly standing in a great roaring silence, and it was shocking. Narcissus spoke at a level where I could hear him, but people nearby couldn't. He'd known the music would stop. "I know your reputation, Ms. Blake. I must have the gun."

I glanced at Jean-Claude.

"I did not tell him."

"Come, Ms. Blake, I can smell the gun, even over . . ." He sniffed the air, head tilted back just a little, "your Oscar de la Renta."

"I went to a different oil for cleaning, one with less odor," I said.

"It's not the oil. The gun is new, I can smell the . . . metal, like you would smell a new car."

Oh. "Did Jean-Claude explain the situation to you?"

Narcissus nodded. "Yes, but we do not play favorites in dominance struggles between different groups. We are neutral territory, and if we are to remain so, then no guns. If it is any comfort, we didn't let the ones who have your cats bring guns into the club either."

I widened my eyes at that. "Most shapeshifters don't carry guns."

"No, they do not." Narcissus's handsome face told me nothing. He was neither upset nor concerned. It was all just business to him—like Marco's voice on the phone.

I turned back to Jean-Claude. "I'm not getting into the club with my gun, am I?"

"I fear not, *ma petite.*"

I sighed and turned back to the waiting—what had Jean-Claude called them—werehyenas. They were the first I'd met, as far as I knew. There was no clue from looking at them what they became when the moon was full. "I'll give it up, but I'm not happy about this."

"That is not my problem," Narcissus said.

I met his eyes and felt my face slip into that look that could make a good cop flinch—my monster peeking out. Ulysses and Ajax started to move in front of Narcissus, but he waved them back. "Ms. Blake will behave herself. Won't you, Ms. Blake?"

I nodded, but said, "If my people get hurt because I don't have a gun, I can make it your problem."

"*Ma petite,*" Jean-Claude said, his voice warning me.

I shook my head. "I know, I know, they're like Switzerland, neutral. Personally, I think neutral is just another way of saving your own ass at the expense of someone else's."

Narcissus took a step closer, until only a few inches separated us. His otherworldly energy danced along my skin, and as had happened in New Mexico with a very different wereanimal, it called that piece of Richard's beast that seemed to live inside me. It brought that power in a rush down my skin, to jump the distance between us, and mingle with Narcissus's power. It startled me. I hadn't thought it could happen with shields in place. Marianne had said that my abilities lay with the dead, and that was why I couldn't control Richard's power as easily as I could Jean-Claude's. But I should have been able to shield against a stranger. It scared me a little that I couldn't.

It had been wereleopards and werejaguars in New Mexico. They had mistaken me for another lycanthrope. Narcissus made the same mistake. I saw his eyes widen, then narrow. He glanced at Jean-Claude, and he laughed. "Everyone says you're human, Anita." He raised a hand and caressed the air just above my face, touching the swirl of energy. "I think you should come out of the closet before someone gets hurt."

"I never said I was human, Narcissus. But I'm not a shapeshifter either."

He rubbed his hand along the front of his dress, as if trying to get the feeling of my power off his skin. "Then what are you?"

"If things go badly tonight, you'll find out."

His eyes narrowed again. "If you cannot protect your people without guns, then you should step down as their Nimir-Ra and let someone else have the job."

"I've got an interview set up day after tomorrow with a potential Nimir-Raj."

He looked genuinely surprised. "You know that you don't have the power to rule them?"

I nodded. "Oh, yeah, I'm only temporary until I can find someone else. If the rest of you weren't so damn species conscious, I'd have farmed them out to another group. But no one wants to play with an animal that isn't the same as them."

"It is our way, it has always been our way."

And I knew the "our" didn't mean just werehyenas but all the shifters. "Yeah, well it sucks."

He smiled then. "I don't know whether I like you, Anita, but you are different, and I always appreciate that. Now give up the gun like a good little girl, and you can enter my territory." He held his hand out.

I stared at the hand. I didn't want to give up my gun. What I'd told Ronnie was true. I couldn't arm wrestle them, and I would lose a fair fight. The gun was my equalizer. I had the two knives, but frankly, they were for emergencies.

"It is your choice, *ma petite.*"

"If it will help you make the choice," Narcissus said, "I have put two of my own personal guards in the room with your leopards. I have forbidden the others from causing further harm to your people until you arrive. Until you enter the upper room where they're waiting, nothing more will happen that they don't want to happen." Knowing Nathaniel, that wasn't as comforting as it could have been.

If anyone would understand the problem, it would be someone who ran a club like this. "Nathaniel is one of those bottoms that will ask for more punishment than he can survive. He has no stopping point, no ability to keep himself safe. Do you understand?"

Narcissus's eyes widened just a touch. "Then what was he doing here without a top of his own?"

"I sent him out with one that was supposed to watch over him tonight. But Gregory said that Elizabeth deserted Nathaniel early in the evening."

"Is she one of your leopards, too?"

I nodded.

"She's defying you."

"I know. The fact that Nathaniel suffers for it doesn't seem to bother her."

He studied my face. "I don't see anger in you about this."

"If I was angry at everything Elizabeth did to piss me off, I'd never be anything else." Truthfully, I was just tired. Tired of having to rescue the pack from one emergency after another. Tired of Elizabeth being up in my face and not taking care of the others, even though she was supposedly dominant to them. I'd avoided punishing her, because I couldn't beat her up, which was what she needed. The only thing I could do was shoot her. I'd been trying to avoid that, but she just may have pushed me far enough that I was out of options. I'd see what actual damage had been done. If anyone died because of her, then she would follow. I hated the fact that I didn't care whether I killed her. I'd known her off and on for over a year. I should have cared, but I didn't. I didn't like her, and she'd been asking for it for as long as I'd known her. My life would be simpler if she were dead. But there had to be a better reason to kill someone than that. Didn't there?

"Some advice," Narcissus said. "All dominance challenges, especially from your own people, must be handled quickly, or the problem will spread."

"Thanks. Actually, I knew that."

"Still she defies you."

"I've been trying to avoid killing her."

We looked at each other very quietly, and he gave a small nod. "Your gun, please."

I sighed and raised the front of my shirt, though the material was stiff enough that I had to roll it back to expose the butt of the gun. I lifted the gun out and checked the safety out of habit, though I knew it was on.

Narcissus took the gun. The two bodyguards had moved, blocking the crowd's view of us. I doubted most people knew what we'd just done. Narcissus smiled as I rolled my shirt back into place over the now-empty holster. "Truthfully, if I didn't know who you were and what your reputation was, I wouldn't have smelled the gun, because I wouldn't have been trying to. Your outfit doesn't look like it could hide a gun this big."

"Paranoia is the mother of invention," I said.

He gave a small bow of his head. "Now enter and enjoy the delights, and the terrors, of my world." With that rather cryptic phrase, he and his bodyguards moved through the crowd, taking my gun with them.

Jean-Claude trailed his fingers down my arm, and that one small movement turned me towards him, my skin shivering. Tonight was complicated enough without this level of sexual tension.

"Your cats are well until you enter the upper room. I suggest we do the mark now, first."

"Why?" I asked, my pulse suddenly in my throat.

"Let us go to our table, and I will explain." He moved off through the crowd, without touching me further. I followed and couldn't stop myself from watching the way the vinyl fit him from behind. I loved watching him walk, whether he was coming or going—a double threat.

The tables were small, and there weren't many of them crowded against the walls. But they'd cleared the dance floor so they could set up for some sort of show or demonstration. Men and women dressed in leather were setting up a framework of metal with lots of leather straps. I was reeeally hoping to be elsewhere before the show started.

Jean-Claude took me to one side before we got to the table that Jason and three complete strangers were gathered around. He stepped in so close to me that a hard thought would have made our bodies touch. I pressed myself against the wall and tried not to breathe. He put his mouth against my ear and spoke so low what came out was merely the soft sound of his breath against my skin. "We will all be safer when the marks are married, but there are other . . . benefits to it. I have many lesser vampires that I have brought into my territory in the last few months, *ma petite*. Without you at my side, I dared not bring in greater powers, for fear that I could not hold them. Once the marks are married between us, you will be able to sense those vampires that are mine. The exception, as always, is a Master Vampire. They can hide their allegiances better than the rest. The marriage of marks will also let my people know who you are, and what will happen to them if they overstep their bounds with you."

I spoke, lips barely moving, lower than he had spoken, because he could still hear me. "You've had to be very careful, haven't you?"

He rested his cheek against my face for a moment. "It has been a delicate dance to choreograph."

I had gone into this evening with my metaphysical shield tight in place. Marianne had taught me that with my aura ruptured, the other shielding was of paramount importance. I shielded with stone tonight, perfect, seamless stone. Nothing could get in, or out, without my permission. Except Narcissus's power had already danced inside my shields. I was afraid that touching Jean-Claude would be enough to shatter the stone, but it wasn't. I wasn't even aware of the shielding, unless I really concentrated. It could stay in place even when I slept. Only when you were attacked did you have to concentrate, if you were good at shielding. I'd spent a week at the beginning of the month in Tennessee with Marianne, working on nothing but this. I wasn't great at it, but I wasn't bad either.

My shields were in place. My emotions were drowning in Jean-Claude, but my psyche wasn't, which meant that Marianne was right. I could hold the dead outside my shield easier than the living. This gave me the courage to do a little more. I leaned my face against Jean-Claude's, and nothing happened. Oh, the feel of his skin against mine sent a thrill through my body, but my shields never wavered. I felt some tension that I hadn't even known was there ease out of me. I wanted him to hold me. It wasn't just sex. If that was all it was, I could have been rid of him long ago. He must have felt it, too, because his hands rested lightly on my bare arms. When I didn't protest, his hands caressed my skin, and that small movement brought my breath to a sigh.

I leaned into him, wrapping my arms around his waist, pressing the lines of our bodies together. I rested my head on his chest, and I could hear his heart beating. It didn't always beat, but tonight it did. We held each other, and it was nearly chaste, just a renewal of the fact that we were touching again. I'd worked on the metaphysical stuff so I could do this and not lose myself. It had been worth the effort.

He pulled back first, enough to look into my face. "We can marry the marks here, or find somewhere more private." He wasn't whispering as much as before. Apparently he didn't care now if others knew what we were doing.

"I'm not clear on what marrying the marks means."

"I thought your Marianne had explained it to you."

"She said we'll fit together like puzzle pieces and there'll be a release of power when it happens. But she also said that the manner in which it is done is individual to the participants."

"You sound as if you are quoting."

"I am."

He frowned, and even that small movement was somehow fascinating. "I do not want you to be unpleasantly surprised, *ma petite*. I am striving for honesty, since you value it so highly. I have never done this with anyone, but most things are sexual between us, whether we will or no, so it is likely this will be, too."

"I can't leave the leopards here long enough to grab a hotel room, Jean-Claude."

"They will not be harmed. Until you go upstairs, they will be safe."

I shook my head and pulled away from him. "I'm sorry,

but I am not leaving here without them. If you want to do this afterwards, that's fine with me, but the leopards are priority. They're waiting for me to rescue them. I can't go off and have what amounts to metaphysical sex while they're afraid and bleeding somewhere."

"No, it cannot wait. I want us to have this done before the fight begins. I do not like that your gun is gone."

"Will this marriage of the marks give me more . . . abilities?"

"Yes."

"And you, what do you get out of it?" I was standing against the wall now, not touching him.

"My own defenses will be strong once more, and I will gain power, as well. You know that."

"Are there any surprises connected with this that I should know about?"

"As I said, I have never done this with anyone, nor have I seen it done. It will be as much a surprise to me as to you."

I stared up into his lovely eyes and wished I believed that.

"I see the distrust in your eyes, *ma petite.* But it is not me that you do not trust. It is your power. Nothing ever goes as it should with you, *ma petite,* because you are like no power come before you. You are wild magic, untamed. You throw the best of plans to the wind."

"I've been learning control, Jean-Claude."

"I hope it is enough."

"You're scaring me."

He sighed. "And that was the last thing I wished to do."

I shook my head. "Look, Jean-Claude, I know everyone keeps saying my people are fine, but I want to see for myself, so let's just get this done."

"This should be something special and mystical, *ma petite.*"

I looked around the club. "Then we need a different setting."

"I agree, but the setting was your choosing, not mine."

"But you're the one insisting on it having to be right now before all the fireworks start."

"True." He sighed and held out his hand to me. "Come, let us at least go to our table."

I actually thought about refusing his hand. Funny how quickly I could go from wanting to jump his bones to wanting to be rid of him. Of course, it wasn't exactly him, but more the complications that came with him. The mystical stuff between us was never simple. He said that was my fault, and maybe it was. Jean-Claude was a pretty standard Master Vampire, and Richard, a pretty standard Ulfric. They were both wonderfully powerful, but there was nothing too terribly extraordinary in their powers. Well, there was one thing about Jean-Claude. He could gain power by feeding off sexual energy. In another century he'd have been called an incubus. It's rare even for a Master Vamp to have a secondary way to gain power outside of blood. So it was impressive, sort of. The only other masters I'd met who could feed off of something other than blood had fed on terror. And of the two, I preferred lust. At least no one had to bleed for it. Usually. But I was the wild card, the one whose powers seemed to fit nothing but legends of necromancers long dead. Legends so old that no one believed they could be true, until I came along. Sad, but true.

The table had cleared out while we were whispering. Now just Jason and one other man were there. The man was dressed in brown leather, from what I could see of his pants to the zipped-front, sleeveless shirt he was wearing. He was also wearing one of those hoods that left your mouth, part of your nose, and your eyes bare, but covered the rest of your face. Frankly, I found the hoods creepy, but hey, it wasn't my bread that was being buttered. As long as he didn't try anything with me, we were cool. It wasn't until he looked up into my face that I recognized those pale, pale blue eyes—the startling ice blue eyes of a Siberian Husky. No human I'd ever met had eyes like that.

"Asher," I said.

He smiled then, and I recognized the curve of his lips. I knew why he'd worn the hood. It wasn't sexual preference, or at least I didn't think so. It was to hide the scars. Once, about two hundred years ago, some well-meaning church officials had tried to burn the devil out of Asher. They'd done it with holy water. Holy water is like acid on vampire flesh. He'd once been, in his own way, as breathtaking as Jean-Claude. Now half his face was a melted ruin, half his chest, most of the one thigh I'd seen. What I'd seen of the rest of him was perfect, as perfect as the day he died. And the parts I hadn't seen, I wasn't sure I wanted to know about. Through Jean-Claude's marks I had memories of Asher before. I knew what his body looked like in smooth perfection—every inch of it. Asher and his human servant, Julianna, had been part of a ménage à trois with Jean-Claude for about twenty years. She'd been burned as a witch, and Jean-Claude had only been able to save Asher after the damage had been done.

The events were over two hundred years old, yet they both still mourned Julianna, and each other. Asher was now Jean-Claude's second in command, but they were not lovers. And they were uneasy friends, because there was still too much left unspoken between them. Asher still blamed Jean-Claude for failing them, and Jean-Claude had a hard time arguing with that, because deep down he still blamed himself, too.

I leaned down and gave Asher a quick kiss on the leather cheek. "What did you do with all your long hair? Please tell me you haven't cut it."

He raised my hand to his mouth and laid a gentle kiss on it. "It is braided, and longer than ever."

"I can hardly wait to see it," I said. "Thanks for coming."

"I would move all of hell to reach your side, you know that."

"You French guys do talk pretty," I said.

He laughed softly.

Jason interrupted. "I think the show is about to start."

I turned and watched a woman being led towards the framework that had been erected. She was wearing a robe, and I really didn't want to see what was under it.

"Whatever we're going to do, let's do it and go get the leopards."

"You don't want to see the show?" Jason asked. His eyes were all innocent, but his smile was teasing.

I just frowned at him. But his eyes looked behind me, and I knew someone Jason didn't like was coming towards us. I turned to find Ajax standing there. He ignored me and spoke to Jean-Claude. "You have fifteen minutes, then the show starts."

Jean-Claude nodded. "Tell Narcissus I appreciate the notice."

Ajax gave a small head bow, much like his master had done before, then walked off through the tables.

"What was all that about?" I asked.

"It would be considered rude to do something magical during someone else's performance. I told Narcissus that we would be calling some . . . power."

I must have looked as suspicious as I felt. "You are beginning to piss me off with this cloak-and-dagger magic act."

"You are a necromancer, and I am the Master Vampire of this city. Do you really believe that we can merge our powers and not have every undead in this room, and more, notice it? I do not know if the shapeshifters will be able to feel it, but it is likely, since we are also both bound to a werewolf. Everything nonhuman in this club will feel something. I don't know how much, or exactly what, but *something, ma petite*. Narcissus would have taken it as a grave insult if we had interrupted this performance without warning him."

"I don't mean to rush you," Asher said, "but you will use up your time in talking if you are not quick about it."

Jean-Claude looked at him, and the look was not entirely friendly. What was happening between them that Jean-Claude would give such a look to Asher?

Jean-Claude held his hand out to me. I hesitated a second, then slid my hand into his and he led me to the wall near the table. "Now what?" I asked.

"Now you must drop your shields, *ma petite*, that so-strong barrier you have erected between me and your aura."

I just stared at him. "I don't want to do that."

"I would not ask if it were not necessary, *ma petite*. But even if I were able to do it, neither of us would enjoy me breaking down your shielding. We cannot merge our auras if my aura cannot touch yours."

I was suddenly scared. Really seriously scared. I didn't know what would happen if I dropped the shields with him right there. In times of crisis our auras flared together forming a unique whole. I didn't want to do this. I am a control freak, and everything about Jean-Claude ate at the part of me that most needed control.

"I'm not sure I can do this."

He sighed. "It is your choice. I will not force it, but I fear the consequences, *ma petite*. I do fear them."

Marianne had given me the lecture, and it was really too late to get cold feet. I could either move forward with this, or eventually one of us would die. Probably me. Part of my job was going up against preternatural monsters—things with enough magic to sense a hole in my defenses. Before I'd ever been able to sense auras, or at least before I knew that I was doing it, my aura had been intact. With my own natural talent, that had been enough. But lately I seemed to be running up against bigger, badder monsters. Eventually, I would lose. That, I might have been able to live with, sort of. But costing Jean-Claude or Richard their lives? That I couldn't handle. I knew all the reasons I should do this, and still I stood there gazing up at Jean-Claude, my heart beating in my throat, my shields tight in place. The front part of my brain knew this needed doing. The back part of my brain wasn't so sure.

"Once I drop my shield, then what?"

"We touch," he said.

I took a deep breath in and blew it out as if I were about to run a race. Then I dropped my shields. It wasn't like tearing down the stone walls; it was like absorbing them back into my psyche. The tower was just suddenly not there, and Jean-Claude's power crashed over me. It wasn't only that I felt the sexual attraction in full force, I could feel his heartbeat in my head. I could taste his skin in my mouth. I knew he'd fed tonight, though intellectually I'd known that when I heard his heart beating. Now, I could feel that he was well fed and full of someone else's blood.

His hand moved towards me, and I flattened against the wall. The hand kept moving, and I pulled away from it. I moved away because more than anything in the world at that moment I wanted him to touch me. I wanted to feel his hand against my bare skin. I wanted to rip the vinyl from his body and watch him, pale and perfect above me. The image was so clear that I closed my eyes against it, as if that would help.

I felt him in front of me, knew he was leaning close. I ducked under his arm and was suddenly standing by the table, leaving him near the wall. I kept backing up, and he kept watching me. Someone touched me, and I screamed.

Asher was holding my arm, gazing up at me with those pale eyes of his. I could feel him, too, feel the weight of his age, the heft of his power in my head. That was my power, but I realized in shielding so strongly from Jean-Claude I'd also cut myself off from some of my own powers. Shielding was a tricky thing. I guess I still didn't have the hang of it.

Jean-Claude moved away from the wall, holding one slender hand out to me. I backed up, Asher's hand sliding over my arm as I pulled away. I was shaking my head back and forth, back and forth.

Jean-Claude walked slowly towards me. His eyes had gone drowning blue, the pupil swallowed by his own power. I knew with a sudden clarity that it wasn't his power or lust that had called his eyes, it was mine. He could feel how my body tightened, moistened, as he moved towards me. It wasn't him I didn't trust. It was me.

I took one step backwards and fell on the small step leading down to the dance floor. Someone caught me before I hit the floor, strong arms around my waist, pressing me against the bare skin of a very masculine chest. I could feel that without looking. I was held effortlessly, feet dangling, and I knew those arms, the feel of that chest, the smell of his skin this close. I craned my head backwards and found myself staring at Richard.

5

I STOPPED BREATHING. To be suddenly inches away from
him after all this time was too much. He leaned that painfully
handsome face over mine, and the thick waves of his brown
hair fell against my skin. His mouth hovered over mine, and
I think I would have said, *no*, or moved, but two things
happened at once. He tightened his one-armed hold around
my waist, a movement that was almost painful. Then his
newly free hand gripped my chin, held my face. The touch
of his hands, the strength in them made me hesitate. One
moment I was staring into his deep brown eyes, the next, his
face was too close and he was kissing me.

I don't know what I expected, a chaste kiss, I think. It
wasn't chaste. He kissed me hard enough to bruise, hard
enough to force my mouth open, then he crawled inside, and
I could feel the muscles in his mouth, his jaw, his neck working as he held me, explored me, possessed me. I should have
been angry, pissed, but I wasn't. If he hadn't held me immobile I'd have turned in his arms, pressed the front of my
body against his. But all I could do was taste his mouth, feel
his lips, try to drink him down my throat, as if he were the
finest of wines and I was dying of thirst.

He finally drew back from me, enough for me to see his
face. I stared breathlessly at him, as if my eyes were hungry
for the sight of those perfect cheekbones, the dimple that
softened an utterly masculine face. There was nothing feminine about Richard. He was the ultimate male in so many
ways. The electric lights caught strands of gold and copper,
like metallic wire through the deep brown of his hair.

He lowered me slowly to the ground from his height of
six one. His shoulders were broad, chest deep, waist tight
and narrow, stomach flat, with a fine line of dark hair running

down the middle of it and vanishing into the black vinyl pants he was wearing. More black vinyl! I was sensing a theme here, but my gaze traveled down his body just the same. Tracing the narrow hips, lingering where I shouldn't have been, noticing things I wished I hadn't, because we were in public, and I wasn't planning on seeing him naked tonight. Knee-high leather boots completed his outfit. The only things he was wearing on his upper body were leather and metal-studded "bracelets" and a matching collar.

A hand touched my back, and I jumped and whirled around, turning so I could face them both, because I knew who was behind me. Jean-Claude stood there, eyes having bled back to normal.

I finally found my voice. "You called him."

"We had an arrangement that whoever you called first would contact the other."

"You should have told me," I said.

Jean-Claude put his hands on his hips. "I am not taking the blame for this. He wished to be a surprise, against *my* wishes."

I looked at Richard. "Is that true?"

Richard nodded. "Yes."

"Why?"

"Because if I'd played fair I still wouldn't have gotten a kiss. I couldn't stand the thought of seeing you tonight and not touching you."

It wasn't so much his words as the look in his eyes, the heat in his face, that made me blush.

"I have played you fair tonight, *ma petite,* and yet I am punished, rather than rewarded." Jean-Claude held out his hand to me. "Shall we begin with a kiss?"

I was suddenly aware that we were standing on the dance floor near the metal framework and the waiting "actors." We had the audience's attention, and I didn't want that. I realized something I hadn't with the stone shield in place. Almost everyone in the room was a shapeshifter. I could feel their energy like the brush of warm electric fur, and they could feel ours.

I nodded. I suddenly wanted the privacy that Jean-Claude

had offered earlier. But staring from Jean-Claude to Richard, I realized I didn't trust myself alone with them. If we had a room to ourselves I couldn't guarantee that the sex would be merely metaphysical. Admitting that even to myself was embarrassing. As uncomfortable as it was to do what we had to do in public, it was still better than in private. Here I knew I'd say *stop*, anywhere else I just wasn't sure. I wasn't thinking about the wereleopards. I was thinking about how large and bare my skin felt. Shit.

"A kiss, why not?"

"We can get a room," Richard said, voice low.

I shook my head. "No, no rooms."

He reached out as if to touch me, and one look was enough to make his hand drop. "You don't trust us."

"Or me," I said, softly.

Jean-Claude held out his hand to me. "Come, *ma petite,* we delay their show."

I stared at his hand for a space of heartbeats, then took it. I expected him to pull me in against his body, but he didn't. He stopped with the width of a handspan between us. I looked a question at him, and he touched my face, gently, tentatively, fingers hovering on either side of my face, like hesitant butterflies, as if he were afraid to touch me. He lowered his face towards me, as his fingertips found my skin. His hands slid on either side of my face, cupping it like something delicate and breakable.

I'd never felt him so tentative around me, so unsure. Even as his lips hovered over mine I wondered if he was doing it this way on purpose to contrast with Richard's forcefulness. Then his lips touched mine, and I stopped thinking. It was the barest of brushes, his mouth over mine. Then, softly, he kissed me. I kissed him back, being as tentative as he, my hands raising, covering his hands as they cradled my face. He'd thrown that surprisingly long black hair over one shoulder so that the right side of his face was bare to the lights and the hair didn't get in the way of the kiss. I ran one hand down the side of his jaw, tracing the shape of his face, ever so gently, as we kissed. He shuddered under that light brush of my hand, and the feel of him trembling under my hand brought a soft sound from low in my throat. Jean-Claude's mouth pressed against mine hard enough that I could feel the press of his fangs against my lip. I opened my mouth and let him inside me, ran my tongue between the delicate points. I'd learned how to French kiss a vampire, but it was a hazardous pleasure, one to be done with care, and I was out of practice.

In slipping my tongue between his fangs, I nicked myself. It was a quick, sharp pain, and Jean-Claude made a soft guttural sound, a heartbeat before I tasted blood.

His hands were suddenly at my back, pulling me against his body. The kiss never stopped, and the urgency of it grew, until it was as if he were feeding from my mouth, trying to drink me down.

I might have pulled away, I might not have, but the moment the front of our bodies touched, it was too late. There was no going back, no saying no, nothing but sensation. I felt that cool, shimmering wind that was his aura touch mine. For one trembling moment we were pressed together, our energy breathing against each other like the sides of two great beasts. Then the boundaries that held our auras in place gave way. Think of it as if you were making love and suddenly your skin slid away, spilling you against your partner, into your partner, giving you an intimacy that was never imagined, never planned, never wanted.

I screamed, and he echoed me. I felt us begin to fall to the floor, but Richard caught us, cradled us against his body, laid us gently on the floor. The power did not leap across to him, and I didn't know why.

Jean-Claude's body was on top of mine, pinning me to the floor, his groin pressed over mine. He drove his hips in against me, forcing my legs apart around the slick covering of his legs. I wanted him inside me, wanted him to ride me while the power rode us.

He struggled up on his arms, leaning up and away from me, forcing his lower body tighter against mine. And the power built in a skin-tingling rush, building, building, like that shining edge of orgasm when you can feel it growing large and overwhelming but can't quite reach it.

I saw Richard leaning over me like a dark shadow against the haze of the lights. I think I tried to say, *no, don't,* but no sound came. He kissed me, and the power flared, but still he wasn't part of it. He kissed my cheek, my chin, my neck, working lower, and I suddenly knew what he was doing. He was kissing his way down to the hole over my heart chakra, my energy center. Jean-Claude had already covered the one at my base, my groin. Richard's chest stretched above me, smooth, firm, so temptingly close, and I raised my mouth to his skin, so that as he kissed down my body he drew his naked chest across my tongue. I licked a wet line down his body. He buried his mouth inside the halter top and touched over my heart, and my mouth found his heart at the same moment.

The power didn't just build, it exploded. It was like lying at ground zero of a nuclear explosion, the shock waves shooting out, out, out into the room, while we melted together in the center. For one shining moment I felt both of them inside me, through me, as if they were wind, pure power, pouring through me, through us. Richard's electric warmth buzzed over us; Jean-Claude's cool power poured over and through like a chill wind; and I was something large and growing, holding the warmth of the living and the cold of the dead. I was both and neither. We were all and none.

I don't know if I passed out or if I just lost time for some metaphysical reason. All I remembered was that I was suddenly lying on the floor with Richard collapsed beside me, pinning one of my arms, his body curled around my chest and head, his legs touching down the other side of my body. Jean-Claude was collapsed on top of me, his body pressing the length of mine, with his head to one side resting on Richard's leg. They both had their eyes closed, their breath coming in ragged pants, just like mine.

It took me two tries to say a breathless, "Get off me."

Jean-Claude rolled to one side without ever opening his eyes. The fall of his body forced Richard's legs to move a little farther out, so that Jean-Claude and I both lay in the semicircle of Richard's body.

The room was so quiet I thought we were the only ones

left in it. As if all the others had fled in terror of what we'd done. Then the room thundered in applause and howling and other animal noises that I didn't have words for. The noise was deafening, beating against my body in waves as if I had nerves in places where I'd never had nerves before.

Asher was suddenly standing over us. He knelt beside me, touching the pulse in my neck. "Blink if you can hear me, Anita."

I blinked.

"Can you speak?"

"Yes."

He nodded and touched Jean-Claude next, stroking a hand down his cheek. Jean-Claude opened his eyes at the touch. He gave a smile that seemed to mean more to Asher than to me, because it made Asher laugh. The laugh was a very masculine one, as if they'd shared some dirty joke that I didn't understand. Asher crawled around me until he was kneeling by Richard's head. He lifted a handful of thick hair so he could see Richard's face clearly. Richard blinked at him, but didn't seem to be focusing.

Asher bent low over Richard, and I heard him say, "Can you hear me, *mon ami*?"

Richard swallowed, coughed, and said, "Yes."

"Bon, bon."

It took me two tries but I had a smart-aleck comment, and I was going to make it. "Now, everyone who can stand, raise their hands." None of us moved. I felt distant, floating, my body too heavy to move. Or maybe my mind was too overwhelmed to make it move.

"Have no fears, *ma cherie,* we will attend you." Asher stood, and it was as if it were a signal. Figures moved out of the crowd. I recognized three of them. Jamil's waist length cornrows looked right at home with his black leather outfit. He was Richard's lead enforcer, or Sköff. Shang-Da didn't look comfortable in black leather, but the six-foot-plus Chinese never looked comfortable outside of nice dress clothes with polished wing tips. Shang-Da was the other enforcer for the pack, the Hati. Sylvie knelt beside me, looking splendid in vinyl, her short brown hair touched with burgundy highlights. Though it looked good, I knew she was conservative enough that it was probably a temporary color. She sold insurance when she wasn't being Richard's second in command, his Freki, and insurance salespeople didn't have hair the color of a good red wine.

She smiled at me, wearing more makeup than I'd ever seen her in. It looked great, but it didn't really look like Sylvie. For the first time I thought how pretty she was, and that she was almost as delicate-looking as me.

"I owed you a rescue," she said. Once upon a time a bunch of nasty vampires had come to town to teach Jean-Claude, Richard, and me a lesson. They'd taken prisoners along the way. Sylvie had been one of them. I'd gotten her out, and I'd kept my promise to see everyone who touched her dead. She did the actual killing, but I delivered them up to her for punishment. She kept a few bones as souvenirs. Sylvie would never complain that I was too violent. Maybe she could be my new best friend.

The werewolves took up positions around us, facing outward like good bodyguards. None of them were as physically imposing as Narcissus's bodyguards had been, but I'd seen the wolves fight, and muscles aren't everything. Skill counts, and a certain level of ruthlessness.

Two vampires came to stand with Asher and the wolves. I didn't recognize either of them. The woman was Asian, with shining black hair that fell barely to her shoulders. The hair was nearly the same color and brilliance as the vinyl cat suit that clung to nearly every inch of her body. The suit made sure you were aware of her high, tight breasts, her tiny waist, the swell of her shapely hips. She gave me an unfriendly look with her dark eyes, before she turned her back on me and stood, hands at her side, waiting. Waiting for what, I wasn't sure.

The second vampire was male, not much taller than the woman, with thick brown hair that had been shaved close to his head, except for a layer left on top that came about halfway to his eyes, shining and straight. He gazed down on me with a smile, eyes the color of new pennies, as if his brown eyes held just a trace of blood in them.

He turned his attention outward, arms crossed over the black leather of his chest. They too faced outward like good bodyguards, letting the crowd know that even though we couldn't stand up, we weren't helpless. Comforting, I guess.

Jason crawled in between their legs, head hanging down, as if he were almost too tired to move. He raised his blue eyes to me, and the look was almost as unfocused as I felt.

He gave a pale version of his usual grin and said, "Was it good for you?"

I was feeling better enough to try and sit up, but failed. Jean-Claude said, "Lie a little longer, *ma petite*."

Since I had no choice, I did what he suggested. I lay staring up at the dark, distant ceiling with its rows of lights. They'd turned off most of them, so that the club was nearly dark. Like the soft gloom that comes when you close the drapes during the day.

I felt Jason lay down on the other side of me, head resting on my thigh. Not long ago I'd have made him move, but I'd spent my time away learning how to be comfortable being close with the wereleopards. It had made me more tolerant of everyone, apparently. "Why are *you* tired?"

He rolled his head up to look at me without raising it from my leg, one hand curving over my calf as if to keep his balance. "You spill sex and magic through the whole club and you ask why I'm tired? You are such a tease."

I frowned at him. "One more comment like that and you'll have to move."

He snuggled his head on my hose. "I can see that your underwear matches."

"Get off of me, Jason."

He slid to the floor without being told twice. He could never leave well enough alone, our Jason. He always had to get the last joke, the last comment, that one bit too many. I worried that someday with someone else that little quirk might get him hurt, or worse.

Richard propped himself up on one elbow, moving slowly as if he wasn't sure everything was working. "I don't know if that felt better than anything else we've ever done, or worse."

"It feels like a combination of a hangover and mild flu to me," I said.

"And yet it feels good," Jean-Claude said.

I finally got upright and found that they both had a hand at my back to support me, as if their movements had been simultaneous.

I actually leaned in against their hands, rather than telling them to move. One, I was still shaky; two, I just didn't find the physical contact unpleasant. All these months of trying to forge the wereleopards into a cohesive, friendly unit, and it was me that had learned to be cohesive and friendly. Me that had learned that not every helping hand is a threat to my independence. Me that had learned that not every offer of physical closeness is a trap or a lie.

Richard sat up first, slowly, keeping his hand on my back. Then Jean-Claude sat up, keeping his hand very still against me. I felt them exchange glances. This was the moment that I usually pulled away. We'd have some fantastic sex, metaphysical or otherwise, and that was my cue to close down, hide. We were in public, all the more reason to do it.

I didn't pull away. Richard's arm slid cautiously up my back, over my shoulders. Jean-Claude's arm moved lower around my waist. They both pulled me into the curve of their bodies as if they were some huge, warm vinyl-covered chair with a pulse.

Some say that that moment during sex when you both have an orgasm your auras drop, you blend your energies, yourselves together. You share so much more than just your body during sex, it's one of the reasons you should be careful who you do it with. Just sitting there on the floor with them was like that. I could feel their energies moving through me, like a low-level current, a distant hum. In time I was pretty sure it would become white noise—something you can ignore, like psychic shielding when you no longer have to concentrate on it. But now it was like we would always walk, move, through that dreamy afterglow where you were still connected, still not quite back in your own skin. I didn't push them away, because I didn't want to. Pushing them away would have been redundant. We didn't need to touch to breach the barriers anymore. And that should have scared me more than anything else, but it didn't.

Narcissus walked out into the middle of the floor and a soft light fell upon him, growing ever so gradually brighter. "Well, my friends, we have had a treat tonight, have we not?"

More applause, screams, and animal noises filled the dimness. Narcissus held up his hands until the crowd fell quiet. "I think we have had our climax for the night." A smattering of laughter at that. "We will save our show until tomorrow, for to do less would be to dishonor what we have been offered here tonight."

The woman, who was still standing to the back of the dance floor in her robe, said, "I can't compete with that."

Narcissus blew her a kiss. "It is not a competition, sweet Miranda, it is that we all have our gifts. Some are merely more rare than others." He turned and stared at us as he said the last. His eyes were pale and oddly colored, and it took me a second or two to realize that Narcissus's eyes had bled to his beast. Hyena eyes, I guess, though truthfully, I didn't know what hyena eyes looked like. I just knew they weren't human eyes.

He knelt beside us, smoothing his dress down in an automatic and strangely odd gesture that I'd never seen a man make before. Of course, he was also the first man I'd ever seen in a dress. There was probably a cause and effect.

Narcissus lowered his voice. "I would love to speak with you in private about this."

"Of course," Jean-Claude said, "but first we have other business."

Narcissus leaned in close, lowering his voice until it was necessary to lean forward to hear him. "As I have two of my guards waiting with her leopards so no harm will come, there is time to talk. Or should I say, *your* leopards, for surely now, what belongs to one, belongs to all." He had leaned so far over that his cheek nearly touched Jean-Claude on one side and my face on the other.

"No," I said, "the leopards are mine."

"Really," Narcissus said. He turned his face that fraction of an inch and brushed his lips against mine. It might have been an accident, but I doubted it. "You don't share every-thing, then?"

I moved my face just far enough away so we weren't touching. "No."

"So good to know," he whispered. He leaned forward and pressed his mouth to Jean-Claude's lips. I was startled, frozen for a second wondering exactly what to do.

Jean-Claude knew exactly what to do. He put one finger in the man's chest and pushed, not with muscle, but with power. The power of the marks, the power that we had all just moments before solidified. Jean-Claude drew on it as if he'd done it a thousand times before, effortlessly, gracefully, commandingly.

Narcissus was pushed back from him by a rush of invis-ible power that I could feel tugging on my body. And I knew that most of the people in the room could feel it, as well. Narcissus stayed crouched on the floor, staring at Jean-Claude, staring at all of us. The look on his face was angry, but there was more hunger in it than rage, a hunger denied.

"We need to talk in private," Narcissus insisted.

Jean-Claude nodded. "That would be best, I think."

There was a weight of things left unsaid in that short exchange. I felt Richard's puzzlement mirror my own, before I turned my head to glance back at him. The movement put our faces close enough so that we could almost have kissed. I could tell just by the expression in his eyes that he didn't know what was going on. And he seemed to know that I could tell, because he didn't bother to shrug or make any outward acknowledgment. It wasn't telepathy, though to an outsider it might look that way. It was more extreme empa-thy, as if I could read every nuance on his face, the smallest change, and know what it meant.

I was still pressed in the circle of Richard's and Jean-Claude's arms, a strange amount of bare skin touching all of us—my back, Richard's chest and stomach, Jean-Claude's arm. There was something incredibly right about the touch-ing, the closeness. I felt Jean-Claude's attention turn, before I moved my head to meet his eyes.

The look in those drowning eyes held worlds of things

unsaid, unasked, all so tremblingly close. Because for once he didn't see in my eyes the barriers that kept all those words trapped. It had to be the marriage of the marks affecting me, but that night I think he could have asked me anything, anything, and I wasn't sure I'd say no.

What he finally said was, "Shall we retire to privacy to discuss business with Narcissus?" His voice had its usual smoothness. Only his eyes held uncertainty and a need so large he almost had no words for it. We'd all waited so long for my surrender. I knew that the phrasing wasn't mine. It sounded more like something Jean-Claude would think, but with Richard also pressed against my body I wasn't really sure who was thinking it. I only knew it hadn't been me.

Even before the marks had merged I'd had moments like this. Moments when their thoughts invaded mine, overrode mine. The images had been the worst—nightmare flashes of feeding on the warm bodies of animals, of drinking blood from people I didn't know. It had been this mingling, this loss of self, that had terrified me, sent me running for anything that would keep me whole—keep me myself. Tonight, that just didn't seem important. Definitely an aftereffect of the metaphysical union of marks. But knowing what it was didn't make it go away. It was a dangerous night.

Jean-Claude said, "*Ma petite,* are you well? I am feeling much better, energized in fact. Are you still ill?"

I shook my head. "No, I feel fine." *Fine* didn't really cover it. *Energized* was a good word for it, but there were others. How long could it take to rescue the wereleopards from yet another disaster? The night wasn't young, dawn would come, and I wanted to be alone with them before that. I realized with a jolt that ran all the way down my body, that tonight was it. If we could get some privacy and not be interrupted, all things would suddenly be possible.

Richard and Jean-Claude both stood up, in a boneless movement of grace for the vampire and pure energy for the werewolf. I gazed at them as they stood above me, and I was suddenly eager to have the other business done with. I wasn't as worried about the leopards as I should have been, and that did bother me. Whatever this effect was, it was distracting me from more important things. Saving the leopards was why I'd come. It was the first time I'd really thought of them in a while.

I shook my head trying to clear it of sex and magic and the weight of possibilities in Richard's eyes. Jean-Claude's eyes were more cautious, but I'd taught him caution where I was concerned.

I held my hands up to both of them. I never asked for help to stand unless I was bleeding or something was broken. The two of them exchanged glances, then they held their hands out to me, again in perfect unison, like choreographed dancers who knew what the other would do.

They could feel my desire, but that had always been there; it told them nothing. I took their hands and let them lift me up. They were both still looking unsure, almost suspicious, as if they were waiting for me to recoil from them and run screaming from the intimacy of it all. I had to smile. "If we can get everyone all tucked in safe and sound before dawn, all things will be possible."

They exchanged another look between them. Jean-Claude made a small movement, as if encouraging Richard. It was a tiny, almost-push with his head, as if to say, *Go ahead, ask.* Normally, seeing them plot behind my back pissed me off, but not that night.

"Do you mean . . ." Richard let the thought trail off.

I nodded, and Richard's hand tightened on mine. Jean-Claude's hand was strangely quiet in mine. "You do realize, *ma petite,* that this new . . ." he hesitated, "willingness, may be a by-product of joining the marks tonight. I don't wish you to accuse us later of trickery."

"I know what it is, and I don't care." I should have, but I didn't. It was like being drunk, or drugged, and even thinking that made no difference.

I was looking at Jean-Claude, and I saw him let out the breath he'd been holding. I felt Richard do the same. It was as if a great weight had been taken from both of them. And I knew that I was that burden. I'd try not to be a burden

from now on. "Let's get this over with and go get the leopards," I said.

Jean-Claude raised my hand to his mouth, brushing the
knuckles across his lips. "And be gone from this place."

I nodded. "And be gone from this place," I said.

6

I'D BEEN COMPLAINING to Jean-Claude for years that his decorating scheme was too monochromatic, but one look at Narcissus's bedroom and I knew I owed Jean-Claude an apology. The room was done in black, and I mean *black*. The walls, the hardwood floor, the drawn drapes against one wall, the bed. The only color in the room was the silver chains and the silver-colored implements hanging from the wall. The color of the steel seemed to accentuate the blackness rather than relieve it. Chains dangled from the ceiling above the huge bed. It was bigger than king-sized. The only term that came to mind was *orgy-sized*. The bed was four-postered, with the largest, heaviest, darkest wood I'd ever seen. More chains dangled from the four posts, set in heavy permanent rings. If I'd been on a date, I'd have turned and run for it. But this wasn't a date, and in we all trooped.

My understanding about most people who were into D and S was that their bedrooms were separate from their "dungeons." Nearby perhaps, but not the same room. You needed somewhere to go to actually sleep. Maybe Narcissus just never rested from the fun and games.

There was a door in the opposite wall, and the drapes were drawn over the middle of one wall. Maybe his real bed was behind door number two or the drapes. I hoped so.

The only chair in the room had straps attached to it, so Narcissus offered us the bed to sit on. I don't know if I would have sat down or not, but first Jean-Claude, then Richard did. Jean-Claude settled against the black bedspread as he did everything, with grace, settling his body against the pillows as if he felt utterly comfortable. But it was Richard who surprised me. I expected to see in him some of the discomfort I felt about the room, but he didn't seem in the least uncomfortable. In fact, I realized for the first time that the heavy leather cuffs at his wrists and the collar at his throat had metal hooks in them, so they could be attached to chains or a leash. He'd probably worn them so he could blend into the club scene, as I'd worn the boots. But . . . but I could feel that he was calm about the room and everything in it. I wasn't.

I looked at Jean-Claude and Richard and knew I'd decided to sleep with both of them tonight, however we arranged it. But seeing them on the bed in the middle of all this, watching them at home in it, made me wonder about my decision. It made me think that maybe, after all this time, I still didn't know what I was getting myself into.

Asher was wandering the room looking at the things on the wall. I couldn't read him like I could read the others, but he, too, seemed unruffled, and I didn't think it was an act. Narcissus had swept into the room with Ajax at his back. He'd agreed to leave everyone else in the hallway, or downstairs, in exchange for us leaving our extra wolves outside the room. I guess for true privacy you did need less than a double digit worth of people in a room.

Richard held his hand out to me. "It's okay, Anita. Nothing in this room can hurt you without your permission, and you're not going to give that." That wasn't exactly the comforting comment I'd wanted, but I guess it was the truth. I used to believe that truth was good, but I'd begun to realize that it is neither good, nor bad. It's just the truth. Life had been simpler when I believed in black-and-white absolutes.

I took his hand and let him draw me to the bed, between Jean-Claude and himself. Well, Narcissus had already made a play for Jean-Claude, so I guess we needed to make the hands-off point. But it still bothered me that Richard put me between them, not simply beside him. The warm, fuzzy feeling I'd had from the marriage of the marks seemed to be receding at an alarming rate. Magic does that sometimes.

I felt stiff and uncomfortable on the black bed between my two men. "What is wrong, *ma petite*? You are suddenly very tense."

I looked at Jean-Claude, raising my eyebrows. "Am I the only one here that doesn't like this room?"

"Jean-Claude liked this room very much, once," Narcissus said.

I turned and looked at the werehyena as he paced the room in his stocking feet. "What do you mean?" I asked.

Jean-Claude answered, "Once, I submitted to unwanted advances because I was told to do so. But those days are past."

I stared at him, and he wouldn't meet my gaze. His eyes were all for Narcissus, as the other man paced around the bed.

"I don't remember you being unwilling," Narcissus said. He leaned against the far post of the bed.

"I learned long ago to make a virtue of necessity," Jean-Claude said. "Besides, Nikolaos, the old Master of the City, sent me to you. You remember how she was, Narcissus. Refusal of an order was not allowed."

I'd had the horror of meeting Nikolaos personally. She had been very, very scary.

"So I was an unpleasant duty." He sounded angry.

Jean-Claude shook his head. "Your body is pleasant, Narcissus. What you like doing with your lovers, if they can take the damage, is not . . ." Jean-Claude looked down as if searching for the right word, then raised his midnight blue eyes to Narcissus, and I saw the effect that his gaze had on the shapeshifter. Narcissus looked like he'd been hit between the eyes with a hammer—a handsome, charming hammer.

"Is not *what*?" Narcissus asked, his voice hoarse.

"Is not to my taste," Jean-Claude said. "Besides, I must not have pleased you very much, for you did not do what my late master wished you to do."

I was the reason that Nikolaos was the *late* Master of the City. She'd been trying to kill me, and I'd gotten lucky. She was dead, I wasn't. And now Jean-Claude got to be Master of the City. I hadn't planned that. How much of it Jean-Claude had planned was still up for debate. It is not just prejudice on my part that makes me trust him less than Richard.

Narcissus put one knee on the bed, one hand still around the bedpost. "You pleased me very much." The look on his face was too intimate. They should have been alone for this conversation. But, then again, watching the way Narcissus looked at Jean-Claude, maybe that wouldn't have been such a great idea. From Jean-Claude all I sensed was a desire to soothe any injured feelings. But I was betting if I could peek inside Narcissus's head I'd find a different kind of desire.

"Nikolaos thought I failed her and punished me for it."

"I could not ally myself with her—not even for you as my permanent toy."

Jean-Claude raised an eyebrow at that. "I do not remember that being part of the deal."

"When I first told her *no*, she sweetened the offer." Narcissus crawled onto the bed. He stayed crouched on all fours, as if he were expecting someone to come up behind him.

"In what way did she sweeten the offer?"

Narcissus started to crawl across the bed, slowly, his knees catching on the hem of his dress as he moved. "She offered you to me for always, to do with as I wished."

A thrill of terror ran through me from my toes to the top of my head. It took me a second to realize it wasn't my fear. Richard and I both turned to Jean-Claude. His face showed nothing. It was his usual polite, attractive, almost bored mask. But we could both feel the cold, screaming terror in his mind at the thought of how close he'd come to being Narcissus's permanent . . . guest.

It filled him with a fear that was larger than the shapeshifter. Images flashed through my mind, memories. Chained on my stomach on rough wood, the sound of a whip going back, the shock of it biting into my skin, and the knowledge that it was only the first blow. The wave of utter despair that followed that memory left me blinking back tears. I had a confused image of being tied to a wall, with a hand rotted to green pus caressing my body. Then the images stopped abruptly, like someone had thrown a switch. But the body the hand had been traveling down had been male. They were Jean-Claude's memories, not mine. He'd been projecting his memories on me and when he realized it, he'd blocked it.

I looked at him and couldn't keep the horror out of my eyes. My hair hid my face from Narcissus, and I was glad because I couldn't be blasé about what I'd just seen. Jean-Claude didn't look at me but kept his eyes on Narcissus. I was trying not to cry, and Jean-Claude's face betrayed nothing.

Jean-Claude hadn't been remembering Narcissus's abuse, but others, many, countless others. It wasn't the pain I carried away from the memories, but the despair. The thought that I . . . no, he. He had not owned his own body. He had never been a prostitute, or rather, he had never traded sex for money. But for power, the whim of whoever was his current master, and strangely for safety, he had traded sex for centuries. I'd known that, but I'd pictured him as the seducer. What I'd just seen had nothing to do with seduction.

A small sound came from Richard, and I turned to him. His eyes were shiny with unshed tears, and he had the same look of numb horror that I felt on my own face. We looked at each other for a long frozen moment, then a tear trickled down his face a second before a hot line of tears eased down my own.

He reached for my hand and I took it. And we both turned to Jean-Claude. He was still watching, even talking, though I hadn't heard any of it, with Narcissus. The other man had crawled all the way across that huge bed to be within touching distance of us all. But it wasn't *us all* that he wanted to touch.

"Sweet, sweet, Jean-Claude, I thought I had forgotten you, but seeing you tonight on the floor with the two of them made me remember." He reached out towards Jean-Claude, and Richard grabbed his wrist.

"Don't touch him. Don't ever touch him again."

Narcissus looked from Jean-Claude to Richard and finally back to Richard. "Such possessiveness, it must be true love." I had a ringside seat and watched the muscles in Richard's hands and forearm tense as he squeezed that dainty wrist.

Narcissus laughed, voice shaky, but not with pain. "Such strength, such passion, would he crush my wrist just for trying to touch your hair?" His voice held amusement and what

I finally realized was excitement. Richard touching him, threatening him, hurting him . . . He was enjoying it.

I felt Richard realize it too, but he didn't let go. Instead he jerked the other man off balance until he fell against his body. Narcissus made a small surprised sound. Richard kept one hand on his wrist, and he put the other to the man's neck. Not squeezing, just there, large and dark against Narcissus's pale skin.

The bodyguard, Ajax, had moved away from the wall, and Asher had moved to meet him. Things could go very bad, very quickly here. It was usually me that lost my temper and made things worse, not Richard.

Narcissus had to sense rather than see the movement, because Richard had him facing away from the rest of the room. "It's alright, Ajax, it's alright. Richard is not hurting me." Then Richard did something that made Narcissus's breath stop in his throat and come out harsh. "You may crush my wrist, if it's foreplay, but if it's not, then my people will kill you, all of you." His words were reasonable, his tone was not. You could hear the pain in his voice, but there was also anticipation, as if whichever way Richard answered, it would excite him.

Jean-Claude spoke. "Do not give him an excuse to have us at his mercy, *mon ami*. We are in his territory tonight, his guests. We owe him a guest's duty to his host, as long as he does not forfeit that right."

I wasn't a hundred percent sure what a guest's duties to his host were, but I was willing to bet that crushing their limbs wasn't among them. I touched Richard's shoulder, and he jumped. Narcissus made a small protesting sound, as if Richard had involuntarily tightened his grip.

"Jean-Claude's right, Richard."

"Anita councils you to temperance, Richard, and she is one of the least temperate people I have ever known." Jean-Claude moved forward, laying his hand on Richard's other shoulder, so we both touched him. "Besides, *mon ami*, hurting this one will not undo the harm already done. No drop of blood less will have been spilt; no pound of flesh less will have been lost; no humiliation will have been stopped. It is over, memories cannot harm us."

For the first time I wondered if Richard and I had gotten the same memories in that flash of shared insight. What I'd seen had been horrible, but it hadn't affected me like it had him. Maybe it was a guy thing. Maybe a white, Anglo-Saxon, upper-middle-class male like Richard would take memories of being abused and raped harder than I would. I was a woman. I knew things like that could happen to me. Maybe he had never thought they could happen to him.

Richard spoke low, his voice fallen to a rolling growl, as if his beast lurked just behind that handsome throat. "Never touch him again, Narcissus, or we'll finish this." Then Richard slowly, carefully, slid his hands away from Narcissus. I expected him to scoot away, clutching his injured wrist, but I underestimated him, or maybe overestimated him.

Narcissus did cradle his wrist, but he stayed pressed against Richard's body. "You've torn ligaments in my wrist. They take longer to heal than bone."

"I know," Richard said softly. The level of anger in those two words made me flinch.

"With a thought I can tell my men to leave her wereleopards to the mercy of their captors."

Richard glanced at Jean-Claude, who nodded. "Narcissus can contact his . . . men mind-to-mind."

Richard put his hands on Narcissus's shoulders, to push him away I thought, but Narcissus said, "You've revoked your safe passage by injuring me against my will."

Richard froze, and I could see the tension in his back, feel the sudden uncertainty.

"What is he talking about?" I asked. I wasn't even sure who I was asking.

"Narcissus has a small army of werehyenas within this building and on the surrounding buildings as guards," Jean-Claude said.

"If the werehyenas are so powerful, then why doesn't everyone talk about them in the same breath with the wolves and the rats?" I asked.

"Because Narcissus prefers to be the power behind the

throne, *ma petite*. It means that the other shapeshifters are constantly currying his favor with gifts."

"Like Nikolaos used you," I said.

He nodded.

I looked at Richard. "What have you been giving him?"

Richard eased away from Narcissus. "Nothing."

Narcissus turned on the bed, still cradling his wrist. "That's about to change."

"I don't think so," Richard said.

"Marcus and Raina had an arrangement with me. They and the rats dictated that my hyenas could never rise above fifty in number. To make this happen they used gifts, not threats."

"The threat was always there," Richard said. "War between you, us, and the rats, with you on the losing side."

Narcissus shrugged. "Perhaps, but have you not wondered what I've been doing since Marcus died and you took over? I wondered when the gifts would start arriving, but instead all gifts stopped, even the ones I'd begun to count on." He looked at me then. "Some of those gifts were yours to give, Nimir-Ra."

I must have looked as confused as I felt, because Jean-Claude said, "The wereleopards."

"Yes, Gabriel, their old alpha, was a dear, dear friend of mine," Narcissus said.

Since I'd killed Gabriel, I didn't like the way the conversation was going. "You mean that Gabriel gave some of the wereleopards to you?"

Narcissus's smile made me shiver. "All of them have spent time in my care, except Nathaniel." His smile faded. "I assumed Gabriel kept Nathaniel to himself because he was his personal favorite, but now that you've told me what Nathaniel is, I know that wasn't it." Narcissus leaned forward on his knees. "Gabriel was afraid to give me Nathaniel, afraid of what we might do together."

I swallowed hard. "You covered your reaction really well when I told you."

"I'm an accomplished liar, Anita. Best remember that." He looked up at Richard. "How long has it been since Marcus's death, a little over a year? When the gifts stopped com-ing, I assumed the pact was at an end."

"What are you saying?" Richard asked.

"There are over four hundred werehyenas now, some new, some recruited from out of state. But we rival the wererats and werewolves now. You will have to negotiate with us as equals instead of peons."

Richard said, "What do you . . ."

Jean-Claude interrupted. "Let us come to terms." I felt the fear that was behind his calm words, and so did Richard. You did not ask a sexual sadist what he wanted. You offered what you were willing to give up.

Narcissus looked at Richard. "Are they Jean-Claude's wolves now, Richard? Do you share your kingship?" The tone was mocking.

"I am Ulfric, and I will set the terms, no one else." But his voice was cautious, the temper slowed. I'd never seen Richard like this, and I wasn't sure I liked the change. He was reacting more like me. As I thought of it, I wondered . . . I channeled some of his beast, some of Jean-Claude's hunger, what did they gain from me?

"You know what I want," Narcissus said.

"You would be wise not to ask for it," Jean-Claude said.

"If I cannot have you, Jean-Claude, then perhaps to watch the three of you make love on my bed would be enough to wash this insult clean between us."

Richard and I said together, "No."

He looked at us, and there was something unpleasant in his eyes. "Then give me Nathaniel."

"No," I said.

"For one evening."

"No."

"For an hour," he said.

I shook my head.

"One of the other leopards?"

"I won't give you any of my people."

He looked at Richard. "And you, Ulfric, will you give me one of your wolves?"

"You know the answer, Narcissus," Richard said.

"Then what would you offer me, Ulfric?"

"Name something I'm willing to give."

Narcissus smiled, and I had a sense of Ajax and Asher circling each other as they felt the tension rising. "I want to be included in the conferences that run the shapeshifter community in this town."

Richard nodded. "Fine. Rafael and I thought you had no interest in politics, or you would already have been asked."

"The rat king does not know my heart, nor do the wolves."

Richard stood. "Anita needs to go to her people."

Narcissus smiled and shook his head. "Oh, no, Ulfric, it is not that easy."

Richard frowned. "You're to be included in decision making. That's what you wanted."

"But I still want gifts."

"No gifts pass between the rats and the wolves. We are allies. If you wish to be an ally then there will be no gifts, except that we will come to your aid when you need us."

Narcissus shook his head again. "I do not wish to be allies, to be dragged into every squabble between animals that do not concern me. No, Ulfric, you mistake me. I wish to be included in the conferences that set policy. But I do not wish to tie myself to anyone and be dragged into a war that is not of my own making."

"Then what are you asking?" Richard said.

"Gifts."

"Bribes, you mean," Richard said.

Narcissus shrugged. "Call it what you will."

"No," Richard said.

I felt Jean-Claude tense a moment before Richard said it. *"Mon ami . . ."*

"No," Richard said and turned to Jean-Claude. "Even if he could kill us all, which I doubt, my wolves, your vampires, they would rain down on this club and take it apart brick by brick. He won't risk that. Narcissus is a cautious leader. I learned from watching him deal with Marcus. He puts his own safety and comfort above all else."

"The comfort and safety of my people above all else,"

Narcissus said. He looked at me. "What of you, Nimir-Ra, how confident do you feel? Do you think if I had my people kill your kittens that the werewolves and vampires would lift a finger to avenge them?"

"You forget, Narcissus, she's also my lupa, my mate. The wolves will defend who she tells them to defend."

"Ah, yes, the human lupa, the human leopard queen. But not really human, is she?"

I met his gaze and said, "I need to go collect my leopards. Thanks for the hospitality." I pushed to my feet and stood beside Richard.

Narcissus looked at Jean-Claude, who still lounged on the bed. "Are they really such children?" he asked him.

Jean-Claude gave a graceful shrug. "They are not like us Narcissus. They still believe in right and wrong. And rules."

"Then let me teach them a new rule." He stared up at us, still kneeling on the bed, still wearing the black lace dress, and suddenly his power burst out before him in lines of heat. It slammed into my body like a giant hand, nearly staggering me. Richard reached out to steady me, and the moment we touched, his beast jumped between us, in a rush of warmth that raced through my body in goosebumps and shivers. Richard's body shuddered, and I felt his breath, our breath, catch. That otherworldly power curled between us, and for the first time I realized that the power came both ways. I'd thought what was inside me was an echo of Richard's beast, but it was more than that. Maybe it would have been different if I hadn't separated myself from him for so long. But now the power that had once been his was mine. The warmth spilled between us like two streams converging into a river, two scalding hot streams that spilled into a river that boiled over my skin. It was so hot that I half expected my skin to peel away and reveal the beast underneath.

"If she shifts, then my men are free to enter this fight." Narcissus's voice was shocking. I think I'd forgotten he was there, forgotten everything but the hot, hot power flowing between Richard and me. Narcissus's face began to grow longer. It was like watching sticks move behind clay.

Richard ran his hand just in front of my body, caressing

the power that flowed off of my skin. There was a look of soft wonderment on his face. "She won't shift. You have my word," Richard said.

"Good enough. You always keep your word. I may be a sadist and a masochist, but I am still Oba of this clan." His voice had become a strange high-pitched growl. "You have insulted me and, through me, all that is mine." Claws slid out from his small fingers until he raised curved paws, not hands at all.

Jean-Claude came to stand beside us. "Come, *ma petite,* let them have room to maneuver." He touched my hand, and that scalding power poured from my skin to his. He collapsed to his knees, hand still pressed against my skin, as if the heat had welded it in place.

I knelt by him, and his gaze raised, drowning blue, the pupil lost in a rush of power, but not his power. He opened his mouth to speak, but no sound came out. He stared at me, and, judging by the look on his face, he felt lost, overwhelmed.

"What's wrong?" Asher asked from across the room, still facing Ajax.

"I'm not sure," I said.

"He seems in pain," Narcissus said. It made me glance up at him. Except for his face and hands, he was still in human form. The really powerful alphas could do that, partial changes.

"The power spills over him," Richard said, and his voice held that edge of growl. His throat was hidden behind the leather collar, but I knew if I could see it, that the skin would be smooth and perfect. His voice could howl from his mouth like a dog's without any change in his appearance.

"But he is a vampire," Narcissus said. "The power of the wolves should be closed to him."

"The wolf is his animal to call," Richard said.

I looked into Jean-Claude's face from inches away, watched him struggle through the hot, scalding power and knew why he wasn't dealing well with it. This was primal energy, the life and beat of the earth under our feet, the rush of wind in the trees, the stuff of life. And Jean-Claude for all that he walked and talked and flirted wasn't alive.

Richard knelt beside us, and Jean-Claude let out a low moan, half-collapsing against me. "Jean-Claude!"

Richard rolled him over into his arms, and Jean-Claude's spine bowed, his breath coming in ragged gasps.

Narcissus was above us on the bed. "What's wrong with him?"

"I don't know," Richard said.

I put a hand on Jean-Claude's throat. The pulse wasn't just racing, it was beating like a caged thing. I tried to use the ability I had to sense vampires, but all I could feel was the heat of the beast. There was nothing cold or dead in the circle of our arms.

"Lay him on the floor, Richard."

He looked at me.

"Do it!"

He laid Jean-Claude gently on the floor, hand still touching his shoulder.

"Move away from him." I did what I asked of Richard, standing and moving around the vampire, pushing Richard back with my body until Jean-Claude lay alone beside the bed.

Narcissus's body had re-formed, until he was the graceful man we'd met downstairs. He'd moved off the bed without being told, but moved around so he could still watch.

Jean-Claude rolled slowly onto his side, and moved his head to stare at us. He licked his lips and tried twice before he could speak. "What have you done to me?"

Richard and I still stood in a cocoon of heat. His hands brushed my arms, and I shuddered against him. His arms locked around my waist, and the more of our bodies that touched the more heat rose around us, until I thought the very air should tremble like the heat of a summer's day off a tar road.

"Shared Richard's power with you," I said.

"No," Jean-Claude said, and he rose slowly to sit, propped heavily on his arms. "Not just Richard, but you, *ma petite,* you. Richard and I have shared much, but it never did this. You are the bridge between the two worlds."

Asher spoke. "She bridges life and death."

Jean-Claude looked up at him sharply, a harsh look on his face. *"Exactement."*

Narcissus spoke. "I knew Marcus and Raina could share their power, their beasts, but Anita is not a werewolf. You should not be able to share your beast with each other, wolf to leopard."

"I'm not a wereleopard," I said.

"Me thinks the lady doth protest too much," Narcissus said.

"Or wereanimal to vampire," Asher said.

I looked at Asher. "Don't *you* start."

He smiled at me. "I know that you are not a true shape-shifter, but your . . . magic has changed because of the addition of Richard. There is something about you, that if I did not know better, I would say you were indeed one of them."

"Richard said the wolf is Jean-Claude's animal to call," Narcissus said.

"That doesn't explain this," Asher said. He knelt by Jean-Claude, reaching towards him.

Jean-Claude caught his hand before it could touch his face, and Asher jerked back. "You're hot to the touch. Not just warm, hot."

"It is like the rush after we feed, but more . . . more alive." He gazed up at us, and his eyes were still drowning blue. "Go save your leopards, *ma petite,* and let us retire before dawn. I want to see how hot," he took a deep breath, and I knew he was drawing in the scent of us, "this power will grow."

"It is all very impressive," Narcissus said, "but I will have my pound of flesh."

"You're beginning to get on my nerves," I said.

He smiled. "Be that as it may, I still have a right to ask for the insult to be avenged."

I looked at Richard. He nodded. I sighed. "You know it's usually me that gets us into this kind of trouble."

"We're not in trouble yet," Richard said. "Narcissus is grandstanding. Why do you think I didn't change?" He stared at the smaller man.

Narcissus smiled. "And here I thought you were just decorative muscle standing behind Marcus."

"You won't fight unless you run out of options, Narcissus, so no more games." There was a coldness in Richard's voice, a firmness that could not be crossed or reasoned with. Again it echoed me more than him. Just how tough had the last few months been on him and his wolves? There are only a few things that will harden you this fast. Death of those close to you; police work; or combat where people are actually dying around you. In civilian life, Richard was a junior high science teacher, so it wasn't police work. I think someone would have mentioned if he'd lost family members. That left combat. How many challengers had he fought? How many had he killed? Who had died?

I shook my head to clear away the thoughts. One problem at a time. "You can't have any of us, or our people, Narcissus. You're not going to start a war over the refusal, so where does that leave us?"

"I will take my men out of the room with your cats, Anita. I will do that." He came to stand in front of me, his back to the bedpost, one hand playing with the chains attached to it, making the metal jingle. "The . . . people that have them are not terribly creative, but they have a certain raw talent for pain." He stared at me with human eyes again.

"What do you want, Narcissus?" Richard said.

He wrapped the chain around one wrist over and over. "Something worth having, Richard, *someone* worth having."

Asher said, "Do you merely want someone to dominate, or are you interested in being dominated?"

Narcissus looked back at him. "Why?"

"Answer the question truthfully, Narcissus," Jean-Claude said. "You may find it worthwhile."

Narcissus looked from one vampire to the other, then back to Asher, standing there in his brown leather outfit. "I prefer to dominate, but with the right person I'll allow myself to be topped."

Asher walked towards us, making his tall, slender body sway. "I'll top you."

"You do not have to do this," Jean-Claude said.

"Don't do it, Asher," I said.

"We'll find another way," Richard said.

Asher looked at us with those pale, pale blue eyes. "I thought you'd be happy, Jean-Claude. I've finally agreed to take a lover. Isn't that what you wanted me to do?" His voice was mild, but the mockery came through just the same, the bitterness.

"I have offered you nearly all in my power, and you have refused all. Why him? Why now?" Jean-Claude got to his knees, and I offered him a hand up, not a hundred percent sure that I should.

He looked at the offered hand.

"If you think it's safe," I said.

He wrapped his hand around mine, and the power flowed in a burning rush down my hand over his, down his arm, and I felt it hit his heart like a blow. He closed his eyes, swayed for a second, then looked at me. "It was unexpected the first time." He started to stand, and Richard went to his other side, so that we held him between us.

"I don't know if this is good for you, or not," I said.

"You fill me with life, *ma petite*. You and Richard. How can it be bad?"

I didn't say the obvious, but I thought it really hard. If you could fill the walking dead with life, should you? And if you did, what would happen to that walking dead? So much of what we were doing between us magically had never been done before, or only once before. Unfortunately we'd had to kill the other triumvirate that consisted of a vamp, a werewolf, and a necromancer. They'd been trying to kill us, but still, they might have been able to answer questions that no one else could have answered. Now we were just swinging in the dark, hoping we didn't hurt each other.

"Look at you, Jean-Claude, between them like a candle with two wicks. You will burn yourself up," Asher said.

"That is my concern."

"Yes, and what I do is mine. You ask, 'Why him?' 'Why now?' First, you need me. Which of the three of you would be willing to do this?" Asher moved around Narcissus as if he weren't there, eyes on Jean-Claude, on us. "Oh, I know that you could have topped him. You can do it when you want, and make a virtue of necessity, but he's had you beneath him, and nothing less will satisfy him now." He stood close enough that the energy swirled outward, over him like a lip of hot ocean water. His breath came out in a shuddering sigh. *"Mon Dieu!"* He stepped back until his legs touched the bed, then he sat down on the black sheets. His brown leather didn't match as well as the rest of us had.

"Such power, Jean-Claude, and yet none of you wishes to pay the price for Richard's temper tantrum. But I will pay that price."

"You know my rule, Asher. I never ask of others what I'm not willing to do myself," I said.

He looked at me curiously, face unreadable behind the mask, except for his eyes. "Are you volunteering?"

I shook my head. "No. But you don't have to do this. We will find another way."

"And what if I want to do it?" he asked.

I looked at him for a second, then shrugged. "I don't know what to say to that."

"It disturbs you that I might want to do this, doesn't it?" His eyes were intense.

"Yes," I said.

That intense gaze moved past me to Jean-Claude. "It bothers him, too. He wonders if I am ruined and all that is left for me is pain."

"You once told me that everything worked. That you were scarred, but . . . functional," I said.

He blinked and looked at me. "Did I? Well, a man does not like to admit such things to a pretty woman. Or to a handsome man." He looked up at us, but the only person he was really looking at was Jean-Claude. "I will pay the toll for our handsome Monsieur Zeeman's display of strength. But I will not be the whipping boy. Not this time."

Not ever again, hung heavy in the air, unsaid, but there all the same. Asher had had two hundred years of being at the mercy of the people who had given Jean-Claude the memories that Richard and I had flashed on. Two centuries more of that kind of care and torment. When Asher had first come to us he'd been cruel occasionally. I thought we'd cured him of it. But watching the look in his eyes now, I knew we hadn't.

"And do you know the best part of all?" Asher asked.

Jean-Claude just shook his head.

"It will cause you pain to think of me with Narcissus. And even after I am with him, he will still not answer the question you have been wanting, so desperately, to have answered."

Jean-Claude stiffened, hand tightening on mine. I felt him slam his own shields into place, keeping us out of what he was thinking, feeling, at that moment. The warm, roiling power between us began to dissipate. Jean-Claude had made himself part of our circuit. Now he was shutting us down, though I didn't think it was on purpose. He just couldn't shield himself from us and keep the flow going.

His voice came out calm, his usual bored, yet cultured, tone, "How can you be so sure that he will not talk?"

"I can be sure of what I do. And I will not give him the answer you want."

"What answer?" I asked. "What are you guys talking about?"

The two vampires looked at each other. "Ask Jean-Claude," Asher said.

I looked at Jean-Claude, but he was staring at Asher. In a way, the rest of us were superfluous, an audience for a show that didn't need one.

"You're being petty, Asher," Richard said.

The vampire's gaze moved to the man on my other side, and the anger in those eyes made the blue spill across the pupils in a frosted gleam. He looked blind. "Have I not earned the right to be petty, Richard?"

Richard shook his head. "Just tell him the truth."

"There are three people in his power that I would strip for, that I would allow to touch me, and answer that so important question." He stood in one graceful movement, like a liquid puppet on strings. He stepped close enough for the power to spill around him, bringing his breath shuddering from his lips. The power recognized him, flared stronger, as if he could act as our third, if we weren't careful. Did the power just need a vampire, and not specifically Jean-Claude? Richard shut down his side of the power, clanging a shield in place that made me think of metal, strong and solid, uncompromising.

Asher caressed the air just above Richard's arm and had to step away, rubbing his hands on his arms. "The power fades." He shook himself like a dog coming out of water. "If you would say *yes*, his torment could end."

I frowned at them both, not sure I was following the conversation, not sure I wanted to.

Asher turned those pale, drowning eyes to me. "Or, our fair Anita." He was already shaking his head. "But no, I know better than to ask. I have enjoyed shocking our so heterosexual Richard by my overtures. But Anita is not so easily teased." He came to stand in front of Jean-Claude. "And, of course, if he wanted the answer badly enough he could do it himself."

Jean-Claude's face was at its most arrogant. Its most hidden. "You know why I do not."

Asher moved back to stand in front of me. "He refuses my bed, because he fears that you would . . . what is the American word . . . dump him, if you knew he were sleeping with a man. Would you?"

I had to swallow before I could answer. "Yeah."

Asher smiled, but not like he was happy, more like it had been a predictable answer. "Then I will pleasure myself here with Narcissus, and Jean-Claude will still not know if I stay because I have become a lover of such things, or because this type of love is all that is left for me."

"I haven't agreed to this," Narcissus said. "Before I take second—no *fourth* choice—let me see what I'm buying."

Asher stood, turning so that his left side was towards the werehyena. He unzipped the mask and lifted it over his head. We were standing enough to one side so that I could see that perfect profile. His golden hair—and I mean golden—was braided along the back of his head so that nothing interfered with the view. I was used to looking at Asher through a film of hair. Without it, the lines of his face were like sculpture, something so smooth and lovely that you wanted to touch it, trace the movement of it with your hands, layer it with kisses. Even after the little show he'd put on, he was still beautiful. Nothing seemed to change that when I looked at Asher.

"Very nice," Narcissus said, "very, very nice, but I have many beautiful men at my beck and call. Perhaps not as beautiful, but still . . ."

Asher turned to face the man. Whatever Narcissus was about to say died in his throat. The right side of Asher's face looked like melted candle wax. The scars didn't start until well away from the midline of his face. It was as if his torturers all those centuries ago had wanted him to have enough left to remember the perfection he'd once been. His eyes were still golden-lashed, his nose perfect, his mouth full and kissable, but the rest . . . The rest was scarred. Not ruined, not spoiled, but scarred.

I remembered Asher's smooth perfection, the feel of that perfect body rubbing against mine. Not my memories. I had never seen Asher nude. I had never touched him that way. But Jean-Claude had about two hundred years ago. It made it impossible for me to look at Asher with unprejudiced eyes, because I remembered being in love with him, in fact, was still a little in love with him. Which meant that Jean-Claude was still a little in love with him. My personal life just can't get more complicated.

Narcissus drew a shuddering breath and said in a voice gone hoarse, eyes wide, "Oh, my."

Asher threw the hood on the bed and began to unzip the front of the leather shirt, very slowly. I'd seen his chest before and knew that it was much worse than his face. The right side of his chest was carved with deep runnels, the skin hard to the touch. The left side, like his face, still had that angelic beauty that had attracted the vampires to him long ago.

When the zipper was halfway down his body, baring his chest and upper stomach, Narcissus had to sit down on the bed as if his legs wouldn't hold him.

"I think, Narcissus," Jean-Claude said, "that after tonight you will owe us a favor." His voice was empty when he said

it, devoid of anything. It was the voice he used when he was
at his most careful, or his most pained.

Asher asked in a careful voice that didn't quite match the
striptease he was doing, "What level of pain does Narcissus
enjoy straight—how do you say—out of the box?"

"Rough," Jean-Claude said. "He can control his desire and
not step outside the bounds of his submissive, but if he is to
be topped, then rough, very rough. You do not need a warm-
ing up period for this one." Jean-Claude's voice was still
empty.

Asher looked down at Narcissus. "Is that true? Do you
like to start out with a . . . bang?" That last word was slow,
seductive. One word, and it held worlds of promise within
it.

Narcissus nodded slowly. "You can start with blood, if
you've the balls for it."

"Most people have to work up to that for it to be pleasurable," Asher said.

"I don't," Narcissus said.

Asher finished unzipping and lowered the shirt off his
arms, held it in his hands for a moment, then struck out with
a movement so quick it was only an after-image blur. He
slapped Narcissus across the face with the heavy zipper once,
twice, three times, until blood showed at the corner of his
mouth and his eyes looked unfocused.

I was so startled by all of it that I think I forgot to breathe.
All I could do was stare. Jean-Claude had gone very still
between Richard and me. It wasn't the utter stillness that he
was capable of, that all the old masters were capable of, and
I realized why. He couldn't sink into that black stillness of
death with the lingering touch of the "life" we'd pumped
through him.

Narcissus used the tip of his tongue to taste the blood on
his mouth. "I am an accomplished liar, but I always give fair
trade." He was suddenly more serious than he had been, as
if the flippant tease was just a mask and underneath was a
more solemn, thinking person. When he looked up, there was
a person in his eyes that I knew was dangerous. The flirt was
real, too, but it was partially camouflage to make everyone

underestimate him. Looking into his eyes, I knew that to underestimate him would be a very bad thing.

He turned those newly serious eyes to Asher. "For this, I will owe you a favor, but only one favor, not three."

Asher reached up and undid his hair, letting the heavy sparkling waves fall around his face. He stared down at the smaller man, and I couldn't see the look he gave, but whatever it was, it made Narcissus look like a drowning man. "I am only worth one favor?" Asher said. "I think not."

Narcissus had to swallow twice before he could speak. "Perhaps more." He turned and looked at us, and his eyes were still raw, real. "Go, save your wereleopards, whoever they belong to. But know this, the ones inside are new to our community. They do not know our rules, and their own rules seem harsh by comparison."

"You warn us, Narcissus, thank you," Jean-Claude said.

"I think that this one would not like it if you were hurt, no matter how angry he is with you, Jean-Claude. I am about to let him bind me to this bed, or the wall, and do to me whatever he wishes."

"Whatever I wish?" Asher asked.

Narcissus's gaze flicked back to him. "No, not whatever, but until I use the safety word, yes." There was something almost childlike in the way he said the last, as if he were already thinking of what was to come, and not really concentrating on us.

"Safety word?" I asked.

Narcissus gazed at me. "If the pain grows too much, or if something is proposed that the slave does not want to do, you use the word agreed upon. Once the word is spoken the master must stop."

"But you'll be tied up, you won't be able to make him stop."

Narcissus's eyes were drowning, drowning in things that I didn't understand, and didn't want to. "It is both the trust and the element of uncertainty that makes the event, Anita."

"You trust that he'll stop when you say stop, but you like the thought that he might not stop, that he might just keep going," Richard said.

It made me stare at him, but I caught Narcissus's nod.

"Am I the only one in this room that doesn't understand how this game is played?"

"Remember, Anita," Richard said, "I was a virgin until Raina got me. She was my first lover, and her tastes ran . . . to the exotic."

Narcissus laughed then. "A virgin in Raina's hands, what a frightening image. Even I wouldn't let her top me, because you could see it in her eyes."

"See what?" I asked.

"That she had no stopping point."

Having almost been a star in one of her little bedroom dramas, saved only by the fact that I'd killed her first, I had to agree.

"Raina liked it better if you didn't want to do it," Richard said. "She was a sexual sadist, not a dominant. It took me a long time to realize how big a difference there is between the two."

I looked at his face, but he was safe behind his shields, I couldn't read him. He and Jean-Claude had more practice at shielding than I did. But, frankly, I didn't want to know what was behind the lost look on Richard's face. I realized with a start that I had Jean-Claude's memories but not Richard's. It had never occurred to me to ask why that was. But later, later. Right now I wanted to be out of this room. "I want out of here."

Jean-Claude pulled gently away from both of us to stand on his own. "Yes, the night is running out, and we have much to do."

I didn't look at him, or Richard. I'd pretty much promised that if dawn stayed at bay we'd have sex tonight. But somehow staring at Asher's naked back, with Narcissus gazing up at him with a look somewhere between adoration and terror, I just wasn't in the mood anymore.

7

THE UPPER HALLWAY stretched white and empty. There was a silver wallpaper border high up on the wall; more silver ran in thin lines down the walls, an opulent yet tasteful display. It looked like the hallway of some upscale hotel. I didn't know if it was camouflage or if Narcissus just liked it that way. After downstairs' black techno-punk and Narcissus's own Marquis de Sade bedroom, it was almost startling, as if we'd stepped from some dark nightmare into a quieter, more peaceful dream.

We were the ones who looked out of place. All of us in black, too much skin showing. Jamil paced up the stairs on point, his muscular upper body showing in tantalizing glimpses through a series of black leather straps. The pants fit his narrow hips like a second skin, and I'd learned long ago from watching Jean-Claude undress that you didn't get that smooth line if there was underwear between the skin and the pants. He turned, his waist-length cornrows flaring out around him. He was a contrast in darkness, the black of the leather, the dark, dark brown of his skin. He moved like a shadow in that white hallway.

Faust went next. He was the new male vampire I'd met downstairs. In the better light, his hair was obviously tinted burgundy, like a shade of red gone wrong, but somehow it suited him. His leather pants were covered in more zippers than seemed necessary to get them on and off, and his black shirt had a zipper up the front. It reminded me of Asher's shirt, except for the color. I tried not to think too much about what Asher might be doing right this moment. I still didn't know if Asher was pimping himself out for us or whether he truly wanted to be with Narcissus. I was more comfortable with the idea of self-sacrifice.

I brought up the middle with the two women behind me. Sylvie still didn't look like herself to me. The black skirt was so short that whoever was in back of her couldn't help but get a flash of whatever was under the skirt. The hose climbed her legs all the way up, making them look long and shapely, though she was only three inches taller than me. She was also wearing three-inch black spikes, which may have added to the illusion of long legs. Her leather top showed a very discreet line of flesh from neck to waist where a belt cinched in her tiny waist. Her breasts seemed to stay magically on either side of the line of skin, as if they were held in place by something more than a bra.

She smiled up at me, but her eyes had already bled to that pale wolfish color. They didn't match the careful makeup and the short, curly brown hair.

Meng Die brought up the rear. Where her pale flesh showed around the vinyl cat suit, colorless body glitter sparkled. There was a touch of glitter at the corner of each up-tilted eye, complementing pale eyeshadow and dramatic eyeliner. She was smaller than me, more delicate of bone, smaller of breast, more slender of waist, like a dainty bird. But the look she gave me was more vulture than canary. She didn't like me, and I didn't know why. But Jean-Claude had assured me she'd do the job. Jean-Claude had a lot of faults, but if he trusted Meng Die to keep me safe, then she'd do it. He was never careless with me, not in that way.

Faust just seemed to be amused as hell about it all. Everything made him smile, pleasantly. Most vampires went for arrogance to mask how they felt. He seemed to use mild amusement. Of course, maybe Faust was just a happy guy, and I was being too cynical.

Why weren't Jean-Claude and Richard with me? Because the wereleopards were mine. If I took other dominants with me, it would be seen as weakness. I was planning to interview other alphas to take over the wereleopards, but until I found someone to do that, I was all they had. If people began thinking I was weak, the leopards would be marked as anyone's meat. It wouldn't just be out-of-town shapeshifters that were trying to take them away from me, it would be every shapeshifter in town. It was funny how many shifters could be assholes unless you were strong enough to stop them.

I had to save the leopards, not Richard, not Jean-Claude, me. But I had to stay alive to do that, so I did take backup. I'm stubborn, not stupid. Though I know a few people who might argue that.

Each white door had a silver number on its surface. Again like a very discreet hotel. We were looking for room nine. There was absolutely no sound from behind the doors. The only noises I heard were the distant thud of the music downstairs and the faint whisper of leather and vinyl—our body movements. I'd never been so aware of how loud small noises could be. Maybe it was the eerie silence of the hallway, or maybe I'd gained something new from the marriage of the marks. Better hearing wouldn't be a bad thing, would it? So many of the "gifts" from the vampire marks tended to be double-edged swords, at best.

I shook off the gloomy thoughts and walked with my foursome of bodyguards down the carpeted hallway. I was trusting them to give their lives for mine. That's what a bodyguard does. Jamil had taken two shotgun blasts for me last summer. It hadn't been silver shot, so he'd healed, but he hadn't known that when he put himself between the gun barrel and me. Sylvie owed me one, and a woman her size doesn't get to be second in the pack hierarchy without being one tough werewolf. I didn't really trust the vampires to give up their undead lives for me. It's been my experience that the longer something semi-immortal lives, the more tightly it hugs its existence. So I counted on the wolves, and knew I could work around the vampires. It didn't matter that Jean-Claude trusted them. It mattered that I didn't. I'd have preferred to just bring along more werewolves, except if I showed up with nothing but wolves at my back, it would be like saying that I couldn't do this without Richard's pack. Not true. Or not completely true. We'd see how deep the shit was once we opened the door.

Room nine was nearly at the end of the long hallway. The building had been a warehouse, and the upstairs had simply been divided into long hallways with huge rooms scattered along them. Jamil was standing to one side of the door. Faust was standing in front of it. Not smart.

I stood to the other side of the door and said, "Faust, the werehyenas had to take guns off these guys."

The vampire raised an arched eyebrow at me.

"They may not have found all the guns," I said.

He still looked at me.

I sighed. Over a hundred years of "life," power enough to be a master vamp, and he was still an amateur. "It would be bad to be standing in the center of the door when a shotgun blast went off on the other side."

He blinked, and a little of that humor leaked away, showing that arrogance that most vamps acquire. "I think Narcissus would have found a shotgun."

I leaned my shoulder against the wall and smiled at him. "Do you know what a cop-killer is?"

He raised both eyebrows at me. "A person who kills policemen."

"No, it's a type of ammunition designed to go through body armor. The cops have no defense against it. You can carry armor-piercing bullets in handguns, Faust. I used the shotgun as an example, but it could be so many things. And they would all take out your heart, most of your spine, or all of your head, depending on where the shooter was aiming."

"Get out of the fucking doorway," Meng Die said.

He turned and looked at her, and it was not a friendly look. "You are not my master."

"Nor you mine," she said.

"Children," I said. They both looked at me. Great. "Faust if you're not going to be helpful then go back downstairs."

"What did I do?"

I glanced at Meng Die, shrugged, and said, "Get out of the fucking doorway."

I could see his shoulders tighten, but he gave a graceful bow at odds with the burgundy hair and leather. "As Jean-Claude's lady wishes, so shall it be." He stepped to the side closest to me. Sylvie moved up close to me, not exactly between us, but close. It made me feel better. Bossing around vampires was always chancy. You never knew when they'd try to boss back. I really, really wanted my gun back.

"What now?" Jamil asked. He was watching the vampires like he wasn't any happier with their company than I was. All good bodyguards are paranoid. It goes with the job.

"I guess we knock." I kept my body well to the side, extended just enough arm to get the job done, and gave three solid knocks. If they shot through the door, they'd probably miss me. But no one shot through the door. In fact, nothing happened. We waited for a few moments, but patience has never been my best thing. I started to knock again, but Jamil stopped me and said, "May I?"

I nodded.

He knocked hard and loud enough to shake the door. It was a solid door. If the door didn't open this time, they were deliberately ignoring us.

The door opened, revealing a brown-haired man as muscled as Ajax, but taller. What did Narcissus do, recruit from all the weight-lifting gyms in town? He frowned at us. "Yeah?"

"I'm Nimir-Ra for the wereleopards. I think you've been waiting for me."

"About fucking time," he said. He opened the door wide, pushing it flush against the wall, putting his back to it, arms crossed across his chest. His arms apparently weren't as muscular as they looked, if he could cross his arms that way. But he did demonstrate that there was no one hiding behind the door. Good to know.

The room was white—white floor, white ceiling, white walls—like a room carved of hard snow. There were blades on the walls—knives, swords, daggers, tiny glittering blades, swords the length of a tall man. The bodyguard by the door said, "Welcome to the room of swords." It sounded formal, like he was supposed to say it.

From the door I couldn't see anyone. I took a deep breath, let it out slowly, and walked inside. Jamil followed a step behind at my shoulder, Faust was at my other side. Sylvie and Meng Die brought up the rear.

A figure stepped into the middle of the room. At first glance I thought it was a man, but on second glance, not exactly. He was man-sized, almost six feet, broad shouldered, muscular, but what I'd thought was a golden tan was golden tan fur, very thin and fine. Covering the whole body. The face was almost human, though the bone structure was a little odd. A wide face, a lipless mouth that was almost a round muzzle. The eyes were a dark orange gold with an edge of blue in them, as if they, like the body, were only partly through their change. It was as if his body had frozen, stopping just short of attaining human form. I'd never seen anything like it. Pale skin showed in patches on his bare chest and stomach. I couldn't tell if the dark gold hair and edge of beard that encircled his face was actually hair or what was left of a mane. The longer I stared at him, the more like a lion he looked, until I couldn't see the man I'd thought I'd seen for the light coating of beast that covered him.

He gave a snarling smile. "Do you like what you see?"

"I've never seen anything like you," I said, nice, calm, even empty.

He didn't like that, my lack of reaction. His smile vanished and became only a snarl of very sharp, very white teeth.

"Welcome, Nimir-Ra, I am Marco, we have been waiting for you." He made a sweeping gesture to either side with his clawed human hands. I glanced around at the "we". They were small to medium-sized men with short black hair and dark skin. Most groups, prides, packs, whatever, were mixed ethnically. But there was a sameness to these dark men, almost a family look about them. Two on either side wore hooded cloaks, with the hoods thrown back, the wide cloaks spread like curtains. I glimpsed blond hair behind the blackness to the left. I couldn't see Nathaniel's hair over the blackness but I knew he had to be on the right.

There was blood on the white floor, pooling into a little depression in the concrete. A drain was in the middle so they could hose the floor down when they were finished. There was another guard in the far corner who looked very unhappy to be there. Three women that I did not know were chained to the wall on either side of the door. Two blonds on the right side, a brunette on the left. They weren't wereleopards, or at least none that were mine.

"Let me see my people," I said.

"Will you not greet us formally?" Marco asked.

"You're not the alpha anything, Marco. You get your head lion in here and I'll greet him, but you, I don't have to greet."

Marco gave a small bow, the gaze of those odd tawny eyes never leaving my face. It was the way you bow in martial arts when you're afraid the other person will hit you if you glance away.

Jamil had moved up beside me, not ahead of me, but close enough that our shoulders brushed. I didn't tell him to move back. He'd saved my life once, I'd let him do his job.

"Then greet me, Nimir-Ra." It was another male voice. He stepped out from behind the cloaks to the left. As he stepped out, the cloaks dropped and I could see Gregory clearly.

He was turned towards the wall, nude except for his pants that had been peeled down to his lower thighs, his boots still on. Chains held his wrists above his head, his legs were wide apart. His curling blond hair fell just below his shoulders. His body was slender but muscled, butt tight. You have to take care of your body if you're going to strip professionally. There was no mark on his body that I could see, but blood had spattered on the floor in front of him, below him, pooling, dark, drying. They hadn't cut anything on his back. My stomach clenched tight, my breath squeezing down in my throat.

"Gregory," I said, softly.

"He's gagged," said the man. I finally dragged my gaze away from Gregory, and the sight of the other man, the alpha, made me stare.

He wasn't a lion man, he was a snake man. His head was wider than my shoulders, covered in olive green scales with large black spots. One arm was bare, and it looked very human except for the scales and the hands that ended in twisted claws that would have made any predator proud. He turned his head to look at me with one large copper gold eye. A heavy black stripe stretched back from the corner of his eye to his temple. His movements were vaguely birdlike.

Other black-cloaked figures stepped away from the walls, dropping hoods to show themselves scaled, with the same stripes near metallic eyes and hands with curling claws.

My people fanned out around me, two going to either side. "Who are you?"

"I am Coronus of the Black Water Clan, though I doubt that will mean anything to you."

"Marco mentioned you were new in town. I'm Anita Blake, Nimir-Ra of the Blooddrinkers Clan. By what right do you harm my people?" What I wanted to do was start screaming, but there are rules. I couldn't be furry, or scaly, but I could follow the rules.

Coronus walked to the wall and stood next to the brunette chained to it. She made small panicked sounds as he reached for her. Sylvie moved a little closer to him, to the girl, as if she was waiting for an excuse. Coronus traced a finger down the girl's cheek, the barest of touches, yet she closed her eyes and shivered.

"I came here seeking swanmanes, and I found three of them. They had already tied up the male. We thought it was their leader, their swanking, or we would not have harmed him. By the time we found we had the wrong animal, it was late in the game."

I glanced at the cloaks still held firmly in place, the impassive faces of the men as impossible to read as if they'd already become snakes. I noticed that one of the figures had breasts. It was nearly naked where they showed above a scoop neck T-shirt. I could see the chains reaching for the ceiling and down to the floor. There was more blood, a lot more blood, on that side.

"Let me see Nathaniel."

"Would you not like to see your blond leopard up close and personal first?"

I started to ask why. I didn't like the fact that he seemed reluctant for me to see Nathaniel. "You want me to see Gregory first?"

The man seemed to think about it, head to one side. The movement looked animal-like, yet not exactly snakelike. "Up close and personal, yes, yes, I do."

I didn't like the way he kept saying *personal*, but I let it go. "Then you've made a request of me, Coronus. If I do it, I can make one of you." Sometimes the rules are helpful. Rarely, but sometimes.

"What would you have of me?"

"I want him unchained."

"He was easily taken once by my people. I see no reason why not. Go, gaze upon him, touch him, then we will unchain him."

Jamil stayed at my side as I walked towards Gregory. My gut was tight. What had they done to him? I could still remember the scream over the phone. A glance from Jamil cleared the snake people away. They stood as far away as the room would allow them to, on either side. I had to step over the chains on the floor and under the ones that held Gregory's wrists up. I came around to look in his blue eyes. A black ball gag was stuffed in his mouth, the string tucked under his hair so it hadn't been visible from the back. His eyes were wide, panicked. His face was untouched, and my gaze followed down the line of his body almost against my will, as if I knew what I'd find. His groin was a red ruin, healing, covered in dried blood. They'd ripped him up. If he'd been human he'd have been ruined. I wasn't a hundred percent sure that he wasn't anyway. I had to close my eyes for a second. The room felt hot.

Jamil had let out a hissing breath when he saw what they'd done to Gregory, and his energy burned over my skin, fed by anger and horror. Strong emotions make shapeshifters leak all over you. My voice came out in a squeezed whisper, "Will he heal?"

Jamil had to come closer to inspect the wound. He touched it reluctantly, and Gregory writhed in pain at the gentlest of touches. "I think so, if they allow him to change form soon."

I tried to pull the gag out of Gregory's mouth and couldn't. It was too tight. I broke the leather string that held it in place and threw it on the floor.

Gregory took a sobbing breath and said, "Anita, I thought

you weren't coming." His blue eyes glistened with unshed tears.

We were almost the same size, so I could touch my forehead to his, hands on either side of his face. I couldn't stand to see the tears in his eyes, and I couldn't afford to cry in front of the bad guys. "I'll always come for you Gregory, always." Seeing him like this, I meant it. I needed to find a real wereleopard to protect them. But how was I going to give them away like stray puppies to some stranger? But that was a problem for another night.

"Unchain him," I said.

Jamil moved to the manacles and seemed to know just how they worked. No key was needed. Great. Gregory sagged as soon as the first chain went, and I caught him, holding him under the arms. But when the second wrist restraint opened, his body fell against my leg and he screamed. Jamil undid the last ankle chain, and I lowered Gregory to the ground as gently as I could. I was stroking his hair, his upper body cradled in my arms, across my lap, when I had a sense of movement to either side.

Jamil couldn't guard both sides at the same time. The knives in my boots were trapped under Gregory's body. It was beautifully timed. I rolled over Gregory's body, and felt the cloak rush over me, as talons slashed where I'd been. I went for the boot knife, but never had a chance. I saw the clawed hand coming for me. Everything slowed down, like images caught in crystal so that you see every detail. I seemed to have all the time in the world to draw the knife, or to try and dodge the slashing talons, yet a part of my brain was screaming that there was no time. I threw myself back onto the floor, felt the air rush over me as the snake man stumbled, so sure of its target that it hadn't been prepared for me to move. The rest was instinct. I foot-swept the snake, and it was suddenly on its back. I got a knife in my right hand, but the snake was on its feet, kicking upward like it had springs in its spine.

I felt more than saw something large and dark leap through the air over me, landing behind me. My attention was diverted for a fraction of a second, but that was enough.

The one in front darted in, a movement so fast my eyes couldn't follow it. I put my left arm out, taking the blow, as my right tried to stab forward. My left arm went numb like it had been hit with a baseball bat. I could have stabbed into the stomach, but I caught movement out of the corner of my eye and threw myself on my side on the floor as the second claw swept over me. I slashed at the legs and opened a gash even through the boots. The snake screamed and limped away.

The second snake came for me, claws outstretched. I didn't have time to get off the floor or anything else. I held the knife ready, my left arm only partially useable, and watched the thing fall on me like an iridescent nightmare. A smaller black blur hit it from the side, and they both crashed into the wall. It was Meng Die. The claws ripped into her pale flesh as I watched.

I didn't have time to see more, because Coronus loomed up over me, blood dripping from his neck and shoulder, his shirt shredded. Sylvie was behind him, struggling with Marco, trying to get past him to follow Coronus. Her lovely hands had turned into claws, though the rest of her was still human. The really powerful shapeshifters could do that—partially change at will.

Jamil was in the far corner, fighting with two of the snake men. Gregory was flowing with fur, changing shape, helpless until he was finished. I didn't have time to look at the other half of the room. Coronus was almost on me, and I was out of time. I did the only thing I could think of. I up-ended the knife and threw it at him. I didn't wait to see if it would hit. I was already moving towards the nearest wall and the collection of blades. I had my hand on the hilt of a sword when Coronus slashed my back open. I fell to my knees screaming, but my right hand stayed on the sword, and I jerked it from the wall brackets as I fell. I turned, putting my left side to him. He sliced open my left shoulder, but it didn't hurt like my back had. Either the wound was deeper, or I was losing the feeling in that arm. I used the seconds I had—the ones he used to cut me—and it didn't hurt to turn the sword in my right hand and plunge it backwards, behind me without turning to see where he was. It was as if I could feel him behind me, as if I knew just where he stood. I felt the blade bite into flesh. I shoved upward, coming to my feet with the force of the blow, shoving the blade backwards, inwards, through him, as hard as I could. I had never done anything like that before, but the movement felt like old memory. And I knew it wasn't *my* memory. It wasn't my body that remembered how to turn the sword as I turned my body to do extra damage, scrambling internal organs as I drew the blade out, and raised it over the kneeling figure. I raised the sword one-handed. This I knew how to do. I'd been taking heads off of bodies for years. The blade was on its downward stroke when he screamed, "Enough!" I didn't stop or even hesitate.

It was Jamil who launched himself into me, over the man's bowed head. He pinned me to the wall, one hand on my wrist, while I fought him. "Anita, Anita!"

I looked up at him, and it was as if I was just realizing who he was, or what he was doing. I'd known, but only in theory, my body had been about to take the snake man's head. My body relaxed in Jamil's grip, but he didn't let me go.

"Talk to me, Anita."

"I'm alright."

"He gives. We win. You get your leopards." His hand went to my hand where it still gripped the sword. "Ease down, you won."

I tried to keep the sword, but Jamil wasn't happy until I let him take it. Then he moved slowly away from me, and I was left looking down at Coronus still kneeling on the floor, holding his claws against the blood that was flowing from his side. He looked up at me and coughed, a little blood touching his lips. He licked it off. "You nicked a lung."

"It's not silver. You'll heal."

He laughed, but it seemed to hurt him. "We'll all heal," he said.

"You better hope Gregory heals," I said.

His black eyes flicked up to me, and there was something in that look that I didn't like. "What is it, Coronus, what puts such unease in your eyes?" I went to my knees in front of him. My left arm hung nearly useless at my side, but it wasn't numb anymore. A deep burning pain was working its way from the wounds at my shoulder and lower back. I purposefully didn't look at them. I could feel the blood flowing down my skin in tickling lines. I kept my gaze on Coronus's eyes.

He met my eyes for a minute while Jamil loomed over us, then Coronus's gaze did a small slide to his right. I followed his look and saw Nathaniel across the wide room for the first time clearly. The world swam in streams of color, and I would have fallen to the floor if my right arm hadn't caught me. It was partly from blood loss and shock, but not all of it was from the wounds. I could hear Coronus speaking through the dizziness and the nausea.

His words were tripping over each other. "Remember that it was the hyenas who made us stop. They who decreed that nothing else was to be done until your arrival. We would never have been so cruel unless we intended to kill him."

My vision cleared, and all I could do was stare. Nathaniel was nude, hanging from his wrists, ankles chained like Gregory's had been. But Nathaniel was facing the room. Knives bisected each tricep. Smaller blades had been forced through each hand so he couldn't close his fingers around them. Thin knives had been forced through the bulk of the muscles just above each of his collarbones. Then the swords began.

Sword blades stuck out just below his collarbones. The blades gleamed silver, sprinkled with drying blood. Unlike the knives, the swords had been shoved in from behind so you couldn't see the hilts.

A wide curved sword stuck out of Nathaniel's right side, through the meat of his body. There were more, too big to be knives, too small to be swords, bisecting his thighs, his calves.

I was on my feet and didn't even remember standing up. I was walking towards him, my left arm hanging down, blood spilling from my fingers. The one thing that I hadn't expected when I saw the damage was his eyes. Those lilac eyes of his were open, staring at me, full of things that I didn't want to understand. A gag filled his mouth, cut across that long auburn hair. He watched me with wide eyes as I walked to him.

I stood in front of Nathaniel and tried to get the gag out of his mouth, but I couldn't do it one-handed. Faust was there, breaking the thong, helping me take it out gently. I touched Nathaniel's mouth, trying to stop him from making any noise. I looked down the length of his body. All the blood! All the blood drying, stiff and tacky against his skin. I couldn't not look at the blades, and from inches away I saw something that couldn't be true. I lowered my hand from his mouth towards the sword blade that protruded from his upper chest. I touched the dried blood, rubbed at it with my fingertips. Nathaniel made a small moan. I didn't stop, I had to be sure. I cleared the blood enough to see, enough to feel that his skin had closed around the blades. In the two hours it had taken me to get to this room, his body had reknit itself with the blades inside of him.

I dropped to my knees as if I'd been hit between the eyes. I tried to say something, but no sound came out. Jamil was there, kneeling beside me. I grabbed a handful of the leather straps across his chest. There was fresh blood on him, wounds in his arms and chest.

I finally managed to say, "How, how do we . . . fix this?"

He looked up at Nathaniel. "We pull the blades out."

I shook my head. "Help me up." The blood loss and the sheer horror were catching up with me. I felt sick, dizzy. Jamil helped me stand in front of Nathaniel. "Do you understand what we're going to have to do?"

Nathaniel looked at me with those purple eyes of his. "Yes," he said, softly, almost no sound at all.

I gripped the knife that was in his quadricep, hand wrapping around the hilt. My lower lip was trembling, and my eyes felt hot. I stared into his eyes, no flinching, no looking away. I took a deep breath, and I pulled it out. His eyes closed, his head thrust backwards, breath coming out in a hissing rush. The flesh clung to the blade. It wasn't like taking a knife out of a roast. The flesh hugged the blade as if it had grown around it.

The bloody knife fell from my hand, making a sharp sound on the cement floor. Nathaniel screamed. Jamil was behind him, and one of the swords was missing from Nathaniel's upper chest. The other sword sucked back through his body as I watched. Nathaniel screamed again. Blood welled from the wound and I turned away. I looked back at Coronus still crouched on the floor, two of his people crowded around him. Something in the look on my face must have frightened him, because his eyes widened, and I saw something like human fear cross his reptilian face.

"We would have taken the blades out, but the hyenas ordered us not to touch either of them again until you arrived."

I looked across the room at the guard that was closest to Nathaniel. The one that had looked unhappy to be there. He flinched under my gaze. "I was following orders."

"Is that an excuse or a defense?"

"We don't owe you an excuse," the other guard said, the tall brown-haired one that had let us into the room. He was standing by the closed door. He was arrogant, defiant, and I could taste his fear like candy on my tongue. He was afraid of what I'd do.

Gregory came to stand near me in half-leopard, half-man form. I'd never seen him like this, all spotted fur, taller than his human form, more muscled. His genitalia hung large and healed between his legs.

One of the snake men was on the floor, dragging its legs behind it. Its spine was broken, but it would heal. Another scream tore from behind me, from Nathaniel's throat. Another snake man was huddled against the far wall beside the chained brunette. Its arm was almost torn from its socket. Sylvie's dress was in shreds, baring her breasts to the world. She didn't seem to care, her hands still curled into claws, pale wolf eyes staring back at me.

"Take your leopards," Coronus said, "and go in peace."

Another scream came on the end of his words. "Peace," I said. I felt strangely numb, like part of me was folding away. I couldn't stand in this room and listen to Nathaniel's screams, and feel. Not and stay sane. A quietness that I sunk into when I killed spilled over me, and it felt so much better. There are worse things than emptiness.

"Who are the women?"

"Swanmanes," he said. "No concern of yours, Nimir-Ra."

I looked at him and felt a smile curl my lips. I knew it was an unpleasant smile. "What happens to them when we leave?"

"They'll heal," he said. "We don't want them dead."

My smile widened, I couldn't help it. I laughed, but it was a bad sound, even to me. "You expect me to leave them to your mercy?"

"They are swans not leopards. Why should you care?"

Nathaniel's voice came thick, and when I turned I saw tears sliding down his face. "Don't leave them. Please, don't leave them here."

Jamil pulled another blade out. Only three to go. Nathaniel didn't scream this time, just closed his eyes and shivered. "Please, Anita, they would never have come here if I hadn't asked them."

I looked at the three women, chained naked to the walls, gagged, surrounded by dozens of clean, unused blades. They watched me with wide eyes, their breath coming in quick shallow pants. Their fear slid down my throat as if it were wine and I could drink it down, deep and cool. Fear, like wine, goes good with food. And I knew just by looking that they were food. They were swans, not predators. They were not us. I was channeling Richard now. I was being a smorgasbord of the boys tonight, of their thoughts and feelings. But there was one thing that was my own. Rage. Not the hot rage that the wolves used when they killed. This was something colder and more sure of itself. It was a rage that had nothing to do with blood and everything to do with . . . death. I wanted them all dead for what they'd done to Nathaniel and Gregory. I wanted them dead. By the rules, I couldn't have them dead, but I'd do what I could. I'd cheat them of their other victims. I would not, could not, leave the three women here like this. I could not do it. Simple as that.

"Don't worry, Nathaniel, we won't leave them behind."

"You have no right to them," Coronus said.

Gregory growled at him. I touched Gregory's furred arm. "It's alright." I looked at Coronus surrounded by his snakes. "If I were you I wouldn't tell me what I have a right to. If

I were you, I'd shut the fuck up and let us walk out of here with everyone we came for."

"No, they are ours until their swan king rescues them."

"Hey, he's not here, but I am, and I say to you, Coronus of the Black Water Clan, that I will take the swanmanes with me. I will not leave them behind."

"Why? Why do you care?"

"Why? Partly because I just don't like you. Partly because I want you dead and I can't do that tonight according to lycanthrope law. So I'll cheat you of your prize. That will have to suffice. But don't ever, *ever* get in my way again, because I *will* kill you, Coronus. I will kill you. In fact, I'd enjoy killing you." I realized that was true. I often killed cold, but there was something in me tonight that wanted him dead. Revenge maybe. I didn't question it, I just let it show in my eyes. I let the shapeshifter see it, because I knew he'd understand it. He wasn't human; he knew death when it looked at him.

He did know. I saw the knowledge in his eyes, tasted that fresh spurt of fear like a chemical rush. He looked suddenly tired. "I would give them up if I could, but I cannot. I must have something to show for this night's activities. I was hoping it would be the swans and the leopards, but if I cannot have one, I must have the other."

"Why do you care about either the swans or the leopards?" I asked. "They are nothing to you, you cannot make them part of your tribe."

His eyes shut down, unreadable. But that flash of fear grew, swelling in a rich odor of sweat and bitterness. He was very afraid. And it wasn't of me, not exactly, but of something that would happen if he didn't keep the swans. But what?

"I must keep them, Anita Blake."

"Tell me why?"

"I cannot." The fear was leaving him. Until that moment I never knew that resignation had a scent, but I could smell the quiet bitterness of defeat on him. It flared through me in a fierce wave, and I knew we'd won.

He shook his head. "I cannot give the swans up."

"You've already lost them. I can smell the defeat on you."

He bowed his head. "I would give them up if I could, but please, believe me, I cannot give them to you. I cannot."

"Cannot, or will not?" I asked.

He smiled, and it was bitter like the odor from his skin. "Cannot." Even his voice held reluctance, as if he wanted to just say *yes*, but couldn't.

"Do what's best for your people, Coronus, walk away from this." I knew in some indefinable way that we would win. My will to win was greater than his. We would carry this night in victory. Some of the snakes would die, because their leader had lost his nerve. Without his strength of will to buoy them, they could not win. They didn't want to be here. I looked at each of them, and in turn, they scented the air as I stared at them. Defeat hung over them like smoke; they had no will to win. They didn't want to be here. So why were they here? Their alpha, their leader, was here, and his will was theirs. So why were they all weak, as if something was missing inside their group, something that made them weak?

I realized with a start that this was what everyone had sensed from the leopards before I came to them . . . this smell of weakness and defeat. Nathaniel was weak. But now my will was his, and I was not weak. I turned to stare into his face, his eyes, and I saw through all the pain, the torture, that he was not hopeless. When I first met him, Nathaniel had had the most hopeless eyes I'd ever seen. But he knew I'd come. He'd known with an absolute certainty that I would not leave him here like this. Gregory could doubt, because he thought with that part of him that was human. But Nathaniel trusted me with something that had nothing to do with logic, and everything to do with truth.

I turned back to Coronus. "Run away from this, Coronus, or some of you won't see dawn."

He sighed heavily. "So be it." And then he did what he shouldn't have done. Something that had no logic to it, from a nonhuman point of view. He was going to lose, and he knew it. Yet he did a very human thing. He attacked us anyway. Only humans waste energy like that when they've been given an out.

The two snakes guarding Coronus suddenly launched themselves at me, and I was too close. I'd been so sure with my new werewolf senses that they wouldn't fight us. I'd been careless. I'd forgotten that in the end we're only half animal. And that human half will fuck you every time.

They came in a blur of speed too fast for me to do anything but start for the other boot knife. I knew I'd never reach it. Gregory leaped in a butter-colored streak, taking one snake out in midair, rolling on the floor. But the other one was on me, claws slashing down before I hit the ground with it riding me. I was already going numb; it didn't hurt. The claws ripped at my stomach, diving through the cloth of my shirt to the flesh underneath. I felt it digging for my heart. I raised my right hand to try and grab the wrist, but it felt like I was moving in slow motion. My hand seemed to weigh a thousand pounds, and distantly I knew I was hurt, badly hurt. Something bad had happened in that first blur of claws.

Gregory was suddenly there, pale fur caught between the multicolored snakes. He fell on top of me, with one of the things on top of him ripping him up. He never tried to defend himself; he clawed at the one riding me, tore it away from me, and the three of them fought on top of me. There was a moment when Gregory's eyes and that snarling mouth were inches from mine. We were pressed as close as lovers, and I knew that the claws in me were his. He'd fallen against me, been pushed into my flesh. Then other hands were pulling us all apart. I had a glimpse of Jamil's face, saw his lips move, but there was no sound. Then blackness swirled over my vision and ate everything but a dim, dim spot of light. Then even that vanished, and there was nothing but the dark.

8

I DREAMED I was running, being chased through the woods at night. I could hear them coming closer, closer, and I knew that what chased me wasn't human. Then I fell to the ground and I was running on four feet. I chased the pale thing that fled before me. The soft thing that had no claws, no teeth, and smelled wonderfully of fear. It fell, and its scream was shrill, it hurt my ears, and excited me. My fangs sank into flesh and did not stop until they tore meat. Blood poured scalding hot down my throat, and the dream faded.

I was in Narcissus's bedroom on the black bed. Jean-Claude was tied, standing between the posts at the end of the bed. His chest was bare, covered in claw marks, blood running down his skin. I crawled across the bed towards him, and I wasn't afraid, because all I could smell was the sweet copper scent of blood. He stared at me with eyes gone solid, drowning blue. "Kiss me, *ma petite*."

I rose on my knees, my mouth hovering over his lips. He moved towards me, but I stayed out of reach of those kissable lips. I moved my mouth lower, until it was just above his chest and the fresh wounds that decorated his skin. "Yes, *ma petite*, yes," he sighed.

I pressed my mouth to his chest and drank. I woke, eyes staring, heart thudding. It was Richard above me. He still had the leather collar on. I tried to raise my arms, to hold him, but my left arm was taped to a board. There was an I.V. in my arm. I looked at the darkened room and knew I wasn't in a hospital. I raised my right arm to touch his face, but it was heavy, too heavy to lift. Darkness spilled over my eyes like warm water rushing in, as my fingertips brushed his skin.

I heard his voice. "Rest, Anita, rest." I think he kissed me, gently, then there was nothing.

I was wading in water to my waist, clear, icy water. I knew I had to get out of the water or I'd die, the cold would steal me away. I could see the shore, dead trees, and snow. I ran for those distant trees, struggling in the icy water. Then my feet went out from under me, and I fell into a deep hole. The water closed over my face, and the shock of the cold hit me like a giant fist. I couldn't move, couldn't breathe. The light faded through the clear, shining water. I began to drift down, down into the cold dark water. I should have been scared, but I wasn't. I was so tired, so tired.

Pale hands reached for me, coming from the light. The sleeve of the white shirt billowed around his arm, and I moved my hand towards him. Jean-Claude's hand wrapped around mine, and he pulled me towards the light.

I was back in the dark room, but my skin was wet, and I was cold, so cold. Jean-Claude was cradling me in his lap. He was still wearing the vinyl outfit. Then I remembered the fight. I'd been hurt. Jean-Claude leaned over and kissed my forehead, laying his face against mine. His skin was as cold as I felt—like ice pressed against me. The shivering was worse; my body danced in small involuntary movements.

"Cold," I said.

"I know, *ma petite,* we are both cold."

I frowned at him, because I didn't understand. He was looking at someone else in the room. "I have brought her back, but I cannot give her the warmth she needs to survive."

I managed to turn my head enough to look around the room. Richard was standing there with Jamil and Shang-Da and Gregory. Richard came to the bed; his hand touched my face. It was hot against my skin. It was too much, and I tried to move away from his hand.

"Anita, can you hear me?"

My teeth were chattering so hard, I could hardly get it out, but finally I said, "Yes."

"You've got a high fever, a very high fever. They put you in a shallow ice bath to bring it down. But your body reacted like a shapeshifter's. The low temperature while so much damage was healing almost killed you."

I frowned at him and finally managed to say, "Don't understand." The involuntary jerks were getting stronger, strong enough that it hurt the wounds. I was waking up enough to feel how very hurt I was. Things hurt that I didn't remember getting injured. My muscles ached.

"You need the high temperature to heal, just like we do."

I didn't understand who the "we" was. "Who . . ." and a spasm shook my body, tore a scream from my mouth. My body fell into convulsions and pain smashed through me. If I could have breathed, I'd have screamed more. My vision began to disappear in large gray patches.

"Get the doctor!" Richard's voice.

"You know what must be done, *mon ami*."

"If this works, then I've lost her."

My vision cleared for a few seconds. Richard was stripping out of the tight pants. It was the last thing I saw before the gray swept up over my eyes and sucked me down.

9

I THOUGHT I dreamed, but I wasn't sure. There were faces in the dark, some of them I knew, some of them I didn't. Cherry with her short blond hair, her face free of makeup, making her look years younger than either of us were. Gregory touching my face. Jamil resting beside me, curled like a dark dream. I drifted in and out, from face to face, body to body, because I could feel their bodies pressed against mine. Naked skin against naked skin. It wasn't sexual, or not overtly so. I woke, if I woke, enough to know it was Richard's arms wrapped around me, my body fitting like a spoon against his, his thick hair spilled across my eyes. I slept, knowing I was safe.

I woke slowly, in a cocoon of body heat and that prickling rush of lycanthrope energy. I tried to roll over and found the press of flesh kept me pinned on my side. I opened my eyes. The room was dark, with a small light near the wall like a child's night-light. My night vision was good enough to be able to see color by it. A man I didn't know was curled against the front of my body. His face was pressed into my shoulder just above my breasts, his breath hot against my skin. Normally, it would have been my cue to panic and run for the hills, but I just didn't feel like panicking. I felt warm and safe, and more . . . right than I'd felt in a long time, as if I were wearing a favorite pair of flannel jammies, wrapped in my favorite quilt. It was that kind of comfort, that kind of peacefulness. Even the sight of the arm around my waist from behind didn't disturb me. Maybe Dr. Lillian had slipped me some medicine that made everything feel okay. All I know was that I didn't want to move. It was like when you first wake in the morning and there's nowhere you have to be, nothing you have to do, and you can float in that half-awake, half-asleep, warm-nest-of-blankets feeling.

The arm around my waist was muscled, definitely masculine, but small, not just the hand, but the whole arm. The skin was tanned and looked darker than it should have against the paleness of my skin. I relaxed against the warm bulk of the body, where it lay spooned against mine. The fact that I was okay sleeping in a three-way naked sandwich, with me in the middle, told me beyond a doubt that I was on some kind of drug. I'd woken up wearing a lot more clothes, and been a whole lot more embarrassed.

I assumed they were both werewolves. It was a big pack, and I didn't know everyone on sight. I was bathed in their energy, as if hot invisible water flowed around the three of us. I remembered being hurt, the claws digging under my sternum. My gaze traveled down my own body and found a ragged circle of pinkish scar tissue where the snake had dug for my heart. There was a dull ache, but the scar was already pink and shiny, flat to my skin. How long had I been out?

I kept waiting for the panic to wash over me, the embarrassment. When it didn't, I looked at the first man, truly looking at him this time. He had rich brown curls cut short in the back, but long on top, so the curls tickled my skin as he made a small movement in his sleep. He was tanned so darkly that his skin almost matched his hair. The one eyebrow I could see had a tiny ring piercing it. One of his knees pinned my lower leg, one hand lay limply on my bare thigh. I think it was his leg being raised and a turn of his hips that saved me from seeing the whole show. What little modesty I had left was grateful. Whatever had kept me comfortable was beginning to wear off. Maybe I was simply waking up.

The rest of his front was pressed so close to me I couldn't see any details. The line of his back and buttocks was smooth, flawless. No tan lines. Nude sunbathing? The body looked young—early twenties—if that. He was taller than me—who wasn't?—but not by much. Five seven, maybe less. He stirred, the hand on my thigh flexing as if he dreamed, then suddenly I knew he was awake. A tension ran through his body that hadn't been there seconds before. I was suddenly wide awake, my heart thudding. I had about two seconds to wonder what the hell you say to someone you've never met when you wake up naked in bed beside him. He opened the eye I could see and moved his face enough to blink two solid brown eyes at me.

He gave a slow lazy smile, still half asleep. "I've never seen you awake before."

I said the only thing that came to mind. "I don't remember seeing you at *all* before. Who are you?"

"Caleb. I'm Caleb."

I nodded and started to sit up. I was getting out of this bed. The comforting warmth was still there, but my embarrassment was stronger. I just wasn't cool enough to keep talking to a strange, naked man, while I was naked, too. Nope, just not sophisticated enough for this one.

The arm around my waist tightened, holding me against the second man, and the bed. Caleb's knee on my leg got heavier, sliding farther between mine. I could suddenly feel parts of his body that I couldn't see. I think I'd have rather seen the whole show than had it pressed against my very upper thigh. Alright, groin, just not the right part to make me start hurting him, not yet. The hand that had been lying on my thigh was suddenly gripping it. It made my pulse speed up. It was too close to being trapped.

"Everybody be calm," I said, "but I need to get up and out of this bed now."

The body behind me moved. Even though I wasn't able to see it, I knew he was propped on one elbow, and the arm around my waist tightened. I was suddenly pressed very firmly against his body, and I knew several things. One, he was about my height, because he spooned perfectly against me; two, he was slender, muscular, and very happy to be pressed to my body. Eeek! I turned towards him like I was looking back at a noise in the dark at a horror movie— slowly, half-dreading. His face rose over my shoulder, long hair spilling to one side of his face in a thick mass that was so sleep-tousled I couldn't tell if it was waves or curls, only that it was a dark rich brown, darker than the first man's, almost brunette. His face was too triangular, almost too delicate, crossing that line into androgyny, the nose perky, a little less than perfect, his mouth wide, bottom lip thick and pouting. It was a sensual face. But it was the eyes that made the face, or ruined it. My first thought was that his eyes were yellow. But there was a thick ring of gray green around the pupil; the overall effect was a deep golden yellow-green set in a tanned face. They weren't human eyes, and don't ask me how I knew, but they weren't wolf eyes either.

I scrambled out from between them. My left arm protested the use, but it didn't hurt enough to outweigh my embarrassment. It wasn't a graceful exit, but at least I was standing at the foot of the bed staring down at the two men instead of sandwiched between them. Screw graceful, I wanted some clothes.

"Don't be afraid, Anita. We don't mean you any harm," the second man said.

I was trying to keep an eye on them and still search the dimly lit room for clothes. I didn't see any. The only cloth in the room seemed to be the sheet, and they were lying on that. I had a horrible urge to cover myself, but two hands weren't going to get the job done, and standing there with my hands cupped over my groin seemed somehow more embarrassing than just standing there. I suddenly didn't know what to do with my hands. My left arm ached in a line from my shoulder nearly to my wrist, a tracery of pink, flat scars down my flesh. "Who are you?" My voice came out a little breathy.

"I'm Micah Callahan." His voice was calm, ordinary, as he lay on his side completely naked. No one does comfortable nudity like a shapeshifter. His shoulders were narrow, everything about him slender, almost feminine. But muscles showed under his skin even at rest, lean muscle, not bulk. You knew at a glance he was strong, but if he were wearing clothes, you might not see it. There were other things you wouldn't see if he had his clothes on. And although the rest of him was slender, small, graceful in a way that women are graceful, parts of him were definitely not small, not slender. It seemed incongruous with the rest of him. As if mother nature had tried to make up for the feminine appearance by overcompensating in other areas. Noticing just how overcompensated he was brought heat in a rush up my face, and I glanced away, tried to both keep an eye on them in case they got off the bed and not look at them at the same time. It's hard to look and not to look, but I managed.

"This is Caleb," he said.

Caleb rolled onto his back and stretched like a big cat, making sure that, if I hadn't noticed already, he was naked, too. I had noticed. What looked like a tiny silver dumbbell pierced his belly button. That I hadn't seen. "We already introduced ourselves," Caleb said, that one innocent sentence sounding anything but innocent. Something in the tone he used, an inflection, while he rolled around on his back and waved himself at me, made the words obscene. I was willing to bet I wasn't going to like Caleb.

"Great, nice to meet you both." I still couldn't figure out what to do with my hands. "What are you doing here?"

"Sleeping with you," Caleb said.

The blush that had been almost gone flamed back to life. He laughed. Micah didn't. Point for him.

In fact, Micah sat up, bending a knee to cover himself, which earned him even more points. Caleb stayed on his back, flaunting himself. "There's a robe in the corner there," Micah said.

I glanced back where he was looking, and sure enough there was a robe. It was my robe, a deep, rich burgundy, with satin edgings, very masculine, like a long Victorian smoking jacket. When I lifted it up, there was a weight in one deep pocket. I had to fight the urge to turn my back to slip the robe on. They'd already seen the whole show. It wasn't like I could express my modesty now. When I had the robe belted in place, I slipped my hands into the pockets and my right hand closed around my derringer. Or at least I assumed it was mine; it *was* my robe. The only person I knew who'd think to leave a gun for me was Edward, and he, as far as I knew, was out of state. But someone had thought of it, and I was very glad. I had clothes and a weapon, life was good.

"Hi, Micah Callahan, nice to meet you. But the name doesn't tell me who you are."

"I am Nimir-Raj for the Maneater Clan," Micah said.

I blinked at him, trying to digest that little tidbit. I wasn't embarrassed anymore. Surprised, working on angry, maybe. "I am Nimir-Ra of the Blooddrinkers Clan, and I don't remember inviting you into my territory, Mr. Callahan."

"You didn't."

"Then what the hell are you doing here without my permission?" The first edge of anger threaded through my voice, and I was happy to hear it. Being angry made everything else easier to handle, even talking to two naked strangers.

"Elizabeth invited me," he said.

The anger rushed through me like a warm wind, and it touched that edge of beast that I'd thought was Richard's. I'd learned at the club however many nights ago it was that it was a permanent resident inside me now. Richard's beast, or mine, it flared through my body and raised above my skin like a sheen of invisible sweat. The men reacted to the power. Caleb sat up, his gaze suddenly intent on me, no teasing now. Micah sniffed at the air, nostril's flaring, his tongue running around the edge of his lips as if he could taste it against his skin.

Strong emotions always make the power worse, and I was so angry. I already owed Elizabeth for abandoning Nathaniel at the club. But now . . . she'd finally done something that I could not let slide.

Part of me was almost relieved, because things would be easier with Elizabeth dead. A tiny part of me was hoping not to have to kill her, but I just couldn't see how to avoid it anymore.

It must have shown on my face, because Callahan said, "I didn't know that her pard had a Nimir-Ra when I came here. She was their old alpha's second. It was within her rights to audition a new alpha for her pard."

"She just forgot to mention that the pard already had a Nimir-Ra, is that it?" I asked.

"That's it," he said.

"Really," I said, making sure the sarcasm was thick.

He stood beside the bed. I managed to keep the eye contact pure, but it was harder than it should have been. "I did not know until three nights ago when Cherry knocked on

Elizabeth's door and asked her to come help heal you that you even existed."

"Bullshit," I said.

"I swear it," he said.

My hand closed around the derringer, felt its comforting weight. I had a moment to wonder what ammo it was loaded with; .38 or .22. I hoped it was .38, it had more stopping power. My left arm gave a twinge like the muscle was trying to jump apart. Tension, or had I permanently injured myself? I'd worry about it later, when I wasn't staring at two were-leopards that might, or might not, be my buddies. "You say you really didn't know about me before you hit town. Great, but why are you still here?"

"When I found out that Elizabeth had lied to me, I came here and tried to help, to make up for entering your territory without your permission. All my leopards took a turn in your bed, helping you heal."

"Bully for you."

He held his empty hands out towards me, palms up. A nice traditional gesture to show that you are unarmed and harmless. Yeah, right. "What can I do to make this right between us, Anita? I don't want war between our pards, and I have learned that you are interviewing alphas to take your place with your leopards. I'm a Nimir-Raj. Do you know how rare that is among the wereleopards? The best you're probably going to find elsewhere is a leopard *lionne*, a protector but not a true king."

"You applying for the job?"

He started walking towards me, and the room wasn't that big. "I'd be honored if you'd consider me for the job."

I tried to hold up my left hand, but the arm spasmed too badly to complete the gesture. But Micah got the idea; he stopped moving. "Let's start by you staying over there. I've had about as much up close and personal with the two of you as I can handle."

He just stood there, hands still in that open see-I-mean-no-harm position. "We caught you off guard, I understand."

I doubted he understood, but it was polite for him to pretend. I'd never met a shapeshifter that had a problem sleeping in a big naked pile, like puppies. Of course, I'd never met a brand-new one, yet. Surely, there was a learning curve for this sort of comfort level.

My left arm was twitching badly enough that I took my right hand off the gun, out of my pocket, and tried to calm the involuntary movements.

"You're hurt," he said.

Every jump of muscle sent sharp little pains through my arm. "Getting clawed up will do that to you."

"I can make it feel better."

I rolled eyes at him. "I bet you say that to all the girls."

He didn't even look embarrassed. "I told you, I am a Nimir-Raj. I can call flesh."

I must have looked as blank as I felt, because he explained. "I can heal wounds with my touch."

I just looked at him.

"What would it take to convince you that I'm telling the truth?" he asked.

"How about someone I know to vouch for you?"

"Easily done," he said, and a second later the door opened.

It was another stranger. The man was around six feet, broad shouldered, muscled, well built, and since he was nude, I knew for a fact that every inch of him was well proportioned. At least he wasn't erect. That was refreshing. He was pale, the first of the new ones without a tan. White hair with generous streaks of gray fell around his shoulders. He had a gray mustache and one of those tiny Vandyke beards. The hair was a clue that he was over fifty, probably. But what I could see of him didn't look old, or weak. He looked more like a lifer mercenary that would cut your heart out and take it back to someone in a box, for the right amount of money. A ragged scar nearly bisected his chest and stomach, curving in a vicious half-moon around his belly button and sinking towards his groin. The scar was white and looked old. Either he'd gotten the injury before he became a shapeshifter or—or I didn't know. Shapeshifters could scar, but it was rare; you almost had to do something wrong to the wound to get a scar that bad.

"I don't know him," I said.

"Anita Blake, this is Merle."

It was only after the introductions that Merle's eyes flicked to me. His eyes looked human, some pale gray color. His gaze went back to his Nimir-Raj's face almost immediately, like an obedient dog that wants to watch its master's face.

"Hi, Merle."

He nodded his head.

"Let her people in the room."

Merle shifted, and I knew instantly that he didn't want to do it. "Some, but not all?" he made it a question.

Micah looked at me.

"Why not all?" I asked.

Merle turned those pale eyes to me, and the look in them made me want to squirm. He stared at me as if he could see through to the other side and read everything in between. I knew it wasn't true, but it was a good stare. I managed not to flinch.

"Tell her," Micah said.

"Too many people in too small a room. I can't guarantee Micah's safety in a crowd of strangers."

"You must be his Skoll," I said.

His lips curled back in disgust—I think. "We are not wolves. We do not use their words."

"Fine, to my knowledge there's no equivalent word among the leopards, but you're still Micah's chief bodyguard, right?"

He stared at me, then gave a small nod.

"Okay. Do you really see my people as a threat to Micah?"

"It is my job to see them as a threat."

He had a point. "Fine. How many are you comfortable letting into the room?"

He blinked, that harsh gaze, shielded for a moment, his eyes uncertain. "You're not going to argue about it?" Again he made the statement into a question with the lilt of his voice.

"Why should I?"

"Most alphas will argue so they don't appear weak," he said.

I had to smile. "I'm not that insecure."

That made him smile. "Yes, those that hoard their power are often insecure."

"That's been my experience," I said.

He nodded again, face thoughtful. "Two."

"Fine."

"Do you have a preference who the two shall be?"

I shrugged. "Cherry and whoever else." I put Cherry in because she seemed to give the best after-action reports. Clearheaded was our Cherry, if not necessarily who you'd want at your back in a fight. But I needed information, not battle skills.

Merle gave me a slight bow, then his gaze flicked back to Micah, still standing by the bed. Micah waved him off. The big man opened the door and spoke quietly. Cherry was the first one through the door. She was tall and slender with well-formed breasts that led the eye to a very long waist, a swell of hips, and proof that she was indeed a natural blond. Wasn't anybody wearing clothes today?

Frankly, it was just nice to see another woman. Normally, I don't mind being the only girl, I do that a lot with the police, but nudity always makes me relieved to see another person without a penis.

She smiled when she saw me, relief so large in her eyes, her face, that it was almost embarrassing. She hugged me, and I let her, but I pulled away first. She touched my face as if she couldn't really believe her eyes.

"How do you feel?"

I shrugged, and the small movement tightened the muscles in my left arm until I had to press it against my body to keep it from jumping around. I spoke through the pain, teeth gritted a little. "Arm's giving me trouble, but other than that, I'm okay."

Cherry touched the arm, running her hand lightly over the sleeve of the robe. "The muscles are tightening up from the rapid healing. It will be alright in a few days."

"Am I not going to have the use of my left arm for a few days?"

"The spasms will come and go. Massage helps. Hot compresses may help. There must have been some severe muscle damage for this much spasming." Did I mention that Cherry was a nurse when she wasn't turning furry?

"I can give you the use of your arm today," Micah said.

We both turned and looked at him. "How?" Cherry asked.

"I can call flesh," he said again.

The look on her face said she knew what that meant, and she was impressed. And a second later, she looked doubtful, suspicious. That was my girl. Though truthfully, Cherry had had a hard enough life before I met her that she'd come with an overly active suspicion. I really couldn't take credit for it.

I was trying to remember what "calling the flesh" meant, when Nathaniel stepped through the door. The last time I'd seen him he'd been pierced with blades, his flesh grown around the steel. Now he was perfect—not even a scar.

I must have looked as pleased, and as astonished, as I felt, because he grinned at me. He did a little turn so I could see that back and front he was healed. I touched his upper chest where I'd pulled out one of the blades. The skin was smooth as if I'd only dreamed the knife. "I know you guys heal almost anything, but I never get over the surprise."

"Eventually, you'll get used to it," Merle said. There was something in his voice that made me look at him. Cherry's and Nathaniel's smiles faded. They looked suddenly serious.

"What's wrong?" I asked.

Cherry and Nathaniel exchanged glances, but it was Micah who spoke. "May I fix your arm?"

I turned to tell him to go to hell until I knew what was happening, but my left arm chose that moment to curl up from fingertips to shoulder, one massive, painful, charley horse that bent my knees. Only Cherry catching me kept me standing. My hand looked like that of a strychnine victim, the fingers convulsed, clawlike. It felt like my arm was trying to tear itself apart from the inside out. Cherry was supporting almost all my weight as I tried not to scream.

"Let him fix your arm, Anita, if he can," she said.

The muscles in my arm relaxed by painful inches, until the urge to scream was only a small voice in my head. My voice came out breathy from the strain, but it was clear, no whimpering. "What is calling flesh again?" I was leaning so heavily on Cherry that it was only politeness that kept her from picking me up in her arms. She was holding all my weight.

Micah came to stand by us. Merle hovered behind him like an overly anxious nursemaid. "I can heal damage in my pard with my body," Micah said.

I glanced up at Cherry and saw Nathaniel standing beside her. They both nodded at the same time, as if they'd heard my unasked question. "I've never seen a Nimir-Raj that could call flesh, but I've heard of it," Cherry said. "It is possible."

"You don't sound like you believe him," I said.

She gave a faint smile that left her eyes tired. "I don't believe in much of anyone." She smiled then. "Except you."

I stood, still leaning on her arm, but almost standing on my own. I squeezed her arm with my right hand, trying to put into my eyes what I was feeling. "I'll always do my best for you, Cherry."

She smiled again, and her eyes lightened a little, though that edge of cynicism never quite left them. "I know that."

"We all know that," Nathaniel said.

I smiled at him. I said the prayer I'd been saying since I inherited the wereleopards: Dear God, don't let me fail them.

I kept a tight grip on Cherry's arm, but turned to Micah. "Why is my arm the only thing that's hurting?"

"You don't hurt anywhere else?" he asked.

I started to say no, then had to think about it. "I ache, but nothing like the arm. Nothing else hurts like it does."

He nodded as if that meant something to him. "Your body and our energy healed the life-threatening injuries first, and the smaller ones like the marks on your back."

"I didn't think healing energy could be that selective," I said.

"It can when directed," he said.

"Who directed it?"

His eyes locked with mine. "I did."

I glanced at Cherry, and she nodded. "He is a Nimir-Raj. He was the dominant for us all. Him and Merle."

I glanced at the big man. "Do I owe you guys a thank-you?"

Merle shook his head. "You owe us nothing."

"Nothing," Micah said. "We were the ones who entered your territory without your permission. It was our transgression, not yours."

I looked at them both. "Okay, now what?"

"Can you stand unaided?"

I wasn't really sure, so I let go of Cherry in stages and found that I could stand on my own. Great. "Yeah, I guess I can."

"I need to touch the injuries to heal them."

"I know, I know, bare skin is best for healing among lycanthropes."

He gave a small frown. "Yes, it is."

I used my right hand to slide the robe off my left shoulder. I realized that it didn't bare enough of my arm. I started to wiggle my left arm out of the sleeve, and another spasm hit me. It was Micah who caught me this time as my arm tried to tear itself off my body and my hand gripped something that I could neither see nor feel. It wasn't just that it hurt. It was unnerving, like I had lost total control of my arm.

Micah whispered, "Scream, there's no shame in it."

I just shook my head, afraid to open my mouth, afraid I would scream. He lowered me to the floor. His hands going to the robe's sash. The spasm relaxed in stages again, leaving me gasping on the floor while he bared most of my left side. Once he'd revealed my left arm and shoulder, he pulled the robe back over me, covering everything I cared about, except for my left breast. I appreciated the gesture. Since I was now lying on the ground staring up at him, I also appreciated that he was no longer erect. That was somehow less threatening.

He was on his knees, tracing his fingers just above the skin of my arm. Except he wasn't touching my skin, he was touching that otherworldly energy that spilled off of my skin.

His energy flowed from his hand and mingled with mine in a dance of electricity that sent goosebumps down my skin. For the first time I thought to ask, "Is this going to hurt?"

"No, it shouldn't."

I heard masculine laughter. I was looking up at all the men in the room except for one. I turned my head to see Caleb still sitting on the bed.

"Is there a joke I'm not getting?"

"Ignore him," Merle said.

I looked up at their so-serious eyes, while Caleb's laughter played background music. "Are you sure there isn't something you want to tell me about the calling of flesh?"

Micah shook his head, sending the tangle of curls sliding around his face. I realized that no one had turned on a light. We were still moving in the twilight of the night-light. "Can someone turn on a light?"

There was a flurry of eye flicks, one to the other, to the other, like they were playing hot potato with the glance. "What's wrong?"

"Why do you think anything is wrong?" Micah said.

"Don't fuck with me, I saw the glances. Why can't we turn on the lights?"

"You may be photosensitive because of the rapid healing," Cherry said.

I looked at her and could feel the suspicion on my face. "That's what all those looks were about?" I said.

"We're worried about how your body is . . . reacting to the injuries." She knelt beside me on the side opposite Micah. She stroked my hair like you'd pet a dog to soothe it. "We're worried about you."

"I got that." It was hard to be suspicious with her vibrating sincerity at me. I finally had to smile. "I guess we can do without the lights until after he heals me."

She smiled, and this time it did reach her eyes. "Good."

"You might want to give us some room here," Micah said. "Otherwise the energy can spread."

Cherry gave me a last touch then stood and moved back, taking Nathaniel with her. Micah stared up at Merle. "You, too."

Merle frowned, but he moved across the room with the others. They all ended up by the bed with Caleb. Strangely, I'd come as far across the room as I could get from the bed without leaving the room. Totally unconscious on my part, honest.

Micah stayed kneeling, but leaned back on the balls of his feet, hands open on his thighs, eyes closed, and I felt him open himself. His energy swirled over me like a thread of hot air that closed my throat, made it hard to breathe. He opened those alien eyes and looked at me, face slack, as if he were meditating or dreaming.

I expected him to lay hands on me, but his hands stayed on his thighs. He leaned his upper body towards my shoulder.

I put my right hand on his arm, and the moment I touched him, his beast curled through me. It was almost as if some great invisible cat were sliding in and out of my body, the way they'll entwine themselves around your legs, except this cat went places that not even a lover should be touching. It froze my words in my throat, and from the look on Micah's face, I could tell he was feeling it too. He looked as shell-shocked as I felt. But he continued to lean into me. My hand stayed on his arm, but it didn't stop him, and I couldn't think well enough to question him. His lips brushed my neck where the scars began, and it brought my breath in a shaky sigh. He pressed his mouth to my neck and forced that swirling, living power into me. It made me squirm, but it didn't hurt. In fact it felt so good that I pushed him backwards.

My voice squeezed out, faint, almost a whisper. "Wait a minute. What's with the mouth? I thought you were going to lay *hands* on me?"

"I said I could heal with my body," he said. The power stretched between us like taffy pulled between the hot sticky fingers of children. It was like if we touched we would melt into each other.

I dragged my hand away from him, and it was like my hand was moving through something—something real and almost solid. My voice was steady, and even I was impressed. "I thought that meant hands."

"If I'd meant hands, I would have said so." He lowered

his face towards me, moving through the power, and it felt like waves in water when someone swims towards you. I grabbed a handful of those tangled curls. "Define body for me."

He smiled, and it was at the same time gentle, condescending, and somehow sad. He stayed kneeling over me, his face close enough to kiss, my hand in his hair, the power pulsing around us, building into something large. "Mouth, tongue, some hands, but it is body, my hands alone won't be enough. I am told that you can heal with your body, as well."

I took my hand out of his hair and tried to get some distance between us, but he didn't move back, so it didn't really work. Truth was I could heal with sex, or something so close to it that you didn't want to do it in public.

"Sort of," I said. I looked across the room, past Micah's head and found Cherry. "Is calling flesh like what I do when I call munin?" Munin were sort of the ancestral memories of the werewolves. Except that they were actually more like ghosts, the spirits of the dead. You could gain their knowledge, their skills, and their bad habits if you had the ability to channel them. I was a necromancer—all the dead liked me. The munin that liked me best of all was Raina, the wolf pack's old lupa. I'd been the one who killed her—to keep her from killing me—and she delighted in the fact that she could take me over. I'd gained the power to control Raina when I accepted her, warts and all. When I called her, I didn't fight her anymore. We'd worked out a sort of truce. But calling munin for healing was almost always sexual for me, because it had been sexual for Raina.

"It's not sexual," Cherry said. "Sensual, but not sexual."

I trusted Cherry's judgment on that. "Okay then, do it."

Micah looked at me, those strange yellow-green eyes so terribly close.

"Do it," I said.

He gave that wistful, sad, condescending smile again, like he was laughing at both of us, and crying for us, too. Unnerving, that smile. Then he lowered his mouth to my neck and the first of the scars. The first kiss was gentle against my throat; he breathed power against my skin, and it was suddenly hard to breathe. But the power hovered above my skin like cloth. Then the tip of his tongue slid along my skin, licking a hot, wet line down my neck. The power followed the line of that heat, sinking under my skin as he licked me. But it was when his mouth pressed over my skin, sealing him against me, sucking me into his mouth, between his teeth, that I felt the power shoved into me, forced into the scars. He literally breathed, bit, ate, the healing into me. I made small helpless movements. I couldn't help it. We all have our erogenous zones in addition to the normal ones, places where if we're touched our bodies react whether we want them to, or not. My neck and shoulders are two of my spots.

He leaned back, far enough from my neck to whisper, "Are you alright?" His breath was so hot against my skin.

I nodded, my face turned away from him.

He took me at my word, pressing his mouth back to my neck. There were no preliminaries this time; he bit me, hard enough that I gasped. My stomach knotted, twisting me onto my side, pulling me away from him.

"Anita, what's wrong?"

"My stomach," I said.

He slid the robe open, passing his hand over my stomach. "There was no wound here."

Another wave of pain tore through my gut, bending me over double, to writhe on the floor. The need tore through me like something alive trying to rip its way out from inside my body.

Micah was there, smoothing my hair back from my face, that power that was building between us rolling through my body like a cat wading through me. He bundled me into his arms, his lap, pressed my face against his chest. "Get the doctor."

His chest was smooth, warm. I could hear his heartbeat, feel it against my cheek. I could smell blood under his skin like some exotic candy that would melt on my tongue and glide down my throat. I worked my way up his body until I could see the big pulse in his neck. I watched that pulse like a man dying of thirst; my throat burned with the need, my lips dry, cracked from want of it. I had to feed. I knew in that instant that it wasn't my thought.

I stretched out that part of me that Jean-Claude claimed and found him. Found him sitting in a windowless cell. He looked up as if he could see me standing in front of him. He whispered, *"Ma petite,"* and I knew where he was. I didn't know why, but I knew where. He was in the St. Louis city jail, in the rooms reserved for things that cannot stand the light of day. I stared into his eyes and watched them fill with blue fire, until they cast their own light in the dim cell.

He reached out towards me, as if we could touch, and it was Micah's power, Micah's beast rolling through my body that tore me away from Jean-Claude.

I opened my eyes to find my arms around Micah, my face pressed to his shoulder, my mouth very close to the long warmth of his neck. There was movement in the room, and I knew distantly that someone had run to get a doctor, but what I needed a doctor couldn't give me.

Micah's skin smelled clean, young. It was like I could tell just by scent how old he was. The blood was like icing spread just under the tenderness of his flesh; and the part of me that thought of Micah as meat wasn't Jean-Claude, it was Richard.

I didn't know how to put the need into words. Micah turned his face, looked into my eyes, and I felt something inside me open; some door that I hadn't even known existed swung wide. A wind blew through the door, a wind made of darkness and the stillness of the grave. A wind that held an edge of electric warmth like the rub of fur across bare skin. A wind that tasted of both my men. But I was the center, the thing that could hold both of them inside and not break. Life and death, lust and love.

"What *are* you?" Micah asked, his voice a surprised whisper.

I'd always thought that vampires took their victims—stole their will with their eyes and took them like magical rape. But in that instant I knew it was more complex than that, and more simple. I saw with Jean-Claude's eyes, his power.

I stared into Micah's face from inches away, and I saw, felt, his own need. Lust was there, a horribly unsatisfied lust, and I knew it had been a long time for Micah. But underneath that was a greater need, a need for power and the shelter that power could provide. It was like I could smell his needs, roll them on my tongue. I stared into his yellow-green eyes in that so-human face, and Jean-Claude gave me the keys to Micah's soul.

"I am power, Nimir-Raj. Enough power to warm you on the coldest of nights." Power flowed off his skin like a scalding wind. That hot wind mingled with the power inside me, twisting together until it drove like a knife deep inside me. It tore a gasp from my throat, and Micah echoed it. The power turned into something gentler, something that caressed instead of stabbed, something that you would wait your whole life to have. I saw the sensation flow over Micah's face, knew that he felt it, too.

A wind stirred the edge of his hair. And the wind was moving between us like the point where cold and heat meet and form something larger than either can form alone, something huge and whirling, a wind so strong it can level houses and drive straw through telephone poles.

His arms tightened around me. "I am Nimir-Raj, mind games don't work on me."

I got to my knees still in the circle of his arms, and pressed my body down the front of his. We were almost exactly the same height, the eye contact was terribly intimate. The power pressed around us like a giant hand squeezing us together. His body responded, and he was large again, so hard pressed to my groin and stomach. This was my cue to be embarrassed, to panic, but I didn't. I knew that Jean-Claude fed off of lust as well as blood, but I'd never really understood what that meant until that moment when Micah's flesh touched mine. It wasn't just the naked press of him, hard and firm against my body, that made me shudder against him, it was the need in his body. I felt his hunger quiver through his flesh, as if I could read parts of him that were too primitive for words, needs that had nothing to do with language, and everything to do with naked flesh.

He closed his eyes, and a soft moan escaped him.

"What I offer isn't illusion, Nimir-Raj, it's real."

He shook his head. "Sex isn't enough."

"I'm not offering sex, not now." Even as I said it, I pressed my body against his. His entire body shuddered against me, and a sound very like a whimper crawled out of his throat.

"I'm offering a taste of power, Nimir-Raj, a small taste of all I can offer you." In my head I knew it was a lie, but in my heart I knew it was true. I could offer him power and flesh, the two things he wanted, needed, above all else. It was perfect bait, and it was wrong. I started to back down, to try and cram the power down, but Jean-Claude fought me. He thrust his power into me like an echo of his body, riding me. It was too late for me to feed as humans feed and give him back his strength. He'd avoided me for nights, because I was weak. I had grown strong again, and he had grown weak, and we had enemies in town. We could not afford weakness. All this, I knew in a heartbeat, his mind to mine. And it was that seed of doubt—*could we afford to be weak?*—that made me unable to shut him out.

"What do you want in return?" Micah asked it in a whisper that held an edge of desperation, as if we both knew that whatever I asked, he would do it.

"I want to drink the warm rush of your body, to have you fill my mouth with that hot liquid that beats just below here," and I rubbed my lips across his neck. The scent of blood so near the surface made my stomach twist, but we were close, so close, mustn't rush it, mustn't scare him. We were like fishermen. We had our net, all we needed was for the fish to stop fighting us and lay still.

My lips hovered over his neck as he spoke. "Show me you have enough power to make it worth my while, and I'll give you any body fluid you want."

I swept his hair to one side, and it slid back. I balled my hand into a fist of his curls to keep it out of the way, and even that movement brought a sound from his throat. I bared the long smooth line of his neck. He moved his head to one side as if he knew what I wanted now. I could see the big pulse in his neck, beating against his skin like something small and separate from him, something alive that I had to make free.

I licked my tongue across that throbbing skin. I meant to be gentle, I meant many things, but his skin was slick and flawless against my mouth; the smell of him intoxicated me like the sweetest perfume. His pulse throbbed against my mouth, and I sank my teeth around that frantic movement. I ate at his skin, dug my teeth into the flesh underneath, and into his power, his beast.

I felt my beast rise through my body, like some great shape rising from the ocean depths, a leviathan that grew and grew, swelling up inside me until my skin couldn't hold it, then it touched his beast, and it stopped, hovering in black water, hovering in my body like some huge thing. The two powers floated in that dark water, brushing huge, sleek sides down the length of their bodies, our bodies. It was a sensation like velvet rubbing inside me, except this velvet had muscles, flesh, and was hard even where it was soft. The imagery that kept flowing through my mind was of some great cat rubbing itself inside me, rolling through me, but bigger than that. I'd seen Richard's beast move through his eyes like some great shape half-seen in water, and it felt that large, that overwhelming. I drank Micah's power down but not just through my mouth and down my throat. Everywhere I touched him, I fed. I could feel his heart beating against my naked breasts. I could feel the blood rushing through his body, feel every inch of him pressed against me. Feel his need, his desire, and I ate at him. I fed at his neck as if his pulse were the center of some filled cake, as if once I gnawed away the flesh I would have something unutterably sweet. I drew blood, and with the first touch of sweet metallic flavor in my mouth, all pretense, all prettiness was wiped away, drowned in the scent of fresh blood, the taste of torn flesh, the feel of meat and blood in my mouth. The feel of his hands pressing my body against his, my legs wrapped around his waist, riding him. I was aware like some distant call that he wasn't inside me, that he was still pressed between our bodies, so hard, so ready that he quivered against my stomach. His breath came fast and faster. Someone was making small animal noises, and it was me.

Micah's fingernails dug into my body, an instant before he poured over me in a scalding wave, noises too primitive for words, and not loud enough for screams coming from his mouth.

I felt Jean-Claude down that long metaphysical cord that bonded us together. I felt him grow quiet and well fed, sated. I drew my mouth away from Micah's torn throat, putting my cheek against his bare shoulder, my legs and arms still wrapped around him. His arms still holding me tight. I was covered in fluid, my breasts thick with it. It ran down my body in heavy liquid lines, curling over my stomach, tracing down to my thighs.

He knelt there supporting both our weights, while our breathing quieted, and the massive pulse of our bodies subsided into silence. And in that silence there was nothing but the feel of his flesh, the raw scent of sex, and in the distance, the satisfaction of the vampire.

10

THE SHOWER WAS one of those group ones, like you'd find in a health club. But I was the only one in it. I'd cleaned off, scrubbed myself thoroughly, but I felt like Lady MacBeth screaming "out, out, damned spot!" Like I'd never really be clean again. I sat on the tiles under the hot, beating water, hugging my knees. I hadn't planned on crying, but I was. Slow tears that felt cool compared to the water pounding my body. I wasn't sure why I was crying. My mind was blank. Usually when I try to be blank, I can't, but just then, there was nothing but the water, the heat, the smooth tiles, and the little voice in my head that kept running round and round like a hamster on a wheel. I couldn't hear what the voice was saying—I think I didn't want to. All I knew was that it was screaming.

A noise behind me made me turn. It was Cherry, still naked. None of the leopards ever dressed unless I made them. I turned my head away from her. I didn't want her to see me cry. I was her Nimir-Ra, her rock. Rocks did not cry.

I knew she was standing over me, could feel it, even before the water's rhythm changed. She knelt over me, the water sluicing around her, leaving me shivering in the sudden touch of the cool, waterless air. I kept my face turned away from her. She touched my water-soaked hair. When I didn't protest she hugged me, arms going slowly around me, as if she expected me to complain.

I stayed stiff in her arms, with her body wrapped around me. She just held me, head pressed to the top of mine, her body sheltering me from the water, leaving me colder, even as her body stretched like heat against my wet skin. I leaned into her by painful inches until finally I let her hold me. I cried, and Cherry held me.

The crying never grew, or got loud. It remained slow tears while Cherry held me, and I let her. Finally, there were no more tears, just the sound of the water, the heat, the feel of Cherry's body around mine. There was comfort in the touch of flesh that went beyond sex. I pulled away, and she drew back. I stood and turned the water off. The silence was sudden and complete. I could feel the press of the night outside. Even without a window, I knew it was the wee hours of morning—maybe two, or even three. It would be dawn in a few short hours. I needed to know why Jean-Claude was in jail. Everything else could wait. We had enemies in town, and I needed to know who they were, what they wanted. After that I'd think about what had just happened, but not yet, not yet. Avoidance is one of my best things.

Cherry handed me a towel and kept one for herself. I wound the towel around my hair and retrieved a second towel for my body. We dried off in silence, no eye contact. It wasn't shower protocol; girls aren't as hung up about that as guys. I just didn't want to talk about what had happened. Not yet.

I wrapped the oversized towel securely around my body, and asked, "Why is Jean-Claude in jail?"

"For murdering you," she said.

I stared at her for a few seconds, and when I could talk, I said, "Pass that by me again. Slowly."

"Someone got pictures of Jean-Claude carrying you out of the club. You were covered in blood, Anita. He was covered in your blood." She shrugged, drying off a spot she'd missed on one long leg.

"But I'm alive," I said. It sounded almost silly saying it.

"And how would you explain that in less than a week you were healed of wounds that should have killed you?" She straightened, slinging the towel over one shoulder, not bothering to cover even an inch of her body.

"I don't want him in jail for something he didn't do," I said.

"If you go tonight, the police will want to know how you healed yourself. What are you going to tell them?" Her eyes were very direct. So direct it made me want to squirm.

"You're treating me like a lycanthrope who hasn't come out of the closet yet. I'm not a shapeshifter, Cherry."

She dropped her gaze then, wouldn't meet my eyes. It reminded me of the looks they'd all given each other in the room where I woke up. I touched her chin, having to reach up to do it. "What aren't you guys telling me?"

A man's voice came from outside the showers. "Can I please come in and clean off?" It was Micah. I'd planned on running for the hills the next time I saw him, but there was something in Cherry's eyes that kept me frozen. She was scared. And there was something else, something I couldn't quite read.

I yelled back, "Just a minute!" Then I continued. "Cherry, tell me. Whatever it is, just tell me."

She shook her head. She was afraid, but of what? "Are you afraid of *me*?" I couldn't keep the surprise out of my voice.

She nodded, looking down again, avoiding my gaze.

"I would never hurt you, any of you."

"For this you might," she whispered.

I grabbed her arm. "Cherry, damn it, talk to me."

She opened her mouth, closed it, and turned towards the door a second before Micah Callahan walked through, as if she'd heard him before I had. He was still naked. I expected to be embarrassed, but I wasn't. I was beginning to have the proverbial bad feeling about whatever it was that Cherry didn't want to tell me.

Micah had combed his hair. It was definitely curls, not waves. The curls were tight, but not small. The color was that shade of dark, dark brown—almost black—that comes to people who start out white blond as children, then darken. The curls fell to just below his shoulders, and, following the line of hair, my eyes found his chest. I quickly moved them up so I could concentrate on his face. Eye contact. That was the ticket. I was getting back to the embarrassment.

"I told you we'd be out in a minute." My voice sounded grumpy, and I was glad. The fact that I was sort of clutching the towel to my body was purely coincidental.

"I heard you," he said. His face, voice, were neutral. Not

as neutral as a vampire's can become. They are the champs of blank expression. But Micah was trying.

"Then wait outside until we're finished," I said.

"Cherry is afraid of you," he said.

I frowned at him, then at her. "Why, for God's sake?"

Cherry looked at him, and he gave a small nod. She moved away from me towards the door. She didn't leave the room, but she got as far away from me as she could.

"What in hell is going on?" I asked.

Micah was standing about four feet away, close, but not too close. I could see his eyes better now, and they were *so* not human. I knew at a glance that they didn't belong in his face. "She's afraid you'll kill the messenger," he said, voice soft.

"Look, all this tap dancing is getting old. Just tell me."

He nodded, winced as if it hurt. "The doctors seem to think that you've been infected with lycanthropy."

I shook my head. "Serpentine lycanthropy isn't really lycanthropy. It's not a disease that I can catch. You either are cursed by a witch into snake form, or it's inherited like a swanmane." That made me think of the three women I'd last seen chained to a wall in the room of swords. "By the way, what happened to the swanmanes in the club?"

Micah frowned. "I don't know what you're talking about."

Without warning, Nathaniel entered the shower. I was beginning to feel positively overdressed in my towel. "We rescued them."

"The snake leader changed his mind after I got hurt?"

"He changed it after Sylvie and Jamil nearly killed him."

Ah. "So they're okay," I said.

He nodded, but his face stayed serious, his eyes gentle, like someone who's about to tell you really bad news.

"Don't you start, too. I cannot catch serpentine shit. It doesn't work that way."

"Gregory isn't into serpentine shit," he said, the voice as gentle as his eyes.

I blinked at him. "What are you talking about?"

Nathaniel started to come farther into the room, but

Cherry caught his arm, kept him near the door for a quick getaway—I think. Zane appeared in the doorway behind them. He was still the six-feet, pale, overly thin, but muscular guy I'd met when he was trashing a hospital emergency room. But he'd dyed his hair to an iridescent pale green, cut short, spiked. The fact that he was fully dressed actually looked odd to me. Of course, it was Zane's version of street clothes that ran to leather, no shirt, and vests.

I looked at the three of them in the doorway. They were so solemn. I remembered Gregory falling into me during the fight. His claws piercing me. "I've been cut up a lot worse by a wereleopard, and I didn't catch it," I said.

"Dr. Lillian thinks it may be because the wound was a deep piercing wound, instead of a surface cut," Cherry said, in a voice that was almost shaky. She was scared, scared of how I'd take the news, or scared of something else, but what?

"I am not going to be Nimir-Ra for real, guys. I can't catch lycanthropy. If I could . . . I've already been cut up enough . . . I'd have turned furry already."

The three of them just looked at me with wide eyes. I turned from them to Micah. His face was still neutral, careful, but there was a shadow in his eyes of . . . pity. Pity? I did not do pity, not as the object of it, anyway.

"You're serious," I said.

"You're exhibiting all the secondary symptoms," he said. "Rapid healing to the point that your muscles cramp. A temperature hot enough to boil the brain of a human. Yet when they lowered your temperature you nearly died. You needed to bake in the warmth, the heat of your pard to heal. That's how we healed you. It wouldn't have worked if you weren't one of us."

I shook my head. "I don't believe you."

"That's okay," he said, "you've got two weeks until the full moon. You won't change for the first time until then. You've got time."

"Time for what?" I asked.

"Time to mourn," he said.

I turned away from the compassion in his eyes, the pity.

Shit. I still didn't believe it. "How about a blood test? That should prove it one way or the other."

Cherry answered, "Wolf lycanthropy shows up in the bloodstream anywhere from twenty-four to forty-eight hours, sometimes seventy-two. Leopard lycanthropy, most of the big cat lycanthropies, take anywhere from seventy-two hours to over eight days to show up in the bloodstream. A blood test won't prove anything yet."

I stared at them, trying to wrap my mind around it, and it just wouldn't wrap. I shook my head. "I can't deal with this right now."

"You're going to have to deal with it," Micah said.

I shook my head. "Tonight, I have to get Jean-Claude out of jail. I have to show the police he didn't murder me."

"Your pard told me that you wouldn't want to be outed. That you wouldn't want your police friends to know."

"I am not a wereleopard," I said. It sounded stubborn even to me.

Micah smiled, gently, and that pissed me off. "Don't look at me like that."

"Like what?" he asked.

"Like a poor little deluded girl. There are things you don't understand about me, about where my power comes from."

"You mean the vampire marks," he said.

I looked past him to the three wereleopards in the doorway. Something on my face made them all flinch. "So nice to know that we're just one big happy family with no secrets."

"I was in on the discussions with the doctors on whether your rapid healing could be merely a side effect of the vampire marks," he said.

"Of course it is," I said. But the first thread of doubt was worming its way through my stomach.

"If it will make you feel better," he said.

I stared into that compassionate face and felt anger wash over me in a line of heat, and with the anger came that trembling energy. Richard's beast . . . or mine? I let myself think the thought all the way through for the first time. Was it my beast that I'd felt with Micah? Was that why I hadn't gotten a sense of where Richard was, and what he was doing? I'd thought of him several times during all the hoopla, but had never felt the mark between us open completely. I'd assumed it was Richard's energy, because it was lycanthrope energy. But what if it hadn't been? What if it had been mine?

Someone touched my arm, and I jumped. It was Micah, his fingers barely touching my arm. "You look pale. Do you need to sit down?"

I took a step back and nearly stumbled. He had to grab my arm to keep me from falling on the slick, wet tile. I wanted to jerk away from him, but I was dizzy as if the world wasn't quite solid. He eased me to the floor.

"Put your head between your knees."

I sat Indian fashion on the floor, the wall to my back, my head bent over my folded legs while I waited for the light-headedness to pass. I never fainted. Not just from shock—occasionally from blood loss—but never from shock.

When I could think again, I raised up slowly. Micah was kneeling beside me, all attentive and compassionate, and I hated him. I laid my towel-wrapped head back against the wall, closed my eyes.

"Where are Elizabeth and Gregory?"

"Elizabeth wouldn't come to help," Micah said.

I opened my eyes at that, turning just my head to meet his eyes. "She give a reason for that?"

"She hates you," he said, simply.

"Yeah, she loved Gabriel, their old alpha, and I killed him. Hard to be friends after that."

"That's not why she hates you," he said.

I searched his face. "What do you mean?"

"She hates that you're a better alpha as a human than she is as a wereleopard. You make her feel weak."

"She is weak," I said.

He smiled, and it had humor in it this time. "Yes, she is."

"Where's Gregory?"

"Are you going to punish him for contaminating you?" Micah asked.

I glanced back at the other three waiting in the door, silent. I realized suddenly what the group dynamics meant.

They were treating Micah as their Nimir-Raj, letting him deal with me, like calling in the husband when the wife has had one too many drinks. I didn't like that much. But if I concentrated just on the moment, the question at hand, no speculation, no looking for the future, maybe I'd survive.

"If Gregory hadn't interfered I'd be dead right now. They would have clawed out my heart. It was an accident that he fell into me during the fight." I was watching Micah's face, but I felt the relief sweep through the others, felt it from yards away. I glanced up at them, and it showed in the lines of their bodies.

"So where is he? Where's Gregory?"

The three of them did that hot-potato eye-flick game again. "Did he refuse to come help save me like Elizabeth?"

"No, of course not," Cherry said. But she didn't explain, didn't add to it.

I looked at Nathaniel. He met my gaze, no flinching, but I didn't like what I saw in his eyes. There was more bad news to come, you could smell it in the air.

I turned to Micah. "Fine, you tell me."

"When your Ulfric found out that Gregory had made you their Nimir-Ra in truth, he . . ." Micah spread his hands.

"He freaked." Zane said it.

I glanced at all of them. "What do you mean, he freaked?"

"He took Gregory," Cherry said.

"What do you mean, he took Gregory?"

"He treated Gregory as an enemy of the pack," Micah said.

I looked at him. "Go on."

"If you had been their lupa in truth, if someone injured you it is within the Ulfric's rights to declare them an enemy of the pack, a criminal."

I kept staring into those yellow green eyes. "What exactly does that mean?"

"It means that the wolves have your leopard, and they will pass judgment on him for injuring you."

"No way, I mean, even if I *am* turning into a wereleopard, which I'm not. It doesn't hurt me. I mean, I'm just going to be a shapeshifter like them now."

"Not like them," Micah said, "like us."

I tried to read his face, but I just didn't know him well enough yet. "You have a point, make it."

"You can't be the wolves' lupa *and* the leopard's Nimir-Ra."

"I've been both for a long time."

He shook his head, and again he winced as if his neck hurt. "No, you were a human dating the Ulfric, who declared you lupa. You were a human that was taking care of the wereleopards until you could find a true alpha leopard to take over the job. Now, you're truly Nimir-Ra, and the pack won't accept you as one of them."

"Are you saying Richard dumped me because I'm going to be a wereleopard?"

"No, I'm saying that the pack won't accept you as his lupa." Micah glanced down, then up. I could see him trying to put his thoughts into words. "My understanding of what's been happening with your local wolves is that your Ulfric has taken them from a monarchy where his word was law, to a democracy where the majority rules. He gets a decisive vote, but not the last word."

I nodded. It sounded like what Richard had wanted for the pack. "It sounds like something he'd do. I've sort of been out of touch for the last few months."

"He has succeeded too well. The vote went against him, against you. The pack will not accept you as lupa when you're wereleopard and not werewolf."

I looked past him at the others. "Is that true?"

They all nodded. "I'm so sorry, Anita," Cherry said.

I shook my head, trying to concentrate and not succeeding. "Alright, fine, fine. Richard can't make me lupa. I never wanted to be lupa, just his girlfriend. Fuck the wolves. But what have they done with Gregory?"

"Richard went ape-shit when he found out what Gregory had done," Zane said. "He thought Gregory had done it on purpose, because we were all afraid to lose you as our Nimir-Ra."

"He accused Gregory of doing it on purpose?" I asked.

Zane nodded. "Oh, yeah, then they took him."

"They, who?"

"Jamil, Sylvie, others." He wouldn't meet my eyes.

"Didn't anyone try and argue with him about this?"

"Sylvie tried to tell him it wasn't right, that you wouldn't like it. He hit her, told her never to argue with him again, that he was Ulfric, not her."

"Shit."

"Do not blame your leopards for not fighting the wolves," Micah said. "They are sorely outnumbered."

"They'd get their asses kicked, I know that. Besides, it's my job to deal with Richard, not theirs."

"Because you are their Nimir-Ra," he said.

"Because I am his girlfriend, sort of."

"Of course," he said.

I waved a hand at him. "Look, I can't deal with all of this right now, so I'm just going to concentrate on the important stuff, I mean the immediately important stuff. Where is Gregory, and how do I get him back?"

Micah smiled. "Very practical."

I looked at him and felt my eyes go cold. "You have no idea how practical I can be."

His eyes did change, but it wasn't fear in them, it was more interest, like my reaction intrigued him. "The situation is complex because you are the lupa that was injured. In effect, you must persuade yourself that Gregory meant no harm."

"That's too easy," I said. "I know he meant no harm. So why do I get the feeling that I can't just call Richard up and say, 'Hey, I'm coming to get Gregory'?"

"Because you must convince not just Richard, but the entire pack, that you have the right to Gregory."

"What do you mean 'right to Gregory'? He's my leopard. He's mine, not theirs."

Micah smiled, lowering long lashes over his eyes, as if he didn't want me to read his expression at that moment. "The Ulfric declared Gregory rogue for, in effect, killing their lupa."

"I'm alive, what . . . ?"

Micah held up a finger, and I let him finish. "You are

dead to the pack—as their lupa. In effect, being a leopard makes you dead to them. You may share Richard's bed again, but you will never be their lupa again. They voted on it, and Richard has destroyed his own power structure to the point where he can't force a vote on them."

"You're saying that he is Ulfric but he doesn't really rule them," I said.

Micah seemed to think about that for a second, or two, then started to nod, stopped in mid-motion. "Yes, in fact, very well put."

"Thanks." A thought came to me, and I gripped his arm. "They aren't going to kill Gregory, are they?" Something passed over his face that tightened my grip on his arm. "They haven't killed him?"

"No," Micah said.

I let go of his arm and leaned back against the wall. "What are they doing to him, or what are they planning to do to him?"

"The penalty for killing the lupa is death in any pack. But the circumstances are strange enough that I think you will be allowed a chance to win him back."

"Win him back, how?" I asked.

"For that, you'll need to ask the Ulfric."

"I'll do that." I looked past him. "Someone get my cell phone out of my Jeep." Nathaniel went for the door without another word.

"What are you going to do?" Micah asked.

"I'm going to make sure that Gregory isn't being hurt. If he's okay for tonight, I'll go get Jean-Claude out of jail. If Gregory is in danger, then I get him out first."

"Priorities," he said, softly.

"Damn straight."

He smiled again. "I am very impressed. You've had several shocks in a very short space of time, yet you are clear-headed, and moving forward to solve the problems one at a time."

"I can only solve one problem at a time," I said.

"Most people let themselves be distracted."

"I'm not most people."

He gave that small smile again, shielding his eyes with his long lashes. "I've noticed."

Something about the way he said it made me suddenly aware that he was nude, and I was wearing nothing but a towel. It was time to get on my feet and get dressed. I stood, pushing away his offer of help. "I'm fine, Micah, thanks anyway." I looked past him at Cherry and Zane still standing in the doorway. "Do I have any clothes here?"

Cherry nodded. "Nathaniel brought your stuff from home. I'll go get it." She moved through the door.

"Weapons, too," I called after her.

She poked her head back around the doorway. "I know." That left just Zane standing in the doorway. "Do you have a job for me?"

"Not right now."

He flashed me a smile wide enough to show that he had dainty fangs upper and lower—kitty-cat fangs. Zane had spent a little too much time in animal form to come all the way back. "I'll go help Cherry then." He paused at the doorway. "I'm really glad you didn't die."

"Me too."

He grinned and left.

That left me alone with Micah. I looked into his yellow-green eyes and knew that they were also a sign that he'd spent too much time in animal form. We hadn't kissed, so I didn't know if he had dainty fangs like Zane. I hoped not, and wasn't sure why I cared.

"Do you mind if I start cleaning up?" he asked.

I shook my head. "Help yourself. I'm going to go look for my clothes." But Nathaniel came around the door with my cell phone.

I looked at the slim black phone. I'd only had it a few months. I'd tried not to buy one. If you had a cell phone and a beeper you were never truly free of the office. Of course, I was on vacation. Though, so far, it hadn't been all that relaxing.

I popped the phone open and dialed Richard's number from memory. There was no answer, just his machine. I left a message, then knew what I was going to do. I had to know what was happening with Gregory. I thought about Richard, the feel of his arms, the scent of his neck, the brush of his hair, and that prickling rush of energy rolled over my skin. I reached down the mark that bound me to Richard and found him standing on a podium. He was arguing with someone, but I couldn't see who. I never got as clear a visual through Richard as I did through Jean-Claude. Richard turned as if he could see me standing behind him, then he thrust me out, throwing up a shield so solid I couldn't feel him on the other side.

Nathaniel was holding my arm, steadying me. "Are you alright?"

I nodded. Being thrust out like that was always disorienting. Richard knew that. Fuck. "I'm okay." I pulled away from Nathaniel and had to call information for the number for The Lunatic Cafe. Richard was in the meeting room in the back of the restaurant. Raina had owned the restaurant, and according to pack law, it could have belonged to me, if I hadn't used a gun to kill her. It had to be mano-a-mano, hand-to-hand, or claws, or at least a knife before all that was hers would be mine. Possessions anyway. You can't get anyone's power by killing them. It just doesn't work that way. And anyway, who would want it to? Guns were considered cheating, so I didn't inherit all of Raina's stuff.

Richard picked up on the second ring, as if he'd been expecting the call. "Richard, it's Anita."

"I know." His voice was angry, closed, and tight.

"We need to talk."

"I'm in the middle of something here, Anita."

Fine, if he wanted to play it brusque and hostile, I'd play. "Where's Gregory?"

"I can't tell you that."

"Why?"

"Because, you might try and rescue him, and you're not lupa anymore. The pack would defend itself, and I don't want you shooting holes in my wolves."

"You leave my leopards alone, and I'll leave your wolves alone."

"Anita, it's not that simple."

"I got the explanation, Richard. You freaked when you found out Gregory may have infected me with leopard juice. You had your enforcers grab him, and you've charged him with killing your lupa. Which is just stupid, I'm not dead."

"Do you know what the pack is voting on right now, right this minute?"

"Not a clue."

"Whether I will be picking another lupa from the pack before the next full moon."

"I guess you'll need one," I said, and even hearing myself acknowledge it made my stomach clench.

"A *lover*, Anita, they're wanting to force me to pick a lover from the pack."

"You mean we can't date now?"

"That's the vote."

"Stephen, one of your wolves, and Vivian, one of my leopards, are living together. No one seems to care about that."

"Stephen is one of the least of us. They wouldn't tolerate cross-species dating for a dominant. And they certainly won't tolerate it for their Ulfric."

"Human is good enough to fuck, but not leopard," I said.

"We are human, Anita. But we aren't cats, we're wolves."

"So you won't be dating me, or anything, now?"

"Not if I want to stay Ulfric."

"What happens to the triumvirate?"

"I don't know."

"You're going to give me up just like that." I was suddenly cold, my stomach like a hard frozen knot.

"You've been out of my life for over half a year. How do I know that something else won't scare you off again?"

"I planned on dating you both, Richard, on being with you both." I realized as soon as I said it that I meant it. I'd made a decision and hadn't realized it.

"What about a week from now, or a month, or even a year? What will scare you off next time?"

"I don't plan on running anymore, Richard."

"Nice to know." I could feel his anger like something hot

and touchable over the phone. Either his shield was leaking, or he'd lowered it.

"You don't want to be with me anymore?" My voice was soft, hurt, and I hated it. Hated it.

"I want to be with you, you know that. You drive me crazy, but I still want you."

"But you'll still give me up," I said. My voice was a little stronger, but not much. Richard was dumping me. Fine, it was his prerogative. I was a pain in the ass, I knew that. But my chest ached with it, damn it.

"I don't want to, Anita, but I'll do what I have to do. You taught me that."

My eyes were hot. I'd taught him that. Great. If we were really going to break up for good, then I would not cry or beg. I would not be weak. My voice came out more solid, more sure of itself. My stomach was still in cold knots, but it didn't show in my voice. The effort that it took to just sound normal over the phone made my chest tight. "You're Ulfric, wolf king. Your word is law in the pack."

"I've worked hard to make sure that everyone has an equal voice, Anita. I can't pull rank now. It would undo everything I've tried to change."

"Ideals are great in theory, Richard, but they don't work too well in real life."

"I disagree," he said. His anger was already leaking away. He just sounded tired.

"I'm not going to argue things we've been arguing since we met. I'm going to concentrate on the things I can change. And no matter how much we want to, we can't change each other, Richard. We are what we are." My voice was uncertain again, full of some of the emotion I was feeling. "So, is Gregory okay?"

"He's okay."

"I want him back, you know that."

"I know that." His anger was making a comeback.

"Now that I'm not lupa, not pack, how do I get him back?"

"You have to come to the lupanar tomorrow night and petition for him."

"What do you mean, 'petition for him?' "

"You have to prove yourself worthy. There'll be some kind of test."

"Like multiple choice, essay, what?"

"I don't know yet. We're . . . voting on it."

"Fuck, Richard, there's a reason why we have a representative democracy in this country, not a pure one. Pure one person, one vote, just doesn't work well. You can't decide anything that way."

"They're deciding, Anita. You're just not liking the way it's going."

"How could you take Gregory? How could you do that?"

"As soon as I realized what had happened, I knew that the pack would vote you out. Most of them weren't happy with you even before. You weren't pack, and they didn't like that. The fact that you've avoided them—all of them—for six months didn't help."

"I had to get my shit together before I could come back, Richard."

"And while you were getting your shit together, mine was falling apart."

"I'm sorry, Richard, I am. But I didn't know."

"Tomorrow night at the lupanar, about an hour after dark. You can bring all your wereleopards and any other shapeshifters that are your allies. If it were me, as Ulfric, I'd bring the wererats."

"I'm not lupa anymore, so they aren't my allies, are they?"

"No," he said, and the anger was gone again. Richard never could hold a grudge for long.

"What happens if I don't win Gregory back?"

He didn't answer me, just the sound of his breathing on the phone. "Richard, what happens to Gregory?"

"He'll be judged by the pack."

"And?"

"If he's convicted of killing our lupa, it's a death sentence."

"But I'm right here, Richard. I'm not dead. You can't kill Gregory for killing me, when he didn't do it."

"I delayed the judgment until you were well enough to attend. It was the best I could do."

"You know, Richard, sometimes it's good to be king. A king gets to pardon whomever he wants, a king gets to fuck whomever he wants."

"I know that."

"Then be king, Richard, really be king. Be their Ulfric, not their president."

"I'm doing what I think best for them all."

"Richard, you can't do this."

"It's already done."

"Richard, if I fail your little test, I will not let you execute Gregory. Do you understand me?"

"You won't be allowed to bring guns into the lupanar, just knives." His voice had gone very careful.

"I remember the rule. But Richard, are you listening to me? Are you understanding me?"

"If we try to execute Gregory tomorrow night, you'll fight us, I understand. But understand this, Anita, your leopards are no match for us, not even with Micah and his pard. We outnumber you five to one, maybe more."

"It doesn't matter, Richard. I can't stand by and watch Gregory die, not for something stupid like this."

"Will you try to save one of your cats and risk losing them all? Do you really want to see what would happen if they tried to fight their way out of the lupanar, through the pack? I wouldn't want to see it."

"This is . . . damn it, Richard, don't put me in a corner, you won't like it."

"Is that a threat?"

"Richard . . ." I had to stop in mid-sentence and count slowly under my breath. But counting to ten wasn't going to do it, maybe a bijillion. "Richard," my voice came out calmer, "I will save Gregory, whatever it takes. I will not let the wolves slaughter my leopards, whatever that takes. You lost your temper and took one of my leopards. You made your pack a freaking democracy, where you don't even have presidential veto. Are you really going to compound the mistakes by starting a war between your pack and my pard?"

"I still think that everyone having a voice is a good idea."

"It's a great idea, but it's not working, is it?" He was quiet again. "Richard, don't do this."

"It's out of my hands. I'm sorry, Anita, you don't know how sorry."

"Richard, you won't really let them execute Gregory. I mean, not really."

Silence again.

"Richard, talk to me."

"I'll do what I can, but I've lost the vote on it. I can't change that."

"Can you really stand by and watch him die for something he didn't do?"

"How do you know he didn't infect you on purpose?"

"I was there. He fell on top of me with two of the snake things riding him. It was an accident. He kept them from cutting out my heart. He saved my life, Richard, and this is damn poor payment."

"He couldn't have turned his claws aside at the last minute?" Richard asked.

"No, it all happened too fast."

He laughed, but it was bitter. "You've been around us so long, and you still don't understand what we are. I could turn aside in less than a blink of an eye. Gregory isn't slower than I am. As a leopard he's quicker, more agile."

"Are you saying he did this on purpose?"

"I'm saying that he had a fraction of a second to decide what he'd do, and he decided to keep you as their Nimir-Ra. He made the choice to take you from me."

"And you're going to make him pay for that. Is that it?"

"Yeah, that's it."

"With his life?"

He sighed. "I don't want him dead, Anita. But when I first found out what he'd done, I wanted to kill him myself. I wanted it so badly I didn't trust myself around him, so I had him taken somewhere safe until I could cool down. But Jacob got wind of it, and forced a vote."

"Who's Jacob?"

"My new Geri, third in charge behind Sylvie."

"I've never heard of him before."

"He's new."

"Damn, third in line, and he's new. He's either a very good fighter, or a very vicious one, to win that many fights in less than half a year."

"He's good, and he's vicious."

"Is he ambitious?" I asked.

"Why?"

"If Jacob hadn't forced a vote, would you have given Gregory back to me?"

He remained quiet so long, that I finally asked, "You still there?"

"I'm here. Yes, I would have given him back to you. I can't kill him for what he's done."

"So Jacob set in motion something that's stripped you of a powerful ally—me—and forced you to declare war on another group—the wereleopards. He's been a busy boy."

"He's just doing what he thinks is right."

"Jesus, Richard, how can you still be this naive?"

"You think he wants my job?"

"You *know* he wants your job. I can hear it in your voice."

"If I'm not strong enough to hold the pack, then it's Jacob's prerogative to challenge me. But he's got to defeat Sylvie first, and she's as good as he is—and as vicious."

"How big is Jacob?"

"My size, not as muscled."

"Sylvie is good, but she's five six, and slender, and a woman. And as much as I hate to say it, that makes a difference. Pound for pound you guys have the upper body strength on us. If the skill is equal, a larger person will beat a smaller one."

"Don't underestimate Sylvie," he said.

"Don't overestimate her, either. She's my friend, too, and I don't want her dead just because you're not willing to take care of business."

"What's that supposed to mean?"

"It means until he defeats Sylvie and becomes Freki, your second in command, you can kill him outside of a challenge. You can have him executed."

"And if Marcus had thought that about me, I'd be dead now."

"And Marcus would be alive, Richard. You're not helping your case."

"We aren't animals, Anita, we're people. And I can't just kill him because I think he's after my job."

"You don't just stand down as Ulfric, Richard, you fight to the death for it. I know theoretically if you both agree, it doesn't have to be death. But I've been asking around, and no werewolf I've talked to can remember a fight for Ulfric that wasn't to the death. He's not after your job, Richard, he's after your life."

"I can't control what Jacob does, only what I do."

I was beginning to remember why Richard and I didn't make a go of it as a couple. Oh, there had been a lot of reasons. I'd seen him eat Marcus, and that had made me run away. Then we got back together, and the marks were overwhelming. But there were other reasons. Reasons that made me feel tired and older than Richard, even though he was actually two years older than me. "You're being stupid, Richard."

"It's not really any of your business, Anita. You're not my lupa anymore."

"If you die, the marks may drag Jean-Claude and me down to die with you, so that sort of makes it my business."

"And you don't risk your life every time you go hunting vampires or preternatural creatures with the police? You almost died in New Mexico less than a month ago. You risked all of us."

"I was trying to save people's lives, Richard. You're trying to remake a political system. Ideology is great in a classroom or a debate, but it's flesh and blood that counts, Richard. It's life and death we're talking about here, not some outdated ideal you have in your head about what a better world you can make for the pack."

"If ideals mean nothing, Anita, then we are just animals."

"Richard, if Gregory dies for this, then *I* will kill Jacob, and anyone else who gets in my way. I'll destroy your lupanar and salt the ground, so help me. You explain to Jacob, and anyone else that needs convincing, that if they fuck with me, they will die."

"You can't fight the entire pack, Anita. Not and win."

"If you think the only thing I care about is winning, then you don't know me at all. I will save Gregory because I said I would."

"If you fail the tests, you can't save him."

"What sort of tests are we talking about?"

"Ones that only a shapeshifter could pass."

"Richard, Richard . . ." I wanted to scream and rant at him, but I was suddenly more tired than angry, more discouraged than enraged. "Mark me on this, Richard, if I fail to save Gregory, then I will remake heaven into hell to avenge him. You explain that to Jacob, make sure he understands."

"Tell him yourself." There was silence and the sound of movement. Then a man's voice came on, a voice that I'd never heard before. The voice was pleasant, young, but not too young.

"Hello, I'm Jacob, I've heard a lot about you." His voice made it plain that he hadn't liked what he'd heard.

"Look, Jacob, we don't know each other, but I cannot allow you to kill Gregory for something he didn't do."

"The only way you can stop us is by winning him back."

"Richard explained that I'd have to pass a test to get Gregory back. He also said if I failed that you'd execute Gregory."

"It's pack law."

"Jacob, you don't want to make me your enemy."

"You are Nimir-Ra of a small leopard pard. We are the Thronnos Rokke Clan. We are the lukoi, and you are nothing to us."

"Yeah, I'm coming tomorrow night as Nimir-Ra of the Blooddrinker's Pard. But I'm Anita Blake. Ask the vampires and other shapeshifters around town about me. See what they say. You don't want to fuck with me, Jacob, you really don't."

"I've already asked around. I know your reputation."

"Then why are you pushing this?"

"That's my business," he said.

"Fine, you want to do this, we can do this. If you cause Gregory's death through voting or werewolf politics, I will bury you."

"If you can," he said. "You're a brand-new shapeshifter. You won't even change form until the full moon, and that's weeks away. You are no match for me."

"You say that like I'm going to offer to fight you one-on-one. I'm not. If Gregory dies, you die. Simple as that."

"If you shoot me, it won't reinstate you into the pack. If you could possibly win one-on-one against me, then maybe they'd vote you back to lupa. But if you just shoot me, you'll never be lupa again."

"I'm going to say this nice and slow, Jacob, so we understand each other. I don't give a shit about being lupa. I care about my friends, and the people I've promised to protect. Gregory is one of those people. If he dies, you die."

"I'm not going to kill him, Anita. I just made sure there was a vote about it."

"Do you like John Wayne movies, Jacob?"

He was quiet for a heartbeat. "I guess, I mean, what does that have to do with anything?"

"Your fault, my fault, nobody's fault, if Gregory dies, you die."

"Am I supposed to get the movie reference?" he asked. He sounded angry now.

"I guess not, but the point is this. I will blame you personally if anything happens to Gregory, for any reason. If he comes to harm, so will you. If he bleeds, so do you. If he dies . . ."

"I get the idea. But I don't have a deciding vote on this issue. I'm just one vote."

"Then you better think of something, Jacob. Because I give you my word that I mean everything I say."

"I heard that about you." He was quiet, and we stood on either end of the phone in silence, until he said, "What about Richard?"

"What about him?"

"If something happens to him what will you do?"

"If I tell you that I'll kill *you* if you kill *him*, that under-

cuts his authority as Ulfric. But I'll say this much, if you
defeat him, then it better be a fair fight in a challenge circle.
If you cheat in any way, no matter how small, I'll kill you."
I wanted so badly to just give Richard blanket protection,
but I couldn't. It would weaken his position, and his position
was weak enough already.

"But if it's fair, you'll stay out of it?"

I leaned against the wall and tried to think. "I'll be honest,
Jacob, I love Richard. I don't always understand him, or even
agree with him, but I love him. I'm ready to kill you over
someone who has never been my lover or even a good friend.
So, yeah, you kill Richard, and I'm really, really going to
want to kill you."

"But you won't," he said.

I didn't like how persistent he was about the issue. It made
me nervous. "I'll make you a deal, you don't challenge Richard for Ulfric until after the next full moon, then whatever
happens, as long as it's fair, I'll stay out of it."

"What if it's sooner?" he asked.

"Then I am going to rain all over your parade."

"You're undercutting Richard's authority," he said.

"No, Jacob, no I'm not. I wouldn't be killing you because
I was lupa or any werewolf stuff. I'd be killing you because
I am just that vindictive. Give me a few weeks until after the
full moon, and you're in the clear on this one, if you've got
the *cajones* to finish the job."

"You think Richard will kill me, instead?"

"He killed the last Ulfric, Jacob. That's how he got the
job."

"If I don't agree to this, you'll just shoot me?"

"From a nice, safe distance, oh, yeah."

"I can promise that I won't challenge Richard until after
the full moon, but I can't promise that the vote won't go
against Gregory. He was one that Raina, the old lupa, used
to help punish some members of the pack. There's more than
one woman here that he helped rape."

"I know."

"Then how can you defend him?"

"He did what his old alpha told him to do, and what Raina, the wicked bitch of the west, told him to do. Gregory isn't a dominant, he's lesser, and he does what he's told, like a good submissive shapeshifter. Ever since I took over as his alpha, he's refused to rape and torture. As soon as he had a choice, he stopped doing it. Ask Sylvie. Gregory let himself be tortured instead of helping to rape her."

"She told the story to the pack."

"You don't sound impressed."

"It's not me you have to impress, Anita, it's the others."

"Help me figure out a way to impress them, Jacob."

"Are you serious? You want me to help you save the leopard?"

"Yeah."

"That's ridiculous. I'm Geri of Thronnos Rokke clan. I don't have to help a wereleopard that even *you* admit isn't a dominant."

"Don't go all class conscious on me, Jacob. Remember the early part of our conversation, the part about you dying? I blame you for the mess. And you will help me clean it up, or I will splatter your brains all over the walls."

"You can't bring guns into the lupanar."

I laughed, and even to me it was an unsettling sound, creepy even. "You going to spend the rest of your life inside the lupanar?"

"Jesus," he said, voice soft, "you're talking about assassinating me."

I laughed again. A small voice in my head was screaming at me, telling me I was being a very good sociopath. But Rebecca of Sunnybrook Farm wasn't going to cut it with Jacob. Maybe later I could afford to be soft. "I think we finally understand each other, Jacob. Here's my cell phone number. You call me before tomorrow night with a plan."

"What if I can't come up with one?"

"Not my problem."

"You'll kill me even if I try and save him—really try and save your leopard, but fail. You'll still kill me."

"Yes."

"You cold bitch."

"Sticks and stones will break your bones, but failure will get you killed. Call me, Jacob, make it soon." I hung up the phone.

11

"I SEE WHAT you mean about you being practical," Micah said. He was standing quietly watching me, face carefully neutral, but he couldn't quite keep everything off his face. He was pleased. Pleased with me, I think.

"You not going to run screaming because I'm a blood-thirsty sociopath?"

He smiled, and again his long lashes came down over his eyes. "I don't think you're a sociopath, Anita. I think you do what needs doing to protect your pard." He raised that yellow-green gaze to me. "I find that admirable, not some-thing to criticize."

I sighed. "Good that someone approves."

He smiled, and it was that mixture of condescension, hap-piness, and sorrow, that I'd seen before. A complex smile, that. "The Ulfric means well."

"You know what they say about good intentions, Micah. If he's determined to take himself to hell, fine. But he has no right to drag the rest of us along with him."

"I agree."

It made me tired that Micah agreed with me. I wasn't in love with him. Why couldn't it be Richard who agreed with me? Of course, there was someone else. I needed to get to Jean-Claude while it was still dark.

"I had to put off the shower, first to be a gentleman, and let you go first, then so the noise wouldn't interrupt your phone call. I need to get clean now, if you don't mind."

"I'll give you some privacy." I turned towards the door.

"It wasn't privacy I was asking for, just explaining why I was turning the water on during our conversation," he said.

That turned me around at the door. "What conversation?"

He turned on the shower, testing the water with his hand,

adjusting the heat, talking over his shoulder. "I've never felt another Nimir-Ra with the kind of power you put off. It was amazing."

"Glad you enjoyed it, but I've really got to go."

He turned to face me, stepping back into the water, throwing his head back for a second to wet his hair. The water hit his neck and he let out a hissing breath, bending over at the shoulders like it really hurt.

I went back into the room. "Are you alright?"

He nodded and stopped in mid-motion. "I will be."

I was close enough that when he raised his head I could see the water beaded on his face, clinging in thick drops to his lashes. I stood to one side, getting sprayed with just the faintest mist of the water. I got my first good look at the side of his neck. "Shit." I reached through the water to touch his face, turned him slowly so I could see the bite.

He had a perfect imprint of my teeth in the right side of his neck. The wound was still seeping blood, so the circle of toothmarks was filled with crimson. The tanned flesh of his neck was already bruising, dark colors swirling to the surface of his skin.

"God, Micah, I'm sorry."

"Don't be sorry, it is a love bite."

I dropped my hand from his face. "Yeah, right, it looks like I tried to eat your throat out." I frowned. "Why hasn't it started healing?"

"Wounds made by the teeth and claws of another lycanthrope heal slower than most, not as slow as silver, but slower than say, steel."

"I am sorry."

"And I said, don't be sorry."

"The last Ulfric I bit like this—and it wasn't nearly this bad, I didn't even break the skin—he considered it an insult. He said, it meant I considered myself higher in the pack than he was."

"We are not wolves. To the pard a wound on the neck from a Nimir-Ra is a sign that the sex was good."

That made me blush.

"I didn't mean to embarrass you, just to explain that you don't owe me an apology. I enjoyed it."

I blushed harder.

"Together we could do great things for our pard."

I shook my head. "We won't know for sure that I'm going to be Nimir-Ra for a few days. Let's take it slow until then."

"If you want to." His gaze was too direct, and I was suddenly aware that he was nude in a shower. I was getting better at ignoring, or at least not being bothered, around nudity. But there were moments when you had to be aware of it, when the look in the other person's eyes made you aware of it.

"I want to," I said.

He turned his back, lowering his head so the water beat on his shoulders, back, lower things. The spray widened as he moved through it, spattering on my face, shoulders, arms, legs, across the towel. It was time for me to leave, past time.

I was at the door again when he called after me. "Anita."

I turned back.

He was standing facing me, rubbing liquid soap from one of the wall dispensers on his body. He was doing his arms as I turned around, lathering his chest as he talked. "If you want us to go with you tomorrow, we would be honored."

"I can't let you drag your pard into our mess."

His hands slid downward, trailing white suds over his stomach, his hips, then slid between his legs, working the soap over himself. I knew from my own experience of getting the stuff off me that you had to scrub more where it had touched you, but his hands stayed, until he was slick, thick with bubbles, and partially erect by the time his hands slid to his thighs.

My mouth was dry, and I realized we hadn't said anything in several minutes. I'd just been watching him spread soap on himself. The thought brought heat in a rush up my face. Micah continued to soap his legs slowly, taking more time with each movement than he needed to. He was definitely doing it for my benefit. I needed to leave.

"If you are my Nimir-Ra, then your mess is my mess," he said, head still bent over his legs, face hidden from me, so that all I could see was the line of his body as he stood in the aisle, away from the water so the soap wouldn't rub off.

I had to clear my throat to say, "I don't want to pick out curtains, Micah."

"The power between us is enough that I'll agree to any arrangement you want." He stood up then, stretching his arm back to soap his shoulders. It made him stretch the front of his body in a long line, and I was painfully aware of him. I turned, really meaning to go out the door this time.

"Anita," he said.

I stopped in the doorway, but this time I didn't turn around. "What?" I sounded grumpy.

"It's alright to be attracted to me. You can't help yourself."

That made me laugh, a good normal laugh. "Oh, you don't have a high opinion of yourself, do you?" But I stayed facing away from him.

"It's not a high opinion of myself. You are a Nimir-Ra, and I am the first Nimir-Raj that you've ever met. Our power, our beasts are attracted to each other. We're *meant* to be attracted to each other."

I turned then, slowly, trying for eye contact and failing. He was turned away with the back of his body facing me. He was still spreading soap over his shoulders. The suds slid slowly down his skin towards his slim waist.

"We don't know yet that I'm a were-anything." My voice was breathy.

He managed to reach his entire back, his arms moving effortlessly over his skin, hands smoothing over the tightness of his buttocks. "You feel the call of my body, as I feel yours."

My pulse was beating way too hard. "You're an attractive man, naked, covered in soap. I'm human, so sue me."

He turned around, still soaped and slick. And he was huge.

My mouth went dry. My body tightened so hard and so suddenly, it almost hurt. It deepened my breathing, made me have to swallow my pulse.

"You're *not* human, that's the difference. That's why you keep looking even when you don't want to." He walked towards me, slowly, moving like all leopards could move when they wanted to. Like he had muscles in places that humans didn't. He glided towards me like some great, slinking cat, his nude body glistening with suds and water, his hair plastered in ringlets to his shoulders, around his face. Those huge yellow green eyes suddenly looked perfectly at home in his face.

"You don't understand yet how rare it is for two lycanthropes to share their beasts as we did." He was almost in front of me now. "They flowed in and out of our bodies." He stood there, not touching, not yet. "They were like two great cats, rubbing their furred sides against each other." He ran his hands slick with soap up my bare arms as he said it. I had to close my eyes. He was describing exactly how it had felt, as if he had read my mind, or had felt exactly the same thing.

His hands slid up my arms to my shoulders, to my neck, spreading slick and wet across my skin. His soapy hands cupped my face, and I felt his face moving towards mine before his lips touched me. The kiss was gentle, his body carefully not touching me.

He slid his fingers into the edge of the towel, gripping the cloth, pulling me forward. It made me open my eyes. It took a few steps to realize he was leading me towards the water.

"You'll need to wash the soap off," he said.

I was shaking my head, and finally stopped moving with him. He kept pulling on the towel and it unwrapped, starting to slide down my body. I grabbed it, holding it just below my suddenly bare breasts.

"No," I said, my voice strangled, but I repeated it. "No."

He stepped into me, pressing the slick hardness of him against my lower hand and arm. He tried to uncurl my fingers from the towel, and I held on for dear life. "Touch me, Anita, cup me in your hands."

I wanted to. I wanted to feel him in my hand. It was as if my skin ached for it

"I know you want to. I can smell it," and he moved his face above my skin, drawing his breath in and out against my wet skin. "I can feel it." He rubbed his hands up my arms again, over my shoulders, down towards my breasts, but stopped without touching them. "I can taste it." He licked a slow line along the edge of my cheek. I shivered and wanted to step back, but it was like I was frozen in place. I couldn't move.

I found my voice, shaky, but mine. My hands clutched to my body, because I knew if I touched him we were in trouble. "This isn't like me, Micah. I'm not like this. You're a stranger. I don't do strangers."

"I'm not a stranger. I'm your Nimir-Raj, and you are my Nimir-Ra. We could never be strangers."

He kissed his way down my face to my neck, biting gently at me, and it made my knees weak. He came back up to my lips, and when he kissed me I could taste the soap from my skin. The feel of him pressed against the front of my body, close enough that if I opened my hand I'd be able to hold him, was overwhelming. I realized it was more than just sex. I wanted to feed off of him again, not with my teeth but with my body. I wanted to drink in the energy of him through my skin, my bare skin pressed to his. I wanted it so badly. His hands slid over my breasts, covering them in soap, making them slick, the nipples already tight and hard. My arms slid around his waist, using the pressure of our bodies to keep the towel in place. He moved against my body, and his chest was so slick, so smooth rubbing against my breasts.

He began to walk backwards with his arms locked behind me, moving us back towards the water. My hands moved over the slick hardness of his back, sliding dangerously lower. It was as if I wanted to press every inch of myself to him, to roll his body around me like a sheet and drink him in through the pores of my skin.

I opened that link with Jean-Claude and found him sitting, waiting, patient. I called for help, and distantly I heard his voice in my head. "It is all I can do, *ma petite,* to control my own appetites, you must control your own."

"What's happening to me?" Even as I asked, Micah moved his body that fraction away that allowed the towel to slide down, and when he quickly moved back, he was pressed against my groin and stomach, and it was déjà vu enough to draw a small sound out of my throat.

Jean-Claude looked up, and I knew that he saw what was happening with Micah, that with a thought he could feel what was happening, as if it were his hands sliding down the slick, soaped skin. My hand slid over the thick hardness of Micah. He half-collapsed against me, as I caressed him, and I knew that it hadn't been my idea to touch him. Jean-Claude had wanted to know what it felt like. He drew away enough for me to move my hand, but the damage had been done. Micah dragged me into the water, surer now than ever that I would say yes.

Jean-Claude's voice in my head. "You can feed off his lust, but the price for that is that you will crave his lust, his sex. It is the double-edged sword of being incubus. The sword edge I have walked for centuries."

"Help me!"

"I cannot. You must ride this thing yourself. And you will either conquer it, or be conquered. You felt what happened when I interfered just now. Because I have denied myself feeding through my body. I knew you would not approve, so I denied myself. And being inside your body while you touch me, while you feed, would be my undoing. I crave you more than you will ever crave the man in your arms. I have wanted to take your body in the way that only I could take it. To feed from your sex, not from a vein. But I knew that would frighten you more than blood."

Micah turned me towards the wall, putting my hands up against the tile, pressing his body against my back. Jean-Claude's voice was soft in my head, more intimate than Micah's touch. "I did not know you would gain this demon from me, *ma petite,* and nothing I can say will convince you of that. I know that. I await you here, until you have wrestled the demon, whatever the outcome." And he shielded from me, hid himself away so he would not feel what was happening, left me alone to make my choice, if I was still capable of choosing.

I found I did have a voice and said, "Micah, please," but I was no longer sure what I was asking.

Micah licked the back of my neck, and I shuddered, pressed against the wet wall.

"Please, Micah, I'm not on birth control." A clear thought at last.

He bit softly at the back of my neck. "I had myself fixed two years ago. You're safe with me, Anita."

"Please, Micah, please don't. If we have sex I'll feed on you. Feed on you like some kind of vampire."

"Then feed, if that's what you need, what you want."

He bit harder, just this side of drawing blood, and my body went passive, calm. It was as if he'd hit a switch I didn't know I had. When he pressed himself inside me, he was slick, and I knew that sometime when I'd been paying attention to Jean-Claude inside my head, he'd spread more soap on himself, allowing that thick hardness to slide more easily inside me.

He pinned me to the wall and slid inside me, one tight inch at a time. It wasn't that he was long so much as he was wide—wide enough that it was just this side of pain to have him work himself inside me, even with the soap.

He pushed until most of him was inside me, and there was a stopping point. Then he began to draw himself out, slowly, so slowly. Then in again, slowly, still having to push himself, to work to make room for himself inside me. I stood pinned against the wall, passive, unmoving. It wasn't like me. I moved during sex. But I didn't want to move, didn't want to stop, and there was no thinking, just the feel of him moving in and out of me. I wasn't as tight now, and the soap had given way to my own wetness, so that he began to move more smoothly in and out of me. He was gentle, but he was so big that even gentle was almost overwhelming. He came to the end of my body before the full shaft of him was inside me. I could feel him bumping against my cervix at the end of each stroke. Most women find having their cervix bumped painful, but some women find it pleasurable. His size was intimidating, but when I realized it didn't hurt, in fact that it felt wonderful, a part of me that was still sane, still keeping track of some safety measures, relaxed and shut down. My last measure of control went away. I didn't want sex. That was just a means to an end. I wanted to feed. I wanted to eat his lust, drink his heat, bathe in his energy. The thought brought a sound low in my throat.

Micah braced himself against the wall, his body pinning mine completely, and began to find a rhythm, still gentle, but quicker. He was being so careful of me, and I didn't want him careful.

I heard a voice that didn't quite sound like mine. "Harder."

His voice came out squeezed tight. "It will hurt if I do it harder."

"Try me."

"No."

"Micah, please, just do it, please. If it hurts I'll tell you. Please." He'd been less controlled in the other room, and I realized why. He truly was afraid of hurting me because he was inside me. When he was just rubbing himself on my body, he hadn't had to worry about damaging me. Now he did. It gave him an edge of control that kept me from feeding. He was a Nimir-Raj, and he had enough power to keep me out. Unless he let down his guard. To do that he had to lose more control than this.

Even as I thought it, a part of me was swimming to the surface. I could think again, at least a little. I didn't want to do this. I didn't want to feed off of him. It was wrong, in so many ways it was wrong. I started to say, "Micah, stop, I can't do this." I got as far as, "Micah . . ." and he took me at my word. He thrust into me so hard and fast it tore a scream from my throat and brought that new part of me that was Jean-Claude's hunger in a raging wave of heat that rode my body and spilled out my mouth.

He'd stopped. "Are you alright?"

"Don't stop. Don't stop!"

He never asked again. He drove himself inside me so fast and hard that it left me gasping, unable to catch my breath. Small, helpless noises fell from my lips, spaced with the words, "Oh, God, yes, yes, Micah!" Every time he thrust as far as he could, smashing himself inside me, it rode that fine line between overwhelming pleasure and pain. And just as the pleasure began to turn to pain, he'd withdraw, and I'd be able to breathe again. Then he'd thrust himself inside me again, and it would start all over.

It felt like he filled me up as if I were a cup, until there was nothing inside me but the feel of his body, the feel of his flesh pounding into mine. It was tight, thick, like he'd plugged a hole with his body, and would never let it go. That sense of fullness inside me grew, grew, and spilled over me, through me, inside me, and tore out of my mouth in ragged, frantic screams, as my body spasmed around him. And it was only then that his control slipped away, letting me know that he had still been gentle. His control went when he did, and I drank him into me, through his chest pressed to my back, his hips thrusting against my butt. I drank him in, as he exploded inside me. I fed on him, drew him inside every pore of my skin, until it was as if our skins gave way and we spilled into each other, became for one shining moment one thing, one beast. And I could feel his beast inside mine, as if they were coupling within our bodies as our human shells merged. In that moment, I didn't doubt that I was truly his Nimir-Ra.

When we were finished and had slid to the floor, him still inside me, his arms hugging me to the front of his body, I started to cry. He was afraid he'd hurt me, but that wasn't it. I couldn't explain the tears to him, because I didn't want to say it out loud. But I knew. I'd tried not to be one of the monsters for so long, and now, in one fell swoop I was them, both of them. You couldn't be a bloodsucking vampire and be a lycanthrope at the same time. They canceled each other out as a disease or a curse. But I had felt my beast curl around Micah's. I had felt it like an embryo in a safe warm place, waiting. And I had fed off of him as surely as any vampire. I'd always thought I'd have to drink blood to be one of them. But I had been wrong, wrong about so many things. I let Micah hold me. I felt his heart pounding against my back and wept.

12

NATHANIEL DROVE BECAUSE I was too shaky to concentrate. I was functioning, moving forward, solving the problems one at a time, but it was as if the very ground I walked on, the air I breathed was precarious and new. As if everything had changed, because I had changed. I knew better. I knew that no matter how bad you feel, or what horrible thing happens to you, that the world just keeps on going. That the rest of the world doesn't even realize that the monsters are eating your heart. A long time ago it use to bother me that I could be in such confusion, such pain, and the world just didn't give a shit. The world, the creation as a whole, is designed to move forward, to keep on keeping on without any one individual person. It feels damned impersonal, and it is. But, then, if the world stopped rotating just because one of us was having a bad day, we'd all be floating out in space.

So I huddled in the passenger seat of my Jeep in the late darkness and knew that only I had changed. But it was just such a big change that it felt like the world should have changed its orbit, just a little.

June was back to its normal hot, sticky self. Nathaniel wore a ribbed tank top and silky jogging shorts. He'd tied his nearly ankle-length hair in a loose braid that curled on the seat beside his thigh. He'd found that if he let his hair fall onto the floorboard, sometimes it tangled around the pedals. He had to watch the gear shift between the seats, too. I'd never had hair that long.

Nathaniel had only had his driver's license for a few months, even though he was twenty. Gabriel, their old alpha, had not encouraged them to be independent. I sort of demanded it of them, as far as they were able. At first Nathaniel had been lost when I started to demand that he decide things for himself, but lately, he'd been doing better. It made me hopeful, and I needed some hope right now.

He'd picked out the clothes that he'd brought to the make-shift hospital for me. Black jeans, royal blue scoop neck T-shirt, a black bra that fit low enough to accommodate the low neckline, matching undies, black jogging socks, black Nikes, a short-sleeved black shirt to cover the shoulder rig with the Browning Hi-Power. People kept urging me to go shopping for a new main gun. They were probably right. There was probably something out there that would fit my hand better than the Browning. But I'd been putting it off. The Browning was like a piece of me. I felt incomplete without it, like I was missing a hand. It was going to take something more than a smaller grip to convince me to switch guns. So, for now, it was still me and the Browning.

Nathaniel had also brought my wrist sheaths and the matching silver knives. I was going to leave them in the car since the shirt was short-sleeved. They were a little too aggressive to wear into the police station. I had just replaced the back sheath I had ruined in New Mexico. It had been a special order, and it had cost mucho extra dinero to get a rush job on it, but it had been worth it. There really wasn't anywhere else on my body that I could carry a blade that large and still be able to sit down, without the hilt showing.

We drove in silence. Nathaniel hadn't even turned the radio on, which he liked to do. He rarely moved in silence if he could have music for background. But tonight he let the silence seep into the Jeep.

I finally asked a question I'd been wanting an answer for. "Who put the derringer in my robe pocket?" The derringer was in the glove compartment.

"I did."

"Thanks."

"The two things that you always do first is get dressed and get armed." His smile flashed in an instant of street light. "I'm not sure which is your highest priority."

I had to smile. "I'm not sure either."

"How are you doing?" His voice was very careful when he asked it, quiet in the rushing silence of the car.

"I don't want to talk about it."

"Okay." He was one of the few people that would actually take me at my word and not press. If I told Nathaniel I didn't want to talk, we didn't talk. The silence between us was no longer strained. In fact, silence with Nathaniel was one of the most relaxing sounds of my day.

Nathaniel parked the Jeep and we got out. I had my executioner's license with me, and most people knew me on sight. It occurred to me that they thought I was dead. As we walked towards the door, I realized I should probably have called ahead and given them a heads up, but it was too late now. I was a yard from the door. I wasn't using the cell phone now.

I was a familiar enough sight that I could usually just wave as I went past the desk, but tonight the officer's eyes got big as he waved me on to the left so I didn't have to go through the metal detector. But he was picking up a phone as he did it. I was betting he was calling ahead. You don't see people rise from the dead every night. Well, I guess *I* do, but most cops don't.

I was up the stairs leading to RPIT's headquarters when Detective Clive Perry opened the door and started down the stairs. He was slender, handsome, African-American, and the most unfailingly polite person I'd ever met. He actually missed the step and had to catch himself on the railing. Even then he leaned against the wall like his legs weren't working quite right. He looked shocked—no, scared.

"Anita." His voice was breathy. It was probably the second time in all the years we'd known each other that he had used my first name. It was usually Ms. Blake.

I responded in kind, smiling. "Clive, it's good to see you."

His eyes flicked from me to Nathaniel, then back to me. "You're supposed to be . . ." He straightened on the stairs. "I mean, we heard . . ." I watched him visibly try to rally. By the time we reached the step he was on, he looked almost normal. But his next question wasn't normal. "Did you die?"

I smiled, then felt the smile fade as I stared into his eyes. He was serious. I guess I did raise the dead for a living, so the question wasn't as ridiculous as it sounded, but I was realizing that some of his shock wasn't just from seeing me walking around. It was from his fear of what I was now. He thought I was the walking dead. In some ways he was closer to the mark than was comfortable, in others he was so far off.

"No, Clive, I didn't die."

He nodded, but there was a tightness around his eyes that made me wonder, if I tried to touch his arm, would he flinch? I didn't want to find out, so Nathaniel and I just walked past him, leaving him alone on the stairs.

I pushed into the squad room with its crowded desks and the busy clatter of people. RPIT had some of its busiest hours after three A.M. The noise died gradually like fading water rings, going out into the room, until I moved in silence between the desks and the staring faces. Nathaniel stayed at my back, moving like an attractive shadow.

I finally said, loud enough to carry through the room, "The rumors of my death are greatly exaggerated." And the room exploded into noise. I was suddenly surrounded by men, and a few women, hugging me, slapping me on the back, pumping my hand. Smiling faces, relieved eyes. No one else showed the reservations that Clive Perry had shown on the stairs, and it made me wonder about his religious background, or his metaphysical one. He wasn't a sensitive, but that didn't mean he hadn't grown up around people who were.

It was Zerbrowski who picked me completely off the ground in a huge bear hug. He's only five eight, and not that big, but he spun me around the room, finally putting me down, laughing and a little unsteady on my feet. "Damn, Anita, damn, I thought we were never going to see you come through that door again." He pushed a tangle of dark curls that were beginning to streak with gray from his forehead. He needed a haircut, but then he usually did. His clothes were the usual mismatch, as if he'd chosen his tie and shirt in the dark. He dressed like he was either color-blind or didn't give a shit. I was betting on the latter.

"It's good to see you, too. I hear you're actually holding someone on suspicion of having killed me."

His smile faded around the edges. "Yeah, Count Dracula's in a cell."

"Can you get him out, because as you see, I am very much alive."

Zerbrowski's eyes narrowed. "I saw the pictures, Anita. You were covered in blood."

I shrugged.

His eyes became cool, suspicious cop eyes. "It's been what, four nights? You're looking positively spry for suffering that much blood loss."

I could feel my own face grow neutral, distant, as cool and unreadable as any cop's. "Can you get Jean-Claude out and ready to go? I'd like to take him home before it gets light."

"Dolph's going to want to talk to you before you leave."

"I thought he might. Can you please start processing Jean-Claude while I talk to Dolph?"

"You going to take him to your house?"

"I'm going to drop him off at his place, not that it's any of your business. You're my friend, Zerbrowski, not my dad."

"I've never wanted to be your dad, Anita. That's Dolph's delusion, not mine."

I sighed. "Yeah." I looked up at Zerbrowski. "Will you please get Jean-Claude ready to go?"

He looked at me for a second or two, then nodded. "Okay." He looked past me to Nathaniel, who had moved to the side of the room to let the great reunion take place. "Who's that?"

"Nathaniel, a friend."

He looked back at me. "A little young, isn't he?"

"He's only six years younger than I am, Zerbrowski, but he drove me tonight, so I wouldn't have to."

His eyes looked worried. "You okay?"

"A little shaky, but it'll pass."

He touched my face, staring into my eyes, trying to read them, I think. "I'd like to know what the hell is going on with you."

I met his gaze, face, eyes blank. "So would I."

That seemed to surprise him, because he blinked and dropped his hand. "I'll get Count Dracula out of hock, you go talk to Dolph."

My shoulders hunched a little, and I had to concentrate to square them. I was not looking forward to talking with Dolph. Zerbrowski went to get Jean-Claude, and I left Nathaniel talking to a nice-enough seeming police woman and went to Dolph's office.

He was standing in the doorway like a small mountain. He's six eight and built like a pro wrestler. His dark hair was cut very short, leaving his ears stranded and bare. His suit looked pressed, tie neatly knotted. He'd probably already been on the job for nearly an eight-hour shift, but he still looked fresh out of the box.

His eyes were very careful when they looked at me. "I'm glad you're alive."

"Thanks, me, too."

He waved a hand and walked me down the hallway away from the office, away from the desks, towards the interrogation rooms. I guess he wanted privacy. Privacy that even the glass windows of his office wouldn't give him. It made my stomach tight and a little trickle of fear go through me. I wasn't afraid of Dolph the way I was afraid of a rogue shapeshifter or a vamp I had to kill. He wouldn't hurt me physically. But I was afraid of the tight set of his shoulders, the cautious, cold look of his eyes when he glanced back to make sure I was following.

I could feel how angry he was, almost like the energy off a shapeshifter. What had I done to deserve such rage?

Dolph held the door for me, and I squeezed past his bulk. "Have a seat," he said, as he closed the door behind us.

"I'll stand, thanks. I want to get Jean-Claude out of here before dawn."

"I heard you weren't dating him anymore," Dolph said.

"He's being held without charge on suspicion of killing me. I'm not dead, so I'd like to get him out of here."

Dolph just looked at me, eyes as cold and unreadable as if he were looking at a witness—no a suspect—that he didn't like much.

"Jean-Claude has a damn fine lawyer. How'd you keep him for over seventy-two hours without a charge?" I asked.

"You're a city treasure. I told everyone he'd killed you, and they helped me lose him for a while."

"Damn, Dolph, you're lucky some overzealous officer didn't put him in a cell with a window."

"Yeah, too bad."

I just stared at him not even sure what to say. "I'm alive, Dolph. He didn't hurt me."

"Who did?"

It was my turn to give *him* cool cop eyes.

He walked up to me, towering over me. He wasn't trying to intimidate me with his height; he knew that didn't work anyway. He was just that big. He touched my chin, tried to turn my face to the side. I jerked away.

"You've got scars on your neck that you didn't have a week ago. They're all shiny and nearly healed. How?"

"Would you believe I'm not sure?"

"No."

"Suit yourself."

"Let me see the scars."

I swept my hair to one side and let him trace one large finger down the healed wounds.

"I want to see the rest of the wounds."

"Don't we need a female officer in here for this?"

"Do you really want anyone else to see them?"

He had a point. "Why do you want to see, Dolph?"

"I can't force you to show me, but I need to see them."

"Why?"

"I don't know," he said, and his voice showed strain for the first time.

I shed the outer shirt and laid it on the table. I held my left arm out to him, pushing the sleeve of the T-shirt up.

He traced his finger over the marks. "What is it about your left arm? It's always where you get hit the most."

"I think it's because I'm right-handed. I'll let them chew on my left arm, while I grab a weapon with my right."

"Did you kill what did this to you?"

"No."

He looked at me, and the anger showed for a second. "I wish I believed you."

"Me, too, especially since I'm telling the truth."

"Who, or what, did this to you, Anita?"

I shook my head. "It's been taken care of."

"Damn it, Anita, how can I trust you when you won't talk to me?"

I shrugged.

"Is the arm all of it?"

"Almost."

"I want to see all of it."

There were a lot of men in my life that I'd have accused of just wanting to get my shirt off, but Dolph wasn't one of them. There'd never been that kind of tension between us. I stared at him, hoping he'd back down, but he didn't. I should have known he wouldn't.

I worked the shirt out of my pants and exposed my bra. I had to raise the edge of the underwire to show the round hole—now scar—over my heart.

He touched it like he had all the others, shaking his head. "It's like something tried to scoop your heart out." He raised his eyes to my face. "How the hell did you heal it, Anita?"

"Can I get dressed?"

There was a knock at the door, and Zerbrowski entered without waiting to be asked, while I was still struggling to get my breasts back behind the underwire. His eyes widened. "Am I interrupting?"

"We're finished," I said.

"Gee, and I thought Dolph would have more staying power."

We both glared at him. He grinned. "Count Dracula is processed and ready to go."

"His name is Jean-Claude."

"Whatever you say."

I had to bend over and rearrange my breasts so the bra would fit right again. Those underwires hurt if they ride up. They both watched me do it, and I stubbornly wouldn't turn away. Zerbrowski watched because he was a cheerful lech, Dolph, because he was angry.

"Would you take a blood test?" he asked.

"No."

"We can get a court order."

"On what grounds? I haven't done anything wrong, Dolph, except show up here not dead. If I didn't know better, I'd say you were disappointed."

"I'm glad you're alive," he said.

"But sorry you can't bust Jean-Claude's ass. Is that it?"

He looked away. I'd finally hit on it. "That's it, isn't it? You're sorry that you can't arrest Jean-Claude—get him executed. He didn't kill me, Dolph. Why do you want him dead?"

"He's already dead, Anita. He just doesn't know enough to lie down."

"Is that a threat?"

Dolph made a low exasperated sound. "He's a walking corpse, Anita."

"I know what Jean-Claude is, Dolph, probably better than you do."

"So I keep hearing," he said.

"What, you're angry because I'm dating him? You are not my father, Dolph. I can date who—or what—I want to date."

"How can you let him touch you?" And the anger was there again, rage.

"You want him dead because he's been my lover?" I couldn't keep the surprise out of my voice.

He wouldn't meet my eyes.

"You're not jealous of me, Dolph, I know that for a fact. It just bothers you that he's not human, is that it?"

"He's a vampire, Anita." He met my gaze then. "How can you fuck a corpse?"

The level of animosity was too personal, too intimate. And then it hit me. "What woman in your life is fucking the undead, Dolph?"

He took a step towards me, his entire body trembling, his huge hands balled into fists. The rage rushed up his face in a near purple wave. He spoke through gritted teeth. "Get out!"

I wanted to say something to make it better, but there was nothing to say. I moved carefully past him, keeping my eyes on him, afraid he'd make a grab for me. But he just stood there regaining control of himself. Zerbrowski walked me out and closed the door behind us.

If I'd been with another woman, we'd have talked about what just happened. If I'd been with a lot of men in a different line of work, we'd have talked about it. But Zerbrowski was a cop. And that meant you didn't talk about the personal stuff. If you accidentally learned something truly painful, truly private, you left it the fuck alone—unless the man involved wanted to talk about it. Besides, I didn't know what to say. I didn't want to know that Dolph's wife was cheating on him with a corpse. He had two sons, no daughters, so who else could it be?

Zerbrowski walked me through the squad room in silence. A man turned as we entered the room. He was tall, dark-haired, with gray starting at the temples. The clean, strong lines of his face were beginning to soften around the edges, but it was still a handsome face in a manly man, Marlboro sort of way. He looked vaguely familiar. But it wasn't until he turned his head, exposing the claw scars on the side of his neck, that I recognized him. Orlando King had been one of the premiere bounty hunters in the country until a rogue shapeshifter had nearly killed him. The stories could never agree on what animal did it; some said wolf, others bear or leopard. The story had grown in the telling until I doubt anyone but King himself knew the truth. King and the shapeshifters that had nearly killed him, if they hadn't all died in the attempt, that is. He had a rep that he never lost a bounty, never stopped until his creature was dead. He earned good money lecturing across the country and in other countries. For his finale he'd take his shirt off and show his scars. It smacked a little too much of circus sideshow for my taste, but, hey, it wasn't my body. He also did some consulting with the police.

"Anita Blake, this is Orlando King," Zerbrowski said. "We brought him in to help convict Count Dracula of your murder."

I glared at Zerbrowski, who only smiled wider. He'd keep calling Jean-Claude by his pet names until it stopped getting a rise out of me. The quicker I ignored it the better.

"Ms. Blake," Orlando King said in the deep rolling voice that I remembered from his lectures, "so good to see you alive."

"It's good to be alive, Mr. King. Last I heard you were lecturing on the West Coast. I hope you didn't interrupt your tour to come solve my murder."

He shrugged, and there was something about the way he moved his shoulders that made him seem taller, broader than he was. "There are so few of us that truly pit ourselves against the monsters, how could I *not* come?"

"I'm flattered," I said. "I've heard you lecture."

"You came up and spoke to me afterwards," he said.

"I'm flattered again. You must meet thousands of people a year."

He smiled and touched my left arm, ever so lightly. "But not many with scars to rival mine. And none half so pretty in this line of business."

"Thanks." He was at least two generations removed from me, so I figured his complimenting me wasn't so much flirting as habit.

Zerbrowski was grinning at me, and his grin said he didn't think King was simply being polite. I shrugged and ignored it. I've found that if you pretend not to notice that a man is flirting with you, most of them will eventually grow tired and stop.

"It's good to meet you again, Ms. Blake. Especially alive. But I know that you must be in a hurry if you're going to rescue your vampire boyfriend before dawn." There was the faintest hesitation before the word *boyfriend*. I studied his face and found it neutral. There was no condemnation, nothing but a smile and goodwill. After Dolph's little fit, it was kind of nice.

"Thank you for understanding."

"I'd love a chance to talk to you before I leave town," he said.

Again, I wondered if he was flirting, and I said the only

thing I could think of. "Compare notes, you mean?"

"Exactly," he said.

I just did not understand my effect on men. I wasn't that attractive—or maybe I just couldn't see it. We shook hands, and he didn't hold my hand any longer than necessary, didn't squeeze it, or any of those funky things men do when they're interested. Maybe I was just getting paranoid where men were concerned.

Zerbrowski led me through the sea of desks to fetch Nathaniel. The police woman, Detective Jessica Arnet, one of the newest members of the squad, was still entertaining Nathaniel at her desk. She was gazing into his lilac eyes as if there was some hypnotic power in them. There wasn't, but Nathaniel *was* a good listener. That's rare enough in men for it to be a bigger selling point than an attractive body.

"Come on, Nathaniel, we've got to go."

He stood instantly but tossed a smile towards Detective Arnet that made her eyes sparkle. Nathaniel's real-life job was as a stripper, so he flirted instinctively. He seemed both aware and unaware of his effect on women. When he concentrated, he understood what he was doing. But when he simply walked into a room and heads turned, he was oblivious.

I touched his arm. "Say good-bye to the nice detectives. We've got to hurry."

He said, "Good-bye, nice detectives." I gave him a small push towards the doors.

Zerbrowski followed us out. I think if Nathaniel hadn't been with us he'd have asked more questions. But he'd never met Nathaniel and wasn't sure of him. So we moved in silence to the Prisoner Processing, where Jean-Claude was sitting on one of the three chairs. Normally the processing area was full of people coming in, going out, and since it's the size of a walk-in closet, that makes it seem crowded. The two vending machines took up room, but except for the prisoner processing clerk—the new name since turnkey fell out of fashion—behind his little barred bankteller window, the place was deserted. But it was 3:30 in the morning.

Jean-Claude rose when he saw me; his white shirt was

stained, torn on one sleeve. He didn't look like he'd been beaten, or hurt. But he was usually a fanatic about his clothes. Only something drastic would have changed that. A struggle perhaps?

I did not run to him, but I did wrap my arms around him, press my ear to his chest, hold on to him as if he were the last solid thing in the world. He stroked my hair and murmured to me in French. I understood enough to know he was glad to see me and that he thought I looked beautiful. But beyond that it was just pretty noise.

It wasn't until I felt Zerbrowski behind me that I pulled away, but when Jean-Claude's hand found mine, I welcomed it.

Zerbrowski was looking at me as if he'd never seen me before. "What?" It came out hostile.

"I've never seen you be that . . . soft with anyone before."

It startled me. "You've seen me kiss Richard before."

He nodded. "That was lust. This is . . ." He shook his head, glancing up at Jean-Claude, then back to me. "He makes you feel safe."

I realized with a jolt that he was right. "You're smarter than you look, Zerbrowski."

"Katie reads self-help books to me. I just look at the pictures." He touched my right hand. "I'll talk to Dolph."

"I don't think it's going to help," I said.

He shrugged. "If Orlando King can have a conversion experience where the monsters are concerned, anybody can."

"What do you mean?" I asked.

"Have you ever read, or seen, any of his interviews before his accident?" Zerbrowski made little quote marks with his fingers when he said *accident*.

"No. That was before I was interested in the topic, I think."

He frowned at me. "I keep forgetting, you were still in diapers then."

I just shook my head. "So tell me."

"King was one of the shining lights behind trying to get lycanthropes declared nonhuman, so they could be executed just for existing, without a trial. Then he got cut up, and, lo and behold, he mellowed."

"Nearly dying will do that to you, Zerbrowski."

He grinned at me. "It didn't make me a better man." I'd held my hands over my stomach, kept his insides from spilling out, while we waited for an ambulance. It had happened just before Christmas about two years ago. Zerbrowski alive and well had been all I put on my list to Santa that year.

"If Katie couldn't make you a better man, then nothing could," I said.

He grinned wider, then his face sobered. "I'll talk to the boss for you, see if I can get him to mellow without a near-death experience."

I looked up into his serious face. "Just because you saw me hug Jean-Claude?"

"Yeah."

I gave Zerbrowski a quick hug. "Thank you."

He pushed me back towards Jean-Claude. "Better get him under wraps before dawn." He looked past me to the vampire. "Take care of her."

Jean-Claude gave a small bow from his neck. "I will take care of her as much as she allows it."

Zerbrowski laughed. "Oh, he does know you."

We left with Zerbrowski laughing, the clerk staring, and the night growing soft around us. Dawn was coming, and I had so many questions. Nathaniel drove. Jean-Claude and I rode in back.

13

I BUCKLED MY seat belt out of habit, but Jean-Claude stayed pressed to my side, arm around my shoulders. I'd started to shake and couldn't seem to stop. It was as if I'd been waiting for him so I could finally fall apart. I didn't cry, just let him hold me while I shook.

"It is alright, *ma petite*. We are both safe now."

I shook my head against the stained front of his shirt. "It's not that."

He touched my face, raised it to look at him in the soft-lighted darkness of the car. "Then what is it?"

"I had sex with Micah." I watched his face, waited for the anger, jealousy, something to flash through his eyes. What I saw was sympathy, and I didn't understand it.

"You are like a vampire newly risen. Even those of us who will be masters cannot fight our hunger the first night, or the first few nights. It is overwhelming. It is why many vampires feed on their nearest kin when they first rise. It is who they are thinking of in their hearts, and they are drawn to them. It is only with the aid of a master vampire that the hunger can be directed elsewhere."

"You're not angry?" I asked.

He laughed and hugged me. "I thought *you* would be angry with *me* for giving you the *ardeur*, the fire, the burning hunger."

I pushed back enough to see his face. "Why didn't you warn me that I couldn't control it?"

"I never underestimate you, *ma petite*. If anyone I have ever known in all these centuries could have withstood such a test, it was you. So I did not tell you you would fail, because I no longer try to predict what power will do to you, or through you. You are a law unto yourself so much of the time."

"I was . . . helpless. I . . . I didn't want to control it."

"Of course not."

I shook my head. "Is the *ardeur* permanent?"

"I do not know."

"How long until I can control it?"

"A few weeks. But even after you have control, you will have to be careful around those you most lust after. They will make the hunger flare like fire raging in your veins. There is no shame to it."

"So you say."

He held my face between his hands. "*Ma petite,* it has been over four hundred years since I first woke with the *ardeur* raging in me, but I remember. All these years, and I still remember that the cry for flesh was almost worse than the cry for blood."

I held his wrists, pressed his hands against my face. "I'm scared."

"Of course you are. You should be. But I will help you through this. I will be your guide. It may pass away in a few days, or come and go, I simply do not know. But I will help you through it, whatever happens."

Nathaniel pulled into the Circus of the Damned parking lot, beside the back door. It was still dark as we got out, but the air had that soft feel of predawn. You could taste the coming morning on the tip of your tongue.

Jason opened the outer door as if he'd been waiting for us. He probably had. Jean-Claude hurried past him to the door that led to the stairs. We followed, but Jean-Claude called back over his shoulder, "I must shower before dawn." With that he left us, running in a blur of motion. The rest of us walked more sedately down the stairs, able to walk three abreast, because none of us were large people.

"How are you feeling?" Jason asked.

I shrugged. "I'm pretty much healed."

"You look shook."

I shrugged, again.

"Okay, I can take a hint. You don't want to talk about it."

"No, I don't."

Jason glanced around me at Nathaniel. "You staying the night?"

"Am I?" I knew the question was directed at me.

"Sure, you may need to drive me home tomorrow, or rather, later today."

"Yes, I am staying."

"You can bunk with me then. God knows the bed is big enough and doesn't see many visitors."

I glanced at Jason. "Does Jean-Claude limit your social activities?"

He laughed. "No, not exactly, but the women who come down here are vampire freaks. They want to sleep in a bed under the ground at the Circus of the Damned. They don't want me, they want Jean-Claude's pet werewolf."

"I wouldn't think . . ." I stopped myself because I realized it was an insult.

"Go ahead and say it."

"I wouldn't think that you'd be that picky," I said.

"I wasn't when I first got here. But lately I just don't want to be with someone who just wants me so she can brag to her friends that she slept with a shapeshifter, or got to sleep where the vampires sleep. No matter how good it feels for a few minutes, it still makes me feel like they've just come to look at one of the freaks."

I slipped my arm through his, squeezed his arm. "Don't let anybody make you feel like that, Jason. You're not a freak."

He patted my hand. "Look who's talking."

I pulled away from him. "What's that supposed to mean?"

"Nothing, I'm sorry I said it."

"No, I want you to explain it."

He sighed and hurried down the steps, but I was in Nikes and could keep up. Nathaniel followed a few steps behind without saying a word. "Explain it, Jason."

"You hate the monsters. You hate being different."

"That's not true."

"You accept that you're different, but you don't like it."

I opened my mouth to argue with him, but had to stop myself, had to think. Was he right? Was he? Did I hate being different? Did I hate the monsters because they were different? "Maybe you're right."

He looked back at me, eyes wide. "Anita Blake admitting she may be wrong? Gasp!"

I tried to frown at him, but I could feel it held an edge of smile that ruined the effect. "I better get used to being one of the monsters, or so I hear."

His eyes went serious. "Are you really going to be a were-leopard?"

"We'll find out, won't we."

"You okay with it?"

It was my turn to laugh, but it sounded bitter. "No. No I'm not okay with it, but the damage is done. I can't change it."

"Fatalism," he said.

"Practicality," I said.

"Same thing," he said.

"No, it isn't."

Jason looked past me at Nathaniel who treaded softly a few steps behind me. "How do you feel about her being a wereleopard?"

"I think I'll keep my feelings to myself."

"You're happy about it, aren't you?" And there was an edge of hostility in his voice.

"No, I'm not."

"You get to keep her as your Nimir-Ra now."

"Maybe."

"Doesn't that make you happy?"

"Stop it, Jason. Richard's told me his little theory about Gregory marking me on purpose."

"You talked to Richard?" He made it a question.

"Unfortunately."

"You know what's happened, then?"

"About you guys taking Gregory, yeah. I talked to Jacob on the phone even."

Jason looked surprised. "What did you say to him?"

"Gregory dies, Jacob dies."

"Jacob wants to be Ulfric."

"We discussed that, too," I said.

"What did he say?"

"He won't challenge Richard until after the full moon this month. You better give Sylvie a heads up, because that means Jacob has to defeat her within the next two weeks."

"Why is he waiting for the full moon?"

"Because I told him I'd kill him if he didn't."

"You can't undercut Richard's authority like that."

"I don't need to, Jason, he's doing such a good job all on his own."

We were at the bottom of the stairs, the heavy door hanging open where Jean-Claude had rushed through. "Richard is my Ulfric."

"I'm not asking you to bad-mouth him, Jason. He's destroyed his power structure within the pack. It's not something to debate, it's just the truth."

Jason stopped me at the door. "Maybe if you had been here, you could have talked him out of it."

I was finally angry. "One, you have no right to question what I do, or don't do. Two, Richard is a big boy and makes his own decisions. Three, don't you ever, *ever* question me again."

"You're not my lupa anymore, Anita."

Anger flared through me like a scalding wave, tightening my shoulders, my arms, spilling into my hands. I'd never felt rage so quickly and so completely. I had to close my eyes to concentrate, so I wouldn't take a swing at him. What was wrong with me?

I felt Nathaniel at my back. "Are you alright?" he said.

I shook my head. "I don't think so."

"Look," Jason said, "I'm sorry, but I don't want Jacob in charge of the pack. I don't trust him. Richard may be a bleeding-heart, flag-waving right-winger, but he's also fair, and he really does try to put the best interests of the pack before his own. I don't want to lose that."

I looked at him, trying to swallow past the anger. My voice came out squeezed tight. "You're scared about what will happen to all of you if Jacob takes over."

He nodded. "Yes."

"Me, too," I said.

He looked into my face, studied it. "If Jacob kills Richard in a fair fight, what will you do?"

"Richard isn't my boyfriend anymore, and I'm not lupa. If it's a fair challenge fight, then I can't interfere. I told Jacob if the fight was fair, and after the full moon, I wouldn't take revenge on him."

"You won't avenge Richard's death?"

"If I kill Jacob, and Richard and Sylvie are already dead, who'll take over? I've seen what happens to a group of shapeshifters who don't have an alpha to lead them. I won't let what happened to the leopards happen to the wolves."

"If Jacob died before he fought Sylvie, then you wouldn't have to worry about it," Jason said.

The anger that had been leaking away made a comeback. "You can't have it both ways, Jason. Either I'm not your lupa—not dominant to you—and thus can't help you fix this, or I *am* still your lupa, still dominant to you, still someone you come to for this kind of help. Make up your mind which you want me to be before you get up in my face again."

"You can't be lupa, the pack voted you out. But you're right, it's not your fault. You had to try and fix yourself before you could fix anyone else. I'm sorry I got in your face."

"Apology accepted," I said. I started to go around him through the door, but he caught my arm.

"I didn't ask you to kill Jacob because you were my lupa, or dominant to me. I asked you because I know you've already thought of it. I asked you because I know if you think it's best for the pack, you'll do it."

"Pack business is no longer my concern, so everyone keeps telling me."

"They don't know you like I do," he said.

I pulled away from him, gently. "What's that supposed to mean?"

"It means that once you've given your friendship—your

protection—to someone, you take care of them, even if they don't want you to."

"If I kill Jacob, Richard will never forgive me."

"He dumped you, right? What have you got to lose by killing Jacob? Nothing. But if you don't kill him, then you lose Sylvie and Richard."

I pushed past him. "I am getting really tired of doing everyone's dirty work."

"No one is better at dirty work than you are, Anita."

That stopped me, made me turn back around to face him. "What's *that* supposed to mean?"

"It doesn't mean anything. It's just the truth." I stared into his so-solemn eyes. I would have liked to argue, but I really couldn't.

I'd thought I couldn't feel worse about myself tonight. I'd been wrong. Watching the look in Jason's eyes, hearing him talk about me like that, made me feel worse. This night just couldn't get any more depressing.

14

Dawn was minutes away when Jean-Claude came through the door in a robe. "You may have the bed, *ma petite,* and I will take my coffin. I think your nerves are raw enough without me dying in your arms as the sun rises."

I'd have liked to argue, because I wanted him to hold me in the worst way, but he was right. I'd had enough shocks for one night. "Nathaniel will stay with me," I said.

A look passed over Jean-Claude's face. "And Jason, as well."

"Why?"

"I do not have the time to explain, *ma petite,* but please trust me that Jason should be here, too. It is for the best."

I could feel dawn trembling close, even so deep underground. "Okay, Jason can stay, too."

Jean-Claude was already edging out the door. "I will tell him on my way to the coffin room. I am sorry to leave you like this, *ma petite.*"

"Go, it's almost dawn," I said.

He blew me a kiss then was gone, leaving the door slightly ajar. Nathaniel was sitting on the corner of the bed, neutral in face, eyes, even body language. He was very good at seeming nonthreatening, soothing almost.

I'd been sleeping off and on for almost four days, yet I was tired, unbelievably tired. I wasn't sure it was physical, more like I'd overused my mind, my emotions. I was wrung out. "Let's get some sleep."

He pulled off his tank top without another word, kicked off his shoes, pulled off his socks, and began to unbraid his hair. I knew that would take a while, so I went into the bathroom while he finished. It had been a long time since I'd seen Jean-Claude's bathroom, with its fancy black tub that was big enough for a small orgy. The silver swan that the water came out of always reminded me of a fountain. But no bath tonight. I just wanted to sleep and to forget. Forget everything.

Of course, I hadn't come away with jammies, and the shirt that Nathaniel had picked for me, though attractive and comfortable, was not long enough to be a sleep shirt. I could not sleep in jeans; it just wasn't comfortable. Damn, why should the small things be so important on a night when all the big things had gone to hell?

There was a knock on the bathroom door. "I'll be out in a minute, Nathaniel."

"It's Jason."

"What do you want?"

"Didn't Jean-Claude tell you that I was bunking with you tonight?"

"He mentioned it."

"He also sent me with pajamas for you. He figured you didn't pack an overnight case."

That got me to the door, and opening it. Jason stood there in a pair of blue silk boxers, baggy enough to be acceptable as sleepwear. Acceptable for him to wear while sharing a bed with me, I might add. Jason, left to his own devices, wore men's bikini underwear—or less—to bed.

He held out a folded piece of red satin. I took it and let it spill through my hands. It was actually two pieces, a loose top with spaghetti straps and a pair of shorts. It was obviously meant to be lingerie.

"He said to tell you that, of anything he had that would fit you, it covered the most, end quote," Jason said.

I sighed. "Thanks, Jason, I'll be right out." I closed the door without waiting for a reply. The top that had looked loose actually clung pretty tightly across my breasts. You'd certainly know whether I was cold or not. The shorts were cut so high on the sides that the legs almost met the waistband. It managed to cover everything and still not leave much to the imagination. Lingerie design at its best, I suppose.

I opened the door and turned off the bathroom light as I came out. Jason was already tucked into the covers on the right side of the bed. Nathaniel was still sitting on the other side. He got up as I came out, his unbound hair floating around him like a living curtain. "My turn," he said softly, turning on the bathroom light and closing the door.

"You look wonderful," Jason said.

"No compliments, Jason. I'm uncomfortable enough in the lingerie."

"Then by all means take it off."

I frowned at him.

He patted the bed beside him, grinning at me. "Come to bed."

"Piss me off enough and I'll send you back to your room."

"Jean-Claude told me to stay here today."

"I could insist." I had my gun on top of my folded clothes, tucked under one arm.

"If you'd shoot me just for teasing you, I'd have been dead a long time ago."

"Please, Jason, I have had a very hard night. Please, just behave yourself, just this once."

He raised his hand in the Boy Scout salute. "I won't bite, promise."

That made me think of Micah and caused me to blush, which was embarrassing under the circumstances.

Jason's eyes widened. "That's a better reaction than I've ever gotten from you. I'll have to remember the line."

"You reminded me of something embarrassing, that's all."

The grin faded to a smile. "I knew it wasn't because of me."

"I am not going to baby-sit your ego, too, Jason. You'll have to take care of it yourself."

"Always do." The smile had faded, leaving him serious. With his yellow hair and blue eyes, he looked somehow out of place against all the black silk, as if he needed a different color to frame him to best advantage. Of course, the bed wasn't meant to frame him to best advantage, it was meant to frame Jean-Claude.

The thought was enough. I felt him in his coffin, felt him dead to the world, gone away wherever vampires go when the sun rises. The feel of him so distant, unable to hold me, or help me, made me feel cold, and even more cut adrift.

I leaned against the heavy cherry wood post of the bed, one hand on it. But my hands were not big enough to encircle the wood. It was a big bed—at least king size.

"What's wrong, Anita?"

I shook my head. "I don't want to talk about it."

"I'm sorry. I will be good. I promise."

"No more teasing?" I asked.

He tried to stay serious, but a smile crept through. "I'd promise no more teasing if I thought I could live up to it, but I will promise to try and not tease you anymore today. How's that?"

I had to smile. "Honest, I guess." I sat down on the edge of the bed.

"You seem lost tonight," he said.

It was so close to what I was thinking that I turned and looked at him. "Is it that obvious?"

"Only to someone who knows you."

"Do you know me that well, Jason?"

"Sometimes. And sometimes you are totally confusing to me."

I pulled back the covers and crawled under the sheet, pushing the heavy satin coverlet away from me. I'd left a lot of distance between me and Jason. I slid my gun under the nearest pillow, safety on. And for extra precaution, since I was sleeping with non-gun users, no bullets were in the chamber.

"Honest, Anita, I'll behave myself, you can move closer."

"I know."

"And not just because Jean-Claude and Richard wouldn't like it."

"Richard isn't dating me anymore, Jason. He's not mine anymore." Just saying it out loud made my skin colder, my stomach clench tight.

"He may say that, but if he found out I tried anything tonight, anything serious, he'd make me pay for it."

"What do you mean?"

"He may not be dating you, but I'll bet my favorite body part that he wouldn't tolerate you dating any of the other werewolves. Him not being able to have you isn't the same thing as not wanting you."

I looked at him, sheet-covered knees hugged to my chest. "When did you get so smart?"

"I have my moments."

I had to smile. "Yeah, you do."

We were both smiling when Nathaniel came out of the bathroom. "Hit the lights, Nathaniel."

Nathaniel did what I asked, and the blackness was complete. The lights were on a timer and would come on softly in a few hours. But until then it was a darkness so complete it was like being dropped in ink. I'm not usually bothered by darkness, but just then it was claustrophobic, like some giant black hand pressing against me.

I felt Nathaniel by the bed. "Please, turn on the bathroom light, leave the door ajar." He went back and did it. One of the good things about Nathaniel was he didn't question orders much. It used to bug me. Now I counted on it, sometimes.

He left the door open a crack, just enough to let a slender finger of light fall into the room and slant along the bed.

Nathaniel lifted the sheet and crawled into bed without a word. But him crawling in meant I had to move over closer to Jason. I found the gun and moved it down a pillow with me. But Nathaniel didn't crowd me, and there was still space between us when we all tucked in for the night. Not as much space as I'd have liked, but still space. In fact I was able to roll over onto my side without bumping anyone. Of course, that wasn't how I slept at home. At home Nathaniel and the rest of the wereleopards cuddled into big piles. I'd slept most of the last six months among them. It was, sadly, getting to the point that when I slept alone I felt lonely.

Nathaniel had rolled automatically onto his side, his back to me, waiting for me to close the distance between us. He'd already moved his hair to one side like a blanket that had to be moved out of the way, leaving his back and part of his neck smooth and bare. I lay there for a second or two, then thought, screw it. I moved in against him, pressing myself to the smooth warmth of his body, my arm sliding around his waist. He was just a few inches taller than me, enough that I cuddled down just a little, pressing my face into his back, in the hollow behind his shoulder blade. It was the way we'd gone to sleep for a long time.

"Now I do feel left out," Jason said.

I sighed, clutching Nathaniel a little tighter. "Do you promise not to try anything?"

"I promise to be good."

"That's not what I asked."

He gave a small laugh. "You're better than you used to be at this game. Okay, I promise not to try anything."

"Then you can get closer, if you want to."

"You know I do," he said. I could feel him moving across the bed towards us.

"You also promised to be good."

"You have no idea how good I can be." He was very close when he said the last.

"You're pushing it, Jason."

"Sorry." But he didn't sound sorry. He curled against my back, his body spooning against me, his knees bending into a near perfect line behind mine. We were within an inch of being the same height, which made spooning easy. It also put certain parts of his anatomy up against my butt, and it was hard not to notice that he was happy to be there. Not too long ago, I'd have made him move, but I'd spent months learning shapeshifter etiquette. The men tried their best not to get erections, and not to use them when they did; the women tried to ignore the fact that they had them. That was the rule. It allowed everyone to pretend we were just a bunch of puppies sleeping in a nice friendly pile. To acknowledge anything else meant the system fell apart.

I realized that it didn't bother me. Over the months I'd learned that it was just one of those involuntary things that happened, nothing truly personal. I think Jason was disappointed that he didn't get more of a reaction from me. When I didn't react at all, he moved his hips just a fraction away from me, but snuggled the rest of himself against me more tightly.

I was effectively sandwiched between them, and it reminded me forcibly of waking up between Caleb and Micah. Not a comforting memory. But the smell of Nathaniel's skin was familiar. The vanilla scent of his hair where it edged my face and stretched under his body was comforting. I drew the scent of him around me like a blanket, pulled my body in as close to the warm curve of him as I could go and not come out the other side, and clung. I acknowledged in my head, though never aloud, that tonight I clung. I held him like he was the last solid thing in the world, the way I'd wanted to hold Jean-Claude and couldn't.

Jason's hand smoothed along my hip, but I'd forced his hand up from around my waist when I tucked so tightly against Nathaniel; there was really nowhere else for it to go. His hand was very still against my bare leg, and there was a tension to him, as if he was waiting for me to protest. When I didn't, he relaxed and even moved his entire body back against me. He'd managed to calm himself. Good for him.

Honestly, it was nice having Jason's weight at my back. Normally, I spooned Nathaniel—took the dominant position with my body protecting his—my back bare to the room. But I wasn't feeling particularly dominant. I wanted someone to have my back. And, if it couldn't be Jean-Claude, or Richard, Jason wasn't a bad choice. For all his teasing, he was my friend.

Nathaniel fell asleep first; he usually drifted off faster than I did. Somehow I knew that Jason was still awake pressed against my back, his hand on my thigh. I could feel a tension in him as I began to drift off, and strangely, it was comforting. Jason literally had my back. It meant I could sleep, and between the three of us, whatever came through the door, we could probably handle it. Probably.

15

I WAS DREAMING. Something confusing about bodies and running and a ringing noise that made the crowd run faster. Ringing noise? I woke up enough to feel Nathaniel move beside me. He groped over the side of the bed and came up with my cell phone from my pile of clothes. He handed the ringing phone to me. "It's for you."

Jason mumbled, "God, what time is it?"

I flipped the phone open and put it to my ear before anyone answered his question. "Yeah, it's me." I was only half awake.

"Anita?"

"Yes, who is this?"

"It's Rafael."

That made me sit up. Rafael was the wererat king. Their equivalent of an Ulfric. He was also Richard's ally. "I'm here, what's up?"

"First, my condolences. I hear you may be Nimir-Ra in truth next full moon."

"Gee, news does travel fast," I said, trying not to sound bitter, but failing.

"Second, I know the pack has one of your leopards, and that you must try and win him back from them tonight. You are allowed to bring allies with you, and I would be honored if you would allow the wererats to accompany you."

"I appreciate the gesture, Rafael, you don't know how much I appreciate it, but I'm not lupa anymore. Your treaty is with the pack, and I'm not pack anymore."

"True, but you risked yourself once to save me from torture, and possible death. I told you then that the wererats would not forget what you had done for us."

"What about your treaty with Richard?"

"It's with Richard, not the pack."

"Showing up at my back tonight is still a conflict of interests, don't you think?"

"I don't think so. I think it will make the point that if Richard is no longer Ulfric, the wererats will not be the werewolves' allies."

"You'll show up with me tonight to make it clear that your treaty is with Richard and not the pack?"

Jason sat up in the bed.

"Yes," Rafael said.

"Clever you."

"Thank you."

"So you don't like Jacob either?"

Jason moved closer to me, as if he could hear Rafael's side of the conversation. Maybe he could.

"No," Rafael said.

"Me either."

"So I will meet you at your home tonight before we drive to the lupanar."

"Just you?" I made it a question.

"Oh, no, we will be there in force so the point is not lost on Jacob's supporters."

"I like the way you think," I said.

"I wish Richard did," Rafael said.

"Have you tried to get him to execute Jacob, too?" I asked.

"I knew you would understand both the problem and the needed solution, Anita."

"Oh, I understand. I just wish Richard did."

"Yes," Rafael said, "yes. Jacob is not the man Richard is, but he has some qualities that I would wish on Richard if I could."

"Me too."

"I'll meet you tonight at your house at full dark."

"I'll be there. And Rafael . . ."

"Yes?"

"Thanks."

"No thanks are necessary. The rats owe you a debt. We pay our debts."

"And it allows you to make a threat to Jacob and his supporters without doing anything that could start a war," I said.

"As I said, Anita, you understand things that Richard does not. Until tonight."

"Until tonight," I said. He hung up. I hung up, flipping the phone closed. Jason was practically leaning over my shoulder.

"Did I just hear that Rafael and the wererats are going with you tonight to the lupanar?"

"You going to tattle to Richard?" I asked, staring at his face from inches away, his back touching my shoulder.

"No."

My eyes widened.

"Unless Richard specifically asks, 'Is Rafael going to be there tonight as Anita's ally?' then I don't have to answer. And I'm not volunteering the information."

"That's cutting your oath of obedience pretty close, isn't it?"

"My loyalty is to Richard. And having the rats with you tonight will help Richard, not hurt him."

I nodded. "Sometimes you have to keep things from Richard to help him."

"Unfortunately," Jason said.

I handed the phone to Nathaniel, who put it back on the floor with my clothes. I checked my watch. It was ten o'clock; we'd had a little over six hours of sleep. Time to start the day. Yippee! It was still hours before I could expect Jean-Claude to be awake.

I snuggled down into the covers on my back. Nathaniel rolled onto his side, hand going across my stomach, one leg entwined over my legs. His second favorite sleeping position, though one I often had to move him out of before I could go to sleep. But I wasn't sleeping, I was thinking, so it was okay.

He rubbed his cheek against my shoulder, and a small movement of his lower body pressed him against me. He was hard and firm under the silky shorts. It was morning, he was male, it was normal. Normally, I could ignore it, just one of those things that you pretended didn't happen, but today . . . Today the feel of him pressed against me made things low in my body clench tight. The need rode through my body like fire spilling through me, over me, inside me.

Nathaniel went very still beside me.

Jason was sitting up, rubbing his bare arms. "What was that?"

I tried not to move, not to breathe, to just be as still as Nathaniel. I tried to think of something besides the warmth of his body pressed against the length of mine. Tried not to feel the press of him hard and ready through the satin of the jogging shorts. I grabbed the sheet and jerked it off of us in one violent movement. I gazed down the length of his body, of our bodies, pressed together. The shorts clung like a second skin to the back of him. The *ardeur* rushed through me again like a new pulse I'd never felt before, and my beast rose up through the depths with it. It was as if they were tied together. I hungered, and my beast woke, rolling inside me like a lazy cat, stretching, eyeing the mouse. Except what this cat wanted to do to the mouse was not only against the laws of nature, but physically impossible. The trouble was this mouse smelled of vanilla and fur, and he was warm and full against me. I wanted to roll him over on his back and tear off the shorts and see what I was feeling. I wanted to lick down his chest, down his stomach, and . . . The visual was so strong that I had to close my eyes against the sight of him lying there. But sight wasn't my only problem. The smell of his skin was suddenly overwhelming, sweet. And I had a desire to roll my body on top of his, not for sex exactly, but to paint his scent on my body, to wear it like a dress.

"Anita," it was Jason. "What's happening?"

I opened my eyes to find him bending over me, propped on one elbow, and the *ardeur* widened to include him. It did not discriminate. I touched his face, ran my fingers down the edge of his cheek, traced the fullness of his lower lip with my thumb.

He moved his mouth back just enough to speak. "Jean-Claude said you'd inherited his need, his incubus. I don't think I believed him . . ." My hand traced down his face, his neck, his chest. ". . . until now," he whispered.

My hand stopped over his heart. It beat against my hand, and I could suddenly feel my pulse in my palm beating against his skin, as if my heart had spilled down my arm to cup against his body.

"Ask me why Jean-Claude insisted I stay in here today."

I just looked at him. I couldn't think, couldn't speak. I could feel his heart, almost caress it. His heart sped, beating faster. My heart sped to catch it, until our hearts were beating together, and it was hard to tell where one pulse stopped and the other began. I could taste his heartbeat in my mouth as if it pulsed inside me already, caressing the roof of my mouth as if I had already taken a bite of him.

I closed my eyes and tried to distance myself from the ebb and flow of his body, his warmth, his need.

"Jean-Claude was afraid you'd try to feed on Nathaniel. I'm supposed to keep that from happening." His voice was breathy.

I raised up, and Nathaniel's arms curled around my waist, pressing his face into my side. I sat up beside Jason with Nathaniel like a tempting weight wrapped around my body. My hand stayed on Jason's chest, cupping his heart. He should have moved away, but he didn't. I could feel his desire, feel the need in him. It was a pure desire, not for power, or anything else, just simply for me. It wasn't love, but it was purity of a sort. He simply wanted me. I stared into his blue eyes, and there was no deceit, no agenda. Jason didn't want to secure his power base, or gain mystical energy, he just wanted to have sex with me, to hold me in his arms.

I'd always treated Jason as lesser than a friend, young and amusing, not serious. Jean-Claude's *ardeur* let me see into his heart, and I found it the most pure of any that I'd looked into in a long time.

I stared down at Nathaniel where he lay clinging to me. I knew his heart, too. He wanted me physically, but more, he wanted me to want him. He wanted to belong to me in every way. He longed for safety, a home, someone to take care of him, and to take care of. He saw in me all the things that he'd lost over the years. But he didn't really see me; he saw an ideal of me that he wanted.

I ran my hand down his arm, and he snuggled against me. I looked back at Jason and let my other hand drop away from him, but it was like I pulled something out of him as it moved; his heart still beat inside my body. We didn't have to touch for that.

The fact that Jason wanted me just for me with no ulterior motives made me want to reward him. Made me love him just a little. It overrode the hunger, stilled my beast, helped me think.

"Get out, both of you, get out."

"Anita, is that you?"

"Go, Jason, take him with you, and go."

"I don't want to go," Nathaniel said.

I grabbed a handful of that thick hair and raised him to his knees with it. I expected to see fear in his eyes, or betrayal, but what I saw was eagerness. I used his hair as a handle and drew him to me until our faces almost touched. I felt his heart thudding, the thrill through his body as I drew him into me. Nathaniel would never tell me no.

If someone can't tell you no, it's rape, or something like it. The *ardeur* poured through me, taking my breath in a long shuddering line. I wanted to kiss Nathaniel, to fill his mouth with my tongue. And I knew if I did, it would be too late.

My voice came out strangled. "You will go when I tell you to go, now get out!" I released my hold on him so suddenly that he fell back against the bed.

Jason was on the other side of the bed, pulling Nathaniel away from me, pushing him towards the door. Watching them go made me want to cry, or scream. They were perfect for feeding. The room was thick with mutual desire, and I was sending them away. I could still feel their heartbeats like candy in my mouth, like a double echo of my own heart.

I covered my eyes with my hands and screamed, wordless, pain-filled. It was as if the hunger finally realized that I was truly going to let them go. It raged through me, tearing one ragged scream from my mouth after another, as fast as I could draw breath. I lay on the bed in the silk sheets, writhing, screaming. I had a sudden memory, and it wasn't mine, of this need denied, locked away in the dark where no hand could touch you, where no skin could melt into yours. I felt the faintest edge of Jean-Claude's madness after that particular punishment. He'd healed, but the memory was still raw.

Hands on me, holding me down. I opened my eyes to find Nathaniel and Jason holding me down. They each had a hand on one wrist and one leg. They could bench press small elephants, but as my body writhed against the bed, I raised them up, made them struggle to hold me.

"Anita, you're hurting yourself," Jason said.

I looked down my body and found bloody scratches on my arms and legs. I had to have done it, but I didn't remember doing it. The sight of those bloody scratches calmed me, made me lie still under their hands.

"I'm going to get something to tie you down with just until Jean-Claude rises," Jason said.

I nodded, afraid to speak, afraid of what I'd say.

He told Nathaniel to hold me, but the only way one person could do that was to hold my wrists while pressing against me with his lower body. It wasn't perfect control, but it kept me from hurting myself.

Nathaniel's hair fell around our bodies with a dry rushing sound, until I saw the world through a curtain of his hair. The scent of him was like some warm pressure between his upraised chest and mine. I could smell the fresh scent of blood, too. And my beast wanted to lick the wounds, wanted to feed on my own skin, or better yet, open wounds on Nathaniel and feed off of him. Just the thought tightened my body, made me writhe underneath him, until I'd freed my legs and he slid against me, only our clothing separating us. He made a small sound, half-protest, half-something else.

I raised my wrists off the bed, pushing against his grip on me. I felt his arms strain against me, forcing me back against the bed. It shouldn't have been a struggle for him to hold me here like this. I was gaining other things besides hunger through the marks, or the beast. Nathaniel was still stronger than I was, I could feel that. But there are things besides strength that count when you're struggling. I raised my arms from the bed again, only a few inches, and he forced me down again. But when I had enough room, I rotated my right wrist against his thumb, and my hand was free.

I raised up enough to kiss his chest, and he went very still above me. I knew in that instant that he wouldn't try and regain control of my arm. I bit him, gently, and his breath went out in a soft, sharp sound. I licked my way up his chest, with him still holding my left arm, his lower body still pinning mine. I ran my tongue over his nipple and felt his breathing quicken. I locked my mouth around his nipple and bit into the skin, the flesh underneath. He shuddered above me, his body jerking enough that I had to be careful not to break the skin. But I held on as he moaned above me, and when I drew back, I saw that I had left a near perfect imprint of my teeth behind.

I lay back against the bed and stared at the bite mark on his chest, with his nipple in the center of it, and a thrill went through me, a wave of pleasure at the sight of it, and a feeling of . . . possession. I'd marked him.

I drew my left wrist out of his hand, and he didn't fight me. He stayed propped above me on his arms, his hips pressed against me, his hair in a cascade around us. He stared down at me, and his face was raw with need. I didn't need anything else to tell me how much he wanted me to finish what I'd begun.

I raised up enough to kiss him, and his lips trembled against mine. The kiss was long and full, and a sound came low in his throat, and he suddenly collapsed against me, his full body weight pinning me to the bed, our mouths, our arms, our bodies locked together in a warm, vanilla-scented nest of his hair, like being rolled in warm satin. Nathaniel kissed me as if he would climb inside me through my mouth, and I opened for him, let him explore me, taste me, touch me. It wasn't his hand underneath my top, kneading my breast, that brought me to my senses. It was my hands down the back of his shorts, cupping the smooth curve of his buttocks. It helped me swim back into control, to fight down the desire, the hunger. Where the hell was Jason? I stopped kissing Nathaniel, stopped touching him, while his hands, his mouth, explored my body. His need was so strong, so strong. I could not leave the bed. I could not walk away. I was not that strong.

"Nathaniel, stop."

His mouth was on my breast through the satin of the top. He didn't seem to hear me.

"Nathaniel, stop!" I grabbed a handful of his hair and pulled him away from me. The front of the top was wet where his mouth had been. His eyes didn't seem to focus on me. It was as if he didn't see me at all.

"Nathaniel, can you hear me?"

He finally nodded. "Yes." Anyone else would have protested being stopped, but he simply looked at me, eyes beginning to focus. There was no resentment on his face, no anger. He simply did what I told him to do and waited for me to say more. I didn't understand Nathaniel; even knowing his heart's desires gave me no real understanding of him. We were too different, but today that difference might help us.

I would not, *could* not have sex with Nathaniel. But I couldn't stop completely either. I had to feed. I had to sink my teeth into his flesh, had to bathe in his lust, had to. "Get off me."

He rolled onto his back, gazing up at me, lying in a pool of his hair, like a shining auburn frame around his body. I wanted to see all of him framed against his hair, and all I had to do was drag his shorts down the curve of his hips. The image was so strong I had to close my eyes, take deep breaths. The need to touch him lashed through me, almost painful, as if the *ardeur* could force me to do it. And maybe it could. But I would control how I touched him. I would control at least that much.

I opened my eyes and found him gazing up at me with those impossible lilac eyes. "Roll over onto your stomach," I said, my voice hoarse.

He rolled over without a single question, and I was reminded how absolutely helpless he was with a dominant. He would do what he was told, whatever he was told. It helped steady me, to know that I had to be in charge. I had to have some control, because he would have none.

I picked up handfuls of that thick hair and pushed it to one side like a piled beast. I bared his back, in a clean smooth line. He turned his head to the side and gazed at me through the film of his hair. There was no fear in him, only a vast patience, an eagerness, and need.

I rose on all fours over him, straddling his body, and lowered my mouth to his skin. I licked across his shoulders, but it wasn't enough. I bit him, gently, and he made a small movement underneath me. I bit harder, and a tiny sound escaped his lips. I bit him hard enough that I felt his flesh fill my mouth, felt the grip of him, the meat of him. I wanted to tear at his flesh, to literally feed from him. The desire was almost overwhelming. I collapsed on top of him, my cheek against his back, until I could control myself. But the scent of his flesh, the smoothness of it under my cheek, the rise and fall of his breathing under my body, it was too much. I would not eat him literally, but I had to feed.

I bit the flesh of his back, drew him into my mouth, and this time I did not stop until I tasted the sweet metallic taste of blood. It was the beast that wanted to finish, blood was not enough. But I raised from the wound and moved on. I marked Nathaniel's back with near perfect imprints of my teeth, and more and more of them held blood. It was as if the longer I did it, the harder it was to control.

The scent of fresh blood tightened my body, filled me with heat and longings that had to do more with food than sex. I sat straddling his body looking down at his back, at my handy work. Blood ran in tiny drops from some of the wounds, but mostly it looked like tiny mouths pressed into his flesh. And it wasn't enough.

I slid my hands down the back of his shorts, drawing my nails delicately along his flesh. He writhed under the touch, started to rise from the bed, and I pushed him back down. "No, no," I said, and he went still under my hands.

I slid his shorts down his body until he lay nude underneath me. I spread his legs so I could kneel between them, lowered my mouth to that smooth, untouched skin, and marked him. There was more flesh to hold in my mouth here, tight, but more plentiful. I filled my mouth with him, drew blood in red, hot circles, until I heard him making small helpless noises. And I knew they weren't pain noises.

I rose on my knees above him, gazed down at the wounds I'd laid on his body, and I wanted more.

I slid my satin top off and wiggled out of the shorts. I laid my naked body on his and rolled along his back, his buttocks, rubbing the blood from the wounds on my body. Nathaniel was saying, "please, please, please," over and over under his breath. His need was like a pressing weight, a thick cloud that hovered over us. It was chokingly close, so overwhelming. He wanted this so badly. This, not sex, this. He'd waited so very long for me to dominate him, to take him.

Micah had wanted me, but his had been the want of a relative stranger. A man wanting an attractive and powerful mate. But with Nathaniel it was different. His desire had built over years, over a thousand intimacies, a thousand denials. It had built until it was a great weight in his body, in his mind. It was a thing that burdened him down, filled him up, and he could not be free of it. I understood why Jean-Claude had said that we would feed off those we were already attracted to. There was so much more to feed from with Nathaniel. Our history together made it not just a feeding, but a feast.

I worked my way back down his body, biting along his flesh, not drawing blood now. I lay with my cheek pressed against the curve of his buttocks, fighting with myself not to reach my hand around to the front of him. Fighting the growing need. I would not touch him, not like that. When I could trust myself, I spread his legs as far as they would go, and bit down, marking areas untouched, getting ever closer, until I could see him pressed between his body and the bed. I wanted to lick him there, roll his testicles in my mouth. But I didn't trust myself. I'd laid his back and buttocks bloody, I didn't trust myself, couldn't guarantee what I would do. I moved my mouth back without touching him, and the pressure of his lust and mine rode like summer lightning, almost there, almost there. I ran my tongue on the small ridge of skin just in back of his testicles, and Nathaniel cried out.

I sucked the skin, drew it into my mouth in a long line,

working it with tongue and teeth, and the pressure broke over us like a storm released in one long thunderous burst. He called my name, and I raked his thighs with my nails and fought with two different hungers not to bite that delicate bit of skin away from his body. When it was over, I drew back from him just enough to see that I hadn't marked him, not even the mark of my teeth. I lay on the bed, between his legs, one arm on his thigh, the other folded beneath me, listening to the pounding of my heart.

He lay quiet except for his still frantic breathing. A sound raised me up to gaze over Nathaniel's leg, propping myself up on the smooth wounded flesh of his butt.

Jason was standing in the middle of the room with what looked like shackles in his arms. His eyes were wide, his own breathing a little too fast.

I should have been embarrassed, but the *ardeur* was sated, and my beast lay curled inside me like a contented cat. I was too well-pleased with myself to be embarrassed. "How long have you been watching?" Even my voice sounded lazy, content.

He had to clear his throat twice before he could say, "Long enough."

I climbed back up Nathaniel's body, until I was pressed against the length of him. I laid my cheek against his face, and whispered, "Are you alright?"

"Yes." It was a whisper.

"I didn't hurt you?"

"It was . . . wonderful. Oh, God, it was . . . better than I'd imagined it."

I raised up, stroking his hair, turning back to look at Jason, still standing in the middle of the floor. "Why didn't you try and stop me?"

"Jean-Claude was afraid you'd tear out Nathaniel's throat or something messy like that." Jason's voice was returning to normal, only the slightest edge of uncertainty in it. "But I watched you. Every time I thought I'd have to intervene, you drew back. Every time I thought you were going to lose control, you didn't. You rode the hunger, you tamed it."

I felt Jean-Claude waken, felt him take his first breath of

the day. He sensed me, too, felt me still lying naked on Nathaniel's body, smelled the scent of fresh blood, felt that I had fed, and fed well. I felt him coming towards me, hurrying towards me, attracted to the scent of blood, and warm flesh, and sex, and me.

16

"JEAN-CLAUDE'S COMING," JASON said.

"I know," I said.

Jason walked to the foot of the bed and gazed down at us, at me. His eyes lingered on me. Most of my body was hidden beside Nathaniel, but he looked at what was revealed. If I hadn't had that glimpse into his heart, I'd have been mad, or told him to stop, but I didn't know what to say now. He wanted me, just me for me, not forever, but just for a night, a day, a week, just for sometimes. Jason's feelings for me might be the most uncomplicated of all the men in my life. Uncomplicated had its attractions, even with the *ardeur* gone. The moment I thought *gone*, I realized that wasn't true. The hunger was just below the surface; like something simmering in a pot, you have to keep the heat low, or it boils over. I'd had enough heat for one day.

Jason and I looked at each other. I don't know what we would have said, but just then the door opened. It was Asher. His room was closer than the coffin room, but I hadn't expected him. His golden hair lay in perfect waves around the shoulders of his robe. Vampires didn't move in their "sleep" so no morning hair problems. The robe was a rich, deep brown, open over matching pajama bottoms. His chest was bare, and the robe flared around him like a cape as he strode into the room.

He came to stand beside the bed, but his gaze went to Nathaniel's body, to the blood. "I felt . . ." He raised his eyes to my face, and I peered at him over Nathaniel's body. "I felt the call."

"I didn't call you," I said.

"The power did." He dropped to his knees beside the bed. "You did this?"

I nodded.

He reached out towards me, as if to touch my face, then jerked back. It was like he'd touched something in the air in front of me that had startled him. He raised his hand to his face and sniffed it, then licked it, as though there was something there to taste.

"May I taste your *pomme de sang*?" It was French for apple of blood, and it was a nickname for a person that was a regular donor to a particular vampire. Part of me wanted to argue with the phrase, but I had fed off of Nathaniel, even tasted his blood. To demand a different phrase was splitting hairs a little too finely for my conscience. We'd call a spade a spade.

"Define taste." I said.

"Lick the wounds."

The suggestion should have bothered me, but it didn't. I lowered my face enough to see Nathaniel's eyes. "Is it okay with you, Nathaniel?"

He nodded, face still pressed to the bed.

"Help yourself."

Asher lowered his mouth to Nathaniel's back, to a wound just above his waist. He kept those ice blue eyes rolled up towards me, the way you would watch someone on a judo mat—afraid that if you look away, they'll hurt you. It reminded me of watching lions drink from pools, with their eyes rolled up, watching for danger while they drank.

Nathaniel made a small sound as Asher licked the wound. It had stopped bleeding, but as the vampire traced the wound with his tongue, I saw blood well to the surface again. Vampires have an anticoagulant in their saliva, but I'd never seen its use demonstrated quite so well before.

It made me wonder. I curled closer to Nathaniel's body, one leg entwining over his. I didn't ask permission, because he was mine, and I knew him well enough to know he would not only not mind, but he would welcome it. I lowered my mouth to another of the wounds that had nearly stopped bleeding and licked. There was the sweet copper taste of blood, and the thick, rich taste of his skin, and a taste of . . .

meat. As if I could tell what he would taste like if I ate him one bite at a time.

The beast flared over my skin like something trembling and alive. Nathaniel's beast responded to it, flaring, rolling, as if I could see it just below his skin, just below his ribs, as if I could feel where it lay in the heart of his body. In that moment I knew I could call his beast, could coax him to change when the moon was far from full. I was his Nimir-Ra, and that meant so much more than merely being his dominant.

Asher's eyes had drowned in pale blue fire, so he looked blind as he licked at the wound. He gazed into my face, directly across Nathaniel's body, our eyes at the same level as we tasted the wounds. My wound bled a little bit more, but not as much as Asher's did. I was not truly a blood drinker—I fed on other things—and staring across Nathaniel's body, feeling his breathing quicken as the two of us touched him, I knew that those other things were here for the taking.

Asher's hand slid over Nathaniel's body, until he touched my thigh where it curved over Nathaniel's leg. The moment he touched me something rushed between us. It was as if the *ardeur* recognized him, as if it had touched him before.

It made me raise up from the wound, drew me back into myself a little. Something on my face made Asher take his hand back.

Jean-Claude entered then. He was wearing a black robe with black fur at collar, lapel, and sleeves. His black hair melted into the fur, so you couldn't tell where one blackness stopped and the other began. The last time I'd seen him in the robe, I'd told him there better be something under the robe besides skin. Now, I hoped there wasn't.

Seeing him brought the *ardeur* boiling over me again. It made me catch my breath, things lower than my stomach clenching tight enough to draw a sound from my throat.

"She holds your incubus," Asher said, and his voice tore my gaze from Jean-Claude to him.

"*Oui.*" Jean-Claude glided around the room to the opposite side of the bed from where Asher knelt.

"She tastes of you, and of Belle Morte."

"*Oui,*" Jean-Claude said. He walked around the bed to the other side, and I rolled away from Nathaniel so I could see Jean-Claude move. The movement exposed the front of my body, and I had enough of myself left to roll onto my stomach.

Jason said, "Awww."

I ignored him.

Jean-Claude lifted the robe so he could crawl onto the bed. The movement revealed a long, pale line of skin from his shoulders to his stomach. The glimpse of that white flesh caught between the blackness of the fur made me want to untie the sash and expose his entire body. But I stayed where I was, half-leaning against Nathaniel, because I was afraid to move. Afraid to go to Jean-Claude, because I didn't trust myself.

There was just enough of *me* left not to want to make love to Jean-Claude in front of the other men. But it was a razor-thin part, something that glittered in the darkness but didn't quite believe itself anymore.

"The hunger recognizes Asher. Is it because it's yours, or because it's hers?" I asked.

"Hers?" he asked.

"Belle Morte."

"I do not know," he said. And he was close enough now that the edge of the robe brushed my body. I could see a thin line of pale skin below the waist where the robe gaped. A thin, thin line of white, but it was enough to let me know that there was nothing under the robe but Jean-Claude.

I wanted to open the robe, to see all of him. I said it without thinking, as if I hadn't meant to say it out loud. "Open the robe." It startled me as if I didn't know my own voice.

I closed my eyes, tried to think.

"It is alright, *ma petite*. Once taken, blood fills your stomach, but lust . . ." Fur brushed in a teasing line down my arm. "Lust is always there, never vanquished completely, never satisfied." He brushed the edge of his furred cuff down my waist, my hip, my thigh, my calf. When he brushed it along my foot, he started back up, but this time on the back of my body, so that the teasing brush touched my buttocks, my back, my shoulder.

I lay wordless, breathless, under his touch. When he curved the fur around my face, I grabbed the edge of the robe and held him away from me. "Make everyone leave." My voice was barely above a whisper.

"I can do nothing until I have fed, *ma petite,* you know that."

"I know. Blood pressure." I was having a hard time thinking. "Then do it, but . . ."

"Hurry," he said softly.

I nodded.

He drew his sleeve out of my grip and looked down the bed to Jason, who was still standing there, watching the show. "Come, *pomme de sang,* come and enjoy the rewards of your sacrifice."

The phrase was oddly formal, and I'd never heard it put that way before. I expected Jason to go around the bed to the same side as Jean-Claude, but he didn't. He rolled over the foot of the bed in a movement so liquid it was like watching water flow, as if his skin barely contained some elemental energy that had nothing to do with the flesh and bone body I was seeing. He ended on his knees on the opposite side from Jean-Claude. I could taste the movement of his body in my mouth, not just his heart, but as if every throb and beat of him was trying to slide over my tongue and down my throat. I could feel his eagerness, not for me, but for what Jean-Claude had to offer. He came eagerly to the vampire, in that breathless rush that you usually save for sex. They mirrored each other, both on their knees, gazing at each other across my body.

"I will leave you alone with your *pomme de sangs* and each other." Asher was standing next to the bed, belting the sash at his waist, securing the robe around him. He stood very straight with that perfect posture that all the old nobles seemed to have, but still he huddled inside the robe.

I rolled onto my stomach, gazing at him, trying to read his face, his body. The discomfort I could read, and even pain. And it must have shown on my face, because Asher dropped his gaze, that wonderful golden hair sliding over the scarred side of his face, so that when he looked up, you could see nothing but the perfect half of him, that one ice-blue eye.

I had a sudden memory of lying in a different bed in a huge dark room surrounded by dozens of candles until the shadows moved and rippled with every small breath of air, every movement of a pale arm. I lay in that trembling golden darkness in the embrace of a pale, dark-haired woman. I gazed up at her, and her face was like something carved of alabaster, with lips red and perfect, hair like the darkness of night made into furred silk, falling around her nude perfection like a veil. Her eyes were pale brown, like dark honey. I knew it was Belle Morte, as if I'd always known her face.

The door opened, and Asher entered, wearing a robe more elaborate, heavier than the one he wore now. But still he huddled in it, held it around his body, afraid. I saw the scars on his face—fresh, raw—and it was . . . painful. My chest went tight with the sight of his ruin. I went to my knees, reaching out to him, moving a body that I'd never been inside. Jean-Claude reaching out to Asher all those centuries ago. But she lay there nude and perfect showing every curve, every secret place to the candlelight, and turned him away. I couldn't remember the words she used, only the look on her face, the utter arrogance, the distaste. The look on Asher's face as he turned from her to Jean-Claude, to me. The look of pain, and he let that glorious hair fall forward, hiding his face, and it was the first time we'd seen him do that, hide from us.

I felt her hands on our body as she turned back to us, as if Asher were no longer there, but we remembered the look on his face, the line of his body as he left that room. I blinked and was back in Jean-Claude's bedroom, watching Asher in his brown silk robe walking towards the door. And the line of his shoulders, the way he held himself, made my chest tight, closed my throat, made my eyes hot with things unsaid and unshed.

"Don't go." I heard myself say it, and I glanced up at Jean-Claude. His face was careful, unreadable, but for just a moment I saw his eyes, and the pain I was feeling was only an echo of what filled his eyes.

Asher stopped at the door and turned, his hair falling over his face, the robe covering everything else. He said nothing, just looked back at me, at us.

I repeated, "Don't go, Asher, don't go."

"Why not?" he asked, his voice as careful and neutral as he could make it.

I couldn't tell him about the shared memory. It would sound like pity, and it wasn't that—not exactly. I couldn't think of a good lie. But this wasn't really the time for lies, anyway. Only truth would heal this. "I can't stand to watch you walk away like this."

He moved his gaze from me to Jean-Claude, and there was anger in him now. "You had no right to share that memory with her."

"I do not choose what *ma petite* knows and what she does not."

"Very well," Asher said. "Now you know how she cast me out of her bed. How she cast me out of his bed."

"That was your choice," Jean-Claude said.

"How could you bear to touch me? I couldn't bear to touch me." He stayed near the door with his head turned to one side, so all you could see was a wave of golden hair. His voice held bitterness the way it could sometimes hold joy—a bitterness that was hard to swallow, like choking on broken glass. Asher's voice and laugh weren't as good as Jean-Claude's, but he seemed better at sharing sorrow and regret than Jean-Claude.

"Why?" I asked, already knowing the answer.

"Why what?"

"Why did she cast you out?"

Jean-Claude moved beside me, and I realized two things. One, he was shielding from me, from all of us, so I couldn't sense him, and two, his body movement alone let me know he wasn't happy.

Asher grabbed his hair, forced it back from his face, showed the scars to the light. "This, *this*. Our mistress was a collector of beauty, and I am no longer beautiful. It pained her visibly to see me."

"You are beautiful, Asher. That she couldn't see that isn't your fault."

He let his hair fall back. It slid over the scars, hiding them. He had almost stopped doing that when he was here in the Circus. I'd forgotten how, when he first arrived in St. Louis, he had automatically hidden whenever you looked directly at him. He had used every shadow, every fall of light to hide the scars and highlight the beauty that remained untouched. He had stopped doing that around me.

It hurt my heart to see him hide. I tried to keep the sheet over me as I crawled towards the edge of the bed, but it was all tangled and trapped under Jason's and Jean-Claude's weight. Screw it, everyone here had seen the show. I wanted to wipe that hurt look from Asher's face more than I wanted to be modest.

Jason moved out of my way without uttering a single teasing comment. Unheard of! I crawled off the bed and walked towards Asher, and other memories spilled over me like cards thrown in the air. How many times had he watched Jean-Claude and Belle Morte and Julianna and so many others walk towards him nude and eager. Even Jean-Claude had failed him. There had been that shadow in his eyes formed of guilt. Guilt at failing to save Julianna, failing to save Asher. But Asher had assumed it was rejection and that Jean-Claude touched him only out of pity. It hadn't been pity—I had the memory of it—it had been pain. They had become constant reminders of how each had failed the other. A constant reminder of the woman they'd both loved, and lost. Until the pain was all they had left. Asher had turned it into hate, and Jean-Claude had simply turned away.

I walked through the memories like moving through cobwebs, things that brushed me, clung to me, but did not stop me. His hands were behind his back, his body leaning against the door, pinning them, and I knew why. Through Jean-Claude's "gift" I knew that Asher wanted to touch me and didn't trust himself enough to have his hands out in front of him. But it wasn't me he wanted to touch. In a way he was like Nathaniel; he saw in me what he needed to see, not exactly what was there.

I touched his hair where it hid his face. He flinched. I swept the hair back from his face, standing on tip-toe to reach him, putting one hand lightly on his chest for balance. He moved away from me, taking a step into the room. I grabbed his robe, but he stayed turned away as the robe pulled back from the perfect half of his chest. "Look at me, Asher, please."

He stayed turned away, and I finally had to walk those few steps to him. I was short enough that, standing right in front of him, I could look up underneath the hair into his face. He turned away again, and I stretched up, putting a hand on either side of his face, turning him to look at me. It put my body against his just for balance, and I felt the reluctance in his body, the need to move away. But he stayed immobile under my touch. He kept his hands behind his back, as if I'd tied them there.

The skin under one hand was so smooth, the other so rough. He could have fought me, but he didn't. He let me turn his face to me. I wrapped my hands in the thickness of his golden hair, holding it back from his face. I stared into his upturned face. The eyes, that impossible pale blue, were unreal, like the eyes of a husky. His lips were still full and kissable, his nose still a perfect profile. Even the scars that started far on the right side of his face were just another part of Asher—just another piece of him that I loved. I'd always assumed that any emotions I felt for Asher were from Jean-Claude's memories of him when they were lovers, companions for over twenty years. But staring at him now, I realized that that was only part of it.

I held memories of his body smooth and perfect. But that wasn't what I thought of when I thought of Asher. I pictured him as he was now, and I still loved him. It wasn't the way I felt about Jean-Claude, or Richard, but it was real, and it was mine. Maybe it wouldn't have existed if I hadn't had Jean-Claude's memories and emotions to build on, but whatever the foundation, I had feelings for Asher that were all mine, no one else's. I realized with something like a shock that it wasn't just everyone else's heart I could see into. I turned and looked back at Jean-Claude, tried to ask with my eyes what I was thinking.

"To know another's heart, you must first know your own, *ma petite.*" His voice was soft, no reproach.

I turned back to Asher, and there was something in his eyes—half wonderment, half pain—as if he expected me to hurt him in some way. He was probably right. But if so, I wouldn't mean to do it. Sometimes the greatest wounds are the ones we try the hardest not to inflict.

I let what I was feeling fill my eyes, my face. It was the only gift I had to give him. His expression softened, and what I saw in those lovely eyes was at the same time wonderful and painful. He dropped to his knees, one tear trailing down his smooth cheek. The look on his face was full of so many things. "The look in your eyes heals a part of my heart, *ma cherie,* and wounds another."

"Love is such a bitch," I said.

He laughed and hugged me around the waist, the roughness of his right cheek pressed into my belly, and I valued that more than anything else he could have done. I stroked his hair and held him against me. I looked across the room to Jean-Claude, and the look on his face was drowning deep, a longing so immense that there were no words to hold it. He wanted Asher and me. He wanted what he had had so many centuries ago. He'd once told Asher that he'd once almost been happy, and that had been when he was in Asher's and Julianna's arms. Before she died and Asher was saved but no longer Belle Morte's perfect golden boy. Jean-Claude had been forced to take Asher back to the vampire Council to have him healed. Jean-Claude had traded a hundred years of his own freedom to the Council for the favor of them saving Asher's life. Then Jean-Claude had fled, and Asher had stayed behind, blaming Jean-Claude for Julianna's death and for his ruin. Jean-Claude had gone from being in love, and being loved by two people, to losing one lover and having the other one hate him.

We gazed at each other. The look in Jean-Claude's eyes was so raw, like a fresh wound that still bled. He wanted to secure his power base with the triumvirate. He did want that—needed it—but there were other things that he wanted, almost needed. And one of those was hugging my waist, pressing his face to my stomach.

Jean-Claude lowered his eyes as if he couldn't control what was in them. He was the master of blank, careful expression. The fact that what he felt was too strong to hide said more than anything else. He couldn't shield his emotions right now. They were too strong; they shattered all his careful control, and a part of me was glad.

In that moment I wanted to give him what he most desired. I wanted to do it because I loved him, but it was more than that. I suddenly realized that with Richard gone from our bed, other things were suddenly possible. I turned back to Asher, gazing down on the top of his head, and knew that to be held in the circle of both our arms would heal something inside him that might never heal any other way.

The *ardeur* flared through me, hot, so hot, as if my skin must feel feverish. Asher drew back from me, letting his arms drop slowly to his sides. He gazed up at me, and the look in his eyes was enough. I knew he felt the hunger, too.

"It feels hot," I said. "Always before your power has felt cool, or cold even. It's Richard's beast that holds the heat."

"Lust is warm, *ma petite,* even among the cold-blooded."

I turned towards the bed and was suddenly very aware that I was nude. I was really going to have to get a robe. It wasn't Jean-Claude's gaze that made me look away, it was Nathaniel and Jason. Everyone in this room responded to me, in different ways, for very different reasons. But it was all fodder for this . . . need inside me.

Asher made some small movement that drew my attention back to him. I started to reach for him, to push his robe from his shoulders, to watch it fall to the floor. I hugged my arms to me, as if I was cold, but I wasn't cold. It was my turn not to trust where my hands were. The temptation was so thick everywhere I looked that there seemed no place to walk in safety. I felt trapped. Trapped, not in the room, but in the desire.

When I was sure I could talk without sounding as confused as I felt, I asked, "Is this thing permanent, or will it go away when we all adjust to the marks being married?"

"I do not know, *ma petite*. I wish I could tell you something more certain. If you were truly of my get, truly vampire, then I would say, yes, it is permanent. But you are my human servant. You have manifested powers in the past, and some have come and gone." He raised his hands. "There is no way to be sure."

"Is it always like this, never satisfied, never finished?"

"No, you can sate yourself, but it takes much to do it. Usually, one must be content with enough to keep the desire from overwhelming you."

"And you haven't fed like this in months, because you thought I would disapprove?"

"Years. And yes."

I stared at him across the room with Asher still kneeling in front of me. I'd always thought of Jean-Claude as the weaker-willed of the three of us—Richard, him, and me. Now I stood there afraid to move, afraid not to move, wanting to do things that were not me, not mine, not even Jean-Claude's. I'd known that the lycanthropes spoke of their animal half as something separate from them—their beast—but I'd never understood that some of the vampires' powers were the same way. Desires, hungers, so strong and overwhelming that they were like separate beings trapped inside your head, your body, your blood.

Asher made a small movement, and I turned to him. My hand reached out to stroke his hair before I'd turned completely to face him, as if my body had been moving without my eyes or my brain. His hair was thicker textured, more like mine, not the baby-fine curls of Jean-Claude or Jason, or the velvet silk of Nathaniel. I bundled my hands into Asher's hair as if I'd memorize the feel of it. Somewhere between mine and Richard's, somewhere in the middle, but not warm like Richard's was to the touch. Asher hadn't fed today, and he had no warmth to give. His skin was cool under my fingertips as I traced his cheek.

I spoke without looking at Jean-Claude. "How have you stood it? How could you fight the need all this time?"

"You are a fledgling, *ma petite*. Your control will never be weaker than now. I have had centuries to practice my control."

I made myself stop petting Asher. But he took my hand as I moved it back and laid a gentle kiss on my knuckles. Even that small touch made me catch my breath. My voice came out weak. "So you can go without feeding the desire."

"No, *ma petite*."

I turned and stared at him, and Asher rubbed his thumb in small circles on my hand. I remembered that small touch as precious, a habit he had no matter which of us he held hands with. "You said you hadn't fed like this."

"I have had no sex, nor touched anyone in such a complete manner as you have done with Nathaniel. But I must feed the desire, just as I must take blood."

"What happens if you don't?"

"You remember what happened to Sabin when he stopped taking human blood?"

I nodded. Asher's thumb continued its small circle on my hand, and it made things low in my body tighten. "Sabin started to rot while he was still alive." I stared into Jean-Claude's perfect face. "Is that what would happen to you?"

He sat back on the bed in his black robe. Jason had moved against the headboard as if watching a show, and Nathaniel still lay on his stomach where I'd left him, watching us with pale eyes. "There was a vampire of Belle's lineage who renounced the lust. He took only animals, as well, and I believe would have rotted as Sabin did, but he did not have the time. He began to age in a matter of days. When he was a wizened thing, Belle had him killed."

"But you haven't aged, what have you been doing?" It wasn't accusatory. I simply wanted to know, because I could feel Asher on the end of my hand like something huge and . . . like something I couldn't live without. I'd wanted Nathaniel, I'd wanted Jason, I'd wanted Micah, but not like this. I think it was Jean-Claude's feelings that made this so much more.

"It is possible to feed from a distance without touching," Jean-Claude said.

"That's why a strip club was your first business. You were feeding off the lust."

"*Oui, ma petite.*"

"Teach me to feed from a distance." Even as I said *distance* Asher drew my hand to his cheek and rubbed against it like a cat. I had to close my eyes for a second, but I didn't tell him to stop.

"Feeding from a distance is a poor substitute for a true feeding."

I opened my eyes and stared at him across the room, and now I could feel him. I could feel his need—for blood, sex, love, and the touch of our flesh against his. He wrapped his arms around his body, as if he were cold, or didn't trust himself not to leave the bed and come to us.

"Teach me anyway," I said.

"I cannot, not this soon. In a few nights I will instruct you, but your control is not . . . complete enough yet."

I started to say, "try me," but Asher drew my finger into his mouth in one long, wet line, and I suddenly couldn't think.

"Come to bed, *ma petite*," Jean-Claude said. "If you feed here, there is a chance you may be sated enough that you will not press our so-stubborn Richard."

The thought was enough to dim the desire for a moment or two. I drew my hand away from Asher, and he didn't protest. The sheer horror of what I'd be like around Richard with this inside me helped me think. Being around him normally made me want sex, but now . . . "My God, I'll be lucky if I don't just strip down and do him in the lupanar." I stared at Jean-Claude. "What do I do?"

"I say again, *ma petite*, if you feed now off of such rich fare, you may be too full to need to feed again so soon. It is all I can offer you for tonight. You could simply delay the meeting for a few nights."

I shook my head. "They'll kill Gregory. I have to get him out tonight."

"Then come and feed."

"Define feed?"

"Drink their lust," he said.

I looked at Jason and Nathaniel, and they weren't even trying for neutral. The looks on their faces brought heat in a rush up my face. I shook my head.

"You do not have to have intercourse to feed from them, as you have discovered."

"Aww," Jason said, but the look on his face didn't match the light teasing of his voice. They were responding to my need, the way I'd responded for so long to Jean-Claude's, drawn like a moth to a flame. You just couldn't help wanting to touch it, even when you knew it would burn.

Asher stood. "I will leave you alone. But with permission, I would feed on Nathaniel as my *pomme de sang* for the day."

"No," I said.

His eyes widened just a touch, face going neutral, eyes empty and cool as a spring sky. I felt him draw away from me. "As you wish." He turned for the door.

I grabbed his hand, slid my fingers between his. "Come to bed, Asher."

I'd thought his face was as blank and careful as it could get. I was wrong. His voice held nothing when he asked, "What do you mean?"

"I can't give you back what you had. I can't even give you . . ." I stopped and tried again. "But I can let you feed together again."

"How?"

"If Nathaniel says it's okay, you can take blood from him, and Jean-Claude will take blood from Jason. You can feed together."

"Do you know how intimate a thing it is to feed together on your *pomme de sang*? A *pomme de sang* is not a casual feeding, it is intimate, to be shared only with intimate companions."

I entwined my fingers around his hand. "I know." I took a step towards the bed, drawing him with me. "Let us feed on your lust, Asher, as in days of old."

Asher stared past me at Jean-Claude. "The last time two fed from my desire, it was Belle and you."

"I remember," Jean-Claude said softly.

He held his hand out to Asher from across the room, and I was reminded of him reaching for Asher all those centuries ago. "Let it be again as it was before, but better this time. Anita loves you as you are now, not as some ideal thing like a butterfly on a pin to be tossed aside if a wing falls away. Come to us, Asher, come to us both."

Asher smiled, then took a step to be beside me. He offered me his arm in a very old-fashioned gesture. I wanted to take his arm, to have an excuse to rub my body against his as we walked, and that was why I asked, "How about the use of your robe, as well as your hand?"

He gave a low and perfect bow, so low that his hair almost swept the floor. "That you had to prompt me to offer you my robe proves I am not a gentleman." He slipped it off as he stood, and held it for me like a coat. Asher is six feet, so the sleeves hung over my hands and the hem pooled around my feet. I pushed the sleeves up and got the sash tied, but the only thing to do for the length was just to bundle it in one hand like you would an overly long dress. But it covered almost every inch of me, and I felt better for it. The sweet scent of Asher's cologne clung to the robe, and that soft, masculine scent made me turn back to him. Made my eyes seek him out. Seeing Asher with no shirt on didn't make me feel better. I had the urge to caress his bare skin, to lick the scars. I never remembered being this orally fixated before, and wondered if it was the beast talking or the vampire. But to ask the question would be to admit the desire, and I didn't want to know that badly.

I laid my hand in Asher's, partially because he was holding his hand out to me, and partially because even that small touch was satisfying. I wanted to touch him, wanted to wrap myself around him and answer that question that Jean-Claude was so desperate to answer. Was all this beauty and heat ruined? Was Asher unable to function as a man now? I closed my eyes as he led me forward, because the visuals were just too strong. Through Jean-Claude I knew exactly what Asher had looked like nude, before the scars. I held memories of his body bathed in firelight as he lay rampant on a rug in a room in a country that I had never seen. I knew the play of moonlight on his back as I touched him.

I tripped on the hem of the robe, and he had to catch me to keep me from falling. I was suddenly pressed against his chest with the feel of his arms solid against my back. My face was suddenly uptilted, as if I were waiting for a kiss, and there was one of those moments when you become aware of each other— painfully and suddenly aware of the possibilities of the next few seconds. He picked me up in his arms, carrying me easily, smoothly forward. I'd have told him to put me down, but my heart had filled my throat, and I couldn't speak around it.

17

ASHER STRODE TO the bed and laid me on it, leaning over Nathaniel's nude body to do so. I lay on my back and felt movement from every direction. Jean-Claude crawled up beside me, and Jason moved down beside him from the head of the bed. Nathaniel rolled over until we were lying beside each other with him on his side. His eyes told me nothing, except he would not say no, but I asked anyway.

"Do you want Asher to feed from you?"

"Oh, yes," Nathaniel said, and there was something in his voice that I rarely heard—surety. In this moment he knew what he wanted. There was no doubt in him, and the strength of his desire made him . . . stronger.

Asher slid in against Nathaniel's back, so that their bodies spooned together. I turned in time to see Jean-Claude mirror the movement with Jason. Jason reached out, touched my arm, and it was like a door had been burst open. I thought I'd felt desire before this, but it had been a dim echo. It roared over me like something huge and burning, except this fire did not burn, it fed me energy, as if I were not the wood on which it fed, but I was the flame. I was the thing that fed and grew and consumed.

I found Jason's mouth and kissed him, kissed him with lips and tongue and teeth, biting at his lips, pulling him into my mouth. And his body was suddenly pressed against mine, his arms pinning me to him, and Nathaniel slid in behind my back. I was pinned between them, and I didn't care.

My leg slid over Jason's hip, my leg touching Jean-Claude on the other side of him. Jason was suddenly pressed between my legs, with only the silk of his shorts between us. It should have been enough to stop me, but it wasn't. I needed him. Nathaniel raised my hair, bit gently at the back of my neck, and a sound drew from my throat. The two of them fell on me, hands, mouths, bodies, like they were fire to my wood, but this wood drew them in, drank them, almost. Jason pushed against me, and the shorts were baggy enough, the silk thin enough that he entered me. The barest of touches, but it was enough to bring me up for air, to make me draw back from him.

He drew back enough to whisper, "Sorry."

My voice sounded as breathless as his when I said, "I'm not on birth control."

Everyone froze. Jean-Claude peered over Jason's shoulder. "What did you say, *ma petite*?"

"I stopped taking the pill six months ago. I've only been on it for two weeks. No guarantee for another two to four weeks."

"You made love to the Nimir-Raj."

"He's been fixed."

Asher said, "She did what?"

Jean-Claude looked across the bed at him. "Her hunger woke for the first time with the new Nimir-Raj. You have not met him."

"You have," Asher said.

"*Oui.*"

Jason was looking at me, and I had to put a hand over his eyes, close them; And the embarrassment helped, but the *ardeur* only withdrew momentarily, like a wave pulling back from the shore, I could feel it rushing towards us again. Jean-Claude was right, every time I said no, the next time was harder to deny.

Jean-Claude rolled off the bed, and I heard a drawer open. He came back into sight with foil-wrapped packages and wordlessly handed them to Jason and Nathaniel.

That did it. I crawled out from between them to huddle against the headboard. "No, no, no, you said no intercourse."

"I said, that you do not need intercourse to feed."

"No, oh, so no." I tucked the robe around my legs and covered everything I could, which was pretty much all of me.

"We are not planning on them having intercourse with

you, *ma petite.* But I have both fed on desire and been fed off of by Belle Morte. There comes a time in the feeding where you lose yourself and cannot always think clearly. I do not want regrets if we get carried away."

"I am not going to have sex with Nathaniel, or Jason. Keep this up, and you won't even be on the list."

"I would rather have you angry with me and not in my bed than accidentally pregnant by one of them."

"I think I can keep from fucking them." I sounded angry, but it wasn't anger that I felt, it was a seed of doubt. That hesitation made the anger worse. I always hid behind anger when I could.

"And before this morning, you would have sworn even more strongly that you would not fuck a strange man you had just met."

The blush was so hot, it almost hurt. "I didn't mean to." That sounded weak even to me. "I couldn't . . ."

"You could not control yourself, *ma petite,* I know. But if you lose control again, would you not rather be safe?"

I shook my head. "If I can't control myself better than this, we're not going to do this."

"And if you do not feed from the lust in this room, how will you go into the lupanar tonight? How will you see your wereleopard lover tonight when he accompanies you to the lupanar without losing your precious control? How will you stand this close to our Richard and not offer yourself to him? *Ma petite,* you have had sex with a stranger."

"He is her Nimir-Raj," Nathaniel said. "They are meant to be a mated pair."

"Pretty to think so," Jean-Claude said, "but I have been where *ma petite* is right now. I have felt the hunger for centuries, and I tell you that you will not be able to go among the shapeshifters tonight unless you are sated. I ask again, can you delay this meeting for a few nights?"

"I might be able to delay it for a night," I said.

He shook his head. "No, *ma petite,* one night will not suffice. You are drawn to Richard and now to the Nimir-Raj. I think you will be unable to think around them unless you have fed. Your wereleopard's life is at stake. Can you afford to be that distracted? Can you bear the thought of being that out of control in a public setting, among potential enemies?"

"Damn you," I said.

He nodded. "Yes, perhaps, but is anything I have said untrue?"

"No." I shook my head. "I hate it, but no."

"Then let us at least take precautions, *ma petite*. It is luck alone that had the Nimir-Raj made safe. Our lives are complicated enough without that."

I knew what "that" meant. An accidental pregnancy. The thought of it made my blood run colder than anything else had. I hid my face in my hands. "I can't do this."

"Then you must call Richard and tell him you cannot come tonight. You cannot go as you are, *ma petite*. The need will only worsen the longer you deny it."

I raised my face and stared at him. "How much worse?"

He lowered his gaze. "Bad enough."

I crawled across the bed to him, made him look at me. "How bad?"

He tried not to meet my gaze. His shields were back in place, and I couldn't tell what he was feeling. "You would be attracted to all the men. You would . . . I cannot guarantee what you would do, *ma petite*, or who you would do it with."

I just stared at him. "No. No, I would never . . ."

He touched my mouth with his fingertip. "*Ma petite*, if you have not found my memories of my first days with this inside my body, then it is a blessing. I was a wanton thing before I became a vampire. But what I did when the desire first fell upon me . . . The desire did not hit me at once, because I craved blood first, then when that quieted, the desire rose inside me." He took my hands in his, pressed them against the cool flesh of his chest. "I did things, *ma petite*, things that even to a hardened libertine were humiliating. A look, a glance, and it was enough to bring me to them."

"Didn't Belle Morte try to protect you?"

"I did not meet Belle until I had been dead nearly five years."

I stared at him. "I thought Belle was your, whatever, that she made you into a vamp."

"Lissette was my creator. She was of Belle's line, but not a master vampire, not by any stretch of the definition. In France it is customary that every kiss of vampires has at least one vampire belonging to each of the council bloodlines. Lissette was the only one of her kind in a nest descended mostly of far less pleasant vampires. Julian was her Master of the City, and he was my first true master. He brought in people for me, but not people I would have chosen. He brought in . . ." Jean-Claude shook his head. "He amused himself at my expense, because he knew I would take whatever he offered, because I would have no choice. I thought I had no room for embarrassment, but he taught me that there were things I did not want to do, and I did them anyway."

I think if he hadn't been shielding so strongly that I would have seen what he was remembering, but he didn't want me to see.

"Let me spare you such degradation, *ma petite*. You are not as I was. You have never given yourself freely. I fear what you would do, or think of yourself, if you did these things. I do not think your sense of yourself would survive intact."

"You're scaring me," I said.

"Good, you should be frightened. Asher met me before I had mastered the *ardeur*. He can tell you what I was like then."

I just looked at Asher.

"I had seen the *ardeur* rise in others before Jean-Claude, and I have watched it since, but I have never seen anyone so crazed by it," said Asher.

"So you helped him learn how to control the *ardeur*."

"*Non*. Lissette sent to Belle, telling her of Jean-Claude's beauty. I was sent to, how would you say, look him over for Belle. I advised Belle not to bring Jean-Claude and his master to court."

"Why?" I asked.

"I was jealous of his beauty and his prowess. After ten years she was growing bored with me, or so I feared. And I did not wish the competition."

"I learned to control the *ardeur* without the aid of another who had experienced it. For five years I fed on flesh as I fed on blood. Only then did I master the ability to feed from a distance."

"Five years!" I said.

"Belle taught me true control of the *ardeur*, and I was not hers until I had been dead five years. But I will be there for you from the beginning. It will not be as it was for me." Jean-Claude hugged me against him, and that scared me more. "I would never have married the marks with you if I had thought you could inherit my incubus. I would not knowingly have done this to you."

I pushed away from him and found him crying, and the fear sat like stale metal on my tongue. I was so scared my body went quiet, not racing, but almost as if every beat of my body, every breath, had simply stopped, and all there was to fill me was fear.

"What have you done to me?"

"I thought at first that you were not vampire, and it would not be a true hunger. But watching you today, I know that it is as it was for me. You *must* feed. You must not deny yourself. To do so is to court madness, or worse."

"No," I said.

"If you had withstood the Nimir-Raj's advances, then I would say that your strength of will might conquer it. If you had withstood the desire to feed on Nathaniel, I would say you would master it. But you fed on him."

"I did not have sex with Nathaniel."

"No. And wasn't what you did instead more satisfying to some part of you than mere intercourse would have been?"

I started to say no and stopped. I could still feel Nathaniel's flesh in my mouth, the touch of his skin under my hands, the taste of his blood on my tongue. The memory brought the hunger over me in a hot rush. Not merely the lust, but Jean-Claude's craving for blood, and Richard's beast—or my beast—wanting to take that last bite and tear flesh for real, no pretending, no holding back.

I had an awful idea. "If I deny one hunger all of them grow worse, don't they?"

"If I deny the lust, I need more blood, and the reverse is true."

"I don't just have your blood lust, Jean-Claude, I have Richard's beast—or mine. I wanted to tear Nathaniel up. I wanted to feed on him for real, the way an animal does. Will that grow worse, too?"

His face started to slip back into careful, neutral lines. I grabbed his shoulders, shook him. "No! No more hiding. Will it grow worse?"

"I have no way of knowing for certain."

"No more games! Will it grow worse?"

"I believe so." His voice was very soft as he said it.

I drew back from him, huddled against the headboard, stared at him, waiting for him to say, "sorry, just kidding," but he just met my eyes. I stared at him, because I didn't want to see anyone else's face. If I saw pity, it might make me cry. If I saw lust, it'd make me mad.

I finally said, "What am I going to do?" There was no inflection in my voice, just a dragging tiredness.

"You will feed, and we will help you. We will keep you safe."

I finally glanced at the others. Every face was either carefully neutral or, in Nathaniel's case, staring down at the bed, as if he didn't trust me to see his eyes. Probably smart of him.

"Fine, but I think we can do better than condoms."

"What do you mean, *ma petite*?"

"Nathaniel can put his shorts on, and I'll find my jammies."

"I still think . . ."

I held a hand up, and Jean-Claude fell silent. "They can put them on underneath their clothes, just in case, but I know that if I tell Nathaniel not to . . . that he won't." I frowned at Jason.

"I'll be good," he said.

"I am not afraid that Nathaniel will disobey you, *ma petite*."

The tone in his voice turned me from Jason's face to his. "What do you mean?"

"I am worried that he will indeed do everything you tell him to do."

We stared at each other for a long space of my heartbeats. I understood what he meant now. It wasn't the boys he didn't trust, it was me. I would have liked to say, I would never ask them—either of them—to do that to me, but there was something in Jean-Claude's eyes, some knowledge, some sorrow, that kept me from saying it.

"How much control am I going to lose?" I asked finally.

"I do not know."

"I'm getting really tired of hearing you say that."

"And I of saying it."

I finally asked what I had to ask, "What do we do now?"

"Our *pomme de sangs* fetch their clothing and yours, and we feed."

And as much as I hated it, as much as I wanted to deny it, I knew he was right. I'd been trying not to be a sociopath because it made me a monster. I just hadn't known what I was saying. I needed to feed off humans, lust instead of blood and flesh, but it was still feeding. Being a sociopath was beginning not to sound so bad.

18

SOMEWHERE DURING THE dressing process I came to my senses. I stayed up against the headboard, Asher's robe belted securely over the red pajamas, my face averted, forehead pressed to the wood. Control was the heart of who I thought I was. I could do this, or rather not do this. I had to try and let this pass me by, because to do anything else . . . I could not do this.

The bed moved, and just the sensation of the men moving around on the bed was enough to tighten my body, speed my pulse. Dear God, help me. This couldn't be happening. I'd feared ending up as a vampire. I'd come close many times, but I'd never thought it would happen like this. I was still alive, still human, but the hunger rose inside me like some great beast trying to dig its way out of me, and all that kept it from surfacing was my fingers digging into the wood, my forehead pressed against the carvings. I wasn't sure which hunger I was fighting. But the *ardeur* colored all of it, whether I was craving flesh, or blood, the sex was there in all of it. I couldn't separate them, and that was scary all on its own.

I felt someone crawling towards me, and I knew without looking that it was Jean-Claude. I could just feel him.

"*Ma petite,* all is prepared, we need only you."

I spoke with my face still pressed into the wood, my fingers clinging to it. "Well, then you'll just have to do without."

I felt his hand hovering over my shoulder, and I said, "Don't touch me!"

"*Ma petite, ma petite,* I would change this if I could, but I cannot. We must make the best of what is given us."

That made me look at him. His face was too close, eyes

that intense midnight blue, hair a dark glory around his pale face. I flashed on another face just as pale, just as perfect, with a wealth of black hair, but with eyes a rich brown like dark amber. They grew in my vision until the world drowned in the dark honey of her eyes, as if it were poured over my eyes, over my skin, my body, until it filled me, and when I raised my eyes to Jean-Claude's worried face, his hand on my arm, I saw something close to terror in his eyes.

He scrambled back from me, and when I turned and stared at Asher, he spilled off the bed, to stand shaking. Jason and Nathaniel stayed on the bed because they didn't know any better. "What's wrong?" Jason asked.

Nathaniel whispered, "Her eyes."

I turned and caught sight of myself in the standing mirror in the corner. My eyes had filled with pale brown fire, not the darkness of my own eyes, but hers.

"No," I said, softly. I felt her thousands of miles away. Her pleasure at my terror rolled through my body, raised my beast and sent me falling onto the bed. My hands strained for something to hold on to, some help, but there was nothing to fight; it was power and it was inside me.

She explored me, raising my beast until it rolled just under the surface of my skin. She touched that part of Richard that was still inside me and raised his beast, until the two energies entwined and my body started to convulse.

I heard yelling. "She's going to change!" Hands holding me down to the bed.

But Belle had learned what she wanted and let them slide back into my body. She separated out the powers inside me like you'd sort a deck of cards. She touched Jean-Claude's link to me and it puzzled her, I could feel it. Until that moment she'd assumed I was a vampire, and now she knew I wasn't. She let what puzzled her slide back deep inside me, then she called the *ardeur*, the incubus, and the moment I thought it, I realized it was the wrong word. Succubus, she whispered in my head, succubus. The hands that had been holding me down, poured over my body, responding to the *ardeur*. It was like being covered in pure lust, rolled in it, like flour on a piece of meat before you cook it.

Hands slid along my skin, a mouth closed on my mouth, and I couldn't see who was right above me, kissing me. I could feel the weight of their body, another set of hands, but I could see nothing but a shining amber light.

Belle kept the *ardeur* on the surface, because it amused her. I couldn't see whose hands were where, or who was doing what, all I could do was feel them; the brush of silk, the press of flesh, a curtain of hair, the scent of vanilla, but I could not see. Belle Morte was using my eyes for other things. She touched that part of me that allowed me to raise the dead. She caressed my necromancy, tried to bring it to the surface as she had the two; beasts and the *ardeur*, but everything else she had explored was hers to call, it was all in some way part of her lineage, her blood. But the necromancy was all mine.

My magic welled up through me, pushing her back, but I couldn't cast her out, not with just the raw power. It was as if she floated near the surface of some dark pool and I sat at the bottom trying to push her out. I couldn't cast her out, but I could see again, think again.

I was nude from the waist up. Nathaniel's mouth closed on my nipple drawing it in. I cried out, and Jason lowered his mouth to my other breast. There was a moment when I stared down at the two of them pressed to my body, the blond head, the auburn, their mouths working at my breasts, the line of their bodies pressed along mine, the marks of my teeth still visible in Nathaniel's flesh, when the *ardeur*, when Belle Morte spilled over me again. Jason's hand slid down the front of the red silk bottoms, his fingers finding me as if he'd always known just where to touch me. I writhed under his touch, their touch.

I grabbed Jason's wrist, tried to pull his hand away, but he fought me and it was a tender place to fight over. I screamed, "Jean-Claude! Asher!"

"Ma petite?" Jean-Claude made the name a question as if he wasn't sure it was really me. I found the vampires standing beside the bed, not helping, not hindering, just watching. But I understood; the *ardeur* called to them too. They were afraid to touch us.

"Feed," I said.

"Non, ma petite."

"I can't fight her and the hunger. Feed, and let me feed."

"You cannot break free of her, ma petite."

"Help me!"

He looked across the bed at Asher, and I watched something pass between them, something built of sorrow and old regrets. "She is right, *mon ami,* she cannot fight Belle and the *ardeur.*"

"She doesn't understand what she's asking," Jean-Claude said.

"No, but she asks, and if we do not do it, we will always wonder. I would rather try and fail, than regret having never tried at all."

They stared at each other for a second or two, then Asher crawled onto the bed and Jean-Claude followed him. Asher stretched out beside Nathaniel, and Jean-Claude mirrored him with Jason. Belle Morte's joy flared through me, filled my eyes with honey-colored flames, and I lost my grip on Jason's wrist. His hand slid back over me, but when I turned to look, I could see Jean-Claude through the dark glass of her eyes and Asher on the other side. I knew that once they touched either *pomme de sang* they would be caught in the desire, and they would not break free. It was a trap. I opened my mouth to say, don't, but three things happened all at once. They each struck into the neck of the man on their side, as if they'd known exactly what the other would do, and Jason forced me over that shining edge of orgasm. I screamed, body bucking against the bed, and only their weight kept me from sitting up, from clawing the air, because it wasn't just my own pleasure I was feeling. I felt Asher's fangs in Nathaniel's neck, felt Nathaniel's body build, build, and finally release in a rush of pleasure that made him bite down on my breast, made me score not his back, but Asher's with my nails. Jason drew his mouth back from me and screamed. The vampires rode their bodies, and I knew with Belle Morte's awareness that the only reason they didn't orgasm with us was the blood pressure wasn't there yet. But the pleasure was. The five of us were locked into wave after wave of pleasure. Like the heat the *ardeur* was named for, it passed over and through us again and again. It was like floating, skinless, formless, just above the bed, and I could feel their heartbeats inside my body. Finally I could feel Jean-Claude and Asher, feel their hearts give a massive beat and feel the life flood through their bodies and spill in a long, hot, line of pleasure that seemed to be pulled from the soles of their feet to the tops of their heads, as if every piece of their bodies, every atom, exploded in pleasure at once. Nathaniel, Jason, and I screamed for them, because their mouths were still locked on the blood, still drinking, still feeding. Then it was over, and the five of us lay motionless, except for the frantic rise and fall of our chests, trying to breath, trying to remember what it was like to be inside our own skins, with just one heart inside us, instead of five. We melted back into our own skins, only the faint dew of sweat and the panicked thunder of our pulses beating against each other's bodies.

Jean-Claude and Asher pulled back from Nathaniel and Jason just as they'd bitten them—together, in a synchronization as perfect now as it had been two centuries ago. Belle Morte filled my mind with images—images of the two of them making love to her before Asher was scored, when they were her perfectly matched pair. I had a confused image of them making love to her at the same time. The feel of them pushing inside her, as perfectly aware then as now of where each other's bodies were, and of exactly what they would do. She missed them, and it was partially my love of Asher, my seeing him as beautiful, that made her regret. The sharing wasn't only one way; she was getting my feelings, too. But I was myself again. The desire had been well fed, sated, so now I could do what I did best.

I called my magic, pulled it around me like a breath of cool wind against my sweat-soaked skin. Nathaniel and Jason pulled back from me, eyes still unfocused.

Jean-Claude and Asher raised up above each of the smaller men, their eyes as out of focus as the lycanthropes', but Jean-Claude said, "*Ma petite,* what . . ."

I reached for him. "Take my hand."

"Ma petite . . ."

"Now!"

Belle's power cut through me like a whip in a practiced hand. She'd been using it to tickle my skin; now she meant it to hurt. I writhed on the bed, only Jason's and Nathaniel's weight keeping me from flailing. My vision was being consumed by brown flames.

A hand in mine, cool flesh, and the moment Jean-Claude touched me I could see again. I was his human servant, he was my master, we were part of a triumvirate of power. If Richard had been here we could have chased her back to the hell she crawled out of. I sent the call in my head, screaming psychically for Richard, but the answer came against my skin. Jason stared at me, confused. He said, "Anita . . ." I felt Richard's power in Jason, the link of their pack. The power of the triumvirate leaped between Jean-Claude's hand, my hand, and Jason's body. It would work, it had to work, because I could feel Belle Morte rising inside me again, and I wasn't sure I had it in me to chase her back.

I drew my necromancy like a great dark cloud, a storm ready to break, filling the room with the tingling brush of magic. Nathaniel drew back, whispered, "Nimir-Ra."

The power pressed like lightning in a bottle, but the bottle was my body, and there was no release without one more thing . . . blood. The last time we'd done overt triumvirate magic I'd asked the boys to give me blood, watched as Jean-Claude had sunk fangs into Richard for the first time, but not today. Today *I* needed the blood, *I* wanted the blood. I would not share.

I used my free hand to lower Jason's face towards me, but I didn't kiss him. My mouth moved down the side of his cheek, and I whispered, "I need blood, Jason. Say yes."

He'd been holding himself off of me with his arms, but he whispered, "Yes," and collapsed his upper body across my breasts, his hand sliding along my stomach as if he meant to do other things. I could smell the blood just below the surface of his neck, could taste his pulse like candy on my tongue, and I bit him. I wasn't a vampire. There were no mind tricks to make it pleasant. We weren't having sex anymore, there was no distraction, only my teeth tearing his flesh, his blood pouring into my mouth, and the moment the blood poured over me the necromancy flared and I pushed it into that honeyed touch. She laughed at me, at us, then the laughter stopped, because she felt the push of my power. I was a necromancer, and she was just another kind of vampire. My magic didn't differentiate between her and any other corpse. I shoved her out, cast her back, locked her outside us. I'd been training in witchcraft this year, so I bound her from us, bound her from harming us in any way, bound her from contacting us through her power. My last thought to her was, *If you want to find out what the fuck is going on, pick up a phone.* Then she was gone.

19

I WAS NAKED again. It seemed to be a theme that night. The five of us lay in a heap, breathing hard, bodies tingling, with that rush that magic will leave behind sometimes—where you feel both tired and exhilarated at the same time—sort of like sex. Asher and Nathaniel lay on the bed just out of my reach. My mouth, chin, and neck were covered in Jason's blood. He lay with his head on my chest, his head turned so I could see the neck wound. I'd marked Nathaniel and Micah, but there was a piece of meat missing from Jason's neck. It wasn't a big piece, but it was a missing piece of flesh, none-theless.

I swallowed hard, taking deep, even breaths. I would not throw up. I would not throw up. I would not throw up. I was going to throw up. I pushed everyone off the bed and ran for the bathroom. I threw up, and the flesh—about the size of a fifty-cent piece—came up just like it had gone down—whole. There was something about seeing it, about having my worst fears confirmed that brought nausea in a burning wave. I threw up until I thought my head would explode and I was dry heaving.

There was a knock on the door. "*Ma petite,* may I come in?" He hadn't asked if I was alright. Smart vampire. I didn't answer him, just stayed kneeling with my head against the cool bathtub edge, wondering if I was going to throw up again or my head would fall off first. My head hurt worse than my stomach.

I heard the door open. "*Ma petite?*"

"I'm here," I said, my voice sounding thick, as if I'd been crying. I kept my head down. I didn't want to see him, or anyone.

I saw the edge of the black robe, then more of it as he

knelt down in front of me. "Is there anything I can get you?"

A dozen answers flew through my mind, most of them sarcastic, but I settled for, "Some aspirin and a toothbrush."

"You could ask me to cut my heart out at this moment, and I might do it. Instead you ask for aspirin and a toothbrush." He leaned in and laid the gentlest of kisses on the top of my head. "I will get what you ask." He stood, and again I heard a drawer opening and closing.

I looked up and watched him move efficiently around the bathroom, setting out a bottle of aspirin and a toothbrush and a choice of toothpastes. It was absurdly domestic, and the black-furred robe didn't fit the part. Jean-Claude looked like someone who should have servants, and he did. But mostly around me he'd always done for himself, and for me. When I wasn't around he probably had fifty dancing girls waiting on him hand and foot. But with me, it was often just him.

He brought me the aspirin and a glass of water. I took them, and there was a moment when I wasn't sure my stomach would keep them down, but it passed. Jean-Claude helped me stand, and I let him. It wasn't just that my legs were shaky—though they were—it was more like all of me was shaky, uncertain.

I started to shiver and couldn't stop. Jean-Claude held me against his robe in the circle of his arms. My breast hurt where it rubbed against the cloth. I pulled back enough to look down at my body. There was a perfect imprint of Nathaniel's teeth encircling my breast around the areola. He'd only drawn blood in a few places, but the rest was a deep red-purple. It was going to be a hell of a bruise if my body didn't heal it first.

Jean-Claude traced his finger across the upper part of the bite mark, and I winced. "Why is it things like this never hurt while you're doing them?"

"The question is its own answer, *ma petite*."

Strangely, I understood what he meant. "It's almost a mirror of what I did to his chest."

"Nathaniel is being cautious, I think."

"What do you mean?"

"He did nothing to you that you had not done to him first."

"I thought they were both carried away with the *ardeur* and Belle Morte."

"The first time you feel the call of her power it is heady stuff. But the fact that Jason did something that he knew you would not allow, and Nathaniel did not, may mean that Nathaniel has more control of himself than Jason does."

"I would have thought it was the other way around."

"I know," he said, and the way he said it made me look at him.

"What's that supposed to mean?"

"It means, *ma petite,* that you may know Nathaniel's heart's desire, but I do not think you truly know *him*."

"He doesn't know himself," I said.

"In part that is true, but I think he will surprise you."

"Are you hiding something from me?"

"About Nathaniel, no."

I sighed. "You know on another day I'd make you tell me what that cryptic remark meant, but damn it, I want a little comfort from someone right now, and I guess you're it."

His eyebrows raised. "When you ask in so flattering a manner, how can I refuse?"

"No games, please, Jean-Claude, please, just hold me."

He drew me back into the circle of his arms, and I moved so that the bite mark wasn't hurting, or rather wasn't hurting more than it already did. It had turned into a throbbing pain, sharp when touched. It did hurt, but a part of me found that satisfying. It was a comfirmation of what we'd done, a painful souvenir of something that had been amazing. If my morals hadn't gotten in the way, I could have just marveled at the whole thing.

"Why am I pleased that Nathaniel marked me?" I asked it in a small voice, because I wasn't a hundred percent sure Jean-Claude shouldn't have been jealous about it.

He stroked my hair, as his other arm held me close. "I can think of many reasons." His voice vibrated through his chest against my ear, mingling with the sound of his heartbeat.

"One that makes sense to me would be enough," I said.

"Ah, one that makes sense to *you*, now that is a different question."

I squeezed my arms around his waist. "No games, remember, just tell me."

"It could be that you are truly becoming his Nimir-Ra." His arm tightened around me. "I do feel something different in you, *ma petite*, some wildness that was not there before. It does not feel like Richard's beast feels, but it is a difference. It may simply be that as Nathaniel's Nimir-Ra you want closer contact with him."

It made sense. It was hard to argue with the logic of it, but I wanted to. "What could be the other reasons?"

"Belle Morte treated you as a vampire of her line. If through the marks or your necromancy you have some of the powers of a vampire, you may have others. It could be that leopards will be your animal to call. I admit that the first is the more likely reason, but the second is also possible."

I leaned back enough to see his face. "Are you attracted to the wolves?" I asked.

"I find it pleasant to have the wolves around me. It is comforting to touch them like a . . . pet, or lover."

I wasn't sure how I felt about him using pet and lover in the same sentence, but I let it go. "So you want to have sex with the werewolves?"

"Do you want to have sex with Nathaniel?"

"No . . . not exactly."

"But you want to touch him and be touched?"

I had to think about that for a few seconds. "I guess so."

"In a true joining of animal and vampire, there is a desire in both to touch, for one to serve and the other to take care of them."

"Padma, the Master of Beasts, treated his animals like shit."

"One of the many reasons that Padma will always be a secondary power on the Council is his belief that all power must be taken, that all power must come through fear. True power comes when others offer it to you and you merely accept it as a gift, not as the spoils of some personal war."

"So the fact that you treat your wolves better than most is just, what, a political decision?"

He shrugged, still holding me against him. "I do not know how other vampires feel. I know only that Belle Morte felt attracted to her cats and I feel the same for my wolves. Perhaps it is only her line that turns the bond between animal and vampire into something like lovers? Much of her power fed into sex, or at least, attraction, and perhaps that is not how others feel?" He frowned. "I had not truly thought about that before. Perhaps it is another benefit of her lineage—or a shortfall of it—that most of my powers turn to something resembling sex."

"Does Asher feel the same way about his animal to call?"

"He has no animal to call."

I widened my eyes. "I thought all master vamps over a certain age had an animal to call."

"Most of the time they do, but not always. Just as his bite can give true sexual release and mine cannot. We have different powers."

"But not having an animal to call is like a major . . ."

"It means he is weaker than I am."

"But he could still be Master of the City somewhere else. I mean I've met Masters of the City that had no animal to call before."

"If there was a territory vacant in this country, and he would be willing to leave us, then yes, he might rise to Master of the City."

I started to ask, *Then why doesn't he go?* But I was pretty sure I knew the answer, and it was a painful answer, so I left it unsaid. Maybe I was growing up at last. Not every thought that came into my head had to come out of my mouth.

"Or it could simply be that you've wanted Nathaniel for a very long time. There is satisfaction in finally giving in to the desire."

I pushed away from him. "You know, you're not very good at this comforting stuff."

"You said no games. Isn't a lie the same as playing a game?"

I frowned at him. "I did not have sex with Nathaniel."

"Come, *ma petite,* you did not have intercourse, but to say you did not have sex is splitting the hair a little too fine, no?"

I glared at him and tried to be angry, but there was something closer to panic than anger making my heart beat faster. "Are you saying that what we just did qualifies as sex?"

"Are you saying that it did not?"

I turned so I couldn't see his face, hugging my arms around myself. I finally turned back to look at him. I tried leaning against the wall, but the tiles were cold and I was still naked. I needed my clothes, but they were out in the other room, and I was so not ready to see the other men again.

"So you're saying that we had sex—all of us?"

He took a deep breath. "What answer do you want, *ma petite?*"

"Truth would be nice."

"No, you do not want the truth. I thought that you did, or I would have taken better care about what I said." He looked tired. "I am glad you are the woman that you are, but there are moments when I wish that you could simply enjoy something without being chased around the room by your guilt and your morals afterwards. What we did tonight is a glorious thing. A thing to be shared and treasured, not something to be ashamed of."

"I was doing better with it before you told me it counts as sex."

"And the fact that I had to tell you that it counts as sex means you are still lying to yourself more than I have ever tried to lie to you."

"What's that supposed to mean?"

He held up a hand. "I will say no more about this. You do not want the truth, and you told me not to lie. I am out of options."

I hugged myself and frowned at the floor. I tried to wrap my mind around what he'd said, what we'd done, and I just couldn't do it. We needed a change of topic, fast.

"Jason acted like a power substitute for Richard," I said.

"Oui." He let me change the subject without a word or a change in expression.

"I didn't know we could do that."

"Nor did I." He took those few gliding steps that put him beside me again. "If it is comfort that you want, more than truth, then I can do that." He touched my chin, raised my face so that our gazes met. "But you must tell me when you do not want the truth, *ma petite*. It is usually your greatest demand on me."

I stared up into his beautiful face and understood what he was offering—comfort, but not honesty. Comforting lies, because I didn't want to hear the truth. "I don't want you to lie to me, but I'm about at my limit for hard truths for the day. I need a breather."

"You want a space of calm to think about everything. I understand that. I can even give it to you for a few hours, but you have to confront Richard at the lupanar tonight, and I fear that more hard truths await you there."

I put my face against his chest, cuddled into the smoothness of his skin, caught between the furred lapels. "Your bringing up Richard isn't going to make me feel better."

"My apologies." He was rubbing my back with his hands, over and over. The movement made the fur on the sleeves rub up and down my body, from my butt to my shoulders. It was soothing and not soothing at the same time. I looked up at him and didn't know whether to cry or scream. "I thought I fed the *ardeur*."

His hands went still against my body. "You have, and you have fed it well, but it is always just below the surface. Like being full but still admiring a beautifully made dessert."

I didn't really like the analogy, but couldn't think of a better one. I pressed my body into his robe, let him cradle me against his body, and listened to the comforting beat of his heart.

I spoke with my face pressed against his chest, the black furred edge of the lapels tickling my lips. "Why didn't you warn me that she could do that?"

"If you were a vampire of my line, then I would have

warned you, but you are not vampire, you are human, and it should not work that way for you."

I leaned back enough to see his face. "Can she enter any of her . . . children?"

"No, her ability to look in upon her children only lasts for a few nights. Once the new vampire is strong enough to control its own hunger, then she is unable to enter, as if some door closes that was held open before."

"She called my beast, or beasts, or whatever the hell is going on with me. She called it to the surface like she knew what she was doing."

"Her animal to call is all great cats."

"So, leopards," I said.

He nodded. "Among other things."

"I thought only the Master of Beasts could call more than one animal."

"It was the ability he came with from almost the beginning, but many of the oldest grow into a variety of powers. She began, as I understand it, able to call only leopards, then one by one the other great cats answered to her."

"If I really am a wereleopard, will she be able to control me—if she meets me?"

"You cast her out, *ma petite*. You can answer your own question, can you not?"

"You're saying I kicked her butt once, I can do it again."

"Something like that, *oui*."

I pushed away from him, my fingers trailing down his arms under the heavy robe until our hands touched. "Trust me, Jean-Claude, one victory doesn't guarantee you'll win the war."

"This was not a small victory, *ma petite*. Never in all her two thousand years of life has any of her line defied her as you just did." He'd bent at the waist just a little to kiss my hands, showing a long, thin triangle of his chest and upper stomach. My gaze followed that line of pale flesh down into the shadow that hid the rest of him. For once I didn't want to undo the robe. Part of it was that I was well . . . satisfied, and part of it—most of it—was that I had just had sex with four men at once, and my discomfort level was just a little too high to think about any sex for a while.

"I knew that vampires could make the bite pleasant, but I never dreamed it felt like that," I said.

"It is one of Asher's gifts to make his bite orgasmic."

I looked at him.

He nodded. "*Oui, ma petite,* I can make it pleasant, but not that pleasant."

"Asher bit me once, and it wasn't orgasmic."

"He drew back when he realized he had rolled your mind without intending to. He . . . behaved himself."

I raised my eyebrows at that. If tonight was the real thing, he'd more than behaved himself. "You fed off of it, too, and Belle Morte, as well."

"It was a feast, was it not?" And something in the way he said it made me blush. "I do not mean to embarrass you, *ma petite*, but it *was* glorious. I have not shared Asher's gift in over two hundred years. I had almost made myself forget what it was like."

"So you can't do this without Belle Morte."

"One of her gifts is to be a bridge, a connection, between her children. That allowed the sharing of gifts."

"I cast her out, Jean-Claude, it won't be happening again."

"And we are both thrilled. I do not think you understand the risk we all took, *ma petite*. If you had failed to cast her out, then she could have done things to us, even from such a distance. We are the only two of her line that ever left her side willingly. Some were exiled, but none simply left, and she is not a woman that takes rejection well."

That was an understatement. "She saw Asher through my eyes. I felt her regret that she'd let him go, that she hadn't seen him the way I did."

He turned his head to one side. "Then perhaps even a very old dog can learn new tricks."

I swallowed, and something about it made me very aware of the taste of blood and other things in my mouth. I had to get cleaned up.

I went to the sink and watched him in the mirror behind me. I'd known I was nude, but it wasn't until I saw myself

in the mirror that I really noticed it. I'd managed to wipe
most of the blood off my mouth with toilet paper, but it was
still clinging to my chest and my neck. "I really need a robe
of my own," I said.

"I would offer you mine," he said.

I shook my head, reaching for the toothbrush. Normally,
I would have washed the blood off first, but I wanted that
taste out of my mouth more. "You naked around me right
now is not what I need."

"I will send . . ." he hesitated, "Asher for a robe for you."

"You started to say Jason, didn't you?"

He looked at me in the mirror.

"I know he'll heal, but . . . I could have really hurt him,"
I said.

"But you didn't, and that is what matters."

"Pretty to think so," I said.

He smiled, but not like he was happy. "I will send Asher
for a robe."

"Great. Thank you."

I squeezed toothpaste onto the brush as he went for the
door. He stopped with his hand on the doorknob. "Normally
you would owe your *pomme de sangs* some gift or show of
gratitude for serving you."

"I think they've had all the gratitude they're getting from
me for one day."

He laughed, and the sound rode over my body like a caress of silk. "Oh, yes, *ma petite,* and I think they would agree,
but I tell you this for later. You must reward your *pomme
de sang* for his, or her, services."

"Money wouldn't do it?" I asked.

The look on his face said he was truly insulted, outraged,
in fact. "You have just shared something more intimate than
most people will ever know with another being. They have
given us a great gift this day, and they are not whores, Anita." My real name, I was in trouble. "They are *pomme de
sangs,* think of them as beloved mistresses."

I frowned at him.

"Today the sharing of pleasure was reward enough, but
you will need to feed the *ardeur* every day, and unless it is

a feeding worthy of the thirst, more than once a day for a few weeks."

"What are you saying?" I asked.

"I am saying that it would be best if you chose a *pomme de sang* and kept him near you, for you do not truly know yet what your hunger is like. It may be a light thing, easily tended, or it may not."

"You're saying I'll need to do this every day?"

"Yes."

"Fuck."

He shook his head. "Was today so horrible, *ma petite*? Was the pleasure you gained so very small?"

"It's not that. It was glorious, and you know it. But we'll never be able to duplicate that, not without Belle Morte, and I don't want a return visit from her."

"Nor do I. But there are many things that can be done to feed, and when you have some control I will teach you to feed from a distance."

"When?"

"A few weeks."

"Shit." I turned back to the mirror, not looking at him. "How do I pick a *pomme de sang*?"

"I think you already have," he said.

I looked at him. "You mean Nathaniel."

He nodded.

"No, I . . . I don't trust myself not to lose control and . . . you know what I mean."

"He is lovely to the eye, and he cares for you. Would it be so very wrong?"

"Yes, yes, it would be like child molesting. He can't say no. If a person can't say no, then it's the same as rape."

"Perhaps what you do not wish to acknowledge, *ma petite,* is that Nathaniel knows exactly what he wants, and what he wants is you."

"He wants me to dominate him in every sense of the word."

"It is best if a *pomme de sang* is submissive to you."

I shook my head.

"Then who else would you want to risk being carried

away with, your Nimir-Raj?" This time there was something in his voice.

"You are jealous."

"The Nimir-Raj is not a *pomme de sang*, a mistress, a dessert, no matter how delectable. He is an entrée, a very, very main course, and I wish to be the only entrée at your table."

"You were sharing me with Richard, and he certainly wasn't just dessert."

"Very true, but he also had ties to me. He is my wolf to call, and that is a different . . . relationship to me, to you, than some stranger."

"I know it was the *ardeur*, but damn, I've never . . ."

"You are not a woman of casual lusts. No, *ma petite,* you are not. And I fear that this Nimir-Raj is no more casual than the rest of your lusts." He looked so serious when he said it, solemn.

"What do you mean?"

"If you are truly his Nimir-Ra, then you will be drawn to him. There is no help for it. And truthfully, I cannot fault your taste. He is not as fair of face as our Richard, but he does have certain compensations." The look on his face made me blush again.

I turned to the sink and started brushing my teeth, and he took it as a dismissal. He went out laughing. When the door was closed behind him and I was alone I stood for a long time looking at myself in the mirror. It still looked like me. But I could taste Jason's blood underneath the toothpaste. I started scrubbing and spitting and running the cold water, listening to the sound of the water instead of the screaming inside my head.

When Jean-Claude came back into the room I was rinsing the blood out of the washrag I'd used and had three different kinds of mouthwash sitting beside the sink. I'd used all three, and I couldn't taste anything but minty freshness. You could scrub yourself clean of the blood and the taste of it in your mouth, but the stains that really mattered were the ones that no amount of soap or water could touch. I'd have said that things couldn't get any worse, but I knew they could, and rapidly. If I locked myself away for a few days until I could control the *ardeur*, the werewolves would vote without me there, and they'd execute Gregory. If they killed Gregory, it wasn't just Jacob that I'd kill. It would be war between me, my pard, and Richard's pack. Richard was just Boy Scout enough to get in my way, and maybe force me to kill him. Something inside of me would die if Richard died, and if I pulled the trigger . . . some things you recover from, some things you don't. Killing Richard would be one of those things I wouldn't recover from.

Jean-Claude said softly, "Are you alright, *ma petite*?"

I shook my head, but said, "Sure."

He held a bundle of blue satin out to me. "Then you need to get dressed, and I will escort you back outside."

I looked at him. "Is it that obvious that I don't want to go back out there?"

"Jason has been taken to his room. He will heal. But we thought it would upset you to see him. Nathaniel awaits your pleasure, since he did drive you."

"What about Asher?"

"He took Jason away."

"You know we have the answer to the question you've been wanting to know," I said.

We looked at each other. "I felt his release, *ma petite*. I know that he has been tormenting me, allowing me to believe he was ruined. But we still do not know how badly scarred he is, and that is a ruin of a different sort."

"You mean he may feel he's so scarred that he doesn't want anyone to see him, or touch him?"

"*Oui.*"

"Until the two of you touched the boys, the *ardeur* didn't spread to you. Belle Morte didn't spread to you. It's like a disease," I said.

"I have seen that particular disease set loose in a banquet room the size of a football field and spread from person to person until all fell upon each other in a . . . well, orgy is too mild a word."

"What did she gain from making a whole room of humans lose control like that?"

"She gains power from every feeding around her, but it was not that alone. She wished to see if there were limits to the number of people she could spread the desire through."

"Did she find her limit?"

"No."

"So hundreds of people," I said.

He nodded.

"And she fed off of the lust from them all?"

"Oui."

"What did she do with all that power?"

"She helped a marquis seduce a king and changed the trade routes and alliances of three countries."

I widened my eyes. "Well, at least it didn't go to waste."

"Belle has many faults, but the wasting of an advantage is not one of them."

"What did she gain through all the political maneuvering?"

"Land, titles, and a king that adored her. Remember, *ma petite,* that this was at a time in history when to be king of a nation meant to be absolute monarch. His word was life and death, and she ruled him through the sweet secrets of her body."

"No one is that good in bed."

A look passed over his face—a small smile that he tried to hide.

"If she was that wonderful, then why did you and Asher leave her the first time?"

"Asher had been with Belle for many years before I arrived, and more beyond that before he found Julianna. He and I were in the circle of innermost power, where many strived for centuries to get to and failed. We were her favorites until Asher found Julianna. It did not occur to me until decades later that Belle was jealous, but I think in a way that was it. She slept with other men, other vampires, and she was content that Asher and I shared each other's beds, and that we went to the vampires she chose to share us with. But another woman that we chose ourselves—that was different. But it is one of our most sacred laws not to harm another's human servant, so Belle did nothing. Then

Asher offered Julianna to me, and we became a ménage à trois, and that raised the question of Julianna sleeping with others."

He looked down at the floor, then up again. "Arturo was one of her favorites, as well. He desired Julianna, but Asher refused him."

"Asher refused him, not Julianna," I said.

"She was his servant. She could not deny if he had consented."

"Ick," I said.

He shrugged. "It was a different century, *ma petite,* and Julianna was a different woman than you are."

"So why did Asher refuse?" I asked.

"He feared for Julianna's safety. We both did."

"Arturo liked it rough?"

"Mother Nature had made it almost impossible for Arturo to have it any way but rough."

I looked at him. "What do you mean?"

He gave that graceful shrug again. "Arturo is still the most well-endowed man I have ever seen."

It was my turn to shrug. "So?"

He shook his head. "You do not understand, *ma petite.* He is *bien outille,* well tooled. Ah, what is the English? . . . Hung like a horse."

I started to point out that Richard was pretty well-endowed, but it's bad form to point out to boyfriend A that boyfriend B is bigger. Micah was better endowed even than Richard, but again, it didn't seem the thing to mention. I was finally left with, "I've seen two men that were hung like horses, as you say, and it was intimidating, but . . . you're implying that you feared for Julianna's safety because he was so big."

"That is exactly what I am saying."

"No one's *that* big."

"Arturo makes even our Richard and your Nimir-Raj seem ungraced."

I blushed and wished I hadn't. "Those weren't the two men I was referring to."

He raised an eyebrow at me. "Indeed?"

The way he said it made me blush harder. "In New Mexico, one of Edward's backups, and one of the bad guys."

"And how did you happen to see just how well-graced they were, *ma petite*?" There was something in his voice, a hint of warmth, like the beginnings of anger.

"I did not have sex with anyone."

"Then how did you see them nude?" His voice still held that warm edge, and I couldn't really blame him.

"Bernardo, Edward's backup, and I got questioned by a local biker gang, uh club. They didn't believe he was my boyfriend. They asked if he was circumcised, and I said yes. I figured I had a better than fifty-fifty chance in America. They made him drop his pants to prove it."

"Under some threat, I assume." He was looking more amused than angry now.

"Yeah."

"And the other one?"

"He tried to rape me."

Jean-Claude's eyes went wide. "What became of him?"

"I killed him."

He touched my face, gently. "I have only recently understood why I was so very attracted to you from almost the first time I heard you interact with the police."

"Not love at first sight," I said, "but love at first hearing. I don't have that good a voice."

"Do not underestimate the dulcet sounds of your voice, *ma petite,* but it was not the sound of your voice that fascinated me. It was your words. I knew from the moment I heard you, the moment I saw the gun and realized that this lovely, petite woman was the executioner, that you would never die waiting for me to save you—that you would save yourself."

I cupped his hand against my cheek, looked into his eyes and saw again that sorrow for failing to save Julianna that never quite left him. "So you wanted me because I was such a tough broad?"

He let me make the joke. He even smiled, but it never reached his eyes. *"Oui, ma petite."*

My voice was soft when I said, "So Arturo wanted Julianna."

He took his hand back, slowly. "And she feared him, and we feared for her. This is two hundred years ago, a little more now. Asher was not as powerful as he is now, and we feared that his human servant would not survive Arturo's attentions."

"I've got to ask, how big was he?"

Jean-Claude spaced his hands apart like you'd measure a fish. "Like this big." It looked to be about six inches.

"That's not so big."

"That is how wide he was," Jean-Claude said.

I just gaped at him. "You're exaggerating."

"No, *ma petite,* believe me, I remember."

"Then how *long* was he?"

He made another measuring movement. I laughed because I didn't believe him. "Oh, please. You're saying he was what, about six inches wide and over a foot long? No way."

"Yes, way, *ma petite.*"

"You said Arturo was one of Belle's favorites. Does that mean she . . ."

"Had sex with him, *oui.*"

I frowned, couldn't think of a slick way to say it, so just blurted out, "Didn't that hurt her?"

"She was a woman with a large capacity for men in every way."

Gee, that was polite. "Most women wouldn't be able to . . . accommodate that," I said.

"No," he agreed.

"Did she want to kill Julianna?"

"No, she believed Arturo would not harm her."

"Why?"

He licked his lips, which he rarely did, and looked uncomfortable, which he did even less often. "Let us say that something that Belle Morte taught Asher and me to take pleasure in, we also did with Julianna."

I frowned at him, because I so did not have a clue. "If you're hinting, I'm not getting it."

"I would rather not discuss it, now. Perhaps at a later time."

I frowned harder. "What aren't you telling me?"

He shook his head. "I think, *ma petite,* that you would rather not know."

I looked at him. "You know, Jean-Claude, there was a time—not that long ago—that I'd have thrown a fit and made you tell me everything. But now if you tell me I don't want to know, then I'll just believe you. I really am not up to hearing intimate and shocking details about your vampire sex life. I've had enough shocks in that area for one day."

"*Ma petite,* I think you are growing up at last."

"Don't push it. And I'm not growing up, I'm just getting tired."

"As are we all, *ma petite,* as are we all."

I let the royal blue satin robe fall from my hands. It had wide lace sleeves and more lace at what passed for the lapels, to curve in flowers down the sides. It was beautiful and fit me perfectly. Most robes are too long for me. He'd probably bought it with me in mind. I belted it in place and didn't want to ask any more questions about the *ardeur* and sex and vampire stuff. But some things had to be clear between us.

"I need to get this straight, Jean-Claude."

"*Oui, ma petite.*"

"You say that what we did was sex, so in effect I had sex with everyone?"

He just nodded.

"You don't seem at all jealous about that."

"I was participating, *ma petite.* Why should I be jealous?"

The answer confused me more. I frowned up at him. "Okay, let me try this again. You say the *ardeur* may need to be fed more than once a day. We can't count on you being Johnny-on-the-spot when it happens. I can sleep over here, but . . ."

"You may need to feed when I am not awake. This is very possible, in fact, it is likely."

"Okay, then what are the rules?"

It was his turn to frown. "What do you mean, *ma petite?*"

"Rules. I mean like what will make you jealous and what won't? What, or who, am I supposed to stay away from?"

He started to smile, then stopped. "You are one of the most cynical people I have ever met, the most practical in a life-and-death context, and if you knew some of the people I had met, you would understand the compliment that is. But you are also very earnest, like a child. It is a type of innocence that I do not think you will ever outgrow. But I find it hard to deal with."

"It's a fair question."

"Indeed it is, but most people would not need to ask it so blandly. They would either ignore it and do the best they could when the need arose, or they would ask who among my people will I allow you to have sex with, without becoming angry."

It made me wince to hear him say it, but . . . "I like the way I phrased the question better."

"I know. You are simultaneously one of the most direct women I know, and one of the most self-deluding."

"I am really not liking where this conversation's going."

"Fine, but I will answer my question, because it is the truth. If Nathaniel is your *pomme de sang*, then I will let intimacy with him pass. Jason as my *pomme de sang* is within his rights to make love with my human servant. It is considered a great gift for a vampire to share his servant with another, and Jason has earned that. He has served me faithfully for many years."

"I'm not a prize to be given away."

He held up a hand. "Hush, *ma petite,* I will answer the question, and I will try for truth, even though you do not want to hear it today. There are many things I would have told you today, if you had been in the mood for truth. But you are right, this we must have clear between us. I would simply have urged you to keep Nathaniel close at hand and let the cards fall as they may, but if you insist on a list, then I will give it to you, but not without reasons. Because I want it clear that I do not share you lightly, and there are men I will not share you with at all."

He was angry now, and his eyes had bled to sapphire

flame. The rest of his body was very still, but the eyes gave it all away. He was in the grip of some strong emotion, probably anger, but I wasn't sure. And he was shielding like a son of a bitch, so something he was feeling, or thinking, he didn't want me to share.

"Asher is acceptable."

He didn't give the reasons for that one, and I didn't ask, because there were too many of them, most of them painful.

"If Richard comes to his senses, then of course." He smoothed his hands down the front of his robe; he often checked his clothes when he was nervous. "The Nimir-Raj will have to be acceptable, because he calls to you. Richard's beast calls to you through my marks, my ties to him, to it, but the Nimir-Raj, he calls to you, Anita." My real name again. He was not happy. "He calls to something in you, in your power. It may be that you are truly Nimir-Ra, and the full moon will see it true. Or it may be that, as with Nathaniel, you have found your animal to call. If you are drawn more strongly to all the leopards, then it could be for either reason. Be wary if the leopards are yours to call. It may not merely be Nathaniel and the Nimir-Raj that beckon."

"Please, don't tell me that I'm going to turn into slut-girl."

He smiled. "I do not think you need to fear that. You are stronger willed than that."

"You just said I might be tempted by the other wereleopards."

"If the Nimir-Raj or Nathaniel are not near you when the *ardeur* rises, then my advice is to give in to it instantly."

I gave him wide eyes.

"If you fight it, *ma petite,* it grows. If it grows large enough, then you may indeed turn into slut-girl. If you give in and feed immediately, then you will have sex with one person, not several, and it will be more a person of your choosing."

"So the real advice is, keep the men I prefer within easy reach."

"I would make Nathaniel, or someone of your choosing, your constant companion."

I swallowed hard and searched his face, but it was pleasantly blank—his expression when he didn't want me to know what he was thinking. His eyes had bled back to normal.

Something occurred to me. "I haven't seen Damian around."

"I speak of sex, and you think of Damian." His voice was still pleasant but the words held something harsh.

"You give me this list of people to sleep with, and not to sleep with, but you leave him off either list. And he wasn't at the club, and he didn't come to the bedroom, attracted by the power like Asher. Where is he?"

Jean-Claude rubbed his hands over his face. "I was going to tell you, then you decided you wanted no more hard truths today." He lowered his hands and looked at me.

"He's alive, I'd know it if he wasn't."

"Yes, I believe you would. There was a time when my first master made my heart beat. Her power suffused me, made me live. But her power came from her Master of the City, so it was in reality his power that filled me. Each master vampire that I belonged to demanded blood oaths, and each one in turn made my blood course, my heart move. Then Belle, herself, the head of my line, brought me in, and she filled me. She was like the pounding of the ocean, and all others before her were but rivers seeking to drown in her embrace. Gradually, I filled with my own power. But even now it is her lineage that makes me live. The power that made her is what keeps me alive. Damian is descended from her line, not from Belle herself, but from one of her children, as I am. I am Master of the City and the power that animates me, animates Damian. When he took the oaths that bound him to me, that made him loyal to me, it became my power that filled him, my power that made his heart beat. And I broke the tie with She who made him."

"You make all the vampires under you alive?" I made it a question.

"The power comes through me, yes, but only if they are of my line, my lineage. If they are descended from other than Belle's children, then no, the blood oaths do not bind as tightly."

"What about Asher? You don't make his heart beat."

He nodded. "Very good, *ma petite*. No, I do not. A Master Vampire is a vampire that has become enough of a power that they fill themselves up. It is one of the things that being a master means, and one of the reasons that many of the older vampire masters still kill their children when they feel that tie break."

"You're volunteering an awful lot of information, and don't think I'm not grateful, it's fascinating, but what does this all have to do with Damian?"

"You have raised Damian from his coffin once, filling him with your necromancy like a zombie. You have saved his life twice with your necromancy. You have forged a tie between him and you."

Actually, I knew that, but out loud I said, "He said that he couldn't tell me no if I gave him a direct order. That he wanted to serve me. It scared him."

"It should have."

"I didn't mean to do it, Jean-Claude. I didn't even know it was possible."

"Legends speak of necromancers that could control all types of undead, not merely zombies. It was at one time Council policy to slay all necromancers on sight."

"Gee, glad the policy changed."

"Yes," he said. "But you severed my tie with Damian. I did not realize it at first, but when he returned from Tennessee, it was not my power that made his heart beat, it was yours."

I remembered feeling that in Tennessee, feeling the tie between us. "It wasn't done deliberately," I said.

"I know that, but you left me with a problem when you went away for over half a year. Damian is over a thousand years old. Though not a Master Vampire, he is still powerful. He no longer had ties to any vampire hierarchy. It freed him of all blood oaths, of all mystically bound loyalties. He was yours, but you did not come to claim him."

"You should have told me."

"And what would you have done? Taken him home to

live in your basement? You did not have the power or control six months ago to deal with him."

"Now I do. Is that what you're saying?"

"You cast out Belle Morte. One of the most powerful of the Council. If you can do that, *ma petite,* then you can handle Damian."

"This is all great, but where is Damian?"

"I could no longer count on his loyalty. I no longer controlled him, do you understand, *ma petite*? I had a vampire that was more than twice my age, and I could not control him. It both made me look weak in others' eyes when I could not afford to appear weak, and it was dangerous, because he knew when you healed over your aura and shielded so tight. It wasn't only Richard and me who felt the loss of you. You cut Damian off, and he went a little . . . mad."

I was scared now, my heart beginning to climb up my throat. *"Where is Damian?"*

"First, *ma petite,* understand that you cannot take him with you tonight, because to tend him will be a full-time job for the first few hours."

"Just tell me," I said.

"I had to lock him away, *ma petite.*"

I stared at him. "Lock him away, how?"

He just looked at me, and it was eloquent.

"He's been locked in a cross-wrapped coffin for six months?"

"About that, yes."

"You bastard."

"I could have killed him, *ma petite,* that's what others would have done."

"Why didn't you?"

"Because it was partially my fault for exposing him to you. Damian was mine to protect, and I failed him."

"He's mine, mine to protect," I said.

"Yet, you deserted him."

"I didn't know. You should have told me."

"And six months ago would you have believed me? Or would you have thought it was some ploy to get you back into my life?"

I started to tell him, of course I'd have believed him, but I stopped and thought about it. "I don't know if I'd have believed you or not."

"I hoped that I would find a way to reestablish my dominance over him, but he is closed to me."

I swallowed hard and looked at him. "If he's mine, then why didn't I feel him when my shielding broke all to hell in New Mexico?"

"I have been blocking you from sensing him, and it has not been easy."

I closed my eyes and counted to ten, but it didn't help. I was so angry my skin felt hot. "You had no right to do that."

"Without the marks being married, I think Damian would have seduced you. Because you would have been drawn to him as you are drawn to Nathaniel now, or perhaps even the Nimir-Raj."

"I would not have fucked Damian without the *ardeur* helping me, and I didn't have that six months ago."

"You may have your vampire back tomorrow night. I will help you nurse him back to health."

"I'm coming back tonight to get him."

"Talk to Asher, *ma petite.* Ask him what it will take to nurse a vampire back from six months in the coffin. Damian is not a master; he has had no ability to feed or gain energy. He will come out of the coffin a starved, crazed thing. There will be very little left of him, at first." He was so calm while he said it.

I didn't know what to say. I wanted to hit him, but it wouldn't change anything. I wasn't even sure it would make me feel better. "I want him out tonight, when I get back from the lupanar."

"You will not be able to tend both your injured wereleopard and Damian tonight. Ask Asher, and he will tell you how much work goes into such as this. One more night will not make a difference to Damian, and tonight you are trying to prevent war between the leopards and the wolves. More than that, you are trying to make a strong enough show of force to convince Richard's enemies that he is too well-allied to be killed. You must concentrate on these things tonight, *ma petite.*"

"I don't believe you," I said.

He shrugged. "Believe what you like, but it will take hours of care to make Damian sane again. It will take days of care, and blood, and warmth, to bring him back to himself."

"How could you know that and still do this to him?" My voice didn't even sound angry, just tired.

"I learned the lessons of the cross-wrapped coffin personally, *ma petite.* I have not done to Damian anything that has not been done to me."

"You were in it for a few days until I killed the old Master of the City."

He shook his head. "When I returned to the Council with Asher and bargained with them, the price for them saving his life was my freedom. I spent two years inside a coffin, unable to feed, unable to sit up, unable . . ." He was hugging his arms, holding himself. "I know that what I have done to Damian is a terrible thing, but my only alternative was to kill him. Would you have preferred that?"

"No."

"Yet, I see the accusation in your eyes. I am a monster because of what I have done to him. But you would feel me more a monster if I had killed him. Or perhaps you would have preferred that I let him go into the city streets and slaughter people."

"Damian would never do that."

"He went mad, *ma petite.* He became an alien. Do you remember the couple that was slaughtered about six months ago?"

"I saw several slaughtered couples over the last year. You'll need to be more specific."

He was angry now, too. Great, we could be angry together. "They were in a car, at a stoplight. The front of the car was dented as if they had hit a body, but no body was found."

"Yeah, I remember that one. They had their throats torn out. The woman had tried to defend herself. She had wounds on her arms where something had clawed at her."

"Asher found Damian wandering a few blocks from the car. He was covered in blood. He fought Asher, and it took over half a dozen of us to bind him and bring him home. Was I supposed to let him wander the streets after that?"

"You should have called me," I said.

"And what? You would have executed him? If insanity is a viable plea in your court system, then he cannot be held accountable. But your court system does not give us the same privileges it gives humans. We cannot plead insanity and live."

"I saw that crime scene. It didn't look like a vampire did it. It looked more like a shapeshifter, but . . . but the marks were wrong." I shook my head. "It was vicious, a vicious animal."

"*Oui,* and so I locked him away and hoped that you would come home to us, or sense his plight. At first I did nothing to block him from reaching you, but you did not come."

"I didn't know."

"You knew that Damian was yours, and yet you did not ask about him. You cast him away."

"I didn't know," I said, again, each word tight with anger.

"And I had no choice, Anita. I had to put him away."

"Do you think the insanity is permanent?"

He shrugged, arms still hugging his body. "If you were a vampire and he your vampire child, I would say no. But you are not vampire, you are necromancer, and I simply do not know."

"If he stays that crazy . . ."

"He will have to be destroyed," Jean-Claude said, voice soft.

"I didn't mean for this to happen."

"Nor did I."

We stood there for a few moments while I thought about everything and Jean-Claude either thought about it, too, or just stood there. "If all you're saying is true, then you had no choice," I said.

"But you are still angry with me. You will still punish me for it."

I glared up at him. "What do you want me to say? That knowing you've shoved him in a box for six months takes the sparkle out of our relationship? Yeah, it bothers me."

"Under normal circumstances you would rescue Damian and avoid me for a time until your anger cooled."

I nodded. "Yeah, that's about right."

"But you will need me, *ma petite,* in these first few nights. You will need another vampire with the same hungers to teach you control."

"Can't live with you, can't live without you, is that it?"

"I hope your anger cools before you need my help again, but I fear it will not. Remember this, *ma petite,* that the *ardeur* is not bound by morals, or even by your preferences. If you fight it long enough, hard enough, you will eventually give in, and it will be out of your control who it chooses. So do this one thing for me, if you cannot forgive me right away, keep always by your side either Nathaniel or the Nimir-Raj. Not for my sake, but for yours. For I think, of the two of us, I would forgive you sooner for sleeping with strangers than you would."

We pretty much left the conversation there. I found Asher and had him confirm the story. Hell, I waited for Willie Mc-Coy to climb out of his coffin and heard the story from him. Damian had gone ape-shit and killed a couple that apparently hit him with their car. The man had gotten out to check on whoever they hit. They had hurt him and Damian struck out, killing the man. But the woman . . . he'd climbed into the car after her. We might have to kill him, because I hadn't understood what my magic meant to Damian. I hadn't understood a lot of things.

I drove out in the soft summer dusk with Nathaniel riding beside me. It had been a very long day. I was going to go home and pick up Rafael and the wererats, and Micah and his pard. He'd left a number at the shapeshifter hospital, and I'd called for it. I almost didn't call, but we needed backup tonight. My embarrassment was a small price to pay. If I had been in contact with Jean-Claude and Richard for the last half year, I probably could have talked Richard out of doing all the shit he'd done to his pack. I'd come home to try and reestablish a relationship, or two, but I was mostly cleaning up the mess that my absence had made. Richard might be dead at the full moon, and Jacob, Ulfric. Damian might be permanently crazy and have to be destroyed. The couple that had hit him with their car would have been alive if I'd known what the hell my magic was doing.

I'd avoided a lot of Marianne's teachings because it was too much like pure witchcraft for my monotheistic beliefs, but I knew now that I had to understand how my powers worked. I couldn't afford to be squeamish. God kept telling me I was okay with Him. I wasn't evil. But at some level I didn't believe it. At some level I thought that witchcraft, raising the dead, wasn't very Christian. If God was okay with me doing it, then what was my problem? I'd prayed about it often enough and gotten the answer more than once. The answer was to do it, that this was what I needed to be doing. If God was for it, then who was I to question it? Look where my arrogance had gotten us. Two dead, one crazy, and if Richard lost the pack . . . there'd be a lot more dead.

I felt a quietness inside me as I drove. Usually the touch of God is golden and warm, but sometimes when I've been really slow and not picked up on what He's wanted for me, I get this kind of quiet sadness, like a parent watching a child learn a necessary hard lesson. I'd never once prayed to God about Richard and Jean-Claude—not about who to choose anyway. It just hadn't seemed right to ask God to help me choose a lover, especially when I thought I knew who He'd pick. I mean vampires are evil, right?

But driving through the falling darkness, feeling His soft presence fill the car, I realized that I hadn't asked because I'd been afraid of the answer. I drove and I prayed, and I didn't get an answer, but I knew He heard me.

20

It was full dark when we pulled up in front of my house. Almost every light in the house was on, like I was giving a party and no one had bothered to tell me. The driveway was full and overflowing onto the road. One of the reasons I'd rented the house was because I had no near neighbors to get caught up in whatever crisis I was having. My crises usually involved gunfire, so no neighbors to get hurt had been my primary requisite in a house. There was no one around to peek out a window and wonder what the hell was going on next door. Just trees and the lonely road, neither of which cared what I did. Or at least I didn't think the trees cared, though Marianne might tell me I'm wrong on that one. You never know.

I ended up parking quite a ways down from the house, with nothing but trees on either side of the road. I turned off the engine, and Nathaniel and I sat in the dark, listening to the engine tick. He hadn't said much since I came back out of the bathroom at Jean-Claude's—nothing at all on the forty-minute drive here. But then, neither had I.

I'd left Jean-Claude in a huff with a firm date to come back tomorrow night and get Damian out of hock. It wasn't just Damian locked away all these months that made me not want to be with Jean-Claude, it was that he had finally changed me into one of the monsters. I already knew that sex with him bound the marks closer, but now that the marks were married . . . what would sex do to us now? How much closer could the marks bind us all? Was it just changes with Jean-Claude, or did I have mystical surprises coming up tonight with Richard, too? Chances were likely, and Jean-Claude really had no clue what the surprises might be. He didn't know what he was doing. He really didn't. Since I didn't know what the hell *I* was doing either, and Richard had no clue. That left us in a bad place. I'd call Marianne tomorrow on the theory that one magic is much like another, but until then I was on my own. Big surprise.

Of course, I wasn't exactly alone. I looked across the front seat at Nathaniel. He looked back at me, face peaceful, hands in his lap, seat belt still in place. He'd pulled his hair back into a thick braid, leaving his face very plain and unadorned. In the moonlight his eyes looked pale gray, instead of their usual vibrant violet. Without the hair or the eyes showing, he looked closer to normal than I'd ever seen him. He was suddenly a person sitting across from me, and I realized with a shock that I didn't really think of Nathaniel as a person. Not as a grown-up separate human being kind of person anyway. He was more a burden than a person to me. Someone to be rescued, helped. He was a cause, a project, but not a person.

The heat began to press in around the Jeep. If we sat here much longer I'd have to turn the air conditioning back on. If Jean-Claude was right, then I'd had sex with Nathaniel earlier tonight. I was hoping Jean-Claude wasn't right, because I still considered Nathaniel a child, an abused child. You took care of them, you did not have sex with them, not even if they wanted you to.

My breast was aching, faintly, from his teeth marks. We'd shared a bed so often that it felt odd when he wasn't beside me. But I still didn't see him as a grown-up. Sad, but true.

"Jean-Claude is pretty sure that the *ardeur* is well fed enough that it won't be an issue for the rest of the night," I said.

Nathaniel nodded. "You won't need to feed again until you've slept for a few hours. Jean-Claude explained it to me, a little."

That pissed me off. "He did, did he?"

He shook his head. "Anita, he's worried about you."

"I'll bet."

"You really aren't going to sleep at the Circus tonight, are you?"

"No," I said. I was sitting back in the seat with my arms

crossed over my stomach. I'm sure I looked as stubborn as I felt.

"And when you get up tomorrow, what then?" His voice was very soft in the hot, dark car.

"I don't know what you mean."

"Yes, you do," he said.

I sighed. "I don't want to do this, Nathaniel. I don't want to have Jean-Claude's incubus inside me. I'd rather be Nimir-Ra for real than have to feed off of others."

"And if you're both?" he asked, voice even softer.

I shrugged, arms still crossed, but hugging me more than being stubborn now. "I don't know."

"I'll be there for you, Anita."

"Be where?" I looked at him.

"Tomorrow, when you wake."

"What else did Jean-Claude tell you while I was running around trying to find out about Damian?"

Nathaniel's gaze never wavered, never changed. He wasn't embarrassed or bothered in the least about the conversation. "That he wouldn't hold a grudge if you had real sex with me."

I studied his face. "You don't consider what we did today sex?" I made it half-question, half-statement.

"No," he said.

"I don't either, but . . ." I was glad it was dark, because I was blushing, but damn it I wanted someone else to answer this question. "I know why I don't think today was actual sex, but why don't you?"

He smiled and did look away. He answered looking down at the floorboard. "What we did the first time with you marking my back, that was closer to real sex for me."

"So it was the dominance/submission thing?"

"No," he said, still looking down. "If we'd really needed the condoms, then it would have been sex."

"You mean intercourse," I said.

He nodded, still not looking at me.

"That's how I feel too. Jean-Claude said I was fooling myself."

Nathaniel flashed me a small smile, then went back to

staring at nothing. "He told me I was being very American, very male, and very young."

"You are American, male, and twenty," I said. "What else are you supposed to be?"

He looked at me for a moment, then looked away again. He was definitely uncomfortable now.

"What else did Jean-Claude say?" I asked.

"You'll be mad."

"Just tell me, Nathaniel."

He shrugged, the thin straps of the tank top showing most of his shoulders as he did it. "He's hoping you'll choose me as your *pomme de sang*. He said he mentioned it to you."

"He mentioned it."

"Can I undo the seat belt?" he asked.

"Be my guest."

He let the belt slide to one side and turned so he was facing me, one leg drawn up into the seat, his braid curled over one shoulder. "Jean-Claude said that the more you fight the *ardeur* the stronger it grows, but if you feed when it first arises, then it's not such a big deal."

"He told me," I said.

"He's afraid you'll try and tough it out tomorrow without him. He's afraid you'll fight it all day, then only give in when you have to."

"Sounds like a plan to me," I said.

Nathaniel shook his head. "Don't be tough on this one, Anita, don't fight. I'm afraid of what will happen if you do."

"What, I'm supposed to roll over tomorrow morning and fall into your arms?" I couldn't keep the sarcasm out of my voice, though it brought a hurt look to his face, and made me want to apologize. "It's nothing personal, Nathaniel. It's not you, it's having to do it that I don't like."

"I know that." He lowered his face, not meeting my eyes again. "Just promise me that when the hunger rises tomorrow that you'll turn to me, or to someone, early and not try to be so . . . tough."

"What were you really going to say on the end of that sentence?"

He smiled. "Stubborn."

I had to smile. "I don't think I can just roll over the first time the *ardeur* hits me. I just can't give in that quickly, Nathaniel. Do you understand that?"

"You have to prove you're tougher than it is," he said.

"No, I have to be who I am, and who I am doesn't just give in to anyone, or anything."

He grinned at me. "That's an understatement."

"You're making fun of me," I said.

"A little," he said.

"You saw what I did to Jason's neck, Nathaniel. What if I hurt you? I mean really hurt you?"

"Jason will heal, Anita, and he wasn't complaining when Asher took him away." Nathaniel grinned and looked away as if he were trying not to laugh.

"What?"

He shook his head. "You'll get mad, and he didn't mean it that way."

"What did he say, Nathaniel?"

"Ask him yourself. He always seems to be able to say outrageous things to you and you think it's cute. When I say them, you just get mad."

"What if I ordered you to tell me?"

He seemed to think about it for a second, then flashed me another smile. It was a good smile, young, relaxed, real. When I'd first met Nathaniel he'd forgotten how to smile like that. "No, no I wouldn't."

"Some submissive you are," I said.

The smile widened to a grin. "You didn't like me submissive. It made you uncomfortable."

"So you're changing to please me?"

The smile faded, but not like he wasn't happy, more like his expression had shifted from humor to thoughtful. "At first, but lately some of it's to please me, too."

That made me smile. "That's the best news I've had all night."

"I'm glad," he said.

I undid my own seat belt. "Let's get out of this car before we melt." I opened the door and knew he'd do the same. We closed the doors, and I hit the button on my key chain that locked the Jeep. It made the little beeping sound, and I walked around the cars to the road, where the walking was smoother. Nathaniel and I started walking down the line of cars towards my house. His braid fell along his spine like a long, thick tail, moving as he walked.

Cherry and Zane came out from between the cars just ahead of us. "We thought you'd gotten lost," she said, smiling.

"You guys let everyone into the house?" I asked.

Her smile faded. "Yes, I hope that was okay."

I smiled. "It's okay, Cherry, really. If I'd been thinking, I'd have arranged for someone to let them in."

She relaxed visibly and dropped to her knees in front of me. I offered her my left hand. I was keeping my right hand free in case I had to draw my gun. Not likely, but you never know. Cherry gripped my hand in both of hers and rubbed her face against it like a cat marking its scent. The other formal greeting involved licking, but I'd finally convinced all of my cats that face rubbing was about all I was comfy with.

Zane went to his knees beside Cherry but didn't try to grab my right hand. He waited until she was done with my left. I'd also broken them of being grabby with my gun hand. He rubbed his face on my hand, and there was the faintest roughness alongside his jaw, as if he'd missed a spot when he shaved.

Cherry rubbed herself against my legs while Zane greeted me. It was like being body-rubbed by a really big cat that just happened, at the moment, to be in human form. The first few times it had happened, I'd freaked. But it just didn't strike me as that strange anymore. I wasn't sure if that was good or sort of sad.

When the greeting was over, Zane said, "We've got the extra key, so we took care of the company." They were both standing now, like good little people—alright, good *tall* people, whatever.

"Good, though I had no idea we'd have this big a crowd."

They fell into step, one on either side of us, and I could feel Cherry beside me. I could feel her energy like a vibrating

line against my body. I'd never sensed her this strongly before. Just another nail in the coffin on the Nimir-Ra question.
The evidence was getting thick enough that if I hadn't been
so damn good at self-delusion, I'd have had to admit it by
now. But I'd had enough for one day. I needed a pass on
this one tonight. So I ignored it, and if Cherry felt anything
different, she didn't say.

It was Zane who put his face next to Nathaniel and sniffed
him as we walked. "You smell like fresh wounds." He
touched Nathaniel's back where it showed above the tank
top. I knew there were bite marks up around his shoulders,
all the way up to his neck. I should have known we couldn't
hide it. Hell, even with clothes covering it, they'd have
smelled it.

"What have you been doing?" Zane asked. "Or should I
say who?"

Nathaniel didn't even glance at me. He was going to leave
it all to me—what was said and what wasn't. Smart of him.
Or maybe he just didn't know what to say either. I tried to
think of a lie that would explain it, and nothing that didn't
make Nathaniel sound slutty came to mind. Either he'd had
sex with some strange woman, or . . . or what? The truth? I
didn't want to tell the truth until I was sure how I felt about
it. Knowing me, that could take at least a couple of days.

Cherry and Zane circled Nathaniel in ever-tightening circles, until their bodies brushed him as they moved around
him. They bumped him continuously, like a shark testing to
see if you're good to eat.

"Come on guys, we don't have time for this. We need to
get to the lupanar and rescue Gregory."

Zane dropped to his knees beside Nathaniel, running his
hands over the smaller man's body. Zane's hands slid under
Nathaniel's tank top.

"Zane, get up," I said.

Cherry stepped very close to Nathaniel, looking down at
him, putting a hand under his chin to lift his face to her, as
if she meant to kiss him. "Who was it?"

"That's Nathaniel's business," I said. Nathaniel glanced
at me, sort of sideways. The look was enough. I was being

a coward. My pulse was going way too fast in my neck, like I'd tried to swallow something while it was still trying to get away.

"If it were Zane, or me, yes," Cherry said. "But while you were in the hospital these last few days we decided that Nathaniel has to run all girlfriends past the pard before he does anything intimate with them."

"As Nimir-Ra, don't I have like presidential veto?"

Cherry looked at me. "Of course, but you have to agree with checking out people for Nathaniel. He nearly got you killed again."

I did agree, but just not that night. That night, of all nights, I wanted everyone to mind their own business. No one cared a damn who slept with whom—until now. It figures. I make my first indiscreet move with one of them, and I was going to have to confess, even though I still didn't know how I felt about it. I opened my mouth to say, *It was me,* but I stopped when I saw the next wereleopard coming down the street. Of all of them, she was the one I least wanted to talk in front of about intimate matters.

It was Elizabeth. Her walk was always a cross between a strut and a glide, the ultimate hooker's walk. She strode from between the cars on Caleb's arm, and there was a self-satisfied smile on her face that said either she didn't know I was angry with her or she was confident I couldn't do anything about it. She was taller than Caleb by nearly five inches. Her hair fell in curls to her waist, a brunette so dark you would have called it black if you didn't have my hair to compare it to. She was pretty in a pouting, lush sort of way, like some sort of tropical plant with thick, fleshy leaves and beautiful but deadly blossoms.

She was wearing a skirt so short the tops of her black hose and the garters that held them up showed. Her shoes were black sandals with a lower heel than she usually wore. After all, we were going to be tramping through the woods. The shirt was sheer enough that even by starlight you could see she wasn't wearing a bra, and she, like me, was a woman who needed one.

Caleb was wearing a pair of bell-bottom jeans, no shoes,

no shirt. The jeans were cut low enough to show off his belly-button ring. I was too young to remember wearing bell-bottoms personally, but I did remember my older cousins competing to see who could get the widest bell. Even as a child I'd thought the pants were ugly. Time had not changed my opinion.

Caleb looked pretty satisfied himself. I was betting they'd had sex together, but it wasn't any of my business who they fucked. Honest it wasn't.

"I'm glad you've had a good night, Elizabeth."

She squeezed Caleb's arm. "Oh, it's been a very, *very* good night."

"I'm glad, because it's about to get very, very bad," I said.

She fake-pouted at me. "Oh, did our little Nimir-Ra get her feelings hurt because I wouldn't come and sleep naked beside her?"

I had to laugh.

"What's so funny?" she asked. Caleb started moving away from her, pulling free.

"Why is it that you don't think I'll kill you, Elizabeth?"

"For what?" she asked.

"Oh, maybe for deserting Nathaniel at the club and letting the bad guys get him, which led to *me* nearly getting killed, and maybe becoming Nimir-Ra for real."

"I'm tired of baby-sitting him," she said. "He used to be a lot of fun, but not anymore. He's got standards now."

"Meaning that he won't fuck you anymore," I said.

The first touch of real anger slid across her face. "We used to have some real good times, Nathaniel and me."

"Not good enough, apparently," I said.

She strode up to stand beside Cherry, which put her very close to me. She truly wasn't afraid of me, and I knew why—or thought I did. She'd been insulting, arrogant, and a down-right pain in the ass since I took over the pard and I hadn't hurt her. I'd let it all slide, because, as she was so happy to point out, I could shoot her, but I couldn't really punish her. *Punish* to a shapeshifter means either beat the shit out of them or do some mystical crap that scares the shit out of them. She was right. I couldn't do the shapeshifter stuff. It had taken me a while to realize why I let Elizabeth slide so much. I'd killed her sweetie, the man she loved. It made me feel bad. Gabriel had earned death, but she had loved him, and I sympathized. But she'd used up the last of my sympathy when I saw Nathaniel hanging from those chains with the swords grown into his flesh. The rules had changed, and Elizabeth didn't know it. Yet.

The other wereleopards glided out of the trees, trailed down the road. Merle's hair gleamed white in the darkness, his beard and mustache silvered. He was wearing straight-legged jeans and cowboy boots with silver-tipped toes. An open leather jacket did more to frame his chest than cover it. He had a woman with him.

She was tall—six feet or maybe a little over. She was wearing jogging shoes, jeans, and a baggy T-shirt that hung to mid-thigh. The baggy T-shirt couldn't hide the fact that she was leggy and well built. Her hair was almost black, straight, thick, cut just above her shoulders. She wore no makeup, and the bones of her face made her look sculpted—almost harsh. Her eyes were pale, her lips, thin. She had one of those faces that would have been beautiful with a little makeup, but was still striking. It was a face you wouldn't forget or grow tired of. Merle was holding her hand, but not like they were a couple, more like a father holds a daughter's hand—a comforting gesture.

She vibrated with that otherworldly energy that all the leopards had to some degree. But this one made my skin dance from yards away. When they got close enough for me to see that her eyes were pale, I could also see that she was afraid. Her eyes had that wincing look of a person who's been abused once too often.

Merle introduced her, "This is Gina."

"Hi, Gina," I said.

She looked at me, and the fear in her eyes was replaced by disdain. "She's a little short for a Nimir-Ra."

"Micah and I are the same height," I said.

She shrugged. "Like I said." But her bravado didn't ring

true. It was more like someone whistling in the dark. But I let it go. Gina wasn't my problem tonight.

Vivian was the last of my leopards, and she came alone down the street. She was one of the few women who made me feel protective and made me think of adjectives like *doll-like* and *delicate*. She was simply one of the most beautiful women I'd ever seen, and the casual shorts and striped tank top with sandals couldn't hide that. She was African-American by way of Ireland, and her skin was that flawless pale cocoa shade that you only get with that particular mixture. She looked sort of lost, and I realized why. I hadn't seen her without Stephen at her side in over a year. Stephen was Gregory's identical twin, also a stripper at Guilty Pleasures. Stephen and Vivian were living together and seemed very happy doing it. But Stephen was at the lupanar tonight like all good werewolves, and she was here with the leopards. Poor Vivian. Poor Stephen. I hadn't really thought until that moment that Stephen might lose a brother tonight. Shit.

Vivian dropped to her knees in front of me, and I offered her my hands. She took them in her hands, then rubbed her face against them, as Cherry and Zane had done. Elizabeth hadn't offered a greeting, and it was an insult. The others weren't my leopards, but she was. And she'd deliberately snubbed me. It was the first time in front of company. I didn't usually insist on it, because I didn't like Elizabeth touching me, but I watched Caleb's face as Vivian rose from her greeting. He'd noticed the oversight.

"How you doing, Vivian?"

"A real Nimir-Ra wouldn't have to ask," Elizabeth said.

I squeezed Vivian's hands and helped her stand. "Are you going to help us rescue Gregory, or just be a big pain in the ass?" I asked Elizabeth.

"I want Gregory safe," she said.

"Then shut the fuck up."

She started to say something, and Cherry gripped her arm. "That's enough, Elizabeth."

"You're not dominant to me," Elizabeth said.

"I'm trying to be your friend," Cherry said.

"You want me to leave her alone?"

"Please," Cherry said.

"Fine," Elizabeth said. She turned back to Nathaniel. "I can smell fresh blood on you, Nathaniel." She put her arms on either side of his neck, hands clasped together, her body pressed the length of his, moving Cherry back. "You finally find someone to top you?"

"Yes," he said.

"Who?" Cherry asked.

"We really don't have time for this," I said. "We need to get to the lupanar."

Merle had to add his two cents worth. "The only reason that Elizabeth treats you the way she does is that you let her. Disobedience must be punished immediately, or the power structure cannot survive—much like your local Ulfric and his pack."

"I control my leopards," I said.

Elizabeth laughed, planting a big kiss on Nathaniel's forehead and leaving a red lipstick print behind. "He fucked someone tonight, when he'd been forbidden to be with anyone without pard approval. And you're going to let *that* slide, too. You are *so* weak."

I took a deep breath and let it out. "He didn't fuck anyone tonight."

Caleb had joined the others crawling around Nathaniel. He plunged his face into Nathaniel's groin. Elizabeth moved back so he could do it. "I smell sperm, but not pussy." This after I knew that Nathaniel had washed thoroughly. Caleb stood, and Elizabeth moved back. He put his hand behind Nathaniel's neck and moved their faces together as if they were going to kiss, but he stopped just short of their lips touching. "I don't smell pussy here either. I don't think he had sex."

Zane raised Nathaniel's shirt as far as he could reach from his knees, then stood pushing the shirt up to Nathaniel's neck. The bite marks were almost black in the starlight. There was a bite mark on almost every inch of his back; the edges didn't touch, but I hadn't missed much. It made me blush.

Vivian looked at me, and I realized that she could probably smell the blood rushing to my cheeks.

Zane said, "He might not have had sex, but he had something."

Caleb came around to gaze at Nathaniel's naked back. "Someone had fun."

"Look at this," Elizabeth said. She drew them around to the front and the bite mark around his nipple. They ran their fingers over it, and Zane pulled Nathaniel's shirt off and threw it on the hood of the nearest car. Everyone but Merle, Gina, and Vivian swarmed Nathaniel, touching the wounds with fingers, hands, and tongues. Nathaniel's head went back, eyes closed, and I knew he wasn't exactly having a bad time, but . . .

"That's enough," I said.

Elizabeth pulled Nathaniel's shorts down, and I got a glimpse of just how not-unhappy he was.

I yelled, "That's enough!"

Elizabeth turned on her knees, her hands on his butt. "Whoever did this could have just as easily done more damage. They could have cut him up bad, and he would have let them do it. Wouldn't you have, Nathaniel?"

"I would have let her do anything she wanted," he said. Shit.

"You can't let him do this," Cherry said, standing and coming to me. "You can't let him skate on this, Anita. Or the next time whoever she is might just kill him."

"She won't kill him," I said.

"You know who it is?" she asked.

I nodded.

"Why didn't you say so?" Merle asked.

I took a deep breath and blew it out. "Because I'm not comfortable with it yet. But that's my problem not Nathaniel's." I held my hand out to him. "Nathaniel."

He pulled his shorts up so he could walk and came to me, squeezing my hand as he took it. I put him behind me, the line of our bodies touching. Physical contact was a way of saying he was under my protection. "I marked him."

Elizabeth laughed still on her knees. "I know he's your

favorite, but I never thought you'd outright lie for him."

"At least some of you can smell it if I lie. I marked his body, my teeth marks."

"Your anxiety level has been high since we got here. I can't tell if you're lying," Merle said. "And if I can't tell, then no one else here is alpha enough to be sure."

"It's gotten so that your scent doesn't change when you lie," Cherry said.

I'd heard of lying with your eyes, but never with your scent. "I didn't know you could do that, lie with your smell."

"I think lying just doesn't make you anxious anymore," she said.

Oh. "Being a sociopath does have its benefits," I said.

Caleb crawled towards us, in that gliding crawl the leopards could do. It was inhumanly graceful. He came close enough to put his face against my leg. I let him, because I figured that they'd get around to smelling me if I claimed Nathaniel. I just hadn't planned on it being one of Micah's cats first.

"He does have her scent on his skin."

"They sleep in the same bed most nights," Elizabeth said. She was on her feet, hadn't even snagged her hose.

Caleb rubbed his face against my leg. "She smells of wolf and . . . vampire." He gazed up at me. "Did you do your Ulfric and your master last night? Is that why Nathaniel doesn't smell like pussy, because there wasn't a hole left for him?"

I'd tried to keep my version of an open mind, but I decided then and there that I didn't like Caleb. "The pard has a right to question who Nathaniel sleeps with, because he doesn't have good judgment. None of you have the right to question me."

Caleb moved in one of those too-fast-to-see motions and shoved his face into my groin, hard enough that it almost hurt. I pulled the Browning without thinking about it and had it pressed against his skull before I realized it. Faster than normal—even for me.

Caleb raised his head back so that his forehead was pressed against the end of the gun. He stared up at me. "You don't smell like dick. Don't tell me you had at least three men with you in a bed and nobody got to fuck you."

"Caleb, I'm really beginning not to like you."

He grinned. "But you won't shoot me, because that would make Micah mad."

"You're right, I shouldn't have pulled the gun. I'm just not used to being able to draw a gun before I have time to think about it."

"I've never seen you move that fast," Zane said.

I shrugged. "Benefits of the change, I guess." I put the Browning back. I wasn't going to shoot him for just being obnoxious.

Caleb rested his cheek against my thigh, and I let him. My struggling would just amuse him, and he was behaving himself, relatively speaking.

Vivian touched my arm. "Are you really going to be one of us?"

"We'll know in about two weeks," I said.

"I am sorry," she said.

I smiled at her. "Thanks."

"You didn't top Nathaniel," Elizabeth said. "You're too squeamish to use your teeth on him like that."

I looked at her, and I let the darkness fill my eyes that was my own version of a beast. The look that said just how far down the well I'd fallen. "I'm not as squeamish as I used to be, Elizabeth. You might want to remember that."

"No," she said, "no, you're protecting him. He's been teacher's pet since day one. You're just afraid of what Micah will do. Afraid of what a real Nimir-Raj will do to him now that he's disobeyed a direct order." She stalked over to us. "And you should be afraid, Anita, you should be very afraid, because Micah's strong, strong the way Gabriel was strong. He doesn't flinch."

"I've heard enough about Gabriel to wonder if that's a compliment." Micah came out of the woods with a tall man beside him. Before Micah, I'd never slept with a man that I'd just met. I'd never slept with anyone that didn't make my heart beat faster, my skin react to the sight of him. As Micah glided from the trees, he was graceful and handsome, but I wasn't in love with him, and my body didn't react like I was.

I was both relieved and a little ashamed of that.

He was wearing shorts that had been cut off and allowed to go ragged at the hem. A white tank top seemed to glow in the dark, making his tan look even darker. A wide leather belt encircled his slender waist. He'd tied his hair back in a ponytail, but it was so curly that it didn't give the illusion of short hair; you knew even from the front that there was a lot more hair behind him. He seemed more delicate in clothes than he had without them. Maybe I just hadn't been paying attention to how small boned he was. There was something graceful in the way he was made, fine bones, smooth skin, very . . . refined, especially for a man. Jean-Claude was prettier, but he was too tall to ever be called delicate. Micah was delicate. The only thing that saved him from looking fragile was the play of muscles in his arms, the way he walked, like the world was his and everywhere he moved he was the center of the universe. It wasn't so much confidence as surety. So much potential in such a small package. He reminded me of somebody.

The man trailing behind Micah was dark complected, with very short, close cut hair, and there was something about his skin tone, even by starlight, that didn't look tan. He was handsome in a young, almost preppy sort of way, but muscled and very alert. That explained why Merle hadn't been glued to Micah's side. We'd had a change of guard. Micah introduced him as Noah.

I'd dreaded seeing Micah again—wondered what I'd say, how I'd feel. I wasn't nearly as uncomfortable as I'd thought I'd be. Maybe I'd have been more so if I hadn't been trying to defend Nathaniel's honor. Maybe because I didn't give any sign of what we'd done, Micah didn't either. Or maybe he was as confused as I was about it. Or maybe that's how casual sex works. I just didn't know.

"What is everyone so tense about?" Micah asked.

"Show him, Nathaniel."

Nathaniel never questioned, just stepped out from behind me and showed his back to the two men.

The bodyguard gave a sharp whistle. Micah's eyes widened, and he looked over Nathaniel's shoulder at me.

"You did this?"

I nodded.

"She didn't," Elizabeth said.

Caleb had risen as far as he could on his knees and was sniffing my stomach, his face pointed towards other things, but he was careful not to touch them. I don't think he would have sniffed my groin in front of Micah. Elizabeth was right on one thing. The leopards just weren't as afraid of me as they were of Micah.

"She smells of blood, too," Caleb said.

"Get away from me," I said.

He smirked, but he crawled away.

"Are you saying she has a wound on her like what he has on his back?" Elizabeth asked.

Caleb nodded as he crawled.

"Then she's lying. Whoever did his back, did her, too."

I sighed. "Am I really going to have to prove this?"

"I would take your word," Micah said, "but apparently your pard won't."

"It's just that we've wanted you to take one of us like this for so long," Cherry said. "And now . . . I think we'd have believed sex but not this. It just doesn't look like your work, and Elizabeth's right about one thing. Nathaniel is your favorite, and you do protect him."

Great, no one believed me. "Fine, just fine," I said. I started sliding out of the shoulder holster to let it flop at my back. Pulling my shirt out of my jeans wasn't a problem, even taking it off and laying it beside Nathaniel's shirt on the car hood wasn't a problem. I was wearing a very nice black bra. It was meant to be seen. Jean-Claude had been a very bad influence on my wardrobe. The problem was taking off the bra. I really didn't want to do that.

I undid the back, but held the front in place. "What happens when you see the bite mark?"

"If you show me a bite mark on your breast that doesn't have fang marks in it, I'll believe it was Nathaniel," Micah said.

Everyone had crowded close. I never liked being the center of attention, not for this kind of thing. "Give me a little breathing space guys."

They moved back a fraction of a step, and I thought, screw it. Everyone here, except Elizabeth and maybe the new bodyguard, had seen me naked. Oh, hell. I slipped the bra off and laid it on the hood with my shirt. I made absolutely no eye contact.

A hand came into view, and I grabbed the wrist. It was Caleb. "Nathaniel gets to take a bite, and I can't even touch it."

"No, you can't," I said.

Micah didn't come any closer. "Why did you mark him?"

I met his eyes, expecting to see accusation, or disdain, or something negative. But his face was very still. "I needed to sink my teeth into something. I needed . . ." I shook my head and looked away. "It wasn't sex I wanted. I wanted to feed."

"No." Elizabeth came crowding close. "No, you can't be Nimir-Ra for real, not for real." There was something close to panic on her face. I could smell her fear. She moved close enough that our bodies almost touched, and I could hear her heart thundering.

"Be afraid, Elizabeth, be very afraid," I said.

She half-turned away from me, and Micah said something at the same time, which is my only excuse for not seeing her fist coming. She rocked me back against the side of the Jeep, filling my mouth with blood and making my knees go weak. Only Cherry catching me around the waist kept me standing. The world swam in black and white streamers for a second. When my vision cleared, Elizabeth was being held by Micah and Noah, the bodyguard.

I pushed myself upright and stepped away from Cherry. She kept hold of my arm, and I let her for a second while I let the last of the vertigo slip away. I put a hand to my mouth and came away with blood.

Merle moved up to take Elizabeth's arm, and Micah came to stand in front of me. "Are you alright?"

"I'll be okay."

He touched my bare arms. It was the lightest brush of fingertips, but it made me shiver. My nipples grew hard, and there was nothing I could do to hide the sudden reaction.

I looked at him, and I didn't have to look up for it, not even an inch. "I don't know you, why . . ."

His arms slid behind my back, pressed our bodies together, and I suddenly couldn't get enough air. "I am your Nimir-Raj, Anita. There is no shame in that."

"You say *Nimir-Raj* like other people say *husband*."

He ran one hand through my hair, until his fingers were tight to my scalp, the other hand at the small of my back. "Our souls resonate like the sound of two perfect bells," he whispered, as his mouth hovered over mine. The comment was so romantic it was stupid, and I should have laughed at it, but I didn't.

He kissed me, a push of his lips, then his tongue slipped into my mouth. I knew when he tasted my blood, because his hands tightened on my body and his body reacted against me. He was too large for me not to feel him grow hard between our bodies.

I ran my hands over his arms, his shirt, and it wasn't enough. I wanted to touch his bare skin to mine, to drink in every inch of him, into every inch of me.

He kissed me as if he would drink me in, and I knew that part of the excitement was the fresh blood. I pulled his shirt out of his pants and ran my hands up his back. But it wasn't enough.

He drew back from the kiss, and I pulled his shirt over his head. Just pressing our bare chests against each other was better. It was as if my skin craved his skin. I'd never felt anything like it.

We held each other, both breathing too hard, our arms locked around each other, faces pressed to each other's shoulders, his breath hot on my neck.

"We don't have time for more," he whispered.

I nodded, my head still against his neck. It wasn't like I'd been planning on more, but . . . "I had to touch my skin to yours, why?"

"I told you, you are my Nimir-Ra, and I am your Nimir-Raj."

I pulled back enough to see his face. "That doesn't explain it to me."

He held my face in his hands, making very serious eye contact. "We are a mated pair, Anita. It's legend among the leopards that you can find your perfect mate, and from the first moment you have sex you're bound, more than marriage, more than law. We will always crave each other. Our souls will always call to each other. Our beasts will always hunt together."

It should have scared me, but it didn't. It should have made me angry, but it didn't. I should have felt a lot of things, but all I really felt was that he was right, and I didn't even want to try and talk him out of it.

"Richard's going to *love* this," Elizabeth said.

Merle and Noah took her down to her knees, in an abrupt gesture that had to hurt a little. I looked at her. "Thanks for reminding me what I was about to do, Elizabeth. I got distracted." I drew away from Micah, my fingers trailing down his arm, as if I couldn't quite bare to let go of him.

"Let her go, boys. She's my problem, not yours."

They looked to Micah, who nodded. Elizabeth stayed on her knees, as if uncertain what to do. She tried to get one of them to help her to her feet, but they ignored her and left her to stand on her own.

I took time to put my bra on as I walked back to my Jeep, the shoulder holster still flapping around my waist. I slipped it over my naked skin, and it was not comfortable, but I didn't want to take the time to put my shirt on. I knew what I was going to do now.

I walked to my Jeep, and everyone waited in the dark while I unlocked the door, scooted into the passenger seat, opened my glove compartment, and got out a spare clip of lead bullets. I'd started carrying an extra clip of lead bullets in the Jeep since I ran afoul of a few rogue fairies. You can shoot the fey with silver all day and it won't do much. But lead, they didn't like lead. Lead also had other uses, because it wouldn't kill a wereanimal. Only silver would do that. I walked back towards them, popping out the clip that was in the gun as I moved. I put the clip in my pocket, though it didn't fit well, and shoved the new clip home until it clicked.

Elizabeth finally started looking worried when I was about two cars away. Anyone else would probably have been running, but common sense wasn't one of Elizabeth's strong suits. I had actually pointed the gun at her while I very calmly walked closer, before she said, "You wouldn't dare."

I stared down the barrel of the gun at her, and I felt nothing. It was a big, cold empty place inside me—utterly calm, peaceful. But at the center of that empty peacefulness was a tiny kernel of satisfaction. I'd been wanting to do this for a long time.

I shot her twice in the chest, while she was still telling me I wouldn't shoot her. She went over backwards, spine bowing, hands scrabbling at the road, legs kicking while she tried to breathe.

Everyone had cleared a big space around her. I stood over her and stared down while she tried to breathe, and her heart struggled to beat around the hole I'd put in it. "You keep saying I can't kill you like a real Nimir-Ra by tearing your throat out, or gutting you. Maybe that's going to change soon, but until then I can shoot you, and you'll be just as dead."

Her eyes rolled desperately, while her body tried to cope with the damage. Blood welled out of her mouth.

"This time it wasn't silver. But fail me again, Elizabeth, in anything large or small, fail any member of this pard, and I will kill you."

She'd finally gotten enough air to talk. She spat out blood and the words, "Bitch, you don't even . . ." more blood, "have the guts . . ." dark blood from her mouth, "to shoot me for real."

Staring down at her, I realized something I hadn't before. Elizabeth wanted me to kill her. She wanted me to send her to wherever Gabriel was. She probably didn't realize that's what she wanted, but if it wasn't a death wish, it was close enough.

She lay there and healed, and cursed me, and told me how weak I was. I shot her in the chest again. She writhed and jerked, and the pool of blood just grew wider underneath her body.

I let the ammo clip fall into my hand from the gun, put it in my other pocket and got my main clip back in the gun. "Silver now, Elizabeth. Any more smart remarks?" I waited until she had healed enough to talk. "Answer me, Elizabeth."

She stared up at me, and there was something in her eyes, something that said we finally had an understanding. She was afraid of me, and sometimes that's the best you can do with people. I'd tried kindness. I'd tried friendship. I'd tried respect. But when all else fails, fear will do the job.

"Good, Elizabeth, I'm glad we understand each other." I turned to the others. They were staring at me like I'd sprouted a second head—a nasty one. Micah held out my clothes to me, and I slipped the shoulder holster off and the clothes on. No one said anything while I dressed.

When everything was back in place, I said, "Shall we go to the house now?"

Caleb looked positively ill. Micah looked pleased. So did Merle, and Gina, and all my leopards.

"You will not be allowed guns tonight in the lupanar," Merle said.

"That's what the knives are for," I said.

He looked at me as if he wasn't sure whether I was serious or not.

"Smile, Merle, she'll heal."

"I'm beginning to agree with what the wererats said."

"And what was that?"

"That you were scary enough all on your own without being Nimir-Ra."

"This isn't even close to as scary as I get," I said.

He raised his eyebrows at me. "Really?"

It was Nathaniel who said, "Really." My other cats echoed him, nodding.

"Then why aren't you afraid of her?" Gina asked.

"Because she doesn't try to be scary to us," Zane said. He looked down at Elizabeth on the ground, still unable to move much. "Of course, maybe the rules have changed."

"Only for bad little leopards," I said, "Let's get to the rats and go see the wolves."

"And the swans," Micah said.

"Swans?" I asked.

He smiled. "You just keep making conquests, Anita, even when you don't mean to do it." He held his hand out to me. I hesitated, then, slowly, I took it. Our fingers interlaced, and we walked together hand-in-hand down the road, and it felt good, and right, like I'd found a piece of myself that was missing. I left Zane behind to make sure Elizabeth didn't get run over by a car. We'd send Dr. Lillian back for her. The rest of the leopards followed behind Micah and me, and for the first time since I'd inherited the cats, I felt like I really was Nimir-Ra. And maybe, just maybe, I wouldn't fail them.

21

RAFAEL THE RAT king had a black limo. He'd never struck me as a limo kind of guy, and I said as much. He said, "Marcus and Raina used to put on quite a show for things like this. I and my rats are not willing to make a spectacle of ourselves, so the limo."

"Hey, I wore makeup," I said. That had made him smile.

We were riding in the back of the limo, with one of his wererats driving. Merle and Zane were in the front with the driver. Merle, because he'd objected to us all being split up among people he didn't know, and Zane, because I just didn't completely trust Merle yet. Though I had no illusions about which of them would win the fight, if it came to that. Richard had a werewolf or two that I would have bet on against Merle, but there was something downright scary about Micah's head bodyguard, a "something" that all of my leopards lacked. Not ruthlessness, more an ultimate practicality. You just knew Merle would do whatever needed to be done, no hesitation, no sympathy, just business. When that's pretty much how you operate yourself, you begin to recognize it in other people, and you watch them closely.

All the leaders got to ride in the back of the limo, which smacked of elitism to me, but it did allow us all to talk together, and no one else seemed to have a problem with it. I wasn't sure why it bugged me, but it did.

Rafael was tall, dark, handsome, and strongly Mexican. He spoke with no trace of an accent, or rather he sounded like he was from Missouri. He sat facing us. Yes, us. Micah and I sat across from him. We were not holding hands. We were not casting longing glances at each other. In fact, strangely, once I was away from the other leopards, I was uncomfortable around him. Maybe it was my usual discom-

fort that always set in after intimacy. But I wasn't sure, it
felt different. Or maybe it was the closer we got to seeing
Richard, the more I wondered what the hell I was doing.
Was I really going to tell Richard that I'd taken a lover,
another shapeshifter? We'd broken up before and gotten back
together, but if Richard thought I'd taken a permanent lover
besides Jean-Claude, it was over. I didn't want it to be over,
though part of me wasn't at all sure that dating Richard was
healthy for either of us. We weren't really good for each
other. Love is like that sometimes.

I pushed away serious thoughts and looked at the last
member of our little party. Donovan Reece was the new swan
king in town. He was about six feet tall, though it was hard
to tell exactly while he was sitting down. His skin was that
flawless milk and cream complexion that the beauty aids
promise when tan is out for a year or two, but Donovan's
was the real deal. He was whiter than I was, as white as
Jean-Claude, but there was a slight pink flush to Donovan's
cheeks, like perfectly applied blush. You could almost see
the blood flowing under his skin, as if it were nearly tran-
sluscent. He not only looked alive, but *very* alive, as if he'd
be hot to the touch.

His eyes were a pale blue-gray that shifted with his moods
like a summer sky that couldn't make up its mind whether
it wanted to be peaceful with fluffy white clouds or rain all
over your head. He was handsome in a clean-cut, preppy sort
of way, as if he should have been on a college campus somewhere pledging to a frat and chugging beers. Instead he was
going with us into a gathering of werewolves where he would
be the only nonpredator there. That didn't sound like a good
idea to me.

"You saved my swanmanes, Ms. Blake. You nearly got
yourself killed doing it. I couldn't risk the girls coming, they
are not . . ." He looked down at his folded hands, then raised
those changeable eyes to me. "They are like your Nathaniel—
victims."

"Nathaniel is driving my Jeep with the rest of my people
in it," I said.

Reece nodded. "Yes, but the shape of his beast is a pred-

ator. My girls are not. If they lost control and changed during
the meeting, they would be meat."

"I agree with you, Mr. Reece, but doesn't the same logic
apply to you?"

"I am a swan king, Ms. Blake, I will not change shape
unless I will it so."

Will it so. I'd never heard anyone put it quite that way.
Donovan Reece had a bad case of arrogance. I wasn't going
to talk him out of this. Rafael had been trying to before I
arrived. Micah never offered. He'd been very good about
letting me do all the talking. I liked that in a man.

"Can you fight?" I asked.

"I will not be a burden, Ms. Blake, don't worry."

I was worried, because I could smell the blood just under
his skin. I could almost see it flowing under his flesh. He
smelled like meat and blood, and heat. He smelled like food.
I'd been around shapeshifters that were prey animals, but I'd
never realized you could tell by smell what wasn't a predator.
I knew by the gentle scent of him that Reece's beast was
something soft and easily killed. Something that would struggle but not hurt me. I had to swallow hard, trying to slow
my pulse, but it would not slow. I wanted to drop on my
knees in front of him and sniff his skin, rub my face against
his bare arms until the short sleeves of his button-up shirt
stopped me. A white undershirt peeked out the top of the
blue and white striped shirt. I wanted to rip the shirt open,
send the buttons popping through the air, take a knife from
my wrist sheath and slit the undershirt, bare his naked chest
and stomach. But it wasn't the *ardeur*, it wasn't sex I was
thinking about. I wanted to see his stomach bare, to feel the
soft tissue under my mouth, my teeth, to bite into . . .

I covered my eyes with my hands, and shook my head.
What was wrong with me?

Micah touched my arm, gently. "Anita, what's wrong?"

I lowered my hands and looked at him. "He smells like
food."

Micah nodded. "Yes."

I shook my head again. "You don't understand what I'm
thinking. It's . . . frightening." I couldn't say it out loud. I

wanted to feed on him, or at least sink my teeth into his flesh. I think I could keep from actually feeding, but the urge to mark that flawless skin was so strong that I almost didn't trust myself.

"When you told me why you marked Nathaniel I knew it was the hunger." Micah said the last word like it should have been in capital letters. "It usually takes a few days, or weeks, before your first full moon, to have the hunger become a problem. It's okay to have thoughts, images in your head about feeding. It's normal."

"Normal." I laughed, but it was a harsh sound. "What I'm thinking isn't even close to normal." Again I couldn't bring myself to say it out loud.

"What do you want to do to Reece?" Rafael asked.

I looked across the seat at him. I opened my mouth to say, then glanced at Reece and stopped. "No, it's like telling a sexual fantasy in front of the stranger you just had the fantasy about. It feels that intimate."

"It *is* that intimate," Rafael said.

I looked back at him, and his dark eyes held my gaze. "If you tell Mr. Reece what you're wanting to do to him, then maybe he'll fly home."

"A rat is a prey animal, too," Reece said.

"Everything that is smaller is a prey animal," Rafael said, "but rats are omniverous. They eat anything that crosses their path, including humans, if they can't get away. A wererat is not a small thing, Mr. Reece, we are large enough to be the predators that our namesakes cannot be."

Reece was scowling at us all now. He shook his head angrily and leaned forward and shoved his wrist into my face. "Get a good whiff, all of you seem to like it."

"I wouldn't do that, if I were you," Rafael said.

"Listen to him, Reece," Micah said.

I didn't say anything because the scent of his flesh so close was intoxicating. It was like the most exotic perfume spread across silk sheets, with an undertone of fresh baked bread and some sweet jelly spread over flesh. I had no words for it, but it smelled better than anything I'd ever smelled in my life.

I was holding his wrist, pressing the thin skin against my lips, before I realized what I was doing. The skin was so tender, and I could smell the blood under that paper-thin layer of skin. I wanted to do more than smell it. I wanted to taste it, to feel his flesh give under my teeth, to have the blood gush warm in my mouth, to . . . I jerked away from him and crawled across Micah, across the seat to huddle in the far corner as far away from the swan king as I could get and not jump out the door.

There must have been something on my face, in my eyes that scared him, because his eyes widened, his full mouth opened slightly. "My God, your control really is that bad."

I managed to say, "Sorry."

"Do you really want to put yourself in the midst of hundreds of us?" Rafael asked.

"I won't be bluffed," Reece said. "You won't hurt me. From everything I've heard about Anita, and you, Rafael, you're the good guys." His gaze flicked to Micah. "Him, I don't know, but I do know that the swans have never thrown their allegiance to anyone. We've been autonomous. The fact that I'm supporting Anita and her pard will mean something to the wolves. We are weak as battle allies, but that any animal other than her own would ally with her pard will mean something to their Ulfric."

I huddled on the far corner of the seat, arms hugging my legs to my chest, a position not really meant to be performed while wearing a shoulder holster. But I was literally holding on to myself, hugging my control and my body. How was I ever going to get through tonight without doing something embarrassing, or deadly? How much worse was my control going to get?

"Your last swan king answered to their now-deceased lupa," Rafael said.

"So I've heard. Though technically he was a swan prince, not a king. I don't know what he owed the old lupa, but I'd guess it was something blackmailable, because I've found some polaroids that would make you blush."

I had to clear my throat twice before I could talk. "Kaspar refused to be in Raina's dirty movies, but the price for that was that he helped audition people for the films."

Reece looked at me. "Audition, what do you mean?"

I huddled and talked, but I was talking over the pulse in my head, the rush of blood in my body. I wanted to be next to Reece. I wanted to take a bite. Instead, I talked. "Kaspar could change form from swan to man at will. Raina used him to see if non-shapeshifters freaked when he changed in the middle of sex."

I felt Micah's reaction even from a distance. Reece looked horrified. "You saw this?"

"No, but Raina took great delight in telling me about it in detail. She tried to get me to watch one of his auditions, but I had better things to do."

"He did this willingly?" Reece asked.

"No," I said. "It was most definitely not his choice. He seemed to hate it."

"We see the fact that we can change forms at will as a great gift. We're one of the few shapeshifters that can do it with ease."

"Is that because your gift is either a curse or a born talent, rather than a disease?"

"We think so," he said.

"Kaspar was under a curse," I said.

"Are you wondering about me?"

Actually I was watching the way his Adam's apple bobbed when he talked, and wondering what it would feel like to fix teeth in his throat, but that was probably a fact best kept to myself. I kept talking, but I think both Micah and Rafael knew how ragged my control was. I hugged myself and kept talking, because silence filled with awful images, terrible desires.

"Yeah, I'm wondering," I said.

"I was born a swan king."

"You were born a swan king, not a swanmane. Does that mean you're male? Is swanmane only used for women?"

He looked at me, studying my face. "I was born to be their king. I'm the first king in over a century."

"Everybody else is chosen to lead, or fights for the right, but you make it sound like a hereditary monarchy," I said.

"It is, but it's not bloodlines that makes the difference, though being a swanmane either runs in your family or it doesn't. But I didn't inherit the title."

"Then how did you know?" I asked.

His eyes had gotten dark, dark gray like storm clouds. "The answer to that is somewhat intimate."

"I'm sorry, I didn't know."

"I'll give you the answer you seek, if you answer a rather delicate question for me."

We stared at each other. My heart rate was almost normal again. I could look at him without smelling the blood under his skin. Talking, listening, doing somewhat normal things had helped. I was a *person*, with speech and higher functions, not an animal. I could do this. Really. I eased out of my little ball, slowly.

"Ask and I'll let you know," I said.

"Did you kill Kaspar Gunderson, the last swan king?"

I blinked at him. That was unexpected. The sheer surprise made my pulse rate speed up a touch. "No, no, I didn't."

"Do you know who did?"

I blinked at him again. I wondered if I could lie and if he would be able to tell, or not. I finally stuck to the truth. "Yes."

"Who?"

I shook my head. "That I won't answer."

"Why not?"

"Because I would have killed Kaspar myself if he hadn't gotten away."

"I know he was responsible for several deaths, and that he tried to kill you and some of your friends," Reece said.

"It was a little more diabolical than that," I said. "He was taking money from hunters and supplying them with shifters."

Reece nodded. "He also made the swanmanes in his care into victims. I think that's what he and the old lupa shared—sexual sadism."

"That's why your girls, as you put it, were at the club with Nathaniel."

"Yes, I don't play those sorts of games, and they've grown to crave it."

I nodded. "I sympathize," I said.

"You've answered my questions truthfully, I can do no less." He started unbuttoning his shirt.

I looked at Micah, who shrugged. I looked at Rafael, who shook his head. Nice that none of us knew why he was undressing.

He left the overshirt tucked in but started pulling the undershirt out of his pants. He was about to bare his soft underbelly, and I wasn't a hundred percent sure my control was up to seeing it. My pulse was in my throat again. Since apparently neither of the men was going to ask, I asked, "Why are you undressing?"

"To show you the symbol of my kingship."

I stared at him. "Excuse me?"

Reece frowned at me. "Don't worry, Ms. Blake, I'm not about to flash you."

"I'm not worried about you flashing me, Reece, it's that . . ." but I never finished, because he'd bared the white, white skin of his stomach. In the darkened car I could still see the pulse just behind his belly button. Hell, I could almost taste it in my mouth, as if I'd already sunk teeth into that tender flesh, as if I was already eating my way through to more vital things. Something was odd about the hair on his chest. It was almost too fine, too thin, too delicate, running in a dainty white line down the center of his chest and spreading in an upside down triangle around his belly button then down into his pants.

I was on the floorboard crawling towards him, and I didn't remember getting there. I stopped, pressed against Micah's legs. "I don't remember leaving my seat. I'm losing time."

Micah put his hands on my shoulders. "It happens when your beast controls you, at first. The first few full moons will be almost complete blackouts, until you can begin to access the memories, and that will take work."

Reece had leaned back across the seat, half-reclining, and started to undo his belt.

This close I could see, or thought I saw what was wrong

with the hair on his chest and stomach. I tried to move forward, but Micah held me, hands tightening on my shoulders. I stretched out my hand and could brush fingertips over Reece's stomach. The light touch of my fingers over his skin made him stop fussing with his belt, made him look at me.

It wasn't hair. "Feathers," I said, softly, "like the down on a baby chicken, so soft." I wanted to run my hands over the surprising texture of it, to roll my body across the feathers and the heat of his skin. I could hear his heart in his chest pounding, and when I looked up, I met his gaze. His pulse was in his neck, like a trapped thing, and I could taste his fear. That one touch of my hand, the soft, dreamy quality of my voice had frightened him.

Micah's arms wrapped around my neck and shoulders and drew me in against his body with his legs on either side of me. He leaned over me, his face pressed to mine, and said, "Ssshhh, Anita, ssshhh." But it was more than a soothing voice. I could feel his beast calling to mine, as if he'd rolled his hand through my body, but so much larger. And that touch made my body tighten, grow wet. It brought my own pulse into my throat.

"What did you do?" I sounded breathless.

"The hunger can be turned to sex," Micah said.

"I wasn't going to feed," I said.

"Your skin went hot. Our bodies spike a temperature just before we change, like a human before a seizure."

I turned, still held in his arms, half-pinned between his knees. "You thought I was going to change?"

"It usually takes weeks, or at least the first full moon, for the first shape change. But you seem to be gaining problems faster than normal. If you changed for the first time here, I don't think either Rafael or I would be able to keep you from tearing Reece up."

"The first change is very violent," Rafael said, "and even the backseat of a limo doesn't have much room to hide or to run in."

Reece looked at me from only inches away, held in Micah's arms, his body, and I knew that it wasn't romantic. He was holding on in case the sex as distraction didn't work.

"She's been Nimir-Ra for over a year," Reece said.

"But still human, until recently," Rafael said.

Reece stared at me for a second or two, then said, "Very well, I have a birthmark in the shape of a swan. My family knew from my birth what I was meant to be."

"I've heard of such things," Micah said, "but I thought it was legend."

Reece shook his head. "It's very true." He sat back in his seat, tucking his undershirt down in front.

"Kaspar had feathers instead of hair on his head," I said.

"I'm told that if I live long enough that gradually that will happen to me." There was something in his voice that said he wasn't looking forward to the prospect.

"You don't sound happy," I said.

He frowned at me, rebuttoning his shirt. "You were human once, Ms. Blake, I've never been human. I was born a swan king. I was raised to take my place as their king from my earliest memories. You have no idea what that's like. I insisted on going to college, on getting a degree, but I may never get to use it, because going from place to place caring for the other swans keeps me very busy."

I stayed in the circle of Micah's body, but the tension was draining away. "I saw my first soul when I was ten, and my first ghost earlier than that, Reece. At thirteen I accidentally raised my dog that had died. I've never been human, Reece, trust me on that."

"You sound bitter about it," he said.

I nodded. "Oh, yeah."

"You must both accept who and what you are, or you will make yourselves miserable," Rafael said.

We both looked at him, and I don't think either look was friendly. "Give me a week or two to come to terms with being a kitty cat," I said.

"I am not referring to you being Nimir-Ra for real," Rafael said. "From the moment I met you, Anita, you have half hated what you are. As Richard has run from his beast, so you have run from your own gifts."

"I don't need a philosophy lesson, Rafael."

"I think you do, and badly, but I'll let that go, if it bothers you so very much."

"Don't even start on me," Reece said. "I've had people preach to me all my life that I'm blessed and not cursed. If my entire family couldn't convince me of it, you might as well not even try."

Rafael shrugged, then turned back to me. "Let's pick a different topic, because we are only minutes away from the lupanar, and I saw Micah's beast—his energy—pass through you, and your beast responded."

"You saw it?" I asked.

He nodded. "His energy is very blue, and yours is very red, and they mingled."

"So you got what, purple?" I said.

Micah hugged me a little tighter, a warning I think not to be flippant, but Rafael was more direct. "No jokes, Anita, if I saw it, so will Richard."

"He's my Nimir-Raj," I said.

"You don't understand, Anita. Micah said he thought birthmarks in the shape of your beast was legend. Well, until just now, I believed talk of a perfect mate was legend. Like true fated love, just a romantic story." Rafael's already serious face got even more solemn. "You recognize some bond from the beginning, so the stories go, but it's only after you have sex for the first time that your beasts can roll through each other's bodies. Only physical intimacy will allow such metaphysical intimacy."

I glanced down from those hard, demanding eyes, but finally made myself look back up. "What are you asking, Rafael?"

"Not really asking, telling. Telling you that I know you had sex with Micah, and that, even though Richard has dumped you and publicly declared that you and he are no longer a couple, he won't like it."

That was an understatement. I pulled away from Micah, and he let me go, no lingering touches. I moved away, and he allowed it. It earned him brownie points. "Richard dumped me, Rafael, not the other way around. He doesn't have any right to bitch about what I do."

"If he dumped her, then she's free to do what she wants," Reece said. "The Ulfric has only himself to blame."

"Logically, you're right, but when has logic dictated how a man acts when he sees the love of his life in someone else's arms?" The bitter way Rafael said it made me look at him, study his face. He sounded like he was speaking from experience.

"As Ulfric to my Nimir-Ra, he has no authority over me."

"Tonight is going to be dangerous enough, Anita. You don't need to make Richard angry."

"I don't want to make things worse. God knows they're bad enough as they are."

"You're angry with him for dumping you," Rafael said.

I started to say *no*, then realized he might be right. "Maybe."

"You want to hurt him."

I started to say *no*, then stopped and tried to think—really think—about how I felt. I was angry and hurt that he could just cast me aside. Okay, it hadn't been that simple, but still . . . "Yeah, I'm hurt, and maybe a part of me wants to punish Richard for that, but it's not just him dumping me. It's the mess he's made of the pack. He's endangered people I care about, and he's doing his usual Boy Scout shit that doesn't even work well in the human world, let alone with a bunch of werewolves. I'm tired, Rafael, I'm tired of it, and him."

"It sounds like you might have dumped him if he hadn't beat you to it."

"I came back to make it work. To see if we could make some sense of it all. But he has to give up that moral code of his that has never worked for him or anyone around him."

"To give up his moral code is to give up being who he is."

I nodded. "I know." And just saying that made me feel worse. "He can't change, and staying who he is is going to get him killed."

"And maybe you and Jean-Claude with him," Rafael said.

"Does everyone know that part?"

"It's standard that if you kill a vampire's human servant, the vampire may not survive the death. And if you kill a vampire, their human servants either die or go crazy. Logic dictates that killing either of you endangers the other."

I still didn't like that everyone knew that to kill one of us might kill all of us. Made it too damn easy for assassins. "What do you want me to say, Rafael? That Richard and I have a fundamental difference of philosophy in nearly every important area? There's more than one reason we didn't get married and live happily ever after. That maybe he's going to have to choose between survival or his morals? That I'm afraid he'd almost rather die than compromise those morals? Yeah, I'm afraid. It's going to kill a little piece of him to see me with Micah. I'd spare him if I could, but I didn't choose any of this."

"You take no blame in this," Rafael said.

I sighed. "If I hadn't left for six months maybe I could have talked him out of the democracy with his pack. Maybe if I'd been here a lot of things would be different, but I wasn't here, and I can't change that. All I can do is try and fix what got broke."

"You think you can fix this, all of it?" Rafael asked.

I shrugged. "Ask me again after I've met Jacob and seen how Richard deals as Ulfric with all of them. I need a feel for the dynamics before I say if it's fixable."

"How would you fix it?" Micah asked.

I glanced back at him. "If Jacob and a few others are the problem, then it's fixable."

"Killing the ones who stand against Richard won't fix things, Anita," Rafael said. "The experiment in democracy must end. Richard must begin being harsher to those who would stand against him. He must be frightening to them, or there will be another Jacob, and another after that."

I nodded. "You're preaching to the choir here, Rafael."

"If you are not his girlfriend, or his lover, then I fear that your influence over Richard will be slight."

"I'm not sure I had a lot of influence over him when we were dating."

"If you cannot talk sense into him, then eventually Richard will die and someone else, probably Jacob, will take over the pack. The first thing any good conqueror does is kill those closest and most loyal to the executed leader."

"You think Jacob is that practical?" I asked.

"Yes," Rafael said.

"What do you want me to do?"

"I want you to hide the fact that you and Micah are lovers."

I glanced behind me at Micah. He shrugged, face peaceful. "I told you I wanted you on any terms that you wished, Anita. What do I have to do to convince you I meant that?"

I searched his face, tried to find something false in it, and couldn't. Maybe he was that good a liar. Maybe I was just being too suspicious. "When we were with the leopards, just the leopards, I was completely comfortable with you. It felt right and . . . why doesn't it feel that way now?"

"You're having second thoughts," Reece said.

"No," Rafael said. He looked at Micah, and the two of them had major eye contact.

The staring contest went on so long that I had to interrupt. "One of you better start talking," I said.

Rafael inclined his head at Micah, as if to say, go ahead. I turned to Micah. "Alright," he said, and he seemed to be choosing his words carefully. I was almost positive I wasn't going to like this conversation. "Every pard, every group of shifters that is healthy has a group mind."

"You mean a group identity?" I asked.

"Not exactly. It's more . . ." He frowned. "It's more like a coven that's worked magic together for a while. They begin to be parts of a whole when it comes to working magic or healing. Together they form more than they form separately."

"Okay, but what's that have to do with why I felt more comfortable when it was just us leopards?"

"If you feel differently when the leopards are around you, then we're forming a group mind. It usually takes months to forge that kind of bond between shifters. Maybe it's just a bond with your own leopards. The change coming on could have set it in motion."

"But you think it's more than that, don't you?"

He nodded. "I think you're forming a group mind with

my pard, that in effect, the decision to join our pards into one unit has already been made."

"I haven't decided anything."

"Haven't you?" he asked. He looked so reasonable sitting there, hands clasped in front of him, leaning a little towards me. So earnest.

"Look, the sex was great. But I'm not ready to pick out china patterns here, you do understand that?" There was a feeling very close to panic in the pit of my stomach.

"Sometimes your beast picks for you," Rafael said.

I looked at him. "What does that mean?"

"If you are already a part of a group mind with his pard, then your beast has chosen for you, Anita. It's more intimate than being his lover, because it's not just him that you have a commitment to."

I gave him wide eyes. "Are you saying that I'm going to feel responsible for the safety and well-being of all his were-leopards as well as my own?"

Rafael nodded. "Probably."

I looked back at Micah. "How about you? You feel responsible for my people?"

He sighed, and it was heavy, not happy at all. "I didn't expect to form a bond this quickly. I've never seen it work this fast."

"And?" I said.

His mouth moved, almost a smile. "And, if we've really formed a group mind, then yes, I'll feel responsible for your people."

"You don't sound happy about that."

"Nothing personal, but your cats are a mess."

"Yours are so much healthier," I said, "Gina looks like someone who's been kicked once too often."

Micah's eyes hardened, and he searched my face. "No one talked to you. They wouldn't dare."

"No one tattled, Micah, but I could see it on her, smell the defeat. Someone's damn near broken her, and it's recent, or ongoing. She got a bad boyfriend?"

His face closed down. He didn't like that I'd figured that out. "Something like that." But his pulse had sped up, and I knew he was hiding something from me, something that scared him.

"What aren't you telling me, Micah?"

His gaze flicked past me to Rafael. "Will she be able to read my people more easily as time goes on."

"And you hers," Rafael said.

"Her people are pretty easy to read now," he said.

I was watching his face. He was controlling his body, keeping the tension out of it, but I could taste the speed of his pulse, and the fear. It wasn't just a small fear either. The thought that I could read his people so completely almost terrified him.

I laid my hand over his clasped ones, and he turned serious, guarded eyes to me. "Why does it scare you that I knew that Gina is being abused?"

He tensed under my hand and pulled away, gently, but he definitely didn't want me to touch him. "Gina wouldn't like it if you knew."

"As her Nimir-Raj, aren't you supposed to protect her from abusive assholes?"

"I've done my best for her," he said, but it sounded defensive.

"Kick the guy's ass and forbid her to see him again. It's a simple problem, don't complicate it. Or is she in love with him?"

He shook his head, eyes down, his hands clutching so tight that the skin mottled. His voice came out even, normal, but that terrible tension shook through his hands. "No, she's not in love with him."

"Then what's the problem?"

"It's more complicated than you could ever imagine." He looked up, and there was anger in his eyes now.

I started to reach out, to touch him, then let my hand fall back. "If we really are forming one pard. If I really am her Nimir-Raj, then no one's allowed to hurt her. No one hurts my people."

"The wolves took your Gregory," he said. The anger was still in his eyes, trembling down his hands.

"And we're going to get him back."

"I know you've had a hard life. I've heard some of the stories, but you talk as if you're young and naive. Sometimes no matter how hard you try, you can't save everyone."

It was my turn to look down. "I've lost people. I've failed people, and they've gotten hurt, and dead." I raised my eyes to meet his gaze. "But the people who hurt them, killed them, they're dead too. Maybe I can't keep everyone safe, but I'm damn fine at revenge."

"But the harm still happens. The dead don't really walk again. Zombies are just corpses, Anita. They aren't the people you lost."

"I know that last better than you do, Micah."

He nodded. Some of the terrible tension had eased away from him, but it left his eyes haunted with some old pain that was still raw.

"I've done everything I can for Gina and the others, and it's still not enough. It will never be enough."

I touched his hands, and this time he let me slide my hands over his. "Maybe together we can be enough for them all."

He searched my face. "You really mean that, don't you?"

"Anita rarely says anything she doesn't mean," Rafael said, "but if I were her, I'd ask first what the problems are before I promised to fix them."

I had to smile. "I was just about to ask, what is Gina into that's got you so terrified?"

He turned his hands so he was holding mine tight. He looked into my eyes. The look was not love, or even lust, but so serious. "Let's save your leopard first, then ask me again, and I'll tell you all of it."

The car slowed and turned. Gravel sounded under the tires. It was the turnoff to the farm that fronted the woods around the lupanar.

"Tell me some of it now, Micah. I need something here, now."

He sighed, looked down at his clasped hands, then up, slowly to meet my eyes. "Once we were taken over by a very bad man. He still wants us, and I'm searching for a home strong enough to keep us safe."

"Why are you afraid to tell me?"

His eyes widened a little. "Most pards don't want that kind of trouble."

I smiled. "*Trouble* is my middle name."

He looked a little puzzled. I guess I was the only one who liked film noir. "I'm not going to kick you guys out because of some asshole alpha. Let me know which way the danger's coming from, and I'll deal with it."

"I wish I had your confidence."

There was a weight to his gaze of such sorrow, such horrible loss. It made me shiver to see it, and he let go of my hands, sliding away from me just before Merle opened the door and offered a hand out. He didn't take the hand, but he slid out into the dark.

Reece followed him with a look at Rafael, as if the rat king had told him to get out and give us some privacy. I turned to Rafael. "You have something to say?"

"Be careful of that one, Anita. None of us know him, or his people."

"Funny, I was pretty much thinking the same thing."

"Even though he can make your beast roil through your body?"

I met his dark, dark eyes. "Maybe especially because of that."

Rafael smiled. "I should know by now that you are not a person to let her affections cloud her vision."

"Oh, it can be clouded, but never for long."

"You sound wistful," he said.

"Sometimes I wonder what it would be like to actually be able to just fall in love and not weigh the risks first."

"If it works out, it's the best thing in the world. If it doesn't work out, it's like having your heart torn out and chopped up into little pieces while you watch. It leaves a big hollow space that never really heals."

I looked at him, unsure what to say, but finally, "You sound like experience talking."

"I've got an ex-wife and a son. They live in a different state, as far away from me as she could drag him."

"What went wrong, if you don't mind me asking?"

"She wasn't strong enough to handle what I am. I didn't hide anything from her. She knew everything before we married. If I hadn't been so much in love with her, I'd have seen that she was weak. It's my job as king to know who's strong and who isn't. But she fooled me, because I wanted to be fooled. I know that now. She is what she is—not her fault. I can't even regret her getting pregnant right away. I love my son."

"Do you ever get to see him?"

He shook his head. "I get to fly in twice a year and have supervised visits. She's made him afraid of me."

I started to reach out to him, hesitated, then thought, what the hell. I took his hand, and he looked startled, then smiled. "I'm sorry, Rafael, more than I can ever say."

He squeezed my hand then moved back from me. "Just thought you ought to know that falling blindly in love isn't at all the way all those poems and songs make it sound. It hurts like hell."

"I did fall in love like that once," I said.

He raised his eyebrows at me. "Not since I've known you."

"No, in college. I was engaged, thought it was true love."

"What happened?"

"His mom found out my mother was Mexican, and she didn't want her little blond-haired, blue-eyed, family tree getting contaminated."

"You were engaged before they'd met your family?"

"They'd met my father and his second wife, but they are both good little Aryans, very nordic. My stepmother didn't like pictures of my mother being out, so they were all in my room. I wasn't hiding it, but that's how my almost mother-in-law took it. Funny thing, her son knew. I'd told him the whole story. It hadn't mattered until his mom threatened to cut him off from the family money."

"Now *I'm* sorry."

"Your story is more pitiful."

"That doesn't make me feel better," he said, smiling.

I smiled back, but neither of us really looked happy. "Ain't love grand?" I said.

"You can answer your own question after you see Richard and Micah in the lupanar together."

I shook my head. "I don't love Micah, not really, not yet."

"But," he said.

I sighed. "But I almost wish I did. It would make seeing Richard less painful. I don't know how I'm going to feel seeing him tonight and knowing that he's not mine anymore."

"Probably about the same way he'll feel when he sees you."

"Is that supposed to make me feel better?"

"No, it's just the truth. Remember that cutting you out of his life was forced on him. He loves you, Anita, for better or worse."

"I love him, but I won't let him kill Gregory. And I won't let him cost Sylvie her life. I won't let him take the pack down to wrack and ruin because of some idealistic set of rules that only he is paying attention to."

"If you kill Jacob and his followers without Richard's permission, then he may send the pack after you and your leopards. If you are not lukoi, not lupa, then to let their deaths go unpunished would make him appear so weak you might as well let Jacob kill him."

"Then what am I supposed to do?"

"I don't know."

Merle stuck his head in the car. "We've got wolves out here. Your rats are holding them back, but they're getting impatient."

"We're coming," Rafael said. He looked across the seat at me. "Shall we?"

I nodded. "I guess it'd be silly not to get out of the car."

He slid out to the edge of the seat, then hesitated, holding his arm out for me. Normally, I wouldn't have taken it, but tonight we were trying for a show of solidarity and style. So I stepped out of the car on the rat king's arm, like a trophy wife—except for the wrist sheaths and the two folding knives hidden in my clothing. Somehow I think trophy wives wear more makeup and less cutlery. But, hey, I haven't ever met a trophy wife, maybe I'm wrong. Maybe they know what I know, that the true way to a man's heart is six inches of metal between his ribs. Sometimes four inches will do the job, but to be really sure, I like to have six. Funny how phallic objects are always more useful the bigger they are. Anyone who tells you size doesn't matter has been seeing too many small knives.

22

THE CLEARING WAS huge, but not huge enough. The cars, trucks, and vans filled most of the available ground; some parked so far under the trees that the paint jobs had to have gotten scratched all to hell. There wasn't room for all the wererats to park, and the cars filled the gravel drive, until it was just another parking lot. Some people ended up parked beside the road, or so they said, as they drifted up through the trees. Rafael had brought all his rats—about two hundred of them. The treaty between the rats and wolves dictated that their numbers had to top at two hundred. Rafael had agreed to that on the understanding that the much larger werewolf pack—six hundred or so—would come to his aid if needed. No questions asked. Your enemies are my enemies sort of thing. He'd explained that in the last few minutes, and it meant that he was risking a great deal tonight. Made me feel guilty. Made me wish I'd found a way to sneak a gun into the lupanar. Truthfully, I hadn't even tried. Was I growing soft, overconfident, or just tired?

The tallest woman I'd ever seen came to stand beside Rafael and me. She was at least six feet six inches, broad-shouldered, and had the muscles that only serious weight lifting will give you. She was wearing a black sports bra across her tanned chest and a pair of faded black jeans. Her dark hair was caught back in a tight ponytail, leaving her face clean and startling with not a touch of makeup on it.

"This is Claudia. She's going to be one of your enforcers for the night," Rafael said.

I opened my mouth to protest, but he stared me into silence. His face so serious. "You have wereleopards, but only Micah has bodyguards. We can't afford to lose you Anita, not for something stupid like this."

"If I can't take care of myself, then what good is my threat?"

"Richard will have his Skoll and Hati. I will have my guards. Micah has his. Only you are without escort. Raina kept the wereleopards as an adjunct to the werewolves. They never really grew into a full pard, not really. Even Micah's people added to yours don't have the right personnel for a working pard. You have too many submissives and not enough dominants. So tonight you will have Claudia and Igor."

Zane said, "We can take care of Anita."

"No we can't," Nathaniel said.

I stared at him. He touched my arm. "Take the help, Anita, please."

"We can protect her," Micah said.

Merle echoed him.

"And if you have to choose between saving Micah, or saving Anita, which one will you choose?" Rafael asked.

Merle looked away, but Noah said, "Micah."

"Exactly."

"Won't your rats feel just as torn between you and Anita as my leopards would?" Micah asked.

"No, because I'll have bodyguards. My rodere, my gang, runs high to enforcers and professional soldiers. Why do you think that Raina and Marcus agreed to the treaty when Richard brought it to them? They'd never have allied with us if we weren't stronger than just our numbers."

"I don't . . ."

He actually touched my mouth with his finger. "No, Anita. When this is over, and you are truly Nimir-Ra, then you will need to advertise for enforcers of your own. Until then, I'll share."

I moved his hand away from my mouth. "I don't think this is necessary."

"I do," he said.

"I agree," Cherry said.

Finally, Micah said, "Agreed." Merle and Noah both gave him a funny look, then exchanged glances with each other.

"I haven't agreed to this," I said.

Nathaniel leaned into me, and said, "If you don't give in on this we'll still be standing here an hour from now."

I frowned at him.

He smiled and shrugged.

I turned to the bodyguard in question. She just looked at me, face impassive, as if it didn't matter to her one way or another. A man moved up beside her. He was about two inches shorter than she was, broader through the shoulders, and had so many tattoos that for a second I thought he was wearing a colorful long-sleeved shirt. His tank top was small and strained over the swell of his chest. Jeans and work boots completed his outfit. He was bald, with a tattoo of a dragon curling around his ears and the back of his skull. Even by starlight you could see the design of the tat was oriental and well done.

"How do you guys feel about putting your life on the line for someone you just met?"

"You saved our king's life," the man said. "We owe you a life."

"Even if it's your own," I said.

"Them's the breaks," he said.

I stared up at the woman. "You agree with that?"

"Like Igor says, we owe you one."

It always made me uncomfortable when people were willing to put my safety ahead of their own. I just wasn't really comfy with the concept of bodyguards, but, what the hell? I put my hand out. They exchanged glances between them, then shook my hand. Igor touched me like he was afraid I'd break, and Claudia tried to squeeze hard enough to make me cry uncle. I didn't. I smiled pleasantly at her, because I knew she wouldn't really hurt me. She just wanted to see if I'd squirm. My pleasant smile made her frown, but she let go of my hand. My hand actually ached just a little, and if my healing powers weren't up to it, I'd be bruised in the morning. Damn.

Rafael turned to some of his rats, giving instructions, leaving me alone with the two bodyguards. "Is Igor your real name?" I asked.

"Nickname," he said.

"What's your real name?"

He smiled and shook his head.

"What could be worse than Igor?" I asked.

His smile widened to a grin. "Wouldn't you like to know?"

It made me smile, and some tightness in my chest eased. You'd almost think I was relieved to have bodyguards of my own. Naw, not me. I didn't need no stinking bodyguards. I probably wouldn't need them, but extra muscle is like extra ammunition. If you need it, it's good to have it, if you don't need it, then it can always go back in the box.

Truth was, I felt more protective of my leopards than protected by them. Sad, but true. And I didn't entirely trust Merle, or Noah, or even Micah. He was keeping things from me, and I didn't like that. Some women are just never satisfied.

Rafael moved off through his people, giving them soft-voiced instructions. Micah moved up closer to me, with Merle and Noah at a very attentive distance. I looked at Micah and suddenly couldn't be this close and not touch him. I reached my hand out to him, his eyes widened, but he took my hand. His hand slid over mine in a play of pulsing warmth that almost took my breath away. I watched a similar reaction play on his face. What was going on? I drew my hand out of his, and it was like pulling it through melted taffy, so thick.

I looked up to find that, except for Claudia and Igor, we were surrounded by wereleopards, his and mine. The moment I met Nathaniel's eyes the power jolted through me. I turned from him to Cherry, and her pale eyes widened. The power was so thick it was like trying to breath something liquid, as if it hurt for the air to go down. The power leaped between me and Zane, Vivian, and Caleb, who was next in the circle. Caleb, who I didn't particularly like. But as soon as I searched his face, the power leaped between us, just as it had with the others.

He gasped, hand going to his chest, as if he'd felt it like a blow there. His voice came out strangled. "What are you doing?"

"She is being Nimir-Ra," Micah said.

I turned back to him, but in the turning crossed Noah's gaze first. The power stretched between me and this stranger, and the fear showed on his face. I was strangely calm; it felt right, good. Gina moved closer to Merle, and that drew my gaze. The power swung through her, from me. We were all like some great circuit of energy, sharing, flowing, growing. Tears trailed down Gina's face; she cried softly, clinging to Merle's arm. I met his eyes last, as if I was supposed to, and he tried to turn away, but it wasn't a matter of locking gazes, it was a matter of my attention going to him. The power, my power, my beast, noticing him.

The power lashed through him, because he fought it. He tried to shield, but he couldn't shield from this. It wasn't that I was strong enough to force him. I didn't try to push. It was more that the power recognized him, and something, maybe his beast, resonated with the power. He turned slowly to stare at me, and the look on his face was pained. It didn't hurt, it felt warm and good and frightening.

The power grew, wound tight and tighter, until it filled the air around us.

Claudia said, "What the hell are you doing?"

"Bonding," Rafael said, and he drew the two wererats out of our circle. The instant they were gone, the circle tightened, and it was like the pressure of a storm; my ears needed to pop, as if the pressure of the air had changed.

Micah moved to stand in front of me. The others formed a circle around us as if someone had choreographed it. We stared at each other and then reached a hand towards each other. It was hard to move forward, as if the air had grown solid and we had to push our way through. Our fingertips touched, and our hands slid together, quickly, easily, like a fish breaking through water into open air. We spilled around each other, our arms, our bodies touching completely, as if we could walk into the other's body like it was an open door. His mouth hovered over mine, and the power was there, breathing, pulsing, hot against my lips. I tried to be afraid. Tried to draw back, but I didn't want to. It was as if a part of me that I hadn't even known existed was in charge, and no amount of common sense—or doubts—could stop it.

It wasn't a kiss, it was a melding. The power poured in a scalding wave from his mouth to mine, from my mouth to his. I could feel the others, like lines of heat running out like spokes of a wheel, and Micah and I were the hub of that wheel. The power ran between us all, back and forth, liquid, burning, growing, growing, and melting. Melting boundaries, borders that kept us separate as people. It was as if Micah's body and mine were a door and we stepped into each other, closer than flesh could touch, closer than hearts could beat, and I felt his beast and mine roll through us, around us, as if the two great animals bound us together like a rope that ran through our flesh, our skin, our minds. And the beasts flared outward, traveled down those lines of power and smashed into each of the others. I felt it as a physical blow, felt them stagger as our twinned beasts traveled the circle and caressed their beasts in turn. And our beasts came home in a rush of heat, like standing in the middle of a bonfire, but it was also a glorious rush, a joyousness like nothing I'd ever felt. I caught, with that rush of power, glimpses into all the others.

I saw Gina tied to a bed and a man above her like a shadow, something evil that the power could not see clearly; Merle covered in wounds and blood, huddled against a wall, weeping; Caleb standing alone, covered in blood, his eyes haunted; Noah running down a hallway with screams chasing him, making him run faster; Cherry lying in a huge heap of warm bodies, beside Zane and Nathaniel and me; Zane's memory was of sitting at my kitchen table eating, laughing with Nathaniel; Vivian lying in Stephen's arms in their bed; Nathaniel's memory was of me marking his back, but the sense of peace I got from him with the memory was stronger than the sense of sex, as if some great burden had lifted from him; and I saw Gregory bound wrist-to-ankle behind his back, gagged, blindfolded, terrifed. He lay naked on a bed of bones. I knew this was not a memory, this was what was happening to Gregory right this minute. And I could see it, feel his terror, and I still didn't know where he was.

The power burst over us all in a wave of skin-rushing,

nerve-caressing contentment, as if we'd all walked into a strange room and suddenly realized that everything in it was familiar, every corner of the room was a key to our hearts, and the word that washed over me, was *home*.

Micah drew back first, shaking. I was crying, and didn't remember when it had started. I heard other people crying in the dark, and I looked beyond us and found that it wasn't just our people. Some of the wererats were crying, faces turned towards us with something like awe—or fear—in their eyes.

Something made me look past all of them to the wood's edge. Richard stood shirtless, dressed in nothing but jeans and whatever shoes he was wearing. The sight of him there painted with starlight and shadows made me catch my breath, not because he was beautiful, or because I wanted him—that always went without saying with Richard—but because he was suddenly, for the first time, wild. It wasn't his anger that made the difference. I saw him at the edge of the woods, the way you'd come unexpectedly upon a wild animal, like glimpsing deer in the twilight, or that flash as something large and furred raced in front of your headlights, and you knew it wasn't a dog and it was too big to be a fox. Richard stood there, and when our eyes met, it sent a jolt through me from the top of my head to the soles of my feet, and into the ground beyond. Whatever else Richard had been doing to screw up his pack's structure, one thing he'd done right, he'd embraced his beast. You could see it on him like a coat that he'd finally grown into, something that fit him, tailor-made.

Marcus, the old Ulfric, had always insisted on dressing up, so at a glance you'd know he was king. Richard stood there with no clothes to distinguish him, yet you knew he was king. Power makes you a monarch, and all the fancy robes in the world won't do the job without it.

We stared at each other across the clearing. Underneath that new veneer of comfortable power, the look on his face made my chest so tight it hurt. If I could have thought of anything to say that would have made things less painful, I'd have said it, but I couldn't think of any words that would help.

Jamil and Shang-Da came up on either side of him, and there was a look of anger on Shang-Da's face. Anger at me, I think. Jamil looked at Richard, as if he wished there was some way for him to guard Richard from this, as well as from bullets and claws. But with some things, even a really good bodyguard can't take the hit for you. This was one of those things.

Richard's voice came deep, loud, clear, untouched by the look on his face. "Welcome rat king of the Dark Crown Clan. Welcome Nimir-Ra and Nimir-Raj of the Blooddrinkers Clan. Welcome to the lands of the Thronnos Rokke Clan. The leopards have shown us this night what it truly means to be a clan, be they pard, lukoi, or rodere. They show us what we all strive for—a true melding of all our parts into a whole." Bitterness crept in at the last, but on the whole, it was a lovely speech, and more heartfelt than pleasant.

"Now join us at our lupanar, and we will see if you can win back your lost cat." There was anger in his voice, and I wondered if Gregory was about to pay the price for Richard's anger with me.

Richard turned and melted into the trees with Shang-Da at his side. Jamil spared a glance back at me, then followed.

Micah leaned close and whispered, "I owe you several apologies. I'm sorry your Ulfric had to see us this way."

"Me, too," I said.

"I said your cats were a mess, and I was wrong. You have made a home for your cats, and mine have nowhere to hide."

"What is wrong with all of you?" It wasn't perhaps the most diplomatic question, but it covered things.

"That is a very long story."

Merle leaned over us. He spoke so low that I almost couldn't hear him. "Be very careful for all our sakes."

They had some very serious eye contact. I said, "What is going on?"

Micah raised my hand and laid a brief kiss on the knuckles. "Let's save your Gregory. That has to be priority tonight, right?"

He smiled and tried to charm his way out of the stare I was giving him. I stared at him until the smile faded from his face and he dropped my hand. "Yeah, saving Gregory is priority for tonight, but I want to know what's going on."

"One problem at a time," Micah said.

I was getting the very distinct feeling that if they all could have lied to me forever, they would have. It wasn't lying, as much as hiding things from me. Things that had to do with blood and pain, and no matter how powerful they all were, Micah's pard wasn't a family, wasn't whole. Strangely, as messed up as me and my leopards were, we were a family. More so than Richard and his wolves, even. Richard was so busy fighting his moral battles and his power structure problems that there wasn't time for mending other things.

"Give me the *Reader's Digest* condensed version, Micah," I said.

"Gregory is waiting for you to rescue him."

"So give me a couple of sentences, but make it the truth, Micah."

"Micah," Merle said softly, but with force to his voice. It was a warning.

I looked at the big man. "What are you guys hiding, Merle?"

Micah touched my arm, brought my attention back to his face. "I told you that once we were taken over by a very bad man, who still wants us. I'm searching for someplace strong enough to keep us safe."

"Are you saying this guy will come looking for you here in St. Louis?"

"Yes," he said.

"Most alphas can take a hint," I said.

Micah shook his head. "This one won't. He will never give us up." He gripped my arm. "If you take us on, you'll have to deal with him eventually."

"Is he bulletproof?" I asked.

The question seemed to confuse him, because he frowned. "No, I mean, no, I guess not."

I shrugged. "Not a problem then."

He looked at me. "What do you mean? That you'll just kill him?"

It was my turn to look at him. "Is there any reason I shouldn't?"

He almost smiled, stopped, then frowned again. "Just kill him, just like that." It was almost as if he were thinking it over, as if it had never occurred to him.

Merle said, "He's a hard man to kill."

"Unless he's faster than a silver bullet, Merle, nobody's that hard to kill."

Rafael came slowly through the leopards, Claudia and Igor trailing him. "We've all been thinking of your leopards as lesser than us. What I just saw makes me envious."

"I know how the wolves work," I said. "And I know that they don't have a sense of home. First Raina and Marcus made them afraid of each other, now Richard's morals have him struggling to be safe. But you and yours seem pretty secure. How different is what I've done with my leopards from what everyone else is doing?"

"I've benefited from your loyalty, your sheer stubbornness. What I didn't realize until tonight is that you didn't save me just because I was your friend, or just because it was the right thing to do. You didn't risk yourself and your people to save me from torture because of the kind of moral rightness that Richard is fond of. You saved me because you could not bear the thought of leaving me behind." He touched my face, very gently. "Not from a sense of right and wrong, but because you are just that tenderhearted."

I looked at him. "I've been called a lot of things, but never that."

He chucked me under the chin like you would a child. "Don't make light of one of your better qualities. You love your people like a mother is supposed to love her children. You want what's best for them, even if that makes you uncomfortable, even if you don't like their choices."

I had to look away from the wonderment on his face, like he was looking at somebody else that couldn't be me. "You have never been their leopard queen in body, but you shamed us all tonight. It's not seeing your closeness to Micah that will torment Richard, though that will burn. It's that you gave us a glimpse of what we are all striving for, for our clans.

Richard believes his moral rightness will get him where your leopards already are."

I looked up at him. "My pard is not a democracy, and I have a hell of a lot more than just presidential veto when it comes to decisions."

"Richard knows that, better probably than anyone, and that will gall him, Anita. It will make him doubt himself."

I shook my head. "Richard always doubts himself when it comes to the lukoi. He'll never have surety about them until he has surety about who and what he is."

"First I have to accept the fact that you're kindhearted, now I have to accept the fact that you're insightful as well. I knew you were powerful, ruthless, and pretty, but that you have a mind and a heart besides is going to take some getting used to."

"Does everyone pretty much think I'm just a sociopath who happens to have magical abilities?"

"It's all you let people see," he said, "until now." He gazed out towards the circle of faces still turned to us. I saw a kind of hunger in their faces, and I knew that they had felt what I'd felt, a sense of true belonging, of being home within the circle—not of bricks or mortar—but of flesh, of hands to grasp, arms to hold, smiles to share. So simple, so rare.

All these months I'd been worried I'd fail the wereleo-pards. I thought failure meant them dying, or getting hurt. What I realized suddenly was that the true failure would have been if I hadn't given a damn. You can bandage a wound, set a broken bone, but not caring . . . you can't cure that, and you can't recover from it.

23

THE LUPANAR WAS a large clearing 100 yards by 150 yards. The clearing appeared to be flat, but actually it sat in a large smooth valley between hills. You couldn't notice it at night, but I knew that just beyond the trees that ringed the far side of the lupanar were steep hills. It had taken me more than one visit to find what lay beyond the trees.

Now all vision stopped at the far edge of the clearing. Torches that rose man-high were stuck into the ground on either side of the stone throne. The throne was a huge chair carved of rock, so old that there were places on the arms where countless generations of Ulfrics had touched it and worn away the stone. Probably the back and seat of the chair were worn as well, but they were covered by a spill of purple silk, suitably royal. There was something very primitive about the huge stone chair and its spill of cloth caught between the wavering golden light of the torches. It looked like a throne for some ancient barbaric king, someone who should wear animal skins and a crown of iron.

Werewolves, most—but not all—in human form, stood or crouched in a huge circle. There was one opening in the circle, which we walked through. The werewolves flowed behind us, like a door of flesh closing. The wererats spread around behind us and to either side, but we all knew if it came to a fight, we were outmatched, and outflanked.

Rafael and two very large wererats stood to one side of me. Donovan Reece, the swan king, was on the other side. Rafael had kindly given him a quartet of bodyguards. Micah stood just a little behind me, and my newly acquired bodyguards were just behind him. Our leopards had spilled out in a rough knot behind us, like a line of defense, before the main show of wererats.

Someone had hung cloth in the trees to one side of the throne. Black cloth, like a curtain, and it took a movement of the wind to draw my attention to it. It was held aside, and Sylvie came through, followed by a tall man I didn't know. Her face was less refined with no makeup, less soft. Her short hair curled neatly, but carelessly. She was dressed in the first pair of jeans I'd ever seen her in, with a pale blue tanktop and white jogging shoes.

The tall man was thin the way basketball players are thin—all arms and legs and lanky muscle. Most of that lanky muscle showed because all he wore was a pair of cutoff jean shorts. But he, like Richard, didn't need finery. He moved in a circle of his own grace and power, like a tiger stalking into view. Except there were no bars to hide behind, and I'd had to leave my gun at home.

He had short, dark hair that curled a little thicker than Sylvie's. His face was one of those that you couldn't decide was attractive or plain. It was made up of strong bones, long lines, thin lips on a wide mouth. I'd just about decided he was plain when he looked at me, and the moment I saw those dark eyes I knew I was wrong. Intelligence burned in there, intelligence and some dark emotion. He let anger flow over his face, and I realized the very force of his personality made him so striking that he *was* handsome, though it was the kind of handsome that would never come across in a still photo, because it needed movement, his vibrating energy to make it work.

I knew without being told that this was Jacob, and I knew something else. We were in trouble.

Richard came next, and he moved in his own vibrating spill of power. He glided as gracefully, filled with as much anger as Jacob, but he still lacked something, some edge that the other man had. An edge of darkness, maybe. All I knew for sure was that Jacob was ruthless. I could almost smell it on him. And Richard, for better, or worse, still was not.

I sighed. I'd thought if he could just once embrace his beast he'd be alright. He sat on the throne with the firelight playing in the loose waves of his hair, turning it to spun copper and burnished gold, the fire shadows playing on the

muscles of his chest, shoulders, arms. He looked the part of
the barbarian king, but there was still something in him,
something . . . soft. And if I could taste it, then so could Jacob.

I had one of those moments of clarity that comes sometimes. There was nothing that any of us could do to Richard
to make him truly harsh. He might act in anger, like he'd
taken Gregory, but no matter what the world did to him, there
would still be something in him that flinched. His only hope
for survival was to surround himself with loyal people who
wouldn't flinch.

Jamil and Shang-Da stood together to one side of the
throne, not too close, but not too far either. Shang-Da was
back in his usual monochrome black business dress: black
slacks, black shirt, black suit jacket, and the polished black
shoes. He always looked very *GQ*, even in the woods.

Jamil could dress up with the best of them, but he tried
to be appropriate to the situation. He had on jeans that looked
freshly pressed and a red muscle tank top that looked splendid against the darkness of his skin. He'd changed the beads
in his waist-length cornrowed hair to red and black. The
beads gleamed softly in the torchlight, as if they might be
made of semiprecious stones.

Jamil caught my glance. He didn't exactly nod, but he
acknowledged me with his eyes. Shang-Da avoided my gaze,
searching the crowd, but never quite looking at me. I think
if Richard would have allowed it the two of them would have
done whatever was necessary to secure his throne. But they
were hamstrung by Richard, and the best they could do was
work within his honorable trap.

Sylvie and I stared at each other for a few heartbeats. I'd
seen her collection of bones of her enemies. She got them
out periodically and handled them. She said it was comforting to run her hands over them. I personally liked a good
stuffed toy and some really fine coffee, but, hey, whatever
makes you feel better. Sylvie would do whatever needed doing, if Richard would only let her.

And if I'd still been lupa, hell, we had enough ruthless
people to get the job done, if Richard would just get out of

our way. We were so close, and at the same time we weren't even in the ballpark. It was more than frustrating. It was like watching a train race towards Richard, and we were all yelling, "Get off the tracks, get off the tracks!" Hell, we were trying to drag him off the tracks, and he was fighting us.

If Jacob was the train, then I could kill him and Richard would be safe. But Rafael was right. If it wasn't Jacob, it'd be someone else. Jacob wasn't the train hurtling to destroy Richard. Richard was.

His voice filled the clearing. "We gather here tonight to say good-bye to our lupa and to choose another."

There was a rash of howls and applause from about half of the pack. But dozens of the werewolves stood silent, watching. It didn't mean they were on my side. Maybe they were neutral, but it was good to notice who wasn't a rousing supporter of my being kicked out of the pack.

"We are here to stand in final judgment for one who has wronged our pack by taking our lupa from us."

There was less applause, fewer howls. It looked like the vote to condemn Gregory had been a close one. That made me feel better, not much, but a little. Though if Gregory died, I guess it really didn't matter.

"We are also here to give the leopards' Nimir-Ra a last chance to win back her cat."

The howls and applause stayed at about fifty–fifty, but the general atmosphere was definitely cooler. The pack wasn't lost, and it certainly wasn't wholeheartedly on Jacob's side. I said a little prayer for guidance, because this was more a political problem, and that wasn't one of my best things.

"It is business between the lukoi and the pard. Why are the rodere here, Rafael?" Richard asked. He talked like he didn't know us, very political, very distant.

"The Nimir-Ra saved my life once. The rodere owe her a great debt."

"Does this mean that your treaty with us is null and void?"

"I formed a treaty with you, Richard, and I will hold to that, because I know you are a man that honors his obligations and remembers his duty to his allies, but I owe Anita a personal debt, and I am honor-bound to uphold that as well."

"If it comes to fighting, who will you fight with, us or the leopards?"

"I hope most sincerely that it does not come to that, but I came with the leopards, and we will go with them, under whatever circumstances that leave-taking will be."

"You have destroyed your people," Jacob said.

Richard turned on him. "I am Ulfric here, Jacob, not you. I say what will be destroyed and what will not."

"I meant no offense, Ulfric." But his voice made the words a lie. "I meant only that if it comes to a fight the rats cannot defeat us. Perhaps their king would like to reconsider who he owes a debt of honor to."

"A debt of honor exists whether you want it to or not," Rafael said. "Richard understands what it means to owe an honor-debt. That is why I know that Richard will honor our treaty. I have no such assurances when it comes to other members of this pack."

There, he'd said it. It was as close to saying, *I don't trust you, Jacob,* as he could get. A spreading well of silence filled the clearing, so that the brush of cloth, the shift of a furred body was suddenly loud.

Richard's hands tightened on the arms of his throne. I watched him, because he was shielding so tight against me that I couldn't feel him, but I could watch, watch him think. "Are you saying that if I am no longer Ulfric that the treaty no longer holds?"

"Yes, that is what I'm saying."

Richard and Rafael stared at each other for a long time, then the faintest of smiles played on Richard's lips. "I have no plans to step down as Ulfric, so the treaty should be secure for a while, unless Jacob has other plans."

That one statement sent a wave of unease through the waiting werewolves. You could feel it, see it spreading out through them, as if they smelled a trap of some kind.

Jacob looked surprised, shocked. He was a perfect stranger, but I watched the confusion play over his face, as he tried to think of what to say. If he said he had no designs on the throne, then he would be foresworn, and the shapeshifters were a little touchy about things like that.

Jacob was either going to have to lie or declare his intentions, and the look on his face said clearly he wasn't ready to do that.

A woman's voice came from the right, clear and ringing like she'd had stage training. "Aren't we getting distracted from the business at hand? I for one am very interested in choosing the new lupa."

The woman was tall, but built all of curves, voluptuous the way that movie stars in the fifties had been. She seemed soft, feminine, yet she stalked over the ground in a swaying glide, half sex on the hoof and half predatory, like she'd lure you in by playing victim, fuck you till you cried for mercy, then eat your face off.

She was even wearing a dress, one that clung to her curves and had a neckline so low that you knew she had to be wearing a bra. Breasts that size didn't do perky without some help. She stalked barefoot, her deep red hair styled and perfect, falling just above her shoulders in a burnished shine.

"We'll get around to choosing the new lupa," Richard said.

She dropped to her knees in front of the throne, folding the dress under her thighs, very ladylike, though making sure to lean forward enough for Richard to look straight down her cleavage. I didn't like her much.

"You can't blame us for being eager, Ulfric. One of us," and she hesitated, making it clear that the "us" was for politeness' sake, "will be chosen lupa and become your mate all in one glorious night." Her voice had dropped to a sultry murmur, still loud enough to be heard.

Nope, didn't like her. I had no room to bitch with Micah standing beside me, but that didn't matter. Logic had nothing to do with it. I wanted to grab a handful of that bottle-dyed red hair and hurt her. It wasn't until Micah touched my arm that I realized I'd been caressing one of the knives in its wrist sheath. Sometimes I touch my weapons when I'm nervous; sometimes my body just betrays my thoughts. I forced my hands to be still, but I was so not happy.

"Go back with the other candidates, Paris," Richard said. He was carefully not looking at her, as if he were afraid to. That didn't make it better; it made it worse.

She leaned forward, putting a hand on his knee. He jumped. "You can't blame us for being eager, Ulfric. We've all wanted you for so *very* long."

Richard's face had thinned down with anger. "Sylvie," he said.

Sylvie smiled, and it was a smile of pure evil pleasure. She grabbed Paris's wrist and dragged her, none too gently, to her feet. Paris was a good two inches taller, but Sylvie's power, her beast, made her seem ten feet tall.

"The Ulfric told you to go back and stand with the other candidates. Do it." She gave Paris a little shove towards the crowd. The woman stumbled, but regained her composure, smoothing the tight dress down over her thighs.

Sylvie had turned to walk back to her place at Richard's side, when Paris said, "I heard you liked it rough."

Sylvie froze, and I didn't need to see her face to feel the instant rage that radiated from her. I knew before she turned, slowly, muscles tense, that her eyes had bled to wolf amber. "What did you say?"

"Sylvie," Richard said, voice soft. It wasn't a command, it was a request. I think if he'd made it a command, she'd have fought it, demanded some sort of satisfaction. But it was a request . . . She turned back to Richard.

"Yes, Ulfric."

"Take your place, please."

She went back to take her place as Freki on his right side. But the anger boiled around her like nearly visible heat off a summer road.

"I apologize to the swan king, for not recognizing him sooner, but we've only met once."

"Yes," Donovon Reece said, "I remember."

"Welcome to our lupanar. I would give you safe passage among us, but I have to know why you are here before I can do that."

"I am here because the Nimir-Ra rescued my swanmanes from the people that nearly killed her. She risked her life for them. I am here at her side tonight as an ally."

"I can't grant you safe passage, Donovan, because if things go badly it will be a fight. If you're Anita's ally, you'll be in the middle of it."

"She risked her life for my people, I can do no less."

Richard nodded, and I watched an understanding pass between them. Birds of an honorable feather, so to speak.

"Does she save every shapeshifter she comes across in trouble?" Jacob asked, and he made it derisive.

Richard started to say something, and Sylvie stepped forward, touching his arm. He gave a small nod, and let her speak. "How many of us has Anita saved from torture or death?" She raised her own hand.

Jamil stepped out from around the throne and raised his own. All my leopards raised their hands like a small forest of gratitude. Rafael raised his hand. I finally spotted Louie, his lieutenant, and Ronnie's boyfriend. He gave a small nod to me and raised his own hand.

Richard stood and raised his hand. There were other hands here and there. Then Irving Griswold, mild-mannered reporter—and werewolf—stepped forward. His glasses reflected the firelight so that he looked blind. He looked like a tall, slightly balding cherub with eyes of flame.

"What would have happened if Anita hadn't saved Sylvie from the vampire council's torture? Sylvie's strong, but what if she had broken? She's dominant enough to call most of us in, to have forced us to give ourselves over to the vampire council." Irving raised his hand. "She saved us all."

Hands went up among the werewolves until nearly half of them were holding a hand up. It made my throat tight, my eyes burn. I wasn't going to cry, but if someone hugged me, I couldn't be sure of that.

Louie stepped forward, small, dark, and handsome, with his short black hair cut neat. "Rafael is a strong king, so strong that if the vampire council had broken him, none of us could have refused his call. We would all have been at their mercy. You all saw what they did to him and how long it took him to heal. Anita saved all the rodere in this city."

The rats raised their hands—all of them.

Sylvie said, "Look around you, do you really want to lose Anita as our lupa? Most of you remember what it was like with Raina. Do you want to go back to that?"

"She's not lukoi," Jacob said.

A few others said the same thing, but not many. "If your only objection to her is that she's not a werewolf," Sylvie said, "then that's a poor excuse for losing Anita."

"Losing her," Jacob said, "this is the first time I've ever seen her. I've been with this pack for five months and this is the first time I've set eyes on your precious lupa. We can't lose something we never had."

There was a lot of support for that, a lot of howls, cries of *yeah*, applause even. I couldn't blame them on this one. I stepped forward, moving until I stood alone between my allies and the throne. Silence fell around the clearing, until you could hear the torches sizzling.

Richard stared down at me. I could meet his eyes now. I made sure my voice carried when I said, "Jacob's right."

Sylvie looked startled. So did Jacob. And there was movement behind me as people startled. "I haven't been much of a lupa to the Thronnos Rokke Clan, but I didn't know I was supposed to be. I was just the Ulfric's girlfriend. I had my hands full with the wereleopards, and I trusted Richard to take care of the wolves. The leopards had no one but me." I turned and faced the crowd. "I was human, not fit to be lupa, or Nimir-Ra." The crowd's murmur was louder this time.

"I don't know if you've all heard, but there was an accident in the fight that saved the swanmanes. I may be Nimir-Ra for real in a few weeks. We won't know for sure, but it seems likely."

They were quiet now, watching me, human eyes, wolf eyes, rats, leopards, but every face held intelligence, a burning concentration. "There's nothing I can do about that. We'll just have to wait and see, but my leopard did not injure me on purpose. I will stake my word of honor on that. I'm told that Gregory stands accused of killing your lupa." I raised my hands out from my body. "Here I stand, alive and well. If you lose me as your lupa, it won't be because Gregory took me from you, it will be because you choose to let me go. If that's what you want, fine. I don't blame you. Until tonight, until just a few minutes ago, I didn't think I was doing a very good job as Nimir-Ra, let alone trying to be human lupa. Now, I think maybe I was wrong. Maybe if I'd stayed around more, things would be better. I did what I thought was right at the time. If you don't want me as lupa, that's your right, but don't punish a fellow shapeshifter for an accident that happened during a fight where he saved me from getting my heart dug out of my chest."

"A pretty speech," Jacob said, "but we've already voted, and your leopard has to pay the price, unless you're shapeshifter enough to win him back."

I looked back, not at Jacob, but at Richard. "Richard, please."

He shook his head. "I can't undo the vote, Anita. I would if I could." He sounded tired.

I sighed. "Fine, how do I win Gregory back?"

"She needs to stop being lupa, before she can be Nimir-Ra." This from Paris, who though back in the crowd, still managed to make her voice ring over the clearing.

"I thought you voted me out as lupa," I said.

"They have," Richard said, "but to make it official by our laws, there's a ceremony that will sever your ties to us."

"Is it a long ceremony?" I asked.

"It can be," he said.

"Let me get Gregory out first, then I'll do whatever lukoi ceremony you want me to do."

"You have the right to refuse to step down," Sylvie said.

I looked at Richard.

"You have that right." His face, his voice, were neutral as he said it. I couldn't tell if he was happy or sad about the idea.

"What happens if I refuse?"

"You'd have to defend your right to be lupa, either by one-on-one combat with any dominant that wants the job . . ." And he stopped there.

Sylvie looked at him, but it was Jacob who finished. "Or

you can prove that you're lupa enough to keep the job by annointing the throne."

I just looked at him and shrugged. "Annointing the throne—what does that mean?"

"You fuck the Ulfric on the throne in front of all of us."

I was already shaking my head. "Somehow I don't think either Richard or I are up to public sex."

"It's a little more complicated than that," Richard said. He looked at me, and there was so much in his eyes—anger, pain—that it hurt to hold his gaze.

"Sex alone isn't enough. We'd have to have a mystical connection between our beasts." He was quiet, and I thought he'd finished, but he hadn't. "Like you have with your Nimir-Raj."

We stared at each other. I couldn't think of anything good to say, but I had to say something. "I'm sorry." My voice came out soft, almost sad.

"Don't apologize," he said.

"Why not?"

"It's not your fault, it's mine."

That made me widen my eyes at him. "How so?"

"I should have known you'd have that kind of bond with your mate. You're more powerful as a human than most true lupas."

I looked at him. "What are you saying, Richard? That you wish you'd made me one of you while you had the chance?"

He lowered his eyes as if he couldn't bear for me to see his expression anymore. I stepped closer, close enough to touch him, close enough so that his vibrating energy spilled like a march of insects across my skin. It made me shiver. But I felt something else, something I'd never felt before, not with Richard.

My beast spilled over my skin and reached out like a playful kitten to swat at Richard's power. The energies sparked against each other, and I could almost see the play of colors in my head, like flint and steel being struck against one another, except in technicolor.

I heard Richard catch his breath; his eyes were very wide.

His voice came hoarse, almost strangled. "Did you do that on purpose?"

I shook my head. I didn't trust myself to speak. The sparks had quieted, and it was as if I were leaning against a nearly solid wall of power, his and mine, as if I could have leaned against that energy and it alone would have kept us from touching. I finally found my voice, but it was a whisper. "What's happening?"

"The marriage of the marks, I think," he said, voice almost equally soft.

I wanted so badly to reach through that power and touch him, to see if the beasts would roll through each other like they did for Micah and me. I knew it was silly, he was wolf, and apparently I was leopard, so our beasts wouldn't recognize each other. But I'd loved Richard for so long, and we were bound to each other by Jean-Claude's marks, and I carried a piece of his beast inside me. I had to know. I had to know if I could have with Richard what I had with Micah.

My hand moved through the power, and it was like shoving it into an electric socket. The energy was so strong, it bit along my skin. I was reaching for his shoulder, a nice neutral place to touch someone, when he rolled off the side of the throne and was suddenly standing beside it. He'd moved so fast I couldn't follow with my eyes. I'd seen the beginning of the movement and the end, but the middle—I'd blinked and missed it.

"No, Anita," he said, "no, if we can't ever touch again, I don't want to feel your beast. We may not be the same animal, but it will be more than anything we've ever had between us. I couldn't bear it."

I let my hand fall to my side and stepped back far enough from the throne for him to regain his seat. I wasn't apologizing again, but I wanted to. I wanted to cry for both of us, or scream. I know the universe has a sense of irony, and sometimes you get reminded just how sadistic that can be.

I would finally have to accept his furry half, because I'd have one of my own. I could be Richard's nearly perfect lover, at long last, and we could never touch each other again.

24

RICHARD WAS SITTING on his throne again, and I was standing back far enough for him to feel safe. Rafael, Micah, and Reece had all moved up beside me, a half-circle of kings at my back. It should have made me feel secure. It didn't. I was tired, so terribly tired, so terribly sad. Even with Micah at my back, I couldn't stop looking at Richard, couldn't stop wondering, *what if.* Oh, I knew, I'd never have allowed him to make me a werewolf on purpose, but a small part of me wondered. But I told that small part to shut up, and I got down to business.

"I want Gregory back unharmed. How do I do that, according to lukoi law?"

Richard said, "Jacob." That one word sounded as tired as I felt.

Jacob stepped forward, obviously pleased with himself. "Your leopard is here on our land, and we've done nothing to hide his scent trail. If you can track him, you can take him home."

I raised my eyebrows at him. "I have to follow a scent trail like a dog?"

"If you were a true shapeshifter, you could do it," Jacob said.

"This isn't a fair test," Rafael said. "She hasn't had her first change. Most of our secondary powers don't appear until after our first full moon."

"It doesn't have to be scenting," Richard said, "but it must be something that only a shapeshifter could do. Something that only a shifter powerful enough to truly be Nimir-Ra, or lupa, could do." He was looking at me when he said it, and there was something in his eyes, something he was trying to tell me.

"That doesn't sound very fair either," Micah said.

Richard kept looking at me, willing me to understand him. I didn't know why he didn't just drop his shields and let me see his mind.

Almost as if Richard had read my mind, he said, "No werewolf or wererat or wereleopard, no one can aid you in finding your leopard. If anyone interferes in any way, then the test is invalid, and he'll die."

"Even if that help is metaphysical?" I asked.

Richard nodded. "Even if."

I looked at him, studied his face, and frowned. I finally shook my head. I'd had a vision of where Gregory was, and under what circumstances, but it gave me no real clue. All I really needed to do was ask someone where a hole was with bones at the bottom. But I couldn't ask anyone there. Then I had an idea.

"Can I use my own metaphysical abilities to aid me?"

Richard nodded.

I looked at Jacob, because I knew the objection would come from him, if anyone. "I don't think your necromancy is going to help you locate your leopard."

Actually, it might have. If the bones Gregory was lying on were the largest burial sight in the area, then I might be able to track the bones and find him. Or I might spend all night chasing after piles of buried animals or old Indian graves. I had a faster way, maybe not better, but faster.

I sat down on the ground, Indian fashion, resting my hands lightly on my knees.

"What are you doing?" Jacob asked.

"I'm going to call the munin," I said.

He laughed, a loud bray of sound. "Oh, this should be good."

I closed my eyes, and I opened that part of me that dealt with the dead. I've heard Marianne and her friends describe it to be like opening a door, but it's so much a part of me that it's more like unclenching a hand, like opening something in my body that is as natural as reaching across the table for the salt. That might sound like an awfully mundane description of something mystical, but the mystical stuff truly is a part of everyday life. It's always there, we just choose to ignore it.

The munin are the spirits of the dead, put into a sort of racial memory bank that can be accessed by lukoi who have the ability to speak with them. It's a rare ability; to my knowledge no one in Richard's pack could do it. But I could. The munin are just another type of dead, and I'm good with the dead.

In Tennessee, the munin of Verne and Marianne's pack had come quickly and eagerly—so very close to being real ghosts, crowding around me, eager to speak. I'd practiced until I could pick and choose who would join with me and be able to communicate. It was close enough to channeling or mediumship that Marianne had suggested I could probably do this with normal ghosts, if I wanted. I didn't want to. I didn't like sharing my body with another being, dead or alive. Creeped me out, yes it did.

I waited to feel the press of the munin spreading around me, like a ghostly card deck that I could shuffle and pick the very card I wanted. Nothing happened. The munin did not come. Or rather a gathering of munin did not come. There was always one munin that came when I called, and sometimes when I didn't.

Raina was the only munin of Richard's pack that traveled with me always. Even in Tennessee, surrounded by munin from a different clan line, Raina was still there. Marianne said that Raina and I had an etheric bond, though she wasn't sure why. I'd managed to call munin hundreds of years old, and Raina, the very recently dead, came with more than ease. But Marcus, the previous Ulfric, remained elusive. I'd thought with my newfound control I'd be able to call him, but not only was Marcus not there, no one was there. The clearing was empty of spirits. It shouldn't have been. This was the spot where they consumed their dead, each pack member eating the flesh to take on the memories and courage, or faults, of the recently dead. They could choose not to feed, but it was like the ultimate excommunication. Raina had been a bad person, and I wondered sometimes what exactly you had to do to get excommunicated from the lukoi.

Raina had been so bad that I would have let her go, but she was powerful. Maybe that's why she was still hanging around.

Though hanging around implied she was like the phantoms of Verne's pack, and she wasn't. She was internal to me, as if she poured out from inside my body, rather than pouring into me from outside. Marianne still couldn't explain why it worked that way for Raina and me. Some things you just accept and work around, because to do anything else is to butt your head against a brick wall; the wall will not break first.

Raina filled me like a hand inside a glove, and I was the glove. But I'd worked a long time to be able to control her. We'd worked out a deal of sorts. I used her memories and powers, and I let her have some fun. The problem was that Raina had been a sexually sadistic nymphomaniac when alive, and death hadn't changed her much.

I opened my eyes and felt her smile curve my lips, felt my face take on her expression. I rose to my feet in a graceful line, and even my walk was different. Once I'd hated that; now I shrugged it off as the price of doing business.

She laughed, full throated, the kind of laugh that makes a man look in a bar. Her laugh was deeper than mine, contralto, a practiced seduction of sound.

Richard went pale, hands gripping the arms of his throne. "Anita?" he made it a question.

"Guess again, my honey wolf."

He flinched at the nickname. In wolf form Richard is a ginger color, like red honey, though I'd never really thought of it like that before. Trust Raina to think of something thick and sticky when she looked at a man.

Her words came out of my mouth. "Don't be bitchy, when you called me for help."

I nodded, and it was my voice that explained to Richard's confused frown. "I was thinking something less than charitable about her. She didn't like it."

Jacob walked towards me and stopped when I looked at him with Raina's expression. "You can't have called munin. You're not lukoi."

Strange, but it hadn't even occurred to me that being a leopard might mean I couldn't call munin. It might explain why the other munin hadn't come when I called. "You said my necromancy wouldn't help me, Jacob, can't have it both ways. Either I'm lukoi enough to call the munin, or I'm necromancer enough to help myself."

We—Raina and me—stalked towards the tall, shirtless man. Raina liked him. Raina liked most men. Especially if the man was someone she'd never had sex with, and among the pack that had been a short list. But Jacob and more than twenty others were new. She looked out over the pack and picked out the new faces. She hesitated over Paris and didn't like her either. You can't have too many alpha bitches in one pack without them fighting amongst themselves.

I felt something I hadn't felt before from Raina—caution. She didn't like how many new people Richard had allowed into the pack in such a short space of time. It worried her. I realized for the first time that it hadn't just been love that made Marcus put up with her as lupa. She was powerful, but more than that, in her own twisted way she did care about the pack, and she and I were in perfect agreement on one thing: Richard had been careless with it. But we both felt we could fix it. It was almost scary that the wicked bitch of the west and I were in such perfect agreement. Either I had been corrupted, or Raina had never been quite as corrupt as I thought. I wasn't sure which idea bothered me more.

Of course, she thought we should seduce Richard into letting us kill a few select people, and I was still hoping that a slightly less sweet reason would prevail. Raina thought I was a fool, and I wasn't sure I didn't agree with her. Scarier and scarier.

"Anita." Richard said my name again, hesitant, as if he wasn't sure I was in there.

I turned, one hand coming up to my hair, flinging it back from my face. It was Raina's gesture, and I watched that one movement make not only Richard, but Sylvie and Jamil behind her, nervous. No, frightened.

I could smell their fear. Raina's laugh bubbled out of my mouth, because she liked it. I didn't. I never liked it when my friends were afraid of me. My enemies, fine, but not my friends.

"I'm here, Richard, I'm here."

He stared at me. "The last time I saw you call Raina's munin you weren't able to think like yourself with her inside you."

"I really didn't leave you for all these months just because I was afraid of how close we all were. I left to get my shit together, and part of that was learning how to control the munin."

Raina said, "Control me? You wish." She hadn't said it aloud, only in my head. It had taken me a long time to realize that some things were said out loud and some things weren't. It was confusing, but you got used to it.

I said aloud what I'd seen in vision. "I saw Gregory in a hole, naked, tied up, lying on a bed of bones. Where is it?"

Raina showed me in images. It was like a fast-forward picture show, but the images came with emotions, smashing into me, one after the other. I saw a metal cap that screwed down with a tiny airway on top that let in enough light for you to see, if the sun was high enough. There was a rope ladder that spilled down into the dark and was taken up when it wasn't needed. I was Raina kneeling on a bed of bones, a human skull next to my knee. I had a syringe and injected its contents into a dark-haired man that was chained like I'd seen Gregory chained, ankles to wrists. He was gagged and blindfolded. When the needle went in, he whimpered and started to cry. The drugs were to keep him from changing.

I turned him over on his side and saw that a bone fragment had cut into his naked groin. I bent towards the smell of fresh blood, fresh meat, and the absolutely intoxicating stink of fear that came off the man. Not man, lukoi. I clawed my way up from my memory before Raina pressed our lips over him. I shoved it away from me, but I could still smell the fear, the drugs sweated out on his skin, the smell of soap from where Raina had cleaned him up, daily, before the abuse began. I knew his name had been Todd, and he'd talked to a reporter about the lukoi, helped them set up a blind with a camera on a full moon, for money. Maybe he had deserved to die, but not like that. No one deserved to die like that.

I came to myself lying on the ground in front of the throne, tears drying on my face. Jamil and Shang-Da were standing between me and the crowd that had moved to help me. Claudia and Igor were facing off with them, and Rafael had Micah by the arm, trying to convince him not to fight his way to me. Merle and Noah were moving up to join Claudia and Igor. This was all about to go to hell.

I propped myself up on my arms, and that small movement froze everyone in place. My voice came out hoarse, but mine. "I'm okay. I'm okay."

I'm not sure they believed me, but the tension level started to drop almost immediately. Good, I had enough problems tonight without a free-for-all breaking out.

I looked up at Richard, and all I could feel was anger. "Is that how you're going to kill Gregory, just leave him down in the oubliette until he rots?" My voice came out soft, because if I lost control of it, I wasn't sure how much other control I'd lose. I knew Raina. She wasn't gone. She'd want her "reward" first. She'd done her job. I knew where Gregory was. I even knew how to get there. She'd earned her prize. I didn't dare lose control of myself with her waiting like a shark just under the water.

"I told them to put Gregory some place far away from me. I didn't tell them to put him there."

I got to my feet slowly, even my body movements controlled, muscles almost stiff with adrenaline and the need to lash out. "But you left him there. Who's been going down and pumping him full of drugs to keep him from turning? You don't have Raina to do the dirty work anymore. Who was it? WHO WAS IT!" I screamed it into his face, and the rage was all she needed. She poured over me, and the last control I might have had drowned because I wanted to hurt Richard. I wanted to do it.

I hit him, closed-fist, turning my body into it, twisting my hand at the end, putting all I had into it. I did what they taught us to do in martial arts class if it was for real. I aimed not at Richard's face, but at a point two inches inside his face; that was the real goal.

I was back in a protective stance before Jamil and Shang-Da had time to react. I felt them move towards me and felt others move forward, too. The very thing I'd been trying to avoid, and I'd set it off. Raina was laughing in my head, laughing at us all.

25

RICHARD WAS LEANING over the arm of his throne, hair covering his face, when Sylvie grabbed me. I didn't fight her. Her fingers dug into my arms, and I knew I'd be bruised in the morning. Or maybe not. Maybe I'd heal it. Jacob was watching it all astonished and pleased.

I glanced back and found the bodyguards fighting. The leopards and rats were spreading out, the wolves beginning to close around them. I opened my mouth to yell something, but Richard's voice boomed over the clearing.

"Enough!" That one word froze us all, and we turned shocked faces to him. He was standing in front of his throne, blood spattered across one shoulder and on his upper chest. One side of his mouth was a red ruin. I'd never been able to do that kind of damage before.

He spat blood and said, "I'm not hurt. Some of you here have been inside the oubliette. You know what it was when Raina still lived. Can you blame the Nimir-Ra for hating me for putting her leopard down there?"

You could feel the tension begin to ease as the wolves pulled back. Richard had to order Jamil and Shang-Da to back off, and they and Claudia and Igor pushed at each other, like bullies that still didn't know who was tougher. I hadn't realized that Claudia was nearly six inches taller than Jamil, until they drew away from each other and he had to stare up at her to glare into her eyes.

Sylvie whispered in my ear, "Are you okay?"

I looked up at Richard. He was still bleeding. "Other than embarrassed, yeah."

She let me go, slowly, as if not sure that I was safe to let loose. She hovered right next to me, between me and Richard, until he motioned her back.

He stood in front of me, and we stared at each other. Blood still dripped from his mouth. "You pack a hell of a punch now," he said.

I nodded. "If you'd been human, what would that have done to you?"

"Broken my jaw, or maybe my neck."

"I didn't mean it," I said.

"Your Nimir-Raj will teach you how to judge your strength. You might stop going to your martial arts classes for a while, until you understand how your body works now."

"Good advice," I said.

He put his hand to his mouth, and it came away bright with blood. I had the urge to take his hand and lick the blood off of it. I wanted to climb his body and press my mouth to his and drink him down. The image was so vivid that I had to shut my eyes, so I couldn't see him standing there half-naked, bloodied, as if that would help me not want him. It didn't. I could smell his skin, the scent of him, and the fresh blood, like icing on a cake that I couldn't have.

"Go get your leopard, Anita."

I opened my eyes and looked up at him. "The oubliette was one of the things you fought against under Marcus. You said it was inhuman. I don't understand how you could use it."

"He was in there for nearly a day before I asked where they'd put him. That was my fault."

"But who's idea was it to put him there?" I asked.

Richard looked at Jacob. The look said it all.

I walked over to the tall man. "You never called me, Jacob."

"You got your leopard back, so what does it matter?"

"If you ever touch one of my people again, I'll kill you."

"You going to pit your kitty-cats against our pack?"

I shook my head. "No, Jacob, this is personal, between me and you. I know the rules. I make this a personal challenge between you and me, and that means that no one can help you."

"Or you," he said. He stared down at me trying to use his height to intimidate me. It didn't work. I was used to being short. I gave him dead eyes until the smirk on his face faltered and he took one step back, which pissed him off. But he didn't retake that step. Jacob might be able to kill Richard in a fair fight for dominance, but he'd never be a true Ulfric.

I stepped up close to him, close enough that a good insult would have made us touch. "There's something weak in you Jacob. I can smell it, and so can they. You may challenge Richard and win, but the pack will never accept you as Ulfric. You winning will tear them apart—it'll be a civil war."

Something flashed through his eyes.

"That doesn't scare you. You don't care," I said.

He stepped back from me, averting his eyes, his face. "You heard the Ulfric. Go fetch your cat before we change our minds."

"You couldn't change your mind with a hundred watt bulb and a team of helpers."

He frowned at me then. Sometimes my humor is a little esoteric, or maybe it's just not funny. Jacob didn't find it funny.

"Go with her, Sylvie, make sure she gets everything she needs to get him out of there and back to the cars safely," Richard said.

"Are you sure you want me to go?" she asked.

"We'll stay with him," Jamil said. None of them tried to hide the fact that they were looking at Jacob while they said it. Not only didn't they not trust him, but they didn't care that he knew that they didn't trust him. How had things downgraded to that? What had been happening in the pack that no one had told me about yet? Plenty, from the looks on everyone's faces.

"She can't go home until after the ceremony to break her ties with the pack," Jacob said.

"She will go home when I say she goes home," Richard said, voice low and full of that deep tone he got just before his voice crawled to something growling and inhuman.

"The candidates have all come prepared tonight, Ulfric, dressed to please you."

"Then they can dress to please me another night."

"You disappoint . . ."

"You are about to overstep yourself, Jacob." There must have been something in the way he said it, because Jacob finally shut up and gave a small bow. But he managed to make the movement mocking, and even from a distance you could tell he didn't mean it. But he lowered his eyes with his head, as he bent at the waist. It's a mistake to take your eyes off your opponent.

I asked, "Am I still lupa until the ceremony?"

"I suppose," Richard said.

"Yes," Sylvie said. And they looked at each other.

"Good." I kicked Jacob in the face, though not as hard as I'd hit Richard. You didn't have to kick as hard to do the same kind of damage.

I watched who in the pack made movements towards us and who didn't. I didn't see what everybody did, but I saw enough. Nobody near the throne made a single move to stop me, or help him.

Jacob staggered to his feet. His nose had burst like a piece of overripe fruit. Blood poured from his face, over his hands, like crimson water. He yelled at me, voice thick with the blood running down his throat. "You broke my nose!"

I was in a defensive stance, the one I'd learned in kenpo, just in case, but he didn't try to hit me back. I think he knew that there were too many people close at hand aching for an excuse to hurt him. Jacob was weak, but he was smarter than he looked, and not quite as arrogant.

"I am lupa of the Thronnos Rokke Clan. Maybe just for tonight, but I am lupa here. And he is Ulfric, and you will by God show some respect!"

"You have no right to question the Geri of this clan. I've *earned* my place. You just fucked the Ulfric."

I laughed, and it startled him, made him unsure. "I know pack law, Jacob. It doesn't matter how I got the job. All that matters is that I am lupa, and that means that except for the Ulfric, my word is law."

His eyes looked uncertain, and the first faint trace of fear showed, like a bitter scent on the wind. "You are about to be dethroned as lupa. Your word means nothing here."

"I am Ulfric here, Jacob, not you, and I say whose word

means something and whose does not. Until we have the ceremony breaking her ties with our pack, Anita is still lupa, and I will support what she says."

"And I," Sylvie said.

"And I," Jamil said.

Shang-Da said, "I support my Ulfric in all things."

"Then let's have a little irony," I said. "Since it was Jacob's idea to put Gregory down in the oubliette, let him take Gregory's place."

Jacob started to protest, hands still trying to stop the blood flow from his nose. "You can't do that."

"Oh, but she can," Richard said, and there was a coldness in him that I'd never seen before. He wouldn't have come up with the idea himself, but he liked it. It let me know just how frustrated he'd been with Jacob.

"Great," I said. "Shall we all walk like civilized wereanimals to the oubliette and rescue Gregory?"

"I will not go willingly down in that hole," Jacob said. His voice sounded a little funny, what with all the blood and his nose smashed to hell, but he sounded sure of himself. He shouldn't have been.

"Your Ulfric and your lupa have both decreed you will go," Sylvie said. "To refuse the order is to refuse their authority."

Jamil continued, "To refuse their authority is to be declared outlaw from the clan."

Jacob glared at me when he said, "I will obey my Ulfric, but I do not acknowledge the Nimir-Ra as my lupa."

"If I say she is lupa, then to deny that is to question my authority as Ulfric," Richard said.

Jacob's eyes flicked to Richard. "We voted her out as our lupa."

"I'm voting her back in," Richard said, voice deep and quiet, but loud enough that it carried.

"Take another vote," Jacob said, still trying to slow the blood from his face. "It will go against her again."

"No, Jacob, you misunderstand me. I said, I am voting her back in, not you, not anyone else, just me."

Jacob's eyes widened. "You've preached about democracy in action since I joined this clan. Are you going back on all of it now?"

"Not on all of it, but we don't vote for Freki, or Geri, or for Hati and Skoll. We don't vote for Ulfric. Why should we vote for lupa?"

"She's fucking the Nimir-Raj. For that alone she should be cast out as lupa."

"That's my problem, not yours, not the pack's."

"You going to fuck her, too? You think the Nimir-Raj will share?"

Richard started to say something, but Micah spoke first, taking a step from the rest, his guards flanking him. "Why don't you ask the Nimir-Raj?"

Richard looked at me, a question in his eyes. I shrugged.

"Ask him, Jacob," Richard said. The blood had almost stopped dripping from Richard's mouth.

"You mind if the Ulfric fucks your Nimir-Ra?" Jacob was still bleeding like a stuck pig. His chest, stomach, even the front of his shorts were soaked with blood.

"I've agreed to any arrangement that Anita wishes, as long as she remains my Nimir-Ra and lover."

"You'd share her with another man?" Jacob said, voice thick with disbelief.

"With two other men," Micah said.

That got almost everybody staring at him. I glanced at him, but mostly watched everyone else's reaction, especially Richard's. The others looked shocked, Richard looked thoughtful, as if Micah had finally done something he didn't hate.

"She is the Master of the City's human servant. Being my Nimir-Ra has not changed that. I've felt the mark that binds them together, and it is not something that will break, as, apparently, the mark that binds her to the Ulfric will not break."

"Nothing binds her to the Ulfric but her stubbornness, and his," Jacob said.

"You think so?" Micah made it a question.

Jacob looked uncertain. The blood from his nose was finally beginning to slow. "You've seen more than I've seen, if you think they still have a special bond."

"More than any of us have seen." This from Paris, who had pushed her way to the front of the crowd.

"I am Nimir-Raj, of course I see more than you do." His voice made it so logical, so matter of fact.

"I am Geri, third in line to the throne."

"Noah is my third in line. I think if you ask him he will say he did not see what I saw either. Third in line to be Nimir-Raj, or Ulfric, is not the same as being the real thing."

I fought not to give Micah the look of gratitude that I wanted to give him. We were still deep in bluff territory, and not safely out the other side yet.

"You can't mean to share your lupa with two other men," Paris said. She'd pushed her way to stand in front of Richard, with her back to me. She was either being insulting, or stupid. Maybe both.

Richard looked down at her, and it wasn't a friendly look. Somehow I didn't think Paris ever had a very good shot at being lupa, not with Richard in charge anyway. "What I and my lupa do, or don't do, is none of your business."

I saw her back stiffen, as if he'd hit her, and maybe he had hit her pride. She'd really believed she could seduce him into picking her. I could have told her that sex wasn't the key to Richard's heart. He liked it well enough, but it wasn't one of his top priorities, not if it interfered with other things that were. It had been the same mistake that Raina had made with him, or one of the mistakes she'd made with him. Raina had never really understood Richard, either.

"You can't just arbitrarily decide you don't need a vote for this," Jacob said.

"Yes," Richard said, "I can."

I stepped up beside Jacob. "That's what being Ulfric means, Jacob."

"You're going back to a dictatorship after all the high-minded talk," Jacob said.

"For tonight, it's sufficient that Anita is my lupa, and that's not going to change. We'll discuss everything else later."

"I say we put it to a vote whether the pack wants to go back to being a dictatorship," Jacob said.

"If you don't have someone set that nose, it may heal crooked," I said.

He glared at me. "You stay out of this."

Richard called up a man with short brown hair and a neat mustache. He shrugged a backpack off his shoulders and began taking out medical supplies. "Fix his nose," Richard said and then turned to Sylvie. "When he's bandaged up, pick some people and escort Jacob to the oubliette."

There were murmurings in the crowd. One clear voice that I hadn't heard before said, "You can't do that."

Richard looked up, searching the crowd, and they fell silent under his gaze. His power rolled out from him like a burning invisible fog, something that clung to your skin and made it hard to breath. They avoided his eyes; some even dropped down into submissive postures, their bodies low to the ground, eyes rolled up, arms and legs held close, making themselves seem small and defenseless, clearly asking not to be hurt.

"I am Ulfric here. If there is any among you that disagree with that, then you are free to challenge the next in line, and the next after that, until you are Freki, then declare yourself Fenrir, and you can challenge me. If you kill me then you can be Ulfric, and you can set any damn policy you want. Until that time, shut the fuck up and follow my orders."

I don't think I'd ever heard Richard cuss. The silence was thick enough to cut. It was Jacob who cut it, like I knew he would. He pushed the mustached doctor away impatiently, while the shorter man tried to pack his nose with what looked like gauze. "Anita shows back up, and so does your backbone. Does she kill and torture for you like Raina did for Marcus?"

Richard's fist struck out in a blur that I couldn't follow. It was almost magical. One moment Jacob was standing, the next moment he was on the ground with his eyes rolled back inside his head.

Richard turned to the rest of them, the dried blood decorating his nude upper body, his hair turned to spun bronze in the torchlight. His eyes had gone wolf amber, and looked more gold than normal against his darker than usual summer tan. "I thought we were people, not animals. I thought we could change the old ways and make something better. But we all felt it tonight when Anita and her leopards melded. Something safe and good. I've tried to be temperate and kind, and look where it's gotten us. Jacob said Anita is my backbone. No, but she's doing something right, something that I've missed. If you won't take kindness, then we'll have to try something else." He looked at me with those alien eyes, and said, "Let's go get your leopard. We need to get him out of the oubliette before Jacob comes to." And he stalked off through the trees and left the rest of us to trail after. There was no question about what to do next. We followed Richard into the trees. We followed the Ulfric, because you're supposed to follow your king, if he's worthy of the name. For the first time ever I thought maybe, just maybe, Richard was going to be Ulfric after all.

26

THE OUBLIETTE WAS a rounded metal lid set in the ground. The metal lid sat in the middle of a clearing scattered with tall, thin trees. Honeysuckle bushes ringed the lid on one side; leaves were so thick on the ground that the area looked untouched. I would never have found it if I hadn't known it was there.

Oubliette is French for a little place of forgetting, but that's not a direct translation. Oubliette simply means little forgetting, but what it is, is a place where you put people when you don't plan on ever letting them out. Traditionally it's a hole where once you push someone in they can't get out. You don't feed them, or water them, or talk to them, or anything to them. You just walk away. There's a Scottish castle where they found an oubliette that had literally been walled up and forgotten, discovered only during modern remodeling. The floor was littered with bones and had an eighteenth-century pocket watch in among the debris. It had an opening where you could see the main dining hall, could have smelled the food, while you starved to death. I remembered wondering if you could hear the person screaming from the dining hall while you ate. Most oubliettes are more isolated, so that once you put him away, you never have to worry about the prisoner again.

Two of the werewolves in nice human form knelt by the metal and began unscrewing two huge bolts in the lid. There was no key. You screwed the lid in place and just walked away. Fuck.

The lid lifted off, and it took both of them to carry it away. Heavy, just in case the drugs didn't keep the adrenaline from pumping enough and cause the change. Even in animal form you'd still have a hard time getting through the lid.

I walked to the edge of the hole, and the smell drove me back. It smelled like an outhouse. I don't know why it surprised me. Gregory had been down there for what, three days, four? In the movies they talk about you starving to death, the romantic stuff—if such horror is really romantic— but no one ever talks about your bowels moving, or the fact that when you have to go, you have to go. It's not romantic, it's just humiliating.

Jamil brought a rope ladder and attached it with large metal clips to the side of the hole. The ladder fell away into the darkness with a dry, slithery sound. I forced myself to crawl back to the edge of the oubliette. I was prepared now for the smell, and underneath the ripe smell of life in too small a space was a dry smell, a dry, dusty smell. The smell of old bones, old death.

Gregory wasn't the strongest person I knew, not even one of the top hundred. What had it done to him to lie there in the dark with the stench of old bones, old death, pressed against his body? Had they explained to him how they'd leave him there to die? Had they told him every time they screwed the lid back in place that they weren't coming back, except to drug him?

The hole was like a perfect blackness, darker than the star-filled night sky, darker than anything I'd seen in a long time. It was wide enough for Richard's broad shoulders to have scooted down into the dark, but barely. The longer I stared at it, the narrower it seemed to become, as if it were some great black mouth waiting to swallow me down. Have I mentioned that I'm claustrophobic?

Richard came to stand beside me, peering down into the hole. He had an unlit flashlight in his hand. Something must have shown on my face, because he said, "Even we need some light to see by."

I held my hand out for the flashlight.

He shook his head. "I let this happen. I'll get him out."

I shook my head. "No. He's mine."

He knelt beside me and spoke softly, "I can smell your fear. I know you don't like close places."

I stared back into the hole and let myself acknowledge just how afraid I was. So afraid that I could taste something flat and metallic on my tongue. So afraid that my pulse was hammering in my throat, like a trapped thing. My voice came out calm, normal. I was glad. "It doesn't matter that I'm afraid." I touched the flashlight, tried to pull it from his hand, but he held on. And, short of playing tug of war—which I would probably lose—I wasn't getting it away from him.

"Why do you have to be the toughest, the bravest? Why can't you, just once, let me do something for you? Going down in the hole doesn't scare me. Let me do this for you. Please." His voice was still soft, and he was leaning into me enough so that I could smell the drying blood on him, the richness of fresh blood in his mouth, as if some small cut had not healed completely.

I shook my head. "I have to do it, Richard."

"Why?" and his voice held the first hint of anger, like a slap of warmth.

"Because it scares me, and I have to know if I can."

"Can what?"

"If I can crawl down into that hole."

"Why? Why do you need to know that? You've proven to me and everyone here that you're tough. You don't have anything left to prove to us."

"To me, Richard, I have something left to prove to me."

"What difference would it make if you couldn't climb down in that stinking hole? You'll never have to do it again, Anita. Just don't do it."

I looked at him, at the puzzlement in his face, his eyes, which had bled back to their normal, perfect brown. I'd been trying to explain shit like this to Richard for a few years now. I finally realized that he would never understand and I was tired of trying to explain myself, not just to Richard, to everybody.

"Give me the flashlight, Richard."

He held on with both hands. "Why do you have to do

this? Just tell me that. You're so scared your mouth is dry. I can taste it on your breath."

"And I can taste fresh blood on yours, but I have to do it because it scares me."

He shook his head. "This isn't courage, Anita, this is stubbornness."

I shrugged. "Maybe, but I still have to do it."

He clutched the flashlight tighter. "Why?" And somehow I thought the question was about more than the oubliette and why I had to climb inside it.

I sighed. "Less and less scares me, Richard. So when I find something that does bother me, I have to test it. I have to see if I can do it."

"Why?" He studied my face like he'd memorize it.

"Just to see if I can."

"Why?" and the anger was more than a faint hint now.

I shook my head. "I'm not competing with you, Richard, or anyone else. I don't give a shit who's better or faster or braver."

"Then why do it?"

"The only person I compete against is me, Richard, and I'll think less of me if I let you, or anyone else, climb down in that hole first. Gregory is my boy, not yours, and I have to rescue him."

"You've already rescued him, Anita. It doesn't matter who climbs in the damn hole."

I almost smiled, but not like it was funny. "Give me the flashlight, please, Richard. I can't explain this to you."

"Does your Nimir-Raj understand it?" The anger burned along my skin, like a swarm of stings. It damn near hurt.

I frowned at him. "Ask him yourself, now give me the damn flashlight." If you get angry at me, it never takes me long to respond.

"I want to be your Ulfric, Anita, your guy, whatever the hell that means. Why won't you let me be . . . ?" He stopped talking, looking away from me.

The man. Was that what you were going to say?"

He looked back at me and nodded.

"Look, if we keep dating, or whatever the hell we're going to do, we have to get one thing straight. Your ego is no longer my problem. Don't be the man for me, Richard, be the person I need. You don't have to be bigger and braver than I am to be my man. I've got male friends that spend most of their time trying to prove they have bigger, brassier balls than I do. I don't need that from you."

"What if I need to be braver than you for myself, not for you?"

I thought about that for a second or two, then said, "You're not afraid of going down into the oubliette, are you?"

"I don't want to go down, and I don't want to see what they've done to Gregory, but I'm not as afraid as you are, no."

"Then it doesn't make you braver than me to go down into the hole, does it? Because it doesn't cost you anything to go down there."

He leaned very, very close to my ear, then breathed the barest of sounds against my skin. "Like it would cost you nothing to kill Jacob for me."

I stiffened beside him, then turned, trying to keep the shock off my face.

"I knew that was what you were thinking the moment I saw you look at him," Richard said.

"You'd let me do that?" I asked, voice soft, but not as soft as his had been.

"I don't know yet. But wouldn't your reasoning be that it would cost you nothing to do it and it would cost me dear?"

We stared at each other. I finally nodded.

He smiled. "Then let me go down the fucking hole."

"When did you start using the F-word?"

"While you were away. I think I missed hearing it." He grinned at me suddenly, a bright flash of smile in the dark.

I couldn't not smile back. Kneeling by that horrible black opening, fear still flat on my tongue, his anger still riding the air between us, and we smiled at each other. "I'll let you go down the hole first," I said.

The smile widened until it filled his eyes, and even by starlight I could see them gleam with humor. "Okay."

I leaned into him and gave him a quick kiss. Too quick for the powers to move between us, too quick to taste the blood in his mouth, too quick to find out if our beasts would roil through each other's bodies. I kissed him just because I wanted to, because for the first time I thought we might both be willing to bend a little. Would it be enough? Who the hell knew? But I was hopeful. For the first time in a long time, I was truly hopeful. Without hope, love dies and parts of you wither. I didn't know what it meant for Micah that I had hope for Richard and me. We'd talked openly about sharing, but I didn't know how much of that had been for public show and how much had been real. But right that second, I didn't care, I clutched that positive emotion to me and held on. Later, later, we'd worry about other things. I'd let Richard climb down first, but I'd still be going down, and I wanted that small warm hope inside my chest along with the fear.

27

RICHARD'S WEIGHT ON the rope ladder kept it tight under my hands. He'd put his flashlight on a strap around his wrist. I watched the pool of yellow light vanishing down into that narrow darkness and realized that I was still barely on the ladder, my head still aboveground.

Micah was kneeling beside the hole. "It'll be alright," he said.

I swallowed and looked at him, knowing my eyes were just a little wide. "I know," but my voice came out breathy.

"You really don't have to do this," he said, voice soft, and as neutral as he could make it.

I frowned at him. "Don't *you* start."

"Then you better catch up with him." His voice was a little less neutral, but I couldn't tell what tone it held.

I started climbing down the soft roughness of the rope ladder, moving quickly, angrily. I wasn't angry with Micah, not really. I was angry with me. The anger got me well down into the dark where the light from the flashlight below me seemed very yellow and very stark against the earthen walls.

I clung there for a second or two, staring at that hard-packed earth. I gazed up slowly and found Micah staring down at me from a distance so far away that I couldn't tell what color his eyes or hair were. I knew it was him from the shape of his face and shoulders. My God, how deep did this pit go?

It seemed like the earthen walls were curving in towards me, like a hand about to close into a fist and crush me, so that I couldn't breath enough of the stale, flat air to fill my lungs. I closed my eyes and forced myself to move one hand off the ladder and touch the wall. It was farther away than I'd thought, and when I finally touched it, it startled me. The earth was surprisingly cool against my hand, and I realized it was cool in the pit, even with early summer heat up above. I opened my eyes, and the walls were still about six feet circular, just like they'd always been. The earth wasn't closing in around me, only my phobia was doing that.

I started climbing down again, and this time I didn't stop until I felt the ladder loosen under my body and it was suddenly harder to climb down without bumping into the dirt walls. Richard's weight was no longer steadying the ladder for me. If I hadn't been such a pain in the ass, I might have asked for him to hold it steady until I got down to the end. Instead I hugged the ladder frantically and kept moving downward. It's hard to cling to something while you're climbing down it, but I managed.

The world narrowed down to the feel of the rope under my hands, my feet trying to find purchase—just the simple act of moving downward. It got to the point that I stopped jumping every time my body bumped the walls. Hands touched my waist, and I let out that little yip that is only a girl sound. I always hated when I did it.

They were Richard's hands around my waist, of course. He steadied me the last few feet, while my heart tried to jump out of my chest. I stepped down onto a floor that crunched and rolled with bones. They were deep yet you didn't sink into them, rather walked on top of them like a saint treading on water.

The narrow shaft opened into a small, cramped, cave-like hole in the earth. Richard had to stand bent almost in two. I could stand up if I was careful, though the top of my hair brushed the ceiling solidly enough that ducking a little was a good idea.

Micah called from way, way above us, "Are you alright?"

It took me two tries to be able to say, "Fine, we're fine."

Micah pulled back from the opening, a dark dot against the paler grayness. "My God, how far down are we?"

"Sixty feet, give or take." There was something in his voice that made me turn to him.

He shook his head and looked to one side, shining the flashlight on something small and hunched. It was Gregory.

He was on his stomach, hog-tied, his arms and legs at such acute angles that I couldn't imagine lying there like that for three days. He was nude, a white cloth blindfold cutting across his face, knotted in a tangle of long blond hair, as if even that had been done to hurt, and not merely to blind. As Richard's light played over Gregory's body, he made small helpless sounds. He could see the light through the cloth, if nothing else. I knelt beside him, seeing where the silver chains had dug into his wrists and ankles. The wounds were raw and bloody where he'd struggled against them.

"The chains have rubbed him raw," Richard said, voice soft.

"He struggled," I said.

"No, he's not powerful enough to take this much silver against his skin. The chains ate their way into his skin."

I stared at the raw wounds and didn't know what to say. I touched Gregory's shoulder, and he screamed through the gag I hadn't seen. His hair had hidden it. But there was a dark rag stuffed in his mouth. He screamed again and tried to worm away from me.

"Gregory, Gregory, it's Anita." I touched him as gently as I could, and he screamed once more. I looked up at Richard. "He doesn't seem to hear me."

Richard knelt and raised a tangle of Gregory's hair. Gregory struggled harder, and Richard handed me the flashlight so he could use one hand to steady the smaller man's face and the other to keep the hair out of the way. There was more cloth stuffed in his ears. Richard pulled out the cloth and found a black earplug deeper in the channel. They were never meant to be pushed in that far, and when Richard pulled it free, fresh blood trickled from his ear.

I just stared, my mind frozen for a second, not wanting to understand. But finally, I heard myself say it. "They burst his eardrums. Why, for God's sake? Wasn't the blindfold and gag enough sensory deprivation?"

Richard held the earplug up to the light. I had to shine the flashlight directly on it to see that it had a metal point.

"What is that?"

"Silver," he said.

"Oh, God, they were designed for this?"

"Remember, Marcus was a doctor. He knew all kinds of medical supply places. Places that would make things." The look on Richard's face told me he was lost in memory and something darker.

I glanced back at the marks on Gregory's arms and legs. "Dear God, did the silver tear up his ear canals the way it did his skin?"

"I don't know. It's good that it's still bleeding. It means if he shapeshifts soon, he'll probably heal." Richard's voice was thick.

I wasn't close to crying, the horror too overwhelming for tears. I wanted Jacob down here, and whoever had helped him, because you didn't do this to a shapeshifter without help, not one-on-one.

Richard tried to take off the blindfold, but it was tied so tight he couldn't get a good hold on it. I handed him the flashlight and drew the knife from my left wrist sheath. "Hold him, the knives are sharp, I don't want to cut him if he struggles."

Richard held Gregory's head between his two hands like a vise, and Gregory struggled harder, screaming through the gag. But Richard held him firm while I slid the knife carefully between the cloth and Gregory's hair. One quick slice downward and the blindfold eased away from his skin, but it had been tied so tight for so long that Richard had to peel it away.

Gregory blinked at the light and saw Richard and screamed more. Something died on Richard's face when he did it, like it had killed something inside him to have anyone be that terrified of him.

I leaned over, placing my hand carefully on the pile of bones and watched Gregory's eyes finally see me. He stopped screaming, but he didn't look relieved enough. I pulled the gag out of his mouth, and it peeled away, taking bits of lip skin with it. He worked his mouth slowly, and for some odd reason I was reminded of the scene from *The Wizard of Oz* where Dorothy puts oil on the Tin Man's jaw after he'd been rusted. The image should have made me smile, but it didn't.

There was a padlock on the chains around each of his limbs. Richard crawled around me, letting me stay where Gregory could see me. I was saying over and over again, "It's going to be alright. It's going to be alright." He couldn't hear me, but it was the best I knew how to do.

Richard snapped the lock on one wrist, and pain showed on Gregory's face like it hurt for the arm to move at all. Richard freed both wrists and then began to slowly uncurl Gregory's body.

Gregory screamed, but not from fear this time, from pain. I tried to cradle him, but moving at all seemed to hurt. It took both of us crawling around to get him unbent enough to lay in my lap. He was never going to be able to climb the ladder.

The bends of both of his arms were covered in needle marks; none of them had healed. "The needle marks, why haven't they healed?"

"Silver needles in direct contact with the bloodstream. A sedative to keep the adrenaline low so you can't change, but not so much that you can't feel, or know where you are, and what's happening. That's how Raina used to do it."

"This is how she used to tie them up and exactly what she used to do to them. How did Jacob know that?" I asked.

"One of my people told him," Richard said. He stayed on his knees rather than stand bent over. His face was calm, almost serene.

"I want them down here. Whoever helped Jacob. Whoever brought out those damn earplugs. I want them down here."

He turned those calm eyes to me, and I saw the anger at the bottom of that calm. "Could you do this to someone? Could you plunge these things in their ears? Could you do all this to *anyone*?"

I thought about that, really thought about it. I was angry, sickened. I wanted to punish someone, but . . . "No, no, I could shoot them, kill them, but I couldn't do this."

"Neither could I," he said.

"You knew Gregory was in the oubliette, but you didn't know what they'd done to him, did you?"

He shook his head, kneeling on the bones, still staring down at the bloody earplug, like it held answers to questions too hard to ask out loud. "Jacob knew."

"You're Ulfric, Richard, you should know what's done in your pack's name."

The anger flared so hot and tight that it filled the little cave like water just this side of boiling. Gregory whimpered and watched Richard with fearful eyes.

"I know, Anita, I know."

"So you're not going to put Jacob down here?"

"I am, but not like this. He can stay down here, but not chained, not tortured." Richard glanced around the tiny space. "Being down here at all is torture enough."

I didn't even try to argue that one. "What about whoever helped him?"

Richard looked at me. "I'll find out who helped him."

"Then what?"

He closed his eyes, and it wasn't until he opened his hand and I saw the flash of blood that I realized he'd pressed the silver point into his palm. He pulled it out and stared at the bright flash of blood.

"You just keep pushing, don't you, Anita."

"The pack knows you well enough, Richard. They know you didn't mean for anyone to be put down here, especially not with all Raina's old accoutrements. Doing this at all was a challenge to your authority."

"I know that."

"I don't want to fight, Richard, but you have to punish them for this. If you don't, then you lose more ground to Jacob. Even if you put him down here, it won't stop things. Everyone that touched this has to suffer."

"You're not angry now," he said, and he looked puzzled. "I thought you wanted revenge, but you seem cold about it all, now."

"I wanted revenge, but you're right, I couldn't do this to anyone, and I can't order done what I wouldn't do myself. Just a rule I've got. But the pack is a mess, and if you want to stop the downward slide and keep them from a civil war, werewolf against werewolf, you must be harsh. You must make it clear that is not acceptable."

"It isn't," he said.

"There's only one way for them to know that, Richard."

"Punishment," he said, and he made the word sound like a curse.

"Yes," I said.

"I've worked for months—no, years—to try and get away from a punitive system. You want me to throw away all that I've worked for and go back to the way it was."

Gregory's hand came up, slowly, painfully, to clutch weakly at my arm. I stroked his matted hair, and his voice came out hoarse, abused, as if even through the gag, he'd been screaming for days. "I want . . . out of . . . here. Please."

I nodded my head so he could see it, and a relief so large it was beyond words flashed through his eyes.

I looked up at Richard. "If your system worked better than the old one, then I'd support it, but it's not working. I'm sorry that it's not working, Richard, but it's not. If you continue this . . . experiment in democracy and gentler, kinder laws, people are going to die. Not just you, but Sylvie, and Jamil, and Shang-Da, and every wolf that supports you. But it's worse than that, Richard. I watched the pack. They're divided almost evenly. It will be civil war, and they will tear each other to bits—Jacob's followers and the ones who won't follow him. Hundreds will die, and the Thronnos Rokke Clan may die with it. Look at the throne you're sitting on as Ulfric. It's ancient, you can feel it. Don't let everything that it stands for be destroyed."

He stared down at the still-bleeding wound in his hand. "Let's get Gregory out of here."

"You'll punish Jacob, but not the others," I said, and my voice was tired.

"I'll find out who they are first, then we'll see."

I shook my head. "I love you, Richard."

"I hear a 'but,' coming."

"But I value the people who count on me for their safety

more than I value that love." It felt cold and awful saying it out loud, but it was true.

"What does that say about your love?" he asked.

"Don't go all sanctimonious on me, Richard. You dropped me like yesterday's news when the pack voted me out. You could have said, screw it, take the throne, I want Anita more, but you didn't."

"You really think Jacob would have let me walk away?"

"I don't know, but you didn't make the offer. It didn't even occur to you to make the offer, did it?"

He looked away, then back, and his eyes held such sadness that I wanted to take it back, but I couldn't. It was time we talked. It was like the old joke about the elephant in the living room. No one acknowledged it existed until the shit was so deep they couldn't walk. Glancing down at Gregory, I knew the shit was too deep to ignore. We were out of options except for the truth, no matter how brutal.

"If I'd stepped down as Ulfric, even if Jacob had let me do it, it would still have been civil war. He'd have still executed those closest to me. It would have been deserting them. I'd rather die, than just walk away and leave them to be slaughtered."

"If that's how you really feel, Richard, then I've got a better plan. Make an example of Jacob and his followers."

"It's not that simple, Anita. Jacob's got enough support that it might still be war."

"Not if it's bloody enough."

"What are you saying?"

"Make them fear you, Richard. Make them fear you. Machiavelli said it nearly six hundred years ago, but it's still true. Every ruler should strive for his people to love him. But if they cannot love you, then make them fear you. Love is better, but fear will do the job."

He swallowed hard, and there was something close to fear in his eyes. "I think I could kill Jacob, and even execute one or two of his people, but you don't think that's enough, do you?"

"Depends on how you execute them."

"What are you asking me to do, Anita?"

I sighed and stroked Gregory's cheek. "I'm asking you to do what needs doing, Richard. If you want to hold this pack together and save hundreds of lives, then I'm telling you how you can do it with the minimum amount of bloodshed."

"I can kill Jacob, but I can't do what you're asking. I can't do something so terrible that the entire pack would fear me." He looked at me, and there was a wildness, a panic in his face, like a trapped thing that finally realizes there is no escape.

I could feel my face grow calm, and I felt myself sinking into that place where there is nothing but white noise and the solid, almost comforting surety that I felt nothing. I said, softly, "I can."

He turned away from me, as if I hadn't spoken, and called up for them to lower the harness. We slid the harness around Gregory, talking only about the task at hand—no metaphysics, no politics. There was a second harness on the rope, and Richard made me put it on. I'd get to cradle Gregory, protecting him with my body so he didn't get scraped up too badly.

"I've never done this before," I said.

"I'm too broad through the shoulders to add Gregory's bulk to mine. It has to be you. Besides, you'll keep him safe, I know you will." There was something in his eyes that made me want to say something, but he jerked on the rope and we started rising into the air.

Richard watched us, face upturned, his flashlight casting odd shadows around the small room as he knelt on the bones. Then we were up inside the tunnel, and I couldn't see him anymore. I had my arms full, literally and figuratively, trying to keep Gregory from crashing into the walls. His arms and legs were still almost useless. I wasn't sure if it was because of the long confinement or the drugs he'd been given, or both. Probably both.

Gregory kept saying "thank you, thank you, thank you" under his breath.

By the time we reached the top, there were tears drying on my cheeks. Regardless of what Richard decided, someone was going to pay.

Jacob was there, already bound in silver chains, carried like a piece of struggling luggage between three werewolves. They let him keep his cutoff shorts. No nudity for the good guys. I guess there has to be some differences, or how do you tell which side you're on?

Cherry was already checking Gregory over. She had to keep chasing the other leopards back. They kept trying to touch him.

I stared across the clearing at Jacob. The look in his eyes was enough. Richard could be squeamish if he wanted to be, but if I let what had been done to Gregory stand unchallenged, then Jacob and his followers would see it as weakness. They'd turn and destroy us once Jacob secured his power base. Because there was one way for Jacob to avoid a civil war, and that was by doing what I was encouraging Richard to do. If he did something so terrible that the others were afraid to fight, then he could be Ulfric without a bloodbath. I'd seen what he'd done to Gregory. Call it a hunch, but I was willing to bet Jacob would do what needed doing. He didn't strike me as the squeamish sort.

Richard climbed out of the hole. "Put him in."

"Do you want the drugs used?" Sylvie asked.

Richard nodded.

"What about the blindfold and the rest?"

Richard shook his head. "Not necessary."

Jacob started struggling again. "You can't do this!"

Richard knelt in front of him, holding him by his thick hair. The grip looked painful. "Who showed you where these were?" He held his hand out with the silver-tipped earplugs in his palm.

"Oh, my God," Sylvie whispered.

Others asked, "What is it?"

"Who, Jacob? Who told you our dirty little secrets?"

Jacob just stared at him.

"I could have them used on you," Richard said.

Jacob paled a little, but he didn't answer. His jaw was so tense that I could see the muscles pulsing, but he didn't give up who'd helped him. He didn't even ask if answering the

question would save him from the oubliette. I had to admire
that, at least, but I didn't have to like it.

"You wouldn't do that." It was Paris, looking a lot less
confident than she had by the throne. She looked downright
unsure of herself in her skintight dress.

Richard looked at her for a long time, or maybe it just
seemed long, and something in his eyes made her look away.

"You're right, I can't use them on Jacob, or anyone." He
looked around the clearing at the scattered wolves and at the
ones waiting in the trees beyond. "But hear me, if there are
anymore of these things around, I want them destroyed.
When Jacob comes out of the oubliette, it is to be sealed up
forever. You have learned nothing from me, if any of you
could do this, you have learned nothing." He signaled Sylvie,
and she came forward with a syringe.

The three werewolves had to hold Jacob against the
ground for her to give him the shot. They held him until his
limbs went limp and his eyes fluttered shut.

"He'll wake up in the oubliette," Richard said. His voice
held not just tiredness, but defeat. He turned to me as they
carried Jacob towards the hole. "Take your leopards, and
your allies, and go home, Anita."

"I'm lupa, remember, you can't kick me out of pack business."

He smiled, but it left his eyes empty and tired. "You're
still lupa, but for tonight you're also Nimir-Ra, and your
leopards need you. Take care of Gregory, and for what it's
worth, I'm sorry about all of this."

"Sorry is worth something, Richard, but it doesn't change
things."

"It never does," he said.

I couldn't read his mood. He wasn't sad exactly, or worried, or, anything I had a name for, except defeated. It was
like he'd already lost the battle.

"What are you going to do?" I asked.

"I'm going to find out who helped Jacob do this."

"How?" I asked.

He smiled and shook his head. "Go home, Anita."

I stood and looked at him for a heartbeat or two, then

turned back to my leopards. Gregory was on a stretcher, and Zane and Noah were carrying it. Cherry was talking to the werewolf doctor that had packed Jacob's nose. She was doing a lot of nodding. Instructions, maybe.

Micah was standing at the edge of the group watching me. I met his eyes, but neither of us smiled. I looked back but Richard was already moving off through the trees with Jamil and Shang-Da at his back. Micah's face was very neutral as I walked towards him. I wasn't hopeful anymore. I could have played it cool, but I didn't want to. I was tired, so terribly tired. My clothes smelled like an outhouse, and probably so did my skin. I wanted a shower, clean clothes, and to make the lost look in Gregory's eyes go away. The shower and clothes were the easy part. I didn't even know how to begin to make Gregory's pain go away.

I held out my hand to Micah, not because of otherworldly energy, apparently depression dampens that, but because I wanted the touch of another hand. I wanted the comfort, and I didn't want to have to think about it. I just wanted to be held.

He widened his eyes, but took my hand, squeezing it gently. I started walking towards the trees, leading him by the hand. The others followed us. Even the swan king and the wererats. Anita Blake, preternatural pied piper. The thought should have made me smile. But it didn't.

28

TWO HOURS LATER I'd had a shower and Gregory had had a bath, though I'd showered by myself, and Gregory had had company. He still didn't have complete use of his arms and legs. I didn't think that Cherry, Zane, and Nathaniel needed to get naked and in the tub with him, but, hey, I wasn't offering to help, so who was I to complain? Besides, it never became sexual; it was as if the touch of their flesh on his was necessary, part of the healing process. Maybe it was.

I was sitting at my new kitchen table. My old two-seater table just hadn't been roomy enough for all the wereleopards to have bagels and cream cheese at the same time. The new table was pale pine, varnished to a golden glow. There still wasn't enough room at the table for everyone to sit and drink coffee, but it was closer. I'd have needed a banquet table to have that much room, and the kitchen wasn't long enough for it. There was more than one reason that feudal lords had had great big castles—you needed the room just to feed and care for all your people.

The only person sitting in the dimly lit kitchen was Dr. Lillian. Elizabeth had been transported to the secret hospital that the shapeshifters kept in St. Louis. All my other leopards were tending to Gregory. Micah and his cats wandered around the periphery of it all. Caleb had tried to include himself in the bath and had been refused. The rest of Micah's pard seemed unsettled, nervous, not knowing what to do with themselves. I had my priority for the evening—taking care of Gregory. Everything else could wait. One disaster at a time, or you lose your way, and your mind.

Dr. Lillian was a small woman with gray hair cut straight just above her shoulders. Her hair was longer than the first time I met her, but everything else was the same. I'd never seen her wear makeup, and her face still looked pleasant and attractive in a fifty-plus sort of way—though I'd discovered she was actually well over sixty. She certainly didn't look it.

"The drugs are still in his system," Dr. Lillian said.

"Drugs, plural?" I asked.

She nodded. "Our metabolism is so fast that it takes quite a cocktail of chemicals to keep us sedated for any length of time."

"Gregory wasn't sedated. He seemed very much aware of everything that was happening," I said.

"But his heart, his breathing, his involuntary reflexes were all subdued. If you can't access the full effects of an adrenaline rush, you can't change shape."

"Why not?"

Lillian shrugged, taking a small sip of her coffee. "We don't know, but there is something in the extremes of the fight or flight response that opens the way for our beast. If you can deprive a shapeshifter of that response, then you can keep them from shifting."

"Indefinitely?" I asked.

"No, the full moon will bring it on, no matter what drugs you pump into someone."

"How long until Gregory's back to normal?"

Her eyes flicked downward, then up, and I didn't like that she'd needed that second to school her eyes, as if something bad were coming.

"The drugs will probably wear off in about eight hours, maybe more, maybe less. It depends on so many things."

"So he stays here until the drugs wear off, then he shapeshifts and he's fine, right?" I put a lilt at the end, making it a question, because I knew the atmosphere was too serious for it to be that easy.

"I'm afraid not," she said.

"What's wrong, doc, why so solemn?"

She gave a small smile. "In eight hours the damage to Gregory's ears may be permanent."

I blinked at her. "You mean he'll stay deaf?"

"Yes."

"That's not acceptable," I said.

Her smile widened. "You say that as if by sheer will you can change things, Anita. It makes you seem very young."

"Are you telling me that there's nothing we can do to heal him?"

"No, I'm not saying that."

"Please, doc, just tell me."

"If you were truly Nimir-Ra, then you might be able to call his beast out of his flesh and force the change, even with the drugs in his system."

"If someone can tell me how to do it, I'm willing to give it a shot."

"So you believe that you will be Nimir-Ra in truth come full moon?" Lillian asked.

I shrugged and sipped my coffee. "Not a hundred percent sure, no, but the evidence is sort of mounting up."

"How do you feel about that?"

"Being Nimir-Ra for real?" I asked.

She nodded.

"I'm trying really hard not to think too much about it."

"Ignoring it won't make it go away, Anita."

"I know that, but worrying about it won't change things either."

"Very practical of you, if you can pull it off."

"What, not worrying?"

She nodded again.

I shrugged. "I'll worry about each disaster as it happens."

"Can you really compartmentalize to that degree?"

"How do we fix Gregory?"

"I take that as a yes," she said.

I smiled. "Yes."

"As I said, if you were a Nimir-Ra in full power, you might be able to call his beast, even through the drugs."

"But since I haven't shifted yet, I can't?"

"I doubt it. It's a rather specialized skill, even among full shapeshifters."

"Can Rafael do it?"

She smiled, the smile that most of the wererats got when you asked about their king. It was a smile that held warmth and pride. They liked and respected him. Let's hear it for good leadership.

"No."

That surprised me, and it must have shown on my face.

"I told you, it is a rare talent. Your Ulfric can do it."

I looked at her. "You mean Richard?"

"Do you have another Ulfric?" she asked, smiling.

I almost smiled back. "No, but we need someone who can call leopards, right?"

She nodded.

"How about Micah?"

"I've already asked him. Neither he nor Merle can call another's beast. Micah did offer to try and heal Gregory by calling flesh, but the injuries are beyond him."

"When did Micah try and heal Gregory?"

"While you were cleaning up," she said.

"I took a quick shower."

"It didn't take long for him to be certain that Gregory's injuries were above his abilities."

"You wouldn't be belaboring the point if there wasn't some hope."

"I can use other drugs to try and overcome the effects."

"But . . ." I said.

"But the mix of the drugs could explode his heart or rupture enough blood vessels in other major organs to kill him."

I stared at her for a heartbeat or two. "How bad are the odds?"

"Bad enough that I need his Nimir-Ra's permission before trying."

"Has Gregory given his permission?"

"He's terrified. He wants to be able to hear again. Of course he wants me to try, but I'm not sure he's thinking clearly."

"So you're coming to me like you'd go to a parent for a child," I said.

"I need someone who is thinking clearly to make a decision on Gregory's behalf."

"He has a brother." I frowned, because I realized I hadn't seen Stephen at the lupanar. "Where *is* Stephen?"

"I've been told that the Ulfric ordered Gregory's brother not to attend tonight. Something about it being unfair for him to watch his own brother be executed. Vivian has gone to get him."

"My, that was big of Richard."

"You sound bitter."

"Do I?" And that sounded bitter even to me. I sighed. "I'm just frustrated, Lillian. Richard is going to get people I care about slaughtered, not to mention himself."

"Which risks both you and the Master of the City."

I frowned at her. "I guess everyone does know that part."

"I think so," she said.

"Yeah, he's risking us all for his high moral ideals."

"Ideals are worth sacrifice, Anita."

"Maybe, but I'm not a hundred percent sure I've ever held an ideal close enough to trade the people I love for it. Ideals can die, but they don't breathe, they don't bleed, they don't cry."

"So you would trade all your ideals for the people you care about?" she asked.

"I'm not sure I have any ideals anymore."

"You're still Christian, aren't you?"

"My religion isn't an ideal. Ideals are abstract things that you can't touch or see. My religion isn't abstract, it's very 'stract,' very real."

"You can't see God," she said. "You can't hold Him in your hand."

"How many angels can dance on the head of a pin, huh?" She smiled. "Something like that."

"I've held a cross while it flared so bright it blinded me until all the world was just white fire. I've seen a copy of the Talmud go up in flames in a vampire's hands, and even after the book had burned to ash, the vampire kept burning until it died. I've stood in the presence of a demon and re-cited holy script, and the demon could not touch me." I shook my head. "Religion isn't an abstract thing, Dr. Lillian, it is a living, breathing, growing, organic thing."

"Organic sounds more Wiccan than Christian," she said.

I shrugged. "I've been studying with a psychic and some

of her Wiccan friends for about a year, hard not to soak some of it up."

"Doesn't studying Wicca put you in an awkward position?"

"You mean because I'm a monotheist?"

She nodded.

"I have God-given abilities and not enough training to control those abilities. Most denominations of the church frown on psychics, let alone someone who raises the dead. I need training, so I've found people to train me. The fact that they're not Christian I see as a failing of the church, not a failing of theirs."

"There are Christian witches," she said.

"I've met some of them. They all seem to be zealots, as if they have to be more Christian than anyone else to prove that they're good enough to be Christian at all. I don't like zealots."

"Neither do I," she said.

We looked at each other in the darkened kitchen. She raised her coffee mug. I'd given her the one with a tiny knight and a large dragon that said, "No guts, no glory."

Lillian said, "Down with zealots."

I raised my own mug in the air. It was the baby penguin mug, still a favorite. "Down with zealots."

We drank. She set her mug on the coaster and said, "Do I have your permission to try the drugs on Gregory?"

I took a deep breath and let it out slowly, then nodded. "If he agrees, do it."

She pushed back from the table and stood. "I'll get everything ready."

I nodded, but stayed sitting. I was praying when I felt someone come into the room. Without opening my eyes, I knew it was Micah.

He waited until I raised my head, opened my eyes. "I didn't mean to interrupt," he said.

"I'm finished," I said.

He nodded and gave that smile of his that was part amusement, part sorrow, and part something else. "You were praying?" He made it a question.

"Yes."

Some trick of the light made his eyes gleam in the dark, like there was a spark of hidden fire down deep in their green gold depths. The illusion lost his eyes and most of his face to shadow and darkness. Only that shimmering gleam remained, as if the color dancing in his eyes was more real than the rest of him.

Without seeing his face, I knew he was upset. I could feel it like a tension down my spine. "What's wrong?" I asked.

"I can't remember the last time I prayed."

I shrugged. "A lot of people don't pray."

"Why does it surprise me that you do?" he asked.

I shrugged again.

He took a step forward, and the light fell upon his face and that odd, mixed smile of his.

"I have to go."

"What's wrong?" I asked.

"What makes you think anything's wrong?"

"Tension level between you and your cats. What's up, Micah?"

He pressed his thumb and forefinger against his eyes, rubbing, as if he were tired. He blinked those jewel-like eyes at me. "A pard emergency. We've got one member that couldn't come tonight, and she's got herself in trouble."

"What kind of trouble?"

"Violet is our version of your Nathaniel, the least dominant of us." He left it at that, as if it explained everything. It did, and it didn't.

"And?" I said.

"And I have to go help her."

"I don't like secrets, Micah."

He sighed, running his fingers through his hair. He ripped the ponytail holder out, threw it on the floor, ran his hands through the shoulder-length curls, over and over, as if he'd been wanting to do it all night. The movement was harsh, frantic with tension.

He looked down at me, dark brown hair in disarray around his face, eyes gleaming. In an instant he went from being this nice, attractive man to something feral and alien.

It wasn't just the hair or the kitty-cat eyes. His beast bubbled against my skin like boiling water. I'd felt his power, but not like this, almost hot enough to scald. Then I realized that I could see that heat, *see* it. It flowed over him, invisible, but almost not, like something half-seen out of the corner of your eye. I could almost see the shape of something monstrous looming around him, like heat rising off of summer pavement, a rippling thing. I'd been around shapeshifters for years and never seen anything like it.

Merle appeared in the doorway. "Nimir-Raj, is anything wrong?"

Micah turned, and I got a swimming afterimage, as if something large and almost invisible moved around and just above his body. His voice came out low and growling. "Wrong, what could possibly be wrong?"

Gina pushed past Merle. "We've got to go, Micah."

Micah put his hands up, and the afterimage moved with him. I couldn't actually see claws and fur, just hints of it, swimming around him. He covered his eyes with his hands, and I saw those ghostly claws go through, into, *past* his face. Watching it made me dizzy, and I looked down at the table-top to steady myself and reality.

I'd heard Marianne say she could see auras of power around people and lycanthropes, but I'd never been able to see one before.

I felt his power folding away, the heat, the skin-ruffling sensation pulling away, like the ocean going back from the shore. I raised my face to see, and that seen-not-seen shape was gone, swallowed back into his body.

He stared down at me. "You look like you've seen a ghost."

"You're closer than you think," I said.

"She's afraid of your power," Gina said, and there was scorn in her voice.

I looked up at her. "I saw his aura, saw it like a white phantom around his body."

"You say that like you've never seen it before," Micah said.

"I haven't, not a visual."

Gina took his arm, gently but firmly, and tried pulling him towards the door. He just looked at her, and I felt his presence, his personality, for lack of a better word, like something almost touchable. She dropped to the floor, gripping his hand, rubbing her cheek against it. "I meant no offense, Micah."

The look on his face was cold. His power, his force began to trickle through the room again.

"Nimir-Raj," Merle said, "if you are going, then you must go. If you are not going . . ." His voice was careful, almost gentle, a pitying tone of voice, and I didn't understand why.

Micah growled at Merle, I think. Then his voice came out normal, human. "I know my duty as Nimir-Raj, Merle."

"I would never presume to tell you the duties of a Nimir-Raj, Micah," he said.

Micah suddenly looked tired again, all that energy draining away. He helped Gina to her feet, though it looked awkward since she was more than a head taller. "Let's go."

They all turned towards the door. "I hope your leopard is alright," I said.

Micah glanced back. "Would Nathaniel be, if he'd called for help?"

I shook my head. "No."

He nodded and turned back for the door. "Mine either." He hesitated and said without turning around, "I'll take Noah and Gina with me, but if it's alright I'll leave Merle and Caleb here?"

"Won't you need them with you?"

He looked back, smiling. "I just need to pick up Violet. I don't need muscle for that, and you might want some extra muscle."

"You mean in case Jacob's people get pesky?"

His smile widened. "Pesky, yeah, in case they get pesky."

Then they were gone into the other room, and I was left alone at the table. Lillian came back in, her eyes narrowed.

"What?" I asked.

She just shook her head. "None of my business."

"That's right," I said.

"But if it were . . ."

"But it's not," I said.

She smiled. "But if it were, I'd say two things."

"You're going to say them anyway, aren't you?"

"Yes," she said.

I waved her to go ahead.

"First, it's nice to see you letting yourself follow your heart with someone new. Second, you don't know this man very well. Be careful who you give your heart to, Anita."

"I haven't given anyone my heart, yet."

"Not yet," she said.

I frowned at her. "You do realize that you've told me to follow my heart and not to follow my heart."

She nodded.

"Those are contradictory bits of advice," I said.

"I'm aware of that."

"Then which piece of advice do you want me to follow?"

"Both, of course."

I shook my head. "Let's go save Gregory and worry about my ever-sordid love life later."

"I can't promise that we'll save Gregory, Anita."

I held up a hand. "I remember the odds, doc." I followed her out and into the darkened living room and tried to believe, really believe, in miracles.

29

WE DECIDED TO do it on the deck out back. My deck backed to a couple of acres of mature woodland. No neighbors. No one to see us. The deck was also twice the size of the kitchen, which was the only part of the house without carpeting. Once a shapeshifter changed on carpet it was either steam clean it yourself, or hire it done. I was not the one who suggested that Gregory would ruin the carpet; it was actually Nathaniel. He was, after all, the person most likely to be vacuuming between housekeeper visits. I wasn't even sure I knew where the vacuum was.

Gregory was curled in the center of the deck, his head in his brother's lap, his arms wrapped around the other man's naked waist. Only the curling yellow hair, paled by moonlight, covered Stephen's upper body. He'd stripped to the waist in preparation for the change. He was going to go out into the woods with his brother. This presupposed that Gregory would survive the change. We had a fifty-fifty chance, not bad odds, if all you were about to lose was money, but when it was someone's life, fifty-fifty just didn't sound that good.

Stephen looked up at me. His cornflower blue eyes were silvered with moonlight. He looked pale and ethereal. His face was raw with emotion; his eyes held an intelligence and a demand that Stephen didn't often show. He was submissive, fragile in every walk of his life, but in that moment he laid a demand on me with his eyes, his face, the pain that showed in the set of his shoulders, the fierce way he touched his brother, who was still huddled in his lap, just a fall of long pale curls and paler skin. Gregory was naked in the hot summer night, and until that moment I hadn't noticed. The nudity didn't make me think of sex, it made me think how terribly vulnerable he was.

Stephen looked up at me and asked with every line of his body, the desperation in his eyes, what he was too submissive to say out loud. I didn't need to be telepathic to know what he wanted. Save him, save my brother, he screamed at me from his eyes. To say it out loud would have been redundant.

Vivian, who was as fragile as Stephen, as submissive, said it out loud anyway. "Please, try and call his beast, at least try before they use the drugs."

I looked at her, and there must have been something in my face that frightened her, because she dropped to her knees and crawled towards me. It wasn't that graceful stalk that the leopards could do. It was like a human crawling, awkward, slow, head down, eyes rolled up. She was displaying the leopard version of submissive behavior, and I hated it. Hated her feeling the need, like I was some ogre that needed placating, but I let her do it. Richard had shown me what happened in a were-group when the dominant refused to be dominant.

She leaned against my legs, pushing her body against me, head down. Normally, leopards would roll around my legs like huge cats, but tonight Vivian just pressed against my legs more like a frightened dog than a luxuriating cat. I leaned over to touch her hair and heard her murmuring under her breath, so soft, "Please, please, please." You would have had to be colder than even I was to ignore that soft pleading.

"It's okay, Vivian, I'll try."

Rubbing her cheek along my jeans as she raised her head, her eyes rolled up to me, again like a frightened dog. Vivian had always been timid around me, but I'd never seen this level of fear before. I didn't think it was Gregory's torture that had made the difference. I think it was the fact that I'd shot Elizabeth full of holes. Yeah, that probably did it. And I couldn't undermine the lesson by reassuring Vivian now that I wouldn't shoot her. Merle and Caleb were listening, and if we were really going to combine our pards, being feared was not a bad way for me to start.

I looked across the deck and found Merle watching me.

He was still fully dressed, jeans, boots, jean jacket over bare
chest, the scar showing like a flash of moonlit lightning
across his stomach. We stared at each other, and the force in
his gaze, the physical potential that shimmered around him,
made the hair on the back of my neck crawl. I'd spent years
around dangerous men, and dangerous monsters; Merle was
both. If I could make him truly afraid of me, that would be
a good thing.

Caleb on the other hand had started stripping off his
clothes when everyone else did, and only my protest, backed
by Merle, had kept his pants on. He walked barefoot, moonlight catching in the rings in his nipple and the edge of his
belly button. He had to look directly at me for the ring in
his eyebrow to spark. He was circling Cherry, who had never
dressed after helping Gregory in his bath. She stood tall and
comfortably nude, ignoring him.

The fact that he was paying attention to her nudity was a
breach of protocol among the shapeshifters. You only noticed
nudity if you'd been invited to have sex. Short of that, you
pretended everyone was as neuter as a Barbie doll.

Zane stepped between Cherry and the circling Caleb, giving a low growl. Caleb laughed and backed off. I did not
need another pain in the ass in my pard, and that's what
Caleb was.

Dr. Lillian was standing behind us holding a huge needle
all ready to go. The two wererat bodyguards, Claudia and
Igor, were behind her. They'd surprised me by putting on
guns in the car on the way over. Guns weren't allowed in
the lupanar, but they were bodyguards, and guns were a good
thing for bodyguards. Claudia had a 10 millimeter Beretta
tucked behind her back. The fact that she could carry a 10
mil anything said how much larger her hands were than mine.
Igor had a shoulder rig with a Glock 9 mil. They were both
good guns, and the two wererats handled them like they
knew what they were doing. Rafael had insisted that they
stay just in case Jacob, or his allies, got some wild idea about
a preemptive strike.

Claudia and Igor stood in typical bodyguard pose, hands
clasped in front of them, one hand holding the opposite wrist.

It's usually a guy thing to stand like that, or a jock thing, but bodyguards do it too. It's like they hold their own hands for reasurrance.

Their faces were neutral. They were here to protect me, not Gregory. Didn't matter to them, or didn't seem to.

Nathaniel leaned against the railing, wearing a pair of shorts, his hair hanging like a dark curtain around his body, still wet from the bath. It took forever for his hair to dry naturally. His face was serene. It reflected an almost zen-like pleasantness, as if he trusted me to make everything alright. Of all their faces, his was the most unnerving. I was used to people being afraid of me, eventually, but soft adoration—that I was not used to.

I looked back down at Vivian, still pressed against my legs. There was fear in her eyes, but there was also hope.

I touched her face and managed a smile. "I'll do what I can."

She smiled, and it was radiant. She was always beautiful, but when she smiled like that there was a little girl peeking out, someone more joyous and more free than the Vivian I knew. I valued that little girl smile from her, because I saw it so rarely.

I walked the few feet to the two men. Stephen was still kneeling, his brother huddled against him. He watched me with cautious eyes. He was rubbing his hand on Gregory's bare back over and over in small circles, the way you stroke a sick child when they want some touch to let them know they're going to be alright. Looking into Stephen's eyes, I knew he didn't believe that. He didn't believe Gregory would be alright, and it terrified him.

I knelt beside them and was almost the same height as Stephen. I met that pale gaze, that demand, and said, "I'm going to try and heal him."

It was Caleb who said, "If Micah couldn't heal him, why do you think you can?"

I didn't even bother glancing back at him. "It doesn't hurt to try."

"You haven't seen your first full moon," Merle said. "You

can't call flesh and heal him, not yet, maybe not ever. Calling flesh to heal is a rare talent."

I did look at Merle. "I'm not going to call flesh, I'm not even sure how that works."

"Then how will you heal him?" Merle asked.

"With the munin."

"How will a werewolf ghost help you heal a wereleopard?"

I shook my head. "I've healed the leopards before using the munin."

"You've healed Nathaniel," Cherry said, "twice, but no one else."

"If it works for one of you, it should work for all of you," I said.

Cherry was frowning.

"What's wrong?"

"You heal with Raina, everything was sex with her, and you want Nathaniel in that way. You've never been attracted to Gregory."

I shrugged. She was pretty much voicing the same doubts that I had, but hearing them out loud made them sound worse. I felt more doubtful that I could do it and more slutty because I needed sexual attraction to heal. But I was getting over the slutty feeling. If I could save both Gregory's hearing and his life, a little embarrassment wasn't too high a price to pay.

I looked down at Gregory, still huddled in a tight fetal ball around Stephen's lap and waist. He held on as if his brother were the last solid thing in the universe, as if, if he let go he'd swirl away and be lost.

I touched his hair, lightly, and he moved his face so that he could see me through a tangle of pale curls. I swept the curls away from his face. It was a gesture you used for a child. I'd hated Gregory once because of some things he'd done when Raina and Gabriel were still alive. But the moment they were dead and he knew he had a choice, he'd stopped doing most of them. Had he made me Nimir-Ra on purpose? Staring into his wide blue eyes I didn't believe that. It wasn't naïveté, it was a surety that Gregory just wasn't that dominant. To decide, even in a split second, to change the status quo that profoundly was just beyond him. He'd debate, or ask advice, or ask permission, but he wouldn't make a unilateral decision without some feedback. I knew this about Gregory. Richard didn't.

I touched his face, cupping it, raising it so he'd meet my eyes without having to do that eye roll that unnerved me. Just too subservient for my taste. I stared into that beautiful face, let my gaze glide over the fall of curls, the line of his back, the curl of his hip, but I felt nothing. I could appreciate his beauty, but I tried very hard to think of my leopards as neuter. You can be someone's friend and have sex with them. The trick is you have to want their emotional and physical well-being more than you want to fuck them. If you cross that line and want sex more than their happiness, then you aren't their friend. Their lover maybe, but not their friend.

But it was more than that. Cherry was right, Gregory had never moved me in that way. I sighed and moved my hand back from him. "What's wrong?" Stephen asked.

"He's pretty to look at, but . . ."

Stephen almost smiled. "But you need more than just a pretty face to lust after."

I shrugged. "Sometimes my life would be simpler if I didn't, but yeah."

"I remember I had to talk you through the first time you healed Nathaniel," he said, voice soft.

I nodded. "I remember too."

Gregory sat up, watching us both, trying to read our lips, I think. There was something frantic about the way he tried to decipher what we were saying. God, please let me help him. He was so scared.

"I think of him more like a child, no offense."

"You think more like a parent than a seducer; that's a good thing," Stephen said. "Don't apologize for it."

Cherry joined us, kneeling on her heels, long body curved in graceful lines. "You called Raina in the lupanar without any lust, right?"

I nodded. "I can call Raina's munin, sometimes even if I

don't want to, but she always demands a price before she leaves."

"You didn't seduce anyone at the lupanar tonight," she said.

"No, but I damn near started a fight by hitting Richard, and that was part Raina's doing. She enjoyed my loss of control, and . . . and she was worried about the pack tonight. She doesn't like what Richard's done. I think she toned down her demands because of that."

"And she doesn't care about us like she does the wolves."

"No, she doesn't."

"What are you afraid of?" Stephen asked. "That you'll molest Gregory."

I shook my head. "No, I'm afraid Raina will."

"You healed Nathaniel in the woods and didn't do anything awful to him," Cherry said.

"No, but I had Richard and the pack there to balance me, to help me control her through the marks. Without extra help in that area, Raina's idea of payment can get a little messy."

"Define messy," Stephen said.

"Sex, violence—" I shrugged "—messy."

"You have the pard here now," Cherry said. "You can use us for balance."

Truth was, without Micah here I wasn't sure I could do that. Just as Richard was my door to the wolves, Micah was my door to the leopards. Or was he? I was treating this like I treated Richard and Jean-Claude, like I was the outsider and they were my ticket in. But what if I really was the leopard queen? If I really was Nimir-Ra, then I should be able to do this without Micah. I realized the moment I doubted that, I was still hoping I wasn't going to be furry next full moon. No matter how much evidence to the contrary, I still didn't believe it. Maybe I didn't want to believe it. But I wanted to heal Gregory, that I did want.

I looked at them all and knew Cherry was right. If I was Nimir-Ra, then I had all I needed to balance me. If I wasn't Nimir-Ra, then it wouldn't work. What did we have to lose? I looked at Stephen and Gregory, their mirror faces, their frightened eyes, and knew exactly what we had to lose if I didn't try.

I took the Uncle Mike's sidekick holster complete with Firestar out of the front of my jeans and looked around. If I was going to be calling on the leopards, I didn't want them having to worry about the gun. I motioned Claudia the wererat over. Since I was still kneeling, she towered over me, only two inches shorter than Dolph. I had to admit it was impressive, even more so because she was a woman.

I handed the holstered gun to her, and she took it. "Make sure no one gets shot with it."

She frowned down at me. "You think someone is going to try and get the gun?"

"Me, maybe."

The frown deepened. "I don't understand."

"Raina's amused by violence. I don't want to be carrying a gun when I call her munin."

Claudia's eyebrows raised. "You mean she'd try to get you to use it on someone?"

I nodded.

"She's tried before?'

I nodded again. "In Tennessee when I was practicing with the munin, yeah."

Claudia shook her head. "You didn't seem that worried at the lupanar."

"I can call her once and be okay, probably. But if I call her too often, too close together, it's like she grows—" I hesitated "—stronger, or maybe I just get tired of fighting."

"She was a bitch when she was alive," Claudia said.

"Being dead hasn't changed her much," I added.

The tall woman shivered. "I'm glad the wererats don't have anything like the munin. The thought of some entity inside me just creeps me out."

"Me too," I said.

She looked down at me, thoughtful now. "I'll keep the gun safe. Is there anything else Igor and I can do to help?"

I tried to think of something, but only one thing came to mind. "If the leopards can't control me, make sure I don't hurt anyone."

"How bad is this going to be?" she asked.

I shrugged. "Normally, I wouldn't be this worried, but last time I called her she didn't get her bit of flesh, or sex. Hitting Richard made her happy, but . . ." I tried to explain. "I called her three times in a row for practice, without molesting or hurting anyone. My teacher, Marianne, and I both thought it was a sign that I was gaining control of Raina. Then the fourth time I called her, it was worse than it had ever been. You either pay as you go with Raina, or you end up owing her, and owing comes with interest, and the interest is hell to pay."

"Should you give me the knives, too, then?" Claudia asked.

She had a point, no pun intended. I took the wrist sheaths off, folded them up, and handed them to her.

"I thought you could control this shit." Caleb was standing just a little behind and to one side of Claudia. He was looking up at the tall woman as if wondering what she'd do if he tried to climb her. I almost wanted him to try, because I was pretty sure what would happen, and even more sure that I'd enjoy watching it. Caleb needed a good lesson from someone.

"I can."

"Then why all the precautions?"

I could have told him about the time in Tennessee when Raina's munin nearly started a riot among Verne's pack in a sort of game of rape tag, with me as the rapee, but I didn't. Instead, I said, "If you're not going to be helpful, stand over to the side and shut the fuck up."

He opened his mouth as if to protest, but Merle said, "Caleb, do what she says." His voice was quiet, a deep rumble of sound, but that mild tone seemed to work on Caleb like a charm.

"Sure, Merle, anything you say." He went to stand over to one side, near Dr. Lillian and Igor.

I glanced at Merle. "Thanks," I said.

He just bowed his head at me.

Dr. Lillian said, "I take this to mean that you want me to wait on the injection."

I nodded. "Yeah."

She turned and walked back through the sliding glass doors, into the darkened house. Everyone else stayed where they were, looking at me. Even Caleb, sulking by the railing with his arms crossed, was still watching the show.

I slipped my shirt off and felt rather than saw all my people react, like wind through a wheat field, involuntary. I never undressed in front of people unless I absolutely had to. The black bra I was wearing covered more than most swim suits, but there's something about letting people see you in your underwear that just makes all us good little girls squirm.

"Black lace, I like it," Caleb said.

I started to say something, but Merle beat me to it. "Shut up, Caleb, and don't make me tell you again."

Caleb settled back against the rail, arms hugging himself, face crinkled into a sulk that made him look even younger than he was.

"Go on," Merle said, "he won't interrupt again."

I looked at him. It was bad that he kept interfering. It undermined my authority, but since I wasn't entirely sure I had any authority over Caleb, it was okay, I guess. But it bugged me. I just wasn't sure what to do about it.

"I appreciate the help, but if our pards really do merge, then Caleb is going to have to learn to respect me, not you."

"You don't want my help?" He made it a question.

"Priority tonight is Gregory, but Caleb and I are going to have to come to an understanding."

"Are you going to shoot him too?"

I tried to read Merle's face and failed. A sort of blank hostility was all that showed. "You think I'll have to?"

Merle gave a very small smile. "Maybe."

It made me smile, a little. "Great, just what I need, another discipline problem in my pard."

His smile vanished like a hand had wiped it away. "We're not your cats, Anita, not yet."

I shrugged. "Whatever you say."

"We are not yours," he said.

I watched his face and saw something cross it in the

moonlight. Maybe if I'd had better light I could have deciphered it. "Why does the thought of me being in charge bother you so much?"

He shook his head. "It's not you being in charge that bothers me."

"Then what is it?"

He shook his head again. "What bothers me is you trying to be in charge and failing—failing really, really badly."

"I do my best, Merle, that's all I can do."

He nodded. "I believe you, but I've seen a lot of people try their best and still not make it."

I shrugged and let it go. "Be pessimistic on your own time, Merle, we need a little hope here, not negativity."

"I'll just shut up then," he said, which implied that if he couldn't be negative he had nothing to say. Fine by me.

I turned back to Gregory and his wide, frightened eyes. I touched his face, gently, trying to ease some of that fear, but he flinched ever so slightly when I touched him. You get enough abuse in your life, and you begin to think that every offered hand is a blow waiting to strike.

"It'll be alright, Gregory," I said. Since he couldn't hear me, I must have been saying it to reassure myself. It didn't seem to do a damn thing for Gregory.

I tried to see Gregory as a lust object, and I failed. I ran my hands over the smooth skin of his back, I grabbed a handful of those yellow curls, looked into those lovely eyes, but all I could feel was pity. All I could feel was protective towards him and how much I wanted to keep him safe. He was totally nude, sitting in front of me, and he was lovely. There was nothing wrong with the way he looked, except that I didn't see Gregory in that way. Trust me to find a way to make virtue a problem.

I turned to Stephen, who was still kneeling beside us. "I'm sorry, he's beautiful, but I want to hold him, keep him safe, not have sex with him, and protective intincts are not going to get Raina to come out."

Cherry said, "You simply called Raina at the lupanar. Why is this different?"

I looked up at her, standing nude and comfortable against

the deck railing. Zane was next to her, clothed, and just as comfortable.

"I can call Raina, but I can't guarantee she'll help me heal Gregory. The healing usually comes with lust, not without."

"Call her," Stephen said. "Once she's here maybe the rest will come."

"You mean call her munin, then get *her* in the mood, not me."

He looked very solemn, but he nodded.

"You know what her idea of sex is, Stephen."

He nodded again. "Trust me," he said.

Strangely, I did. He wasn't dominant, in fact was very often a victim, but Stephen did what he said he'd do, at almost any cost. There was a desperate stubbornness in him, no matter how often you knocked him down.

"I'll call the munin."

"And I'll make sure that Raina sees Gregory the way she needs to see him."

We looked at each other and had one of those moments of near perfect understanding. Stephen would do anything to save his brother, and I would do almost anything to help him do that.

30

I SAT BACK on my heels in front of Gregory, and I opened myself to the munin, dropped that barrier that kept Raina out, and she spilled up through me like warm water filling a pipe, up, up, riding on a wave of eagerness that she hadn't had at the lupanar. A thrill of fear went through me. I knew it was a bad sign, but I didn't fight her. I let her come, let her fill me up, let her laugh bubble from my throat.

When she looked at Gregory, she had no trouble seeing him as a sexual object, but then Raina saw almost everyone as a sexual object, so no big surprise.

I touched his face, caressed the line of his jaw. Gregory's eyes widened. I realized in that moment that he might not know what the hell we were doing, or what had changed. I could call Raina and think rationally. I'd fought long and hard to be able to do that. I could be distant while my hand glided down Gregory's bare chest. I could stop my hand—our hand—at his slender waist, and Raina couldn't force me lower. She snarled in my head, giving me a visual of her in wolf shape, snapping at me. But it was just a visual, like a dream; it couldn't hurt me, or anyone.

Raina spoke in my head. "This wolf still has teeth, Anita."

"You know the rules," I said.

"What?" Stephen asked.

I shook my head. "I'm talking to Raina."

"That is just creepy," Zane said.

I agreed with him, wholeheartedly, but Raina was already talking in my head, and I couldn't answer him. "I know the rules, Anita, do you?"

"Yeah."

"I do whatever I please . . ."

"And I try to stop you," I finished for her.

"Like old times," the voice in my head said.

It did sound like the relationship we'd had when she was alive. She wanted to kiss Gregory, and I didn't fight it. The kiss was openmouthed, but soft, nothing that would scare me too badly. In her own way Raina was learning how to work me, too.

I'd never kissed Gregory before, never wanted to. I still didn't want to. Kissing, in some ways, is more intimate than intercourse, more special. I pulled away from his lips, and Raina was just as happy to kiss the side of his neck. His skin was warm and smelled like soap. I buried my face under his hair at the back of his ear and found the hair still damp, smelling of my shampoo.

I tried to call healing from Raina, but she fought me. "No, not until after my reward."

I actually had leaned back from Gregory, and must have said it out loud, because Stephen asked, "What reward?"

I shook my head. "Raina won't heal him until after she's been . . . fed." It was a type of feeding; in her own way Raina was like the *ardeur*, except she only needed feeding when I called her—her craving, not mine.

"What do you want?" I asked it out loud, because I still wasn't comfortable with having silent conversations in my head.

She gave me a visual of kissing down his chest, of forcing him onto his back on the deck, and the next thing I remembered clearly was laying a gentle kiss beside Gregory's belly button. He was lying on his back, watching me with unfocused eyes. I was lying across his body, pinning his legs, my nearly naked chest pressed over his groin. I didn't remember getting there. Shit.

I rolled off of him, and Raina came like heat, racing through my body, drawing my mouth down to his hip, licking along that small hollow just where the waist meets groin. Gregory writhed under the stroke of my mouth, and as much as I'd tried to ignore it, drew our gaze to his groin.

He was hard, ready, but the sight of him pushed Raina back, left me in control, not because it was embarrassing, but because I had never seen Gregory erect before. He was still lovely to look at, but he was an odd shape, almost hooked at the end. I didn't know that men could be made that way, and it stopped me cold.

Raina screamed in my head, roared over me in a rush of body memory. The memory was of being on all fours with a man riding me from behind, riding Raina. I couldn't see who it was; all I could do was feel. They'd found that spot in a woman's body, and the rush of orgasm was close. Raina threw her—our—head back, a rush of auburn hair flinging free of our face, and I saw Gregory's reflection in the room's mirror.

Raina whispered in my head, "It's always like that with him from behind, because of his shape."

I tore free of the memory and found myself on all fours beside Gregory, one hand on his body. I fell back from him, because the shared memories didn't work without body contact.

I turned my face away so I wouldn't see him nude and ready, because I could still feel the memory of him inside my body, Raina's body. A hand touched my bare arm, and the rush of memories this time was overwhelming. I was there.

He filled my mouth, my throat, came inside me in a spill of thick heat, and with his body trembling, thrashing, teeth tore into thick, tender flesh, and we ate him. Blood poured upwards, and Raina bathed in it.

I fought free of it, screaming, shrieking, and someone else was screaming. It was Gregory. For one awful second I opened my eyes, because the memory was so strong I couldn't tell the difference between it and reality. But when I could see again, he was whole, crawling away from me, from the shared memory. Because that was one of Raina's gifts, the ability to share the horror.

I could still feel the thickness of meat in my mouth, taste blood and thicker things. I crawled to the railing, pulled myself up and lost everything I'd eaten that day.

Someone came up behind me, and I put out a hand, head still dangling over the dark edge of the deck. "Don't touch me."

"Anita, it's Merle. Nathaniel said that no one was to touch you that had ever shared a . . ." he hesitated, "moment with the old lupa. I didn't know her. She can't hurt you through me."

I held my head in my hands. It felt like it was going to split apart. "He's right."

His grip on my shoulders was as hesitant as his words. I pushed away from the railing and the world swam. Merle caught me, held me against his chest. "It's alright."

"I can still taste meat and blood and . . . oh, God! God!" I screamed it, and it didn't help, not for this. Merle held me against his chest, tight, my hands pinned to my sides, as if I'd tried to hurt myself. I didn't think I had, but I didn't know anymore. Months of practice, and Raina could still do this to me.

I screamed wordlessly over and over again, as if I could scream the memory out of me. Every time I drew breath I could hear Merle whispering, "It's alright, it's alright, Anita, it's alright."

But it wasn't alright. What Raina had just shown me would never be alright. Merle carried me into the bathroom, and I didn't protest. Caleb wet a cloth and put it on my forehead without a word of teasing. A small miracle, but not the one we needed.

31

RAINA HAD GONE, fled laughing, pleased with herself. God, I hated that woman. I'd already killed her; it wasn't like I could do anything else to her, but I wanted to. I wanted her to hurt like she'd hurt so many others, but I guess it was a little late for that.

Dr. Lillian was shining a tiny light in my eyes and trying to get me to follow her fingers. I wasn't doing a good enough job apparently, because she wasn't happy. "You are in shock, Anita, and so is Gregory. He was a little shocky before you began, but damn it."

I blinked and tried to focus on her. My eyes just couldn't settle on anything, as if the world were trembling, but that made no sense. Maybe I was the one that was trembling? I couldn't tell. I clutched the cover they'd put around me, huddling on my white couch amid the multicolored pillows, and couldn't get warm. "What are you saying, doc?"

"I'm saying that Gregory's chances are worse than fifty-fifty now."

I blinked and fought to look at her, meet her eyes, to think. "How bad?"

"Seventy-thirty, maybe. He's curled on the deck in a blanket, shivering worse than you are."

I shook my head, and couldn't seem to stop. I closed my eyes, forced myself to be still for a second, a heartbeat. I spoke without opening my eyes. "I saw . . . how did Gregory heal . . ." I stopped, tried again. "How did he survive . . . what she did to him?"

"We can regrow any body part short of decapitation, unless fire is added to the wound to close it. We can't heal burns, unless the burned flesh is completely removed, in effect making a new wound." Her voice was bitter, fierce. I'd never heard her so angry.

I looked up at her. "What's wrong with you?"

Lillian looked down, wouldn't meet my eyes. "I was the doctor on call the night she did that to Gregory. I saw the reality, not just a memory."

I shook my head, and had to bury my chin on my knees to stop the movement. "It isn't a memory with the munin, doc, it's real. It's like . . . it's like a live-action movie, but with me in the movie." I hugged my knees and tried desperately not to think, not to revisit what I'd experienced. I was actually having some luck being absolutely blank. Even my mind had finally found something so terrible it couldn't cope with it. In a bizarre way, it was comforting. I'd finally found a line that I could not cross.

"If I try to force Gregory into animal form now, it'll probably kill him," Dr. Lillian said.

I buried my face into my knees, hiding. I spoke with my mouth buried against the thick covers. "I can't try again."

"No one is asking you to call that bitch again."

"Anita." It was Nathaniel.

It wasn't his voice that made me look up, it was the rich, bitter smell of coffee. I found him holding my baby penguin mug full of fresh coffee. It was very pale, lots of sugar, lots of cream; good for shock. Hell, good for everything.

He helped me rescue my hands from the blanket and wrap them around the mug. I held the mug tight, and it took several seconds to realize I was burning my hands. I didn't panic, just handed the mug back to Nathaniel. He took it, and I stared at my pink, red hands. I had first-degree burns, and I hadn't felt the heat until it was too late.

"Damn," I said, softly.

Lillian sighed. "I'll get some ice." She left us alone.

Nathaniel knelt in front of me, being careful not to spill the coffee. Merle and Cherry glided into the living room while I was still staring at my reddened hands. Cherry sat beside me on the couch. She was still nude, but it didn't matter. Nothing seemed to matter. Merle stayed standing, and

I didn't even bother trying to look up at him. All I could see were the silver toes of his boots.

"Nathaniel said that you touched his beast when you marked his back," Cherry said.

I blinked at her, meeting her pale eyes. I nodded. I remembered a shining moment, after I'd marked his back actually, where I'd felt his beast roiling under the touch of my power, and I'd been sure I could call that part of him, make him shapeshift for me. I was still nodding, and made myself stop, saying, "I remember."

Lillian came back out and applied bags of ice wrapped in a small towel to my hands. "Try not to hurt yourself for a few minutes. I'm going back to check on Gregory." She left me with the three leopards and my ice.

"If you touched Nathaniel's beast, there's a chance you could call Gregory's now."

I shook my head. "I don't think so."

Cherry gripped my arm. "Don't fall apart on us now, Anita, Gregory needs you."

The first flare of anger pushed through the shock. "I have done my fucking best for him tonight."

She dropped her hand away from my arm, but didn't look away. "Anita, please, Merle thinks you may be strong enough to call Gregory's beast, even before your first full moon."

I clutched the towel-covered ice to my chest. The sudden cold across my nearly naked chest helped clear my head. "I thought that wasn't possible before I shifted for the first time."

"With you, Anita," Merle said, "I would be a fool to say what you can and can't do."

I let the ice fall on the coverlet in my lap and looked up at the big man. "Why the change of heart? I failed Gregory out there on the deck."

"You risked yourself for one of your cats. It is the very best a Nimira-Ra, or -Raj, has in them, to take great risks for their people."

I touched the towel, found one corner wet, and knew the plastic bag hadn't sealed completely. I moved the bag right-side up so it wouldn't spill anymore. "What do you want from me?" My voice sounded as tired as I felt.

Merle knelt in front of me, and I met his eyes. There was a look in them that I didn't want right now. He seemed to trust me, and I didn't feel trustworthy. I felt scared.

"Call Gregory's beast."

"I don't know how. When I was with Nathaniel, it was . . ." I sighed.

"It was sexual," Cherry finished for me.

I nodded. "I am not trying for that kind of mood with Gregory again tonight. I don't think either he, or I, could handle it if it went wrong again."

"Calling the beast doesn't have to be sexual," Merle said.

I met his strangely trusting gaze. I was beyond tired. I just didn't have anything left tonight, not for Gregory. I did not want to touch him again tonight. Part of me was afraid that Raina would make an unplanned appearance, though I knew that was almost impossible for her now. I did have better control than that. But . . . "How can I ever touch Gregory again and not remember that?"

"I don't know," Cherry said, "but please, Anita, please help him."

"How do I call his beast without getting in the mood?" I asked.

"You need to talk to someone who can call the beast from their people," Merle said.

I looked at him. "You got someone in mind?"

"I am told your Ulfric can call the beast from his wolves."

I nodded. "So I hear."

"If he called a wolf into form, while you watched, then he might be able to show you how to do it."

"You really think it will work?" I asked him.

"I don't know," he said, "but isn't it worth trying?"

I handed him the leaking bag of ice. "Sure, if Richard will come."

Nathaniel answered that one. "Richard blames himself for Gregory's injuries. If we offer him a chance to heal him, he'll come."

I stared at Nathaniel, watched the intelligence in those flower-colored eyes. It was one of the most insightful things

I'd ever heard him say. It gave me just a little hope, that indeed Nathaniel could be made whole—that he was getting better. I needed some hope just then, but it was still unnerving for Nathaniel to know Richard so well, to be that observant. It meant that I'd underestimated Nathaniel. I kept equating submissiveness with being inferior, and that wasn't really the case. Some people choose to be bottoms, to serve; it doesn't make them less, just different. I looked into his face and wondered what else I'd missed, or what else he'd show me? It was a night for revelations, so why the hell not have Richard join us? How much worse could it get? Please, no one answer that.

32

I BRUSHED MY teeth and sat at the kitchen table in the dark, drinking coffee while we waited. Nathaniel padded barefoot into the room, his hair swinging loose around his bare chest and the jean shorts he'd put on.

"How's Gregory?" I asked.

"Dr. Lillian put an IV in him, to help with the shock, she said." He stopped beside the table, not quite in front of me.

"An IV. Richard will be here within an hour or less. If she put an IV in then . . ." I let my voice trail off.

Nathaniel finished for me. "Gregory's very hurt."

I looked up at him in the darkened kitchen. The only light was the small one over the sink. It left most of the room in thick shadows. "You don't mean the injuries he got from the wolves, do you?"

He shook his head, all that hair sliding around his body. A long heavy strand slid over one shoulder, and he tossed his head to flip it back behind him. I'd never been around a man that had such long hair, who was so comfortable with it.

"He kept talking about Raina," Nathaniel said, "kept swearing under his breath." His voice had dropped low, almost a whisper. He was staring over my head at things I couldn't see, and probably didn't want to.

I touched his arm. "You alright?"

He looked down at me, smiled, but not like he was happy. He moved his hand so he was holding mine. His grip was tight like he needed the comfort.

"Talk to me, Nathaniel."

"I gave you copies of three of my movies." He smiled, wide this time, before I could say anything. "I know you've never watched them. When I gave them to you, I still thought you were like Gabriel and Raina, that it had to be sex, that you would like that they were porn. I understand now that you'll take care of us no matter what, not because you lust after us or because you love one of us, but just—because." He went to his knees, still holding my hand, pressing it against his chest with both his own. He laid his head on my lap, his face turned away from me. I moved a thick line of hair away from his face, so I could see his profile as he leaned against me.

We sat there for a few moments, me waiting for him to continue, him maybe waiting for me to prompt him, but the silence wasn't strained. One of us would fill it when we were ready, and we both knew that. He was the one who sighed, keeping one hand on my hand, pressed to him, his other hand curling around my leg. I could feel the beat of his heart against the back of my hand.

"I did more movies than just those three. Most of them with Raina. Gabriel wouldn't let her have me as a lover, or a slave. I think he knew she'd kill me, but on film where things could be controlled . . ." He hugged his body against mine, clinging.

"What happened?" I said, softly.

"She did that to Gregory on her own, as a kind of . . . fun. But when he survived it, she wanted to do a version of it on film."

I went very still for a second or two. I think I stopped breathing, because when my breath finally did come out, it shook. "You?" I made it a question.

He nodded his head, cheek still pressed to my thigh. "Me."

I stroked his hair, stared down into that young face. He was six years younger than me, almost seven, but it seemed like there should have been decades between us. He was so much a victim, so much anyone's meat.

"Gregory wouldn't do it again, said he'd kill himself first, and Gabriel must have believed him."

I kept petting his hair because I didn't know what else to do. What do you say while someone whispers horrors in your ear, tells you their most intimate, nightmarish secrets? You sit and you listen. And you give them the only thing you can—the silence and the safety to talk and to be heard.

His voice dropped soft, softer, until I had to lean my face over his to hear him. "They chained me down, and I knew the script. I knew what was about to happen, and I was excited. The fear made the anticipation almost unbearable."

I laid my cheek against his, felt his mouth move as he spoke, and I kept very, very quiet. I had nothing to offer but my silence, and my touch.

He whispered, "I like teeth, biting, I like a lot of damage. It was wonderful until . . ." He closed his eyes, turned his face into my jeans, as if even now he couldn't look at the memory. I had lifted my head up when he moved, but laid a gentle kiss on the back of his head. "It's okay, Nathaniel, it's okay."

He said something, but I couldn't understand it.

"What?"

He moved his head just enough so that his mouth wasn't buried against my leg. "God; it hurt. She took it in pieces, wanted it to last longer than it had with Gregory."

His whole body gave one great shiver, and I leaned over him, my free hand across his back, smoothing the hair away so I could reach his skin. I stroked over his back, and found all the little bite marks I'd left in his skin. I hadn't felt bad for marking him, until now. Now I felt like I'd used him like everyone else had.

I curled my body over his, hugging him into my lap, holding him as close as I could. "I am sorry, Nathaniel, so sorry."

"You don't have anything to be sorry about, Anita. You've never hurt me."

"Yes, I have."

He raised up enough to meet my eyes. He looked so young, eyes wide. "I love that you've marked me, don't be sorry about that." He gave a small smile. "If you start feeling guilty about it, you won't do it again, and I want you to, I want that very much."

"If I feed on you, Nathaniel, for the *ardeur*, or the flesh, or whatever, I'm using you. I don't use people."

He held my hand so tight that it almost hurt. "Don't do this to me."

"Do what?"

"Don't punish me for telling you about how Raina hurt me."

"I'm not punishing you."

"I tell you this horrible thing, and you start feeling protective of me, and guilty. I know you, Anita, you'll let your head get in the way of what we both need."

"And what exactly is that?" And even I could hear the impatience, almost anger, in my voice.

He raised up farther, bringing his face close to mine, because I'd sat up, distancing myself from him. "You need to feed the *ardeur*, and I need to have a place to belong."

"You are welcome in my house as long as you need it, Nathaniel."

He shook his head, pushing the hair back impatiently, letting go of my hand, putting his hands on my knees, half-crawling under the table so that he was kneeling between my legs, though only his hands touched the tops of my knees. He stared up at me. "No, you tolerate me. I do some housework, errands, but I don't belong. You don't go through your day thinking about me. I'm here, but I'm not part of your life, I know that. If I am your *pomme de sang*, then I will be. I'll finally belong to you in a way that both of us can live with."

I shook my head. "No, Nathaniel, no."

He grabbed the legs of the chair and picked the entire thing up with me on it from a kneeling position and moved it backwards with a bump, so he could fit under the table better. He hadn't even strained when he did it. He put his hands on the chair arms, slid his lower body against the chair, putting my knees on either side of his hips.

"And who else are you going to feed off of every day? Richard? Jean-Claude? Micah?"

"The *ardeur* may be temporary," I said.

He put a hand on either side of my waist. "If it's temporary, then feed on me until it goes away. If it's permanent . . ."

"I don't want to feed on anyone."

His hands slid around my waist, his head going to my lap, and I realized he was crying. "Please, don't do this, Anita, please don't do this."

I stroked his hair, his face, and didn't know what to say. What was I going to do if the *ardeur* was permanent? Richard didn't let anyone feed off of him for any reason—same rule I had. Jean-Claude would be literally dead to the world when I most needed to feed. Micah was still a question mark. But in some ways, feeding off of Nathaniel because he was the only one that would let me, was almost worse.

I lifted his face from my lap, a hand on either side. Tears glittered on his cheeks in the faint light. I kissed his forehead, kissed his closed eyes, the way you would a child's.

"Did I get here just in time, or am I interrupting?" It was Richard standing in the doorway. Perfect fucking timing, as always.

33

I FROZE WITH Nathaniel's face cradled in my hands, him kneeling between my legs with the table hiding most of him, having just risen from kissing him, and knew how it looked. I wasn't sure I could explain it to Richard's satisfaction. To my knowledge Richard didn't know about the *ardeur* yet, and right then I didn't want to tell him.

I laid another gentle kiss on Nathaniel's forehead and leaned back. I wasn't going to act like I'd done something wrong when I hadn't. Nathaniel took his cue from me, laying his head back in my lap, which I realized meant he was invisible from the doorway, the table hiding what he was doing.

Richard strode into the kitchen like an angry wind, his power biting along my skin. He came to stand where he could see that Nathaniel had his cheek against my thigh, gazing up at the larger man, as he towered over both of us.

Jamil and Shang-Da were hanging back by the doorway. They were good bodyguards, but some things bodyguards can't keep you safe from.

I felt my face go neutral, empty, vaguely pleasant. "I was comforting one of my leopards, something wrong with that?"

"He looks very comfortable," Richard said, voice mild enough, but his power was hot, like opening the door to an oven.

I licked my lips. I was going to have to explain the ardeur, sooner or later, and since I wanted him to help us save Gregory, tonight was probably the right time. "Nathaniel and I were discussing some side effects of marrying the vampire marks."

"You mean the *ardeur*," he said.

I was surprised and let it show. "Who told you?"

"Jean-Claude thought I should know. He encouraged me to come over and be here for you in the morning."

"And you said?" I kept my voice as neutral as I could, but not as neutral as I wanted it to be.

"I don't let him, or Asher, or any of them, feed off of me, blood or anything else. I don't see why I should change that rule just because it's you and it's sex instead of blood."

"Did he explain that if I don't feed off of you, or him, I still have to feed off of someone?"

"There's always your Nimir-Raj." The contempt in his voice was thick enough to walk on.

"Micah's been called away on pard business."

"You really think he won't be back before morning so you can fuck him? I do."

I stared up at him, still sitting in the face of his burning power and the sheer physical presence of him. Richard was one of those big men who never seemed big unless he was angry. He seemed big now, and I wasn't impressed.

I started petting Nathaniel's hair, and he snuggled in against my legs, letting the tension ease out of his body. "You dumped me, remember?"

"And did you fuck him for the first time before or after you found out I'd dumped you?"

I had to think about that for a second or two. "After," I said.

"You mourned my loss for, what, half a second?"

I felt heat crawl up my face. I was out of moral high ground, and explaining that it was the *ardeur* just wasn't good enough for Richard.

"It took all three of us to get into this mess, don't make it worse."

"Don't you mean four of us, or is it five now?"

I must have looked as blank as I felt. "I don't know what you're talking about."

He grabbed the table and shoved it backwards with a scream of wood on wood. Nathaniel stayed curled around my legs and just looked up at him. I'd never gotten my gun back from the wererats. I had gotten my knives back, but I wasn't really willing to cut Richard up, not yet, not for this.

I couldn't arm wrestle Richard, not and win, so really my only option was to sit, look perfectly calm, and tell him by my facial expression what a fucking asshole he was being.

He shoved the table again, making the wood scream, then he knelt beside Nathaniel and pushed his long hair back. He bared his back and stared at the bite marks.

"Is that all?" he asked, voice fierce, his power so high it was like treading in boiling water, up to my chin, and still rising.

"No," I said.

Richard gripped the back of Nathaniel's shorts and pulled, the movement so violent that Nathaniel's entire body moved with it. I heard the button from the top of the shorts bounce along the floor. Richard jerked down the shorts and stared at the bite marks, where they trailed ever lower.

Richard leaned over Nathaniel, not quite touching, but he was like some huge presence, and I felt Nathaniel cower against me.

Richard hissed into his ear, "Did she suck you off? She's good at that."

"That's enough, Richard."

Nathaniel answered, "No."

"You're so scared of me I can't tell if you're lying or not." He grabbed a handful of Nathaniel's hair and pulled him backwards, peeling him away from me. I had one of the wrist sheath knives in my hand and didn't remember drawing it. The point was pressed against the long line of Richard's throat, and even I was breathless at the speed of it. It must have been a blur of movement. It wasn't human speed.

Everything froze.

Shang-Da and Jamil moved into the room. I pressed the point deeper against Richard's neck. "Don't interfere, boys."

They stopped moving. I met Richard's gaze and found his eyes had gone wolf amber. "Let go of him, Richard." My voice was low, but it seemed to fill the room.

"You wouldn't kill me for this." His voice was low, careful, too.

"Kill, no, but bleed? Oh, yes."

"You need me to help you save Gregory."

I could feel his pulse beating against the tip of my knife. "I won't let you hurt Nathaniel to save Gregory."

His grip actually tightened on Nathaniel's hair, and I pressed the point in enough to draw the first crimson drop. "Would you be this upset if it wasn't Nathaniel?" he said.

"This is the only warning I will ever give you, Richard. Never touch one of my people again."

"Or what? You'll kill me? I don't think you'll do it."

I realized in that moment that if I wasn't willing to kill him, I had no threat. And I really wasn't willing to kill him, not over this, not yet.

I drew the blade back from his neck and watched him relax, the tension easing away from him, his hand still in Nathaniel's hair. I moved without thinking, and I was fast enough that the knife cut across his forearm before he could react. He jerked away, came to his feet, and took a step back, holding his bleeding arm. The cut was deeper than I'd meant for it to be, because I'd rushed it. Blood dripped from between his fingers. Jamil and Shang-Da moved into the room.

I stood and drew Nathaniel with me, as he pulled up his shorts to cover himself. I put the French doors at our backs. "You are never to lay a hand in anger on my leopards, Richard, you or any of your wolves."

Jamil was helping Richard press a towel to the wound. Shang-Da had gone for Dr. Lillian. "It would serve you right if I just walked out and left you and your leopards to fend for yourselves."

"You'd leave Gregory to be permanently deaf, or dead, because we had a fight? He's in danger because you couldn't control your temper, or your wolves."

"It's my fault, right, all my fault."

I just looked at him, Nathaniel behind me, the bloody knife still in my hand.

Richard gave a laugh that sounded more out of pain than humor. "I've let everyone down tonight." He looked at me, and there was something fierce in his face that wasn't his beast but just sheer emotion. Anger, pain, so deep it was like anquish. "I'll help you save Gregory, because you're right, it *is* my fault. I'll take this," he raised the wounded arm, while Jamil still held it, "because you're right again, I had no right to touch one of your people. I wouldn't have let you abuse one of my wolves either."

Dr. Lillian came in, took one look and started scolding us for being children who couldn't play well together. "He's going to need stitches. Shame on you both."

Richard stared over her head as she cleaned the wound. I think he wasn't really glaring at me, he was glaring at Nathaniel. He was genuinely jealous. Jealous in a way that he shouldn't have been. What had Jean-Claude told him about the *ardeur* and about Nathaniel, and about what we'd all done together at the Circus? Jean-Claude wouldn't actually lie, but he might make things sound worse if it suited his purposes. But what purpose did it serve to make Richard jealous of Nathaniel? I would have to ask Jean-Claude about that. I had time to call while Richard got stitched up.

34

JEAN-CLAUDE ADMITTED ONLY to telling the absolute truth. But, he added, if because of that Monsieur Zeeman was jealous of Nathaniel, this wasn't an altogether bad thing. "He will share you with me, because he must, and he will share you with Micah also, because he must, but we are both alphas, dominants. To share you with someone like Nathaniel—that is different."

"You changed something about the story to make Nathaniel sound like more of a threat, didn't you?"

"No, *ma petite,* I merely told the truth without leaving anything out. He is not entirely happy with Jason either."

"Jean-Claude, you can't do this to Richard. You'll drive him mad."

"Mad enough, perhaps, to finally acknowledge that he cannot live without you, and that he must come to terms with our triumvirate."

"You Machiavellian shithead, you're playing with him."

"I am trying to maneuver him into doing what must be done if we are to survive. If that be Machiavellian, so be it."

"You are making things worse," I said.

"I don't believe so. I think, *ma petite,* that you still do not understand men. Many men will give up a woman if they are unhappy with her. But let another man try to claim her, and often, they find they still do want her."

"You and Micah aren't competition enough?" I asked.

"As I explained, we are his equals. Nathaniel is lesser, and that will prick his pride more."

"I didn't think Richard had that kind of destructive guy pride."

"I think there are many things you do not know about our Richard."

"And you do?"

"I am, after all, a man, *ma petite*. I believe I understand the male psyche a tiny bit better than you do."

I couldn't argue with that. "Well, give me a heads-up next time you plan to do any maneuvering. You could have gotten one of us killed."

He sighed. "I do keep underestimating the stubbornness of both of you. My apologies for that."

I leaned my forehead against the kitchen wall. "Jean-Claude . . ."

"Yes, *ma petite*."

I closed my eyes. "Tell me exactly what you think Richard thinks about Nathaniel and me."

"I told him the absolute truth, *ma petite,* nothing more, and nothing less."

I turned around, put my back to the wall, looked out at the empty kitchen. Richard was in the downstairs bathroom getting stitched up. Nathaniel was with the other leopards. I'd given strict orders that he was not to be left alone. I just wasn't up to Richard and him actually having a fight. It would be too . . . ridiculous, or pathetic.

"And what does that mean, that you told the truth, no more, no less?"

"You will not like it."

"I don't like it now, just tell me, Jean-Claude."

"I told him what had happened with the *ardeur*, and added my own belief that the reason you so often find Nathaniel around when sex is in the air is that you find him sexually attractive."

"That did not make Richard come over here and start a fight."

"I do remember adding that you might find a less-demanding male refreshing after the two of us. Someone who did not make so many demands on you, someone who merely accepted you as you are."

"You do that," I said.

"So good of you to notice," he said. "But it is not I that has been living in your home for months, and from what I smell on Nathaniel when he comes into work, sharing your bed."

"Any of the wereleopards are welcome in the bedroom when they stay here. It's like a big pile of puppies—it's not sexual."

"If you say so." His voice was soft, mocking.

"Damn you, Jean-Claude, you know I don't see Nathaniel that way."

He sighed, and it was heavy. "I think it is not me that you lie to, *ma petite*, but yourself."

"I am not in love with Nathaniel."

"Did I ever say you were?"

"Then what are you talking about?"

He made a small exasperated sound. "*Ma petite*, you still believe that you must love every man that you come to physically. It is not so. You can have very pleasant, even wondrous sex with a friend. It does not have to be love."

I was shaking my head, realized he couldn't see it, and said, "I don't do casual sex, Jean-Claude, you know that."

"Whatever you are doing with Nathaniel, *ma petite*, it is not casual."

"I can't use him as my *pomme de sang*. I can't."

"Your morals have reared their ugly heads, *ma petite*, do not let them make you foolish."

I opened my mouth to protest everything he'd said, but closed it and just thought about what he'd said for a few seconds. Did I find Nathaniel attractive? Well, yeah. But I found a lot of men attractive. That didn't mean I had to be intimate with them.

"*Ma petite*, I can hear you breathing. What are you thinking?"

What he said made me think a new thought. "When we first married the marks I could almost read your mind, unless you concentrated to keep me out. Now it's not like that. Maybe the *ardeur* will be temporary, too."

"Perhaps, we can but hope."

"If I have the *ardeur*, I'll have to have sex. Isn't that what you wanted?"

"I would be a fool to deny that your enforced chastity is

burdensome, but I would never willingly inflict the *ardeur* on anyone. It is a . . . curse, *ma petite*. The blood lust that I feel can be sated. My body can only hold so much. But the *ardeur*, oh, *ma petite,* it is never truly satisfied. There is always that ache, that need. How could I wish that upon you? Though if our Monsieur Zeeman would cooperate, it might be the answer for the two of you to finally reach some permanent arrangement."

"What, move in together?"

"Perhaps." His voice was very careful when he said that one word.

"Richard and I can't be in a room for an hour without arguing, unless we are having sex. Somehow I don't think that makes for domestic bliss."

I felt the first emotion he'd let me feel over the phone—relief. He was relieved. "I want what is best for all of us, *ma petite,* but as things grow more complex, I am no longer certain what 'best' would be."

"Don't tell me your machinations didn't include some backup plan to cover every eventuality. You are the ultimate plotter, don't tell me you missed a trick."

"I watched Belle Morte fill your eyes with her fire. You are acquiring powers as if you were a Master Vampire, or a Master Lycanthrope. How could I have planned for any of this?"

There was a cold knot of fear in the center of my gut. "So you finally admit that you don't know what the hell is going on either."

"*Oui*, does that please you?" I heard the first stirrings of anger in his voice. "Are you happy now, *ma petite*? I am well and truly out of my depth. No one has ever tried to forge an alliance such as we have, an alliance not of master and two slaves, but of three equals. I do not think you appreciate how gentle I am when it comes to hoarding my power. The wolves are my animal to call. Many masters would have forced them to simply be an adjunct to their own vampires."

"Nikolaos's animal to call was rats, not wolves," I said. "By the time you took over as Master of the City, Marcus and Raina's pack was too strong for you to make them an adjunct to your power. Hell, until you replenished the vamps that I killed, they were probably more powerful than you and your vampires."

"Are you implying that the only reason I am not a tyrant is because I didn't have the strength of arms to make it so?"

I thought about that for a second, then said, "I'm not implying it, I'm saying it."

"You think so little of me?"

"I know what you were like two, almost three years ago, and I think then you would have consolidated your power base with very little regard for anyone that got in your way."

"Are you saying I am ruthless?"

"Practical," I said.

It was his turn to be quiet for a second or two, then, "Practical, yes, I am that, as are you, *ma petite*."

"I know what I am, Jean-Claude, it's you I'm not sure of."

"I would never willingly hurt you, *ma petite*."

"I believe you," I said.

"I am not sure the same can be said of you," he said, quietly.

"I don't want to hurt either of you. But Richard cannot harm my leopards, and if you do anything stupid, don't blame me for what happens next."

"I would never underestimate your level of . . . practicality, *ma petite,* though I think Richard might."

"He told me I wouldn't kill him just for roughing up Nathaniel."

"How rough was Richard to little Nathaniel?"

"Don't talk about him like he's a child, Jean-Claude, and rough enough that I cut Richard's arm open."

"How badly?"

"The doc's stitching him up, even as we speak."

"Oh, dear," he said, and sighed, and this time the sound eased down my skin. I realized that he'd been behaving himself until now, at least about using his voice.

"No more games, Jean-Claude. I want to put Richard on the phone, and you tell him you did this on purpose."

"But I cannot tell him that I lied about Nathaniel, now can I?"

"You fix this, Jean-Claude, now, tonight. I need Richard to teach me how to call Gregory's beast. I don't have time for him to sulk."

"What am I to tell him, *ma petite*? What surety can I give him that you will not be in Nathaniel's arms tomorrow morning? I believe that I can maneuver Richard into staying the night, having him there at your side when the *ardeur* rises."

"Richard's already made his position clear, Jean-Claude. He doesn't let you, or Asher, or anyone, feed off of him. He doesn't see why the rules change just because it's me and sex, instead of blood."

"He said that?" Jean-Claude gave a questioning lilt to his voice.

"Yeah, he said that, almost word-for-word."

Jean-Claude sighed, and it sounded tired. "What am I to do with the two of you?"

"Don't ask me," I said, "I just work here."

"And what, exactly, does that mean, *ma petite*?"

"It means that we don't have a boss. It's great being equals, if that's what we are, but none of us knows what the hell is going on, and that isn't good, Jean-Claude. We are messing with some very serious stuff here, metaphysically and emotionally and just plain physically. We need some clue as to what we should be doing with all of it."

"And who should we be asking advice of, *ma petite*? If any vampire on the Council were to suspect that I have not given you both the fourth mark, they would destroy us, for fear that with the fourth mark we would become an even greater power."

"I've talked to Marianne and her friends. They're witches, Wiccan."

"So we find, what, a local coven, and ask their guidance?" He sounded patronizing.

"I resent the tone, Jean-Claude, especially since I don't hear you offering any better suggestions. Don't criticize unless you can do better."

"Very true, *ma petite,* and very wise. My deepest and

most sincere apologies. You are quite right. I do not have a suggestion for whom we might turn to for advice, or guidance. I will think upon your suggestion to find a friendly witch to speak with."

"I have a friendly one to speak to. She just might need to see the three of us together to see how things work."

"You mean your Marianne?"

"Yeah."

"I thought she was more psychic than witch."

"There's not all that much difference," I said.

"I will take your word on that. I do not have much business with either."

I realized I'd been planning to call Marianne since I woke up sandwiched between Caleb and Micah. Funny how it had slipped my mind.

"Is there anything you can say to Richard that will help smooth things on this end?"

"Do you wish me to lie?"

"Damn it, Jean-Claude . . ."

"I can point out to him that if he does not meet the *ardeur*'s appetite that someone else must."

"I've already pointed that out to him." I thought about that for a few heartbeats. "He accused me of having . . ." I found I couldn't quite say it. "He accused me of doing worse with Nathaniel than I've done, and he was crude about it. I'm not sure I want to have sex with him right now."

"You are angry with him," Jean-Claude said.

"Oh, yeah."

"So angry that if he asked, you would refuse his bed?"

I started to say *yes*, then stopped myself. I was tired. Tired of all of it, of both of them, if the truth be known. Couldn't live with them, or without them. I wanted Richard's body like an ache in my heart, but when he wanted to be, he could be ugly, and his mood tonight was ugly. I didn't want to have sex with him when he was like this. Hell, I didn't want to be around him when he was like this.

"I don't know," I said.

"Well, that was honest, and does not bode well. If you refuse Richard, and Nathaniel, and your Nimir-Raj does not return tonight, what will you do in the morning, *ma petite*? Please, think carefully on this. I beg you to choose the lesser evil, whatever that may be, rather than wait until the hunger overrides your common sense, or even your need for survival."

"What are you saying?"

"I am saying what I have said before—that to deny the *ardeur* is to worsen it. Deny it long enough and hard enough, and it will begin to erode all that you are, or thought yourself to be. I survived what I did to feed it in those first weeks, but my moral degradation had been accomplished years before I died. I say again, *ma petite,* that you will not take it as well as I did. I believe it will compromise your sense of who you are."

"And fucking Nathaniel isn't going to compromise me?"

He sighed. "Put that way, I do see your point. But how much more compromising would it be to seduce a stranger?"

"I would never do that."

"Is that not exactly what you did with the Nimir-Raj?" His voice was very quiet as he said it, very careful not to be accusatory.

I would have loved to have argued the point, but I hate to lose, and I was going to lose this one. "Alright, you've made your point."

"I hope so, Anita, I do hope so." He never used my name unless something was very wrong. Damn.

"You know, just once it might be nice to have normal problems."

"And what, exactly, is a normal problem, *ma petite*?"

Another point for Jean-Claude. "I don't know anymore."

"You sound tired, *ma petite*."

"It's only a few hours until dawn. I've been up all night, so yeah, I'm tired." Just acknowledging it seemed to bring it on in a rush that left me rubbing my eyes, which smeared the eye shadow I'd put on onto my fingers and probably around my eyelids. I wore makeup so seldomly that I often forgot I was wearing it.

Richard came back into the kitchen with his bodyguards

and the wererats in tow. He gave me a look, and it was not a friendly one.

"I've got to go," I said to Jean-Claude.

"Do you wish me to speak to Richard?"

"No, I think you've done enough damage for one night."

"I meant only to help."

"Sure you did."

"*Ma petite.*"

"Yes."

"Be careful, and remember what I have said about the *ardeur*. There is no shame in it."

"Even you don't believe that," I said.

"Ah, you have found me out. There is no shame in feeding, if you feed immediately on a person of your own choosing. If you fight, then you will find yourself feeding on someone not of your choosing, in a place not of your choosing. I do not think you would enjoy that, *ma petite.*"

He was right about that anyway. "I'll talk to you tomorrow after you get up. I haven't forgotten Damian, you know."

"I did not think that you had, *ma petite.* I will look forward to your call."

I hung up without saying good-bye, mainly because I was angry, and scared. Not only did I have Richard to deal with tonight and Gregory to save, but tomorrow morning when I woke up, the *ardeur* would be there, waiting. There was a chance that it wouldn't be, that the one day was the only time I'd have it, but I couldn't count on that. I had to plan for the worst-case scenario. Worst case was I would wake up tomorrow and need to feed just like I had this morning. The big question was, who would I feed on, and could I live with myself after I'd done it?

35

I HATE BEING awake at three in the morning. It is the god-forsaken heart of darkness when the body runs slow, and the brain runs slower, and all you want to do is sleep. But I had promises to keep, and miles to go before I could sleep. Or at least a couple of miracles to perform before I could go to bed.

Dr. Lillian had unhooked Gregory's IV, but he was still bundled in the quilts. He sat on the picnic table on the deck, cradled between Zane and Cherry. Dr. Lillian kept touching Gregory, checking his pulse, how clammy his skin was. She was frowning and clearly not happy. Nathaniel stayed by them, keeping the picnic table between him and Richard. Richard hadn't tried to hurt him again; in fact, he'd ignored him studiously. The other cats milled around near the sliding glass doors. The two wererat bodyguards, Claudia and Igor, were standing to one side of me as I leaned on the railing. They started following me around when Richard came out with his bandaged arm and Jamil and Shang-Da at his back.

Richard's power crept on the summer darkness like close thunder, making the hot, sticky night even thicker and making it harder to breathe. I think it was the press of his power, the edge of his anger, that made the wererats start acting like bodyguards. I'd tried telling them that Richard wouldn't hurt me, but Claudia had shrugged, and said, "Rafael told us to keep you safe, and that's what we're going to do."

"Even if I tell you that there is no threat?"

She shrugged again. "I'd say, you're a little too close to this one to make a sound judgment call."

I'd glanced at Igor. "You agree with her?"

"I never argue with a lady, especially one that can beat me at arm wrestling."

Igor's logic was hard to argue with, but it meant that I had acquired two tall, muscular shadows, and it irritated me. But neither of them gave a damn whether I was happy or not. They were following Rafael's orders, and my wishes didn't count.

So Richard and his bodyguards, and me, with mine, stood on the deck, facing Stephen, who had stripped off in preparation for the change. If you made the change with clothes on, you ruined them. Shapeshifters either haunted the thrift shops, looking for old clothes to wear on the night of the full moon, or went nude.

We all stood there in the circle of Richard's power. The energy built around us like invisible lightning lashing around us. The power literally crackled, raising the hair on our arms, raising the hair on our heads, like the hackles on a dog.

Jamil said, "Richard . . ." But one glance from Richard stopped him in mid-sentence. The power rose another notch, squeezing around us like some kind of giant hand.

"What's wrong, Richard? What's with the power display?" I asked.

He turned to me, and the anger in his face made me want to step back, but I didn't. I stood my ground, but it took effort.

"Do you want to save your cat?" he asked, voice thick with the emotion that showed on his face, that crackled in his power.

My voice was almost a whisper, "Yes."

"Then watch," he said.

He spread his hands in front of Stephen, keeping them about eight inches away from the smaller man's shoulders. The energy squeezed tight, and tighter, until I had to swallow to try and clear my ears, as if there'd been a pressure change. But swallowing didn't help. It wasn't that kind of pressure.

Richard's hands convulsed, as if his fingers were digging into something invisible just in front of Stephen. He staggered towards Richard, one step, and I was close enough to hear a small pained sound come from him. Richard balled his hands into fists, and something shimmered between them like heat caught in the close summer darkness. The bones in my face ached with the building power. The air was almost too thick to breathe, as if it had weight.

Richard made one abrupt movement with his hands and the pressure broke, like a storm finally bursting to life. For a second or two, I thought the heavy, clear liquid that burst around us was rain, but it was hot like blood, and it didn't fall from the sky. It burst from Stephen's body. I'd seen dozens of shapeshifters change, but nothing like this. It was as if Stephen's body blew apart in a rain of hot, thick fluids and small bits of flesh. The beast usually pulls itself from the human body, like a butterfly from a chrysalis, but not this time. Stephen's body folded over on itself, and his man-wolf shape was just suddenly standing there. It collapsed to its knees, panting, shivering.

I was left standing, not even breathing, covered in the rapidly cooling bits and pieces of Stephen's body. When I could breathe again, I gasped. "Jesus Christ."

Stephen's fur was the color of dark, golden honey. He crouched, shivering at Richard's feet. Again, the change may hurt while the person is going through it, but once it's over, they usually stand up and start moving around. Stephen seemed disoriented, almost like he was in pain. What the hell was happening?

He crawled the last few steps to Richard, laying his long, teeth-filled snout against his wolf king's jogging shoes. He was almost in a fetal position, great, muscular arms wrapped around golden fur, lying at his Ulfric's feet. It was extreme submissive behavior, and I didn't know why. Stephen hadn't done anything wrong.

I looked up at Richard. His white shirt was plastered to his body with the thick fluids. He turned his face to look at me, and the faint light of stars glistened in the wetness on his face. A thick piece of something slid down his cheek as he glared at me. The look on his face was defiant, as if he expected me to be angry with him.

I raised a shaking hand and wiped the worst of the gunk off of my face, flinging it onto the deck where it hit with a wet splat. I looked at the bodyguards. They too were spattered with the thick stuff, but not nearly as messy as Richard and I. They hadn't been standing as close. They all stared at Richard, stared at him with a mixture of horror and anger and astonishment on their faces, which let me know that something was very, very wrong.

I had to try twice before I could speak, and even then my voice was breathy. "I've seen a lot of shapeshifters change into their beasts, but I've never seen anything like that. Was it different because you called Stephen's beast instead of him doing it on his own?"

"No," Richard said.

I waited for more, but that was all he said, and it looked like all he intended to say. But *no* just didn't cover it. I looked at the others. "Okay, someone tell me what just happened here."

Jamil started to speak, then stopped and looked at Richard. "With my Ulfric's permission." The words were polite, but the tone was angry, almost defiant.

Richard looked at him. I couldn't see his face, but whatever look he gave Jamil, it was something that made the other man flinch. Jamil dropped to one knee in the spreading pool of thick liquid. He bowed his head. "I mean no offense, Ulfric."

"That's a lie," Richard said, and his voice was lower than normal, just a tone or two above a growl.

Jamil darted a glance upward, then bowed his head again. "I don't know what you want me to say, Ulfric. Tell me, and I will say it."

Richard turned back to me, leaving Jamil kneeling. "I didn't just call Stephen's beast, I tore it from his body."

I glanced down at Stephen, who was still crouched at Richard's feet. "Why?" I asked.

"It's usually punishment to do it this way."

"What did Stephen do?"

"Nothing." Richard's voice was harsh, almost as harsh as the look on his face.

"Then why punish him?"

"Because I could." His chin lifted when he said it, and that arrogance was back.

"What the hell is wrong with you, Richard?"

He laughed, and the sound was so inappropriate that it made me jump. He laughed, but it was too loud, too harsh. "Didn't this teach you how to call Gregory's beast?"

"I didn't learn a damn thing except that you're in a foul mood and taking it out on other people."

"You want to know what's wrong? You really want to know?"

"Yeah, I do."

"Get out of the way, Stephen," he said, and Stephen didn't even ask why, he just crawled out from between us.

We were left staring at each other, not quite two feet apart. What he'd done to Stephen seemed to have taken the edge off his power, but it was still there like some great slumbering thing pressing against the surface.

"Open the marks, Anita, feel what I'm feeling."

"I opened the marks already. I figured I had to, to learn how to do this."

"So it's just my shielding?" He made it a question.

I nodded. "I can feel your rage, Richard, I just don't know why."

"Just my shields between us and . . ." He shook his head, almost smiling, then he dropped his shields. It hit me like a physical force, drove me back a step. Anger so raw it filled my throat with bile; a self-loathing so deep that it drew tears down my cheeks in two hot lines. I stood there for a minute feeling Richard's pain, and it was suffocating.

I stared up at him, the tears still wet on my cheeks. "Richard, oh my God."

"Don't feel sorry for me, don't you *dare* feel pity for me!" He grabbed my arms when he said it, and the moment we touched, our beasts poured up from inside us and spread across our skins in a hot dance of power. His beast crashed through me, invisible, metaphysical claws ripping through my body. It was as if Richard's beast was trying to eat his way through my body. I screamed, and thrust my beast into his, and I felt claws ripping into meat. There was nothing to see with the eye, but I could feel it, feel fur and muscle and meat under claws and teeth. I screamed not just from the pain, but from the sensations of cutting Richard up. He hurt me, and I wanted to hurt him back. There was no more reasoning, no more thinking, just reacting.

Our beasts tore through each other, rolling, clawing, tearing. We collapsed on the deck, screaming. Dimly I could still feel Richard's hands locked on my arms as if he couldn't let go.

There was movement all around us. People hovering, but no one interfered, no one touched us. When we fell, they scattered, as if afraid to touch us. Voices shouting above our screams, "What's wrong? What's happening? Anita, Anita! Richard, control it!"

His beast was suddenly like a weight inside me, but it didn't hurt. The two energies lay quiet, leaning against each other, not mingling, just leaning. I could almost feel the solid push of his beast against something inside of me that had bones and fur, and wasn't me. I couldn't hear anything but the thundering of the blood in my own head. I felt Richard's weight on top of me, before I looked down to find him collapsed over me. His head rested on my chest. I could feel the pulse of the blood in his body, his heart racing against the skin of my stomach. I was covered in the cool slime from Stephen's body. One, I was lying in a pool of it; two, Richard had been covered in it, and he'd slid down my body. I was going to have to shower before I could go to bed, even if it was dawn. And I ached, ached as if I'd been beaten. I knew I'd be stiff when I moved.

Everyone was standing in a ring above us, staring down. I found my voice, hoarse, almost raspy, but clear. "Get off of me."

Richard raised his head, slowly, as if he hurt, too. "I'm sorry."

"You're always sorry, Richard, now get off of me."

He didn't move, in fact he settled heavier, hands curving at the edges of my waist. "Do you still want to help Gregory?"

"That's what this whole show is about, so yeah."

"Then let's try again."

I tensed, and started trying to wriggle out from under him.

His hands tightened at my waist. "Easy, Anita, it won't hurt. I don't think."

"Says you. It hurt like a son of a bitch. Let me go, Richard." My voice held the beginnings of anger, and fear. I liked the anger, could have done without the fear.

"You fought me to a standoff. It's over," he said.

I stopped struggling and stared at him. "What are you talking about?"

"We're not the same kind of animal, Anita. They had to find out who's . . . tougher."

I stared down the line of my body into those brown eyes. "Are you saying this was some kind of dominance display?"

"Not exactly."

Strangely, it was Merle who answered. "When two such different beasts meet, and they are both strong dominants—such as a true Nimir-Ra, and a true Ulfric—the two animals must fight and test each other. I have seen it before. It is a type of taming of one beast by the other."

I looked way up at the tall man. "No one tamed anyone."

Merle knelt beside us. "I think you are right. It is as the Ulfric has said, a standoff. He could have kept fighting until one of you won, or lost, but he chose to let it be."

I remembered someone telling Richard to control it, *it* being his beast. I looked at Richard. "You stopped, didn't you?"

"I don't care which of us is more dominant, Anita. Those kind of games have never meant anything to me, unless people forced me to play them."

"You said something about helping Gregory. What did you mean?"

He started working his way a little higher up my body, sliding his body along mine. I could feel the slime from his shirt recoating my bare stomach and nearly bare chest. My disgust must have shown on my face, because he asked, "What's wrong?"

"Your shirt is covered in slime, and I'm lying in a pool of it. I didn't just want you to get off me to be off of me, I wanted to get up out of this mess."

He came to his knees, his legs on either side of mine. I

could feel our beasts stretched between us like something that should have been visible, as if each of their heads was buried in the other's chest. He offered me a hand. I stared up at him.

"I know you don't need the help, Anita. But our beasts are touching now. It's a close connection and physical contact will help us keep it until we finish with Gregory."

I didn't need the earnest look on his face to know he was telling the truth. The marks were still open between us. I knew he was telling the truth.

I took his hand and he lifted me to my feet. Standing up hurt, and either he felt it or saw it on my face. "I hurt you," he said softly.

"We hurt each other." I could feel that he was stiff, aching, but he moved like he wasn't, and I still moved human stiff.

He raised the bottom of his shirt, still holding my hand. "Touch me."

I looked up at him, and he laughed. "Just keep physical contact, Anita. I don't mean anything by it. But I need both my hands."

I laid a hand on his side, very tentatively.

He shook his head. "I'm going to take my shirt off."

If you can't touch a person's hands, arms, or much of their upper body, you run out of polite places to touch. I settled for sliding my hand under the wet shirt, touching the smooth firmness of his side. Even his skin was damp from the shirt having molded to it.

Richard drew the shirt over his head, and I was left standing inches from him as he revealed the flat plains of his stomach, the muscular swell of his chest, and arched his back to draw the shirt over his head. The sight of him, the pull of the lust that always came when I saw him without clothes pushed my beast against his. I felt furred sides roll against each other, a tentative roll of power that felt like someone had taken velvet and caressed the most intimate part of me.

Richard gasped.

I concentrated hard to stop the movement, but that I'd done it without thinking brought heat in a wash up my face.

I looked at the ground; my hand was still only touching his side, just above his jeans, but the touch felt suddenly intimate. I wanted to take my hand away, and his hand covered mine before I could move. He pressed my hand to him, firm, but not forceful.

He touched my chin, raised my face until I had to look at him. "It's alright, Anita. I love the fact that just seeing me moves you like that."

The blush that had been fading, blazed harder. He laughed, soft, low, with that edge that a man's laugh gets when he's thinking intimate things. "I have missed you, Anita."

I looked up at him. "I missed you, too."

His beast moved through me in a wash of power and sensation that left me gasping. My beast responded to his. I couldn't seem to stop it. Maybe I didn't want to. Those shadow forms rolled in and out of each other, through us, until I couldn't breathe, couldn't think. It was Richard who drew back first, and said, "Dear God, I never thought . . ." I felt the effort it cost him to draw back from me, to stop. His face showed a businesslike, no-nonsense look, but I could feel the trembling of other things inside him. His voice came out brisk. "I'll call Jamil's beast, the way it's supposed to be done. Feel what I do, how I use my beast to call his."

My voice was a little breathy. "Then I'll do Gregory."

He nodded. "Or I can call Shang-Da's beast, if you need to see it one more time."

I nodded. "Okay."

He slid a hand around my waist, drawing me against him. It didn't seem as intimate as the roil of our beasts inside us. Jamil stood facing us. He'd stripped off his shirt and shoes, but kept on his pants. It occurred to me for the first time that I'd never seen him nude, except when he'd been injured and near death. Jamil didn't do casual nudity. One of the few modest shapeshifters I knew.

"I'm ready, Ulfric."

After what Richard had done to Stephen I thought Jamil was being awful trusting. But then, everyone trusted Richard;

he was very trustworthy. No, lack of trust wasn't the problem.

"I don't need to physically touch anyone to do this, but it's easier that way, so I'll touch him, so you can understand better how it works."

I nodded, wrapped in the circle of his arm, the firmness of his body, the velvet roll of our beasts like another arm to hold us against each other.

Richard touched Jamil's bare shoulder, and I felt his power move outward like a warm wind. It caressed Jamil's skin, and Richard's beast flowed with it, pulling mine along for the ride. Richard's power teased along Jamil, coaxing, and the best analogy I could think of was like someone trying to lure a cat down out of a tree. Beckoning, talking sweetly, promising caresses, and treats, if only it would come down. But Jamil's beast didn't come down, it came out. It rolled out of the center of his being like a pale golden fog, an almost shape. I saw his beast like I'd seen Micah's earlier, for an instant, then Jamil collapsed to the deck, and his bare back began to ripple like water under a strong wind. The wolf drew out of his back in a long wet line, and his body dissolved into that dark furred shape, so that his human body became the wolf, like flipping over a coin, heads, tails, but still the same coin. I felt the rightness of it, the harmony of it. Jamil embraced what he was; there was no conflict between him and his beast. I'd never seen him in wolf form, man-wolf, but not this pony-sized black beast. He was like Little Red Riding Hood's worst nightmare.

The wolf shook himself, and I realized that his fur was dry. There was more of that clear goop all over the deck, but very little of it had clung to the wolf itself. Yet another metaphysical mystery: How do werewolves stay dry when shapeshifting is such a mess?

I turned without a word, drawing Richard with me. I went to Gregory, still sitting on the picnic table, only Cherry and Dr. Lillian with him now. Zane had come to see what the matter was when Richard and I started writhing on the deck.

Gregory looked at me, blue eyes silvered in the moonlight. I smiled and touched his cheek, cupped the side of his face against my hand. I reached for his beast, not with my hand, but with that shadowy thing that swirled through Richard and me. I sent it shivering across Gregory's skin, and he sat up, letting the quilt fall away from his bare upper body. Cherry moved away just enough so they wouldn't touch, as if she was afraid to touch him now.

I tried to coax his beast, to call it with sweet caresses and gentle persuasion, but it remained stubbornly just under the surface, trapped by the drugs that still made Gregory's body a prison and the shock that had further dampened everything I needed to call. But I knew that it didn't have to be gentle. I might not have been along for the ride when Richard brought Stephen's beast, but I'd seen it, and I knew enough of power to guess what he'd done.

"I'll try not to hurt you," I said, but I thrust my power into Gregory. I felt it hit his chest and sink into him like a large flesh-and-fur blade.

Gregory gasped, back arching, just a little.

I found his beast like a curled cat, asleep, sluggish, and I grabbed it in my hand, sank claws in it and pulled it screaming into the air. I ripped his beast out of him, and Gregory shifted, as Stephen had shifted in an explosion of blood, flesh, and fluid. I was covered in it, so thick I had to scoop it out of my eyes to see. To see that yellow and black spotted man-leopard lying hunched on the table. I watched Stephen come to sniff along his brother's shivering body.

"Gregory, Gregory, can you hear me?" I asked, and my voice was softer than I meant it to be.

Gregory blinked leopard eyes at me, but a growling voice came out of that furred throat. "I can hear you."

Stephen threw his head back and bayed. Jamil echoed him, and the leopards' screams of triumph filled the night.

36

DAWN WAS SLIDING through the trees in a wash of white, white light that left the trees looking like black paper cutouts against the shining sky when I pulled the curtains and filled the bedroom with twilight dimness. I'd put very heavy curtains in the room when Jean-Claude had been a frequent visitor. The bedside lamp seemed dim after the glow of sunrise. Nathaniel sat on the edge of the bed by the lamp. He was wearing the bottoms of silk pajama shorts. They were a pale lavender silk that echoed his eyes and looked too delicate a color for men's sleepwear. I always suspected the shorts were originally designed for a woman, but shorts were shorts.

The lamplight caught red highlights in his auburn hair, where it gleamed down the side of his body like something warm and alive, almost separate. Strangely, in wereleopard form, he was a black panther, so that auburn hair vanished once he left human form.

Nathaniel was the only one of the wereleopards still in human form. So he was the only one that got to share my bed. If they were kitty-cats, they had to sleep elsewhere, but in human form we tried to be a big pile of puppies. Somehow it was less comfy with only Nathaniel than it would have been with more of them. Maybe it was the fact that his right nipple still had a circle of my teeth marks.

"Shouldn't the bite marks have healed by now?" I asked.

"I don't heal as quickly as some," he said softly. "And marks made by another shapeshifter, or even a vampire, heal more slowly."

"Why is that?"

He shrugged. "Why does silver kill us, and steel not?"

"Point taken," I said. I ran my hand through my still-damp

hair. I'd showered and was actually wearing pajamas, not an oversized T-shirt, which was my usual sleep attire. Though *pajamas* may have been too big a word for the emerald green camisole and matching short-shorts. There was a floor-length robe in the same vibrant green, so everything was covered, but Nathaniel knew I hadn't dressed up for him. Or at least I hoped he did.

He watched me pacing the room with careful eyes. We had crossed a line, he and I, and the mark on his chest just kept reminding me of it. I didn't think that Richard would tolerate Nathaniel and me sharing the bed alone, not that I really expected the three of us to bunk together, either. Oh, hell, I didn't know what I expected. I had expected Richard to come to me after his shower. But he was a no-show, and it was dawn, and I was tired.

There was a firm knock on the door. I said, "Come in," with my heart beating a little too fast. Merle opened the door, and I hoped my disappointment didn't show on my face. His own face registered nothing, so I couldn't judge what he saw on mine.

"The Ulfric is in the kitchen." He did look uncomfortable then. "He is crying."

I felt my eyes widen. "Excuse me?"

Merle looked down, then up, almost defiant. "He has ordered his bodyguard out of the room, and he is crying. I do not know why."

I sighed. Although I was tired, I was excited at the thought of Richard being in the house, of him coming to me, maybe. Instead of sex we were going to have another session of hand-holding, and shoulder-crying. Damn it.

I felt my shoulders slump and forced myself to stand upright again. I didn't have to ask why Merle had told me. Who else would Richard take comfort from? I wasn't even a hundred percent sure he'd take comfort from me.

I went for the door. Merle held it open for me, and I walked under his arm without having to duck. "Thanks for telling me, Merle," I muttered as I went out into the darkened living room.

Shang-Da was leaning against the wall by the open doorway that led into the kitchen. He looked as uncomfortable as I'd ever seen him. He wouldn't meet my eyes. What was going on?

Caleb was settled on the couch with a blanket and an extra pillow. He was sitting up, the blanket bunched in his lap. He was nude from the waist up and probably nude from the waist down if no one had made him wear jammies. I hoped someone had remembered to put a sheet on the couch. He watched me walk across the room, and even in the dim light from the kitchen I didn't like the way his eyes followed me.

"Nice robe," he said.

I ignored him and went for the doorway. Richard sat at the kitchen table. He'd opened all the curtains so that the room was filled with the soft light of dawn. His shoulder-length hair had been blow-dried to a soft, fluffy mass. I could never blow-dry my hair without it turning to something thick and awful-looking. The early morning light made his hair look more golden than normal, less brown. He looked up, and I realized the gold glow was a halo effect of the rising sun. It painted a nimbus of shining gold around him, leaving his hair light brown around his face, making the skin at the center of his body look even darker than it was, almost like it was in shadow.

I had a moment to see the shine of tears on his shadowed face, then he lowered his head and twisted in his chair so I couldn't see. The movement placed more of his body in the burning golden light, but the illusion of halos and shadow was gone.

I walked to the table, stood close enough to touch his bare shoulder, not sure if I should. "Richard, what's wrong?"

He shook his head, still not looking at me.

I reached out, touched the smoothness of his shoulder gently. He didn't tell me to go away, and he didn't pull away. Okay. I touched the tears on the cheek closest to me, smoothed them away with my hand. It reminded me of comforting Nathaniel earlier.

I touched Richard's chin, turned his face to me, and dried the tears on his other cheek with the sleeve of my robe. "Talk to me, Richard, please."

He smiled. Maybe it was the "please." I didn't use that word often. "I've never seen this before." He touched the sleeve very gently.

I wasn't going to be distracted, not even by him noticing what I'd worn with him in mind. "You have to be as tired as I am, Richard. What's keeping you up?"

He looked down, then up, and there was such sorrow in his dark eyes, that I almost said, *no, don't,* but he needed to talk. "Louisa is in jail, and Guy is dead."

I frowned. "I don't know the names."

"Louisa is one of our newest wolves." He looked down again, not meeting my eyes. "Guy is her fiancé . . . husband. *Was* her husband." He covered his face with his hands, shaking his head over and over and over.

I held his wrists, lowered his hands so I could see his eyes. "Richard, talk to me."

His hands turned in my grip, holding my hands. We held hands while I watched the pain in his eyes spill out in words. "Louisa killed Guy on their honeymoon, yesterday. I got the call just before I came here."

"I still don't understand. It's awful, tragic, but . . ." I said.

"I was her sponsor. I trained her to control her beast, and she lost that control on her honeymoon in the middle of . . ." He lowered his head, and raised my hands so that his forehead rested against the back of my hands.

"She lost control in the middle of sex," I finished for him.

He nodded, his face still pressed to my hands. "Losing her virginity," he said, voice muffled, low.

"Did you say virginity?"

He pulled away from me then, dropped his hands in his lap, and I noticed for the first time that he was wearing a towel knotted at his waist. "Yes."

"You mean she'd never tried to control her beast during intercourse?" I asked.

He shook his head. "They'd been engaged for more than two years before Louisa was attacked and became one of us. They both wanted to wait for the wedding night."

"Commendable," I said. "And orgasm, to a certain extent, is orgasm. If she could control herself during nonintercourse orgasm, then she should have been able to control herself during intercourse, too." I touched his shoulder again. "You did all you could for her."

He jerked away as if I'd burned him, coming to his feet so suddenly that the chair crashed back against the kitchen island, then the floor. I sensed rather than saw people in the doorway. I said, "We're alright." I turned to see Shang-Da, Merle, and the two wererats, still hesitating in the doorway. "We're alright, go away." They all pulled back, but I knew now that we had an audience, because they wouldn't go far.

Richard stood in the middle of my kitchen wearing nothing but a towel and the golden first light of dawn. Normally it would have distracted me from anything reasonable, but not this morning. The pain in his face was more important than his body right now. Looking at him, standing there so defiant, so hurt, I had an idea, an awful idea.

"Please tell me you don't mean she wanted to wait for *any* sexual contact until the honeymoon?"

His chin raised, and that arrogance tried to slide over him. But it was a mask, and I saw through it now. Underneath he was scared and guilty. "I taught her to control the beast during anger, sadness, fear, pain, every extreme of emotion, but not sex. I respected her convictions."

I stared at him. It was so something Richard would do. Theoretically, I even approved, but theory and practice aren't the same. In real life it had been a bad idea, and Richard should have known that better than I did.

I felt my face go blank, empty. It was a good cop face. I didn't want anything I was thinking to show for this. "So this Louisa shifted in the middle of sex and killed her husband, and the cops caught her." I didn't add that I was surprised they hadn't shot her on sight. Finding the big bad wolf eating the body of the nice little human would be cause enough for shooting to kill.

"Louisa turned herself in. I think if she didn't think suicide was a sin, she'd have killed herself." He turned my way walking to the sliding glass doors, leaning his forehead against the glass, as if he was tired.

I wished I could have said it wasn't his fault, but it was.

He was her sponsor, the one who was supposed to teach her how to be a shapeshifter. I'd learned from dealing with the wereleopards, and Richard, and Verne's pack in Tennessee that orgasm of any kind was one of the true tests of their control. Orgasm was supposed to be a release, but to truly give up all control meant shifting form, and that was the ultimate nightmare when you had a human lover. Richard had lectured me often enough when we were dating that he didn't trust himself the night of the full moon, or even the day before. He didn't fear losing control and killing me, just losing control and scaring me to death. Or more honestly, grossing me out. He had shifted on top of me once, and that had had nothing to do with sex. And that one experience had sent me running to Jean-Claude. Well, Richard changing on top of me and seeing him eat someone.

I didn't know what to say. All I knew was that I had to say something, that silence was almost worse than anything.

He spoke without turning around. "Go ahead, Anita, tell me I'm a fool. Tell me I sacrificed both of them on the altar of my ideals." His voice was bitter enough to choke on, just hearing the pain in it.

"Louisa and her husband wanted to hold true to who they were. You wanted to help them do that. It's perfectly, logically you." My voice was empty, but at least it wasn't reproachful. It was the best I could do. Because it was a waste, a waste because Richard and the girl and her fiancé had been more worried about appearance than reality. Or maybe I'm just cynical, and tired, oh, so tired.

It was like any really good tragedy—entirely dependent on the personalities of the people involved. If Richard had been more practical and less idealistic; if Louisa and her late husband had been less religious, less pure; hell, if the husband really brought her to orgasm with just intercourse, then if he'd only been less talented. So many things had gone into making all the good intentions go horribly wrong.

"Yes, it was perfectly, logically me, and I was wrong. I should have at least forced her to have her first experience with Guy where the pack could oversee it, save him. But Louisa was so . . . delicate about it. I just couldn't insist. I just couldn't make her strip down in front of strangers and have her most intimate moment witnessed. I just couldn't do it."

I didn't know what to say. I did the only thing I could think of to comfort him. I went to him and put my arms around his waist, put my cheek against the smooth firmness of his back, and held him. "I am so sorry, Richard, so very sorry."

His body started to shake, and I realized he was crying again, still soundlessly, but not gently. Great racking sobs shook his body, but the only sound he allowed himself was the harsh shaking of his breath as he gasped, trying to get enough air.

He slid slowly to his knees, his hands making harsh sounds down the glass of the door, as if he were taking skin off as his hand slid down the glass. I stayed standing, leaning over him, cradling his head against my body, my hands on his shoulders and chest, trying to hold him.

He fell backwards, and I was suddenly trying to hold all his weight as he went for the floor. I tripped on the hem of the robe, and we ended in a heap on the floor, with his head and shoulders in my lap and me struggling to sit up. The knot on the towel had loosened, and a long, uninterrupted line of his body showed from his waist down his hip to his foot. The towel was still in place, but it was losing the battle.

His mouth opened in a soundless cry, then suddenly there was sound. He gave one ragged, tear-choked scream, and the sound seemed to free something inside him. Because the sobbing was suddenly loud, full of small, awful, painful sounds. He sobbed, and whimpered, and screamed, and clutched at my arms, hard enough that I knew I'd be bruised. And all I could do was hold on, touch him, rock him, until he quieted. He finally lay on his side, his upper body as far into my lap as he would fit, the rest of him curled up so that one thigh covered him. The towel formed a heap on the floor underneath him. I didn't even know when the towel had fallen away. I was sort of proud of that, because usually when I see Richard naked, I lose about forty points of IQ and most of my reasoning ability. But now, his pain was so raw, that

that took precedence. It was comfort he needed, not sex.

He finally lay quiet in my arms, his breathing slowed almost to normal. His eyelids had fluttered shut, and for a moment I thought he was asleep. Then he spoke, eyes still closed. "I appointed an Eros and Eranthe for the pack." His voice was still thick with all the crying.

Eros was the Greek god of love, or lust, and Eranthe was the muse of erotic poetry; in werewolf lore they were the names for sexual surrogates. A man and a woman that did what needed doing when a werewolf's sponsor was too squeamish. Verne's pack had them, because Verne's lupa was very jealous of her Ulfric, and sometimes you just needed someone who isn't emotionally involved.

"That's good, Richard. I think it will make things easier."

He opened his eyes, and they were bleak. It made my chest ache to see that look in his eyes. "There are other positions that would make a lot of things easier," he said, voice thick and low.

I tensed up. I couldn't help it, because I knew that there were titles among the lukoi that would make all the problems he'd created in the pack fixable. There were titles that amounted to executioners, torturers. The lukoi have a long history through some very harsh times. Very few packs fill these slots anymore. Most don't see the need, but then most Ulfrics are good little tyrants; they don't need to delegate the rough stuff.

"Do you know what Bolverk means?" Richard asked softly.

"It's one of the names of Odin. It means worker of evil." My voice was almost as soft as his.

"You didn't remember that from a semester of comparative religion back in college."

"No," I said. My pulse had sped up. I couldn't help it. Bolverk was the title for what amounted to someone who did the Ulfric's evil deeds. It could be anything from trickery, to lies, to murder.

"You asked Verne about it, didn't you?"

"Yes." I kept my voice low. I was afraid to be loud, afraid

he'd stop talking. I thought I knew where the conversation was going, and I wanted to get there.

"Jacob is going to challenge Sylvie," Richard said, and his voice was growing stronger, "and he'll kill her. She's good, but I've seen Jacob fight. She can't win."

"I haven't seen him fight, but I think you're right."

"If I made you Bolverk . . ." He stopped. I wanted to yell at him to finish, but I didn't dare. All I could do was sit there, very still, and try not to do anything that would change his mind.

He started over. "If I made you Bolverk, what would you do?" That last was soft again, as if he couldn't quite believe he was saying it.

I let out a breath I hadn't even realized I was holding and tried to think. Think before I spoke, because I'd only get one shot at this. I knew Richard, and if what I said didn't meet with his approval, the offer would go away, and he might never be willing to ask for this kind of help again. I'd seldom been so eager to speak and so afraid at the same time. I prayed for wisdom, diplomacy, help.

"First, you'd need to announce my new title to the pack, then I'd choose some helpers. I'm allowed three, Baugi, Suttung, and Guunlod."

Richard said, "The two giants Bolverk tricked to get the mead of poetry, and Guunlod, the giant's daughter, who he seduced for it."

"Yes."

He rolled his upper body over, so he was looking up at me. "You spent almost every weekend of the last six months in Tennessee. I thought you were just studying with Marianne, learning how to use your talents, but you were studying the lukoi, too, weren't you?"

I tried to be very careful, as I said, "Verne's pack runs very smoothly. He's helped me make the wereleopards into a true pard."

"You don't need a Bolverk or a Guunlod to make the leopards into a pard." His gaze was very direct, and I couldn't lie to him.

"I was still your lupa, but not a werewolf, the least I could do was learn about your culture."

He smiled then, and it reached his eyes, just a little—chased that lost look away. "You didn't care about the culture."

That pissed me off. "Yes, I did."

His smile widened, his eyes filling with light, the way the sun filled the sky as it rose above the edge of the world. "Alright, you cared about the culture, but that wasn't why you wanted to know about Bolverk, the evildoer."

I looked down, feeling just a little embarrassed. "Maybe not."

He touched my face lightly, turning me to look down at him again, to meet his gaze. "You said you didn't know about Jacob before you talked with him on the phone."

"I didn't," I said.

"Then why ask Verne about Bolverk?"

I stared down into those true-brown eyes and spoke the truth. "Because you are kind and fair and just, and those are lovely things to have in a king, but the world is not kind, or fair, or just. The reason Verne's pack runs smoothly, the reason my pard runs smoothly, is because Verne and I are ruthless when we need to be. I don't know if you could be ruthless if you had to be. But I think it would break you, if you managed to pull it off."

"Having you be ruthless for me is going to break something inside of me, Anita. Something that's important to me."

I stroked his hair, feeling the thick softness of it. "But me doing it won't break as much, or as badly, as you doing it, Richard."

He nodded slowly. "I know, and I hate myself for that."

I leaned over and kissed his forehead, very gently. I spoke with my lips touching his skin. "The only true happiness, Richard, lies in knowing who you are—what you are—and making peace with it."

His arm curved up around me, holding me against him. He spoke with his mouth against the hollow of my throat. "And are you at peace with what you are?"

"I'm working on it," I said.

He kissed my throat, very softly. "Me too."

I drew back enough to see his face, and his hand thrust upward through my hair, pulled my face down to his. We kissed, soft, then harder, his lips, his tongue, his mouth working at mine. I cupped his face in my hands and kissed him— kissed him long and hard. When I drew back, breathless, I found that he'd rolled his lower body over and lay on his back, nude. He laughed at the expression on my face and pulled me down towards him. I lost that forty points of intelligence and all my reasoning skills as he undid my robe and I ran my hands down the long line of his body.

I had just enough self-possession left to say, "Not here. We've got an audience in the living room."

His hand slid under the green satin of the camisole, curving around to my back, pulling me against him. "There's no place in the house that they won't hear us, smell us."

I pulled back from him before he could kiss me. "Gee, Richard, that makes me feel a lot better."

He propped himself up on one arm, staring down at me. "We can go into the bedroom if you want, but we won't be fooling anybody."

I didn't like that, and it must have shown on my face, because Richard drew his hand out from under my top, and said, "Do you want to stop?"

We hadn't really gotten started, but I knew what he meant. I looked into the solid brown of his eyes, traced the edge of his jaw with my gaze, the fullness of his lips, the curve of his throat, the spread of his shoulders, the way his hair fell around him, catching the early morning light, bringing out shades of gold and copper in his hair, the swell of his chest, his nipples already dark and hard, the flat line of his stomach with that thin, dark line of hair that went from his belly button to . . . the skin was darker, richer, you could almost smell the blood that pumped him full and hard. He looked ripe, like he was something full to bursting with life. I wanted to touch him, to squeeze, oh so delicately. I lay on the floor with my hands at my sides, my pulse beating in my throat, and said, "No, I don't want to stop." My voice was almost a whisper.

His eyes filled with that dark heat that spills into a man's face when he's almost a hundred percent sure of what's about to happen. His voice was deeper, that low note that most men's voices get when the excitement runs deep. "Here, or the bedroom?"

I tore my gaze away from him to look at the open doorway to the living room. There was no door to close. I needed more privacy than this. Even if they could hear us, even smell us in the bedroom, at least they wouldn't be able to see us. Maybe it was only an illusion of delicacy, but sometimes illusion is all you've got.

I looked back at him. "Bedroom."

"Good choice," he said, and got to his knees, taking my hand, so that when he got to his feet, he half-pulled me to mine. The movement startled me, and I fell against him. The height difference was enough that it put my hand on his hip and so very close to other things. It embarrassed me how very much I wanted to touch him, hold him. I started to pull away, because I was so close to losing all decorum and groping him right there in the kitchen. I wasn't entirely sure that if I grabbed him we'd make it to the bedroom. I wanted that door between us and everyone else.

He put his arms around my waist and lifted me off my feet, until our faces were even and I didn't know what to do with my legs. If I'd been sure we wouldn't be using the kitchen table I'd have wrapped my legs around his waist, but I didn't trust either of us that far. He put his arms under my butt, so that my head was slightly above his, and I rested in his arms almost like I was in a swing. I could still feel him pressed hard and firm against my body, but it had a certain decorum to it that straddling his waist lacked. He started walking for the door, carrying me, his eyes so intent on my face that he almost tripped on a chair. It made me laugh, until his eyes came back to meet mine, and I saw the need in those dark eyes. That one look robbed me of speech, and all I could do was stare into his eyes as he carried me into the bedroom.

37

THE BEDROOM WAS empty when he kicked the door shut behind us. I didn't know if the living room was empty or not. I couldn't remember anything but Richard's eyes from the kitchen to the bedroom. Every room might have been empty, for all I'd seen.

We kissed just inside the door; my hands were full of the rich thickness of his hair, the firm warmth of his neck. I explored his face with my hands, my mouth, tasted, teased, caressed, just his face.

He drew back from my mouth enough to say, "If I don't sit down, I'm going to fall down. My knees are weak."

I laughed, full-throated, and said, "Then put me down."

He half-walked, half-staggered to the bed, laying me on it, going to his knees beside it. He was laughing as he crawled onto the bed beside me. He lay beside me, his knees hanging over the side of the bed, though since he was tall enough for his feet to actually touch the floor when he lay like that, maybe *hanging* wasn't the right word. We lay beside each other on the bed, laughing softly, not touching.

We turned our heads to look at each other at the same moment. His eyes sparkled with the laughter, his whole face almost shining with it. I reached out and traced the lines of laughter around his mouth. The laughter began to fade as soon as I touched him, his eyes filling up with something darker, more serious, but no less precious. He rolled onto his side. The movement put my hand along the side of his face. He rubbed his face into my hand, eyes closed, lips half parted.

I rolled onto my stomach, and moved towards him, my hand still on his face. He opened his eyes, watching me crawl towards him. I propped myself up on hands and knees and watched his eyes as I leaned in towards his mouth. There was eagerness there, but there was also something else, something fragile. Did my eyes mirror that look, half-eager, half-fearful, wanting, afraid to want, needing, and afraid to need?

My mouth hovered over his, our lips touching, delicate as butterflies blown by a warm summer wind, touching, not touching, sliding along each other, gliding away. His hand grabbed the back of my neck, forced my mouth to press against his, hard, firm. He used his tongue and lips to force my mouth open. I opened to him, and we took turns exploring each other's mouths. He came to his knees, hand still pressed to the back of my neck, our mouths still locked together. He drew back, crawling backwards to the head of the bed, leaving me kneeling alone in the center of the bed. He reached under the covers, drew out pillows, propped himself up, watching me. There was something almost decadent about him naked, propped up, watching me.

I knelt looking back at him, having a little trouble focusing, thinking. I finally managed to say, "What's wrong?"

"Nothing," he said, voice deep, lower than normal. It wasn't the growl of his beast, it was a peculiarly male sound. "I want to run my beast through you, Anita."

For a split second, I thought it was a euphemism, then I realized he meant exactly what he'd said. "Richard, I don't know."

"I know you don't like otherworldly stuff during sex, but Anita . . ." he settled into the pillows in a strange smoothing motion that somehow reminded me that he wasn't human, "I felt your beast. It rolled through me."

Just hearing it out loud took a little of the glow off for me. I slumped back against the bed, still on my knees, but no longer upright, hands limp in my lap. "Richard, I haven't had time to think this through. I don't know how I feel about it yet."

"It's not all bad, Anita. Some of it can be wondrous."

This from the man who had hated his beast for the entire time I'd known him. But I didn't say that out loud. I just looked at him.

He smiled. "I know how strange that sounds coming from me."

I looked at him harder.

He laughed, settling lower on the pillows until he was sprawled in front of me. One leg bent up so he wouldn't touch me, but close enough that I could have touched him. He lay there unself-consciously nude, which I'd seen before, but it was more than that. He seemed bathed in a comfortableness that was rare for Richard. I'd seen it at the lupanar, that he'd accepted his beast. But it was more than that; he'd accepted himself.

"What do you want from me, Richard?"

This was his cue to get serious, to demand I be less bloodthirsty, or a half dozen other impossible things. He didn't. "I want this," he said, and I felt the prickling rush of his power a second before it passed through me like a warm ghost.

I shuddered with it. "I don't know, Richard. I don't know if this is a good idea." It would have sounded better if my voice hadn't had a tremble in it.

I expected him to question, or talk, but he didn't. I felt his power like a brush of thunder a second before it smashed into me. I had a second of panic, a moment to wonder if his beast and mine would claw me apart, then his power rubbed through me like a velvet glove. My beast rose as if from a great, warm, wet depth, up, up to meet the warm, burning rush of Richard's energy. He pushed his beast through me, and I could feel it, impossibly huge, the brush of fur so deep inside me that I cried out. I felt his beast as if it had crawled inside me and was caressing things from the inside that his hands would never have touched. My power seemed less certain than his, less solid. But it rose around the hard, muscled fur like velvet mist, swirling through his power, through my own body. Until it felt as if something huge was growing inside me, something I'd never felt before, swelling inside me. It felt larger than my body, as if I couldn't hold it inside myself, like a cup filled to the brim with something hot and scalding, but the liquid kept pouring in, and still I held it, held it, held it, until it burst over me, through me, out of me, in a roar of power that turned the world golden and slow, drew my body to its knees, curved my back, sent my hands clawing at the air trying to hold on to something, anything, while my body spilled apart and remade itself on the bed. For a space of labored heartbeats I thought he'd brought on the change, and I had slipped my skin for real, but it wasn't that. I felt like I was floating and only gradually felt my body again. I lay on my back, my knees folded under me, hands limp at my sides, so relaxed it was like being drugged.

I felt the bed move under me, and a moment later, Richard appeared above me. He was on all fours, looming over me, and I had trouble focusing on his face. He cradled my face, staring into my eyes, while I tried to look at him. "Anita, are you alright?"

I laughed then, slow and lazy. "Help me get my knees straightened out, and I'll be fine."

He helped me straighten my legs, and even then all I wanted to do was just lay there. "What did you do to me?"

He lay down beside me, propped on one elbow. "I brought you, using the beasts."

I blinked at him, licked my lips, and tried to think of an intelligent question, gave up, and settled for what I wanted to know. "Is it always like that between lycanthropes?"

"No," he said and leaned over me, until his face filled my vision. "No, only a true lupa, or a true Nimir-Ra, can respond to my Ulfric the way you just did."

I touched his chest enough to back him up so I could see his face clearly. "You've never done that with anyone before?"

He looked down then, a curtain of his hair sliding over his face, hiding it from me. I pushed his hair back so I could see that nearly perfect profile. "Who?" I asked.

Heat washed up his neck and face. I wasn't sure I'd ever seen him blush before. "It was Raina, wasn't it?"

He nodded. "Yes."

I let his hair fall back in place and lay there for a few seconds thinking about it. Then I was laughing, laughing and couldn't stop.

He was back at my shoulder, peering down at me. "Anita?"

The laughter faded as I looked into his worried eyes. "When you forced Raina to give you up all those years ago, did you know that she was the only one that could do this with you?"

He nodded, face solemn. "Raina pointed out the downside to not being her pet."

I took his hand and slid it down the front of my satin bottoms. His fingertips found the wetness that had soaked through the satin, and I didn't have to guide his hand anymore. He cupped that big hand of his over my groin, and the cloth was soaked through. He traced fingertips across my inner thigh and the skin was wet, wet down to my knees.

"How did you give it up?" My voice came out in a whisper.

His finger slid up the inside of my thigh, in the hollow just below. He leaned in to kiss me as his finger slid slowly, slowly, upward across the moist skin, under the wet satin. His mouth stayed just above mine, so close that a sharp breath would have made us touch. He spoke, his breath warm on my skin, as his finger caressed the edge of me. "No amount of pleasure was worth her price." Two things happened at once; he kissed me, and his finger slid inside of me. I screamed against his mouth, back arching, fingernails digging into his shoulder, as his finger found that small spot and thrust over and over it, until he brought me again. The world had soft, white edges, like seeing through gauze.

I felt the bed move, but couldn't focus, couldn't see, wasn't sure I cared what was happening. Hands fumbled at my shorts. I blinked up to see Richard kneeling over me. He slid my shorts down, spread my legs, and knelt between them. He leaned over me raising the satin camisole, baring my breasts. He ran his hands across them, made me writhe, then moved his hands down the line of my body, his hands gripping my thighs, bringing me in a harsh jerk against his body.

The moment he rubbed against the outside of me, I felt the rubbery latex of the condom. I looked up at his face, and asked, "How did you know?"

He moved so that his lower body was lying between my legs, but still pressed against the outside of my body. Most of his weight was supported by his arms like a modified push-up position. "Do you really think Jean-Claude would warn me about the *ardeur* and not warn me that you weren't on birth control?"

"Good point," I said.

"No," he said, "this is." I felt the movement of his hips, seconds before he thrust inside me, in one powerful motion that drove sounds from my mouth, somewhere between a scream and a shout.

He lowered his head enough to see my face. I lay gasping under him, but whatever he saw there reassured him, because he arched his back, his face looking somewhere in the distance, and drew himself out of me, slowly, inch by inch, until I made small noises. He drew himself out until he was barely touching inside me. I gazed down the length of my body to see him stretched hard and ready. He'd always been careful of me, because he wasn't small; that one first thrust had been more force than he'd ever before allowed himself. He, like Micah, filled me up, hit that point deep inside that was either pain or pleasure. I saw his back and hips flex a second before he thrust into me. I watched him thrust into me, saw every inch of him plunge into me, until it bowed my back, my neck, and I couldn't watch because I was writhing underneath him, my hands scrambling at the bedspread, digging fingers into the covers.

He drew himself out of me again, and I stopped him with a hand on his stomach. "Wait, wait." I was having trouble breathing.

"It's not hurting you. I can tell by your face, your eyes, your body."

I swallowed, took a shaky breath, and said, "No, it's not hurting me. It feels wonderful, but you've always been so careful, even when I asked you not to be. What's changed?"

He looked down at me, his hair falling around his face like a silken frame. "I was always afraid of hurting you before. But I felt your beast."

"I haven't changed yet, Richard, we don't know for sure."

"Anita," he said softly, and I knew he was chiding me. Maybe it was a case of the lady protesting too much, but still . . .

"I'm still human, Richard, I haven't changed yet."

He leaned over me, his hair gliding around my face as he kissed me gently on the cheek. "Even before the first full moon, we can take more damage. The change has already begun, Anita."

I pushed against his chest until he drew back enough for me to see his face. "You've always been holding back, haven't you?"

"Yes," he said.

I searched his face and saw such need in his eyes, and I knew why he'd been so angry at Gregory. He'd said that he almost regretted not making me his lupa in truth, now that he'd seen me be Nimir-Ra, but it was more than that. I looked into his brown eyes in the spill of early morning light and knew that he'd wanted me to be what he was, even though he hated it, that at some level he'd been tempted to make me his lupa for real. Somewhere in the lovemaking where he had to be so careful, he'd thought of it, more than once. It was there in his eyes, his face. He started to look away as if he could feel that I saw it all, but he made himself look back, meet my gaze. He was almost defiant.

"How careful have you been of me, Richard?"

He did look away then, using his hair as a shield. I reached through that thick hair to touch his face, to turn him to look at me. "Richard, how careful have you been of me?"

There was something close to pain in his eyes. He whispered, "Very."

I held his face between my hands. "You don't have to be careful anymore."

A look of soft wonderment crossed his face, and he bent his head down, and we kissed, kissed as we had earlier, propping, exploring, taking turns at thrusting into each other. He drew slowly back from the kiss, and I felt the tip of him touch my opening. I stared down the length of our bodies so I could watch as his body flexed above me, and he thrust himself inside me harder this time, quicker. It brought my breath in a soundless scream.

"Anita . . ."

I opened my eyes, not realizing I'd closed them. I gazed up at him. "Don't be careful anymore, Richard, don't be careful."

He smiled, gave me a quick kiss, then he was back, arched

above me, and this time he didn't stop. He thrust every inch of himself into me as hard and as fast as he could. The sound of flesh into flesh became a constant sound, a wet hammering. I realized it hadn't been just his size that made him careful, but his strength. He could have bench-pressed the bed we lay on, and that strength lay not just in his arms, or back, but in his legs, his thighs, in the body he was pressing inside me, over and over again. For the first time ever, I began to appreciate the full power of him.

I'd felt the strength in his hands, his arms, when he held me, but it was nothing to this. He made of our bodies one body, one pounding, sweating, soaking, drenching piece of flesh. I was vaguely aware that it did hurt, that I was bruising, and I didn't care.

I called out his name as my body tightened around his, squeezing, and I spasmed underneath him, body slamming against the bed, not from Richard's thrusts, but from the power of the orgasm itself; screams spilled from my throat as my body rocked underneath him. It felt good, better than almost anything, but it was almost violence, almost pain, almost frightening. Somewhere in the midst of it all I was aware that he came, too. He screamed my name, but held his place, while I continued to writhe and fight underneath him. It wasn't until I lay quiet that he allowed himself to collapse on top of me, slightly to one side, so my face wouldn't be pressed into his chest.

We lay in a sweating, breathless heap, waiting for our hearts to slow enough to speak. He found his voice first. "Thank you, thank you for trusting me."

I laughed. "You're thanking me." I raised his hand to my mouth and kissed the palm, then rested his hand against my face. "Trust me, Richard, it was my pleasure."

He laughed, that rich throaty sound that is purely male, and purely sexual. "We're going to need another shower."

"Whichever of us can walk first can have the first shower," I said.

He laughed and hugged me. I wasn't even sure my legs would work enough to shower at all. Maybe a bath.

38

I WOKE JUST enough to feel the weight of someone at my back. I snuggled against that warmth, wrapping sleep back around me. An arm spilled over my shoulder, and I wriggled into the circle of arm and body. It wasn't the warmth, or the feel of him that woke me; the wereleopards had gotten me used to all that. It was the scent of his skin. By the scent alone, I knew it was Richard. I opened my eyes and snuggled deeper against him, curling that dark, muscled arm tighter around my body like drawing a cozy blanket around me. Of course, a blanket didn't have the hard weight of Richard, or the silken glide of his naked skin against mine, or the ability to cuddle back, to use hands to pull my body tighter in against him. He closed the distance, worked until, even with the height difference, his chest, stomach, and hips were curled around me. He gave one last movement, and I could feel him pressed hard and ready against the back of my body. It was morning, he was male, but it wasn't something embarrassing to be ignored. I could pay as much, or as little, attention to it as I wanted, and I wanted.

I started to roll over in the almost tight circle of his body and found I was stiff. My lower body felt bruised, aching, but in a good way. I laughed as he opened his arms enough for me to roll onto my back.

"What's so funny?" Richard asked.

I stared up at him, still laughing, I think to keep from groaning. "I'm stiff."

He wiggled his eyebrows at me. "So am I."

I blushed, and he kissed my nose, then my mouth, but still chaste, still not really sexual. It made me laugh. If it had been anyone but me, I'd have said I giggled.

The next kiss wasn't chaste, and the one after that pressed

me back against the bed. He slid his leg between my thighs, until his knee touched me, and I winced.

He drew back. "Are you too sore for this?"

"I'm willing to give it the ol' college try," I said, "but honestly, maybe."

He stayed propped above me, fingers moving a lock of my hair from my cheek. "What I did last night would have broken things inside an ordinary human."

I didn't need a mirror to feel my eyes go cool. I'd really been trying not to think about it.

"I'm sorry," he said. "I didn't mean to ruin the mood." He smiled suddenly and looked younger, more relaxed than I'd seen him in a long time. "I'm just glad to be with someone I don't have to worry about hurting."

I had to smile at him. "I'm not hurt, but we might have to try something a little more gentle this morning."

The humor faded, and something else filled his eyes, as he lowered his face for another kiss. He spoke as he moved towards me. "I think we can come up with something." He kissed my lips, then worked one kiss at a time down my neck, my shoulders. He got distracted at my breasts, covering them in kisses, his tongue licking a quick, wet line across one nipple. He cupped one breast in his hands, holding it in the circle of his warmth, sliding his mouth over the nipple, taking as much of the breast into his mouth as he could. He sucked me into his mouth until he held over half my breast in the wet warmth. And with that touch, the *ardeur* flared up through my body from wherever it had been hiding.

Richard drew back from my breast, hands still cradling it. "What was that?" There were goosebumps on his arms.

"The *ardeur*," I said, voice soft.

He licked his lips, and I saw real fear in his eyes. "Jean-Claude told me about it, even let me feel his own version of it, but I didn't really believe it. I don't think I wanted to believe it."

My beast had awoken with the *ardeur*, as if one hunger fed the other. I felt it uncurl inside me and stretch for all the world, like some great cat waking from a nap. It rolled through me, reaching out to Richard, and his beast woke to it. One hand was on the solid warmth of his chest, but I could feel something else in there, something moving around as if his chest were hollow and there was something caged inside.

He gripped my hand, moved it back from his chest. "What are you doing?"

"The *ardeur* calls to our beasts, Richard." I snuggled down underneath him, my hand sliding down his body, tracing the flatness of his stomach, the curve of his hip. He grabbed my hand just before I could touch him. He had both my hands now, trapped in his larger ones. It didn't bother me, because I knew that I could touch him with things other than my hands, or even my body. I remembered the feel of his beast thrusting through me, and I spilled mine into him in a hot push of energy.

He jumped off of me, rolled out of the bed in a movement that was almost too quick to follow with the eyes. He stood by the bed, breath coming in ragged gasps, as if he'd been running. I could feel his fear like fine champagne. It added to the sex, brought me to my knees, to crawl from the tangle of covers to the edge of the bed. I could smell how warm he was; the scent of his skin came to me on the air, the faint sweetness of the cologne he'd put on the day before. My gaze wandered over the beauty of him. His sleep-tousled hair hung in a heavy mass over one side of his face. He brushed the thickness of it back from his face with one hand and a toss of his head, and that one simple movement made things low in my body tighten. But underneath the sex was the thought of what all that smooth, hard skin would feel like under my teeth. I wanted to mark him as I'd marked Nathaniel. I wanted to sink my teeth into his flesh and bite. I had a flash of what it felt like to taste him like so much meat, to feel his body respond, not just to the sex but to the hunger, and I knew for the first time why shapeshifters spoke of the hunger like it should be in all capital letters. Raina had risen her lascivious head. The *ardeur* overrode, or overpowered her, but she was there, supplying images to the things I was feeling. I slid off the bed, and Richard backed up.

I could see his pulse in his neck, beating like a trapped

thing. His beast was trapped, too, trapped by his control, his fear. I could feel it, as if it were literally pacing inside his body, like a wolf in a cage at the zoo; pacing, pacing, never free. It might be a large, roomy cage, but it was still a cage. Raina gave me a visual that drove me to my knees. I saw Richard pinned under my body, chained to a bed, and when he came inside me, he shifted at the same moment. That was release for the shapeshifters; anything else was holding back.

Richard knelt in front of me. "Are you alright?" He touched my arm, and that was a bad thing. My beast roared across our skins, hit his in a blow that I felt physically in my stomach and ribs, like a punch. It staggered Richard, made him fall forward into me, and we clung for a second, arms around each other, our bodies pressed together. The *ardeur* flared over us like invisible flame, and we knelt in the heart of that fire like the wick of a candle. His heart beat against my arms, where they lay pressed to his chest, as if my skin had become a drum and he beat inside me, filled me with the rhythm of his body. My own heartbeat found a home inside Richard's body. We were filled with the rise and fall, the pulse and beat of each other, until I couldn't tell whose heart was in my chest, whose blood rushed through us. For a trembling moment we pressed above one another, as if our skin would give way and we would finally be what the marks had promised—one being, one body, one soul. The power broke apart, as Richard struggled against it, like a drowning man, breaking apart the power like arms shatter water; you can move it, disrupt it, but it flows back around you, swells over you, engulfs you. Richard screamed, and I felt him fall back.

I opened my eyes as his hand pulled away, and my hand tried to hold him. His hand was almost free, only his fingers still caught in mine, when the *ardeur* pressed around us, and I knew his control was fragile enough that I would feed. I felt his confusion, felt him struggling to decide what to hold on to and what to let go. I realized that the shields had come down long ago, because he couldn't hold the marks closed, keep himself in human form, and keep me from feeding, all at the same time. He screamed again, and I felt Richard decide, felt the conscious choice of the lesser evil. He shoved his beast down, down, deep inside himself, and he shut the marks between us like slamming a door. It was so sudden that it felt like the world had lurched. I had a moment of dizziness, was almost sick, then the *ardeur* rode over us, through us, like a thundering thing to trample us both underfoot, until we were just flesh, bone, blood, just meat, just need. I saw Richard's back arch, his head fling back, and through the *ardeur* I felt the growing pressure, tightness in his body, seconds before that hot release spilled over him, and I held his hand while his body rocked with the strength of it, and the pleasure of it drew me to my knees, almost as if the power itself lifted me up for a second, held me, rocked me, and I fed, I fed, and fed, and fed, until we were left lying on the floor, sweat-covered, breathing in gasps, our hands still locked together.

Richard pulled away first. He lay there, eyes unfocused, breathing labored, his heart beating too fast, filling his throat. He swallowed hard enough that it sounded like it hurt. I felt weighted, heavy with the feeding, almost like I could sleep again, like a snake after a big meal.

Richard found his voice first. "You had no right to feed off me."

"I thought that was the idea of you staying until morning," I said.

He sat up slowly, as if he were stiff now. "It was."

"You never said *no*." I rolled onto my side, but didn't try and sit up yet.

He nodded. "I know that. I'm not blaming you."

He was, but at least he was trying not to. "You could have stopped me, Richard. All you had to do was either leave the marks open between us or let your beast go. You could have held the *ardeur* out. You made your choice on what to control."

"I know that, too." But he wouldn't look at me.

I propped myself up on my arms, almost sitting. "Then what's wrong?"

He shook his head and got to his feet. He was a little unsteady, but he went for the door. "I'm leaving, Anita."

"You make that sound awfully permanent, Richard."

He turned and looked at me. "No one feeds off me, no one."

He'd closed himself so tight that I couldn't tell what he was feeling, but it was plain on his face. Pain. His eyes held some deep pain, and he'd pulled so far away in his mind, his heart, that I couldn't tell what it was, only that it hurt him.

"So, you won't be here tomorrow morning when the *ardeur* comes again?" My voice sounded almost neutral when I asked.

He shook his head, all that heavy hair sliding around his shoulders. His hand was on the doorknob, his body turned away enough that he hid himself from me as much as he could. "I can't do this again, Anita. For God's sake, you have the same rule. No one feeds on you either."

I sat up, arms wrapping around my knees, holding them tight to my chest. I guess I was covering my nakedness, too. "You've felt the *ardeur* now, Richard. If I can't feed off of you, then who? Who do you want me to share this with?"

"Jean-Claude . . ." But his voice dropped off before he could finish.

"It's a little after noon and he's still dead to the world. He won't wake in time to share the *ardeur* with me."

His hand tightened on the doorknob hard enough for me to see the muscles in his arm tense. "The Nimir-Raj, then. I'm told you've already fed on him once anyway."

"I don't know Micah that well, Richard." I took a deep breath and said, "I don't love him, Richard. I love you. I want you."

"You want to feed off me? You want me to be your cow?"

"No," I said, "no."

"I am not food, Anita, not for you or anyone else. I am Ulfric of the Thronnos Rokke Clan, and I am not cattle. I am the thing that eats the cattle."

"If you had shifted, then you could have blocked the *ardeur*, kept me from feeding, why didn't you?"

He leaned his forehead against the door. "I don't know."

"Honesty, Richard, at least with yourself."

He turned then, and his anger flared across my skin like a whip. "You want honesty, fine, we can have honesty. I hate what I am. I want a life, Anita. I want a real life. I want free of all this shit. I don't want to be Ulfric. I don't want to be a werewolf. I just want a life."

"You have a life, Richard, it's just not the life you thought it would be."

"And I don't want to love someone who is more at home with the monsters than I am."

I just looked at him, hugging my knees to my bare chest, my back pressed up against the bed. I looked at him, because I couldn't think of a damned thing to say.

"I'm sorry, Anita, but I can't ... *won't* do this." He opened the door then. He opened the door, and he walked out, closing it behind him. The door closed with a soft, firm click. I sat there for a few seconds not moving. I don't even think I was breathing, then slowly the tears squeezed out, and my first breath was a ragged gasp that hurt my throat. I rolled slowly to the floor, lying in a tight, tight ball. I lay on the floor and cried until I was cold and shivering.

That's how Nathaniel found me. He pulled the blanket from the bed and wrapped it around me, picked me up, and climbed onto the bed with me in his arms. He held me in the curve of his body, spooned against me, and I couldn't feel him through the thick blanket. He held me and stroked my hair. I felt the bed move and opened my eyes to find Cherry and Zane crawling around me. They touched my face, took my tears with the tips of their fingers, and curled around me on the other side until I was cupped in their warmth.

Gregory and Vivian came next and climbed onto the bed until we all lay in a warm, thick nest of bodies and covers. And I was hot and had to peel the blanket back, and their hands spilled over me, touching, holding. I realized that I was still naked and so were they. No one ever put on clothes unless I made them. But the touching wasn't sexual, it was comfort, the warm pile of puppies, and everyone in that pile loved me in their way. Maybe it wasn't the way I wanted to be loved, but love is love and sometimes I think I'd thrown away more love than most people ever get a chance at. I was trying to be more careful lately.

They held me until I fell asleep, exhausted with crying, skin hot. But down in the center of my being was a cold, icy spot that they couldn't touch. It was the place where I loved Richard, had always loved Richard, almost from the first time I'd seen him. But he was right on one thing. We couldn't keep doing this. I wouldn't keep doing this. It was over. It had to be over. He hated what he was, and now he hated what I was. He said he wanted someone that he wouldn't have to worry about hurting, and he did want that, but he also wanted someone human, ordinary. He couldn't have both, but that didn't keep him from wanting both. I couldn't be ordinary, and I wasn't sure I'd ever been human. I couldn't be what Richard wanted me to be, and he couldn't stop wanting it. Richard was a riddle with no answer, and I was tired of playing a game I couldn't win.

39

I SLEPT LIKE I was drugged, heavy, with harsh, fragmented dreams, or nothingness. I don't know when I would have woken, but someone was licking my cheek. If they'd shaken me or called my name, I might have been able to ignore it, but someone was licking my cheek in long languorous movements that I couldn't ignore.

I opened my eyes and found Cherry's face so close I couldn't focus on it. She moved back just enough so I wouldn't feel cross-eyed looking at her, then said, "You were having a nightmare. I thought we should wake you."

Her voice was neutral, her face blank, cheerful in an anonymous sort of way. It was her nurse face, cheerful, comforting, telling you nothing. The fact that she was naked, lying on her side, propped up on one elbow so that her body showed in one long line didn't seem to distract from her professionalism. I could never pull that off naked. No matter what else was happening I was always aware that I didn't have clothes on.

"I don't remember what I was dreaming," I said. I raised a hand to smooth the wetness along my cheek.

"You taste salty from all the crying," she said.

The bed moved, and Zane peeked around my other shoulder. "Can I lick the other cheek?"

It made me laugh, and that was almost miracle enough to let him do it, almost. I sat up and instantly regretted it. My whole body felt stiff and abused, aching, as if I'd been beaten. Hell, I'd felt better after some of the beatings I'd taken over the years. I hugged the blanket to me, partially to cover my nakedness, partially because I was cold.

I leaned against the head of the bed, frowning. "You said nightmare. What time is it?"

"About five," Cherry said. "I could say *daymare*, if you like, but either way, you were —" she hesitated "—whimpering in your sleep."

I hugged the blanket tighter. "I don't remember."

She sat up, patting my knee under the blanket. "Are you hungry?"

I shook my head.

She and Zane exchanged one of those looks that say just how worried about you people are. It made me angry.

"Look, I'm okay."

They both looked at me.

I frowned at them. "I'll be okay, alright."

They didn't look convinced.

"I need to get dressed."

They both just lay there staring at me.

"Which means get out and give me some space."

They exchanged another of those looks, which bugged me, but at a nod from Cherry, they both got up off the bed and went for the door. "And put some clothes on," I said.

"If it'll make you feel better," Cherry said.

"It will," I said.

Zane gave a little salute. "Your wish is our command."

That was actually a little too close to the truth, but I let it go. When they were gone, I picked out some clothes, some weapons, and made it to the bathroom without seeing anyone. I wouldn't have put it past Cherry to make sure I had a clear shot to the bathroom. They were managing me, but this morning, make that afternoon, I didn't care enough to complain.

I was as quick in the bathroom as I could be, and for some reason I didn't like looking in the mirror. I was trying not to think, and seeing my eyes staring back at me like those of a shock victim made it hard not to think about why I looked so pale, so shell-shocked.

I put on my usual black undies and matching bra. It was getting to the point where I didn't own a white bra. Jean-Claude's fault. Black jogging socks, black jeans, black polo shirt, shoulder rig, complete with Browning Hi-Power, the Firestar in its interpants holster in front almost lost against the black shirt. I even added the wrist sheaths and the two silver knives. I didn't need this much firepower for walking around the house, especially with so many shapeshifters running around, but I was feeling shaky, as if my world was less solid today than yesterday. I'd always thought that Richard and I would work something out. I wasn't sure what, but something. Now, I didn't believe that. We weren't going to work anything out. We weren't going to be anything, except the bare miniumum to each other. I wasn't even sure his invitation to be Bolverk was still on the table. I hoped so. I could lose him as my lover, but I couldn't let him send the pack to rack and ruin. If he didn't cooperate, I wasn't sure how I was going to stop it, but that was a problem for another day. Today my goal was just to survive, just to get through the day. I huddled my weapons around me like comfort objects. If I'd been alone in the house, or if it had just been Nathaniel, I would have carried Sigmund, my stuffed toy penguin, around with me. That was how bad a day it was.

I did have a moment when I caught a glimpse of myself in the mirror in my bedroom where I stopped and had to smile. I looked like I was dressed in casual assassin chic. I'd teased some of my friends who were assassins or bounty hunters about assassin chic, but sometimes you gotta go with the stereotypes. Besides, I look great in black. The black-on-black look made my skin look almost translucent, like it should have glowed. My eyes were swimmingly dark. I looked almost ethereal, like a wingless angel on a bad day. Alright, maybe a fallen angel, but the effect was still striking. I'd learned long ago that if you're feeling unloved by the man in your life, the best revenge is to look good. If I'd really wanted to follow the strategy completely, I'd have put on makeup, but screw that. I was still on vacation. I didn't wear makeup on vacation.

There was a crowd in the kitchen. The order for everyone to wear clothes had been taken to heart. Cherry had on cutoff jean shorts and a white men's shirt with the sleeves torn off, so that little bits of thread decorated the arm holes. She'd tied the ends of the shirt so her stomach showed as she moved around the kitchen. Zane's gaze followed her

wherever she moved. I wasn't sure how Cherry felt about
him, but Zane was beginning to act like a man in love, or at
least very serious lust. He sat at the table wearing the leather
pants he'd taken off last night, ignoring his coffee and watching Cherry.

Caleb leaned against the counter in his jeans, with the top
button unbuttoned so that his belly-button ring showed. He
sipped coffee and watched Zane watch Cherry with an odd
look on his face. I couldn't decipher it, but I didn't like it,
as if he were trying to think how to cause trouble between
them. Caleb struck me as one of those who liked to cause
trouble.

Nathaniel was sitting at the table, his long hair in a braid
down his back, chest bare, but I knew without checking that
he'd have something on. He knew me well enough to know
I liked my houseguests clothed.

Igor and Claudia stood when I came into the room. His
tattoos were even more striking in the full light of day. They
graced his arms, what I could see of his chest through the
white tank top, and the sides of his neck, like liquid jewels,
brilliant, eye-catching. Even from a distance they were beautiful against his pale skin. I wasn't much into tattoos but I
couldn't picture Igor without them—the look just worked for
him. He'd put on the shoulder rig, and it still looked like it
should chaff with the tank top, but, hey, it wasn't my skin.
The Glock sat under his arm, a black spot on all that pretty
color, like an imperfection on a Picasso.

Claudia looked positively ordinary beside him—if a
woman that was so damn close to seven feet and muscled
better than most men could look ordinary. The gun at the
small of her back wasn't nearly as noticeable as Igor's. Her
black hair was still pulled back in a tight ponytail, leaving
her face clean and empty, and that included her eyes. Claudia
had cop eyes, or bad-guy eyes, the eyes of someone who
doesn't let you see what's inside. I didn't meet many women
with eyes like that, outside of the police. If her face had been
a little softer, she'd have been beautiful. But there was something in the set of her jaw, the way she held that full mouth
that said, back off, no touching. It robbed her of something

that would have changed everything about her.

The two of them came to take up posts to either side and a little behind me. I would have protested, but I'd discovered last night that it didn't do much good. They took orders from Rafael, not me. He'd said, "Keep her safe," and that was what they were going to do. I was too . . . whatever the hell I was to waste energy on telling them to back off. They could follow me around if it made them feel better. This afternoon I just didn't care.

Merle was standing in the corner of the cabinets, near enough to the coffeemaker that Igor crowded him while I poured my coffee. I didn't know who had made a fresh pot, and I didn't care; just the sight and smell of it made me feel better.

Merle was wearing the cowboy boots, jeans, and jean jacket over bare chest that he'd had on last night. He was sipping coffee out of one of the few plain mugs I owned. The scar on his chest was very white, ragged, pitted in one spot as if that had been the deepest part of the wound. It did look like lightning carved into his chest and stomach. I wanted to ask what had happened, but there was a look to his eyes as he watched the kitchen that said he probably wouldn't tell me, and he'd definitely see it as intrusive. None of my business anyway.

The only chairs open at the table gave their backs to the bay window and the sliding glass door. I hated sitting with my back to a window or a door—especially a door. Nathaniel touched Zane's arm. He glanced back at me then got up, coffee cup and all, and went around to the chair that backed the door. Cherry sat beside him, though her chair had been Claudia's, and it was turned so that she had the view of both doors. Cherry moved the chair closer to Zane, giving her back to all that glass.

There'd been a time when I wasn't this careful, especially at home, but today was going to be one of my paranoid days. Insecurity had that effect on me, even emotional insecurity.

Claudia sat beside me. Igor leaned against the island behind me, keeping an eye on Merle, I think. They didn't seem to like each other.

I took the first sip of coffee, hot, black, and let the warmth fill me for a few seconds, before I asked, "Where's Gregory?"

"Stephen and Vivian took him back to their apartment," Cherry said.

"But he's alright?" I asked.

She nodded, smiling that smile that made her look years younger than we both were. "He's healed, Anita. You healed him."

"I called his beast, I didn't heal him."

She shrugged. "Same difference."

I shook my head. "No, I couldn't heal him last night."

She frowned, and even that was pretty. She was buzzed today, shining with it. I glanced at Zane, who was still gazing at her. Maybe it was love for both of them. Something had certainly put a twinkle in her eye.

"For heaven's sake, Anita, you saved him, does it really matter how you did it?"

It was my turn to shrug. "I just don't like the fact that Raina's munin seems to be interfering more and more when I try to heal."

The doorbell rang, and I jumped like I'd been shot. Nervous—who me?

"I ordered take-out," Nathaniel said.

I looked at him. "Please tell me it's Chinese."

He nodded, smiling, I think at my pleased expression. We'd discovered that though no Chinese restaurant would ordinarily deliver out this far, that for a sizable tip, and I mean sizable, they'd make an exception for us. Nathaniel got up, but Caleb pushed away from the door. "I'll get it. I don't seem to be much use for anything else." He set his mug on the island and threaded his way between us to vanish into the living room.

"What's his problem today?" I asked.

Igor answered, "He tried to get friendly with Claudia."

"And me," Cherry said.

I looked from Cherry's smiling face to Claudia's frown. "And he's not bleeding or bruised?"

"It wasn't necessary to hurt him," Claudia said, "only to

be very, very clear." The tone in her voice and the look in her eyes made my own eyes go cold. I don't know if I'd ever met a woman that had that effect on me. It made me feel sexist to say that it was more unnerving because she was a woman, but it was still true.

Her nostrils flared, and I watched all of them sniff the air. Everyone moved at once, scattering around the room. Claudia stood, grabbed my arm—my gun arm—and pulled me back towards the far side of the kitchen and the wall. She already had her gun out in her right hand. I jerked my gun arm free as Igor moved with her and they stood in front of me, blocking my view. Igor had his gun out, too. I was about to ask what the hell was going on, when I smelled it. The acrid, musty scent of snakes.

I had the Browning out and pointed at the door, sighted two-handed when the first snake man came through the kitchen doorway with Caleb in front of him, a sawed-off shotgun pressed into the angle of his jaw. "Anyone moves, and he dies."

40

EVERYONE FROZE, AS if we'd all taken a collective breath and held it. "No one has to die here," the snake man said. He looked at me with a huge copper-colored eye. The strong black stripe that edged the eyes looked like dramatic makeup. There were no scars on this one's face. He was shorter and seemed younger. His scaled face almost managed a smile, but the jaw of a snake is just not made for smiling. His eyes were as empty and alien as the rest of him. "Our boss just wants to talk to Ms. Blake, that's all."

"Have him pick up the damn phone and make an appointment," I said. I was staring down the barrel of the Browning at a point near the center of his chest, far enough up from Caleb's head that I wasn't worried about shooting him, but close enough to the throat that with the ammo I had in the gun it might pretty much decapitate him. If he ever moved the gun barrel out of Caleb's jaw. A sawed-off shotgun, with silver shot at touching range, and Caleb would be gone. I didn't much like him, but I couldn't let the bad guys blow his head off, could I?

"He didn't think you'd come," the snake man said.

"You go away, have him call, and I promise to give it the consideration it deserves." My voice was quiet because I was stilling my breath as much as I could, waiting for that one shot, if it ever came.

The snake man ground the barrel into Caleb's neck, until he forced a small pain sound from him. "This is silver shot, Ms. Blake. At this range it'll take his head."

"The second after he dies, so do you." Claudia said it, her voice as quiet and steady as the arm that held the gun that was pointed at the snake man's head.

He gave a hissing laugh, and it was echoed from behind

him. More of the things started to move up in the open doorway. I caught a flash of silver metal, more guns. "No one
else comes through that doorway, or I'll blow you away and
let Caleb take his chances."

He pushed the barrel of the shotgun into Caleb's jaw until
the smaller man had to rise on tiptoe, and I saw the first hints
of panic on his face. "I don't think she likes you very much,"
the snake man hissed.

"Doesn't matter," I said. "I'm not letting you bring more
guns into this room."

"You promise not to hurt Anita." It was Merle. I'd almost
forgotten him standing to one side and behind us.

"We won't harm a hair on her head."

"We can smell that you're lying," Claudia said.

The snake head turned to one side, birdlike. "Most people
can't smell changes in us, can't smell anything but the stink
of snake."

Cherry's voice. "Anita."

My eyes flickered to her, and I saw movement outside the
sliding glass doors. They were trying to flank us. "We've got
movement on this side," Igor said.

For once other people had guns, and they seemed to know
what they were doing. How refreshing. My gaze turned back
to the snake man in time to see him motion with the barrel
of the gun towards the glass. "We have the house surrounded.
There is no need for all of you to die."

Claudia fired a second before I did. Her bullet hit him in
the face, mine took him high on the chest, low on the neck.
His head vanished in a welter of blood and thicker things.
My ears rang with the shots in the small space. The snake's
body jerked back; the shotgun went off as his hand convulsed. Caleb threw himself to the floor towards us. Two
more snake men came through the door shoulder-to-shoulder,
both with shotguns. Claudia said, "Left."

I shot the one on the right, and she took the one on the
left. Both of us hit what we aimed at, and the two fell to the
floor, one shotgun skidding across the floor towards us.

Another shotgun blast exploded to our left. I turned towards the noise, I couldn't help it. The sliding glass door

had shattered, and I hadn't heard the sound of falling glass, just the shotgun roaring. Igor was kneeling, using the island as cover, as he put two shots into the chest of a man. The man fell to his knees, abruptly, like a puppet whose strings had been cut.

"Incoming," Claudia said, and I turned back to the other door. I could see the barrel of a shiny revolver, something nickel plated. Claudia was standing with her body pressed to the cabinets on the near wall, almost hidden from the door. She fired twice at that shiny barrel, and there was a scream that overrode the ringing in my ears. A screaming that went on and on like the squeal of a baby rabbit when a cat gets it. Dimly, I heard someone yell, "Shut up, Felix!"

Shots showered into the room from the side of the inner door that neither Claudia nor I could see and still stay hidden. Someone touched my arm, and I whirled, smacking into Nathaniel with the barrel of the Browning. He pointed. Igor was on the floor, on his side, with the first hint of crimson trickling across the floor. I saw Zane and Cherry under the table, hugging the ground. I caught a glimpse of Merle farther back, tucked into the corner of the cabinets, probably better hidden than any of us. What do you do in a gunfight if you have no gun, hide? I had a moment of meeting Merle's eyes, before I turned back to the wreckage.

A man stepped through the broken sliding glass door, a pump-action shotgun in his hands. He pumped a round in as he stepped through the door. I shot him three times before his knees collapsed from under him. He should have had the round pumped in before he stepped through the door.

Claudia was putting bullets into the inner door. I don't think she was hitting anything now, but she was keeping them from rushing us. Nothing else moved in the broken door, but I stayed crouched, gun aimed two-handed at the opening.

Bullets rained down from the inner door, and Claudia and I hugged the cabinets. I kept an eye on the far door, but I couldn't keep aimed and take cover at the same time. Another shotgun blast roared through the room from the little window above the sink. It took a big bite out of the island cabinets. I was as low to the ground as I could get, on my butt, pressed to the cabinets, but I kept the Browning on the sliding glass door. The shotgun sent another blast through the little window, and the shots from the living room came one after the other, not aiming, just keeping us where we were. I kept my eyes and my gun on the far door. They were shooting to cover something, and that was the only door left.

Three of them came through the sliding door, and everything slowed down. I was seeing the world through crystal, everything sharp edged. I had all the time in the world to see the two snakes and the lion man Marco come through in a blur of movement that was so fast I knew that none of them was human. I saw the shotguns, long and black, barrels impossibly long; the lion, Marco, had a 9 mil in each hand. I had an impression of blond and golden fur, before my first bullet took him in the side, spun him around. Claudia fired into one of the snakes, dropped him, but the other shotgun roared, and I felt her stagger above me.

I put two shots into the man's chest, and he collapsed on the kitchen table, shotgun falling soundlessly to the floor.

A bullet hit right next to me, and I saw Marco aiming from a prone position. I brought the Browning around to aim at him, but I was going to be too late. I watched him squeezing off the shot and knew he had me. There wasn't time to be scared, just a calm thought, that he was going to shoot me, and I couldn't stop him. Then a black blur was on his back, jerking him backwards, as the shot skidded along the floor in front of me. A wereleopard in man form threw the man out of the door and vanished after him.

I kept my eye on the door, but nothing moved. Something dripped on my face, warm, almost hot. Claudia slumped down the cabinets, to sit, legs sprawled out in front of her, gun still gripped in her hand, but loosely. I gave myself a second to see that her right shoulder and arm was a mass of red, then I turned back to the sliding glass door. I hugged the cabinet beside her. If they came through from the living room, then I could get some of them. If they rushed us from both doors at once, it was over.

I saw movement in the far corner and found Merle on his

feet with a shotgun in one hand and a snake in the other.
He'd pulled him through the window. It was another pump,
and he pumped a round in the chamber with one hand, tearing his fingers through the throat of the snake with the other.

I saw his mouth move more than heard him and knew the
lack of sound wasn't just shock, it was too much gunfire in
a small room. I thought he said, "I've got this door." I eased
around Claudia and tried to cover the living room, having to
trust that Merle really could handle the other door. Claudia's
eyes rolled as I moved around her. Her mouth moved, but I
couldn't hear her. She began to reach her left hand towards
her motionless right, as if the right hand couldn't move. I
kept an eye on the door, but felt her painfully slow movements as she transferred the gun to her left hand. Since I was
pressed just above her body, I hoped that she practiced left-
handed. I'd hate to get shot by accident, when I was so much
more likely to get shot on purpose.

Nothing happened for what seemed like forever; the silence was utterly still. My hearing came back in stages. I
heard Caleb muttering over and over again, "Mother fucking
son of a bitch, mother fucking son of a bitch." He was curled
against the far cabinets behind me, making as small a target
of himself as he could. Nathaniel actually had Igor's dropped
handgun and was pointing it at the sliding glass door. I'd
taught Nathaniel the basics of guns. I had too many around
for him not to know something about them, but watching
him lean against the island cabinets above Igor's body, the
gun held two-handed, his left arm steadied against the cabinet
edge, I knew he'd shoot whoever came through that door. If
he was actually going to start picking up guns during fights,
I was going to have to take him out to the range with me
more.

Of course, that presupposed we would all live to do anything else. The silence stretched, until the wind sighing
through the trees outside the broken glass seemed loud.

A voice came from the direction of the deck. "It's me,
it's Micah." The voice was a deep, growling bass.

"It doesn't sound like Micah," I called back.

"It sounds like me when I'm not in human form," the voice said.

I said, "Merle?"

"It's Micah," he said.

"Come into the doorway, slowly," I said.

The black wereleopard eased through the broken doorway, claws held in the air. The dark shape seemed to fill the doorway. In leopardman form he was over six feet, broader through the shoulders, bulkier all over, as if he had muscles in this shape that he didn't have in human form. His fur gleamed like ebony, sunlight caressed his side, bringing out black-on-black rosettes like sable flowers crushed into velvet. Pale skin showed through at his chest, stomach, lower. In the movies the wolfmen are sexless, smooth as a Barbie doll. In real life, they are very much male. Somehow it was easier to see him naked in half-human form and not be the least bit embarrassed. I just didn't see the shapeshifters as sex objects once the fur started to flow.

"Where's the guy you threw out the door?" I asked.

"He got away."

"I don't hear anyone in the living room," Merle said.

"They all went out the front door," Zane said, "or at least the room looks clear." He and Cherry were still crouched under the kitchen table, flat to the ground.

"I'll check the living room," Micah said.

"These bad guys have silver bullets. I wouldn't be so cavalier about it," I said.

He nodded and his head was mostly leopard, very little left of the man he was, except, strangely, those chartreuse eyes. They marked him as alien, other, in human form, but as that furred and muscled body stalked past me, those same eyes marked him as Micah. The color was richer. Encircled with black fur, the eyes were even more striking. He hesitated in the doorway, then crept through, going low, making as small a target of himself as he could. It was rare to see a lycanthrope that took advantage of cover. Most of them seemed to see themselves as invulnerable, which was usually true, but not today. Igor was very still on the floor, and Claudia's shoulder looked like so much meat. She was slumped against the cabinets. Her left hand still gripped the gun, though the hand was motionless on the floor, as if she had no use of the arm.

When I glanced down, the gun was pointed somewhere in the direction of the sliding glass doors. The hand wavered enough that I was nervous crouching over her, but she fought that shaking limb so that she never quite compromised the line of my body. The right side of her body was soaked with blood, and her eyes were having trouble focusing. I think only shear stubbornness was keeping her conscious.

My gaze flicked to Igor's still form and the bodies piled in the doorways. If Igor was breathing, I couldn't see it. "Check his pulse, Nathaniel."

Nathaniel glanced down at the man, gave me a second of eye contact, then turned back to staring at the broken sliding door. "I'd hear his heart if it was still beating. Hear the blood in his body if it was still moving. It's not." He said all that with his head turned away from me. It made it somehow worse, more unnerving.

Micah appeared in the far doorway. "There's no one left alive in here." He stepped over the pile of bodies in the door, and even that movement was gliding, his balance forward on the feet, which were somewhere between human and leopard. Was I really going to be a leopard when the moon came full this month? Was this dark, graceful shape, this muscular shadow, what I had inside of me?

I pushed the question away; we had other more pressing problems, like the wounded. I'd concentrate on the emergencies and try to let everything else go. It was one of my specialties. I put my fingers against Claudia's neck, trying to check her pulse. She shrugged her shoulders, moving just enough so I couldn't check it. "I'm fine," she said, voice harsh. "I'm fine."

That was so obviously not true, I didn't even argue. Until I checked the house personally, I wouldn't believe we had the all-clear, but my industrial size first-aid kit was in the pantry, and I knew the immediate area was safe. "Cherry crawl out from under the table on this side and get the first-aid kit." I stood up and moved around the cabinets so I'd be able to see both the living room and the sliding glass door, not to mention the bay window over the breakfast nook.

Cherry glanced once at Zane, then crawled out from among the chair legs. She stayed low until she got to the pantry closet. She had to make Caleb move, scooting at him, gently, with her feet. He finally unwound from his tight fetal position and crawled about a foot away so Cherry could get the kit.

Cherry went to Igor first. She was a wereleopard; her hearing was just as good as Nathaniel's, but she went through all the motions, then turned to Claudia. Claudia tried to push her away with her left hand, gun still in it.

"Claudia, let Cherry help you," I said.

"Damn it!"

Cherry took that for a yes and started inspecting the shoulder. Claudia didn't fight her anymore, and I was glad. Shock can make you do and say funny things. I didn't really want to arm wrestle the wererat, wounded or not. Of course, Micah was here and he could probably arm wrestle Claudia and win, at least while she was wounded.

I was still keeping a peripheral sense of the open spaces, but as the time dragged on quietly, there was only the wind in the trees, the noise of summer locusts thrumming through the open living room door and the splintered glass of the back door. I began to relax by inches. That tension in my shoulders that I always get during a fight and never really notice until the adrenaline lets down, let me know that I thought we were safe, for now.

Then I heard something over the summer silence—sirens. Police sirens wailing, getting closer. I didn't have any near neighbors. You heard gunshots in Jefferson County pretty regularly, so who the hell reported the gunshots?

Micah turned that strangely rounded face towards me. "Are they coming here?"

I shrugged. "I don't know for sure, but it seems likely."

We both glanced down at the bodies on the floor, then looked at each other. "We don't have time to hide the bodies," he said.

"No, we don't," I said. I looked at everybody. Merle was

still watching the kitchen window, the borrowed shotgun in his big hands. Zane had crawled out from under the table to play nurse for Cherry, handing her things as she asked for them. She had packed Claudia's arm.

Cherry looked up at me. "She could partially heal herself if she shapeshifted, but she'd still need medical attention."

"The police tend to shoot shapeshifters in animal form," I said.

"I'll stay," Claudia said, teeth gritted just a little. "The more wounded we have on our side, the better the police will like it."

She had a point. I looked at Micah. The sirens were very near now, almost in front of the house.

"You better go, Micah."

"Why?"

"The police are about to burst in here, see a lot of bodies, a lot of blood. Anything in animal form stands a good chance of getting shot."

"That's not a problem," he said. The fur began to recede, like water pulling back from the shore. As human skin was revealed, his bones slid out of sight into it, like hard things thrown in wax, covered, melted. I'd never seen anyone change so casually, so easily. It was almost as if he were merely changing clothes, except for the clear fluid that ran down his body like a liquid sheet, the sound of bones popping, reforming, even the sound of flesh boiling over him. Only his eyes remained the same, unchanging, like two jewels fixed in the center of the universe. Then he was suddenly human again, body covered in that thick, watery fluid. I'd never seen so much of the liquid before from only one change. I was standing in a pool of it and hadn't noticed.

He slumped suddenly, trying to catch himself on the cabinet, but I was in the way and had to grab him around the waist to keep him from falling to the floor. "Rapid change comes with a price."

"I've never seen anyone change back that quickly," Cherry said.

"And he won't fall into a coma-sleep either," Merle said. "Give him a few minutes and he'll be fine, messy, but fine."

There was admiration in the big man's voice, and something else—almost jealousy.

The sirens wailed to a stop outside the house, then silence. "Everybody put the guns down. Don't want to get shot by accident," I said.

Nathaniel did as I asked, instantly. I had to press Micah closer into my body, one-handed, so I could put my own gun back on the cabinet. Micah's body shuddered against me. I looked at him, about to ask if he was alright, but the look in his eyes stopped me. It wasn't pain I saw in his eyes. I slid my other hand around his waist so that I held him more securely against me. His skin was slick under my hands. He managed to put a hand on the cabinet behind us. I stared into his eyes from inches away, and there were worlds to drown in, in those eyes, needs and hopes, everything.

A man's voice yelled, "Police!"

I yelled back, "Don't shoot, the bad guys are gone. We've got wounded." I moved Micah so he could prop himself against the cabinet, then put my hands on my head and moved carefully into the doorway. I had to step over the bodies in the kitchen door to come into the line of sight of the two officers crouched in the doorway. If I'd been a large imposing man, they might still have fired, not on purpose exactly, but you don't see three bodies in a doorway in Jefferson County, Missouri, every day. But I was small, female, and looked fairly benign, unarmed. But I kept talking as I moved anyway. Things like, "They attacked us. We've got wounded. We need an ambulance. Thank God you guys came when you did. The sirens scared them away." I kept babbling until I was sure that they weren't going to shoot me, then the really hard part started. How do you explain five bodies in your kitchen, some of which even in death didn't look very human? Beats the hell out of me.

41

Two hours later I was sitting on my couch, talking to Zerbrowski. He looked, as he usually did, like he'd dressed in a hurry, in the dark, so that nothing quite matched, and he'd grabbed the tie with the stain on it, instead of the one that he probably meant to wear. His wife, Katie, was a neat, orderly sort of person, and I'd never figured out why she allowed Zerbrowski to leave the house dressed like a walking disaster. Of course, maybe it wasn't a matter of allowing him to do anything; maybe it was just one of those battles you just gave up on after a few years.

Caleb sat on the far end of the couch huddled in a blanket we'd gotten off the bed. The paramedics that had taken Claudia away had said he was in shock. I was betting that this was the first time he'd been on the wrong end of a shotgun. Only the top of his curls and a thin slit of brown eyes showed above the blanket. He looked about ten years old, huddled like that. I would have offered comfort but Zerbrowski wouldn't let me talk to him or anyone else. Merle stood against the wall at the end of the couch, watching everything with unreadable eyes. The cops kept giving him little eye flicks as they moved around the room. He made most of them uncomfortable for the same reason he made me uncomfortable; he wore the potential for violence like an expensive cologne.

Zerbrowski pushed his glasses more firmly on his nose, shoved his hands in his pants pockets, and looked down at me. He was standing, I was sitting, the looking down part was easy. "So let me get this straight, these guys just burst in here, and you don't have the first idea why."

"That's right," I said.

He stared at me. I stared back. If he thought I was going

to break under the pressure of his steely gaze, he was wrong. It helped that I really didn't have the faintest idea what was going on. I sat. He stood. We stared at each other. Caleb shuddered on his end of the couch. Merle watched all the people scurrying back and forth.

There were a lot of people. They moved around the house behind Zerbrowski, going in and out of the kitchen, like huge, ambitious ants. There's always too many people at a crime scene, not gawkers either. You always have too many cops around, way more than you need. But you never know which pair of eyes or hands will find that vital clue. Frankly, I thought more evidence was probably lost with all the traffic than found with the extra help, but that was me. I'm just not the social type.

We stood in our own little well of silence. The bedroom door opened behind us. I glanced back to see Micah come out of the room. He was wearing a pair of my sweatpants. Since they were men's sweats anyway and we were the same height, they fit perfectly. I'd never had a boyfriend that I could trade clothes with before. You just didn't find that many grown men my size.

The police hadn't let him shower, so his long hair had dried in messy clumps to his shoulders. The drying liquid was beginning to flake off in patches. His chartreuse eyes flicked towards me, but they stayed neutral. Dolph came right behind him, looming over Micah the way he loomed over me. Dolph's eyes weren't neutral; they were angry. He'd been angry since he stepped through the door. He'd separated us all into different rooms. Nathaniel was being questioned by his friend from the police station, Detective Jessica Arnet. They were in the guest room upstairs. Detective Perry had questioned Caleb and was still questioning Zane. Dolph had done Merle and Micah. Zerbrowski hadn't so much questioned me as simply stood there and made sure I didn't talk to any of the others. Call it a hunch, but I was betting Dolph planned on questioning me personally.

We did have five bodies on the ground, three of which even in death hadn't changed back to human form. The three snake things had stayed snakey. Shapeshifters always change back to their original form in death. Always. Which raised the question, if they weren't shapeshifters, what the hell were they?

"Anita," Dolph said. One word, but I knew what he meant. I got up and went for the bedroom. Micah brushed his fingertips across my hand as I passed him. Dolph's eyes tightened, and I knew he'd noticed.

He held the door for me, and I walked past him into my bedroom. I resented them using my house, my bedroom, to question me, but it beat the hell out of going downtown. So I kept my complaints to myself. Dolph had every reason to take us all downtown. We had dead bodies, and I wasn't even denying I had killed them. Oh, I might have tried to deny it if I thought I could get away with it, but I couldn't, so I didn't.

He motioned me to the kitchen chair that had been moved into the bedroom. He stayed standing, all six-feet-eight of him. "Tell me," he said.

I told him exactly what had happened. I told the truth, all of it. Of course, I didn't know enough to need to lie. They'd carted Igor's body away, all those bright tattoos still vibrant, more alive than the rest of him. We had one dead and one wounded. It was my house. It was obviously a case of self-defense. The only difference from the other two times I'd had to kill people in my house was the number of bodies and that some of them were so not-human. Other than that, I'd walked on much more questionable occasions. So why was Dolph treating this one more seriously? I didn't have a clue.

Dolph stared down at me. He has a much better steely gaze than Zerbrowski, but I gave him calm, blank eyes. I could look innocent this time, because I was.

"And you don't know why they wanted to take you?"

Actually, I had a thought on that one, but I didn't share it, couldn't. They might have come hunting me because I nearly killed their leader. One of the problems with withholding evidence from the police is that later you can't always explain yourself without confessing that you've withheld evidence. This was one of those moments. I hadn't told Dolph about the half-men half-snakes taking Nathaniel and the fight afterwards. I could have told him now, but . . . but there were too many things that I'd have had to tell him, like that maybe I was going to be a wereleopard. Dolph hated the monsters. I wasn't ready to share that with him.

I gave him an innocent face and said, "Nope."

"They wanted you pretty damn bad, Anita, to come in here with this kind of firepower."

I shrugged. "I guess so."

The anger filled his eyes, thinned his lips to a tight line. "You are lying to me."

I widened my eyes. "Would I do that?"

He whirled and slammed his hand into the top of my dresser, hard enough that the mirror thudded against the wall. The glass shivered, and for a second I thought it might shatter. It didn't, but the door opened and Zerbrowski stuck his head in the door. "Everything alright in here?"

Dolph glared at him, but Zerbrowski didn't flinch. "Maybe I should finish questioning Anita."

Dolph shook his head. "Get out, Zerbrowski."

Brave man that he was, he looked at me. "You okay with that, Anita?"

I nodded, but Dolph was already yelling, "Get the fuck out!"

Zerbrowski gave us both a last look and closed the door, saying, "Yell if you need anything." The door closed, and in the sudden silence I could hear Dolph's breathing, heavy, labored. I could smell the sweat on his skin, faint, not unpleasant, but a sure sign that he was in distress. What was going on?

"Dolph?" I made his name a question.

He spoke without turning around. "I am taking a lot of heat for you, Anita."

"Not on this you're not," I said. "Everybody that you took out of this house won't be human. The laws may cover shapeshifters as human, but I know how it works. What's one more dead monster?"

He turned then, leaning his big body against the dresser, arms crossed. "I thought that shapeshifters changed back to human form when they died."

"They do," I said.

"The snake things didn't."

"No, they didn't."

We looked at each other. "You're saying they weren't shapeshifters?"

"No, I'm saying I don't know what the hell they are. There are snake men in a lot of different mythologies. Hindu, vaudun. They could be something that was never human to begin with."

"You mean like the naga you pulled out of the river two years ago?" he said.

"The naga was truly immortal. These things, whatever they are, couldn't stand up to silver bullets."

He closed his eyes for a second, and when he looked at me again, I saw how tired he was. Not a physical tiredness, but a tiredness of the heart, as if he'd been carrying some emotional burden around a little too long.

"What's wrong, Dolph? What's got you so . . . riled up?"

He gave a small smile. "Riled up." He shook his head and pushed away from the dresser. He sat on the edge of the bed, and I turned in the chair, so I was straddling the back of it and could see him better.

"You asked what woman in my life was sleeping with the undead."

"I shouldn't have said that. I'm sorry."

He shook his head. "No, I was being a bastard." His eyes were fierce again. "I don't understand how you can let that . . . thing touch you." His revulsion was so strong that I could almost feel it against my skin.

"We've had this discussion before. You're not my father."

"But I am Darrin's father."

I gave him wide eyes. "Your oldest, the lawyer?" I asked. He nodded.

I watched his face, tried to catch a clue, afraid to say anything. Afraid I'd misunderstood him. "What about Darrin?"

"He's engaged."

I watched the terrible seriousness of his face. "Why do I get the idea that congratulations aren't in order?"

"She's a vampire, Anita, a fucking vampire."

I blinked at him. I didn't know what to say.

Those angry eyes glared at me. "Say something."

"I don't know what you want me to say, Dolph. Darrin's older than I am. He's a big boy. He has the right to be with whoever he wants to be with."

"She's a corpse, Anita. She is a walking corpse."

I nodded. "Yeah."

He stood, pacing the room in long angry strides. "She's dead, Anita, she's fucking dead, and you can't get grandchildren from a corpse."

I almost laughed at that, but my sense of self-preservation is stronger than that. I finally said, "I'm sorry, Dolph, I . . . it's true that, as far as I know, female vamps can't carry a baby to term. But your youngest, Paul, the engineer, he's married."

Dolph shook his head. "They can't have kids."

I watched him pace the room, back and forth, back and forth. "I didn't know. I'm sorry."

He sat back down on the bed, broad shoulders slumping suddenly. "No grandchildren, Anita."

I didn't know what to say, again. I couldn't remember Dolph ever sharing this much of his personal life with me, or anyone for that matter. I was both flattered and almost panicked. I am not a natural caregiver, and I just didn't know what to do. If he had been Nathaniel or one of the leopards, or even one of the wolves, I'd have hugged him, petted him, but he was Dolph, and I just wasn't sure he was a petting kind of guy.

He just sat there staring blindly at the floor, his big hands limp in his lap. He looked so lost. I got up from the chair and went to stand beside him. He never moved. I touched his shoulder. "I'm so sorry, Dolph."

He nodded. "Lucille cried herself to sleep after Darrin made his little announcement."

"Is it the vampire issue or the no-grandchildren issue?" I asked.

"She says she's too young to be a grandmother, but . . ." He looked up suddenly, and what I saw in his eyes was so raw, I wanted to look away. I had to force myself to meet that pained gaze, to hold it and take in everything that he was offering. Dolph was letting me see further inside him than ever before, and I had to honor that. I had to look at him, let him see that I saw it all. If he had been a girlfriend, I'd have hugged him. If he had been most any of my male friends, I'd have hugged him, but he was Dolph, and I just wasn't sure.

He turned his face away, and only then, when he'd given me all the pain in his eyes, did I try to hug him. He didn't let me do it. He stood up, moving away from me. But I'd tried, and that was the best I could do.

When he turned back towards me, his eyes were blank, his face set in that mask he usually wore, his cop face. "If you are holding out on me, Anita, I will bust your ass."

I nodded, my own face falling back into a mask as empty as his. The moment of sharing was over, and he was uncomfortable with it, so we'd go back to familiar ground. Fine with me. I hadn't known what to say anyway. But I'd remember he let me see inside. I'd remember, though I wasn't sure what good it would do either of us.

"A group of shapeshifters, or whatever, attacks me in my own home, kills one of my guests, wounds another, and you'll bust *me*. What the hell for?"

He shook his head. "You are holding out on me, Anita. Sometimes I think you do it out of habit, sometimes just to be a pain in the ass, but you don't tell me everything anymore."

I shrugged again. "I'm not saying I'm holding out anything about today, but I tell you what I can, Dolph, when I can."

"How about the new boyfriend with the cat eyes?"

I blinked at him. "I don't know what you mean."

"Micah Callahan. I saw him touch you."

"He brushed my hand, Dolph."

He shook his head. "It was the way he touched you, the way your face softened when he did it."

It was my turn to look down. I didn't look up until I was

sure I could keep an empty face. "I'm not sure I'd call Micah my boyfriend."

"What would you call him?"

"I appreciate you sharing your personal life with me, Dolph, I really do, but I don't have to return the favor."

His eyes hardened. "What is it with you and the monsters, Anita? Us poor humans not good enough for you?"

"It's none of your business who I date, Dolph."

"I don't mind the dating, but I still don't know how you can stand for them to touch you."

"If it's none of your business who I date, it sure as hell isn't any of your business who I have sex with."

"You fucking Micah Callahan?" he asked.

I met his angry eyes with my own, and said, "Yeah, yeah I am."

He stood trembling in front of me, big hands in fists at his side, and for just a second, I thought he might do something, something violent, something we'd both regret. Then he turned his back on me. "Get out, Anita, just get out."

I started to reach out, to touch him, then let my hand drop. I wanted to apologize, but that would have made it worse. I was uncomfortable with the fact that I had sex with Micah, and that made me touchy. Dolph deserved better. I did the best I could to make up for it. "The heart wants what the heart wants, Dolph. You don't plan on making your life complicated, it just happens, and you don't do it on purpose, and you don't do it to hurt the people who love you. It just turns out that way sometimes."

He nodded, still turned away from me. "Lucille wants to call you and talk about vampires sometime—wants to understand them better."

"I'd be happy to answer any questions she has."

He nodded again, but wouldn't look at me. "I'll tell her to call."

"I'll look for the call."

We both stood there, him still not looking at me. The silence stretched between us, and it wasn't companionable, it was strained. "I don't have any more questions, Anita. Go on out."

I stopped at the door, looked back at him. He was still carefully turned away, and I wondered if he was crying. I might have been able to sniff the air and use my newfound leopard senses to answer the question, but I didn't. He'd turned away so I wouldn't see, wouldn't know. I respected that. I opened the door and closed it quietly behind me, leaving him alone with his grief and his anger. Whether Dolph cried or not was his business, not mine.

42

WHEN THE LAST policeman had wandered away, the last emergency vehicle driven off, the summer silence settled over the house. The kitchen was a mess—broken glass ground into the floor, blood drying to black-red puddles on the polished wood. I'd never get all the blood out from the crevices in the wood. It would be there forever, a reminder that superior fire power had prevailed, but not without cost.

I was going to have to call Rafael and tell him I'd gotten his man killed and his woman wounded. I had to admit that it had been a damn good thing I'd had them. The two extra guns had made the difference. If I'd been the only one armed, things might have gone differently. Okay, I might be dead.

A noise behind me whirled me around. Nathaniel stood in the doorway with a broom, a dustpan, and a small bucket. "I thought I'd clean up the glass."

I nodded, my heart in my throat too much to talk. I hadn't heard him come up behind me. He was only in the doorway, not so close, but close enough if he'd been a bad guy with a gun.

I had been utterly calm through everything. I hadn't fallen apart when the police were here, but suddenly I was shaking, a faint trembling. A nice delayed reaction, damn.

Nathaniel set the dustpan and the bucket on the table, propped the broom against a chair, and walked slowly to me. He peered into my face, lilac eyes concerned. "Are you alright?"

I started to open my mouth and lie, but a small sound came out when my lips parted, almost a whimper. I closed my mouth tight to hold the sounds in, but the shaking got worse. If you're too damn stubborn to let yourself cry, then your body finds other ways to let it out.

Nathaniel touched my shoulder, tentatively, as if not sure he was welcome. For some reason that made my eyes burn, my chest tighten. I clutched my arms tight around myself, as if by holding tight I could keep the tears squeezed inside. He started to move in, started to hug me. I pulled away, because I knew that if he held me I'd cry. I'd already cried once today; that was all I was allowed. Hell, if I cried every time someone tried to kill me, I'd have drowned in my tears by now.

Nathaniel sighed. "If you found me like this, you'd hold me, make me feel better. Let me do the same for you."

My voice came out squeezed tight. "I fell apart once today. Once is enough."

He grabbed my arm. Almost anyone else I'd have been watching for it, but not Nathaniel. I thought of him as safe. His fingers squeezed my arm, not hard enough to hurt, but hard enough to let me know he was serious. I stopped shaking, like a switch had been thrown. I was focused, not even close to tears.

He shook me by the arm, hard enough to have me glare at him. "You wouldn't take a hug. I knew that this," he squeezed the arm a little harder, "would help."

"Let go of me, Nathaniel, now." My voice was low and careful, purring with anger. Nathaniel had never laid hands on me before in any way that was close to violent. Underneath the anger was sadness. He was supposed to be safe, and now he wasn't. He was becoming a person, not just a submissive mess, and it hadn't occurred to me until just this moment that I might not like everything that Nathaniel would grow into.

I felt movement, as if the very air had changed current, just before Micah stepped through the doorway of the kitchen. His hair was still wet from the shower, slicked back from his face, giving me the first real glimpse I'd ever had of that face without the curls to distract the eyes.

His face was as delicate as the rest of him. I'd assumed the long curls only made him seem more delicate, but it was bone structure, just him. If you could ignore the broadening of his shoulders, going down into that slender waist, the straight line of his hips, you might almost say, *girl*. He wasn't really anymore feminine looking than Jean-Claude, but he was more delicately boned, slighter. It was just easier to pull off being masculine when you were an inch away from six feet than when you were an inch away from five-feet-five. Only one thing ruined the delicacy of his face. His nose wasn't quite perfectly straight; it had been badly broken once upon a time and not healed quite right. It should have ruined the near-perfection of his face, but it didn't. It, like his eyes, seemed to add to Micah, make him more interesting, not less attractive. Maybe I'd just had my fill of perfect men.

He'd added an oversized T-shirt to the sweatpants. The shirt hit him at mid-thigh, which hid more of his body than it showed, but even covered, I was aware of him. Aware of him in a way that I was aware of Richard and Jean-Claude. I'd always assumed it was love mixed with lust, but I didn't know Micah well enough to love him. Either pure lust felt pretty much like love, or there was more than one kind of love. It was too confusing for me.

"What's wrong?" he asked.

Nathaniel went back to his broom, bucket, and dustpan. He picked them up and began to sweep the glass up, ignoring us.

"Nothing, what's up?"

He frowned at me. "You're both upset."

I shrugged. "We'll get over it."

He closed the distance between us, but the movement was too sudden after Nathaniel's grab, and I backed up.

Micah stopped, looked at me, clearly puzzled. "What happened? You didn't look this spooked when the guns were out."

I glanced at Nathaniel, who was kneeling, sweeping glass into the dustpan. He was studiously avoiding looking at me, at us. "We had a disagreement."

Nathaniel stiffened then, his whole body reacting to what I'd said. He turned slowly around until he looked up at me with those flower-colored eyes. "That wasn't fair, Anita. I've never disagreed with you in anything."

I sighed, not because he was right, but because of the hurt

in his eyes. I went to him, balanced on my heels, because I didn't dare try to kneel in the glass. I touched his bare shoulder, the side of his face. "I'm sorry, Nathaniel, you just caught me off guard."

"Why won't you let me in, Anita, why? I know you want to."

I touched his back where the bite marks had almost healed, dim reddish circles. "I don't let anyone in without a fight, Nathaniel. You should know that by now."

"Not everything has to be a fight," he said. His eyes were very wide, glittering.

"For me it does."

He shook his head, closing his eyes, and tears trailed down his cheeks. I helped him stand, because I was still worried about the glass. When we were standing, I eased my arms around him until my face touched his bare skin, my mouth pressed into the hollow of his shoulder where the collarbone spoons inward. His arms wrapped around me, held me close. His skin was so soft, so warm. I took a deep shaking breath. He smelled of vanilla, like always. I was never sure whether it was soap, shampoo, cologne, or just him. But underneath was a ranker scent—one that no perfume-maker in the world would bottle. Something feral and far too real, the scent of leopard, of pard.

I felt Micah at my back. I knew the feel of his body, like a line of heat before he pressed himself against me. But his arms didn't encircle me, they touched Nathaniel. Micah's body spooned against mine as we stood, but his hands, his arms traced mine, holding Nathaniel to us, embracing him.

Nathaniel let out a trembling breath. A deep, rumbling sound came out of Micah's throat, and it took me a second to realize he was purring, a deep rhythm of contentment. The purr vibrated against my back. Nathaniel started to cry, and I heard myself say, "We're here, Nathaniel, we're here." We're here. Pressed into the rich vanilla of Nathaniel's skin, Micah's purr thrumming against my body, the feel of both their bodies so solid, so real, and I did cry. I held Nathaniel, Micah held both of us, we cried, and it was okay.

43

SOMEONE CLEARED THEIR throat loudly from the doorway.
I blinked through the soft tears and found Zane standing
there. "Sorry to interrupt, but we've got a crowd out here."

"What do you mean?" Micah asked.

"The swan king, his swanmanes, and pretty much at least
one representative from every other wereanimal in the city,
as far as I can tell."

Nathaniel and Micah pulled away from me. We all rubbed
at our faces; even Micah had been crying. I wasn't sure why;
maybe he was just an emotional kind of guy. "What do they
want?" I asked.

"To see you, Anita."

"Why?"

Zane shrugged. "The swan king won't talk to us flunkies.
He insists that he talk to Anita, and her Nimir-Raj, if she
pleases."

Micah and I exchanged glances. We both looked as puzzled as I felt. "Tell Reece that I need a bit more info before
I grant an interview. I'm a little preoccupied."

Zane grinned wide enough to flash his upper and lower
cat fangs. "We deny him entrance to the house until he tells
us peons what he wants. I like it, but he won't."

I sighed. "I don't want to start a fight just because he
shows up without calling. Shit." I started to walk out, but
Micah caught my hand as I went by. I turned back to look
at him.

"May your Nimir-Raj accompany you?"

I smiled, partly because he'd asked, rather than assumed,
and partly because looking at him made me smile. I squeezed
his hand, and his hand closed around mine, pressing back.

What I wanted to say was, "I'd love the company," what came out was, "Sure."

He smiled, and for the first time it wasn't mixed, it was just a smile. He raised my hand to his lips and pressed his mouth against my knuckles. The gesture reminded me of Jean-Claude. How was it going to be to have Micah and Jean-Claude in the same room at the same time with me?

Micah frowned. "You don't look happy now. Did I do something wrong?"

I shook my head, squeezed his hand, and led him towards the living room. He pulled me back towards him. "No, you thought of something that bothered you. What was it?"

I sighed. "Truth?"

He nodded. "Truth."

"Just wondering how awkward it's going to be when you and I are in the same room with Jean-Claude."

He pulled on my hand, drawing me against him. I put a hand up to keep our bodies from touching completely, and found his heartbeat under the palm of my hand. Even through the cotton shirt, I could feel the thud of his body, as if his heart were naked in my hand. I had to raise my head just a little to meet the green gold depths of his eyes.

His voice came out a little breathy. "I told you, I want to be your Nimir-Raj, whatever that means, whatever it takes."

My own voice wasn't doing much better than his. "Even if that means sharing me with someone else?"

"I knew that coming in."

I felt a frown forming between my eyes. "You know what they say about things that are too good to be true, don't you?"

He touched his fingertips to my face and bent towards me, speaking softly as he moved. "Am I too good to be true, Anita?" He whispered my name against my lips, and we kissed. Gentle, soft, wet. His heart was beating so fast under my hand, my pulse was in my throat, and I think I'd forgotten to breathe.

He drew back first. I was breathless and a little disoriented. There was a look on his face—delight, I think—with the effect the kiss had had on me.

It took me two tries to find my voice. "Too good to be true, oh, yeah, definitely."

He laughed then, and I wasn't sure I'd ever heard him laugh before. It was a good sound. "I can't tell you how much it means to see that look in your eyes."

"What look?"

He smiled, and he was suddenly all male, pride, pleased with himself, and something else—almost embarrassed. He touched my face. "I love the way you look at me."

It made me lower my eyes, and I blushed, even though I wasn't thinking a damn thing that was sexual.

He laughed again, a surprised burst of sound that held so much joy. He laughed the way children laugh before they learn to hide how they feel. He picked me up around the waist and swung me around the kitchen.

I would have told him to put me down, but I was laughing too hard.

"I hate to interrupt," Donovan Reece, the swan king, said from the doorway, "but I told them you'd help us." He frowned at us, his pale, pale skin, showing almost no lines, as if his skin was like the water that his alter form swam upon. He had obviously decided not to wait outside.

I asked, still held above the ground in Micah's arms, "Help you do what?"

He shrugged. "Nothing important, just find some missing alphas and try to convince the Kadru of the werecobras that her Kashyapa, her mate, isn't dead, just missing with the rest. Trouble is," Reece said, "I think she's right. I think he's dead."

Micah let me slide back to the ground. I wondered if my face looked as grim as his. Marianne tells me that the universe/deity loves me and wants me to be happy. So why is it that every time I get a little happy all hell breaks loose? The message seems clear, and it's not about love.

44

DONOVAN REECE HAD curled up on the far end of my white couch. He was dressed in blue jeans so faded they were almost white. His pale pink shirt brought out the natural pink and blue undertones of his near translucent skin. He was beautiful, but not in the way a man or woman is beautiful, in the way a statue or a painting is beautiful, as if he wasn't quite real. Maybe it was because I knew that he had baby swan feathers on his chest, but of all the people in the room he seemed the most surrealistic.

A tall woman with hair almost as white as his sat on the arm of the couch by him. Her pants were black leather, her loose-fitting blouse a pink that matched his shirt, almost. I'm not sure I would have remembered the woman if the other two hadn't been kneeling on the floor at their feet. The second blond's hair was pale yellow and matched her long summer dress. The brunette's hair fell like a curtain around a navy blue dress with tiny white daisies all over it. The swan-manes that we'd saved from the club were all looking at me with large, almost fearful eyes.

I only recognized one person other than the swan king and his entourage. I'd met Christine for the first time at the Lunatic Cafe back when Raina still owned it, and Marcus, her Ulfric, was still trying to control all the other wereanimals in town and make himself high supreme commander, whether everyone else agreed or not. Christine's hair was still blond, short, professional. She was dressed in a navy business suit. Her powder blue shirt was partially unbuttoned, as if she'd removed a tie, though I don't think she had. She was perched on the other end of the couch from Donovan, her sensible navy pumps still on. Almost everyone else had gotten casual. There were a pile of shoes near my front door.

"Hi, Christine, it's been a while," I said.

She looked up at me, and it wasn't a friendly look. "I'm impressed you remembered my name."

"I tend to remember people I meet under stressful situations."

I got the tiniest smile out of her. "Well, we do seem to meet under less than pleasant circumstances," she said.

Donovan took over then, introducing me to the man and woman sitting between them. They were both dark-complected. Their bone structure was pure middle America, nothing special, but their eyes were too big, too dark, the hair truly black. There was something exotic about them that straight European just doesn't give you. They also looked amazingly alike, like male and female versions of each other. They were Ethan and Olivia MacNair, respectively.

The man in my white chair was bulky, not muscled, or fat, just big. He had the fullest beard I'd ever seen. The thick hair covered most of his face and neck. He was introduced as Boone, and the moment he turned small dark eyes to me, I knew he was something that would eat me if it could. Not wolf, not cat, but something with teeth.

His voice was a rumbling bass, so low it almost hurt to hear it. "Ms. Blake."

I nodded. "Mr. Boone."

He shook his head, the dark beard rubbing back and forth over his white shirt. "Just Boone, no mister."

"Boone," I said.

Nathaniel, Zane, and Cherry were bringing in kitchen chairs so the last four people could sit down. Two women, two men, were left. One man was slender with golden red hair, and strangely up-tilted green eyes. He sat on the floor, huddled against the side of the couch as if he were hiding.

"That's Gilbert," Donovan said.

"Gil," he said, voice almost too soft to hear.

The woman was tall, nearly six feet, broad-shouldered, strong-looking. Her hair was brown, streaked with gray, pulled back from her face in a loose ponytail. Her face was bare of makeup. She offered me a hand, and gave me one of the best handshakes I've ever had from another woman.

Her brown eyes were deep with worry, as she said, "I'm Janet Talbot. It's good of you to see us all on such short notice."

"I didn't come here to make small talk." This from a woman who was standing on the far side of the room, near the big picture window. She was looking out through the closed sheers, hands gripping her elbows, nervous tension singing along her straight spine, as she turned to face the room. I could see where Ethan and Olivia had gotten the dark skin and their exotic look. Nilisha MacNair was about my size but even more delicately put together, so that she seemed smaller. A man might think words like *birdlike, kittenish,* until he looked in her eyes. Once you looked into those dark, dark eyes, you knew better. The eyes gave the lie to the packaging. She was hell on wheels and used to getting her own way.

A man stood near her, but not too near. He was as tall, as blond, as pale, as she was small, black-haired, and dark. He was also muscled in a way that nature does not do. His shoulders were broad, waist narrow, hands large enough to palm her entire head, yet he was clearly afraid of her. Oh, it was bodyguard deferential, but there was real fear there, too.

Merle was leaning casually near the big blond man. I didn't know where Caleb was, and didn't care.

"I am the Kadra, and the Kashyapa, who is dead, is my husband." Nilisha MacNair let out a sudden breath that shook, then she regained control like a mountain squeezing downward. "*Was* my husband."

"Father is not dead," Olivia said. "I won't let you make him dead by giving up."

Her brother, Ethan, touched her arm, as if trying to soothe her or tell her to shut up. She ignored him.

But the damage was done; the fight was on. "How dare you? How dare you say that I would make him dead? I am merely facing the truth."

Olivia stood up, shaking off her brother's hand. "You just can't stand the fact that he was with another woman when it happened."

The fight went downhill from there. Apparently Henry

MacNair, patriarch of the clan, had been leaving his mistress and fellow werecobra's house, when someone had taken him. No body was found, but a lot of blood was left behind. There had been signs of a struggle, a car on its side, a good-sized tree torn up. When wereanimals struggle, they struggle.

I actually learned quite a bit from the fight, but when it was reduced to the two women screaming at each other from less than a foot away, some of it not even in English, I'd had enough.

I looked across the room at Donovan. He had brought them to my house, after all. He shrugged. Basically, he didn't know what to do either.

I had visions of dumping water over their heads, but decided that it might just work better to leave the room. I motioned the others into the kitchen, and they all trooped out. It was as the last of them were leaving the room that the shouting began to die down. Then Nilisha's voice. "Where are you all going?"

Janet Talbot spoke for all of us. "Some place quieter."

I couldn't see the women's faces, but I could almost smell the embarrassment on the air. Not wereanimal ability, just a good guess.

"Please," Olivia said, "please, I do apologize. Please come back."

Everyone started trickling back into the room. Nilisha actually took a chair with the blond bodyguard behind her. "We are all very worried about my husband."

"Worried about him, Mama?" Olivia said.

The woman nodded, smiled. "Yes, worried."

"He's not dead," the girl said.

"If you can have hope, so can I."

They smiled at each other like bright mirrors, so alike in that one moment. Ethan looked relieved, but he didn't smile.

"Alright, besides Henry MacNair, who else is missing?"

"My son, Andy," Janet Talbot said. She handed me a snapshot of a young man with her brown hair, cut short, but his features were softer than hers. He was handsome, bordering on pretty. "He looks like his father." She said it, as if strangers had remarked on the lack of resemblance before. I wouldn't have said a damn thing.

"Our Ursa," Boone said, "I didn't think to bring a picture."

"Ursa, bear, your queen?" I made it a question.

He nodded that massive, bearded head, and I wondered how I'd missed it. "She went out to pick up a few things at the store and never came back. No signs of a struggle, just gone."

I looked at Gil of the green eyes. "Who'd you misplace?"

He shook his head. "No one, I'm just scared."

I looked at Christine. "How 'bout you?"

"I'm here as a representative for the weres that only have one or two members. Those of us who have chosen St. Louis because there were no others like us. I'm the only weretiger in town, so I haven't lost anybody, but we've lost one werelion."

"I don't suppose the missing lion is named Marco?"

Christine shook her head. "No, Joseph, why?"

Donovan answered, "The lion man was named Marco."

"Oh" she said.

"And," Donovan added, "Joseph isn't able to change that close to human. No one I know of can change that close to human and hold it without changing."

Christine continued as if I hadn't spoken. Focused, Christine was always focused. "Joseph's mate is pregnant. Amber would be here but she's under complete bed rest until the baby is born."

"Until she loses it, you mean," Cherry said.

I glanced at her. "You say that like she's lost some before."

"This is her third try," Cherry said.

"I'm sorry to hear that. Losing her . . . mate must not be helping her stress levels."

"That is an understatement," Christine said.

"She's a fool to keep trying," Cherry said. "We can't carry a baby to term, and that's that."

I looked at her again. "Pass that by me again, slowly."

"The change is too violent, it causes miscarriage." Cherry

said it matter of factly, then I watched her understand what she'd just said, and she whispered, "Anita, I didn't . . . you shouldn't have had to find out this way. I'm sorry."

I shrugged, then shook my head. "But the MacNairs have two children. I'm looking at them. Janet has a son."

"My type of shapeshifting is inherited," Janet said. "It's not tied to the moon. I avoided shapeshifting until after Andy was born."

I looked at Nilisha. "I am a werecobra. I can choose to try and carry a baby like a mammal or like a snake."

"You laid eggs?" I made that one a big question.

She nodded. "I couldn't have carried them in my body. The change is too hard. But I had other options."

The unspoken, *but you don't,* hung on the air. It was too hard to think about. It wasn't like I'd ever considered having children. I mean, get real, with my life? Out loud, I said, "One problem at a time. So who disappeared first?"

Henry MacNair was the first victim, and had had the most struggle. Then, the werelion, Joseph; Andy Talbot, weredog, as it turned out; and last the Ursa of the bears, Rebecca Morton.

The last time we'd had this many wereanimals missing, it had been the old swan king who was delivering them over to be hunted by illegal thrill seekers.

I looked at Donovan Reece. He either read my mind or anticipated it. "Interesting coincidence that I come into town about the same time everyone goes missing, isn't it."

"Gee, Donovan, you read my mind."

"I swear to you that I know nothing of this."

Nilisha said, "I know all about the betrayal of the last swan king. But I am betting my husband's life that Donovan is innocent of all this."

I shrugged. "We'll see."

"You do not trust my judgment," she said.

"I don't trust much of anyone's judgment but mine. Nothing personal."

Olivia touched her arm. "Mother."

Nilisha took a deep breath and calmed down. The day was looking up.

"The first thing I'm going to suggest is that we call in the police."

Nobody liked that idea. "Look, they have resources that I don't, computer searches, forensics."

"No," Nilisha said, "no, we must handle this among ourselves."

"I know the rule is that we don't bring in the human authorities, but guys, we have four missing, and they made a run at the swans and the leopards already."

"You think the snake people and their pet lion are behind this?" Donovan asked.

"It would be too big a coincidence if they weren't," I said.

"I agree," Micah said. He'd been very quiet through everything, carefully not standing or sitting too close, as if he didn't want to confuse things. He was letting me be in charge without hovering.

"Okay, then who are these guys, and what the hell would they want with a variety of shapeshifters?"

We talked for a couple of hours but didn't come up with anything brilliant. The snakemen were behind it. But why? Why would any wereanimals give a shit about other wereanimals that weren't their kind? If it had just been the werecobras targeted, then maybe it could be a reptile turf war, though frankly, it was unusual to have a fight even between two different kinds of snakes. The town was big enough for everybody as long as they weren't the same species.

I thought Nilisha MacNair was right and her husband was dead. If people kidnap someone and don't want money, they want worse things, usually things that include blood, pain, and, eventually, death. They were probably all dead, and if they weren't, we needed the police in on it to keep them alive.

It turned out that everyone had reported their people missing, neglecting to mention the part about being wereanimals. "But don't you see, the police have a twenty-one-year-old college senior missing, a forty-five-year-old husband, a thirty-something single woman, and a thirty-something married man. Other than the fact that they're all Caucasian, there is no common denominator to link up these cases. But if I can tell the police they are all wereanimals, then that's the link. You guys live all over the city. You have different police units working on each case. They'll never make the connection, unless we tell them what the connection is."

Janet Talbot nodded first. "Andy's almost got his pre-med degree. If they find out what he is, he'll never be a doctor, but I want him safe more than I want anything right now. So I agree, go to the police."

"I can't speak for Amber," Christine said, "but I'm pretty sure she'd agree."

"I should ask the others first, but the hell with it, find Rebecca for us, even if that means bringing in the cops," Boone said.

We all turned to Nilisha MacNair. "No, if they find out, we are all ruined."

Olivia took her hand. Ethan knelt in front of her. "Mother, without father, what does it matter?"

I wasn't sure she'd agree since he'd been cheating on her, but she nodded, and she agreed. Love is a funny thing sometimes. But whatever the motive, it meant I could talk to Dolph, and I wouldn't even have to lie.

45

Dolph answered on the second ring. "Dolph." He never said, Regional Preternatural Investigation Team, or even police, just his name, not even his last name, not even his full first name, just "Dolph," or "Dolph, here." Did anyone ever complain? Somehow I doubted it.

He sounded as close to surprised as he ever gets. "Anita, I didn't expect to hear from you until we'd at least finished the paperwork on the last batch of bodies." I heard a man's voice, but couldn't tell what was said. Dolph came back on. "Zerbrowski says that if you killed someone else just hide the body, he's not starting over on the paperwork."

"I know enough about procedure to know that he'd have to start a new report anyway. Separate crime, separate report, right?"

"Do you really have a fresh body out there?" He sounded tired, but not surprised.

"No," I said.

"Then how do we rate a call?"

"I have information pertaining to several crimes and the permission of those involved to tell you the truth, the whole truth. Now, isn't that refreshing?"

I could almost feel him sitting up over the phone. "I'm a cop, truth is always refreshing, so dazzle me."

I told him. As I'd suspected, the MacNair case was already on the roster for Dolph and the gang, but it was the first he'd heard of the others.

"I interviewed the wife personally. She kept saying she had no idea why some monster would attack her husband. It might have helped us find him if we'd known."

"Dolph, they run a restaurant. If it gets out that they're shapeshifters, they may lose it."

"Board of Health can't shut them down for this."

"No, but word will get out, and the customers will start to worry. You know it, and I know it."

"No one will find out from my people. You have my word on it."

"Yeah, but how many other departments are involved? How many nonpolice are at every crime scene, not to mention clerical workers? It'll come out, Dolph, eventually it'll come out."

"I'll keep a lid on it, Anita, but I can only guarantee my people."

"I know, Dolph, but Andy Talbot wants to be a doctor. He'll never get into med school once this comes out. Rebecca Morton is a chiropractor. If they find out what she is, they'll yank her license."

"Why is it that most of these people go in for professions where this is a problem?"

I shrugged, knew he couldn't see it. "Just lucky, I guess."

"I think it's stubbornness," Dolph said.

"What do you mean?"

"Tell anyone that they can't do something, and they'll want to do it."

He had a good point. "Makes sense."

"How do these disappearances tie in to the attack on your house?"

Damn, the whole truth, I'd said. There was my chance to prove it. I took a deep breath and told him almost all of the truth. I told him that Gregory had called for help, leaving out why he'd call me. Dolph never questioned that I'd be a good choice when calling for rescue from the monsters. He did say, "He could have called the police."

"It hasn't been that long since the police killed wereanimals on sight, Dolph. You can't really blame them for being leery of you guys."

"Why didn't you tell me all this when you were in for questioning?"

"You were mad at me," I said, as if that explained it. And it sort of did, though it made me sound childish.

"What are you leaving out?" he asked.

"I tell you the truth, and you still doubt me. That really hurts, Dolph."

"Not as much as it's going to if I find out you withheld evidence on this."

"It's not like you to make threats, Dolph."

"I'm tired," he said.

I was quiet for a second. "You should get some rest, Dolph."

"Yeah, if you can keep from killing anyone else, maybe I'll catch up on the paperwork."

"I'll do my best," I said.

"You do that." I heard him take a deep breath. "Is this all the information you're going to give me on this?"

"Yep."

"I'll go back and interview the families again. Do you know how much extra work this is going to be, just because they fucking lied the first time?"

"They didn't mean to make your job hard, Dolph, they were just scared."

"Yeah, so isn't everyone?" With that, he hung up.

I stared at the buzzing phone. The man was not in a good mood. I knew why, now, and I was probably one of the few outside his family that did know why. I wondered how much grouchier he was going to get, and if it would start affecting his job, if it hadn't already. If his hatred of the monsters took away his objectivity, then he was going to be useless as the head of the Regional Preternatural Investigation Team. Shit. It was a problem for another day. I could add it to the list of things I'd worry about later. At the rate the list was growing, I'd never have time to worry about everything on it. Maybe I could throw a dart and make what it stuck in the problem of the day. Or maybe I could just ignore the list. Yeah, ignoring sounded good.

46

THE MACNAIRS, PLUS bodyguard, promised to drive straight to RPIT's headquarters and give statements. Janet Talbot went with them. Christine didn't really know anything about the werelion's disappearance, so she just went home, promising to be careful. I offered to let her stay at my place until the bad guy, or guys, was caught, but she turned me down flat.

Donovan Reece said, "She is an independent creature."

I could admire that. "I hope her independence doesn't get her hurt."

He shrugged, getting to his feet. I noticed a lump under the front of his pink shirt. "You're armed," I said.

He glanced down at the place where his gun was trying and failing to hide. "I won't let my girls be taken again."

"People, call them people," I said.

He gave me a smile. "They are all girls."

"Humor me," I said.

He gave a small bow of his head. "My people, fine, but I won't let them be taken again."

"Or you either, Donovan. Remember everyone that's vanished has been a leader, not a follower. They chained Nathaniel up because they thought he was you; your people being taken was just incidental."

He met my eyes, suddenly very serious. "You're right. How did you know I was armed?"

"If you're going to tuck a gun into the front of your pants, wear a darker-colored shirt, and maybe one that's a size bigger."

He nodded. "I've never carried a gun before."

"Do you know how to use it?"

"I know how to shoot. I just don't usually carry concealed."

"Do you have a license to carry?"

He blinked at me.

"I take that as a no."

"No," he said.

"Then if you use it and kill someone, it's going to be a headache in court. Carrying concealed without a license will make it an illegal weapon. Depending on the judge, you might see jail time."

"How long does it take to get a license?"

"Longer than you'll want to wait. But check your county and start the process. Or don't start the process, and when you get arrested you can try and claim ignorance of the law. It's not a legal excuse, but it might sway a judge. I don't know. I'd apply for a license and hope it goes through."

"What do I have to do to apply?"

"It differs from county to county. Check with your local police. They'll know who you have to see."

He nodded again. "I'll do that." He looked at me, gray eyes so serious. "Thank you, Anita."

I shrugged. "Just doing my job."

He shook his head. "This isn't your job. You're no one's alpha here. You could have just refused to help us."

"And what good would that have done?" I asked.

"Most of the wereanimals won't help each other."

"You know of all the furry—and feathered—politics, that's the one I understand the least. Just like now, what happens to one group can affect the others. If you guys had been talking to each other, then you'd have known that Henry MacNair went missing, violently missing. It might have put all of you on guard."

"You think it would have prevented the other disappearances?"

"I don't know, but it might have helped. People would have been more cautious, maybe not gone out alone. We might have at least had witnesses."

"It was after my girls—people—got taken and you helped us that Christine came to me. She knew about the bears' Ursa having gone missing. It was Ethan MacNair, not his mother, that told us about his father."

"I bet he paid for going outside his mother's orders," I said.

"Probably," Donovan said, "but you're right, if we'd just bloody talk to each other, we could help each other more."

"Not just in emergencies either," I said.

His eyes narrowed. "You mean a coalition of wereanimals?"

I shrugged. "I hadn't thought that far ahead, but why not? Something where we share information. We've got a lion working with a bunch of snakes. Why should the bad guys get along better than we do?"

"Every time one of the animals talks about joining forces they always mean that they'll be top . . . dog. You want to be everybody's Nimir-Ra, Anita?"

"I'm not talking sharing authority. That'll never work without a war. I'm just saying share information, help each other more. When one of the leopards or wolves gets hurt, he, or she, has a place to stay until they're well. That kind of thing."

"Someone would need to be in charge of it."

I felt like grabbing him by the front of the shirt and shaking him. "Why, Donovan, why does anyone have to be in charge? Something happens to one of your swans, you pick up the phone and call me, or Ethan, or Christine. We call someone else. We try to help each other. We don't need a hierarchy, just a willingness to cooperate."

He looked unhappy, almost suspicious. "You don't want to be in charge."

I shook my head. "Donovan, I don't even want to be in charge of what I'm in charge of now. I sure as hell don't want to add to it."

It was Micah, who had been leaning against the wall, so still, so calm that you forgot he was there, who said, "She's offering you friendship, Donovan."

"Friendship?" He made it sound like a foreign concept.

Micah nodded, pushing away from the wall to stand beside me. "If something goes wrong and you need help, you call your friends."

Donovan frowned hard enough that he formed lines in

that flawless skin. "Wereanimals aren't even friends with each other, let alone across species lines."

"That's not true," I said. "Richard," I paused after I'd said his name, as if it hurt, or I was waiting for it to hurt. Micah touched my shoulder, and I put my hand over his, held on. I tried again. "Richard's best friend is one of Rafael's rats. My leopard Vivian is living with, and in love with, Stephen, one of Richard's wolves."

"That's different."

"Why?"

"Because the wolves and rats have a treaty, and through you the leopards and the wolves are joined."

I shook my head. "You're quibbling, Donovan, or deliberately missing the point. Let's just agree to try and help each other, that's all. I don't have any ulterior motives. I'm just trying to keep the damage to a minimum."

"It's true you didn't have to save my girls. It nearly cost you your life."

"And you didn't have to go to the lupanar with me. But you did. That's how it works, cooperation."

He thought for a moment, then nodded. "Agreed. I'll try to get the others to agree also. You're right, you are right. If we'd just talk to each other, we could prevent a lot of bad things from happening."

"Great," I said, and let out a breath I hadn't realized I was holding. I wanted this. I wanted them to talk to each other, to help each other.

Someone cleared their throat, softly. It made us all look at Gil. He was still huddled beside the couch, where he'd been the entire time. "You have something to say?" Donovan asked.

"How far does this new spirit of cooperation go?" he asked. His uptilted green eyes were almost round with anxiety. He gripped his knees so hard his hands were mottled. He was scared; you could smell it on him, that and a neckruffling scent that I didn't recognize.

"What do you mean?" Donovan asked.

"I'm actually talking to Anita," Gil said.

I glanced at Micah then back to the man huddled on the floor. "What do you want to know?" I asked.

"I'm the only werefox in town. I don't have an alpha, or any family." He stopped there and licked his lips nervously.

"And?" I said.

"How much help are you willing to give?"

"How much do you need?"

"Can I stay with you until this thing, or whatever, is caught?"

I felt my eyes go wide. I opened my mouth, closed it, exchanged a look with Micah. He shrugged. "It has to be your call. It's your house."

Point. I turned back to Gil. "I don't know you at all. If you are a bad person, and you do bad things to my people, I will kill you, but if you really just want someplace to hide for a few days, you can stay."

He seemed to get smaller, more huddled. "I won't hurt anybody. I just want to feel safe again, that's all."

I looked at Donovan. "Do you know anything about him?"

"He's scared of his own shadow. I wouldn't trust him to help in an emergency. I think he'd save himself first."

Gil didn't argue with Donovan's estimation of him, he just huddled, trembling. "If we only help the strong ones, then we're not helping ourselves," I said.

"You'll take him in, knowing he can't help you in a fight, and would probably run to save his own skin?" Donovan asked.

I looked at those wide, terror-filled eyes and saw something besides fear, a pleading. They said, "Please, please help me."

"You can stay, and we'll protect you, but if there is an emergency I expect you to do your best. You don't have to fight, but don't be a hindrance."

"What's that mean?" he asked.

"It means if the guns come out, hide under something, get low to the ground. Don't make yourself a target. If my people get hurt and you have a chance to drag them to safety but leave them to die instead, you'll be next."

"I'm not brave, Anita, I'm not even a little bit brave."

"Don't be brave, Gil, just do what you're told, do your best whatever that is, but understand the rules. Keep yourself out of the line of fire because we won't have time to worry about you when the fighting starts. Help if you can, stay out of the way if you can't. Simple."

He nodded, rubbing his chin between his knees, over and over. "Simple," he whispered, "I wish life were simple."

"Life isn't simple, Gil, but a fight is." I knelt in front of him, and I hated the weakness that radiated from him. Dear God, the last thing I needed was another emotional cripple following me around. But I couldn't kick him out. Anita the bleeding heart. Who'd have thought it? I stared at him, until his frightened eyes met mine. "A fight is simple, Gil. You protect yourself, your people, and you kill the bad guys. You do whatever it takes to get yourself and your people out alive."

"How do you know who the bad guys are?" he asked, voice almost a whisper.

"Anyone in the room that isn't us," I said.

"And you kill them, just like that?"

I nodded. "Exactly," I said.

"I don't think I could kill anyone."

"Then hide."

He did that chin-rubbing nod thing again, like he was scent marking his own knees. "I can hide, I know how to do that."

I touched his face very gently. He flinched, then relaxed a little. All the animals liked to be touched. "I'm not very good at hiding, maybe you can teach me."

"Why would you need to know how to hide?" he asked.

"Because there's always someone, or something, bigger and badder than you are."

"I can teach you how to hide, but I don't know if I can learn how to kill."

Where had I heard that before? Oh, I knew—Richard. But even he had learned how, in the end. "You'd be surprised what you can learn, Gil, if you have to."

He hugged himself again. "I don't think I want to learn how to kill people."

"Now that," I said, "is a different problem altogether."

"I don't want to," he said.

I stared down at him. "Then don't, but don't let your squeamishness get any of my people killed."

"It's more likely to kill me."

"True, but that's your choice—get yourself killed if you want, but don't bring harm to me or mine because of some moral high ground."

"Would you really kill me for it?"

I knelt back in front of him. "You can stay with me and I'll keep you safe, or die trying, but if you fuck up and cause the death of one of my leopards, or my friends, I will kill you. I don't want you to be crying later and saying you didn't understand. Because if you've earned it, I will shoot you while you beg me not to."

"But who decides whether I deserve it?" he asked.

"I do."

He stared up at me as if he weren't sure if he was safer with me or without me. I watched him think it through and felt nothing, no pity. Because Gil the werefox was a liability. In a combat situation he was a fucking casualty waiting to happen. I was civilized enough to give him protection when he asked, but not civilized enough to pay in the blood of those I held dear. In that moment I knew I wasn't a sociopath, because if I had been, I'd have kicked his ass out the door. Oh, hell, I'd have shot him and put him out of everyone's misery. Instead I offered him a hand, and pulled him to his feet.

"Do you understand the rules?" I asked.

"I understand," he whispered.

"You willing to live by them?"

He gave one small nod.

"You willing to die by them?"

He took a shaky breath, then gave another nod.

I smiled and knew it never reached my eyes. "Then welcome to the club, and keep your head down. There's some business we have to take care of tonight. You can come along." Even I wasn't sure if that was an invitation or a threat.

47

THERE WAS STILL a thread of light in the sky, like a slender golden ribbon, glowing against the push of dark, dark clouds when we parked in the back of the Circus of the Damned. The back parking lot was for employees. It was dark, bare, not the least bit entertaining, unlike the front, which was like a carnival. I'd driven past the bright lights and dramatic posters without a second glance.

"Did the clowns up front have fangs?" Caleb asked.

It wasn't until he asked that that I realized that none of them had ever been to the Circus. I undid my seat belt and leaned around so I could see him in the middle section of seats. He was sitting pressed against the door with Merle's broad shoulders crowding him. Nathaniel was on the other side of Merle. Cherry and Zane were in the back seats with Gil. Micah was sitting up front with me. Until we knew my house wasn't a free-fire zone we'd keep everybody together. Rafael had sent two new bodyguards over, but they'd arrived just as we were leaving, and I wouldn't make anyone in the Jeep move. They followed us, not happy, but taking orders, which was good.

I answered Caleb's question. "Yeah, the big spinning clowns on top of the sign have fangs."

"I saw a poster for zombie raisings. Do you do that?" Merle asked.

I shook my head. "I don't believe in using God-given gifts for entertainment purposes."

"I didn't mean to insult you," he said.

I shrugged. "Sorry, I'm a little touchy about shit like that. I don't approve of a lot of things some of my fellow animators do for money."

"You raise the dead for money," Caleb said.

I nodded. "Yeah, but I've turned down more money than I've taken."

"Turned down, why?" he asked.

I shrugged. "Local money who wanted to have his Halloween party in a cemetery so I could raise zombies at midnight. Or the guy that had offered a million if I could raise Marilyn Monroe and guarantee that she'd do anything he asked for a night." I shuddered. "I told that one if I even heard a rumor that he'd gotten someone to do the job, I'd see his ass in prison."

Caleb's eyes were a little wide. I think I'd shocked him. Good to know that I could. "You're deeply moral," Merle said, a tone in his voice like he was surprised.

"My own version of it, yeah."

"You hold to your own rules no matter what?" Merle made it a question.

I nodded. "Most of the time."

"What will make you break your own moral code?"

"Harm to my people, survival, the usual."

Merle's eyes flicked to Micah, sitting beside me. It was a small movement. If I hadn't been looking directly at him, I'd have missed it.

"What?" I asked, glancing from one to the other.

Merle answered, "You sound like Micah."

"You make that sound like a bad thing," I said.

He shook his head. "Not a bad thing, Anita, not a bad thing at all, just . . . unexpected."

"You still don't sound entirely happy about it," I said.

"Merle worries too much," Micah said.

I glanced at him, but he was watching the big man. Micah had tied his hair back while it was still wet, so that it lay flat to his head, utterly straight until it spilled out into the long ponytail, where the curls spilled like froth along his spine. His hair lay like brown velvet against the charcoal gray of his shirt.

"What does Merle worry about?" I asked.

"Taking care of me, mostly, and now, I think, you."

I looked at the big man. "Is that what you're worrying about?"

"Something like that," Merle said. He'd put a clean white T-shirt underneath his jean jacket, but other than that, he was wearing an identical outfit to the first one I'd ever seen him in. If he'd been wearing more leather, he'd have looked like an aging biker.

Micah turned towards me. His shirt made that rich, slithery sound that silk makes against leather seats. The dark gray shirt was short-sleeved, button-up, dressy. The color brought out the gold-green of his eyes, made his skin look even darker. He'd matched the shirt with black jeans, black belt, silver buckle, soft black tie-up shoes. It occurred to me for the first time that he looked like he'd dressed for a date. Had he dressed to impress me or Jean-Claude? It was a semiformal occasion for any alpha to meet the Master of the City. But especially one that was fucking the Master's human servant. I just wasn't sure how to handle the whole situation. Jean-Claude had taken Micah in stride in theory, but how would he react to seeing him in the flesh? How would Micah react to seeing Jean-Claude?

Damn it, I had enough to worry about without having to juggle male egos.

"You're frowning again," Micah said.

I shook my head. "It's nothing. Let's get this over with."

"Why do you sound less than thrilled?"

I had my door open and turned back around to say, "We're here to rescue Damian. I don't know what shape he's going to be in. Why would I be thrilled?"

"I know you're worried about your friend, but are you sure that that's really what's bothering you?"

I frowned at him. "What are you talking about?"

"I'm nervous about meeting the Master of the City, too."

It was almost like he'd read my mind. We didn't know each other well enough for him to really read me, but . . . he was either telepathic, which I didn't believe, or he *could* read me that well. I wasn't sure which thought bothered me more.

I let out a breath and half slumped in the seat. "Yeah, I'm a little nervous about introducing you to Jean-Claude. He was cool about you in the abstract, even knowing that we've been together, but seeing you in the flesh . . . " I tried to think how to word it. "I don't know how he'll feel about that."

"Will it make you feel any better if I promise to behave myself."

"Maybe, if you can pull it off."

"I can pull it off," he said, giving me very serious eye contact. He certainly vibrated sincerity.

"Don't take this wrong, Micah, but I've been disappointed pretty badly recently by the men in my life. It's a little hard to trust that anyone can pull it off."

He reached out to touch me, then let his hand fall back, as if something in my face hadn't been friendly. "I'll do my best tonight, Anita, that I can promise."

I sighed. "I believe you."

"But," he said.

I had to smile. "Your intentions are good, my intentions are good, Jean-Claude's intentions are probably good." I shrugged. "You know what they say about good intentions."

"My best is all I can offer," he said.

"And it's all I can ask, but let's say I'm not exactly sure how to handle this. I'd barely gotten to where I could deal with Richard and Jean-Claude at the same time, and now here *you* are. I just don't know."

"I can go back to your house," he said.

"No, Jean-Claude asked to meet you."

Micah looked at me. "And that makes you nervous."

I half-laughed. "Oh, yeah."

"Why?"

"If Jean-Claude were having sex with someone else, I wouldn't want to meet them."

Micah shrugged. "Do you think he means me harm?"

"No," I said, "no, nothing like that." I tried to put it into words and couldn't. Maybe it was just my lack of sophistication. How do you introduce boyfriend C to boyfriend A, after boyfriend A has been such a good sport, of late, about boyfriend B, who is no longer in the picture? Or maybe it was the way Jean-Claude had asked for him. "Bring your Nimir-Raj, *ma petite,* I would like to meet him."

"Why?" I'd asked.

"Am I not entitled to meet the other man in your bed?"

It had made me blush. But here Micah was, and here we were outside the Circus. Jean-Claude was inside, waiting. I was actually more scared about introducing the two of them than I was worried about Damian. If Jean-Claude didn't try and kill Micah, *then* I'd worry about Damian. I was ninety-nine percent sure that Jean-Claude wouldn't start a fight. It was the last one percent that clenched my gut into a tight knot as we moved out into the darkness.

The two new bodyguards came up to flank me as I walked towards the back door. They were both over six feet, male, and radiated bodyguard badass. Other than that they were almost opposites. Cris (no h, it's short for Cristiano) was mid-twenty-something, skin tanned a soft gold, eyes a pale shade of gray blue. His hair was that shade of pale brown that some people call blond. Bobby Lee was over forty, very short hair, gone white gray, eyebrows still black above star- tling blue eyes, like bits of water-blue sapphires. He had a neatly trimmed mustache and beard that were also black, with the first streaks of white and gray running through them.

Cris had no accent whatsoever, but Bobby Lee's voice was thick as hominy, and twice as Southern.

Nathaniel tried to stand next to me, and Cris moved to keep him away. "He's with me," I said.

"We were ordered to keep you safe. I don't know him."

"Look, both of you, we don't have time for major intro- ductions here. He's one of my wereleopards, so are the two blonds. Micah's the one with the ponytail, the two men with him his leopards."

"Who's the redhead?" Bobby Lee asked.

"Gil, he's a werefox, and he's under my protection, too."

"They're like walking cannon fodder," Cris said.

I frowned up at him. "Most of this cannon fodder are friends, or more, to me. If the shit hits the fan and you save me at the expense of their lives, you will follow them."

"Our orders are to keep you safe, ma'am, no one else," Bobby Lee said.

I shook my head and drew Nathaniel into the crook of my arm. "What would Rafael do if you protected him but got his people slaughtered?"

They glanced at each other. Bobby Lee finally spoke. "It would depend on the situation."

"Yeah, maybe, but I'm armed, and can take care of myself most of the time. I need backup, not interference."

"We weren't told to be backup," Bobby Lee said.

"I know, but tonight there may be a certain amount of grandstanding. Jean-Claude won't let me get hurt, but he might play with some of the others, even me. Don't over-react, okay."

"You're making it so we can't do our job," Cris said.

I shrugged, hugging Nathaniel to me. "I appreciate you being here. I appreciate the help. I might be dead right now if Igor and Claudia hadn't been with me. But there are people who I would risk my life to keep safe, and some of them are with me tonight. All I'm saying is keep cool, don't overreact, don't jump the gun."

Again they looked at each other. I sighed. Bobby Lee was wearing a sleeveless jean jacket over his T-shirt. Cris wore a short-sleeved dress shirt and oversized black tank top un-tucked, sloppy over his khaki pants. It was too hot to wear a coat. But I was wearing a black silk shirt, open over a black tank top myself. I had my shirt tucked in, and the Firestar 9mm in a front draw across the front of all that black. Most people wouldn't see it, black on black. But the long-sleeved shirt was hiding guns and knives. I was betting that Bobby Lee had at least one gun under his jacket, probably at the small of his back, because there was no bulge, no matter how slight, under either arm. It was hard to see the bulge under Cris's left arm. He'd chosen a shirt with a lot of print on it, bright patterns to distract the eye, but a hot wind blew his shirt back, and I caught a glimpse of his shoul-der holster. I couldn't be sure what was under the untucked tank top, but I was betting at least one more gun, in front for a cross-draw, just like mine.

"You cannot shoot anyone tonight unless I say so, how's that for clear?"

"We have our orders," Bobby Lee said, "and they aren't from you."

"Then you can go back to Rafael and tell him I refused your help."

Cris's eyes widened a touch. Bobby Lee's expression never changed. Those pretty blue eyes were as empty as glass, no one home. "Why are you so afraid of taking us inside?" he asked.

I sighed again and tried to put it into words they'd understand and I was willing to share. I couldn't come up with anything, so I tried the truth. "I am about to introduce my Nimir-Raj to the Master of the City for the first time."

"You fucking both of them?" Bobby Lee asked, and the phrase seemed wrong with that Scarlett O'Hara accent.

I started to protest, or bitch, but let it go. "Yeah, I am, and I'm a little worried about how the introduction's going to go."

"You think the Master will try and kill your Nimir-Raj?" Cris asked.

"No, but he may want to play with him, and a vampire's idea of fun and games can get a little odd."

Bobby Lee laughed. "Odd, she says, odd." He laughed again, and it sounded warm and deep and rumbly. The laughter filled his eyes, made them more real. "What she is trying to say, Cris, is that we are about to be entertained just like when the rats meet the hyenas. A show of force with no danger, but maybe a little discomfort."

"Yeah, what he just said."

Cris nodded. "So tonight isn't real."

"It's real," I said, "but it's just not dangerous in any way you can protect me from."

"We're supposed to protect you, period," Cris said.

Bobby Lee clamped him on the shoulder. "We can't protect her from her own love life, Cris. We're supposed to keep her body intact, not her heart."

"Oh," Cris said, and he looked suddenly much younger—early twenties, at best.

Bobby Lee turned to me. "We'll hang back tonight, unless you're in real physical danger."

"I'm glad we understand each other."

His eyes went empty again, the smile still curving his lips.

"Oh, we don't understand each other at all, ma'am, I can almost guarantee that, but we'll do what we're told, until we decide not to."

I didn't exactly like the sound of that, but, looking into his empty blue eyes, I knew it was the best I was going to get.

48

THE STEPS LEADING down into the bowels of the Circus are wide enough for three small people to walk abreast, but the steps themselves are oddly spaced, as if whatever the steps were originally built for wasn't two-legged, or at least wasn't human sized.

We were following Ernie down the steps. The first time I'd met him he'd had one of those long hair cuts with the sides shaved. The sides had grown out, and he'd cut the rest, so he had a fairly standard short haircut, with a little more on top, so he could gel it into soft spikes, sort of executive punk. The short hair also left his neck bare so you could see two fang marks on the right side.

He wasn't feeding Jean-Claude. I don't think the Master of the City fed off humans anymore, not when he could have lycanthrope. But there were other vampires under the Circus, and they had to eat, too.

Micah walked beside me. Merle, Bobby Lee, and Cris had a disagreement about exactly where they were going to walk. They finally settled on Cris walking with Ernie ahead of us and Merle and Bobby Lee walking just behind us. Everyone else sort of trailed behind, including Caleb. None of the bodyguards seemed to give a shit if the others lived or died. I was pretty sure that the bodyguard thing was going to get on my nerves soon, like tonight.

The huge metal door at the end of the stairs was open, waiting. It was usually kept locked for security purposes. My stomach clenched so tight that it hurt. I just didn't know how to handle this. Did I kiss Jean-Claude hello? Did I touch Micah in front of him? Oh, hell.

"Did you say something?" Micah asked.

"Not on purpose," I said.

He looked a question at me, and that did it. I would behave like I always did. I would do exactly what I'd do if the other one wasn't there. To do anything else was going to have us all walking on pins and needles. Besides, I'd been careful with Richard and Jean-Claude, and look where that ended up. I didn't want the same mistakes again. Maybe we could make new ones.

49

THERE WERE SILVER drapes just inside the door. That was new. Ernie parted the drapes and led us into Jean-Claude's living room. Once upon a time it had been black and white drapes, and a smaller area, but now it was white, silver, and gold. White drapes, silk and sheer, hung like a hallway that led into something that looked like a huge fairytale tent. The stone walls and ceiling that I knew were there, were hidden by yards and yards of gold and silver cloth. It was like standing in the middle of a jewel box. The coffee table had been painted gold and white and made to look antique, or maybe it was the real deal. A crystal bowl sat in the center of the table with a spill of white carnations and baby's breath.

A huge white couch sat against the far drapes, so covered in silver and gold pillows that some of the pillows had fallen to the white carpeted floor. Two overstuffed chairs were in opposite corners, one gold, one silver, with white pillows on each.

The fireplace looked real, but I knew it wasn't because it had been added later, but it was everything a fireplace should have been, except it was painted white. There was even a new marble mantel that was white with veins of silver and gold, ordered to match.

The only thing that hadn't changed was the portrait above the fireplace. The first thing you saw was Julianna, sitting, dressed in silver and white, half-laughing, brown hair done in careful ringlets. Asher stood behind her in gold and white, his face still perfect, his gold hair in ringlets longer than hers, his mustache and Vandyke beard a blond so dark it was almost brown. Jean-Claude sat behind Julianna, the only one of the three not smiling, solemn, dressed in black and silver.

He'd designed the room around the painting—silver and gold and white.

"Wow." Caleb said it for us all.

I'd seen Jean-Claude's sense of style before, but every once in a while he'd amaze even me. Then I felt him coming towards us. I felt him coming and that wasn't a good thing. I'd expected anger, jealousy, but what was moving towards me was simply lust, need. He could shield better than this. Was this my punishment, to be drowned in his lust? If so, he'd misjudged me, because it was just going to piss me off.

He pushed through white and silver drapes, and for a moment I couldn't see where his clothes began and the cloth ended. He was wearing a silver frock coat with white edging, white buttons. His shirt was a spill of white froth, the pants, what I could see of them, were white, but the white leather boots covered almost all of his long legs. The leather looked soft, pettable, held in place with small silver buckles going from just above his ankles to his very upper thigh.

I stared because I couldn't do anything else. Even if he hadn't been projecting sex inside my head, he'd have made me think of it. His hair fell in loose curls nearly to his waist, a black glory on all that silver and white.

Bobby Lee said, "Well, aren't you just pretty as a picture."

Jean-Claude didn't even look at him. He looked at me, and I was walking towards him across the so-soft carpet without a thought, except that I had to touch him.

He closed his eyes, held out his hand. "No, *ma petite,* do not come closer."

I hesitated for a second, then started walking again. I could already smell his cologne, sweet, spicy. I wanted to run my hands through his hair, wrap the scent of him on my hands.

He stumbled back, half-tripping in the drapes. There was something like panic on his face. "*Ma petite,* I thought I could shield you from the *ardeur,* but I cannot."

That did stop me. I had to frown at him. I couldn't seem to think. That kept me where I was, almost close enough to touch him, but not quite. "What's happening, Jean-Claude?"

"I have fed this night, but I have not fed the *ardeur*."

"That's what I'm feeling," I said, "the *ardeur*."

"*Oui*, I am shielding as hard as I can, yet you are picking up on it. That has never happened before."

"Is it because I've got my own *ardeur*?"

"That is all that has changed, so yes, I believe so."

"You're not going to be in any shape to help with Damian, are you?"

He sighed and looked down. "I need to feed all my hungers, *ma petite*. I have not had this much difficulty with the *ardeur* in centuries. Something about sharing it with you has affected me. I did not know until I felt you enter the building that it had changed."

"You mean your control is better farther away from me?"

He nodded.

"What the hell is this 'ardoo-whatever'?" Bobby Lee asked.

I glanced back at him. "When we want to share, I'll let you know."

Bobby Lee raised his eyebrows at that, then made a small pushing motion. "You're the boss, ma'am . . . for now."

I let that slide and turned back to Jean-Claude. "What do we do?"

Nathaniel offered a suggestion. "Feed him."

I looked back at him, and the look must have been enough, because he put his hands out empty, and went to stand by the fireplace. Everyone else had taken a seat, except for Gil, who was huddled beside one of the chairs on the floor, clutching a pillow.

I turned to Jean-Claude, and it was Micah's voice that turned me back again. "I've seen Anita in the—" he changed whatever he was going to say—"grip of the *ardeur*, and this doesn't look like it. She's way too calm."

Jean-Claude looked past me at him, seeing him, I think, for the first time, at least in person. His gaze traveled up and down his body, an assessing look, like he was thinking of buying or was trying to be deliberately insulting.

Micah either didn't catch the insult or was proof against it, because he started walking towards us. He moved in a well of his own power, as if even here, surrounded by Jean-Claude's things, he was supremely confident, totally at ease. He moved like a dancer, compact, graceful, strong. The sight of him tightened things low in my body. Jean-Claude made a small sound. I started to turn towards him, but it was too late, his shields shattered and the *ardeur* roared over me. My skin ran with heat, my breath stopped, my vision was gone in streamers of color. Jean-Claude's need marched over me, through me, inside me. It screamed in my head, danced down my nerves, flowed through my veins. In that instant if he had asked anything, anything at all, I would have said *yes*.

My vision cleared and I found Jean-Claude on the floor, half-caught in a spill of draperies that he'd pulled from their hangers, so that he sat in a nest of white and silver. His face was almost slack with need, his eyes already a spill of blind blue fire.

I was on my knees, too, and didn't remember falling. Micah was there, taking my arm, I think to help me stand, but the moment he touched me the *ardeur* leaped, and he fell to the floor beside me, like someone had struck him with a hammer; his legs just stopped holding him. He whispered, "Oh, my God."

The bodyguards moved in then, and I had to scream, "No!" There must have been something in my voice, because all three of them froze in mid-motion. "No one touches us, no one." My voice was high, frantic. There was a very real chance that the *ardeur* could spread through the whole room, one touch at a time. We had enough problems without that.

Micah had released my arm, his hands nerveless in his lap, but the tie had been made, and the act of touching, or not, didn't change it.

Jean-Claude crawled from the bed of glittering cloth, slowly, every move something graceful and dangerous. He'd never looked more predatory than he did at that moment.

"Jean-Claude," I whispered, "don't." But I couldn't move. I watched him like a tiny bird fascinated as the serpent glides closer, caught between terror and the sheer beauty of him.

Asher was suddenly there in the space between the cloth. Jean-Claude froze, but it wasn't that stillness that the old vampires could fall into, there was a thrumming energy to him, more like a big cat about to pounce than something cold and reptilian.

"Jean-Claude, you must control the *ardeur* better than this." He was hugging his arms as if he felt at least a brush of it himself. He'd noticed the new faces and used a practiced shake of his head to spill his golden hair across the scars, only revealing the perfect half.

Jean-Claude's voice came low and harsh. "I cannot."

I'd been afraid; now it was sheer terror. I looked up at Asher and saw him through a film of all the times we'd touched him, all that beauty, all the beauty that I still saw. I whispered, "Help us!"

Asher was shaking his head. "If I am dragged in as well, it will help no one."

"Asher, please!"

"Once he feeds, all will be well, simply let him feed."

I shook my head. "Not here, not like this."

Micah said, "If it will help, why not let him feed?"

I looked at him, and just turning to him made my mouth part, my breath catch. It was almost like the *ardeur* remembered him, like a succulent food that it wanted to taste again.

It took two tries to say, "You don't understand."

Zane said, "Anita doesn't let Jean-Claude feed off of her." He and Cherry were sitting on the far edge of the couch, watching with wide eyes, not coming near us.

"I thought she was his human servant," Micah said.

"She is." Jean-Claude whispered it.

Something in those two words made me look at him, made me stare into those glittering blue eyes. He couldn't trap me with his gaze anymore, because I was his human servant, but tonight there was a pull to those eyes. I wanted to cradle his face in my hands, wanted to taste those half-parted lips.

"Anita!" Asher's voice jerked me around, made me look at him.

"Help me."

"He can feed on me." Micah said it, voice soft. We all turned and stared at him.

He looked a little less sure. I think something he saw on our faces made him hesitate, but he said it again. "If a little blood will cure this, then I'm willing."

"He has fed on blood tonight already," Asher said. "It is not blood he needs but . . . *voir les anges*."

"English, Asher, even I didn't understand that one," I said.

He waved his hands as if erasing what he'd said. "He needs release, a . . ." He said several things in rapid French, and I couldn't follow it. Asher was in great distress if his English had abandoned him.

I was careful not to look at Micah when I tried to explain. "It's the *ardeur* that Jean-Claude needs fed."

"He needs sex, not blood," Nathaniel said. His voice was soft, but a glance showed him standing as far across the room as he could get. I didn't blame him a bit.

"The first time you fed on me it wasn't intercourse, just contact," he said.

I nodded, still trying not to look at any of the men. "I remember."

"Contact is okay," Micah said.

I had to look at him, and the surprise was great enough that for just a second I almost fought free of the ardeur, I could almost think. "What kind of contact?"

"Sexual contact." His face was very serious, eyes solemn, as if he, too, could think again. "I said I would do anything to be your Nimir-Raj, Anita. What do I have to do to convince you I mean it?"

"What are you offering, Micah?"

"Whatever you need." He looked past me to Jean-Claude. "Whatever you both need."

I felt Jean-Claude's attention sharpen, almost like a physical force, and the *ardeur* was back, thick enough to drown in. My breath froze in my throat, my pulse was too fast to swallow. Jean-Claude's voice came, I think in my head, because his lips never moved. "Be careful what you offer, *mon ami,* my control is poor tonight."

Micah answered, as if he'd heard Jean-Claude too. "You were a ménage à trois with the Ulfric. He's gone. I'm here, and I'm staying. I will be Anita's Nimir-Raj, whatever that means."

I managed to say, "Who said that we were a ménage à trois?"

"Everyone," he said.

I wondered who everyone was, because I knew it *wasn't* everyone.

Jean-Claude was moving forward again, painfully slow, every movement so full of energy, so full of potential violence and grace, that it almost hurt to watch. It made my pulse race, my breath hard to take—made my body run moist. Oh, shit, oh, shit, oh, shit.

"Jean-Claude, no," but my voice was a whisper.

His mouth hovered over mine, then his face turned for a second to Micah. I watched the two of them gaze at each other from inches away and felt the power pulsing in the air between. Jean-Claude moved so slowly to close the distance between them that it was like watching slow motion. Micah sat there, waiting. He didn't move in to him, but he didn't move away either. I thought at first they'd kissed, then some trick of the light let me see a thin line of space between their mouths. Not touching, not yet. I watched their lips so tremblingly close, and part of me wanted them to touch, but Jean-Claude held his place, held his place until Micah closed his eyes, as if he couldn't stand to meet those glowing orbs, like looking away from the sun, too brilliant to bear.

And still Jean-Claude did not close that small distance. It was the distance of a breath, the flick of a tongue and still he held himself almost touching, almost there, but not quite. The tension grew, grew, grew, until I wanted to scream. I didn't realize that I'd moved in towards them, until they both turned at once and looked at me from inches away. My eyes flicked from one to the other. Eyes like blue fire; eyes like yellow-green clouds. Micah's eyes grew more green as I watched, until they were pale, pale green, like spring leaves. He focused on me. I couldn't explain it, but I knew that this was the look he hunted with, that sharp focus, the pupil nearly lost in the color of his eyes.

I realized that I'd pushed the *ardeur* back. I was attracted to both, but I could think again, feel something besides the burn. You practice one kind of metaphysical control, and I guess it gives you an edge on all of them. The relief made me feel weak, as if I could have curled on the floor and slept. We weren't going to fall on each other like ravening lust-monsters. Yippee.

I eased away, started to crawl backwards. Jean-Claude's gaze followed me, but he made no move to touch me. There was something about the way he stayed on all fours that let me know the *ardeur* was still riding him. But if I could keep from touching him, we'd be alright. He watched me, like a starving man, who was watching his first meal in days crawl away. But he played fair, he stayed where he was, he let me crawl away. He knew the rules. Micah didn't.

He reached for me, and I threw myself back to the floor in a blur of speed that I'd never had before, but Micah wasn't human either. He followed me in a movement that was too fast for my eyes to follow, so that he was above me before my mind could see that he'd moved. It was magical.

He was frozen just above me, his body balanced on hands and feet, almost like he was doing a push-up. I reached out, around him, trying not to touch him. I had time to say, "No, don't," then two things happened at once. Micah dropped his body on top of mine, and Jean-Claude took my outreached hand. Maybe he thought I was reaching for him, I don't know. But the moment we touched the heat ran over us, through us, and there was nothing but the need.

50

WE KISSED, AND it was like melting from the mouth down. My hands slid over the silk of Micah's shirt, and it wasn't enough. I ripped at it, tore it from his body until my hands spilled over the solid smoothness of his chest, his skin like warm satin under my fingers. Micah was suddenly grinding me into the floor, so heavy. I opened my eyes and found Jean-Claude above us, over Micah, pressing us both into the floor. I had a moment of meeting his eyes, a moment to see the rage in that blind blue fire, then his arms were around Micah, and he was jerking the smaller man backwards.

I sat up, watching them roll across the floor, fighting. Anger, frustration, and just sheer tiredness welled up inside me until there was no room for the *ardeur*. I was tired of fighting, so tired of it.

I smelled blood like a hot spike through the center of my body; the smell was almost sexual. That was enough. I drew the Browning and sighted around the room. For a split second, I had the two of them at the end of the barrel. For a split second it occurred to me. Then I moved the gun around the room, registering for the first time that there was no one left in the room but us. Good to know we didn't have an audience. I pointed the gun at the overstuffed white couch and fired. One of the small gold and silver pillows jumped upward with the impact. The noise was thunderous in the stone room, as if the heavy drapes caught the sound, held it around us.

They froze. Micah's hands were claws, shredding across Jean-Claude's back, because that was all he could reach. Jean-Claude's face was buried in Micah's neck, his body wrapped around him, so that everything vital was hidden while he tried to tear Micah's throat out.

I sighted on them. "Stop it, stop it, both of you, or the next one goes in one of you. I swear, by God, that I will shoot you."

Jean-Claude raised up, blood in a crimson wash across his mouth, chin, down his neck. There was so much blood, it made me afraid to look at Micah's neck. Micah's claws stayed in Jean-Claude's back. I could see the tension as if every muscle were poised to drive the claws farther in.

"The Nimir-Raj holds me in place, *ma petite*. I cannot move."

"Micah, let him up."

Micah didn't move, and I guess I couldn't blame him, but . . . I aimed the gun at his head because that was the only clear shot I had. I had a small spurt of panic that I might have to pull the trigger, then a calmness welled over me, and I stood in that well of silence, that buzzing white noise that I went to when I killed. There was no feeling here, there was almost nothing here.

"I . . . will . . . kill you, Micah." My voice sounded as empty as I felt.

Micah turned his head slowly to look at me. Blood flowed from the left side of his neck down his shoulder, his chest. He was drenched in his own blood. I could see more of it welling up, sliding down, but not constant; the blood pumped out with his pulse. Shit.

"Let him up, Micah, he's pierced your carotid." I lowered the gun and started to close the distance between them.

Micah looked up at the vampire, still poised with his claws in Jean-Claude's flesh. "If I die, I want him to go with me."

"It should be simple enough for a Nimir-Raj of your power to heal such a small wound," Jean-Claude said, still pressed around the other man's body, intimate.

Micah withdrew the claws from Jean-Claude's back. Jean-Claude moved enough to prop himself up on his hands. I saw Micah tense a second before his arm swung in that unbelievable speed, so fast, so fast. Jean-Claude's throat hadn't even started to bleed when Micah's hand was back at his side. Then blood spilled in a fountain from Jean-Claude's throat.

"Heal *that*," Micah said.

I was left standing there, watching them both bleed to death. Mother fucking son of a bitch.

51

Jean-Claude half fell, half moved off of Micah. Blood sprayed in a red rain as he knelt on all fours, coughing, as if he were trying to clear his throat. It made the blood pump faster.

I screamed, at first wordless, then I thought of something better. I screamed, "Asher!"

Micah was already rolling in black fur, bones sliding in and out, muscles rolling in glimpses of pinkish flesh. He'd shapeshift and heal himself, but Jean-Claude couldn't shapeshift.

I grabbed Jean-Claude's arm, and the moment I touched him the marks flared between us. I was choking on my own blood, drowning in it. Strong hands were digging into my arms, fingers like cold stone. I blinked and found Jean-Claude's face glowing like carved alabaster with white light inside it. His skin glowed behind the coating of blood on his lower face, like rubies spread across diamonds. His eyes were pools of molten sapphire flame, if fire could be cold, achingly cold. A wind sprang from his body, from our bodies, and it was the cold of the grave that danced around us, fluttered our hair around our faces. We reached that cold power out, out, to find Richard, and as before the answer came against our skin. Jason was kneeling beside us. I didn't have time to marvel that he was healed. He touched us and the mark that was Richard flared through his body, a warmth to dance with our coldness. And I knew Micah was kneeling behind me, furred and clawed. I felt him at my back the way I felt Jason, as if he were tied to us.

Micah fell back, screaming, "Nooo!" The tie was cut and for a second I swayed, as if part of my support was gone, then Nathaniel was there, and the world was solid again.

We knelt, bound by flesh, magic, and blood. I watched the flesh in Jean-Claude's throat reknit, reform, remake, re-shape itself until the flesh was perfect and white, surrounded by a coating of wet blood. He'd healed so fast that the blood hadn't had time to dry.

I smelled roses, not the faint perfume of potpourri, but thick, melt-on-your-tongue, old-fashioned garden roses, as if I were drowning in the cloying sweetness of them. It was like being dipped in honey that you knew had poison in it.

Honey, honey brown eyes. I remembered the pale honey brown of Belle Morte's eyes. "Do you smell the roses?" I asked.

Jean-Claude turned drowning blue eyes to me. "Roses? I smell nothing but the scent of your perfume, and skin." He scented the air, "And blood."

Nathaniel and Jason were lost in the wonder of the power rush, but no one smelled roses but me. Once upon a time I'd smelled perfume when a certain Master Vampire had been using her magic. My friend and fellow animator, Larry Kirkland, had smelled the perfume, too, but no one else around us had been able to scent it.

I looked into Jean-Claude's eyes, not with my sight, but with my magic, and found something, something that wasn't him. It was subtle. What she'd done with me earlier had been like a sledgehammer between the eyes; this was a stiletto in the dark.

I found the thread of her power coiled in him, and the moment my magic, my necromancy, hit it, the power un-coiled, opened, and it was like a window thrown wide. I saw her sitting in her room by fire and candlelight, as if electricity hadn't been invented. She was dressed in a white lace dress-ing gown, all that black hair falling around her, and a bowl of pink roses next to her pale hand. She turned those huge pale brown eyes to me, and I saw the surprise on her face, the shock. She saw me kneeling with the men, as I saw her before her dressing table with her roses.

I cut her off, cast her out of Jean-Claude, as I'd cast her out of me earlier. It was easier, because she hadn't tried to possess him, only to tamper with him, to be that dark voice in his ear that pushed him a little over the edge.

Jean-Claude slumped suddenly, as if dizzy. He raised eyes to me that were as normal as they ever got, his usual midnight blue. There was fear on his face, no hiding it. "I thought I saw Belle, sitting before her mirror."

I nodded. "You did."

He looked at me, and I think that only all our hands on him kept him from falling to the floor. "She weakened my control of the *ardeur*."

"And your control of your temper," I said.

"What has happened?" Asher asked.

I looked up to find that everyone was back in the room. "Any of this blood yours, ma'am?" Bobby Lee asked.

I shook my head. "Not a scratch on me."

"Then I guess we won't get blacklisted from the bodyguard union for leaving you alone with a shapeshifter and a vampire, so they could fight over you." He was shaking his head. "The next time you ask us to leave you alone because it's your love life, we aren't going to listen to you."

I shook my head, again. "We'll talk about it later."

"No, ma'am," he said, "we won't."

I let the argument go. There was always time to fight later. Besides, he was too close to right. If I'd gotten between them at the wrong moment, who knew what accident might have happened?

Jean-Claude spoke softly, voice urgent, to Asher. They were speaking French and I still didn't know enough to catch more than a word here and there. I heard Belle, clearly, several times.

In English Asher said, "Do you remember Marcel?"

"*Oui*. He went mad one night and slew his entire household."

"Including his human servant," Asher said, "which is what killed him."

The two vampires stared at each other. "No one ever understood what had caused it," Jean-Claude said.

"So fortuitous," Asher said, "only two nights before he would have fought Belle for her Council seat."

Jean-Claude took Asher's offered hand and let him help

him to his feet. Asher had to steady Jean-Claude with a hand on his elbow. "So fortuitous that many tried to prove she had poisoned him, or some such," Asher said.

Jean-Claude nodded, passing a hand over his face, as if he were still dizzy. I felt nothing, as if my necromancy protected me from whatever Belle had done to him. "The Council themselves tried to prove her at fault and failed," Jean-Claude said.

"Did they hire a witch to look into the magic angle?" I asked. I stood on my own, just fine. Nathaniel and Jason got to their feet, again with no ill-effects, except for Jason's stupid grin, which he often wore after a power rush.

The vampires looked at me. *"Non,"* Asher said, "no one thought of it."

"Why the hell not?"

"Because, *ma petite,* she should not be able to do what she did to a Master of the City, even one of her own bloodline. That she could do this to a Master of the City that was *not* her bloodline would be unthinkable."

"Impossible," Asher added.

"I think it's like real possible," I said. "I caught her in the act."

"Who's Belle?" Micah asked in his growling leopard voice.

I turned to him, slowly, and something must have shown on my face, because Merle moved in front of him, and suddenly the two wererats were alert, starting to move up beside me. I don't know what I was about to say, probably something really angry, because Micah beat me to it.

"He pierced my jugular vein, Anita. I'm allowed to defend myself when someone tries to eat my throat out."

"Remember I'm his human servant. He dies, so might I."

He stalked around Merle, gliding on bent legs and kitty-cat feet. "So I'm just supposed to let him kill me?"

"No," I said, "no, but your wound wasn't life-threatening. You proved that already. There's not a scratch on you now."

"I healed it, yes, but not every shapeshifter could have healed it. A vampire wound is a lot like silver, it can kill, and most of us heal from those wounds like we were human."

He was standing very close to me, those green-gold eyes sparkling with anger. "He meant to kill me, Anita, don't think he didn't."

"He is right, *ma petite,* if he had not held me off more, I would have torn his throat out."

I turned back to Jean-Claude. "What are you saying?"

"I saw him on top of you, and I was drowning in jealousy. I meant him harm, *ma petite.* He defended himself."

"He didn't have to do that last blow. The fight had stopped."

Jean-Claude looked past me at Micah, and there was something on his face—respect, I think. "If he had done to me what I did to him, then I would have had no choice but to make my point," he seemed to consider several words and settled for, "strongly."

"Strongly? He damn near slit your throat."

"After I had tried to do the same to him."

I was shaking my head. "No, no, I don't . . ."

"What, *ma petite,* are you truly saying that if someone had torn your throat out, tried for your life that you wouldn't have shot them?"

I opened my mouth to argue, closed it, tried again, and stopped. I looked at him, then back at Micah, then back to Jean-Claude. "Well, damn."

"The Nimir-Raj has made his point, *ma petite.* He is willing to be accommodating up to a point—beyond that point there is no compromise."

Micah nodded, and the movement looked awkward in his furred body. "Yes."

"You have the same rule, *ma petite,* as do I. The three of us merely have different places where the line is drawn. But the line is there for all of us."

"How can you both be so reasonable about this? You both nearly just killed each other?"

They looked at each other, around me, again, and there was something in that look. It was something masculine and arcane, as if the fact that I was a girl meant I wouldn't get it, and they couldn't explain it to me. Which did explain it to me.

"Oh, great, great, you guys nearly kill each other, and that makes you buddies."

Jean-Claude gave that wonderful Gallic shrug, his face still covered in Micah's blood. "Let us say we have an understanding."

Micah agreed.

"Jesus, only men could get a friendship out of something like this."

"You are friends with Monsieur Edward. Did you not both begin by trying to kill each other?" Jean-Claude asked.

"That's different," I said.

"How?"

I tried to argue, but stopped because I would have looked silly. "Fine, fine, so what, the two of you kiss and make up?"

They looked at each other, and again there was weight to the gaze, but it was a different weight. "Shit," I said.

"I think we begin by apologizing," Jean-Claude said. "I am truly sorry for my lack of control."

"Me, too," Micah said, then added, "and I'm sorry that I had to try and kill you." It was interesting phrasing, not I'm sorry I nearly killed you, but sorry I had to try and kill you. I was seeing Micah's ruthless streak. It wasn't really any bigger than my own, but it bothered me anyway. Wasn't sure why, but it did.

I didn't know what to do, so I decided to move on, we had other business. "Are you well enough to help get Damian out of his coffin?"

"I have used up all my reserves, *ma petite.* I will need to feed again." He raised a hand. "But not the *ardeur,* merely blood."

Merely, he says.

"I offered to let you feed on me earlier. The offer still stands," Micah said.

"No, Micah," Merle said.

Micah touched the taller man's arm. "It's alright."

"Are you not afraid I will try and tear your throat out again? I would listen to your bodyguard."

"You said we had an understanding."

"That is true."

They were watching each other, and I could almost feel the testosterone rise.

Micah smiled, or tried to. In the half-leopard form it was a snarl of white fangs in black fur. "Besides, the next time you bite me like that, it better be foreplay, or I will kill you."

"If it pleases you, my pleasure," Jean-Claude said. He laughed then, that touchable sound that caressed my skin, made me shiver. Micah reacted to it, eyes wide. He'd never heard Jean-Claude's laugh before. If he thought the *laugh* was something special, well, the best truly was yet to come.

"I thank you for your most generous offer," Jean-Claude said, "but I prefer my food without fur."

"No problem," Micah said. Micah released Merle's arm, and did that magically quick change. His tanned skin seemed to absorb the fur like rocks sinking into water. He stood naked and perfect, no mark of the fight on that smooth skin. Neither his clothing nor the tie in his hair had survived the change. But strangely the hair fell straight around his face, as if it were affected by the fact that he'd pulled it back tight while it was still wet. The hair was still thick, but it framed his face better, was less overwhelming, so that you could still see the delicate bone structure, those wondrous eyes.

I heard someone catch their breath, and it wasn't me. I don't think it was Jean-Claude, but I wasn't sure. Didn't matter, didn't want to know.

"You are not even dizzy, are you?" Jean-Claude asked.

Micah shook his head.

Jean-Claude raised his eyebrows, lowered his eyes, fought to control his face, until he could give a perfect blank expression, but it took him a few seconds. "I will clean this," he made a vague motion at his gore-soaked clothes, "before taking such a bounty, if that is alright?"

Micah gave a small nod.

"You are not taking a bath," I said.

"I will be quick, *ma petite.*"

"You have never taken a quick bath in your entire life."

Asher laughed, then tried to smother it, but was only partially successful. He spread his hands. "*Mon cheri,* she is right."

"Would I touch that for the first time covered in this?"

Asher's face sobered instantly, like someone had thrown a switch. He turned that serious, blank face to stare at Micah, who stared back. If he was uncomfortable under the scrutiny, it didn't show.

Asher sighed. "I suppose not."

"And what are we supposed to do for the hour that it takes you to soak in the tub?" I asked.

"I will be quick, *ma petite,* my word on it."

I crossed my arms over my stomach. "I'll believe it when I see it."

"*Ma petite,* I have given my word."

"On important stuff, your word is great, but when it comes to primping, you have no sense of time."

"I thought that was the man's line," Bobby Lee said.

I glanced at him then back to the vampire. "Couldn't prove it by me."

Bobby Lee laughed, but no one else did.

52

I SAT ON the white couch with its brand-new bullet hole. Micah sat down beside me, and since he was naked, that was . . . interesting. Uncomfortable, and sort of titillating all at the same time. He kept insisting on trying to talk to me, and I found it hard to keep eye contact, and that was embarrassing.

Bobby Lee and Cris stayed near me, hovering behind and to one side, because I made them move from right behind me. I just don't like armed people at my back, not unless I know them really well. The wererats were there to protect me. I believed they'd do the job, because Rafael told them to, but I still didn't want them standing armed at my back. Merle lounged near the fireplace, keeping an eye on Micah and the other bodyguards. Gil was actually hiding in the corner, or nearly—not a stable guy—the others milled around the room. Except for Asher.

He sat in the chair opposite the couch and watched us. He had shaken that glorious hair over his face so that only the perfect side was visible, and only one pale blue eye looked at us. His face showed nothing, but I could still feel the weight of his gaze, like a hand pushing. His face may have shown nothing, but he was giving us way too much attention.

I might have asked why, but Jean-Claude walked back through the gap in the drapes. I had to check my watch. Only twenty minutes had passed. I'd dated him off and on for nearly three years; a twenty-minute cleanup was nothing short of miraculous. Of course, his black hair was still wet and heavy; he hadn't taken time to blow-dry it. He was wearing one of my favorite robes, the black one with the black furred edging. The fur outlined a wonderful expanse of pale perfect chest. The robe was open enough that the cross-shaped burn scar showed, and as he glided into the room you caught glimpses of his upper stomach through the fur. The robe was very loosely tied, not at all the way he usually wore it.

He had that smile on his face that said he knew he looked wonderful, and he knew just what effect he had on me, then his gaze slid to Micah. I was close enough to see Micah's pulse speed up, jumping under the skin of his neck. He tried to meet Jean-Claude's eyes, but finally had to look down, and he blushed.

His reaction made *my* pulse speed up. I looked back at Jean-Claude gliding towards us, catching a glimpse of his pale feet under the black robe, against the white carpet. The look on his face was all for Micah. It made me go up on one knee, my butt against the arm of the couch. I felt oddly possessive, almost jealous, as if I should be defending Micah's honor. I'd never felt like this with Richard and Jean-Claude, but then, Jean-Claude had never looked at Richard in quite that way. Because Richard would have hurt him.

Micah had nearly killed Jean-Claude over an insult that Richard would not have fought back over, yet here he sat blushing, uncomfortable, but not angry.

Jean-Claude was standing in front of us, so close that the furred hem of the robe brushed Micah's bare leg. "Have you changed your mind, *mon minet?*"

Micah shook his head, then raised his face up to look at the vampire. There was both vulnerability and warning in that look. "I haven't changed my mind."

"Bon." Jean-Claude went to his knees in front of him. "You are powerful in your own right, and you are not my animal to call. I may not be able to cloud your mind and make this tasting a pleasure. You may be able to keep me out of your mind."

Micah nodded, thick hair falling around his face. "I understand."

"Do you have a preference on where the blood is taken from?"

"The neck hurts less," Micah said.

Jean-Claude raised an eyebrow. "You've done this before?"

Micah gave a smile that managed not to be happy. "I've done a lot of things before."

Jean-Claude raised both eyebrows at that and looked at me. I shrugged.

"Very well, *mon minet*." He stood in one graceful movement, swinging the robe around him like a dress, giving the slightest glimpse of bare legs as he stalked behind the couch. He stopped just behind Micah, putting a hand on either of his shoulders. He didn't caress, or squeeze, just rested his hands on that smooth, warm flesh for a moment.

"Get on with it," Merle said.

Micah turned his head to look at the other wereleopard. "Merle." One word, but it made the big man lean back harder on the fireplace, arms crossed over his chest, face sullen, a very unhappy bodyguard. But he did what he was told.

Jean-Claude slid one arm around the front of Micah's shoulders, across his very upper chest. He used his free hand to smooth Micah's hair back, exposing the side of his face and the long clean line of his throat. Micah moved his head a little to the side, giving Jean-Claude a better angle. The small movement was like a woman coming to her tiptoes for a kiss, a helpful movement.

"Maybe we could have a little privacy," I said, and it made both men look at me.

"As you like, *ma petite*." Everyone left except Merle, Bobby Lee, and Asher. They were the minimum that might be needed to keep us from killing each other. After what had just happened, I really couldn't work up a good argument for leaving us completely alone. When everyone had settled down, Jean-Claude turned back to Micah.

Jean-Claude's fingers stroked Micah's hair so that it fell behind his ear, exposing the entire side of his face, the shape of his ear. He pressed the back of Micah's head gently against his chest, drawing the exposed neck in an even longer line. Micah was utterly passive, eyes closed, face peaceful; only the pulse in his neck beating like a trapped thing gave lie to all that calmness.

Jean-Claude bent over him, mouth open, lips going back, but even this close I got only the barest glimpse of teeth. He

bit down, sharp, sudden. Micah gasped, breath catching in
his throat. Jean-Claude's grip tightened at Micah's head, his
shoulders, pressing him in against his body. I could see the
muscles in Jean-Claude's jaws working, his throat swallowing convulsively. One of them was making small noises low
in his throat, and I wasn't sure who it was.

Jean-Claude reared back, bringing Micah with him, drawing him half over the couch. Micah cried out, his hands going
to Jean-Claude's arm, holding on, as the vampire rocked his
body backwards. Jean-Claude moved his hand from Micah's
face to his waist, as if he knew the other man wouldn't move
away now. He held Micah, arms across his chest and waist,
Micah's hands on Jean-Claude's arm. He stretched Micah's
body backwards as he'd lengthened the man's neck earlier,
so that Micah's body showed in a long, clean line, back
curved against Jean-Claude's body, so that both of them were
bowed backwards.

I was left kneeling on the couch, staring up the line of
Micah's nude body, seeing without doubt that what was happening was making his body happy. His face was slack with
need, pleasure. His hands convulsed over Jean-Claude's arm,
and he half-screamed, half-shouted, "God!"

Jean-Claude's body began to straighten up, slowly. He
eased Micah back over the couch. He raised his mouth from
Micah's neck; his eyes were drowning blue, sightless, inhuman. His lips were full, red, but not with spilled blood, red
like someone who's been kissing too much. He released Micah slowly, letting his body slide against the back of the
couch, until the wereleopard half-collapsed on his side. His
head spilled into my lap, and I jumped. Micah raised his
head, slowly, heavy. He propped himself up on one arm and
turned unfocused eyes to me. His pupils were enormous,
drowning black in the circle of his green-yellow eyes. I
watched his pupils spiral downward to small dots so that the
color almost overwhelmed them, like a vampire's eyes. I
could feel him staring at me, the weight of his gaze like
something pushing against me. He leaned in towards me,
slowly, lips half-parted.

I stayed where I was, frozen, unsure what to do. It wasn't

that he was any less lovely than he had been. It was just . . . oh, hell, I didn't know what to do. I didn't even know what I wanted to do.

"Didn't you need to get Damian out of his coffin?" Asher's voice came dry, making me draw back from Micah.

Jean-Claude snarled at him, looking more inhuman than the entire time he was feeding.

Asher stood in one smooth motion, like a puppet pulled up by strings. "Fine, but if you are going to have sex, then I don't have to watch."

I stood, Micah's hands sliding down my body as I moved away from the couch. I faced Asher. "Look, I am so far over my comfort zone right now that I can't think, but I'll tell you one thing. I am not going to salve your male ego while the little voice in my brain is still screaming, run away, run away. So, put the attitude on ice, Asher, I can't deal with it right now."

He was suddenly vibrating with anger, his eyes like icy blue pools. "So sorry that my discomfort annoys you."

"Fuck you, Asher."

He was suddenly moving forward in a blur of speed. I backed up so fast that I fell against the couch. Micah caught me, or I'd have fallen to the floor. I had time to draw a gun, or a knife, but I didn't even try. Asher wasn't trying to hurt my body, just my feelings. He bent at the waist, looming over me and Micah, though I think that part was accidental. He put a hand on either side of us and leaned into my face, so close that I had to pull back to focus on those chilling blue eyes. "Don't offer things you're not willing to do, *ma cherie,* because that is annoying."

He stood up abruptly and stalked from the room.

Micah's voice was soft. "What was all that about?" His hands were still on my arms, half-holding me, protective.

I shook my head. "Ask Jean-Claude." I pushed to my feet. "I'm going to go get Damian."

"I will accompany you, *ma petite.*"

"Fine." I started walking. I could feel them following me, feel them both behind me. I almost turned around to see if they were holding hands, but if they were, I wasn't ready to see it.

Bobby Lee trailed behind without a word. Smart man.

53

THE ROOM WAS bare stone walls. There was no pretense of comfort. It was the vampire's version of prison, and it looked like one. There were half a dozen coffins sitting on bare, raised platforms with silver chains around them, waiting to be raised and locked in place with crosses. The only crosses in the room were on the two closed coffins. Two? Two chained coffins. Damian was in one. Who the hell was in the other?

"Which one is your boy?" Bobby Lee asked.

I shook my head. "Don't know."

"I thought you were supposed to be this boy's master."

"That's the theory."

"Then shouldn't you be able to tell which box is which?"

I glanced at him, gave a small nod. "Point." I looked back at the door but it was still empty, just us. I didn't know where everyone had gone to, and I was so trying not to speculate on what might have distracted Micah and Jean-Claude.

I tried to concentrate on who was in the coffins, but I couldn't. Once upon a time I could sense Damian even before he woke in his coffin, but I got nothing from either coffin, except that there were vampires in them. I went to the closest coffin. The wood was pale and smooth. Not the most expensive, but not cheap either, heavy, well made. I passed my hands across the smooth wood, fingers caressing the coolness of the chains. Something banged against the lid of the coffin. I jumped.

Bobby Lee laughed.

I frowned at him, then turned back to the coffin, but I wasn't touching it anymore. I knew it wasn't possible with a blessed cross attached to the lid, but I'd had this sudden image of an arm tearing through the wood and grabbing me.

Damian was supposed to be homicidally crazy. Better cautious than dead.

I put my hands just above the coffin, not quite touching. I drew my necromancy, like drawing a breath, and breathed it out through my body, not exactly through my hands, but everywhere. The necromancy was part of *what* I was, not just who I was. I started to push my power into the coffin, but it was pulled in, like water pouring into a hole. The water falls down because gravity pulls it down, and there is no stopping it; it's natural, automatic. My necromancy spilled into that coffin, and into Damian. I felt him lying in the dark, his body pressed against the thin satin. I saw his eyes stare up into mine, felt something flare inside him, something that recognized my power, but I couldn't feel him. There was no personality there, no Damian. I knew it was him, but there was no thought in him, nothing but that tiny spark of recognition, and barely that. I tried to reconcile the thing I felt to what I knew Damian had been, and it was like he had become something else. I said a quick prayer, and I didn't even feel odd praying to God about a vampire. I'd had to give up my narrow ideas of God a long time ago, or give up church and everything I held dear about my religion. The deal was, if God was okay with what I was doing, then I had to be, too.

"Where is everybody?" I asked it aloud, so Bobby Lee answered.

"I don't know, but if you come with me, we'll go look."

I shook my head staring at the other coffin. Who was in there locked in the dark? I had to know, and if I could, I'd get them out. I didn't approve of torture, and being locked in a coffin where you would never starve to death, but always go hungry, never die of thirst, but burn with the need for liquid, be trapped in a space so small you couldn't even turn onto your side, were all good definitions of torture in my book. I liked most of Jean-Claude's vamps, and I wouldn't leave them like this, not if I could presuade him that they'd been punished enough. I was pretty stubborn about things like that, and Jean-Claude was wanting to please me right now; I could probably get whoever it was out. I'd do my best. But who was it? Admittedly, there were vampires that I'd make more of an effort to save, just like people.

I went to stand beside the other coffin and pushed my magic into it. I had to push this time; it wasn't like Damian. Whatever was in this box didn't welcome me in. It wasn't anyone I had a connection with. I felt something, and I knew it was a kind of undead, but it didn't feel like a vampire. It felt emptier than that. It was fully dark outside; there should have been movement, life, of a sort, but there was nothing. I pushed farther into the thing, and found the faintest answering pulse. It was as if whatever was in there was a lot more dead than alive, yet not truly dead.

A sound turned me towards the door. Jean-Claude glided into the room, his robe tied tight now, like a signal that he was ready to get down to business. He was alone.

"Where's Micah?" I asked.

"Jason has taken him to get some clothing. They should be able to find something that will fit him."

"Who is in this coffin?" I'd almost said, *what*, but I was betting it was a vampire, just not like one I'd ever sensed before.

His face was already careful, neutral. "I would think, *ma petite,* that you have enough to be concerned over with Damian?"

"You know and I know that I am not moving until I know who's in here."

He sighed. "Yes, I know." He actually looked down at the floor, as if he were tired, and because his face showed nothing, the gesture looked half-finished, like bad acting. But I knew that for him to be working so hard at keeping anything off his face, only to let his body betray him meant he was very unhappy. Which meant that I was really not going to like the answer.

"Who, Jean-Claude?"

"Gretchen," he said, finally meeting my eyes. His face told me nothing, the one word empty.

Once upon a time Gretchen had tried to kill me because she wanted Jean-Claude for herself. "When did she get back in town?"

"Back?" He gave it that little lilt that made it a question.

"Don't be coy, Jean-Claude. She came back to town still out for my blood, and you put her in here, so when?"

His face became like a sculpture, except with less movement in it. He was hiding as much of himself as he could, and the shields were like armor. "I say again, *ma petite,* she had gone nowhere."

"What's that supposed to mean?"

He looked at me with that perfect face, so unreadable. "It means that from the moment you watched me put her in the coffin in my office at Guilty Pleasures, she has always been here."

I blinked, frowned, opened my mouth, closed it, tried again, failed. I must have looked like a landed fish, because I couldn't think of a damn thing to say. He just stood there, not helping.

I found my voice, and it was breathy. "You're saying that Gretchen has been in a coffin for two, no three years?"

He just looked at me. He'd stopped breathing. There was no sense of movement to him at all, as if, if I looked away I'd never find him again; he'd be invisible.

"Answer me, damn it! Has she been in a coffin for three years?"

He gave the smallest of nods.

"Jesus, Jesus." I paced the room, because if I didn't do something physical, I was going to hit him or start screaming. I finally ended up standing in front of him, hands in fists at my sides. "You bastard." My voice was a hoarse whisper, squeezed out of my throat because to do anything else would have had me ranting at him.

"She tried to kill my human servant, who I also loved. Most masters would have simply killed her."

"That would have been better than this," I said, voice still a hissing whisper.

"I doubt Gretchen would agree."

"Let's open the coffin and see," I said.

He shook his head. "Not tonight, *ma petite.* I knew you would feel this way, and we can try and release her, though I have poor hope for it."

"What's that supposed to mean?"

"She was not the most stable of women when she went in. This will not have strengthened her grasp of reality."

"How could you have done this to her?"

"I told you before, *ma petite,* she earned her punishment."

"Not three years," I said. My voice was beginning to sound normal again. I wasn't going to hit him, great.

"Three years for nearly killing you. I could leave her in for three more years, and it would not be punishment enough."

"I'm not going to argue whether the punishment was justified or excessive, or anything. All I can say is that I want her out of there. I won't let her stay in there another night. There's barely anything left now."

He glanced at the coffin. "You have not opened it, how do you know what is inside?"

"I wanted to know how Damian was. I used a little magic to explore what was inside both coffins."

"And what did you discover?" he asked.

"That my necromancy recognizes Damian. That Damian isn't there. It's like his personality is missing. Whatever made him, him, is missing."

Jean-Claude nodded. "With the vampires that are not master strength and never will be, it is often the Master of the City, or their creator, that enables them to exist as strong presences. Cut off from that, they often fade."

Fade, he called it, like he was talking about curtains that had been in sunlight too long, instead of a living being. Well, a sort-of-living being.

"Well, Gretchen is way past faded. There's almost nothing left. We leave her in even one more night and she may not be there."

"She cannot die."

"Maybe not, but the damage . . ." I shook my head. "We have to get her out now, tonight, or we might as well put a bullet in her."

"Leave Damian in for one more night, and I will agree to release Gretchen."

"No," I said. "Damian is like one of those feral vamps.

The longer he's like this, the greater the likelihood that he'll never be anything else."

"Do you really believe that one more night will damage him irreparably?" Jean-Claude asked.

"I don't know, but I know that if I wait until tomorrow night to get him out and the damage is permanent, I'll always wonder if that one extra night made the difference."

"Then we have a problem, *ma petite*. A hot bath is being run now in preparation for one released vampire. We only have one place suitable here at the Circus for such a recovery."

"Why a bath?" I asked.

"They must be brought back to life, to warmth. The process must be done carefully, or the risk is one of true death."

"Wait a minute. A vamp can be in the coffin locked away forever and never die, but getting them out can kill them? That doesn't make sense."

"They have adjusted to the coffin, *ma petite*. To bring them out after a length of time is a shock to their system. I have seen vampires die of it."

I knew he wouldn't lie; he was too unhappy about having to say it. "So we throw them both in the same tub, no big."

"But it is a big, *ma petite*. The attention and power needed to bring one back must not be divided between them. It will take all that I have to bring one at a time back. I cannot divide my efforts without risking them both."

"I know that you made Gretchen, but you didn't make Damian. His ties to you as Master of the City broke when he became mine, so you aren't his master in any way. I am."

"Yes," he said.

"Then isn't it my job to bring Damian back—my mystical connection with him, not yours?"

"If you were truly his master, another vampire, I would agree. But you are, for all your talents, still human. There are things you cannot do for him, and there are many things you will not know to do for him."

"Like what?"

He shook his head. "It is a complex process, requiring specialized skills."

"And you have those skills," I said.

"Do not sound so skeptical, *ma petite*. I was part of our mistress's emergency . . . crew," he said. "She would punish others and we would be left to deal with the aftermath. It was often her way."

"We?" I asked.

"Asher and myself."

"So Asher knows how to do this," I said.

"*Oui,* but he is not Damian's master either."

"No, but I am. If Damian still has one, I'm it. So you take care of Gretchen, you loan me Asher, and he tells me what to do for Damian."

"After his little display in the other room, you would trust him?"

"I'd trust him with my life, and so would you."

"But not our hearts," Jean-Claude said.

"Why did it bother him so much to see you with Micah?" I asked. "He's seen almost as bad with Richard, and me."

"I believe that you as my human servant and Richard as my wolf to call were possessions, mine by right, and you were already in place when Asher arrived in St. Louis. Micah is not my animal to call. He has no ties directly to me. He is your Nimir-Raj, but nothing to me."

"And?" I asked.

"Asher was willing to share me with you and Richard because you were mine. But this Nimir-Raj is simply another man that has my favor when Asher does not."

"Micah doesn't have your favor, exactly, yet."

Jean-Claude gave a small smile. "True, but Asher does not see it that way."

"If it weren't for my . . . social qualms would you be doing Asher right now?"

He laughed, an abrupt sound that didn't dance along my body; it just filled his face with glee. The closest I'd ever seen to real laughter from him. "Social qualms—ah, *ma petite,* that is precious."

I frowned at him. "Just answer the question."

The laughter faded, almost like a person, instead of that abrupt change he usually did. "Asher and I would likely have come to an understanding if it would not have cost me you, *ma petite.*"

"An understanding. Now who's being coy?" I said.

He gave that Gallic shrug that meant everything and nothing. "You would not be comfortable with brutal honesty, *ma petite.*"

"Fine, if I could have stomached it, would you have taken Asher back as your lover by now?"

He thought about it, then finally, "I do not know, *ma petite.*"

"I know you love him."

"*Oui,* but that does not mean we could be lovers again. When he and I were happiest, it was with Julianna. You might be able to stand us as lovers out of your sight, as long as we did not act like lovers in front of you. I do not think you would like watching Asher and me hold hands in front of you."

Put that way, he was right. "What are you saying?"

"I am saying that Asher deserves better than a hidden relationship where we could never show public affection for fear of hurting you. I would rather give him up completely to someone else, male or female, than force him to play second—or lower—to you forever."

I opened my mouth to say that I liked Asher, even loved him in a way, but I didn't, because I didn't want to raise the possibility of a true ménage à trois. What I'd seen with Micah and Jean-Claude had already bugged me a lot. I just couldn't deal with two men and me. Yeah, yeah, it was the Midwestern, middle-class value system, but it was the way I looked at the world. I couldn't change that, could I? And if I could, did I want to?

I didn't know. I just didn't know. The fact that the thought didn't make me run screaming into the night bothered me, but not as much as I thought it should have.

54

Jean-Claude gave Jason the keys to the locks on the silver chains. He'd spent the last hour explaining everyone's job. Jason would be the appetizer, oh, sorry, Gretchen's first feeding. It couldn't be someone human because the first feeding after being in the box could be quite . . . *traumatic.* Jean-Claude's choice of words, not mine. So basically Jason got to be point man and take the first damage. Then it was Jean-Claude's turn to donate blood. The vamp's master gave a feeding and rebound the vamp to the blood oaths that connected them either to the Master of the City, their bloodline, their maker, or, in Jean-Claude's case, all three. All three was better; the stronger the original connection, the greater chance the vampire had of healing the damage.

That last part made me worry for Damian. I wasn't his maker, I wasn't his bloodline, or his Master of the City. I wasn't sure exactly what I was to him. To that question, Jean-Claude had said, "You are his master, *ma petite.* Whatever that means for a necromancer, that is what you are to him. If taking blood from you doesn't reconnect him, then Asher will try. Failing that, they will fetch me from Gretchen. Damian must rebind his ties to one of us, or he is lost."

"Define lost," I said.

"The madness may be permanent."

"Shit."

"Oui."

But first Gretchen, so that I could see it done, understand the process better.

Jason unlocked the chains. They fell off the coffin and clunked against the wood, a dull, harsh sound. It made me jump. Gretchen had tried to kill me when she only *thought* I was dating Jean-Claude. She might rise from the coffin bent on killing me. I'd been her advocate, demanding Jean-Claude let her out. Now as Jason undid the locks on the lid itself, my chest was tight, and I had to fight to keep my hand away from my gun. It would be stupid—not to mention ironic—if I had to kill her the moment she rose. I could just hear Jean-Claude's dry, *And this is an improvement, ma petite*? I said a quick prayer that it wouldn't come to that. I didn't want to kill her, I wanted to save her. Wanting to do the last didn't mean I wouldn't do the first, but it did mean I would try to avoid it.

Jason raised the lid, slowly. Not because it was heavy, but because, I think, he was scared, too. The idea of being Gretchen's first meal had made him laugh, that anticipatory sound that is half grown-up male, and half little boy. The sound that men reserve for things that combine sex and usually sports, cars, technology, or danger—depends on your man. I'm sure there are men out there that would give that purring, excited laugh at the thought of gardening, or poetry, but I haven't met them. Might be an interesting change, though.

The lid went back in that halfway position that coffin lids do. Nothing moved. There was just Jason standing there in his cutoff jean shorts, bare back to the room. Gretchen didn't come bounding out and eat anybody, and I let out a breath I hadn't known I was holding.

Jason stayed there, gazing down, unmoving, hands frozen on the lid. He finally turned towards the rest of us, and there was a look on his face that I'd never seen. It was a mixture of horror and pity. His spring blue eyes were wide, and there was a glitter of tears, I thought. Jason and Gretchen hadn't been close. The reaction couldn't be personal. What was in that coffin to put that look on Jason's face?

I was moving forward without realizing it. "*Ma petite,* do not go closer."

I looked at him. "What's the matter with her? Why does Jason look so . . . stricken?"

Jason answered, "I've never seen anything like this."

I had to see now, I had to. I kept walking towards the

coffin. Jean-Claude met me, blocked my path. "Please, *ma petite,* do not go closer."

"I'm supposed to watch the process, right? I'm going to have to see what she looks like sooner or later, Jean-Claude. Might as well be sooner."

He studied my face, as if he'd memorize it. "I did not anticipate that she would be so . . ." He shook his head. "You will not be happy with me after you see her."

"You don't know what she looks like either," I said.

"No, but Jason's reaction tells me many things I do not wish to know."

"What's that supposed to mean?"

He just stepped aside. "Gaze upon her, *ma petite,* and when you have forgiven me, come back to me."

Forgiven him? I did not like the phrasing. I'd been scared of Gretchen pouncing out and trying to kill me; now I was more frightened of looking at her, of what horror awaited me inside that coffin. My pulse was trying to climb out my throat, and I couldn't breathe past it. Jason's face, Jean-Claude's sorrow, and the utter stillness from the coffin had left me so scared my mouth was dry.

Jason moved to one side, turning away from the coffin, leaning his butt against it, arms hugging his sides. He looked pale and ill. I wondered if he'd changed his mind about letting Gretchen touch him.

I stood just far enough back that I couldn't see into the coffin. I didn't want to see something so horrible that it made Jason pale. I didn't want to see it, but I had to.

I stepped up to the coffin, like stepping up to the plate, knowing that the ball coming at you is going a hundred-plus miles an hour and you have no chance to swing. My eyes couldn't make sense of what I saw at first. My mind simply refused to understand. It's a safety feature that we all have. If something is too horrendous, sometimes our brain just says, nope, not going to see this, not going to record this, nope, it would break us. But if you stare long enough, the mind says, well damn, we're not turning away, and finally, finally, you'll see it, and once you see it, you'll never be able to unsee it.

It lay against white satin so that the dry, brown color was very stark, painfully outlined. It looked like a wizened mummy, one of those bodies they find every once in a while in the desert, where the dryness makes natural mummies. The brown skin had molded to the bones, there was no muscle under it, just bones and skin. The mouth was open wide, as if the jaw hinge had broken. The fangs were dry, but white like a skull. The entire head had dried down to just the skull covered by a light coating of brown skin. Patches of bright blond hair clung to that skull, and the bright color made it worse, more obscene somehow. The eyes opened. I jumped, but the eyes that stared back at me were filled with something brown and dried, like big raisins. They blinked once, slowly, and a sound like wind sighing came out of the mouth.

I fell back from the coffin, fell to my knees. Jason grabbed my arm, drew me to my feet. I shook his hand off and went for Jean-Claude. He stood there, face patient, empty. I hit him without ever breaking stride. Maybe he expected me to stop, take a stance, but I hit him in the face, closed fist, like it was a continuation of the movement of my body. I twisted my fist—my whole body—into it, and he was suddenly on the floor, looking up at me, with blood on his face.

55

"YOU BASTARD, YOU fed off her energy while she was in there." I had to stalk away from him to keep from kicking him. Some things you did not do; some lines you did not cross.

He touched the back of his hand to his mouth. "What if I had nothing to do with it?"

"What if?" I came to stand over him. "What if? Are you really going to try and tell me that you didn't feed off of her?" I pointed back towards the coffin and must have glanced back, because the next thing I knew he had my legs, and I was suddenly falling towards the ground. I slapped the hard stones with my arms like I'd been taught in Judo. That took some of the impact, kept my head from hitting the stone floor, but it took concentration. By the time my body hit the ground, Jean-Claude was on top of me, pinning my arms to the floor with his forearms, the rest of his body trapping the rest of mine.

"Get off of me."

"*Non, ma petite,* not until you hear me out."

I tried to raise my arms, not because I thought I could outmuscle him, but because I had to try. I've never been able not to struggle even when I know it's a lost cause.

I was able to raise my arms a little—not enough to get away, but enough to make him bear down, enough to widen his eyes, enough to make him tense. Good to know the marks were helping me gain useful things like strength and not just crap.

Blood was a bright surprise against that pale skin. The blood dripped from an open cut on his mouth. "How do you know that this is not what all vampires would be reduced to after years?"

I glared up at him because I couldn't do much else. "Liar."

"How are you so certain?" He pressed himself harder against me for emphasis I think because he wasn't happy to be there; his body was all about anger not sex. "How do you know, Anita?"

He'd used my real name. "I'm a necromancer, remember?"

His face clearly said he didn't believe the answer was that simple, and he was right. I was remembering my visit to New Mexico and what I'd learned there. A monster rising above the bar in a club in Albuquerque. It rose above the bar in a thin line of pale flesh, like the rising of a crescent moon, then a face came into view. It was a woman's face with one eye gone stiff and dry like some kind of mummy. Face after face rose brown and withered, like a string of monstrous beads strung together with pieces of body, arms, legs, and thick black thread like gigantic stitches holding it all together, holding the magic inside. It rose up and up until it towered against the ceiling, curving like a giant snake to stare down at me. I estimated forty heads, more, before I lost count, or lost the heart to count anymore.

There had been another club in that town, and it had been worse in some ways, because the torture was part of the entertainment . . . Lines had appeared on the man's skin. The muscles under his skin began to shrink, as though he had a wasting disease, but what should have taken months was happening in seconds. No matter how willing the sacrifice, it can still hurt. The man started screaming as fast as he could draw breath. His lungs were working better than the first man's, and he drew breath so fast, it was like one continuous shriek. His skin darkened as it drew in and in, like something was sucking him dry. It was like watching a balloon shrivel. Except there was muscle, and when the muscle vanished, there was bone, and finally there was nothing but dried skin over bones. And still he screamed.

The last insult, or gift, or horror, had been the Master of the City of Albuquerque's power. Her power had beat against me like frantic wings, birds crying that they've been shut out in the dark and they want inside to the light and the warmth. How could I leave them crying in the dark, when all I had to do was open and they would be safe? I'd fought it, but in the end the wings erupted into a torrent of birds. My body seemed to open, though I knew it didn't. And the winged things—only half-glimpsed—spilled into that opening. The power flowed into me, through me, and out again. I was part of some great circuit, and I felt the connection with every vampire she'd touched. It was as if I flowed through them, and they through me, like water coming together to form something larger. Then I was floating in the soothing dark, and there were stars, distant and glittering.

Images then, and they had force to them like things slamming into my body. I saw the Master of the City standing on the top of a pyramid temple surrounded by trees, jungle. I could smell the rich greenness of it and hear the night call of a monkey, the scream of a jaguar. Her human servant knelt and fed from the bloody wound on her chest. He became her servant, and he gained power, many powers. And one of them was this—how to take the life force of something, someone, and feed upon it, without killing it. And I understood how he'd taken the man's essence, during that terrible entertainment. More than that, I understood how it was done, and how it was undone. I knew how to unmake the creature in the bar, though what had been done, being sewn together into a Frankenstein nightmare, might mean that to bring them back to flesh would kill them. I didn't need the necromancer who had trapped them to undo the spell; I could do it myself.

The memories were so vivid, it was like reliving them. I came back to the present almost with a jolt, staring up into Jean-Claude's eyes, still trapped under his body, still in the punishment room thousands of miles away from Obsidian Butterfly and her small army. But it was the look on Jean-Claude's face that caught my breath in my throat.

His eyes were wide, and I knew in that moment that he'd seen my memories, that he'd shared them the way I sometimes shared his. Fuck.

His voice had a shakiness to it that I rarely heard. "*Ma petite,* you were a busy girl while you were away from us."

"You saw what I saw, and you know how I feel about what you did to Gretchen."

His hands tightened on my arms, fingers digging into my skin just a little. "I know how you feel, *ma petite.* But I will not take this blame gently. I am the Master of the City, my vampires live through me. Unless they are masters themselves, their life force comes through the line that bred them, until they take blood oath to a Master of the City. Then that master makes their hearts beat. If I run short of power, then some will simply not wake in the night, or they will become revenants, animals to be destroyed as Damian has become."

I moved under him. "I don't . . ."

"Shhh, *ma petite,* I will not be condemned without a hearing, not this time. Perhaps you can save Damian, but he is over a thousand years old. Even though not a master, that is a long time, long enough to accumulate power enough to survive. But vampires like Willie and Hannah who are not masters and not that old, they would fade or go mad, and there would be no saving them." He shook me, digging into my arms, raising his elbows so that I could have gone for a weapon if I'd wanted, but I just watched him and listened.

"Is that what you want, Anita? Which of them would you sacrifice to save Gretchen? Gretchen whom you hate. I took power from her because you denied it to me."

"Don't blame this on me," I said.

He moved suddenly, sitting up on his knees, his body straddling my legs. He lifted me into a sitting position, fingers brushing against my arms. "The system of master and servant has worked well for thousands of years, but you keep fighting it, and you keep forcing me to do things I do not wish to do." He raised me up close to his face, and I watched his eyes bleed to burning blue from inches away. He shook me more violently this time, almost hard enough to scare me.

"If I could have fed the *ardeur* as it was meant to be fed, then this would not have been necessary. If I could have fed through my human servant, this would not have been necessary. If I could have fed through my animal to call, this would not have been necessary. But you and Richard bind me 'round with rules, you cripple me with your morality, and you force me to do such as I swore I would never do. I have been in the box and been food for my master, and it was the worst thing I have ever endured. And now because you and he had your moral high ground to keep you pure, you have forced me to be more practical than I have ever wanted to be."

He released me so suddenly I fell back against the floor, slamming an elbow into the stones. He stood over me, as angry as I'd ever seen him, and I had no anger to give back. I finally said, "I didn't know."

"That is becoming a poor excuse, *ma petite*." He went to the coffin and gazed down at what lay inside. "I gave her my protection once, and this is not protection." He turned and glared at me. "I do what I must, *ma petite*, but I take no pleasure from it, and I tire of the necessity of it. If you would but meet me even halfway, we could avoid so much pain."

I sat up, fighting the urge to rub my elbow. "Do you want me to say I'm sorry? I am. Do you want permission to feed off of me, is that it?"

"The *ardeur*, yes," he said. "But in truth, if you are in the mood for it, simply having the marks open and married gains me much."

He held his hand out to Jason, and for one of only a few times, I saw Jason hesitate before taking Jean-Claude's hand. Jean-Claude didn't even look at him, as if his obedience was simply a fact, like gravity. "If she were stronger it would be a more dangerous feeding, but she is very weak, so it will not be so very bad." The words were comforting, but he never looked at Jason as he lowered the younger man's wrist towards what lay in that coffin.

I got to my feet, watching Jason's face. He was pale, eyes wide, breath coming too short, too fast. He didn't normally have a problem letting vamps feed on him, but I understood. What lay in that coffin was something out of a nightmare. Most of the time if you saw a vamp looking like something made of dried sticks, it was well and truly dead.

Jason pulled on his arm, keeping himself just out of reach, I think. Jean-Claude turned to him, but there was no anger. He kept the one hand on Jason's arm, and the other he touched to his face, gently. "Would you have me take your mind, before she strikes?"

Jason nodded, wordlessly.

Jean-Claude cradled his hand against Jason's face. They stared into each other's eyes, one of those long, lingering stares, like lovers, except I felt the moment that Jason slipped away. I felt his mind release, his will evaporate. His face went slack, his mouth half-parted, eyes fluttering. Jean-Claude kept his hand on the other man's face, as he guided the wrist into the coffin.

Jason's body tensed, and I knew that Gretchen had bitten him. But his eyes stayed closed, his face pleasant. I found myself beside the coffin without meaning to be. The dried stick hands raised as I watched, clutching at Jason's arm, holding him against the mouth. Jean-Claude moved his hand back, as the thing in the coffin pressed Jason's wrist to its mouth. Blood flowed over that brown skin, soaked the white satin pillow, and still that lipless mouth fed.

The room was suddenly too warm, almost hot. I turned away and found Micah watching me. I couldn't read his expression, wasn't sure I wanted to. I looked away from whatever was in his eyes. I didn't want to meet anyone's eyes right now. I'd fought so long and so hard not to be what I was. Not to be Jean-Claude's human servant, not to be Richard's lupa, not to be anything to anyone. Everyone seemed to be paying the price for that. I hated having other people pay the price for my problems. It was against the rules somehow.

Jean-Claude's voice drew me back to the coffin. "Drink, Gretchen, drink of my blood. I gave you life once, let it be so again." Jason was sitting slumped beside the coffin, cradling his bloody wrist with a beatific expression on his face. The dried thing was sitting up with Jean-Claude's arm behind its shoulders. It looked . . . better, but still not alive, not even quite real. He offered the pale flesh of his wrist to that lipless mouth, still red with Jason's blood, and it bit down. I heard Jean-Claude sigh, but that was the only sign that it might hurt.

"Blood to blood, flesh to flesh." Jean-Claude spoke the

words, and with each word, with each suck of blood, I felt
the power grow, felt it curl in my stomach, shorten my
breath. Gretchen's body began to stretch and fill. The pieces
of hair thickened and began to flow around her. The dried
things in her eye sockets filled and began to have a hint of
blue to them. When Jean-Claude moved his wrist from her
mouth, they were full-pouting lips. She had blue eyes and a
wealth of yellow hair. She was thin, her bones showing under
the near translucent paleness of her skin. Her eyes were filled
with fire, nothing human. Her hands were still painfully thin,
her body fragile, but she looked almost like the vampire that
had tried to kill me years ago.

He picked her up in his arms; her body didn't fill out the
clothes that hung from her frame. "Breath to breath," he said
and leaned in towards her. They kissed, and I felt the power
pass between them. I knew that that kiss could have drained
her life away again, but it didn't. When he raised back from
her, her face was full and rounded, human looking. It was
like Prince Charming waking Sleeping Beauty, except that
this beauty's eyes found me, and the hatred in them was a
burning thing.

I sighed. Some people never learn. I met that hateful gaze
and said, "Gretchen, I promise you two things, you'll never
have to go back in that box, and if you try to hurt me or
mine again, I'll kill you. And that would be a damn shame
since I'm the one who persuaded Jean-Claude to let you out
in the first place."

She just looked at me the way that tigers behind bars
watch the visitors, biding their time. Jean-Claude hugged her
to him. "If you try and harm my human servant again, I will
see you destroyed, Gretal." *Gretal* had been her original
name, so I'd been told.

"I hear you, Jean-Claude." Her voice sounded rough, as
if the time in the coffin had damaged it.

"Come, Jason, we need to warm this one." Jason got to
his feet like an obedient puppy, still bleeding, still happy.

Jean-Claude paused in the doorway looking, not at me,
but at Asher. "I must take this one to the bath, or all the
work will be undone. But Damian is a revenant now."

Asher raised a hand, which had been hidden along his body. He had a gun, a .10-millimeter Browning, the big brother of my own gun. "I will do what needs doing."

"We are not going to kill Damian," I said.

Jean-Claude looked at me, then at Micah, and Nathaniel, and Gil, and the other wereleopards, and even the body-guards. His gaze seemed to take everyone in, then he looked at me again. "I ask again, *ma petite,* who will you sacrifice for your high ideals?"

"You think he can't be saved, don't you?"

"I know that once the madness takes a vampire, even the master who bore him cannot always bring him back to his senses."

"Is there anything I can do that might bring him back to himself?"

"Let him feed, try to see he does not kill that which he eats, and hope when he tastes your blood, he regains his senses. If your blood does not sate him, then Asher will try to feed him. If that fails . . ." He gave that shrug that meant everything and nothing; even holding Gretchen it looked graceful.

"I don't want him to die because of me."

"If he dies, *ma petite,* it will be because he tried to kill someone in this room." With that he walked out, Jason trailing behind.

I think, perhaps, I'd used up Jean-Claude's patience with me, or maybe seeing what he'd done to Gretchen had bothered him that much. Whatever the cause, he left me in the room with everyone looking to me as to how to proceed. And I didn't have a clue. Who was I willing to put next to the coffin? Who was I willing to risk?

56

THE ANSWER, OF course, was no one, but we finally decided who got to be the first victim. I was pretty useless for the discussion, because I would have put myself first in line. Never ask of anyone what you're not willing to do yourself. But Asher pointed out that I couldn't be the first feed if I had any chance of being Damian's master. So they decided among themselves, and it was Zane left standing next to the coffin.

Everybody but me that had a gun had it out with a round chambered. I needed my hands free to offer up a body part to get gnawed on. Come to think of it, I didn't much like that job description either. But it wasn't watching Zane's pale back as he unfastened the chain that bothered me, it was watching Cherry's face as she watched him do it. That much fear for someone's safety, that much importance attached to one other being meant that it was love for her, too. They loved each other, and he was about to cry, cry for help, and loose the carrion birds to feed, and feed, and feed.

The lid of the coffin was only half raised when Zane jerked forward and pale hands showed around him, holding him. Blood sprayed the white satin of the coffin, spattered over Zane's shoulders, and the only thing we could see of Damian was pale hands and arms latched around Zane's back. There was no shot to take.

Someone was screaming. I think it was Cherry. I had my gun out, but there was no way to fire without killing Zane first. Micah and Merle were at the coffin, trying to pry Zane free. Zane fell back, his throat a gaping wound, and something that was all bloody fangs and wild red hair grabbed Merle and folded around him, tearing at the big man's throat. The wererats and Asher were standing back, waiting for a clear shot, but there wasn't going to be one, not before someone else died.

I pushed forward, trying to shove Micah out of the way while I pressed the gun to Damian's face, but Micah was trying to pry the vampire off of Merle, and in the struggle I couldn't get my gun steady. The barrel slipped in the blood against Damian's skin, and suddenly green eyes turned to me, and there was nothing in them but hunger. Damian was already dead. I just hadn't pulled the trigger yet.

Then he was on me, faster than anything I'd ever seen. I was pressed back against the satin of the coffin, my hips and legs sticking out. He didn't go for my neck; he buried his fangs in my upper chest. I screamed past the pain and pressed the barrel of the Browning against his temple. Asher was yelling, "Don't fire, you'll hit Anita!"

I screamed again and had to adjust the angle of the gun, because if I'd pulled the trigger, the bullet would have gone through his head into my chest. I moved the gun a fraction while he savaged me. My finger curled on the trigger when he raised his green eyes to me. I watched his eyes fill up with knowledge, intelligence—with him. He raised his mouth back from my chest. He looked scared. "Anita, what's happening?" He seemed to see my bloody chest for the first time, and his eyes went wide. "What's happening to me?"

The moment he spoke, the moment there was something in him besides monster, I felt the connection between us click into place, like a perfectly tuned string on a harp. The power flowed between us like warm water, filling him up, filling me up, and I drew him down to me, my blood still on his lips.

I heard Asher saying, "Stay back, it's alright, let her finish."

I whispered as I drew Damian down to me, "Blood of my blood, flesh of my flesh, breath to breath, my heart to yours."

And just before our lips met and his fate was sealed, he whispered, "Yes, oh, yes."

57

I WAS SHOULDER-DEEP in water so hot it made my skin pink. I was so hot I was almost ill, because I was still fully dressed, including all my guns. Damian leaned up against the front of my body, my arms wrapped around him, holding him close. His body folded in against mine, his arms holding mine across his bare chest.

How did I end up being guardian of the bathtub for Damian once we reached my house? He'd gone into convulsions, and only my touch had calmed him. We'd gotten him to my house with Nathaniel riding in the back, cradling Damian. They'd filled the bathtub with hot, hot water, and I'd left Asher in charge of Damian's care. I'd done my part, I'd brought him back to himself. I had a bandage over my left breast to prove that I'd donated my piece of flesh and blood for the night. Zane and Merle were on their way to the lycanthrope hospital, with Micah and Cherry to oversee them. Everyone else had trooped back to my house, and everything had seemed fine, until screams from the bathroom brought me running.

Damian had been beating himself against the floor, convulsing like he'd tear himself apart, vomiting blood on the tile. Asher and Nathaniel had been fighting to hold him down, to keep him from hurting himself, but they couldn't hold him. I knelt to help, and the moment I touched him, he quieted. I'd withdrawn my hand, and his body had bucked again, hands scrambling at the slick tile. I'd touched his shoulder, and he calmed. We'd tried letting him take blood from Caleb, but the moment I stopped touching him, his body rejected the blood, and everything else. The last time I'd stopped touching him, Damian had simply gone quiet, and I had felt him beginning to fade, to die.

We'd dragged Damian into the steaming bath water, and I'd held him. He had recovered, but only with me holding him while my clothes stuck to my body.

"What's wrong with him?" I asked.

Asher had answered, "I've only seen this reaction between master and servant."

"I'm Damian's master, so what? It shouldn't cause this, should it?"

"No, *ma cherie,* not merely master, but master vampire and human servant."

"Damian is not my master," I said.

"Damian is no one's master," Asher said quietly, gazing down at us from the edge of the tub. He was sitting in a pool of the blood that had poured out of Damian.

"What are you saying, Asher?"

"You have made him your servant."

"He can't be a human servant, he's a vampire," I said.

"I did not say human servant, *ma cherie.*"

"Then what are you talking about?"

"A . . . vampire servant for a master necromancer, I think."

"You think?" I made it a question.

"We are dealing with things of legend, *ma cherie,* things that should not be possible. I am having to . . . guess at this."

"Guess?" I said.

He sighed. "If I said that I knew for certain what has happened, it would be a lie. I would never lie to you on purpose."

I had protested, demanded, but nothing I could do or say made it untrue. I had a vampire servant, and that was impossible. But impossible or not, Damian lay against my body, clinging to me, like I was the last hope he had.

Asher glided back into the bathroom, wearing a beach towel wrapped around him. The towel was big enough to cover him from armpits to mid-calf, effectively hiding his body. Hiding the scars. "My clothes are covered in blood. I hope you do not mind."

I hated wearing bloody clothes myself, so, "Fine, glad you found a towel you liked."

He glanced down at the colorful towel. "I do not fit in your robe."

I was sorry Asher felt like he had to hide himself away, but I had other things to worry about. "I think if I don't get cooler soon I'm either going to throw up or pass out."

He knelt by the tub, smoothing the long towel under his knees in a gesture that you don't see much in men. He touched my face lightly. "You are flushed." He touched Damian. "His skin is still cooler than it should be." He frowned. "You need to take off some of your clothing, especially the jeans, I would think."

Normally, I go to great lengths not to be unclothed in front of all the boys, but tonight I was willing to strip down a little. "How do I undress and still hold him?"

"I believe that one of us could hold him against you while you disrobed."

"You really think that he'll go into convulsions again?"

"You could release him, and we could find out," Asher said, voice soft.

I shook my head. "I'm tired of cleaning up blood. Just help me hold him."

Asher's eyes went a little wide. "I will call Nathaniel."

The heat had gone to my head in a pounding headache. "Just jump in, Asher, I promise not to peek."

He curled beside the tub, tucking every piece of him he could underneath the towel. "If I dropped this towel to the floor, would you really not look?"

His question stopped me. I opened my mouth, closed it, and tried to think through the heat, the headache, the growing nausea, and finally just said the truth. "I wouldn't mean to look, but no, you're right. If you're naked I'm going to look. I don't think I could stop myself."

"Like a car accident, you cannot turn away," he said.

I looked up then and found he'd turned away, hiding his face with that fall of golden hair. Damn it, I didn't have time to hold everybody's hand. "Asher, please, I didn't mean that."

He wouldn't look at me. I extracted one arm from Damian, who moved around the remaining arm like a child settling in his sleep around his favorite Teddy bear. I grabbed Asher's arm through the towel. "Yes, I'd look just for sheer curiosity's sake, how could I help it? You've teased and taunted about how bad your injuries are. You've set it up so that I'll have to look, have to see."

He was looking at me now, those pale eyes, empty, hidden from me.

I dug my fingers into his arm, trying to grip him through the towel, and finding mostly cloth. "But if you don't know by now that I just want to see you nude, then you haven't been paying attention."

His face told me nothing, that blank politeness that both he and Jean-Claude could pull off when they wanted to. "Now help me get some of these clothes off before I melt."

He gave a low chuckling laugh that danced over my skin and brought my pulse to my throat. I was too hot to have goosebumps. "You offering to disrobe without any magic to push you, I believe that is a first."

I had to laugh, because he was right. But the laugh forced me to close my eyes, because it felt like the pulsing of the headache was going to shove my eyeballs out of their sockets. I let go of his arm and pressed my hand to my forehead to try and keep my head from falling into pieces. "Please, Asher, I am going to be sick."

I heard the water splashing, felt it push against me as someone climbed into the tub. I opened my eyes slowly, trying to hold the headache inside and found Nathaniel kneeling in the water. His hair was still bound in a loose braid that trailed behind him, curling through the water like something separate and alive. The swirling braid brought my gaze low on his body, and I had a peripheral sense that Nathaniel wasn't getting any clothes wet whatsoever, but I didn't care. The headache had reached a point where I was afraid I was going to start throwing up if I didn't get cooler.

He answered my question without me asking it. "Asher wants Damian to try to take blood again, see if it will stay down."

Asher was still perched on the edge of the tub wrapped in the towel. "Damian must be able to keep down blood, or he will perish. I believe that if you stay in constant contact with him that he will be able to keep a feeding down."

"If I have to stay in constant contact then I have to get cooler first."

"Nathaniel will help you," he said.

I glanced up at Asher, and even in the dim glow of a night light, it hurt my head. "Fine."

Damian made small protesting movements as Nathaniel tried to take some of his weight off of me. We finally leaned him up against the edge of the tub with Asher supporting some of his weight, but letting him keep my arm pressed to his chest. Nathaniel undid my belt and helped me slip the shoulder holster off one arm, but I needed the other arm free to slip it out of the other strap. Damian fought us, slowly, stubbornly, as if he were sleepwalking. But he was a vampire; he could have torn his way through the wall of my bathroom with his bare hands. If he didn't want to let go of my arm, we couldn't make him, not unless we were willing to break his fingers one at a time, and we weren't willing to do that.

"What do we do?" Nathaniel asked.

"I have to get out of this heat," I said. "Can we like run cold water in the tub, or something?"

"No," Asher said, "we must keep him as warm as possible, until after he has retained some of the blood. We don't dare allow him to be chilled."

"Then get these clothes off me."

I felt rather than saw the two of them exchange glances. "How do you want me to do it?" Nathaniel asked.

I leaned my head forward, resting against the top of Damian's wet hair. His skin was the coldest thing in the tub. I was so hot I was about to be sick, yet Damian's skin was still cool to the touch. The headache overwhelmed me and spilled out my mouth. I did my best to crawl out on the edge of the tub before I vomited. Damian had managed to miss the water every time he threw up; at least I could do the same. But he clung to me, and only Asher's hand on my arm kept me high enough from the water to keep it clean.

My head was screaming, the pain so strong that it impacted my vision in explosions of color. Asher got me a cool cloth and wiped my mouth. He laid another cool cloth across my forehead. Then Nathaniel gripped the back of my shirt and ripped. He tore it off of me in pieces. Asher draped a wet towel over my shoulders that was so cold it made me whisper, "Shit."

Asher and Nathaniel took my weight and Damian's and moved us back to the far edge of the tub, as Gil came in and started cleaning up the mess. Gil had cleaned up a lot of messes tonight, and he'd never bitched, not once. He did a double take at the pieces of my shirt floating in the water, but never commented aloud. He made a good flunkie. Did what he was told and didn't ask questions.

Nathaniel tried to tear my jeans off the way he'd done the shirt. He managed to rip the top, but Damian's weight kept pushing me under the water, and he couldn't get the leverage he needed. Asher fastened the towel as securely as he could and climbed gingerly into the water. He knelt and slid his arms around Damian and me and lifted, standing, holding us both upright. I was still touching bottom, but he was still holding both our weights, because my legs still weren't working quite right. He held us both effortlessly.

Nathaniel put a hand on either side of the rip he'd made in my jeans and pulled. The heavy wet cloth came apart under his hands with a sound like tearing flesh, but heavier— a wet, harsh sound. The force of it jerked my body, and only Asher's strength kept me standing.

I felt the air on my bare skin and realized that in ripping away the jeans he'd taken my undies with them, but I didn't care. The air on my skin was still suffocatingly hot. I couldn't breathe. The last thing I remember thinking was, I'm going to pass out, then nothing.

58

I WOKE LYING on the edge of the tub with only one arm in the water with Damian. Cold towels covered me from head to foot. The one on my face lifted, and I saw that Nathaniel was in the water, holding Damian upright. I blinked up through a strand of wet hair and found Asher spreading a fresh cold towel against my face. He left enough of my face uncovered so I could look at him, sideways.

"How are you feeling?"

I had to think about that. "Better." He replaced the towels down the length of my body, and I realized I was completely nude. I shivered with the cold cloth and didn't care about anything except that I was finally cool. "How long was I out?"

"Not long," Asher said, smoothing the towel so that it molded to my legs.

I looked at Nathaniel, kneeling in the tub, pinning Damian to the edge, so the vampire could hold on to me. "I've never seen a shapeshifter pass out from heat exhaustion before," he said.

"A first time for everything," I said.

Damian turned his head slowly to look at me. His eyes were clear, bright, alive again. His eyes were the color of emeralds, and it wasn't caused by vampire powers, it was his natural eye color, as if his mother had fooled around with a cat to get him here. People just didn't have that color of eyes.

I smiled at him. "You look better."

"I fed."

I glanced at Nathaniel. He turned his head so I could see the neat bite marks in the side of his throat.

"I think I can support myself," Damian said.

Nathaniel looked a question at Asher, who must have nodded, because Nathaniel backed off. Damian settled against me, still holding my arm across his chest, but lightly now. One hand gently on my wrist, the other hand stroked my arm.

"I hear you're my master."

I looked into those calm eyes. "You don't seem upset."

He rubbed his chin and cheek against my arm. It was catlike, and intimate, a lover's gesture. I studied his face, tried to read past those peaceful emerald eyes. Then I realized I didn't have to read his face. The barest thought and I knew that the peacefulness in his eyes went all the way through. He was filled with a great calmness, a sense of rightness. Calm and peace had never been my reaction to Jean-Claude binding *me* closer to him.

I could feel what Damian was feeling, knew his heart almost better than my own, but I didn't understand him. In that moment staring into those beautiful, peaceful eyes, I simply had no clue. I would have run for the hills, fought, screamed, hated. I would not have gone quietly into any kind of servitude, no matter how potentially beneficent the ruler. Truthfully, I wasn't a hundred percent sure I was a beneficent ruler. I mean I was easy to get along with as long as everything went my way, but cross me, and I wasn't easy. I was close to being the hardest person I knew, and I know some hard people. I was trying to be softer lately, but trying to be softer and actually being softer, aren't the same. I looked into Damian's eyes and knew that if it were me, tied to me as master, I'd be scared.

Damian turned in the water, kneeling at the tub edge. He leaned in and laid a gentle kiss on my forehead. "You saved me, again."

He was right, but as his lips touched my skin, I wondered how long he'd be grateful and when he'd finally realize how screwed we both were.

59

ASHER TOOK DAMIAN down to the basement for the day, settling them both in just before dawn. Micah had called, saying that both Merle and Zane would survive. Cherry was going to stay there with Zane, and he had to go check on the rest of his wereleopards. I invited him to bring his leopards over to my house, and he said he'd ask. We didn't say "I love you" at the end of the conversation, which was unnerving. I wasn't used to sleeping with someone that I didn't love or didn't say I love you to. But I was too tired to think that hard, so I pushed it down where all the other things I don't want to think about live. The place is getting damned crowded. Nathaniel helped me dress in the coolest jammies I had—a silky spaghetti strap nightshirt that would have been too revealing if I hadn't been so damn short. Then Nathaniel cuddled in beside me in a pair of jogging shorts. Gil slept in the guest room. The two wererat bodyguards divided the night up between the couch and sleeping on the floor in front of the door of my bedroom, which meant if I had to go to the bathroom after we bedded down I'd have to step over them. Bobby Lee said, "It'll wake us up, make sure you don't go wandering around alone."

I couldn't persuade Bobby Lee or Cris that I didn't need that much watching, but truthfully I was too tired to do much arguing. So we all settled down for a long summer's nap. Nathaniel had closed the heavy curtains so that the room lay in a heavy gray twilight.

I settled down in the air-conditioned hush of the bedroom with Nathaniel curled up against my side and fell almost immediately into a deep, dreamless sleep. When the bedside phone shrilled, I knew what it was, but it took me several seconds to wake up enough to move. Nathaniel had actually reached across me and answered, "Blake residence," before I opened my eyes.

He was quiet, face very serious, then he cupped his hand over the receiver and said, "It's Ulysses, Narcissus's body-guard. He wants to speak with you."

I took the phone, still lying flat on my back. "This is Anita, what do you want?"

"My Oba wishes to meet with you."

I moved my head enough to see the clock and groaned. I'd barely had two hours of sleep. I could manage an hour nap and feel okay, or go without sleep, but somewhere between two and three hours just felt worse. "I work the night shift, Ulysses, whatever Narcissus wants can wait until later in the day."

"The word went out yesterday that any information about the missing lycanthropes was to go through you."

That woke me up a little. I blinked and tried to be more awake than I felt. "What information?"

"He will only talk directly to you."

"Then put him on the phone, I'm all ears."

"He insists that you come down to his club, now."

"I have had less than two hours of sleep, Ulysses. I am not dragging my ass over to the Illinois side of the river at the crack of dawn. If he has information that can help us save shapeshifters' lives, just give it to me, and I'll see that the info gets to where it needs to go."

"My Oba insists that if you do not come down to the club now, he will not share the information at all."

I sat up, leaning against the headboard, closing my eyes. "Why now?"

"It is not my way to question my orders."

"Maybe you should work on that," I said.

There was silence on the other end of the phone. I didn't know if he was puzzled and didn't get my comment, or if it had struck too close to home. He finally said in a quiet voice, "Right now the lions' Rex is alive. That may not be the case in a few hours."

I sat up, eyes wide, completely awake at last. "How do you know that?"

"My Oba knows many things."

"Narcissus would really let the lions' Rex die, just because I won't come down to the club at the ass crack of dawn?"

"My master is very insistent."

"Shit," I said softly and with feeling. "Tell him I'll be down, but tell him this, too. The next time he's in trouble, maybe no one will help him either."

"This is more help than he has ever been to any other animal clan."

There was something in Ulysses's voice now, something. He was lying. I could hear it in his voice. I didn't know if it was vampire powers or werewolf, or wereleopard, and I didn't care. The question was, why lie about the fact that the werehyenas had helped no other shapeshifter group more than this? Why was that worth a lie at all?

"Narcissus helps out more than he wants people to know, doesn't he?" I said.

"What makes you say that?" There was a thread of fear, almost panic, in Ulysses's voice.

"What would it hurt if the lycanthrope community knew that the werehyenas were helping other animals out?" I asked.

His breath came out in a long sigh. "Narcissus would never want anyone to think that about the werehyenas. It would . . ." he hesitated, "be bad for business."

"If Narcissus is so concerned about Joseph the lion, then why not give me the info over the phone?"

Ulysses laughed, abrupt, amused. "Narcissus has never given anything away for nothing. There's always a price with him."

"So my dragging down to his club on no sleep is the price?"

"Something like that."

"Can I bring my people?"

"My master would love to see any of your people you care to bring."

I didn't like the phrasing on that. "How big of him."

"When will you be here?" Ulysses asked.

"How do you know I'm coming?"

"Because you know that he's enough of an egotist that if you don't come now he may not share the information at all. You know he'd let the lions' Rex die just because he's not the same animal we are, and you not coming down now would be an insult."

"This clannish shit has got to stop, Ulysses. We need to start helping each other more."

"Not my place to change the system, Anita. I'm just trying to survive in it."

He sounded sad. "I don't mean to yell at the messenger, Ulysses, I'm just tired of the system."

He laughed again, but not like he was happy. "*You're* tired of the system. Jesus, you have no idea. When can I tell him to expect you?"

"An hour. Less, if I can manage it. I want Joseph alive to see his baby."

"His mate will probably lose it like all the others."

"I thought you hyenas didn't talk to the lions or anyone else. How do you know about Joseph's baby woes?"

"Narcissus keeps track of things like that."

"Why would he care?"

"He wants a baby."

That made me raise my eyebrows. "I've never pictured Narcissus as the paternal type."

"Try maternal."

"What?"

"We'll be waiting for you, Anita. Don't keep him waiting. He doesn't like to be kept waiting." I heard sorrow in his voice, sorrow bordering on grief. I almost asked what was wrong, but he'd already hung up. What had Narcissus done to him to put that tone in his voice? Did I really want to know? Probably not. Not unless there was something I could do about it, and there wasn't. If I started a war with every harsh lycanthrope master in town, I'd have to kill them all, or almost. The only one who wasn't harsh was Richard, and that was going to get *him* killed. I complained about Narcissus being too harsh and Richard being too soft. I guess I was just never satisfied.

I hung up the phone and told Nathaniel what was happening while I picked out clothes. Nathaniel threw a tank top over the jogging shorts he'd slept in, added jogging shoes, no socks. He knew better than to try and dress, because he'd insist on unbraiding his hair and combing it out, which would take all the time the rest of us would need to get dressed. I was wrong. Nathaniel wasn't even close to done with his hair when the rest of us were dressed and ready to go. Bobby Lee and Cris just threw on their shirts and shoes, ran fingers through their short hair, put the holsters back on, and they were ready to go. Gil came down in jeans, jogging shoes, and an untucked men's dress shirt. The shirt looked new, but he didn't keep us waiting. Caleb came down in jeans and nothing else. I didn't bother to tell him to throw a shirt on, or shoes. Somehow I didn't think that Narcissus would deny us service because Caleb was underdressed.

I actually took the longest getting dressed: black jeans, red polo shirt, black Nikes, every blade I had, including the new back sheath I'd had made for the largest knife that ran along my spine. The first sheath had gotten cut to pieces by emergency room personnel, while they were trying to save my life. I also brought my two handguns, though I wasn't sure that any of us would be allowed to bring guns into the club. But just in case I brought them, and I warned Cris and Bobby Lee about the no-guns rule. They flashed their own set of wicked-looking blades—about three apiece—and we were ready to go.

I thought about calling Christine the weretiger, but figured since it wasn't quite seven that I'd let somebody sleep in today. Besides, I didn't know shit yet. When I knew something worth sharing, I'd share.

I was halfway to the club when I realized that the *ardeur* hadn't set in. It was morning. I was awake. There wasn't a stir from the *ardeur*. Hope flared through me in a warm, fuzzy wash. Maybe the *ardeur* was going to be temporary. Dear God, I hoped so. I said a brief prayer of thanks and kept monitoring myself for the first hints of unbridled lust.

We arrived at Narcissus in Chains with me grumpy, but not the least bit lustful. It was a good day.

60

I WAS ABLE to park right in front of Narcissus in Chains. Not only was there no line at 8:00 A.M., there were no other people in front of the club. The wide sidewalk stretched empty, almost golden, in the early morning light. If I'd had time for coffee, I might even have said it was pretty, but I hadn't had time for coffee, so the sunlight was just bright. I had finally broken down and bought sunglasses a few weeks ago. I huddled behind them, wishing I was still in bed. I was so tired, I felt fuzzy-headed. I'm usually pretty good at going without sleep. The only thing I could blame the fuzziness on was the heat exhaustion from the night before. Maybe I needed more than three hours to recover from it. It made me wonder how bad off I'd have been if I hadn't had all my preternatural powers. A person can die of heatstroke.

Nathaniel was at my side, Bobby Lee and Cris, a step behind and to either side. Gil and Caleb brought up the rear. The door opened before we could knock. Ulysses ushered us into the darkened club. He was still wearing his leather and metal harness. The smell of it made me wonder if it was the exact same outfit he'd been wearing, was it five or six days ago? The tall, dark, and handsome man that I'd met looked hollow-eyed. His strong hands gripped his elbows, hugging his body. When he moved a hand to motion us inside, it shook. What the hell had been going on?

Half a dozen other muscular men of varying races and heights stood in the shadows waiting for Ulysses to tell them what to do. The tension in the room was so thick you could have choked on it.

Cris made a hissing sound at my back, and I couldn't blame him. I decided then and there that unless we got some really good explanations, we were keeping the guns. There was an air of desperation about all the werehyenas, as if something really bad had happened.

The door was shut behind us, but we were close to it, and no one was between us and it. I wanted to save the lion Joseph, but not enough to risk myself and my people. If it was a choice, I knew who I'd choose. Cold, maybe, but I'd never met Joseph the werelion. He wasn't real to me yet, and everyone with me was.

Ulysses must have seen, or smelled, something on us, because he explained. "Our master has seen fit to punish us."

"What for?" I asked.

He shook his head. "That is personal."

"Fine, let's talk to Narcissus, and you guys can get back to punishing yourselves."

"We are not punishing ourselves," Ulysses said.

I shrugged. "Look, I don't believe in letting anyone push me around to this degree, but it's not my deal, it's yours. So let's share information and let us get out of here."

Something crossed Ulysses's face, some emotion that I couldn't read. "No guns in the club, that's the rule."

"I think we'll keep our guns," Bobby Lee said.

I glanced at him, and the look was enough. He shut up but smiled at me. "Actually, I agree with him. We're not giving up our guns today."

Ulysses shook his head. "I can't fail my master in this, Anita. You have no idea what he'll do to us if we let you inside with guns."

I glanced at the men standing around in the shadowed room. Fear rolled off of them in waves; their bodies were tight with tension. I'd never seen so many men so thoroughly whipped before. They would do exactly what they were told to do, because they were terrified to do anything else. I'd been told that a good dominant was a caring partner. Maybe Narcissus wasn't a good dom, maybe he was a bad one.

"I'm sorry, Ulysses, really, I don't want to cause you pain, but if Narcissus has gone crazy enough to make all of you this scared, then we keep the guns."

"Please, Anita, please." He must have seen something on my face that let him know I wasn't going to give in, because he dropped to his knees in front of me. The sound of his knees hitting the floor was sharp, made me wince. He'd kept his hands wrapped on his arms, so that he just dropped without catching himself at all. "Please, Anita."

I shook my head, staring into those haunted eyes.

Tears glimmered down his cheeks. "Please, Anita, please, you don't know what he'll do to our lovers if we fail him."

"Lovers?" I made it a question.

It took him two tries to say, "Ajax is my . . . lover. We've been together four years. Please, Anita. I don't have any right to ask this, but please give up your guns."

I shook my head. "I'm sorry, Ulysses, really I am, but the more you talk the more I want to keep my guns."

He moved so suddenly that I didn't have time to react, and Cris and Bobby Lee both cleared their guns, but Ulysses wasn't trying to hurt me. He wrapped his arms around me, buried his face in my chest, and wept and begged. He stank of fear and blood and worse things.

"Put up the guns, boys, he's not trying to hurt me."

They put their guns up, but they didn't look happy. But then, neither, I suppose, did I. I touched Ulysses's head, but he just kept saying, "Please, please, please."

"You guys can all come with us, just walk out with us."

Bobby Lee whispered, "This is not a good idea."

"I don't care. Nobody deserves to be treated like this."

"What'cha gonna do, Anita, offer them all sanctuary? We didn't bring that many guns," he said.

"If the other werehyenas object, we leave them. I didn't bring us out here to get killed, but if we can, we take them with us."

Bobby Lee shook his head. "You make your life hard, Anita, you make your life very hard."

"So I've been told."

Ulysses just clung to me, crying, begging. I had to grab his face and make him look at me, and even then his eyes didn't focus. It took almost a full minute for him to see me. "You can come with us, Ulysses, all of you, just walk out."

He shook his head. "They have our lovers. You don't know what they'll do, you can't know."

"They?"

A rifle shot exploded from somewhere in the room. I had the Browning halfway out of its holster when Cris staggered backwards. Blood sprayed out his back onto Caleb and Gil. Gil started screaming. I had to turn away before Cris hit the floor.

Bobby Lee said, "Three on the catwalk with rifles. Fuck, girl, we've walked into it."

I looked where he was looking and could barely make out the shapes. If I was supposed to be the kitty-cat, why did the rat have better night vision?

Ulysses was whispering over and over, "I'm sorry, I'm sorry, I'm sorry."

I put the barrel against his forehead. "Whatever else happens, Ulysses, you die next."

A man's voice came out of the darkness. He was speaking over a sound system, that much I could tell. "If you pull the trigger, we will kill your other bodyguard. Rifles with silver shot, Ms. Blake, and I assure you that my people are dead shots. Now, put your guns down, and we'll talk."

I kept my gun and told Ulysses, "Get away from me, now!" He crawled away, still crying.

I picked out the shadowy form on my side of the catwalk. Bobby Lee was aimed to the other side, which left one man in the middle without a gun on him. But from this distance, with them above us, we had to make each shot count, which meant that we had to kill what we could, then hope we could do something with the last one. "Who the hell are you?" I asked.

"Drop your guns, Ms. Blake, and I'll tell you."

"We keep our guns, girl," Bobby Lee said. "He's going to kill us either way."

I agreed.

"We don't want you dead, Ms. Blake, but we don't give a shit about your friends. We can just keep picking them off until you change your mind."

I moved to stand in front of everyone, so that the middle shot was harder. From the above angle, I couldn't block them completely, but it was the best I could do. "Everybody get down." Only Bobby Lee hesitated. "They don't want me dead, and I need your gun." He glanced at me, then dropped to one knee, using me to shield himself from the middle gunman. He'd grasped my plan. Everyone else was hugging the floor. There was no cover, and the door was close but not close enough, what with three rifles on us.

"What are you doing, Ms. Blake?" the voice asked.

"Just testing a theory," I said.

"Don't be stupid, Ms. Blake."

"Bobby Lee," I said.

"Yes, ma'am."

"How good are you?"

"Give the word, we'll find out."

I felt my body go very, very still, so that the world narrowed down to the end of my gun and that shape crouched on the catwalk. It was about ten yards. I'd hit targets farther away than that. But that was target shooting. I'd never tried to drop a man with a handgun from this distance. I let out the last of my breath so that I was just stillness, just the gun, just the point of the gun, just the aim of the gun, and with the last, barest touch of my voice, I whispered, "Word."

Our guns went off almost simultaneously. I didn't shoot just once, I fired as fast as I could pull the trigger. My figure jerked, the target came out of his crouch, then fell slowly off the catwalk. I turned my gun before the body hit the ground and found the man in the middle standing up. I saw the shadow of his rifle. I heard the voice shouting over the explosion of gunshots, "Don't hit her, don't you dare."

The rifle plowed up the floor inches from me—two shots—trying to get me to move and give him a shot at Bobby Lee, but I stood my ground and fired back. Bobby was firing with me, and the shadow form jerked, staggered, then slumped forward, his rifle falling to land on the floor with the other two bodies of the now-dead riflemen.

The voice said, "Boys, do not disappoint me."

The werehyenas rushed us. Bobby Lee and I started shooting. We divided the six werehyenas up between us, smooth, no cross fires, no taking the other's hit—my side of the room, his side of the room. I took two, I think he took one, and we both clicked empty. I drew the Firestar left-handed, which made it about two seconds slower than it needed to be, but it was probably faster than popping the clip on the Browning and reloading. If I survived, I'd have to time which one was faster.

It was Ulysses who was almost upon me like a dark shape of doom. A gun exploded at my back, and Ulysses fell backwards onto the floor. I whirled to find Nathaniel with a gun. His eyes were wide, his lips parted, a look of astonishment on his face. He'd picked up Cris's dropped weapon. Movement turned me back to the fight. Metal flashed as Bobby Lee waded into the last two werehyenas. The fight was too intense. I couldn't get a clear shot.

The far doors opened, and men poured out. I rushed the fight around Bobby Lee and fired almost point blank into someone's back. The man shuddered and dropped, putting me face-to-face with Bobby Lee. It had startled him, and I had to fire across his body into the last of the fightees. I pointed the Firestar at the werehyenas pouring towards us. I emptied the gun into them, as we all started backing for the door. I wasn't as good left-handed. I don't think I killed anyone, but I wounded someone with every shot, and it slowed them, made them hesitate.

Gil, Caleb, and Nathaniel were already at the doors. Daylight spilled in, and I was dazzled for a second, because my sunglasses were still tucked across the front of my shirt. I dropped the Firestar, popped the empty clip from the Browning and had the second clip pounded home before we made the sidewalk. I still couldn't hear the noise of the clips hitting home, but I saw Bobby Lee making the same movement with his gun that I'd made with mine. I knew he was locked and loaded.

I yelled, "Nathaniel! Jeep, get it running!" I knew he knew where the extra set of keys were. I remembered Narcissus saying that there were over five hundred werehyenas. We had to get out of there before they decided to pick up more guns or just overwhelm us with numbers. Shooting them would slow them down, but whoever that voice had been, he had them terrified. I could kill them, but I couldn't terrorize them. Whether they poured out of that door in a wave would depend on whether they feared death or terror more.

I glanced back to find Nathaniel in the Jeep, with Caleb and Gil in the back. The engine roared to life. Bobby Lee and I started for the Jeep, and the werehyenas rolled out into the sunlight, too many to count, almost too many to aim at. I fired into the mass of bodies, and I yelled, "Run!"

Bobby Lee and I were running for the Jeep, which meant our aim wasn't what it should have been, but the men were packed so tight that we kept hitting them anyway. They'd fall, then there'd be screams, sounds, a chittering laughter that raised the hair at the back of my neck, and the wounded rose as hyenamen, muscled, pale-furred, spotted, with a muzzle full of fangs and claws like black knives. We weren't whittling them down, we were giving them better weapons to use against us.

Nathaniel yelled, "Get in!"

I glanced back to find the doors open front and middle. I slid into the rear seat, Bobby Lee slid in front. The doors were shut, locked, and Nathaniel was pulling away from the curb when they poured over us. They swarmed the car, covering the windows. Nathaniel hit the gas and the Jeep roared forward. An arm smashed through the window beside me. The sound of breaking glass was everywhere. They were trying to hold on and get inside. I fired through my window into the man beyond, and he fell away. Bobby Lee was firing into the hyenaman that was trying to crawl through the windshield.

But there were at least three others smashing at the glass, trying to crawl through. I fired the Browning into the one on the opposite window from mine. It took four shots before he fell away. The Browning had to be close to empty, but I'd lost count. The last two werehyenas were halfway through the windows; one of them spilled into the back of the Jeep. He launched himself at me, and I fired two more bullets almost point blank into him. The gun clicked empty. The man fell, apparently dead at my knees, because I was kneeling in the back of the Jeep, which meant that I'd crawled over the seat to meet his charge. I didn't remember doing it.

The last one was in half-man form. He was having trouble tearing his way through the window. I think he'd caught something painful on the glass. I drew the blade that I wore down my back. My right knee was down, leg flat to the floorboard, my left, raised on the ball of my foot. It was a swordsman's stance for when you couldn't stand—balanced. I struck in a blur of speed, feeling the strength in my body like nothing I'd ever felt before. He looked up at the last second just before the blade bit into the side of his face and split his head open. Blood splattered on my arms, across my face. The body slumped forward, most of its lower parts still dangling out the window. The upper part of his head from just above the jaw was gone, spilling out onto the carpet, soaking into the leg of my jeans. I had a heartbeat to think, holy shit, then I heard the sounds on the roof.

Bobby Lee said, "Persistent bastards."

I didn't answer, just knelt by the wheel well opposite the bodies. Edward, assassin to the undead, and the only person I knew of with a higher kill count for monsters than me, had talked me into letting a friend of his remodel my Jeep. The wheel well held a secret compartment. Inside there was an extra Browning Hi-Power, two extra clips, and a mini-Uzi with a mushroom clip. The clip barely fit inside the compartment, but it nearly tripled the round capacity, so it was worth the tight fit.

Claws ripped through the roof of the Jeep and started peeling it back, like opening a tin can. I threw myself onto my back and fired up into the roof. Animal howls, one body fell past the windows, but the other one stayed on the roof, the half-animal arm shoved through the metal. I went to my knees, firing just in back of the arm. The hyenaman rolled off the back of the Jeep and bounced in the road. The arm stayed in the hole in the roof, caught on the metal.

When the ringing in my ears toned down enough for me to hear something besides the pounding of my own blood, I could hear Caleb saying, "Fuck, fuck, fuck," over and over. Gil was huddled beside him on the floorboard, screaming, a high piteous sound, his hands over his ears, eyes closed. I leaned on the seat, but didn't try to climb back over. My back was covered in blood and worse things from rolling around on the floor.

I yelled, "Gil, Gil!"

He just kept screaming. I tapped the top of his head with the gun barrel. That made him open his eyes. I pointed the gun at the ceiling while he stared at me. "Stop screaming."

He nodded, hands lowering slowly. He kept nodding over and over again. Caleb had stopped cursing under his breath. He was breathing so hard I thought he might hyperventilate, but I had other things to worry about.

"What kind of clip ya got on that Uzi?" Bobby Lee asked.

"It's called a mushroom clip. It about triples the ammo capacity."

He shook his head. "Damn, girl, where have you been living that you need that kind of firepower?"

"Welcome to my life," I said. I looked down at Gil. "Next time I tell you to stay home, stay home."

"Yes, ma'am," he whispered.

"Slow it down, boy," Bobby Lee said, "we don't want to get picked up by the cops with bodies in the car."

"The damage may be a tip-off," I said.

The arm dangling from the ceiling had changed back to human shape. It flopped bonelessly as Nathaniel turned a corner. I looked away from it and found the now-human with his head bisected. His brains had leaked out in pieces. I was suddenly hot, dizzy. I couldn't remember what I'd done with the big blade. I must have dropped it, but I didn't remember doing it. I wedged myself into a corner, the Uzi raised to the ceiling, my body held on three sides by metal and the seat back. It was as close to being held as I could manage. I closed my eyes, so I couldn't see what I'd done. But the smell was still there: fresh blood, butchered meat, and that outhouse smell that let you know someone's bowels had let loose. I started to choke, and the Jeep pulled off the road. That made me look up, gave me something else to concentrate on.

Nathaniel was pulling onto a gravel road in the middle of nowhere. There were trees, a floodplain, green grass, and beyond that, the shine of the river. It was a peaceful spot. He drove until we weren't easily visible from the road, then stopped.

"What's going on?" I asked.

Bobby Lee answered, "I think if we drive around in traffic with legs sticking out, someone will notify the police."

I nodded. It was a good point. "I should have thought of it," I said.

"No, you've done your work for the day. Let me do the thinking 'til your head clears."

"My head's clear," I said.

He climbed out of the car and spoke through one of the broken windows as he moved towards the legs. "I know pangs of conscience when I see them, girl."

"Stop calling me 'girl'."

He grinned at me. "Yes, ma'am." He grabbed the legs and shoved the body through the glass. It landed with a thick sound on top of the first body. A sound came out of the body on the bottom. It might have just been air escaping—it happened sometimes—but then again . . .

I was on my knees, Uzi pointed at the bodies. Bobby Lee said, "Don't hit the gas tank, ma'am, we don't want to blow ourselves up." He had his gun back out.

I shifted my angle so that I'd shoot through the dark head that lay at the bottom of the pile. Did two bodies constitute a pile? Did it matter? Something brushed my hair and I jerked the gun up, only to find that I'd brushed the fingers on the arm hanging from the ceiling. It was coming loose, sliding lower on its own. Great.

I pressed the barrel of the Uzi against the top of the head. "If you're alive, don't move, if you're dead, don't worry about it."

Bobby Lee opened the back of the Jeep, his gun angled down for a shot at the "body."

"If I fire into the top of his head, the bullets may cut your legs out from under you."

He moved off to one side, gun steady. "My deepest apologies, ma'am, I know better than that."

I pressed the gun barrel more securely into the top of the

head and began to reach slowly towards the neck that was just visible under the very dead top body.

"I'm alive." The voice made me jump and nearly made me squeeze the trigger.

"Shit," I said.

"Why don't you finish it?" the man asked. His voice was pain-filled, but not thick. I'd missed heart and lungs. Careless of me.

"Because that wasn't Narcissus's voice over the speaker system, and Ulysses said they had your lovers. That we didn't know what they'd do to your lovers if you guys failed them. Who is the guy over the speaker? Who is 'they'? Where the fuck is Narcissus? Why would the werehyenas let anyone take them over like this?"

"You're not going to kill me?" He made it a question.

"You answer our questions, and I give you my word that we won't kill you."

"May I move?"

"If you can."

He moved slowly, painfully onto his side. His hair was curly, dark, cut very short, skin pale. He turned until he could see my eyes, and the effort left him shaking, his lips blue, which made me think maybe we didn't have much time to ask our questions, that maybe we'd already killed him, just not fast enough.

His eyes were a strange shade of gold. "I'm Bacchus," he said in that pain-filled voice.

"Nice to meet you. I'm Anita, that's Bobby Lee, now start talking."

"Ask me anything."

I started asking. Bacchus started answering. He didn't die. By the time we crossed the bridge into Missouri, his lips were pink and healthy and the dazed look had left his eyes. I was really going to have to start packing better ammo.

61

BACCHUS ACTUALLY DIDN'T know all that much. Narcissus had introduced his new gentleman fair, Chimera, and they'd seemed to be having a wonderful time together. If not true love, then the rough trade they both wanted. Then Narcissus had gone into one of the rooms and not come back out. For twenty-four hours the werehyenas had thought it was just sex, but after that, they stopped believing Chimera's assurances that Narcissus was alright. Ajax had managed to get inside, and that's when it went bad.

"Ajax told us Narcissus was being tortured, really tortured."

"Why didn't you rescue him?" I asked.

"Chimera came with his own bodyguards. They took . . ." Bacchus had to stop and fight to take a deep breath, as if something inside him was hurting. "You don't know what they've done to our people. You don't know what they've threatened to do to them if we fail them."

"Tell us, then we'll know," I said.

"Have you met Ajax?" he asked.

I nodded.

"They cut his arms and legs off and burned the ends of the wounds so he couldn't heal the damage. Chimera said they'd put him in a metal box and just get him out on special occasions." Bacchus choked, and I wasn't sure if it was from injuries or horror.

Bobby Lee said, "He's upset enough that I can't tell if he's lying or not, but I think he's telling the truth." His voice was a little hoarse, as if he were seeing the images in his head that I was trying very hard not to imagine. I'd gotten better lately at simply refusing to let my imagination run away with me. Maybe it had something to do with being a sociopath; if so, let's hear it for dementia. I sat there in the Jeep, my mind carefully blank, no visuals. Bobby Lee looked ill.

"How many bodyguards does this Chimera have?" I asked.

"About twenty-five, before you started killing them."

"I thought there were like five hundred of you guys. How could twenty-five men keep you down?"

Bacchus looked at me with stricken eyes. "If someone had your Ulfric, Richard, and was cutting pieces off of him, crippling him, wouldn't you do anything to save him?"

I stayed quiet and thought about that one. I gave the only truthful answer that I could. "I don't know. It would depend on what 'anything' covered. I see your point, but why didn't you just rush them?"

Bacchus propped himself up against the side of the Jeep. Nathaniel took a corner a little fast, and Bacchus tried to grab something so he wouldn't slide. I gave him my hand, caught him, and he looked both grateful and uncertain. He kept hold of my hand and gave really good eye contact. "We didn't have an alpha. Ajax and Ulysses were the next in command, and once they started cutting up Ajax, Ulysses told us to do what they said." He squeezed my hand, not too tight. "The rest of us aren't leaders, Anita. Our alphas were all telling us to cooperate with Chimera. We're followers, that's it, that's all. We need an alpha with a plan."

My eyes widened. "What are you saying, Bacchus?"

He drew me close to him with our clasped hands. "There are still almost one hundred and fifty ablebodied hyenas. God knows what they'll do to the prisoners now that we've failed them."

"Why do they want Ms. Blake?" Bobby Lee asked.

"Chimera wants Anita for his mate."

That raised my eyebrows. "What are you talking about?"

"He's got a real hard-on where you're concerned. I don't know why."

I tried to draw my hand out of Bacchus's grip, but he kept me close. "He's tried to kill me at least twice. That doesn't sound so friendly."

"He wanted you dead, now he doesn't, I don't know why. Chimera's crazy, he doesn't need a reason to change his mind." He gazed up at me, still holding my hand. "Please help us."

"Can you guarantee that the other hyenas will follow Ms. Blake?" Bobby Lee asked.

Bacchus looked down, his grip loosened, then it tightened, and he looked up again. "I know that if we'd had any alphas that would have stood up for us all, we'd have taken these guys out by now. But Ulysses loves Ajax, really loves him. He didn't know what to do."

"What about Narcissus? He's not still all mushy about Chimera, right?" I said.

"No, but the only time we've been allowed to see Narcissus, he was gagged."

"Narcissus has a reputation," Bobby Lee said, "of being a tough bastard. I don't think he would have rolled over for them."

Bacchus shrugged, and I finally freed my hand. "I don't know," the werehyena said, "but he couldn't tell us to attack them. For all I know Chimera may have taken his tongue. He did that to Dionysus, my . . . lover." He hugged himself, head down, eyes closed. "He gave me the tongue in a box wrapped with a ribbon."

I'd been given a box once with pieces of people I cared about in it. I'd killed the ones who'd hurt them, killed them all. But the damage done to my friends had been permanent. Nothing I could do would fix it, because they'd been human; they didn't grow back lost body parts.

Bacchus kept his eyes closed, his face very still, as if he were holding himself tight, afraid to lose control. I didn't know what to say in the face of his pain. How did I go from trying to kill him to feeling bad for him? Maybe it was a girl thing, or maybe I'd been oversocialized as a child. Whatever the reason, I found myself wanting to help him, but not wanting to risk any of my own people. Cris was dead on the floor of Narcissus in Chains. I hadn't known Cris long; his loss wasn't that great to me, it just wasn't. But if I went in there in force, I'd be risking people I would miss.

Still . . . "Can you draw a plan, a layout of the club, mark where everybody is being held?"

He opened his eyes, his expression surprised, the tears he'd been holding back trailing down his cheeks, forgotten. "You'll help us?"

I shrugged, uncomfortable at the frantic relief in his eyes. "I'm not sure yet, but it doesn't hurt to find out what we'd be up against."

Bacchus took my hand again, pressed it to his cheek. I thought at first it was going to be some kind of hyena greeting, but he laid a soft kiss on my hand and let me go. "Thank you."

"Don't thank me yet, Bacchus, don't thank me yet." I didn't say out loud that if the club looked too hard to take, like it would cost too many lives, I wouldn't do it. I kept it to myself, because he might lie, make it seem easier. The person he loved was being tortured. People will do a lot of things for the person they love, even stupid things.

62

.

BOBBY LEE INSISTED on calling Rafael first thing. Nathaniel and Caleb helped me get Bacchus settled in the kitchen. He was still walking like things hurt. Gil had sat down at the end of the couch first thing, huddling. He'd been withdrawn since I told him to stop screaming. Normally, I'd have asked what was wrong, but screw it, I didn't have time to baby-sit him right now.

The kitchen was dim and depressing with all the windows and the sliding glass door boarded over. We had to turn on all the lights. My sunny kitchen had been turned into a cave.

An hour later we had a fair map of the inside of the club. Bacchus knew the guard schedule for the hyenas but not for Chimera's men. He did the best he could but said, "Chimera changes his routine, sometimes every day, at least every three days. One day he kept changing his orders every hour or so. It was weird, weirder even than normal for Chimera."

"How unstable is he?" Bobby Lee asked.

Bacchus actually seemed to think about that for a second or two. I'd thought it was a rhetorical question; maybe I was wrong. "Sometimes he seems fine. Sometimes he's so crazy it scares me. I think it even scares his own people." Bacchus frowned then said, "I heard them say things, like he literally was getting crazier and they were afraid of him, too."

The doorbell rang. It made me jump. Nathaniel jumped off the kitchen counter, where he'd been sitting. "I'll get it."

"Check and see who it is first," I said.

He looked back over his shoulder, the look on his face clearly saying that I was telling him something he already knew. After months of sharing room and board with me, he knew to check the door before he opened it.

"You used to just open the door," I said.

"I know better now," he said and vanished into the living room.

He came back almost immediately. "It's the werewolf that was at Narcissus in Chains, the one called Zeke." Nathaniel looked a little pale.

Bobby Lee and I both had guns in our hands. I didn't really remember drawing mine. I was looking at the boarded-up windows. The wood was a little more protection than the glass had been, but we couldn't see through the wood either. The bad guys could sneak up on us better. "Is he alone?" I asked.

"He's the only one standing on the porch," Nathaniel said, "but that doesn't mean he's alone." His eyes were a touch wide when he said, "I don't smell snakes or lions." I could see the pulse in his neck jumping under his skin.

"It's going to be alright, Nathaniel," I said.

He nodded, but the look on his face told me he wasn't convinced. Gil joined us in the kitchen. "What's happening?"

"Bad guys," I said.

"More of them?" he said, voice plaintive.

"You might have been safer on your own, Gil," I said.

He nodded. "I'm beginning to see that." His eyes were so wide it looked painful.

I had brought the mini-Uzi in from the car and had re-loaded it from the gun safe upstairs. I took it off the kitchen cabinet and debated between it and the Browning. The door-bell rang again. I didn't jump this time. I hung the Uzi over my shoulder by its strap and settled the Browning more comfortably in my hand. The Uzi was really an emergency weapon. The fact that I'd even thought about answering my door with it on my person was probably a bad sign. If I needed more than a 9mm to answer my own front door, I should just leave town.

I peered out at the living room, but there was nothing to see but the closed front door. I was going to have to look out the side window to see what was waiting on the porch. I approached the door with the Browning in a two-handed grip, staying to one side of the door. I was ready in case they started shooting through the door. Of course, last time they'd shot through the windows, too, but the drapes were drawn, and it was the best I was going to be able to do, as far as safety went.

I knelt by the window, because most people shoot for the chest or head, and on my knees I'm a lot shorter. I eased the drape to one side, and something slapped against the glass. I jumped back, bringing the gun up, but nothing else happened. I had an image in my head of what it had been, and it hadn't been a gun. I thought it had been a picture. I eased the drape back and found myself staring at a Polaroid of a man chained to a wall. He was nude, covered in bloody scratches, blood covering most of his body so it was hard to see at first exactly who it was. Then gradually my eyes made sense of it, and I realized it was Micah. I sat back abruptly on the floor, almost like I'd fallen. My hand dragged at the drape, keeping it open. The gun wasn't where it was supposed to be, but hovered in the air, half-forgotten. A gag cut across that wide mouth, the delicate face covered in blood and swollen flesh. The long hair was mounded to one side, as if it were so sticky with blood that it no longer moved freely. His eyes were closed, and I wondered for a second that lasted forever if he was dead. But there was something about the way he hung in the chains that said *alive*. Even in a picture there is a stillness to death that the live cannot mimic. Or maybe I'd just seen enough bodies to know.

Bobby Lee was beside me. "What is it, what's wrong?" Then he saw the picture, and I heard his breath go in sharp. "That's your Nimir-Raj, isn't it?"

I nodded, because I still wasn't breathing, which made it hard to talk. I closed my eyes for a moment, took a deep cleansing breath, and let it out slowly. It shook as it left my body. I cursed silently. "Get a handle on it, Anita, you can do better than this."

"What?" Bobby Lee asked.

I realized I'd said the last aloud and shook my head, letting the drape fall back into place. I got to my feet. "Let him in, let's see what he's got to say."

Bobby Lee was giving me a funny look. "You can't shoot him until after we know what's happening."

I nodded. "I know."

He touched my shoulder, turned me to look at him. "There is a look on your face, girl, that is as bleak as a winter's dawn. People kill other people while they're wearing that look. I don't want you to let your emotions get in the way of business."

Something that was almost a smile touched my lips. "Don't worry, Bobby Lee, I won't let anything interfere with business."

His hand dropped away slowly. "Girl, the look in your eyes now scares me."

"Then don't look," I said, "and *don't* call me 'girl'."

He nodded. "Yes, ma'am."

"Now open the damn door, and let's get this done."

He didn't argue again. He just went for the door and let the big, bad wolf inside.

63

WHEN WE OPENED the door, Zeke had a picture of Cherry in front of his chest. His first words were, "Shoot me and they both are worse than dead."

So he took a seat on my white couch, still breathing, though if he said the wrong thing, I was hoping to change that.

"What do you want?" I asked.

"I was sent to fetch you for my master."

"Define 'fetch'," I said. I was sitting on the low wood coffee table in front of him. Bobby Lee was standing in back of him with a gun pressed to his spine. At that range with silver ammo there wasn't an alpha in the world that would survive, or at least none that I'd met, and I'd met a few.

"He wants you to be his mate."

I shook my head. "I heard that, but didn't he try, twice, to have you guys kill me?"

Zeke nodded. "Yes."

"And he suddenly wants me to be his honey bun."

Zeke nodded again. The gesture looked odd in the wolf-man form, kind of like a golden retriever that was nodding sagely.

"Why the change of heart?" I asked. The fact that I was asking calm questions while the Polaroids of Cherry and Micah sat beside me on the coffee table was a testament to both my patience and my lack of sanity. If I'd really been sane I couldn't have been calm, but I'd hit that switch in my head that let me think when awful things were happening. The same switch that let me kill without much remorse. Being able to divorce myself from my emotions kept me from shooting pieces off Zeke's body until he told me where Micah and Cherry were. Besides, there was always the very real possibility that we could do it later. Talk reasonably first, torture only if you had to, conservation of energy.

"Chimera was told that you would be a panwere like himself."

I raised eyebrows at that. "Panwere, what the hell is that?"

"A lycanthrope that can take more than one form," Zeke said.

"Not possible," I said.

Bacchus spoke from the kitchen doorway. He'd stayed as far away from Zeke as he could and remain in the room. "Chimera can take more than one form, I've seen it."

I looked back at Zeke. "Okay, fine, he's a panwere. Why would someone tell him that I was one, too?"

"Before I answer that question, I have someone waiting in a nearby car. I would like her to come in and speak with you."

"Who?" For a wild moment I thought he might mean Cherry, but he didn't.

"Gina."

"Micah's Gina?" I asked.

Zeke nodded.

I looked behind him at Bobby Lee. "Do we trust him to go back out and come back in without reinforcements?"

Bobby Lee shook his head.

I shook my head, too. "Sorry, Zeke, but we don't trust you."

"Send Caleb then." He looked at the wereleopard, who had been very quiet throughout everything. Caleb was sitting in the far corner of the room, keeping away from Zeke, a lot like Bacchus, come to think of it. But then Gil was huddled in a different corner. I'd assumed I was surrounded by scaredy-cats, hyenas, and foxes, but now . . .

"How did you know his name?" I asked.

"I know a lot of things about Caleb."

"Explain," I said.

The doorbell rang again. I didn't jump this time. I was in that faraway place where I didn't get nerves, though the Browning was pointed at the door. Did that count as nerves?

I went to the door, and Bobby Lee stayed with his gun

pressed to Zeke's back. "Y'all better hope that that is some-one friendly," Bobby Lee drawled.

Zeke's wide nose flared, scenting the wind. "It's Gina."

Call me paranoid, but I didn't trust him. I peeked out the window. This time there were no nasty surprises, just Gina standing on the small porch, a thick gray shawl hugged around her upper body. It was nearly ninety outside, what the hell was the shawl for? I let out a deep breath. The shawl was thick enough to hide all sorts of unpleasant surprises. Damn.

"What's she got under the shawl?" I asked Zeke.

"You might say a message from Chimera."

I glanced back at him. "Talk like that isn't going to get the door opened."

Zeke moved his shoulders, and Bobby Lee must have pressed the gun barrel deeper into his back, because he stopped moving abruptly. "She's been tortured. Chimera sent her with me to show what will happen to your leopard if you don't come with me."

"Why the shawl?" I asked again.

Zeke closed his eyes, as if he wanted to look away but was afraid Bobby Lee would take it wrong. "It's to cover her, Anita, just to cover up her nakedness." He sounded weary, not just tired, but weary. "Please, let her inside, she's in a great deal of pain."

"He smells like he's telling the truth," Bobby Lee said.

I sighed. That was probably as good an assurance as we were going to get. I opened the door, gun at the ready, stay-ing out of the sight of anyone who might be watching from the yard. Because I was hiding behind the door, I didn't see Gina until she was well into the room. I closed the door behind her, and she jumped, then gasped, as if the sudden movement had hurt her badly. When she looked at me, it was all I could do to keep from gasping. I thought at first she had two black eyes, then realized it was just hollows under her eyes so deep they looked like bruises. Her skin was so pale with an undertone of gray, and I understood for the first time what they meant by ashen. She was ashen, as if her body was covered by something thinner, more delicate, than skin. Her tall body was hunched in on itself, as if standing upright would hurt. Her lips were nearly bloodless, but it was her eyes that hurt me the most. They were filled with horror as if she were still seeing whatever had been done to her, as if she might always see that awful thing over and over again.

She spoke in a voice that was hollow, hopeless. "I got worried."

I didn't need to see what was under the shawl to believe that she'd been tortured. I didn't need to see anything but her face.

"Can she sit down before she falls down?" Zeke asked.

I nodded a little too rapidly, realizing that I had been staring. "Please, sit down."

Gina looked at Bobby Lee, standing behind Zeke. "Have you told them?"

"I wanted you here to back up my story," Zeke said.

She nodded once, then moved to sit beside him on the couch. She sat close to him, almost touching. If he'd had anything to do with what had happened to her, I don't think she'd have been so cozy.

In fact she was so cozy that I was almost certain she knew Zeke. Knew him not just for Chimera's fun and games, but knew him before. How did one of Micah's cats end up friendly with Chimera's top goon?

I asked. "You two seem to know each other." Alright, maybe that wasn't a question, but it would do.

They exchanged a look, then Zeke turned to me. I wished that he was in human form. Even after years of dealing with lycanthropes, I still had trouble reading their expressions when they were in animal form. The fact that his eyes were human helped some, but you never realize how much of the expression isn't really the eyes but the facial movements around the eyes, until you don't have them as clues.

"Let me start by saying that Chimera wants you alive and well and in his care in less than two hours or he will start doing permanent damage to Micah and your leopard."

I felt my eyes go a little dead. "We have a deadline then," I said. "Talk faster."

"Shortest version that I know is this. Chimera has always been a harsh master, but never sadistic, until the last few weeks. He's unstable, and I believe he's going mad and will kill us all if he remains in charge."

"This is the short version?" Bobby Lee asked.

"I agree," I said, "speed it up."

"I want you to help me stage a palace revolt, Ms. Blake. Is that quick enough for you?"

"Maybe that was a little too quick," I said. "Why do you want to revolt, and why do you want my help?"

"I told you, I fear that Chimera will destroy us all. The only way to prevent that is to kill him."

Well, that was blunt. "So, why my help?"

"You have a certain reputation for deadly force."

"You talk like an English professor," I said, "or an expensive lawyer. Why not just kill him yourself?"

"The others that follow him, fear him, they would not trust that I alone could guarantee his death."

"And I can?"

"You and your people, yes."

"My leopards are not going inside."

Nathaniel said, "Anita . . ."

I shook my head. "No, I won't endanger the rest of you to save one of you."

"What kind of pard would we be if we allowed our Nimir-Ra to go into danger alone?"

"A pard that obeyed orders," I said.

He leaned back against the wall, but there was an unusually stubborn set to his face that said maybe, just maybe, he'd been picking up more than just weapons skill from hanging around with me. Was stubbornness catching?

"Not your leopards, but the wolves, and the rats."

"The rats aren't mine." *And I'm not the wolves' lupa anymore.*

"Rafael is already on his way here with some of our people," Bobby Lee said.

I frowned at him. "Well, nice you mentioned that."

He shrugged. If he was getting tired of pressing the gun

into Zeke's back, it didn't show. "Rafael is my alpha, not you, ma'am."

"I understand that, but if we're going to get along, you still need to keep me informed. I've had enough surprises for one day."

"Amen to that," he said.

"Where are Micah and Cherry being held?" I asked.

Zeke shook his great wolfish head. "No, not until you agree to help us."

"Chimera wanted to blackmail me into being his sweetie, you want to blackmail me into helping you kill him. I don't see much difference."

"The only way to stop Chimera and those still loyal to him is their death. I propose that we pool our resources and accomplish that."

"You talk awful pretty for a goon."

"I am his goon because when he conquered my small pack of wolves, he forced me into this form and kept me in it. When he allowed me to try and change back, this was the best I could do."

I looked into those human eyes. "Only your eyes," I said.

"Only my eyes."

The eyes were usually one of the first things to go animal if you stayed in beast form too long at a time. His eyes being the only thing human was odd. But I didn't ask him to explain, because we were eating up our time and I wanted Micah and Cherry back.

"In this form," Zeke said, "I can be nothing else but a goon, an enforcer. I cannot be human."

I didn't try to argue that he was human. I let it go. "Let's cut to the chase. Bobby Lee, will Rafael help on this?"

"I think so. He's coming with enough soldiers to make a good show."

I looked at Bacchus. "Will the werehyenas join forces with their, what, oppressors? Will you guys help Zeke and his people?"

"Zeke always tried to save us pain. He always spoke for moderation." Bacchus nodded. "I think the others will agree to work with him, but whether they'll agree to let everyone live afterwards, that I can't promise."

"If we help you destroy him," Zeke said, "then you turn around and slaughter us, we have gained nothing."

In looking between Bacchus and Zeke I'd glanced back over the photos. I'd spent the last few minutes not thinking about them. I'd managed to concentrate on other things, but it was as if that one glance had torn through all the barriers that usually kept me from doing stupid shit. I stood up, abruptly enough that everyone looked at me.

"Would you kill Zeke?" I asked.

"No, but Marco, he has to die," Bacchus said.

"Why?" I asked.

"He and the snake men have to die," Bacchus said.

"Agreed," Zeke said. Then he looked up at me. "And I think I know a way to have the wolves involved."

"I'm listening."

"Chimera is wolf, hyena, leopard, lion, bear, and snake."

"He's behind the disappearances of the other alphas," I said.

Zeke nodded.

"Are they alive?"

"The lion and the dog are. Chimera hasn't been able to force them to change form yet. He never kills anyone unless he can break them first."

"Is Narcissus alive?" This from Bacchus.

"Yes," Zeke said. "Chimera has not been able to break him either."

"How will any of this interest the wolves?" I asked. I'd gone to stand on the other side of the kitchen doorway, opposite Bacchus. I couldn't see the pictures from there.

"Chimera's never been able to find a dominant animal group that was weak enough to be taken over by outsiders before, until he heard of your wolf pack."

I stood up straighter, pushing away from the wall. "What do you mean?"

"Jacob, Paris, and a few others are what's left of my pack. Chimera couldn't send me because my condition would raise questions."

"Are you saying that as soon as Jacob becomes Ulfric, he turns the pack over to Chimera?"

"That was the plan," Zeke said.

"And now?" I asked.

"Now either Jacob and the others agree to leave your pack where it is, or they die."

"You'd kill what's left of your own pack, just like that?" I said.

"They stopped being my pack a long time ago."

"So let me get this straight," Bobby Lee said, "you want the rats, the wolves, and the leopards to join forces with the hyenas and whatever people of yours will join you and destroy the rest."

"Yes," Zeke said.

"And if we don't?" Bobby Lee asked.

"You talk as if you have many choices here," Zeke said. "You do not. Chimera will do worse than kill your leopards. What he has allowed done to the hyenas is beyond any civilized tolerance. His sanity is slipping away, and there are those among his people that will do terrible things without a master to tell them no."

"It takes time to arrange an offensive like this," Bobby Lee said.

Zeke said, "I do not see a clock but time is running out. Anita must be in Chimera's presence before two hours is over, or it will go badly for Micah and the leopard."

"You keep saying Micah and the leopard," I said, "like you know Micah." I had an awful thought, and I'd been slow not to think of it before. "Jacob was supposed to get the wolves for Chimera, and Micah was supposed to get the leopards." I said it in an empty voice. My body felt empty, as if I were falling away inside myself, drowning in that great white static that allowed me to kill and not to think.

"We thought their alpha was dead and it would be easy enough." He looked at me. "We didn't know about you, or rather didn't understand what you were."

Gina spoke. "Once Micah met you, he knew it wouldn't work. He tried to get Chimera to leave you and yours alone, but when you went up against Jacob, you became too big a threat. Chimera ordered you killed. Micah didn't find out about the order until after everyone had left to come after you. He saved you."

I just looked at her. My mind was still trying to process the thought that Micah had lied to me the entire time I'd known him.

"Micah told Chimera that you were going to be a panwere like him, and he might never find another one like himself. That's why you can control the leopards and the wolves both."

I blinked at her. "I guess that's one theory." My voice sounded distant even to me.

"Don't you understand, Anita? I don't think Micah believed it, but it was all he could think of to keep you alive and him alive, and not to get the rest of us tortured." She stood up, and pain tore across her face. Zeke steadied her, then she stood straight and she let the shawl fall away.

Burns traced her pale shoulders. The rest of her chest was bare and lovely and unharmed, but as she turned to show her back, Gil gasped. Her back was patterned with burns, no, not burns, brands. Someone had branded her over and over again. The burns were fresh, some of them bloody raw, some with crisp blackened skin, as if the pressure hadn't been even every time. Some of the marks were smeared around the edges, as if she'd moved, struggled.

She turned back to face me, tears glittering in her eyes. "Every time Chimera sent Micah out he had Violet or me with him. If Micah didn't do what he was told to do, then he'd hurt us." She started walking towards me, hands holding her arms, as if to hold herself steady, but every step hurt, and it showed in the flinching of her eyes. "What would you do to keep this from happening to Nathaniel?"

I met her eyes, but it took effort. "I'd do a lot, but I wouldn't betray anyone."

The tears started slowly down her face, as if she were fighting not to cry. "He tortured Micah because Micah refused to help lure you into the ambush. Chimera is going to kill him, because he says that Micah is no longer his cat, but yours, that the wiles of a woman have won his loyalty." She sobbed, and the movement must have hurt, because she bent forward, body spasming. I caught her by the arms to keep her from falling.

"Oh, God," she whispered, "it hurts."

My throat was tight. I held her elbows until she could stand again.

"I'm Chimera's message to you, Anita. He says he'll do this to your leopard if you don't come back with us."

"You're not going back there," I said.

"He still has Cherry and Micah. If I don't go back he'll do this to her. I don't think she'd survive it." I understood what Gina meant. Not Cherry's body, but her mind.

She began to collapse towards the floor, slowly, me supporting her as gently as I could. "Micah knew what would happen to him when he refused to help trap you, but he still did it." She was on her knees now, her hands gripping my arms tight, tight enough to hurt. "I would have lied and agreed to do anything to keep this from happening to me." She sobbed again, and I held her arms to keep her from falling backwards onto her back on the floor. I held her while she shook in pain, and when she quieted, she said, in a voice more tears than noise, "I would have betrayed anyone to stop him from hurting me. But he didn't want anything from me. Nothing I could say, or do, would stop it. Chimera promised Micah that only he would suffer for refusing, then once he was chained up and couldn't get away they brought me in and made him watch." She looked at me, eyes wide, full of awful things. "Chimera would have made Cherry or me take animal form. He said he'd never had a female beast before."

"That's what he calls those of us trapped between forms," Zeke said.

Gina's fingers dug into my arm, just a little. "Micah took our place. He's alpha enough to have kept human form. He risked his human form for us. Merle was our Nimir-Raj but he wouldn't risk his humanity for us. Micah took his place, our place. He's our Nimir-Raj because he loves us, all of us. Micah offered to betray you to stop them from hurting me, but Chimera said he could smell that Micah was lying and that he would just get away and warn you. So he sent me with Zeke, because he trusts Zeke."

I looked at Zeke over her slowly collapsing form, trying to cradle her as she slid down, and not hurt her, but everything seemed to hurt. She was making small mewling sounds by the time I helped her lower herself to the floor. There was something in Zeke's human eyes that didn't need facial expressions to interpret.

"Chimera must be stopped," Zeke said, softly. "He must be stopped."

"Yes," I said, still holding one of Gina's hands, "yes, he must be stopped."

"Stopped, hell," Bobby Lee said, "we need to kill his ass."

I nodded. "That, too."

64

WE MADE IT back to the club with a little time to spare. The wererats had arrived in force at my house, and I'd left Rafael in charge of the rescue, because that's what it would be. I was letting Zeke take me into the bad guy's lair unarmed. Zeke would be carrying my weapons, and theoretically he'd give them back to me if I needed them, theoretically. But theory and practice aren't always the same thing. Zeke had tried to kill me once; now I was supposed to trust him with my life. It seemed a bad idea, but I was still going to do it. With enough time maybe we could have come up with a better plan, but we didn't have the time. Not if we hoped to save Cherry and Micah.

It seemed like I'd spent most of the last four years arriving too late. Too late to save people, too late to keep the monsters away. I was cleanup crew, someone that came after the bodies were scattered around and mopped up the mess. I killed the monsters, but only after they'd done terrible things. Even now, Chimera had already butchered and tortured, but I could confess to myself, if to no one else, that part of me didn't give a damn about the others. I mean, I was sorry for Gina's pain and Bacchus's lover, and Ajax getting chopped up, but they were abstract to me. Cherry and Micah were real. How very quickly Micah had become that real to me frightened me, but if I didn't look too closely at it, I could keep moving forward, could keep thinking clearly, could keep breathing normally. Thinking too much tended to make my thoughts jump around, my breath come a little too fast.

The main part of the club had been dark and empty. The party, as they say, was upstairs. It was the room at the end of the big white hallway that we'd gone down to rescue Nathaniel and Gregory days ago. Chimera waited outside the door in his black hood, and his eye slits were unzipped so I could see pale gray eyes. He wore a rather ordinary looking suit, complete with tightly knotted tie and white shirt that met oddly with the black leather of the hood. He had his hands behind him, leaning against his arms. He was trying for casual and failing. He was nervous, and I didn't need any lycanthrope powers to notice.

Gina had needed help from two of the werehyenas to make the steps. Zeke and I could have helped her, but he was pretending to guard me, and Gina had a note under her shawl to slip the hyenas. The note was from Bacchus, asking one of them to let him in the secret entrance. Apparently Chimera had never asked if there was a secret entrance to the club, so no one had told him.

Chimera's eyes looked past me to her. "Gina . . ." He shook his head. "Take her away, get her some medical care."

The two hyenas didn't argue, just turned and went back down the hallway. The snake man that had been with them stayed where he was, his black-and-green striped eyes never leaving Chimera's face. I would have said he stood at attention like a good soldier, but it was more than that. There was something on his face that went beyond that, as if standing there waiting for Chimera's orders was the most wonderful thing in the world. That look of patient adoration was creepy all on its own, and I knew why Bacchus had said the snakes had to die. Not because of what they'd done to the hyenas, not revenge, but because people who worship their kings as gods don't participate in palace revolts.

"I wasn't sure you'd come, Ms. Blake."

The voice was familiar, but I couldn't quite place from where. "You didn't give me much choice."

"And for that I am sorry."

"Sorry enough to let me take my leopards and go home?"

He almost smiled, but shook his head. "Micah is not your leopard, he's mine, Ms. Blake."

Again, the voice rang familiar, but I couldn't place it. I shrugged. "You got me down here with the understanding that both Cherry and Micah would be set free, unhurt. Sounds like they're both mine."

He shook his head again. "To give up Micah I would have to give up all my leopards, and I am not willing to do that."

"Then you lied to get me down here."

"No, Ms. Blake." He took his hands out from behind his back. He wore black leather gloves. "Join your pard to ours, strengthen us."

I shook my head. "I came down here to free my people, not to join your club."

He looked at Zeke. "Didn't you explain to her what I wanted?"

Zeke shifted beside me. "You told me that if she came down here unarmed you would free Micah and the other wereleopard. That is all you told me."

Chimera frowned; even through the hood I could see it. He rubbed at his face behind the leather as if something hurt. "I know I told you that I wanted her to join us."

"You have said many things over the last few weeks," Zeke said, voice very careful.

"How long have you been the leopard's Nimir-Ra?" he asked. The voice was normal, ordinary, though his hands kept rubbing at his face.

"About a year."

"Then you must see as I do that there needs to be a joining together of all the different forms. The only thing that has allowed us to move in to every city and take over the smaller groups is the fact that the larger groups won't help them. They're like city neighbors who only call the police if it's their own apartment being robbed. They let anyone who isn't like them go to hell."

"I agree that the lycanthrope community could use a little togetherness, but I'm not sure torture and blackmail is the way to get it done."

He clamped his hands over his eyes, back bowing, as if he were in pain. The snake man touched him with small dark hands. Chimera shuddered, then raised up, the snake man still touching him, comforting him, I think.

Chimera looked at me, eyes very direct. He grasped the leather hood and pulled it over his head. His dark hair stood on end, sweaty, needing to be combed. The touch of gray at the temples wasn't distinguished anymore. It looked more like mad-scientist hair, as if he'd done something awful and it had changed colors over night. I could see the scars at the side of his neck now. Orlando King, alias Chimera, looked down at me.

I just gaped at him. I was too surprised for anything else.

"I see that you didn't recognize me, Ms. Blake."

I shook my head, and tried twice before I could say, "I didn't expect to see you here." That sounded lame even to me, but what I meant was Orlando King, bounty hunter extraordinaire, should not have been the leader of a group of rogue shapeshifters. It wasn't doable somehow.

"That's why you knew about all the shapeshifters in town, because they came to you for help."

He nodded. "I have been known, since my accident, to hunt down rogue lycanthropes and not inform the authorities. A few bad apples don't have to spoil the entire barrel."

I looked at him and tried to think. "People thought your near-death experience had mellowed you, but you contracted lycanthropy, that's why you stopped being a bounty hunter."

"It seemed wrong to hunt other unfortunates," he said. "People who had less to do with the accident that made them what they were than I did. At least I was hunting the werewolf that almost killed me. I was trying to hurt it. Most people who survive an attack are just innocents."

"I know that," I said, voice soft, because knowing Chimera was Orlando King didn't help solve the mystery for me; it deepened it. I was more confused than when I walked in the damn building.

"But my change of heart, as you put it, came later. Wolf lycanthropy showed up in my bloodstream within forty-eight hours of my attack. I decided I would take out as many monsters as I could and let them take me out before the first full moon." He stared past me, eyes distant with remembering. "I took the most dangerous jobs I could find, until I ended up trying to kill an entire tribe of weresnakes in the depths of the Amazon basin." He looked at the small dark man still at his side. "I decided that dozens of any animal would surely kill me, and if not, then at the first full moon

I would be in an area devoid of any human except the people I'd come to kill."

"Logical, I guess," I said, because it seemed appropriate to say something.

His gaze flicked to me. "I had planned my death, Ms. Blake, but every animal I tried to kill just wasn't up to killing me. By the time I had my first full moon I'd been infected by a great many forms of predatory lycanthropy. And on that first moon, I changed into what Abuta and his people are, then a wolf, then a bear, then a leopard, then a lion, so forth, and so on." He was looking at Abuta, and his face held some of the religious fervor that the smaller man seemed to emanate. "They thought I was a god because I could take so many forms. They worshipped me, and they sent half their tribe to accompany me back to civilization." He laughed then. It was abrupt and unpleasant. Something about that laugh raised the hairs on my arms.

"You've killed all but three of them, Anita. I may call you Anita, mightn't I?"

I nodded, almost afraid to speak, because emotions were chasing across King's face, emotions that didn't match his calm words, as if he were feeling things that he wasn't aware of. It was like watching a badly dubbed film, except it was body actions that were out of step, not the words.

A prickling rush of energy came off him like heat, and his eyes turned. One pale greenish leopard, one wolf amber. It wasn't just the colors of the irises that didn't match, it was the shape of the pupils; the entire set of each eye socket was slightly different from the other. I hadn't noticed the bone structure shifting; it had been that fast.

A smile curled his lips. The entire expression of face, body, everything changed, and it wasn't shapeshifting; it was as if another person just settled into King's skin. Chimera's voice was slightly southern, thick and round-voweled. It was the voice I'd heard over the loudspeaker when they tried to ambush us in the club. "Poor Orlando, he just can't cope anymore. He hates what he's become."

I think I stopped breathing for a few heartbeats, which made my next breath harsh. I'd dealt with sociopaths, psychopaths, serial killers, crazies of all ilk, but this was my first multiple personality.

Chimera jerked at the tight tie, tore it off, unbuttoned the collar, rotated his neck, and smiled. "There, that's much better, don't you agree?"

My voice came out breathy. "Always good to be comfortable."

He stepped closer to me, and I backed up, bumping into Zeke. Chimera stepped in very close, almost touching and sniffed just above the skin of my face. This close his power rode over me like thousands of ants biting along my skin.

"You smell of fear, Anita. I didn't think a little eye shift would spook you."

I licked my lips, staring into those mismatched eyes from inches away. "The eyes don't bother me."

"Then what does?" he asked, still hovering over me.

I licked my lips again and didn't know what to say. Or rather, couldn't think of a safe thing to say. I thought of several smart alec remarks, but you should humor crazy people when you're at their mercy; it's a rule. Of course, I also had a rule never to put myself at the mercy of sadistic serial killers suffering from multiple personality disorder. I hoped we all lived to regret my breaking that rule. Truly insane people are often unpredictable and hard to negotiate with.

"I'm waiting for an answer," he said in a sing-song voice.

I just couldn't think of a good lie, so I tried mild truth. "The fact that I was talking to Orlando King and now I'm not, but it's the same body talking at me."

He laughed and stepped back. Then he went very still, as if he were listening to things I couldn't hear. Was it the rescue, this soon? It couldn't be. He looked down at me, smiling that unpleasant smile and ran his hands down his own body. "I make better use of the body than Orlando does."

Okeydokey, things were not improving. I looked up at Zeke and tried to tell him with my eyes that he should have told me that Chimera was this crazy.

Chimera grabbed my wrist, jerked me close. I'd been so busy trying to get eye contact with Zeke that I hadn't even seen it coming. "I was always inside Orlando. I was that part of him that allowed him to slaughter other human beings and feel nothing but hatred. He rarely took a shifter in animal form. It was safer in human form, and Orlando was a very big believer in safety, at least for himself." He drew me against his body using my wrist like a handle. He wasn't hurting me, but the strength in his grip was like a promise, a threat. He could have crushed my wrist and we both knew it.

"King had a reputation for getting the job done," I said.

"The job was to kill other people, women as well as men. Then he'd cut off their heads, burn the bodies, make sure they weren't coming back. I was the part of him that enjoyed the work, and when he became what he hated most in the world, I protected him from himself."

"How?" I asked, softly.

"By doing the things he was too weak to do himself, but still wanted done."

"Like what?" I asked. Rescue was coming; it was just a matter of stalling until help arrived. It had been the original plan, and the fact that Chimera was Orlando King and crazier than a June beetle on crack didn't really change the plan. Just keep him talking. All men love to talk about themselves, even the ones who are completely buggers. Being insane doesn't change that, or at least it never had before. It was just the multiple personality stuff that was freaking me out. If I treated Chimera like any other homicidal maniac, we'd be fine. At least that's what I kept telling myself. My pulse stayed too fast, my chest stayed tight, the fear stayed high; I don't think I believed myself.

"You want to know how I helped Orlando?" he asked.

I nodded "Yeah."

"You really want to know what I've done for him?"

I nodded again, but I was beginning not to like the way he kept phrasing things.

He smiled, and just the smile promised painful, unpleasant things. "You know what they say. Talk is cheap. Let me show you, Anita, let me show you what I've done." With that he reached behind him to the doorknob, turned it, and pulled me into the room beyond.

65

THE ROOM WAS black, utterly black, like being flung into blindness, nothingness, like a cave. Chimera released my arm. It was like being cut adrift, lost in the blackness. I stumbled in the darkness. I reached out blindly to catch myself and touched something. I grabbed at it, trying to hold on to something, anything. Then the flesh gave under my hand, and I realized it was human and not where it should have been. It was too high up to be someone's calf. I jerked back, and something else brushed my back. I let out a little squeal, hands out, stumbling in the dark, and smacked into something else that swung as I hit it. I realized whatever it was, was hanging from the ceiling. I moved away from it and ran face first into the next surprise. The solid smack of flesh on flesh let me know it was a body. The scream let me know it was still alive. I'd hit hard enough that the man swung into me again, and I tried to back away and bumped into another one. That one didn't make any noise. I kept my hands out in front of me and fought to get free of them, but my hand kept touching bodies and body parts—hips, thighs, groins, buttocks. I moved faster, trying to force my way out of the forest of hanging bodies, but moving fast made them start to swing and crash into me. Screams came out of the dark, as if I'd started them all bumping into each other. Men screaming in the dark; by the sound of the voices I knew there were no women. One body hit me hard enough that I fell, and dangling feet brushed against me. I tried to crawl away from them, but they were everywhere, touching me, brushing me, some struggling against my back. I lay down on the floor trying to get away, to get clear, swatting at them with my hands, frantic not to be touched. I crawled on my back, using my feet and hands to try and get under them, but their heights were all different, and I couldn't get free of them.

I felt a scream building in my gut and knew if I screamed once I'd just keep on. My hand landed in a pool of something warm and liquid, and it stopped me. Even in the dark I knew what blood felt like. This was probably the point where most people would have definitely started screaming, but somehow the feel of the blood calmed me. I knew about blood and letting it out of a man until he died. I pressed my hand into that still-warm pool and it steadied me.

I lay back on the floor with my hand in blood and my head resting in God knows what and relearned how to breathe. If I lay very still and didn't try and move, the feet didn't touch me, nothing touched me. So I lay in the dark and closed my eyes and tried to use my other senses, because my eyes were useless. I've got pretty good night vision, but even a cat needs some light, and there was nothing, nothing but the darkness.

The chains creaked as the bodies still swung heavily above me. There were tiny air currents. A warm drop hit my cheek. All the movement had started fresh bleeding from someone. I kept my eyes closed and forced myself to take steady, even breaths. One man was screaming, "God, God, God!" over and over again, as fast as he could draw breath. He'd lost it, and I didn't blame him. I'd come damn close myself, and I wasn't hanging nude from the ceiling, bleeding.

Chimera's voice came out of the darkness. "Shut up, shut the fuck up!"

The man stopped screaming almost instantly, but his breath came in whimpers, as if he had to make some sound.

"Anita," Chimera said. "Anita, where are you?"

Even he couldn't see in the pitch blackness, and the smell of blood, sweat, and flesh masked my odor apparently. Great, he didn't know where I was. I wished I could think of something good to do with that information. But I just lay in the dark on the foul floor, my hand in the pool of cooling blood, another drop of fresh, warm blood hitting my cheek, and did nothing. All I had to do was stall until the cavalry arrived.

I'd tried talking to Chimera and that hadn't worked so well.
I'd try silence.

"Anita, Anita, answer me."

I didn't answer. If he wanted to find me he could damn
well turn on the light. I thought I wanted some light. But
then I thought maybe I didn't really want to see what hung
above me in this room. Maybe it would be one of those sights
that blasts the mind, one you never really recover from. But
I badly wanted to see something, almost anything. I lay in
the dark, the way I used to huddle under the sheets as a child,
afraid of the dark, afraid of what I could not see.

"Answer me, Anita!" He screamed it this time, voice
harsh.

A male voice from above me. "Answer him if you can,
you don't want him angry with you."

Another man gave a sound like a choking laugh. It
sounded thick, as if there were blood in his mouth and throat.

The dark was suddenly full of voices saying, "Answer
him, answer him." It was like the wind had found a voice
and was giving me instructions in the dark.

Another drop of blood fell on my cheek and began to
slide slowly down my skin. I didn't wipe it off. I didn't
move. I was afraid any movement would let Chimera know
where I was, and I didn't want that.

"Shut up!" Chimera yelled, and I heard him move farther
into the room. The voices above me fell silent. But I could
still feel them hanging there like weight above me, like a
rock ceiling pressing down on me. I took a deep breath, let
it out slowly. My claustrophobia was trying to scream in my
head that I couldn't breathe, but it was a lie. The dark did
not have weight to it; that was the fear talking. If Chimera
wanted to let me lie in the dark for the next hour until help
arrived, I'd let him. I would not panic. It wouldn't help anything for me to start crawling frantically across the floor with
feet brushing my back. If I did that, I would start screaming,
and I wouldn't stop for a long, long time.

The blood oozed along my neck into my hair, and I kept
my eyes closed and concentrated on breathing shallow, quiet.

"Answer me, Anita, or I will start cutting on the men

hanging above you," Chimera said. His voice was closer, but not too close. He was still outside the forest of hanging bodies.

I still didn't answer.

"You don't believe me? Let me prove it to you."

A man screamed, high, piteous, hopeless.

"Don't," I said.

"Don't what?"

"Don't hurt them."

"They're nothing to you, not your animal, not your friend. Why do you care?"

"Orlando King knows the answer to your question."

"I'm asking you," Chimera said.

"You already know the answer," I said.

"No, no! Orlando knows the answer. I don't. I don't understand. Why do you care about strangers?" The other man screamed again.

"Stop it, Chimera."

"Or what?" he asked. "What will you do if I don't stop? What will you do if I stand here in the dark and cut pieces off this man? How will you stop me?"

The man was shrieking, "No, don't, not that, nooo!" The scream fell off, which meant the man was either dead, or he'd fainted. I hoped he'd fainted, but either way I couldn't do much about it.

"Can you taste the fear, Anita? Roll it on your tongue like the strong spice it is."

Right then my mouth was so dry I couldn't have tasted a damn thing. But I could sense their fear, smell it on them. All of them were afraid now, fresh terror, pouring out of their skin. "It's easy to scare people in the dark, Chimera. Everybody's afraid of the dark."

"Even you?"

I avoided the question. "I was told if I came down here that you'd let Cherry and Micah go."

"I did tell Zeke that."

And in that moment I knew he had no intention of letting them go. It shouldn't have surprised me, but it did. Had I really expected fair dealings from him? Maybe. It offended some part of me to know that he wasn't going to do what he'd said. It meant all deals were off. I'd gone from having something to bargain with, to nothing. Just on a whim, he could kill Cherry and Micah before help arrived. My pulse was speeding up again, and I fought to keep my breathing steady. I took my hand out of the cooling pool of blood. I might as well move. He'd locate me soon through my voice.

I laid my hands on my stomach and tried to think of what I could do, unarmed, against a man who outweighed me by more than a hundred pounds and was strong enough to break through brick walls. Nothing useful came to mind. Maybe violence wasn't the way to stall. What did that leave? Sex? Sweet reason? Witty repartee? Dear God, a little help here.

"You don't feel the need to talk, do you?" he asked, voice calmer than it had been, more "normal."

"Not unless I have something to say."

"That's unusual in a woman. Most of them can't stand the thought of silence. They talk and talk and talk." He was sounding calmer. In fact, he sounded like we should have been sitting across a table in some nice restaurant on a blind date. Since we were in a pitch-black torture room with blood on the floor, the matter-of-fact voice was more frightening than the ranting had been. He was supposed to rant and rave, but calm small talk, that was really crazy.

His voice got calmer, but it never sounded exactly like Orlando King's. It was as if there was another voice coming out of him, another personality, maybe. I didn't know, and I didn't care. If it kept him from cutting people up, then yea.

"Would you like to see your leopard now?" the calm voice asked.

"Yes."

The lights exploded across my vision, and I was as blind with the brilliance as I had been with the dark. I put a hand over my eyes to shield them, then slowly lowered it as my spotty vision cleared.

I was staring up at a pair of feet, legs. My gaze went up the line of the man's body to find fresh claw marks on his buttocks and thighs. Another drop of blood trailed from his bare foot to land on my hand. My gaze went slowly to the next pair of legs, and the next, and the next . . . Dozens of men hung like obscene ornaments. For the first time I let myself wonder, was Micah hanging somewhere in the forest of bodies?

"Do you want to stand up or are you enjoying the view from there?" The calm voice spoke from only about two feet away from me. It made me jump badly. I rolled my head back to see Chimera standing two hanging men away from me.

"I'll stand, if you don't mind."

"Allow me to help you." He pushed one of the hanging men to the side like you'd move a drape, like the pale blue eyes weren't open, staring, like the man didn't shudder as Chimera touched him.

I was on my feet, carefully avoiding the body nearest me, before Chimera could push aside another one and help me stand. I really didn't want him to touch me.

Chimera's eyes had bled back to human gray. His face was blank, ordinary. That nearly diabolical smile was gone, but I wasn't looking at Orlando King either. It was somebody else. The question was, was the new personality going to be more helpful or more dangerous?

He pushed back the bodies like holding open a door so I could walk out. I let him do it, but I kept my attention on him, as if I expected him to try and grab me. I guess I did. When I stepped out into a clear space a breath went out of me that I hadn't even known I was holding.

Chimera stepped beside me, and I moved just a little away from him. Movement caught my attention but it was only the hanging men swinging slowly from where Chimera had moved them. All of them bore marks of some kind; claws, blades, burns. One of them was missing his legs below the knees. I turned back to the man in front of me, and I knew I looked pale. I couldn't help that. I hadn't screamed. I hadn't panicked, much. I couldn't control the involuntary stuff. I was having enough trouble with the voluntary.

"Where are my leopards?" I asked, and my voice sounded almost normal. I got a zillion brownie points for that.

"Your leopard is here," he said and moved to a heavy

white curtain that took up almost all of the near wall. He
pulled on a cord and the curtain parted. Behind it was an
alcove, and Cherry was chained by her wrists and ankles to
the stone wall. A leather ball gag filled her mouth. Her pale
eyes were wide. Tears stained the dried blood on her face.
Her face looked untouched, but the blood had come from
somewhere.

"She's healed everything we did to her," Chimera said.
Abuta the snake appeared at Chimera's side, as if he'd been
summoned. The bigger man stroked the snake man's head,
like you'd pet a dog that you liked a lot. "Abuta has shown
quite a talent for this sort of thing."

I swallowed hard and tried not to get angry. Anger
wouldn't help anyone. Help was coming. I just had to stall
until it got here. I glanced around the room. There were men
chained to the wall all the way around. I didn't recognize
any of them. There was a certain uniformity to them—
youngish, or at least not old, well built, some slender, some
muscular, all races, all physical types, all attractive. I wondered how long it had taken Narcissus to find this many
good-looking men?

Micah wasn't along the wall. The room in the Polaroid
had looked more like the alcove that Cherry was in. I glanced
at the still unopened part of the curtain. Was he behind there?

I had moved closer to Cherry without realizing it, because
she made a small movement in her chains, and I startled. I
turned back to find her looking at Chimera, not me. He
hadn't moved as far as I could see, but something he'd done
had frightened her, and I finally realized what. His eyes had
gone animal again, and that eerie smile was back. It was
Chimera again, and call it a hunch, but I was betting he did
most of the pain work for the other two personalities.

"Unchain her," I said, like I was positive he'd do what I
asked. I so wasn't sure.

He reached out a hand towards her face, and I grabbed
his wrist. "Unchain her."

He smiled that unpleasant smile at me. "I'd hate to lose
one of the only women we've got up here. Narcissus may
go both ways, but he keeps the women out of his pack. Real

spotted hyenas are matriarchal. He's afraid if he brings women in that instinct will take over and he'll lose his pack, because he's not woman enough to keep it."

"I always enjoy learning new zoological facts," I said, "but let's unchain Cherry and get her out of here."

"But what of your lover? What of Micah?"

I met those mismatched animal eyes and fought to keep the fear out of my face. "I figured you were saving him for last, a sort of finale." My voice had gone from calm to jaded. From the tone, you'd have thought that it didn't matter to me one way or another, but I couldn't stop my pulse from jumping in my neck.

His smile deepened, and I watched a human expression fill those animal eyes. Anticipation, anticipation of my pain, I think.

He opened the curtain slowly, revealing Micah chained by his wrists and ankles to the wall, just like Cherry. But unlike her, his wounds hadn't healed. The right side of his face had been beaten badly. His eye was swollen completely shut, encrusted with dried blood. That delicate curve of jaw was so swollen it didn't look real. The swelling had twisted his lip to one side. It was so swollen that I could see the pink inside of his mouth and glimpse teeth where his mouth no longer closed completely.

I heard a small sound, and it was me. It was close to a sob, and I couldn't afford that. If Chimera knew how much this cut me up, he'd just hurt Micah more. I couldn't stop myself from touching him. I had to touch him, because only then would he be real to me. Seeing was never quite believing with me.

I touched my fingertips to the whole side of his face. His good eye fluttered open. There was a moment of relief, then I think he saw Chimera, and his eye widened. He tried to speak but couldn't open his mouth. He made small hurt noises.

Chimera touched his bruises, lightly, but Micah winced anyway. I grabbed his wrist, as I had for Cherry, and moved my body in between the two men. "Unchain him."

"I broke his jaw personally for lying to me."

"He didn't lie to you," I said.

"He told me you were going to be a panwere like me, but you're not." He leaned into me sniffing. "I'd smell it if you were. You're *something*, and it's not human. It smells of leopard and wolf." He took a deep breath just above the skin of my face. "But it also smells like vampire. You aren't what I am, Anita." He looked at Micah. "He was just trying to keep me from hurting him or his cats after he saved you from my people, when they came to your house."

"So I'm not a panwere. Does that mean you don't want me for your mate?"

He laughed then. "Oh, I don't know, I enjoy rape, adds spice." I think he said it just to shock me, but I wasn't sure. Had he raped Cherry? Had he touched her? I tried to keep the thought off my face, because with the thought came a white, hot wash of anger.

"Oh, you don't like that idea, do you?" He tried to touch my hair, and I stepped away from him out of the alcove so I'd have room to maneuver. Help was on its way, but a glance at my watch showed another twenty minutes of the hour still left. Maybe the troops would come sooner, maybe they wouldn't. I couldn't afford to count on it.

He didn't try and follow me, just let me inch away. "I could rape you in front of Micah. I don't think either of you would like that. Though truthfully I might prefer it the other way around. Orlando is homophobic. I wonder why that would be?"

I spoke as I inched down the curtain, drawing him away from Cherry and Micah. "We dislike most in others what we hate most in ourselves," I said.

"Bravo," Chimera said. "Yes, I keep a lot of Orlando safe from Orlando."

"That must be hard," I said.

"What?" he asked.

"Keeping secrets when you share the same body."

He followed me slowly around the edge of the wall. "At first he didn't want to know what we did, but lately he's become . . . unhappy with us. I think he'd have done himself harm if I hadn't stopped him." Chimera motioned towards the hanging men. "He woke up in the dark in the middle of them. He screamed like a girl." Chimera put his fingers to his lips and said, "Oops, excuse me, you didn't scream at all. He screamed like a baby until I came and rescued him, but he didn't seem all that grateful. Like he blamed me." Chimera looked puzzled, and again I had that impression that he was listening to things I couldn't hear.

He stared at me. "Do you hear that?"

I widened my eyes at him and shrugged. "What?"

He looked off past the hanging men, and I looked around for a weapon. All this damage and cutting people up, there had to be a blade around here somewhere. But the room stretched white and empty, except for the chained men. Weren't there supposed to be pokers, maces, fucking weapons? What kind of dungeon was this, victims but no instruments of torture?

I heard it then, screams, fighting. The battle was on. Though it was still distant. The good news was that help was on its way, the bad news was that Chimera knew what was happening and I was alone with him. Alright, not alone, but nobody chained to the stone was going to be able to help me.

He turned a face so full of rage to me that it was almost bestial, without any shifting of form.

"Why did you take all the alphas?" I asked. I was still going to try and keep him talking; it was all I had.

"So I could rule their groups." His words came out low and growling through clenched teeth.

"Your snakes are anacondas. The alpha you took was a cobra. You can't rule over a type of snake you're not."

"Why not?" he asked, and he started to stalk towards me, still in human form, but with that tense grace that is more animal than human.

I didn't have a good answer for that one. "Are the alphas alive?"

He shook his head. "I hear fighting, Anita. What have you done?"

"I haven't done anything."

"You're lying. I can smell it."

Okay. Maybe truth would help. "The sounds you hear are the cavalry riding to the rescue."

"Who?" he asked, voice almost pure growl. He was still stalking towards me, and I was still backing up.

"Rafael and his wererats, probably the werewolves by now."

"There are hundreds of werehyenas in this building. Your cavalry cannot get through them in time to save you."

I shrugged, afraid to tell the truth, afraid he'd take it out on the werehyenas' lovers. And I didn't dare try to lie; he'd smell it. So I just kept backing up. We were almost to the door. If I could get it open, maybe he'd chase me. Maybe I could lead him into an ambush of my own.

Abuta moved in front of the door. I'd forgotten him, and that was careless. Not fatal, not yet, but careless.

I pressed my back to the wall so I could keep an eye on both of them. Abuta stayed by the door, the message clear that if I kept away from the door he'd keep away from me. Chimera, on the other hand, kept stalking closer. I was between a panwere and a snake—not actually a rock and a hard place, but close.

Chimera flowed into his other form. I've seen shapeshifters change for years, and it was always violent, or messy. But this, this was almost . . . breathtaking. Scales flowed over him as if they were water. There was no clear fluid, no blood, nothing but the change, as if he stepped from one form into another, like Clark Kent changes into Superman. It was so quick it was almost instantaneous. He didn't even miss a step. His clothes folded away like the petals of a flower falling to the earth, and he stepped out in the snake form of Coronus. The big snake man stopped moving. He froze in that stillness that reptiles love. I froze when he did. He finally turned his head so he could look at me with a copper eye. It must have played hell with his depth-perception having to do that.

"I remember you. Chimera told us to kill you." He looked around at the dark room and said slowly, "Where are we?"

Then he bent over as if in pain, and the next form was human but not Orlando's body. He was Boone and before Boone's eyes had lost their confused look, he was a lion man.

For a second I thought it would be Marco, but of course he couldn't be both Marco and Coronus; not even Chimera could pull that one off.

He was golden, tawny, muscled, masculine, with a mane around his half-human face that was almost black. The claws on his hands were like black daggers.

"This form is truly mine," he growled. "The snake and the bear are like Orlando, they still believe in themselves. But I am all there is, and there is nothing but Chimera." He reached for me, and I bolted. I ran towards the hanging men, because I knew they'd slow him down, then turned at the last second, so fast I fell on the ground and skittered away on hands and feet like a monkey. They would slow him down, but he'd cut them up to get at me. I couldn't let that happen.

He cornered me on the far side of the room—farthest away from the door and Micah. I think he could have caught me sooner but he wasn't rushing. I don't know why. The sounds of fighting were closer, but not close enough.

Chimera came at me like grace contained in violence, a mountain of tawny muscle and fur that gleamed in the lights. He opened his mouth and roared, a sound I'd never heard outside of a zoo before. That coughing roar made me stand a little straighter. Zeke and Bacchus had promised to come get us out of here before the rest of the fighting started. They'd failed, or lied, but I wasn't going down without a fight, and I wasn't going down screaming. I watched him come towards me, like a slow-motion nightmare, beautiful and terrible, like some kind of beastial angel.

Suddenly, the *ardeur* rose inside me like a warm wave, spilling along my skin, drawing a gasp from my throat. The last time it had risen because of Richard's nearness. This time . . . maybe it was just time to feed again. The moment I thought *feed* I knew Jean-Claude had awakened, and with his rising, down in the depths of the Circus, the *ardeur* had risen inside me.

Chimera stopped where he was, shaking his great maned head. "What is that?" he growled.

My voice came breathy. "The *ardeur*."

"The what?"

"The *ardeur*, the fire, the need," I said. With each word the *ardeur* grew like a weight, and that weight brushed against my beast. It spilled upward from that tight curled place inside me, and the two separate heats rose up inside, spilling along my body, drawing me forward towards Chimera. I wasn't afraid of him anymore, because I could smell his fear. You never had to be afraid of anything that was afraid of you. Part of me knew that wasn't true, that a scared man with a gun is more likely to shoot you than a brave one, but the parts of me that were able to think were sliding away, leaving behind only instinct. What was left liked the smell of fear. It reminded me of food and sex.

Chimera backed away, and we began a slow walk back the way we'd come, this time with me advancing slowly on him. I stalked him as he'd stalked me, and part of me noticed that I was placing my feet one atop the other, almost stepping in my own footsteps, like a cat. The walk was oddly graceful, swaying my hips. My spine was very straight, shoulders back, arms almost motionless at my sides, but there was a tension running through my upper body, an anticipation of action, of violence. Always before the *ardeur* had overridden the beast's hunger, but as I stalked Chimera, watched that huge muscular form back away from me, it was meat I was thinking of. Teeth and claws, flesh to rend, to bite, to tear. I could almost taste his blood—hot, almost scalding in my mouth, down my throat. It wasn't just my beast's hunger, but Jean-Claude's blood thirst and Richard's craving for flesh. It was all that and the *ardeur* running through all of it, so that one hunger fed into the next in an endless chain, a snake eating its own tail, an Ouroboros of desires.

Chimera stopped running, pressing himself up against the white curtain. We were almost back to Cherry and Micah. There was solid wall behind Chimera, behind the curtain. "What are you?" he asked in a voice that was strangled, full of the fear that rose out of him in waves. He scented the air, nostrils flaring. "You don't even smell the same."

"What do I smell like?" I touched his chest with just my fingertips, not sure what he'd do. But he didn't pull away. I pressed my palm over his heart and felt that thick, heavy beat rise against my hand, as if I could have caressed it, like running your hand over the head of a drum. I knew in that moment what he wanted most of all. He wanted to die. Whoever was at the core, whatever was left of who Orlando King had been, he wanted to end it. He'd been trying to kill himself since the moment he learned he was going to be a werewolf. He'd never changed his mind. He just couldn't bring himself to commit suicide, not directly anyway.

I leaned in close to him, pressing our bodies together, lightly, both hands on his chest. "I'll help you," I whispered.

"Help me, how?" But his voice was fearful, as if he already knew.

Pain lanced through my chest. My knees collapsed and Chimera caught me, carefully, in those clawed hands. I think it was an automatic gesture. I saw through Richard's eyes for a moment, saw a werehyena snarling in his face, felt the claws ripping through his chest. The pain was sharp, bones breaking, then numbness, and Richard didn't fight it. He let the numbness roll over him. I knew in that instant that Richard wanted to die, or rather he didn't want to live as he was. The pain had made him reach out for me, but his hands were slow, slow to defend himself. He would never admit he'd let himself die, but he wanted it, and it made him slow. Slow enough to have the hyena man carve his chest open like cracking a melon.

Shang-Da was there pulling the hyena off of him, then I was back in my own body, airborne, thrown into the curtain and the alcove beyond. The curtain cushioned some of the fall, and the last remnants of Richard's numbness made my body limp, so it didn't really hurt. I lay for a second in a spill of curtain. My hand brushed outward and hit metal. I raised the edge of the curtain and found that this alcove was full of weapons. I'd found the blades. Chimera had thrown me into them, and the shock of Richard's injury had squelched the ardeur. My hand closed on a knife that was longer than my forearm. I raised it to the light and knew silver when I saw it. The *ardeur* was gone without my feeding it, and I was armed. Life was good.

Then I heard the sound of claws, or blades, in flesh; a thick, tearing sound of something sharp going through meat. You hear the sound often enough, you know what it is.

I could see the hanging men from here, and they were untouched. My stomach clenched tight and cold, because I knew where Chimera was. I just didn't know which of them he was cutting up.

I pushed the curtain away from me, started to stand, and Abuta was in front of me. I kept one hand balled in the curtain and flung it at him. He did what anyone would do. He flinched, and I drove the silver blade through the middle of his body, angling up, hunting for the heart.

Abuta screamed, hand reaching back towards where Chimera was cutting up my people. He said something in a language I didn't understand. As his body collapsed, I kept twisting the blade trying to find his damn heart, but the blade was stuck on his ribs and wider than my usual knives. It wouldn't move where I wanted it to go. I got a glimpse of a golden-colored blur moments before Chimera smashed a hand into me and sent me flying back into the hanging men. I hit solid, and they cried out, then I was on the ground trying to relearn how to breathe. His arm had taken me across one shoulder, and it was numb from the impact.

Chimera knelt over the snake man, cradling him in his arms. Movement turned my gaze towards Micah and Cherry. The front of Cherry's body was bloody ribbons, as if he'd racked claws down either side of her as deep as he could go, as much damage as he could do in as little time as possible. Her ruined chest rose and fell frantically; she was alive.

Micah's body was spilled open like something ripe that had been thrown against a wall. His intestines glittered like something separate and alive. I could see things inside his body that were never meant to see the light of day. He convulsed, jerking against the chains.

I screamed, and something about my panic opened me to Richard again. He was lying on the floor downstairs, and he was dying, and more than that I felt that his giving up had hurt the wolves. He was their Ulfric, their heart and their head, and his will was weak, and it made them weak. The hyenas and the halfmen that fought for Chimera were fighting for what they believed in, or fighting for the ones they loved. The wolves had nothing but Richard's willingness to die.

And I knew in that moment that if he died like that it wouldn't just be Jean-Claude and me who would join him, it would be all the wolves. Something had gone terribly wrong with Bacchus and Zeke's plan. The hyenas and the halfmen would slaughter our pack. All of them, all of them would die.

I screamed again, and Chimera was in front of me, one hand balled in my shirt, his claws ripping shallow wounds in my upper chest. He drew the other hand back, and time seemed to slow. I had all the time in the world to decide what to do, and yet, I had no time left. I felt Richard's breath rattling in his chest, felt him begin to die. Micah's body gave one last shudder, then he went very still.

I screamed, wordless, reaching for something, anything to save them. My power came, *my* power, and the one thing I could do to save us all. It was one of the worst things I'd ever seen done and I didn't hesitate.

I didn't call my power—there was no time. I *became* my power. It flowed up, through me, instantly, spilled into my hands. I touched one hand to the furred arm that held me, then blocked his other arm as it swept down towards me in a blur of motion. Blocked the blow and swept my free hand up over Chimera's arm, so that both my hands touched his arms. The moment enough of me touched enough of him, I called the power I'd learned in New Mexico. When I raised a zombie I put energy into the corpse, helped what lay in the grave to be solid and real. This was the reverse of that. I took energy out, sucked it away, made the lion man less real, less alive.

The fur flowed under my hands until I touched human skin. It was Orlando King's body that collapsed to its knees in front of me. Orlando's eyes that raised horrified gray to search my face, to beseech me, maybe. But he never asked me to stop, and truthfully I wasn't sure I knew how to stop.

He started to scream just before his skin began to run

with fine lines, like watching decades catch up with him in one fell swoop. I fed on him, fed on his essence, fed on what he was. It rushed through my body, thrilling along my skin, singing through my bones, cascading in a rush of joy through every fiber of my being, and beyond. I felt the energy flow outward to Micah, down that link that made me want to touch him every time we were close. The power found Richard and made him breathe. It spilled outward to all the wolves, and they were no longer dependent on Richard's broken will, they had mine, and I wanted to live. I wanted us all to live. We would live. We would live, and our enemies would die. I willed it so. I made it so. I used Orlando King's life to fill my leopards, my wolves, and distantly, my vampires, with will. Will to live, to fight, to survive.

And through all of it, Orlando King shrieked. He screamed as his body drained away into my hands. His skin was like dirty tissue paper on skeleton sticks when I finally let him go. He collapsed on his side, that large body turned to something light as air, but still he screamed. One ragged horror of a sound after another, and I felt no pity. I felt only the rush of power like a flight of bird wings inside my head.

Micah was beside me in black, furred leopard man form. The center of his body was whole, healed, only partially due to his shifting. A huge spotted leopard the size of a pony stalked around us, hissing at what was left of Orlando. Cherry was whole in her furred coat, not even bloody.

I must have stood there longer than I knew, draining Orlando King's life away. Long enough for them to tear the chains off, long enough for them to shapeshift and heal. The hanging men were changing form, too. And with the change, they broke their chains, healed most of the damage that had been done to them, and dropped to the ground in spotted fur and claws. They sniffed around what was left of Orlando. They gave strange barking sounds as the thing continued to scream.

Micah's voice came furry, rough with his new shape. "Your eyes are like a night-filled sky with stars in it."

I didn't need to see a mirror to know what he meant. My eyes were black, swimming and dark with the distant glow of stars in that darkness. Obsidian Butterfly's eyes had been like that, and my eyes had mirrored hers after she touched me with her power.

The far door opened and the wolves poured in. Shang-Da and Jamil were holding Richard between them. He was still in human form, still refusing to shift and help the power heal him.

The wolves, some in human form, some not, came to touch me, lick me, abase themselves before me. They growled and snapped at the dried thing that still screamed on the floor.

Jamil and Shang-Da helped Richard around the room until he stood facing me and Micah. It was only when he was that close that I realized his eyes were black with the play of cold stars in them, too. I wondered if Jean-Claude's eyes looked the same, and a thought let me know that it was so. Jean-Claude was basking in the rush of power. Richard stared at me like I'd run over his mother. The pain on his face had nothing to do with the healing wounds. I'd taken just a little bit more of his humanity, or so he felt.

He gazed down at the screaming thing on the floor with those black star-filled eyes and said, "How could you do it?"

"I did what I had to do," I said.

He was shaking his head. "I didn't want to live this badly."

"I did," Micah said.

The two men looked at each other; yellow-green eyes to black. Something seemed to pass between them, then Richard looked back at me. "Is he dying?"

"Not exactly."

He closed his eyes, and I got a glimpse inside him before he threw up his shields. It wasn't the horror that made him blanch, it was the fact that the power rush had felt better than almost anything else he'd ever experienced. Then the shields tightened, but his eyes stayed a swimming blackness.

"Get me out of here," he said.

"Change shape, Richard, heal yourself," I said.

He just shook his head. "No."

"Damn it, Richard."

He just said, "No," then Jamil and Shang-Da helped him towards the door. I watched him go but didn't try and call him back. I did my best to ignore him as I knelt by the skeletal thing that I'd made out of Orlando King. I knew how to give him back his energy, and that too would have been a rush in it's own way, but Orlando wanted to die, and Chimera was too dangerous to be kept alive. I did what Orlando wanted, and I passed judgment on Chimera. I called my magic one more time and spilled it into that struggling, screaming thing, and I released the soul. It fluttered past me like an invisible bird, and the body gave that long harsh breath that is often the very last sound. Orlando King died unrecognizable, unless you had dental records.

Micah helped me to my feet. He was back in human form. Before I'd seen Chimera, I would have said that Micah's change was smoother than anyone's I'd ever seen. He pulled me into the circle of his arms, and I pressed my face against the bare skin of his neck, caught the scent of his skin, and the *ardeur* welled up inside me, as if it had been waiting. Goosebumps ran up his bare arms, and he gave a nervous laugh. "I don't know if I'm up to it. I've had a hard day."

I wrapped my arms around his back, pressed my face against his chest, to hear the beating of his heart strong and steady. And for no reason that I could figure out, I started to cry, and the *ardeur* flowed away on a wash of tears, and hands. Hands not just Micah's, but hands of wolves, hyenas, and the leopards that had disobeyed me and come for the fight. And finally Zeke and the halfmen who had joined him. They all touched me, marked me with their scent, their tears, their laughter. We laughed and cried, howled and roared, made every noise you could make. Richard missed a hell of a victory party.

Epilogue

RICHARD DID MAKE me his Bolverk. But I was no longer his girlfriend. I'm not even sure I'm upset about that. He's free to find another lupa, though I'm not sure the pack will agree with him; they seem to like me just fine. As Bolverk of the Thronnos Rokke Clan, my first order of business was to execute Jacob. Paris is still alive at Richard's insistence. I think it's a mistake, but he is Ulfric. Oh, well.

I did not turn furry with the full moon. Apparently, Jean-Claude was right about the leopards being my animal to call, just as Damian is my vampire servant. I'm gaining powers like a master vampire. Go figure.

The snake men and Marco died during the fighting. The remainder of Chimera's people have joined their appropriate animal groups. We have a shapeshifter coalition to promote better understanding among the groups. I'm chairman, though I tried not to be. Micah and his pard stayed in town.

Micah and I are still dating, if you can call sharing a bed and my house dating. But I haven't left Jean-Claude. I'm dating them both. I am Jean-Claude's human servant, and I can't hide from that anymore. Jean-Claude wasn't horrified by what I did to Orlando King, either. He was pleased. Pleased we won, pleased we all survived. He and Micah seem to be getting along, so far. I keep waiting for the other shoe to drop and all hell to break loose between them, but so far, so good.

We rescued Joseph, the lions' Rex, and his wife is still pregnant, four months and counting—a record. Narcissus turned out to be a hermaphrodite, and he's pregnant, too. I'm not sure Narcissus should be breeding, especially knowing who the father is, but it's not my choice.

The cobras' king and son were both dead. Killed after Chimera had broken them.

I wake up pressed between Micah and Nathaniel. You can't feed the *ardeur* off of the same person every day, not even a lycanthrope. That's why they used to say that succubi and incubuses killed their victims. You can literally love someone to death. So, I feed on Micah and Nathaniel. Micah as my Nimir-Raj, and Nathaniel as my *pomme de sang*. No, I'm not having intercourse with Nathaniel. Both of them seem peaceful with the arrangement, though I'm still a little weirded out by it. I'm still hoping the *ardeur* is temporary.

Belle Morte's people contacted Jean-Claude. They're negotiating for Musette, one of Belle's lieutenants, to come for a visit. The mention of Musette's name made Asher and Jean-Claude go pale.

Ronnie is horrified that I came so close to getting killed, but it hasn't made her any more reasonable on the subject of my love life. We're back to not seeing a whole lot of each other. Maybe Micah can be my new workout partner, no pun intended.

I still love Richard, but it doesn't matter. It won't work. He can't accept what he is, or what I am. Neither of us can change our nature, and I don't even want to anymore. Micah accepts me for what I am, all of me. He loves me, from my toy penguin collection to my cold-blooded practicality. He doesn't mind bodies on the ground, and neither does Jean-Claude. I hope Richard makes peace with himself someday, but it's not really my problem anymore. I'll keep the pack safe with or without him.

As for the rest, if I wake up to silk sheets I know I'm at Jean-Claude's place. If I wake up on pure cotton sheets, I'm at home. But wherever I am, Micah is beside me. I go to sleep against the smooth warmth of him, breathing in the honeyed sweetness of his skin. Sometimes the sheets smell of Jean-Claude's cologne, sometimes they don't. Sometimes Micah's body bears two neat fang marks, and I feel Jean-Claude in his coffin, settling down for the day, content and well-fed, full of my sex and Micah's blood. Life really is good, even if you are dead.

Turn the page
for an exciting preview of

CERULEAN SINS

another Anita Blake, Vampire Hunter novel by

LAURELL K. HAMILTON

My ZOMBIE RAISING equipment was in a gray Nike gym bag. Some animators have elaborate cases. I've even seen one who had a little suitcase that turned into a table like something that might be used by a magician or a street vendor. Me, I made sure everything was packed tight so nothing got broken or scratched up, but other than that I didn't see the point to being fancier than you needed to be. If people wanted a show they could go down to the Circus of the Damned and watch zombies crawl from the grave with actors pretending to be terrified of them. As for me, I wasn't an entertainer, I was an animator, and this was work.

I turned down Halloween parties every year, where people wanted me to raise zombies at the stroke of midnight or some such nonsense. The scarier my reputation got, the more people wanted me to come be scary for them. I'd told Bert I could always go and threaten to shoot all the party-goers, that'd be scary. Bert had not been amused. But he had stopped asking me to do parties.

I'd been trained to use an ointment spread over face, hands, heart. The smell of rosemary, like breathing in a Christmas tree, still held a great nostalgia for me, but I didn't use the ointment anymore. I'd raised the dead in emergencies without it, more than once, so it got me to thinking. Some believed it helped the spirits enter you, so the powers-that-be could use you to raise the dead. Most, in America anyway, believed that the scent and touch of the herbal mixture enhanced your psychic abilities, or even helped activate them so they'd work at all. I never seemed to have any trouble raising the dead. My psychic abilities were always on-line for animating. So I still carried the ointment, just in case, but I didn't use it anymore.

The three things I did still need for animating were steel, fresh blood, and salt. (Though the salt was to put the zombie back in the grave once we were finished with it.) I'd cut my paraphernalia to absolute minimum, and recently, I'd cut it down even more. And I mean that cut part literally.

My left hand was covered in little bandages. I was using those clear ones, so I didn't look like a tan version of the mummy's hand. There were larger bandages on my left forearm. All the wounds were self-inflicted, and it was beginning to piss me off.

I had been learning how to control my growing psychic powers by studying with Marianne, who had been a psychic when I met her, but had become a witch. She was Wiccan now, though not all witches are Wiccan, and if Marianne had been another flavor of witch, I wouldn't have had to cut myself up. Marianne, as my teacher, shared some of my karmic debt, or so her group, read coven, believed. The fact that I killed an animal every time I raised the dead, three, four times a night, almost every night, had made her coven rant, rave, scream, and basically loose it. Blood magic is black magic to a Wiccan, taking a life for magical purposes, any life, even a chicken, is very black magic.

How could Marianne have tied herself to someone who was being so . . . evil?

To help Marianne's karmic burden, and mine, the coven assured me, I'd tried to raise the dead without killing anything. I'd done it before in emergencies, so I was willing to try it. Surprise, surprise I could raise the dead without killing anything—but I could not raise the dead without fresh blood. Blood magic is still black magic to Wiccans, so what to do? The compromise was that I would use only my own blood to raise the dead. I wasn't even sure that would work, usually I needed other blood. But it *did* work, for the recently dead, at least.

I'd started out slicking up my left forearm, but that had rapidly lost its appeal, since I needed to do it three or more times a night. Then I'd taken to pricking my fingers, a little blood seemed to be enough for anyone dead under six months. But I'd run out of fingers, and my arm had enough scars without me adding more. I'd also found that when I practiced left-hand shooting that I was slower, because the cuts freaking hurt. I would not cut up my right hand, because I couldn't afford to be slower with my right. I'd decided I was sorry I had to kill a few chickens or goats to raise the dead, but the animals' lives were not worth my own. There I've said it, a total selfish judgement call.

My left hand hurt, and I was tired of being covered in bandages and Neosporin. And I couldn't raise anything over six months with only a pin prick of blood, the cut needed to be bigger, and that also hurt—a lot. I wasn't masochistic enough to keep doing it.

I was going to have to call Marianne and tell her I'd failed the Wiccan test of goodness. Why should they be any different, most right-wing Christian groups hated me, too?

I glanced behind me at my audience. Two new uniformed police officers had joined Lieutenant. Nicols and Officer Newman. The police stood in the middle of the two groups which had been allowed to come close enough to the grave to hear what the zombie would say. It was way closer than fifty feet, but both parties needed to hear Gordon Bennington, or so the judge had ruled. The judge in question had actually joined us, along with a court reporter and her little machine. He'd also brought along two burly-looking baliffs which made me think the judge was even smarter than he looked, and I'd been pretty impressed before. Not every judge will take zombie testimony.

For tonight, this graveyard was court. I was just glad that Court TV hadn't gotten wind of it. It was just the kind of weird crap that they liked to televise. You know, transsexual's custody case; female teacher rapes thirteen-year-old boy student; pro-football player's murder trial. The O. J. Simpson trial has not been a good influence on American television.

The judge said in his booming, court voice, which echoed strangely in the flat emptiness of the cemetery, "Go ahead Ms. Blake, we're all assembled."

Ordinarily I'd have beheaded a chicken and used its body to sprinkle a blood circle, a circle of power, to contain the zombie once it was raised so it wouldn't go wandering all over the place. The circle also helped focus power and raise energy. The problem was that I was thinking if I'd tried to get enough blood out of my body to walk even a small circle of power, I'd have been finished for the night, too dizzy and too light-headed to do anything else. So what's a morally upright animator supposed to do?

I unsheathed the machete and heard several gasps behind me. It was a big blade, but I'd found that beheading a chicken one-handed needed a big, sharp blade. I stared at my left hand and tried to find a space that was bandage-free. I put the top edge of the blade against my middle finger, the symbolism was not lost on me, and pressed my finger against the blade. I kept the machete too sharp to risk drawing the blade down my finger. It would be a bitch to need stitches because I'd cut too deep.

The cut didn't hurt immediately which meant I'd probably cut deeper than I wanted. I raised my hand so the moonlight fell on it, and saw the first dark welling of blood. The moment I saw it, the cut hurt. Why was it that everything hurt worse when you realized you were bleeding?

I began to walk the circle, holding the steel point downward, my bleeding finger flat to the earth so that occasional drops would hit the ground. I'd never truly felt the machete carving the magic circle through the ground, through me, until I stopped killing animals. It had probably always been like a steel pencil tracing my circle, but I'd never been able to feel it over the stronger rush of the death. I felt each drop of blood that fell, felt the earth almost hungry for it, like rain in a drought, but it wasn't the moisture the earth drank, it was the power. I knew when I'd walked the entire circle around the headstone, because the moment I touched the place where I'd begun the circle closed with a skin-tingling, hair-raising rush.

I turned to face the headstone, feeling the circle around me like an invisible trembling in the air. I went to the headstone which was at the far end of the circle. I tapped the headstone with the machete. "Gordon Bennington, with steel I call you from your grave." I touched my bloody hand to the cold stone. "With blood I call you from your grave." I moved back to the far edge of the circle, at the foot of the grave. "Hear me now, Gordon Bennington, hear and obey. With steel, blood, and power, I command you to rise from your grave. Rise from your grave and walk amongst us."

The earth rolled like heavy water, and just spilled the body upward. In the movies the zombies always crawl from the grave with reaching hands like the ground is trying to keep them prisoner, but most of the time, the earth gives freely, and the zombie just rises to the top, like something floating to the surface. There were no flowers to get in the way this time, nothing for the body to trip over as he sat up and looked around.

One thing I had noticed when I stopped killing the animals was that my zombies weren't as pretty. With a chicken I could have made Gordon Bennington look like his photo in the paper. With only my own blood, he looked like what he was, a reanimated corpse.

He wasn't awful, I'd seen much worse, but his widow screamed, long and loud, and began to sob. There had been more than one reason I wanted Mrs. Bennington to stay home.

The nice dark suit hid the chest wound that had killed him. But we could see the odd color of his skin. The way the flesh had begun to sink into the bones of his face. His eyes left were too round, too large to bare, so they rolled in their sockets barely contained by the waxy flesh. His blond hair was patchy and looked like it had grown, but that was illusion, caused by the shrinking of the meat of his body. Hair and fingernails do not grow after death, contrary to popular rumor.

There was one other thing I had to do to help Gordon Bennington to speak. I walked across the now solid ground and knelt by his puzzled, wizened face. I couldn't smooth my skirt down in back because one hand was full of machete and the other was bleeding. Everyone got a nice long glimpse of thigh, but it didn't really matter, we were about to do the thing that disturbed me the most about not sacrificing a little poultry.

I held out my hand towards Gordon Bennington's face. "Drink, Gordon, drink of my blood and speak to us."

Those round, rolling eyes stared at me, then his sunken nose caught the scent of blood, and he grabbed my hand with both of his, and lowered his mouth to the wound. His hands felt like cold wax with sticks inside it. His mouth was almost lipless, so his teeth pressed close in my flesh as he sucked at my hand. His tongue whipped back and forth on the wound like something separate and alive in his mouth, feeding from me.

I took a deep, steadying breath, breath in and out, in and out. I would not be sick. Nope. I would not embarrass myself in front of this many people.

When I thought he'd had enough, I said, "Gordon Bennington."

He didn't react, just kept his mouth pressed to the wound, his hands clutching my wrist.

I tapped him gently with the side of the machete on top of his head. "Mr. Bennington, people are waiting to talk to you."

I don't know if it was the words or the tap with the blade, but he looked up, and slowly began to pull back from my hand. His eyes held more of him now. The blood always seemed to do that, fill them back up with themselves.

"Are you Gordon Bennington?" I asked. We had to be all formal.

He shook his head.

The judge said, "We need you to answer out loud, Mr. Bennington, for the record."

He just stared up at me. I repeated what the judge had said, and Bennington spoke, "I am, was, Gordon Bennington."

One of the upsides to raising the dead with just my blood was that they always knew they were dead. I'd raised people before where they didn't know that, and that was a bitch, telling someone that they were dead, and you were about to put them back in the grave. Real nightmare stuff, that was.

"How did you die, Mr. Bennington?" I asked.

He sighed, drawing in air, and I heard it whistle, because most of the right side of his chest was missing. The suit hid it, but I'd seen the forensic photos. Besides I knew what a mess a shotgun makes at close range.

"I got shot."

There was a tension behind me, I could feel it over the buzz of the power circle. "How did you get shot?" I asked, voice calm, soothing.

"I shot myself going down the stairs to our basement."

There was a cry of triumph from one side of the crowd and an inarticulate scream from the other.

"Did you shoot yourself on purpose?" I asked.

"No, of course not. I tripped, gun went off, so stupid, really. So stupid."

There was a lot of screaming behind me. Mostly Mrs. Bennington yelling, "I told you so, little bitch . . ."

I turned and called, "Judge, did you hear all that?"

"Most of it," he said. He turned that booming voice on full volume and shouted, "Mrs. Bennington, if you will be quiet long enough to listen, your husband has just said he died by accident."

"Gail," Gordon Bennington's voice was tentative, "Gail, are you there?"

I did not want a tearful reunion on top of the grave. "Are we finished, Judge, can I put him back?"

"No," this from Fidelty Insurance's lawyers. Conroy stepped closer. "We have some questions for Mr. Bennington."

They asked questions, at first I had to repeat them for Bennington to be able to answer, but he got better at answering. He didn't look any better, physically, but he was gathering himself up, being more alert, more aware of his surroundings. He spotted his wife, and said, "Gail, I'm so sorry. You were right about the guns. I wasn't careful enough. I'm so sorry to leave you and the kids."

Mrs. Bennington came towards us, with her lawyers in tow. I thought I'd have to ask them to keep her off the grave, but she stopped outside the circle, as if she could feel it. Sometimes the people that turn out to be psychically gifted surprise you. I doubt if she was even aware of why she stopped. Of course, she was holding her hands tight to her body. She was not reaching out to touch her husband. I don't think she wanted to find out what that waxy-looking skin felt like. I couldn't blame her.

Conroy and the other lawyers tried to keep asking questions, but it was the judge who said, "Gordon Bennington has answered all your questions in detail. It's time to let him get back to . . . rest."

I agreed. Mrs. Bennington was in tears and Gordon would have been too, except his tear ducts had dried up months ago.

I got Gordon Bennington's attention. "Mr. Bennington, I'm going to put you back now."

"Will Gail and the children get the insurance money now?"

I glanced behind me at the judge. He nodded.

"Yes, Mr. Bennington, they will."

He smiled, or tried to. "Thank you, then, I'm ready." He gazed back at his wife who was still kneeling on the grass by his grave. "I'm glad I got to say good-bye."

She was shaking her head, over and over, tears streaming down her face. "Me, too, Gordie, me, too. I miss you."

"I miss you to, my little hell cat."

She burst into sobs at that. Hiding her face in her hands. If one of the lawyers hadn't grabbed her she'd have fallen to the ground.

My little hell cat didn't sound like a term of endearment to me, but hey, it proved Gordon Bennington had really known his wife. It probably also proved that she would miss him for the rest of her life. I could forgive her a few temper tantrams in the face of that much pain.

I squeezed on the wound in my hand and thankfully got a little more blood. Some nights I had to reopen a wound, or make another one, to get the zombie put back. I touched my bloody hand to his forehead, leaving a small dark mark.

"With blood I bind you to your grave, Gordon Bennington." I touched him with the edge of the machete, gently. "With steel I bind you to your grave." I switched the machete to my left hand and picked up the open container of salt that I'd left inside the circle. I sprinkled him with salt, and it sounded like dry sleet as it hit him. "With salt I bind you to your grave, Gordon Bennington, go and rise no more."

With the touch of salt his eyes lost their alertness, he was empty as he lay back on the earth. The ground swallowed him like some great beast had rippled its fur and he was just gone, swallowed back into the grave. Gordon Bennington's corpse was back where it belonged and there was nothing to mark this grave from any other. Not so much as a blade of grass was out of place. Magic.

I still had to walk the circle backwards and uncast it. Normally, I don't have an audience for that part. The zombie goes back in the grave, everyone leaves. But Conroy of Fidelity Insurance was arguing with the judge, who was threatening to cite him with contempt. And Mrs. Bennington was not in a condition to walk, yet.

The police were just standing around watching the show. Lt. Nicols looked at me and shook his head, smiling. He walked over to me as the circle went down and I began to clean my new wound with antiseptic wipes.

He lowered his voice so the truly grieving widow wouldn't hear him. "You could not pay me enough to let that thing suck my blood."

I half-shrugged, holding gauze over my finger so it would stop bleeding. "You'd be surprised what people do pay for this kind of work."

"It ain't enough," he said, an unlit cigarette already in his hand.

I started to give some flip answer when I felt the presence of a vampire, like a chill across my skin. Out there in the dark, someone was waiting. There was a gust of wind, and there was no wind tonight. I looked up, but no one else did, because humans never look up, never expect death to fall upon them from the sky.

I had seconds to say, "Don't shoot, he's a friend," before Asher appeared in our midst, within an arm's length of me, his long hair streaming behind him, his booted feet touching down. He was forced to make a half running step to catch the momentum of his flight, which brought him to my side.

I turned and put myself in front of his body. He was too tall for me to cover all of him, but I did my best, moving us so that if anyone shot at him they'd risk hitting me. Every policemen, every bodyguard had drawn a gun, and every barrel was pointed at Asher, and me.

I stared at the half circle of guns, trying to keep an eye on everyone at once and failing, because there were too many of them. I kept my hands out from my body, fingers spread, universal sign for "I'm harmless." I didn't want anyone thinking I was going for my own gun, that would be bad.

"He's a friend," I said, voice a little high, but otherwise calm.

"Who's friend?" Nicols said.

"Mine," I said.

"Well, he ain't my friend," one of the uniforms said.

"He's not a threat," I said, pressing my body back enough that I could feel Asher in a long line against me.

He said something in French, everybody gripped their guns a little tighter. "English, Asher, English."

He took a deep shuddering breath, as if he wasn't breathing much. "It was not my intent to frighten anyone."

Asher knew better than to fly into the middle of a bunch of mundanes, especially cops. It had only been a few years since the police were allowed to shoot a vampire on sight, just for being a vampire. It had only been four years since Addison V. Clark had made vamps "alive" again, at least to the law. They were citizens with rights now, and shooting them on sight without just cause was murder. But it still happened now and then.

"If you shoot with me in the way, you can all kiss your badges good-bye."

"I don't have a badge to loose." It was Balfour the body-guard, of course, being tough, but he had a big gun to go with his big talk.

I looked at him. "If you shoot, you better kill me, because you won't get a second chance."

"Nobody's shooting anybody," Nicols said, and I was close enough to hear him mutter, "damnit," under his breath.

He'd moved his gun to point at the bodyguards. "Put the guns down, now." The other policemen had followed his lead and suddenly the circle of guns was pointed away from me, and at Balfour and Rex. I let out a breath I hadn't realized I was holding, and sagged a little against Asher.

Asher had taken the risk of freaking out a group of armed humans. He'd also spoken in French, which meant he was scared enough, or angry enough, to have forgotten his English. Something was very wrong, and I couldn't ask him, not yet. First, get out of the line of fire, then fix the rest.

We were standing so close together that his wavy golden hair brushed against my own black curls. He put his hands on my shoulders, and there was a tension to his hands. He *was* scared. What had happened?

The police had convinced the bodyguards to put their guns away. The uniforms divided up and walked the two interested parties back to their respective cars. It left Nicols, the judge, and the court reporter standing near us. At least the court reporter wasn't still typing.

Nicols turned to me, his gun pointed downward, tapping a little against the leg of his slacks. He frowned, eyes flicking to Asher, then to me. He knew enough not to risk staring the vampire in the eyes. They could bespell you with their eyes, if they wanted to. I was immune because I was the human servant of the Master Vampire of the City. Through Jean-Claude I was safe from most of what Asher could do. Not all, but most.

Nicols was obviously unhappy. "Okay, what was so damned urgent that he had to fly in here like that?"

Damn, he was too good a cop. Even though he'd probably dealt very little with vampires, he'd made the logic jump that only an emergency would make Asher appear like he did.

His eyes flicked up to Asher again, then down to my face. "It's a good way to get yourself shot, Mr. . . ."

"Asher," I answered for him.

"I didn't ask you, Ms. Blake. I asked him."

"I am Asher," he said in a voice that fell on the air like a caress. He was using vampire powers to make himself more acceptable. If Nicols figured out what he was doing, it would backfire. But it didn't.

"What's wrong, Mr. Asher?"

"Just Asher," and the voice glided across my skin so soothing. I had some immunity to the voice, but Nicols didn't.

He blinked, then frowned, puzzled. "Fine, Asher, what the hell is the rush?"

Asher's fingers tightened minutely on my shoulders, and I felt him take a breath. I had a second to hope that he wasn't going to try an Obi-Wan on Lieutenant Nicols. You know, "these are not the droids you're looking for." Nicols was stronger willed than that.

"Musette has been gravely injured. I came to take Anita to her side."

I felt the color drain from my face, my breath caught in my throat. Musette was one of Belle Morte's lieutenants. Belle Morte was the fountainhead of Jean-Claude and Asher's bloodline. She was also a member of the Council of Vampires that had a home base somewhere in Europe. Every time council members had visited us people had died. Some of them ours, some of them theirs. But Belle Morte had never sent anyone, until now. There had been some careful negotiations about Musette coming over for a visit. She was due a month from now, just after Thanksgiving. So what the hell was she doing in town a week before Halloween? I didn't for a minute believe Musette was hurt. It was just Asher's sneaky way of telling me how bad things were in front of witnesses.

I didn't have to pretend to be shocked, or scared. My skin was cold with the thought of what Musette might be doing right now to people I cared about . . .